Critical acclaim for Romanitas:

'A thoroughly good read . . . vividly imagined . . . elegant, lively writing'   *Sunday Telegraph*

'A fast-moving, compelling story, brilliantly imagined'
Conn Iggulden

'[A] hugely imaginative debut'   *Daily Mirror*

'*Romanitas*, the first of a three-parter, has the feel of Mary Stewart's "Arthur" books and sets the stage for an absorbing drama'
Sunday Sport (Top Read of the Fortnight)

'A heady blend of almost every established genre, resulting in something that feels fresh and new. *Romanitas* is beautifully written . . . the trilogy may well become something of a modern classic'
Books & Magazine Collector

'Epic in undertaking, *Romanitas* creates a fascinating world that is both contemporary in tone, and yet about as far removed from the world we live in as it is possible to imagine. McDougall's writing style is fresh and light and the involving story ensures you'll gobble up the 400 pages in no time, staying eager to find out how the remainder of the trilogy unfolds'
Dreamwatch

'[An] intriguing debut novel . . . The plot of *Romanitas* gripped me and kept the pages turning. McDougall's setting is original . . . her alternate history feels well researched and believable'   *Starburst*

Sophia McDougall lives in London where she also writes plays and poetry. *Romanitas* is her debut novel.

ROMANITAS

SOPHIA McDOUGALL

An Orion paperback

First published in Great Britain in 2005
by Orion
This paperback edition published in 2006
by Orion Books Ltd,
Orion House, 5 Upper St Martin's Lane,
London WC2H 9EA

1 3 5 7 9 10 8 6 4 2

A CIP catalogue record for this book is available
from the British Library.

ISBN-13: 978-0-7528-7709-9
ISBN-10: 0-7528-7709-7

Typeset at The Spartan Press Ltd,
Lymington, Hants

Printed and bound in Great Britain by
Clays Ltd, St Ives plc

The Orion Publishing Group's policy is to use papers that
are natural, renewable and recyclable products and
made from wood grown in sustainable forests. The logging
and manufacturing processes are expected to conform to
the environmental regulations of the country of origin.

www.orionbooks.co.uk

To my Mother

This is the first of three books set in a Roman Empire which never fell but spread to take in half the world.

[CONTENTS]

THE MAP OF THE WORLD

THE NOVIAN DYNASTY
AN IMPERIAL FAMILY TREE

Gaius Novius Faustus Augustus

[m]

Sextilia Gratiana

Titus Novius
Faustus Augustus
(Emperor of Rome)

[m]

Julia Sabina

Novia Faustina
(**Makaria**)

Lucius Novius
Faustus

[m]

Drusilla Terentia

Drusus Novius
Faustus

Tertius Novius
Faustus **Leo**

[m]

Clodia Aurelia

Marcus Novius
Faustus

[ACKNOWLEDGEMENTS]

I am grateful to Jon Wood, for his cheerful and considerate editing and unfailing belief in the book, Simon Trewin for being such a kind and clear-sighted agent, St John Donald, also at PFD, for taking me on and for setting the whole process of bringing *Romanitas* to publication in motion. Thanks also to Sarah Ballard for her insightful editorial suggestions at an early stage of writing, to Claire Gill for her encouragement on matters concerning the cover and other issues, Alice Dunn for telling me that she wanted to know what happened next, and to Genevieve Pegg for her reassurance during the editorial process.

If my understanding of history, geography, anatomy and politics is still not up to much, nevertheless it is a good deal better than it was before I began to research this trilogy. I continue to be amazed and delighted at the willingness of the people I have encountered to share their knowledge and time. I owe particular gratitude to M Nicolas Ferrer at the Grottes de Gargas, without whose generous help, the chapter 'The Cave of Hands', could not have been written. I must also thank Dr Simon Hawkes, who talked to me about brachial plexopathy and was very tolerant of my extreme slowness in understanding him. I wish I had been polite enough to ask the name of an amused and helpful man at Dovetail Greenhouses whom I cold-called to ask about the plausibility of breaking into and hiding in industrial hot-houses. I thank him anyway. And Alan Samson checked my Latinisation of American and other names, made intelligent comments on my 'History of the Roman

Empire' and maps, and, in general, slightly alleviated my fear of being found out.

My friend Maisie Tomlinson deserves thanks for her continuing patience and help (it is not everyone who will willingly impersonate a victim of crucifixion first thing on coming home from work) as does Eleena Misra for a conversation about poison, Richard Dawson who also helped with my Latin, my father for some suggestions on the construction of the alternative history and its geopolitics, and my mother for being such an acute and imaginative reader of everything I write.

Once, when we were on our way to the place of prayer, we met a slave girl who was possessed by an oracular spirit, and brought large fortunes to her owners by telling fortunes.
Acts, 16.16.

Romulus will rule, and build the walls of Mars
And he will give his people his own name:
Romans. On them I lay no limits.
I set them free from distance and from time,
I have given them an Empire without end.
Aeneid. I

EMBALMED

Marcus' parents had been embalmed for eight days, but though their eyes were closed and their injuries invisible, they did not look asleep, as they were presumably meant to. Their veins were plump with wax, and the clear light lit up a kind of translucent yellowness under the heavy make-up on their skin. The air was syrupy with incense, which successfully masked the scent of the chemicals keeping their tissues moist. Still, Marcus knew the smell was there. The grey had vanished from his father's brown hair, and his mother's lips were painted a russet shade she had never worn in life, although one could now see it suited her. They looked as peaceful as artificial fruit.

There were long black flags hanging between roofs and upper windows in all the streets, but above Leo and Clodia the light pulsed between the basilicas' marble and mirrored walls and the silvered panels on the temple of Saturn, burned in the many lenses and leapt, piercingly, to the east, from the Colosseum's glass roof. But the glaring buildings and statues seemed to be planted deep in a heavy soil of black-dressed people, weighted down, wading. From above, the buildings and the people would look like one static mat, so densely and so nearly motionlessly were the streets filled. The Sacred Way, cleared for the procession to pass, closed inexorably behind it, like a syringe filling with black ink.

The people were not all from Rome or even from Italy: everywhere, over the eight days – right at the Empire's edges – Mexica, India, Gothia, Gaetulia – they must have been struggling for time, and the cost of travel, and beds in Rome, so that they could cut themselves free to be sucked here as on an inward tide. Here, at the very centre of it, Leo and Clodia lay now before the rostra in a kind of wide bay framed with people, and on the empty ground, in the light, the scattered rose petals still showed very white, like shells. From this bare core, held back by the Praetorians, the people brimmed outward a long way, around the Colosseum, into the other Forums, as far as the Pantheon, just to know they were close, although there was nothing to see there except longvision screens, which could have been anywhere.

From the rostra, Marcus Novius Faustus Leo looked down into the cameras. He was squinting because of the light, and he was enough of a Novian – and, therefore, enough of an actor – to hope for a guilty flutter of a second that the effect might be mistaken for blinking back tears. He was instantly disgusted with himself, and he forced himself to forget that he had thought it.

He could not dispel an uneasy awareness of how badly he was handling the speech. The oration he was reading was by one of his uncle's speechwriters, and he had scanned it over only once before. He had meant to do better, and even told himself he would learn it off by heart, but the days had gone by and he had barely been able to bring himself to touch the thing. He could see now that a touching youthful inarticulacy had been written into it. He could feel places where he should stammer, where he shouldn't be able to go on, where there ought to be a poignant tremble in his voice; but he kept reading blandly about his father's selflessness and patriotism. He was delivering it badly because he was not delivering it badly enough.

'My father loved three things more than his own life,' he said. 'My mother, myself, and above all his country.'

There was a slow swell of applause and some sobs, but Marcus simply read through them. The mourners missed some of what he said next, which was anyway only more of the same. He was becoming faintly sickened by it, not least because his father would never have spoken so of himself or anyone else; he would have written the speech himself, and every phrase he spoke would have been perfectly weighted with calculated and irresistible sincerity. Marcus went on, almost in a monotone now, marvelling to himself at how hurt the mourners looked, and how many of the people packed below him were in tears. There could not possibly be so many real tears for his parents, he decided. They had to be crying for themselves, even if they didn't know it. Why were they all so unhappy then? There were two women straining against the cordon: a pretty girl not much older than himself resting her head on her mother's shoulder. They held limp blue flowers, and they were clutching each other and shuddering with such sharp, raw sobs he thought they could barely breathe. They bothered him somehow, and although he went on reading he kept forgetting the sense of what he was saying to look at them. He felt as if they were abusing his own lungs and eyes, as if they were weeping out any ability he might have had to cry himself.

'Poor boy, poor boy!' someone had called at him, as with his uncle and cousins he led the procession through the streets of Rome. He had provided no reason for anyone to shout that, he had been concentrating on keeping in step with his cousins, Drusus and Makaria, and his uncle. In so far as he was thinking anything, he was listening to the choir of women and boys lamenting behind him, and looking at the white petals scattered on the road in front of him, the gold leaf on his parents' bier. He was quietly amazed how much melancholy splendour had been conjured up in so little time – only eight days! Someone had been working very hard.

He had braced himself a little when he came to the section of the speech about his mother, wondering half-excitedly if here the dull, drifting feeling would evaporate at last. As it turned out he had nothing to worry about. The writer had made his mother quite lovely, but even more unrecognisable than the placid figure lying in the Nionian

3

silk dress in the centre of the Forum. In any case, the focus of the speech was squarely on his father. Of course, he knew it would be; his father was the most popular of the Novii, he was a war hero, and he would have been— but Marcus would not think about that yet. But he knew in a tired way that part of the reason it all seemed so unreal – all the tears and incense and flowers and music and the ridiculous archaic black togas he and his family were wearing – was that it was all for his father. And although he felt as if he had been knocked half out of consciousness, or suddenly gone deaf, he knew that sooner or later the feel of things would come back; and then it would be his mother's death that would hurt him most.

He rushed through to the end now, which was about how much his father loved and admired Titus Novius Faustus Augustus, who was Marcus' uncle and the Emperor. Then there was something to do with the gods, and that, merci-fully, was it. He took the pages of the oration with him off the podium, realising too late that it would have looked better to have left them there. He slid into place beside Drusus, who wordlessly pulled the speech out of Marcus' hands – just the faintest contraction of disapproval on his forehead. It was not a moment for a member of the Imperial family to be clutching bits of paper. When Marcus looked again the speech had vanished. His cousin must have passed it silently backwards into the hands of a slave. He had done it as deftly as a conjuror. In any case, Marcus never saw it again.

The Emperor was heading for the podium steps. He was a tall, ponderous man of sixty-one with soft heavy hair and handsome features blurred by fat. As he passed his nephews, he patted Marcus kindly on the shoulder, and then touched Drusus' arm and whispered a word in his ear. A spasm of exasperation twisted Drusus' face.

'What is it?' whispered Marcus, barely moving his lips, as Faustus began his own speech with a promise to love Marcus like a son. Marcus found the words 'I want to go home, I want to go home' were repeating wretchedly in his head. He looked at Drusus. He didn't know him well or like him much, but of all the Novii, his cousin was the closest to him in age, and it was strange to see the length and breadth of his own face there beside him, a straightness and symmetry, except for the deep curve over the eyelids, the slight crookedness at the mouth which they all seemed to have on one side or the other. But Drusus' hair was hazel and his eyes green, and Marcus' colouring was his mother's.

'My father,' answered Drusus in the same way, and 'Don't look, don't draw attention,' as Marcus turned curiously to see what Uncle Lucius was doing. But almost as he said it, someone pushed between them and ran right up to Leo and Clodia's bier. Faustus stopped reading and looked unhappy and uncertain for a moment. He said 'Lucius . . .' almost imploringly, but then, after glancing a furtive command or plea at the attendants on either side of the rostra, he gave up, or decided to wait, composing his face and looking outward with grave authority, as if this was a pause he'd chosen to make.

Leaning over the bier, Uncle Lucius was gnawing at his drooping lips and wringing his hands – something Marcus had never seen anyone do before. He was as tall as Faustus but somehow he didn't look it – he looked shrunken and crouching and pitiful. His white hair stood up in tufts, as though he'd cut it himself. He laid a hand on Marcus' father's calm face and said 'Leo!' once, in an awful splintered old voice.

'Come on,' said Drusus. 'It'll look better if we do it.' Marcus didn't know how to say he didn't want to get any closer either to Uncle Lucius or to the bodies of his parents, and already Drusus was leading him forward into the centre of the forum. He heard a kind of soft sighing from the crowd – and knew that it meant encouragement and approval.

He felt that the quiet of half the world had fallen respectfully still around this space, and, although he had not felt so on the podium, he was horribly conscious of being looked at, not only by the hundreds packed into the forum of course, but by invisible millions; the funeral was the only thing showing on longvision.

Drusus slid an arm round his father's shoulders and said, 'Come on, Dad', as gently as he could, although there was a sawing note of resentment in his voice. 'Yes, come on, Uncle Lucius,' agreed Marcus miserably. Lucius would not even look at Drusus directly. Marcus tried to concentrate on the unusual sympathy and admiration he found himself feeling for his cousin, half-shutting his eyes so he wouldn't have to look at a strand of his mother's fair hair blowing unchecked across her mouth.

Lucius' weak green eyes were wavering and scared. If he didn't recognise Marcus it wasn't surprising; Marcus had seen him perhaps three times before in all his life.

Of course, neither Faustus' oration nor his own had mentioned Lucius, although this was the first time in years he'd been allowed out in public. He was supposed to be having a good spell, and Marcus' father was his brother, after all, just as much as Faustus was.

'No,' said Uncle Lucius. 'Leo!'

Drusus nodded at Marcus and reluctantly he took hold of his uncle's arm, and they tried to chivvy him away from the bier. Oh, I wish I were at home, thought Marcus, tugging at a fold of his uncle's sleeve. Then Drusus must have pushed Lucius too hard, for he stumbled sideways, and leant heavily and unexpectedly against Marcus. Marcus staggered, uselessly put out a hand. He felt thin and futile with obscure shame. He was going to fall over like a little boy, there in front of everybody.

Then, to his amazement, Uncle Lucius' hand closed around his wrist and hauled him upright, so that for a moment after all the loose, weak-eyed face was turned to his, staring at him, the features, under the tremulous lines and the wavering expression, painfully more like his father's face than Drusus' was like his own, the blood of course being that much closer.

Marcus could clearly remember a time before he had known about Uncle Lucius, before having to think about it. He could remember Leo explaining, but he was less sure of why and how it had begun – had he seen Uncle Lucius chewing his lip and refusing to look at people, and asked his father, 'What's wrong with him?' No, he did not have that impression. It had been deliberate, his father had decided to tell him for his own reasons, without prompting and without warning.

First of all, Tertius Novius Faustus Leo told his son about the wars that slowly prised the southern half of Africa out of Rome's hold, especially about the first and bloodiest phase. He said there was a besieged town, near the Congo. There was a Roman battalion sent to relieve it. This was more than two hundred years ago, and the family went into the Senate then, or into the army. They were not Emperors. One of them was there, in Africa, a general; Somebody Novius Something.

So it began as a story, and Marcus thought he could remember listening with interest but also with politely masked strain, even suspecting, already, that his father had some ulterior motive, that the story might be some sort of trap. Perhaps he thought it was going to turn suddenly into a test of history or geography. When Leo mentioned the Congo, Marcus nodded wisely, fumbling through his memory in silent agony to be sure he knew where that was. Had his father really forgotten the full name of this ancestor, or would he be asked to supply it? Was he supposed to work out why they'd lost southern Africa, how they could have kept it? He was eight. He felt ashamed that they hadn't got to this war at school yet.

Anyway, said Leo, the African mutineers had the Roman troops and a pack of civilians holed up in the town, starving and dying of one disease and another. Partly because he really cared for his men, and partly deliberately, to make them love him so that he could get more from them, this Novian had always lived as much like them as possible, eating the same food, taking more than the same risks. And all the time, except during the most acute moments of battle, he was as aware of Rome as if the Senate and the

7

court and his family were ranked around him in a weightless auditorium, in which, at the centre, he was brave almost without remembering that he could really die. It didn't matter; the soldiers did love him, because, as well as everything else, he knew what he was doing. They believed him when he told them they would break the siege quickly, and they did.

Then he crucified as many of the mutineers as were still alive. He was only doing what anyone else would have done. Perhaps he could have spared some of the younger rebels, but Rome had been badly shocked by the siege and Novius knew he had to set an example. So he set rows of crucifixes on the banks of the Congo. Nailed to one of them – this was back when they still used hammers and nails – was a boy of twelve. If Novius thought about this, he might have told himself that the boy had been old enough to kill Roman citizens, or to help kill Roman citizens, or at least to be present when Romans were killed. Or, if someone had forced him really to imagine and understand it, he might have wept for pity and shame. He wasn't a bad man. Or at least, he didn't feel like a bad man to himself. He was kind to his own children. Most likely he didn't think about it at all.

Leo had said this all quite slowly and simply. Often he would stop, almost at the end of every sentence, and look at Marcus, to be sure he had understood it, but not merely checking, trying to push the words further.

That night, though he was exhausted, Novius couldn't sleep in the town he'd saved, but not because he was thinking about the boy – who was still alive, perhaps, dangling from his twisted arms out there in the dark – but because he was grieving for the soldiers he'd lost, because he was homesick for Italy, because he could never get used to the African heat. He had a morbid terror of tropical illnesses, so although a mosquito net was draped over his bed, he couldn't believe it would protect him. The slightest fluting of an insect went through his head like a shriek, and each time that happened he'd have to begin the terrible work of trying to get to sleep all over again.

8

(Marcus knew his father must be making some of this up – he couldn't know about the mosquitoes and not remember this Novian's name.)

The sound Novius heard next was far worse than the insects. At first it was easy to believe the sound was only in his aching brain. Soon, though, he had to admit to himself the footsteps he could just hear, were really moving slowly across the wooden floor. It should have been impossible for anyone to get into his room, and he had not heard the door open. He should have been able to reach out for the pistol in the drawer of the table by his bed, but he couldn't move. It was not that he was paralysed with terror – although he was more afraid than he could understand – he truly was physically powerless to make the least movement. Then suddenly there was silence again, except for the spiralling moan of the mosquitoes, and the silence went on so long that Novius might have dared to hope the footsteps had been a dream after all, except for the fact that he still couldn't stir.

Then there was a whisking sound that seemed to scrape the very breath out of him – and the mosquito net collapsed around him like the end of the world. The wooden hoop that had supported it crashed onto his chest. He lay there, the hoop framing his head and shoulders, his terrified breath sucking the white fabric in and out, and he felt the bed shift and the net tighten as someone lay down beside him.

Through the milkiness of the net he could just make out a woman's silhouette. And his heart clamoured with horror, because although he could not see her features, and although she had not yet spoken, he could feel somehow that she hated him with more force and intent than he had known was possible, and still he could not move.

She was the boy's mother.

He waited for a knife to puncture his chest or to race across his throat, but instead she took his head in her hands, and it seemed that heat struck out from the ten points of her fingers, and swelled through his skull. And he heard a low, susurrating hiss as she began to whisper softly and steadily in his ear. At first he thought he understood the words, and then that he didn't, and then he could no longer hear her because his head was flooding and bubbling with heat, and his pulse roared in his ears like the sea. And he forgot all about her as the bed began to tip and wheel and he was past understanding anything.

In the morning Novius' slaves found him still lying under the net, which was now heavy and transparent with his sweat, his body juddering and trembling underneath it. The woman they found on the floor. She had stabbed herself.

After a day or two, his temperature went down and he explained what he could; he said a witch had put a curse on him in the night. He felt better, and he even laughed weakly about what had happened. But then the heat surged through him again, and his skin went yellow and he began to vomit blood. His doctors were sure he would die. Then suddenly the fever broke again, and this time his body recovered quickly. The jaundice faded from his skin and the hollow shadows between his ribs softened and disappeared. But he dribbled and cried like a child for no reason anyone could understand. Sometimes he attacked his attendants and sometimes he shouted obscenities and exposed himself. The illness had inflamed his brain and damaged it forever, they said. They sent him home to his wife, who looked after him for the rest of her life, poor thing, because every now and then he would get a little better and seem to recognise her.

No one would remember this (said Leo), but then fifteen years later one of his sons fell ill, and when he recovered he was just the same as his father. Even that might have been a terrible coincidence, but nearly thirty years after that, the daughter of the other son went mad, too. Sometimes it seems to lie quiet for a generation or even longer. But it has always come back. Until he was thirty-five, your Uncle Lucius was all right – a shy man, perhaps, he used to say he'd been born into the wrong family. But there was nothing wrong with him. He had a wife and your cousin Drusus, who was just a baby back then. But seven years before you were born, he started to say odd things under his breath, and to look at the ground or the sky when people spoke to him. When one day he began to be ill, he locked himself up in his bedroom and for two days and nights his slaves and his family heard him chattering and laughing and screaming to himself. When at last they broke down the door they found he was as he is now. It all happened just as it has for the last two hundred years.

The crucifixion of the boy and the suicide of his mother were horrible and frightening in a way Marcus could not understand at first, for, of course, he had heard of such things before. Slowly he realised that he was frightened simply because his father had intended him to be. He had not meant Marcus to be merely pleasurably chilled, he had wanted the story to grow indelibly into him, so that no amount of comforting could get it out again, and this was what happened. And over the next few nights, which Marcus had stopped sleeping through, Marcus decided his father had wanted him to feel not only frightened but guilty, and not only guilty but angry. But he didn't see what he had done for his father to want him to feel like that. But the other part of the story was worse, because it wasn't finished and it was to do with him. Soon Marcus began to turn his every thought over and over, looking for anything abnormal or misshapen. He started to force himself to stay awake at nights because he was afraid of his dreams. Dreams seemed real and weren't, and Marcus could see that they were pretty close to madness.

He still remembered the fight his parents had over this: his mother Clodia suddenly tipping a heap of papers onto the floor and shouting, 'You want everyone around you to be miserable.'

'I want him always to remember it,' his father had said. 'In any case, he had to know about Lucius at some point.'

'In that way? At this age?'

'It's a warning. It is a metaphor for Rome,' said Leo, with a grave, noble note in his voice.

'Don't you *attempt* to patronise me. You know I think the same as you. I don't know why you have to force it on a little boy, that's all.'

'If you understood what I'm trying to do, you'd see why.'

'I do understand it, and I can see that you're trying to be self-righteous and sadistic. You always are.'

Later Clodia had come to Marcus and hugged him so that he could feel her body was rigid with anger. She said, 'Your Uncle Lucius is the first case of whatever-it-is anyone can remember. And you're just as much my son as your father's, and there's no curse on my family.'

Marcus let himself sleep again, but he knew, really, that this was no reassurance. He never quite lost the habit of watching his own thoughts and wondering how he would tell if there was anything wrong with them. It was an induction; in the following years he realised gradually that everyone else in the family did the same thing, that his uncle and grandfather and all of them must have clung desperately to their power, in spite of it. And that they all watched each other, too. To accuse someone, to hiss, 'It's you. It's already happening to you. You will be next.' Sometimes it hovered between them, unspeakable and tempting. His mother, not bound by the family contract, must surely have said it to his father at some point.

Now he was sixteen, and his parents' car had ripped free of a road in the Gallic Alps, leaped like a fish and then slithered down sideways onto the rocks. But it wasn't true that he would never see them again. After Faustus' speech, they would be carried to the tomb of the Novii and lie there in state and under glass. He could go and see them whenever he liked.

Even when they got Uncle Lucius back to the ranks of the family, he wouldn't let go of Marcus' wrist, and evidently he did know him after all:

as if his real face were underwater and only half-visible. She believed that she observed all this as coldly as if she were thirty years older than her real age, which was fifteen.

Because she knew it was more or less what the woman was thinking, she added, 'I hope he's the heir. We need a handsome emperor.'

The woman grinned and said, 'I shouldn't be thinking this way, should I? It's all right for you. I'd be cradle-snatching.'

Una gave her a sweet false smile, and saw that she had done it badly and that the woman was beginning to think she was odd. Una went away before the woman began to wonder what she was doing alone and why she was clutching a shopping bag on a day when everything was shut, or guessed from her crumpled clothes and unbrushed hair that she had not been under a roof that night. She did not see the little scuffle by the bier or Marcus' tears.

Afterwards, as she hurried towards London Bridge, she wondered why she had stopped. Of course, there was the need to be inconspicuous, but she could have crossed the square quietly, that was not much of a risk. Why hadn't she done so? She clenched her teeth with sudden self-disgust. She was the last person who ought to be susceptible to Novian glamour.

There was hardly anyone on the bridge. The shops lining it were shut, which was supposed to show respect and meant that the shopkeepers could go and lay flowers on the steps of the temple of Dea Roma. And what good, thought Una acidly, was that going to do anyone? Would it console Leo and his wife for being dead? She indulged herself in scorn so as to get across the bridge; she needed it because with each step she became more giddy with panic, and the near-impossibility of what she meant to do came closer to choking her. She had hated the people in Julian Square, but now she longed for a crowd to hide in. She felt huge and obvious as the boy on the screen had been.

She scowled at herself. No one was particularly looking at her, and there was every reason to hope no one was after her yet: her little bedroom in the house in the Lupanarian District betrayed no signs of any intention. She had taken nothing with her, not even a coat, not even the handful of coins doled out to her two days before. It was all the money she was supposed to have.

As for the difficulty of what she was going to do next, and the appalling consequences of likely failure, they were now irrelevant. There was no possibility of changing her mind.

She didn't look back until she got to the other side of the bridge. Then she turned once and let herself see the steel crosses ranked along the banks of the Thames. They were empty, as she had known they would be, that was supposed to be a mark of respect too. Their reflections shivered blackly in the rain.

She imagined whiteness. It began as a single bright speck in her head, and spread until it bleached her out. It went on spreading until it bleached out everything.

Now she followed the magnetway line pushing through London for the south and Dubris. She crossed an abandoned car park, struggled over a crumbling metal fence, and fell among nettles and blackening buddleias in a patch of waste ground under the magnetway viaduct. She did not stop. She stooped under a buddleia's drooping stems and clawed determinedly at the place where the bricks had been loosened by the roots of weeds. She worked methodically to dispel the irrational certainty that what she was looking for would no longer be there.

But it was. She drew it out slowly: a dusty bundle of plastic, folded over and tied and retied on itself with paranoid care. Una sat down suddenly, holding it loosely with gentle, unbelieving fingers. She was limp with relief and more than relief; a sudden excess of happiness. It was ridiculous because she had scarcely done anything yet, but still, things were going as well as she could have hoped. This was almost the last of her hiding places. As soon as she had begun to find ways of getting money of her own, she had seen that there would be less chance of losing all of it if she divided it into widely separate troves. All that morning she had been touring these places: the holes she had dug under a bench by the statue of Hadrian in Paullinus' Park and in the overgrown forecourt of a derelict wrestling school; the space behind the cracked tiles of an abandoned bath-house. She was astonished that none of her stashes had been disturbed. In fact they had been hidden so carefully in places picked with such obsessive caution, that the only risk would have been if anyone had seen her burying the money, and she had been very sure that no one had.

A slick train shot cleanly overhead. Una laughed weakly. There were hundreds of people just above her, and they didn't know she was there. She could feel the dim chaotic hum of thought and feeling and memory, speeding unknowingly away from her. She lay back against the brick and looked up at the damp buddleia leaves. She remembered how painfully sweet the scent of the purple flowers had been in the early summer, when she had first hidden the pack of sesterces, how helpless the brown and red butterflies had been to free themselves from it. She had the idle thought that she would like to live there forever.

She was very tired. There were hours before she could do much more and it would have been safe, indeed wise, to sleep through some of them. But she didn't sleep, and it was not only that her clothes were still damp and she was cold. She had subdued the terrible vertigo she had felt on London Bridge, but it was not gone altogether.

At last she stood up stiffly and found herself sad at the thought of leaving this invisible place, and at the fact that all the hiding places scattered over London whose preciousness had sustained her for years would soon mean nothing to her. She dropped the packet into her shopping bag with the others. She did not unpick it; she knew what was inside and she was still afraid of attracting the attention of thieves between here and the last cache. There she was going to have to break her habit and hide everything together for a little while. It had to be ready to collect quickly after she found Sulien; if she found him; if there was an after.

She went east towards the Thames again. The funeral was over and a few shops and eating houses had begun to light up. Una ordered herself into one of them, bought lamb stew in a plastic bowl and made herself eat it. She was too possessed by anxiety and determination to feel hungry, but she knew that her stupid body was beginning to weaken, and it mustn't.

The pale London sky was darkening as she followed the long curve of the river towards the docks. She followed a concrete walkway along the water, marching briskly into the wet, dirty little wind, her arms tightly folded. She saw a cormorant plunge suddenly from its nest on a mooring post into the dark green water. She found she was thinking about the house in the Lupanarian District again. They would know she was missing by now, but perhaps they would think she had had an accident or been murdered. It sometimes happened. Maybe they had already given up on finding her.

She passed docks fat with spices, tea and oil. A siren blared somewhere up ahead: they were still unloading the ships. But the sunlight was getting very weak now and she was no longer afraid of being noticed. She pushed her thin body between the loose panels of a rusting mesh fence and stood for a moment looking out at the river. This was a dilapidated wharf, scattered with misshapen crates and empty barrels. The black husk of a warehouse squatted beside her. She crossed the yard and with some difficulty, hauled open the rotting door of a forlorn outbuilding. Inside it was crammed with rubbish; heaps of old rope, long coils of plastic tubing and sheeting, dried-up cans of paint and, for some reason, a bent door resting at an awkward slant on top of everything. She struggled through it all, finding her way by touch and the dim glow from ships on the river. There was a damp, mouldering smell and she heard a sudden skitter of claws behind her on the invisible concrete floor. This was her last and most recent hiding place, furthest from the Lupanarian District and established at the greatest risk. She'd had to be away from the house

18

far longer than was allowed. The lies she'd had to tell that time had felt thin and fragile, and though they'd seemed to believe her she'd been knocked about all the same. But she felt no pleasure at reaching the shed. She pulled a heap of litter away from the cheap black travelling bag she had hidden at the back and stared blankly at it. She wondered how long it would be before anyone found it, and what they would think, if she did not come back.

She put her head on her knees and perhaps this time she did sleep for a while; at any rate it was with a shock that she became aware again of the dark shapes around her and the odd sour smell.

It was raining again when much later that night she darted busily along a little road, trying to look as if she were hurrying somewhere else, never turning her head right or left. She had doubled back on herself and walked a mile or so west. Here the buildings rose right on the edge of the Thames, forcing the thin street around them and away from the water. The river military station was a brown dumpy little building perched with seeming precariousness on the embankment, its rump hanging out over the river. Una only lifted her eyes once towards the building: enough to take in the square, shut doors and the camera roosting above them. She kept straight ahead until she judged she was out of the invisible circle it cast into the street.

Beyond the station the street was open to the river again. She turned towards it, sticking close to the station's blank west wall, and peered back over the water. She saw that from the back of the building a long steel walkway led down to a broad landing stage, dimly lit, where snub patrol boats and long blunt custodial ferries were huddled. There were no cameras that she could see on the quay, which was not so very strange – the only obvious way to the boats was through the military station. Unless perhaps there was a camera on the back wall of the station? She couldn't tell at this angle. She took a breath and held it for a while. From this point on her plan had had to deal with unfamiliar things, it had had to become less precise exactly as it became more dangerous. She did not know which boat was the one she needed, or how to get on board without being caught.

But there was something she could do which gave her a few more chances than she would otherwise have had. Inside the building the men must know which boat was scheduled to collect prisoners from the ship in the Thames estuary: if they knew it, so could she. She could filter through their thoughts and carry out the things she needed. What she was going to do was far more difficult than offering the woman in Julian Square back her own opinions – those scraps of nonsense about Marcus had lain so flimsily on the surface that almost anyone could have picked them up – but it was the same.

Sometimes a stranger's thought would fly at her, fully formed and as bright and sharp as a fierce bird.

More usually it was like a long, soft buzz, a half-meaningless mutter endlessly falling apart and reforming, shot through with sharp threads of intention. That was tolerable and if she tried she could shut it out (but that was something she had not dared to do that day). But behind it always there were louder, more brutal noises: yelps and roars that belonged to pictures, lurid and ugly and bulging dangerously against the shame that contained them. She guessed these things were somehow necessary, or at least could not be helped; she knew, though she hated the thought of it, that her own wintry sharpness was shored up on the same squalor. This made it no easier to quell a disgust that was sometimes almost overpowering. If she wanted to, and often when she didn't, she could know people better than they could bear to know themselves.

People were like clumps of brambles rustling in a high wind, indistinct and making a faint continuous noise and painful to touch. Sometimes – but it was so difficult and so horrible – she could nudge the wind one way or another, turn a leaf over, separate the thorned branches so their shape became clear.

This was what she did now. She stood and pressed her

cold cheek against the wall of the station and pretended her skin was growing into it. Her eyelids fell, so that she saw the flaws in the brick softened and doubled through the film of her own wet lashes. Odd points of mood snagged her already from inside. There was someone . . . yes, there was a man trying to remember the words of a song and wanting to go home. He couldn't remember if the next word was 'regret' or 'forget' and without that he couldn't get onto the next line at all, and though he kept trying not to think about it, the broken song kept rising up in his mind and humming itself over and over, like an insect.

So Una half-shut her eyes and dropped invisibly through him like cold water into warm. She let herself spread out slowly, hesitantly, smoothing away her own shiver, until she as good as owned him. She was through and through him, and could see him as clear as if every piece of him were an eye of hers.

The boats, she whispered outside, pressed against the damp wall, not knowing she was moving her lips. The crosses. The morning.

The half-remembered song flickered away for a moment as the boats at the mooring stage rose suddenly in the man's mind, but at once the thought veered off – he remembered a boat his family had owned when he was a child, and then a bad picnic they'd had on a cold beach when they'd all argued horribly, and then a kind of cake they'd eaten – could you still get it? – and then what food he had in the cupboards at home, and then how he wished he was in his kitchen, about to go to bed.

Una waited patiently, letting the thread of thought spin itself out, hearing the song come back, and then she tried again. The boats. The executions.

This time he followed the thought readily, away from the nag of the song. The executions. Una was startled and unnerved by a shaft of pity for the prisoners. She did not want to see such things, so she pushed it aside and pressed imperceptibly: Which boat, she insisted. Which boat was going? And there she saw what she thought she needed: he hovered between two numbers: three and four; and there was a name: 'Nausicaa'. As soon as it formed the word fragmented and began to circle and reassemble itself meaninglessly: *causi-naa, au-cis-san, cause, nausea.*

She did not wait to see where the pieces settled. She rushed back to herself, sighing and scrubbing her face with her hands, trying to shake the man's personality off like dirty water. She felt soiled and sick. She hated doing what she had done, she hated the dilution of her own self, the residue of other people that clung to her, above all she hated the vile things which were always there and which she always saw. Unconsciously, she made a little raw noise in her throat like a sob and ran.

But even the throbbing revulsion driving her forward was not enough to shake her merciless grip on her purpose. So she stopped suddenly, clasping hold of the railing holding her back from the river, anchoring herself on the wet metal under her palms. It was just as well to be some distance away from the military station. She looked down at the dark water glittering below her and before she had time to think she swung herself over the barrier. But then she did hesitate for a moment, with only her heels on the concrete and her grasp on the railing holding her upright. Already her body was battered and worn out; if she went into the water now she would have to spend what was left of the night soaked in water fouled with chemicals and effluence.

Though her flesh recoiled from what was to be done, she did not seriously consider that there was any choice: giving up was unimaginable. She thought of the cormorant dropping from the mooring post – the river had to be clean enough to keep fish alive. She kept the thought of the bird diving safely after its prey to nerve herself. So Una turned, adjusted her grip on the railing, and lowered herself softly into the Thames.

She was already drenched from the rain, so the river wasn't as cold on her skin as she'd feared. Worse was the thick velvetiness of the floating sludge billowing against her, and the stench that bloomed off the water; a fresher, more vivid version of the smell in the wharfside shed. She swam slowly, just a gathering of black in the black water, letting her limbs hang under the surface so as not to break it.

When she reached the station she swam further out into the river, so that the landing stage was between her and the building. She reached up and hooked her fingertips over the edge of the platform and lifted her head and shoulders out of the water: from here the station looked huge and top-heavy, the walkway a strange thick arm pointing. As she had feared, there was a camera fixed over the station's back door, but she thought she might be safe if she kept to the shadows of the boats: there was so little light.

She let herself down into the water again and swam to the row of custodial ferries, pressing as close to them as she could to read the names and numbers painted on their sides. She hung for a while between two boats: yes, the boat numbered four had the name 'Nausicaa', but the man in the station had thought of the number three, too – perhaps it was the number that was important and the name had come up clinging to it like seaweed on a fishing line. She could do no better than guess, so she stretched up to catch hold of the gunwale, and hauled herself up onto the deck of the boat called Nausicaa, on the side furthest from the station and its camera. Without much hope she tried the door that led down to the cells. It was locked, as she'd expected. Keeping low against the bridge, she crept round to the stern of the boat. She sighed and closed her eyes for a second. She had expected no better, but the deck was stark and bare of places to hide. There was nothing except a large metal box about four feet high, built into the deck, which held gas cylinders and some low plastic tubs whose purpose she couldn't guess.

At last she ducked forward and wedged herself between the box and the bridge and sat there, coiled in an awkward knot, trying to still her shuddering body. The rain was easing, but now the air snatched the warmth off her wet skin.

As a place to hide it was pitiful; all she could do was trust in her ability to flick aside filaments of attention as they settled on her. But already she was almost sick with cold and weariness, soaked through with the man's thoughts and the green Thames.

[III]

STEEL CROSS

Sulien had lived five days longer as a result of the deaths of Marcus' parents, but the morning after their funeral the guards led him out of his cell in the prison ship on the Thames estuary and put him on the low-slung army boat bound for London.

They would already know his height and the span of his arms; they would have adjusted the settings accordingly. They would fix his arms and legs in place with leather straps and tighten them until the backs of his wrists were flat on the metal and his feet pressed hard against each other. Then they would turn a switch on the side of the cross, and three spikes would leap upright as surely as three keys entering three locks, undoing the knots of veins, puncturing the thick nerve that carried the precious feeling in his fingers, splaying the bones of his feet, violating the darkness of the flesh and finding the light again beyond the soft, vulnerable skin. Then a hydraulic pump would slowly raise the steel cross up to face the river, tipping him gently forwards so that his weight was slung between his pierced wrists, tugging the bones of his arms from their sockets, trapping the breath in his lungs. He might hang there fighting the cross for days; watching the barges going back and forth on the Thames, carrying coal and sugar and wine.

Sulien knew a lot about the body, and he could imagine intensely and accurately what was going to happen to him. He even thought that if he shut his eyes and concentrated on his own innocent nerves, he could imagine the pain. And yet he could not believe in it; it was impossible that sitting there, with all his flesh *knowing* it had decades ahead of it, he should really be dying more certainly than of any illness. His body was so convinced it could not happen that he was not even as afraid as he should be. He felt he could hardly move or think, and not really for fear but because he was so hypnotised by the certainty that this wasn't true, that there was more before him than hours of torture and then nothing.

Every half hour one of the officers would open the little hatch in the door and look in to make sure he had not found the one escape from the steel cross, the way through the wall of his own muscle and skin. Every time this happened it reminded Sulien that he really ought to have a go at killing himself. But he could not believe in that either – it was just not the sort of thing he would ever do. He got up and turned in a pointless little half-circle – trying to work himself up to it, or trying to persuade the walls around him of the laughable implausibility of his being about to die. 'Come on. Do it,' he said sternly, aloud. He sat down again and looked speculatively at his wrists. At once, he shuddered and clenched his right hand protectively around his left wrist, clutching so hard that his fingers could just feel the groove between the two thin bones. Gathering himself again he began to pull clumsily at the hem of his shirt, pretending that he would tear off a strip and twist it into a noose, knowing that he wouldn't. He could not think what to fix it to in any case; but people did kill themselves, even on suicide watch, so it must be possible. It was just somehow not possible for him.

The hatch opened again – how could that have been half an hour? It had scarcely felt like time enough to cross the cell.

Sulien had been owned all his life and scarcely noticed it. The word 'slave' was there, yes, but it had seemed to surround him painlessly, without touching him. Or that was not quite true – there were the years when he had still lived with his mother and sister; but they had become so shadowy to him. He saw his first years through a kind of cold, bluish-grey haze – it was the colour of the attic bedroom he had shared with his sister, but he had forgotten that. There had been a white-haired old man – monstrously old he had seemed to Sulien – who owned the house and Sulien's mother. He strode around and Sulien and his sister had to keep out of his way. His mother had shrunk to the impression of a moving pillar of quiet fretfulness – he remembered a voice, hissing anxiously, but scarcely anything it had said.

Just occasionally, it struck him as strange that were it not for a handful of bright, painful memories of his sister, he might almost have believed that he had simply not existed until his tenth year, but had appeared, fully formed, on the day Catavignus had bought him. But he never understood that his childhood was vague because he had made it so; he had made himself so elastic and pliable that his past had flown irretrievably over him like a fierce gale, leaving him intact and unmarked. He was springy and resilient as grass; he had a forceful talent for happiness – but he did not know that he had paid for these things with his memory.

His sister, however, would not fade so tractably. It was not that her appearance had remained very clear to him – she had had long straight hair, he knew that much, and dark brown eyes, and of course she had been smaller than him – it was rather the memory of her *presence*, and how essential that had seemed even when she annoyed him, that was still sharp. For all these years the lack of her, and the wrongness of it, had lasted like a soft but incessant ache. He remembered – oh, what? Fighting with her on the attic stairs, they must have been perhaps seven and six. He had pushed her harder than he meant to, and watched appalled as she fell and fell, and landed ages later crying and bleeding. He rushed down to her, already agonised with guilt: I'm sorry, I'm so sorry. Please don't tell. Please forgive me. His remorse was intense and ridiculous: he was certain she would hate him for the rest of her life. It was a tragedy! She punched him, but he just went on apologising until he was crying harder than she was. All right, I forgive you, she said at last, but he knew it was just to shut him up, so he kept on and on at her until she punched him again, hurting him this time. This seemed deeply unjust to Sulien, and his need for forgiveness diminished significantly. They had stamped upstairs together, silent and aggrieved. Then his memory blurred again, but he remembered trying to wash the blood out of her hair before his mother or the old man saw it, and looking at the edges of the wound on her scalp, and feeling an odd certainty that it ought to be possible for him to close it up, now, at once.

It was not until much later, when he was living with Catavignus and his family, that Sulien realised that the old man must have been not only his mother's owner, but probably his father too. He was faintly disgusted, because his mother was so young and the man so old – but he could summon up no stronger response. Although the old man had treated Sulien and his sister with indifference or at best with impatience, it did not occur to Sulien to resent him; nor did he wonder, as another child might have done, whether the fact that he had not been loved meant that there was something wrong with him. He knew there wasn't. And already that time had become remote and indistinct.

What had happened then? He knew but he couldn't remember. One morning the man, Sulien's father (but the word meant nothing to him) had a stroke. He did not die at once, and at first their lives were scarcely any different, except that Sulien and his sister did not have to be so careful to keep out of sight, and that their mother was more anxious than ever. But he did die, and for a while they had stayed in the house, cleaning it and packing things away, but now it – and they – belonged to someone else. But that was not to be for very long, because the family that was moving in had slaves of their own and could not afford three more. Besides, there would be no room for them. His mother drove himself and his sister to an eating house in Epidian Street and introduced them to a man called Rufius, who, in Sulien's memory, consisted mainly of sweat and beard. Sulien had a feeling his mother had hung around for a few hours, while Rufius showed them their bedroom and the kitchen, and taught them how to load the dishwasher. But then she went. The new family must have decided to keep her after all.

At first their mother visited them. Perhaps it had been quite often, although he did not remember it so; every week at first, maybe, later every month . . . time seems so much slower to children. Perhaps they cried and begged to be taken home every time she came, and in the end that was why she stopped coming. Sulien and his sister wiped tables and dried plates and were very unhappy. Sulien pictured these things happening, and could pity his younger self as he might have pitied a character in a story, but he could no longer distinguish the remembered pictures from imagined ones. And further on there were no images of any kind. There was an utter, pristine blankness, a glacier in the memory he made no attempt to cross. Somewhere in the whiteout was his sister – she went, she was sold off. Perhaps it was from the first day without her that Sulien began to flinch away from knowing how it had happened. There was no good in clinging to what she had been doing the last time he saw her, or the last thing she had said to him. He didn't want to miss her; he wanted to get her back. One day he would be able to. If he had to wait then he would. Having decided this, he let layers of faith grow and harden around it until the certainty was luminous and perfect, like a religious thing, like a pearl.

The first thing was to wait for a way of leaving the eating house. He did not exactly plan, but he prepared himself in other ways.

Among them there was something that for Sulien was more like the memory of a memory than the real thing:

Late one night, when he was almost ten years old, standing with his arms sunk up to his elbows in warm dishwater, he performed an experiment. Without thinking about it in the least, as if it were something he had always been going to do, he dragged a knife – a short, stubby thing they used for carrots – up out of the water, languidly placed its edge against the back of his hand and let it sink, scarcely pressing at all. Blood flowed riotously into the water, and a hot spark of pain lit itself on Sulien's hand. The blood fascinated Sulien as if it was the first or most beautiful thing he had ever seen. But he was shocked at having done such a thing – it was as if his body had acted without his permission. He didn't want to hurt himself. Indeed, though the cut was shallow, he was still a little boy, and the pain was almost enough to bring tears to his eyes. But almost at once the shock vanished, because after all it was quite obvious why he had done it. Of course the pain hadn't been what he was aiming for. It was a test.

Swiftly then, he took his hand out of the water and ruined a dishcloth by wiping the blood off with it. Then he laid his thumb over the cut, hiding it. Although a watery tendril of blood felt its way out from underneath, Sulien didn't see it. His eyes were shut and he was already shrinking down inside his own body until all of him that mattered was knitted into the cut skin and the tissues underneath it. It was almost like being plunged suddenly into a strange hectic town, where everything was bright and loud and volatile – except not really like that because he knew its every inhabitant, its every street. He could see everything, exact and perfect: the tiny blood vessels indignant and betrayed, but still beautiful. Why shouldn't it be easy to put it all right?

When he took his thumb away, the cut hadn't disapeared, of course. But it was only a neat seam of perfectly clotted blood, and it scarcely hurt at all any more. Sulien wasn't surprised.

So now he would wait for the right chance to do this again, in the right way. And one afternoon Rufius scalded himself dramatically, pouring boiling milk over his arm in front of all the customers. Before he could rush for cold water, almost before he could roar and swear, Sulien had begun to draw the heat out of the skin and calm the out-raged nerves.

He repeated his trick twice, three times – until the as-tonishment around him reached the right pitch and Rufius could sell him on for any price he chose. But while doctors and aristocrats and rich businessmen scrapped over him, Sulien knew that he would choose his new owner. When he did not like the look or the voice of the latest wealthy visitor to the eating house, he would simply refuse to perform. He would look at the bruise or blister or the grey sick face or whatever they presented to him, as if it were brick or concrete and nothing to do with him. Rufius would hit him, but somehow he could not hit him hard enough to make him change his mind.

Sulien did not exactly forget, but neither did he quite confront the fact that this – the first, convenient burn – had not been purely accidental. He had been at Rufius' side just before the hot milk surged out of the pan, and suddenly he had stumbled sideways, jostled, pushed. He kept the know-ledge aside from himself, like something dangerously hot. He knew he had hated Rufius, and wouldn't have blamed himself much for wanting to damage him, but he hadn't acted out of hatred. He didn't like to think of himself hurting someone so coolly, as part of a strategy. The thought of the injuries he'd refused to touch troubled him too.

When Catavignus came to the eating house, he did not drag along some wretched patient and wait for Sulien to prove what he could do. Instead, he managed to get Rufius to leave them alone, which was a good start in itself. Sulien looked at him warily. Catavignus sat down at one of the long eating-house tables (the place had been closed to customers since the bidding war over Sulien began). Sulien saw that Catavignus wanted him to sit down opposite him, and his first impulse was to do so, but he stayed standing. He had learnt how to be cautious, even if it wasn't entirely natural to him. Catavignus was a doctor – a famous surgeon, although Sulien did not know that at the time. He was just past fifty, short and burly, with very fair hair, whitening early to an ugly butter-yellow. Behind his elegant silver-framed glasses, his eyes were bright blue and huge like those of a baby.

'How do you do it?' asked Catavignus at last, simply.

The hysteria Sulien's talent provoked had been such that no one had quite asked that before. Rufius had told prospective buyers that Sulien was possessed by a benign but unpredictable demon (which explained the occasions when he wouldn't exhibit his strange ability); sometimes he said that he was inspired by Apollo or Asclepius. Any of these explanations might have been true for all Sulien knew – because how could he tell what such things would feel like? But now he was taken aback by the strength of an unexpected desire to explain the strange, mesmeric process in which sight and touch seemed to merge into a single sense that drew him down into the midst of such intricate beauty.

Catavignus listened intently and courteously, restraining his surprise to an occasional bob of his eyebrows above the silver glasses, and asked Sulien to describe, in detail, the veins and nerves and muscle he saw. Then he stood up, looked at Sulien almost ruefully for a moment and said, 'What's the highest offer on you so far?'

Sulien told him, and added cheerfully, 'but I think you'll have to bid at least another third again, sir.' He had decided both that Catavignus was rich enough to afford him, and that he was glad of it. And he rather liked the thought of being so expensive.

Catavignus smiled, sighed at the cost, and went out. Sulien was happy. Already he was folding up the eating house – and the whole of his childhood – and packing it safely away.

Catavignus' house was beautiful. All of its many rooms glowed quietly with colour and wealth, everything clean and elegant and tasteful under a thin film of friendly disorder. There were attic rooms for the other slaves, but Sulien was not to have one of these. His bedroom looked out onto the trees of Paullinus' Park, and it was as warm and almost as well furnished as the rest of the house. If it was at first just faintly impersonal, that was only because it was so new to Sulien. Over the next few years he would fill it with his own things – pictures and music and books.

If Catavignus became even richer and the house became more beautiful during the years Sulien lived there, and if this was because of Sulien himself and his gift, why should he have minded? He lived in the midst of beauty and affluence; he had almost everything he wanted. Catavignus gave him, if not a salary, regular gifts of money, and taught him, meticulously, to name every organ and bone his curious gift allowed him to see, and to recognise various diseases and injuries, and to understand their treatments. He poured his own learning into Sulien – and Sulien loved it all, both for the sake of the books and the comfort, and because of Catavignus himself.

It was not exactly that he treated Sulien like a son; it was rather that the strain of not doing so was pitifully obvious. He never said or did anything that went beyond the polite friendliness a good assistant deserved, but when he appraised Sulien's absorption of medical history and anatomy, his voice would grow raw with barely restrained affection. When Sulien grew unexpectedly tall, Catavignus blinked up at him, moved and proud, as if Sulien's height somehow reflected well on him. If all this was obvious to Sulien, it must have been far more so to Tancorix, who was Catavignus' daughter. It was for her sake Catavignus tried to pretend he felt nothing but kindly interest for Sulien, but his failure to disguise the daily betrayal of her was wretchedly clear. Both Sulien and Tancorix knew love when they saw it.

Tancorix was a year and a half older than Sulien, and she disliked him as soon as Catavignus brought him home. No – probably it was even before that, for Catavignus showed an enthusiasm about the mere idea of Sulien that he had never quite mustered for Tancorix. When Sulien first saw her she was almost twelve, her father's pale blond hair and blue eyes incongruous on a plump, awkward body and a face assaulted early by acne. She hated her appearance ferociously: she already had little breasts between her hunched shoulders and large stomach, her yellow eyebrows were square and menacing, her mouth was large, her nose seemed to have nothing to do with the rest of her blemished face. She hated these things so much that it was, perversely, a comfort to make herself look worse: she wore huge, tent-like dresses that must have been meant for someone three times her age; and when Sulien arrived she was in the middle of a long campaign of refusing to brush or wash her hair, so that it hung in lank ropes and bunches and smelt faintly rancid. Catavignus' attempts on her hair, and his badly timed suggestion that he or Sulien do something about her spots, provoked violent outpourings of rage and grief. Sulien would slink tactfully from the room whenever this happened, but it made no difference. On one of these occasions he ran into Huctia, the housekeeper, on the stairs. They rolled their eyes at each other knowingly as Tancorix wailed and thundered.

'You might as well have stayed in there,' said Huctia. 'She wants you to hear.'

It was true. Tancorix dealt with her unhappiness as she did her ugliness – by making it violent and spectacular.

'Oh,' Tancorix was howling, 'oh, why do you hate me so much?'

Sulien and Huctia heard the sad murmur which was Catavignus saying that of course he didn't hate her.

'Yes, you do, you do!' shrieked Tancorix. 'You wish I'd never been born. Then you'd be happy and you wouldn't have to look at my face!'

Huctia grimaced and Sulien copied her. It was somehow easiest to get on with the other slaves when they were all hiding away together from Tancorix's outbursts – there was a sense of companionship that was usually impossible. Sulien was aware that they must resent him at least a little – they knew he was a slave only in name. He had to be

34

careful never to forget and order them to do something, as Tancorix or Catavignus might. He wore himself out being charming to them, so they wouldn't hate him. He couldn't stand to think of being hated.

Now they heard Catavignus sighing gustily with mingled exasperation and guilt. He didn't hate Tancorix, of course, but he could not persuade himself to love her very much either, and in any case it was hard to keep the impatience out of his voice when she was like this. 'Do stop being absurd, Tancorix,' he said weakly.

Tancorix roared, ridiculously, 'You are an *intolerable human being*!' and banged out of the room. Sulien ran up the stairs to get out of her way, because Tancorix was quite likely to attack him on these occasions, and he didn't like to fight back. He didn't want more clamour. This time Tancorix only pushed him against the wall as she thudded past him and said, 'And *you* are a horrible little *rodent*, I *hate you*.' Her insults were always overblown and preposterous, like everything else about her.

Sulien didn't hate Tancorix. He felt too sorry for her and had not yet realised that was part of the reason she disliked him so much.

But she was not always there. To Sulien's and Catavignus' guilty relief, she spent half her time with her mother in Gaul. This time, she went early, stepping tight-lipped into the car that would take her to Dubris, and staring rigidly ahead. But she broke her dignified silence to say bitterly to Catavignus, 'You needn't expect to see me again, so start celebrating.'

They would see her again, of course; but the next time she appeared her hair would be short and wild-looking – her mother found the oily mats of hair were too far gone to be combed out, and cut them off.

Released from her presence, Catavignus was free to find Sulien's sister. Of course, Sulien had intended that he should from the minute he saw him, and Catavignus had been fairly quick to promise it, once the boy had made himself so indispensable. After all, with what Sulien had earned in patients' fees, Catavignus could afford to buy him a dozen sisters.

But this one seemed to have dropped out of sight and out of finding. Her name seemed to have been changed at least once, and no one had kept her long. Catavignus found only a number of places where she was said to have been; another eating house, a slave market, a family who had wanted a maid-of-all-work. 'I don't know what you want with *that* one,' said the cook of this last household. 'She didn't last two weeks here. She just *stopped* one day, she wouldn't so much as move a step – she wouldn't even make her own bed, let alone anyone else's. Wouldn't explain herself. It didn't matter what you did to her.' An overseer at a textile plant said that on the contrary, she had been very biddable, they'd have kept her if the business hadn't taken a turn for the worse. Catavignus began to think his inquiries had taken a wrong turning somewhere – surely the cook and the overseer weren't talking about the same girl.

He couldn't help getting tired of the search. He was sick of fruitless treks across London, of handing over little wads of sesterces for information that got him nowhere; and though he wasn't sure whether to believe the cook's story, it had made him worry about the girl's character. Suppose he found her, and realised he did not want such a person in the house? He should never have promised anything so rashly. He felt thoroughly tempted to give up the whole thing, and indeed he couldn't bear to waste another hour on it – but it would be terrible to disappoint Sulien so. As a compromise, he handed responsibility over to Huctia, who wearily followed the lost girl's erratic career until she traced her to a family who denied all knowledge of her, under any name. The spasm of relief Catavignus felt dispersed itself rapidly. He would have to tell Sulien.

Now, in his gently rocking cell on the prison ferry, Sulien was on his feet again, his breath suddenly sharp in his throat, his heartbeat just a raw trembling against his ribs.

His arms and shoulder were bruised. He had flung himself twice – stupidly – against the door almost without realising it. 'Catavignus, *please*,' he found he was saying, and he laughed, startling himself. That would have been no good, even if Catavignus had been there to hear him. But it was so hard to believe; he wanted so badly to be able to forgive him, as he had allowed himself to years before when his sister had not been found. Back then, feeling all his faith breaking down around him, he had wept and shouted as Tancorix would have done; but he let Catavignus comfort him, and he had made the bargain with himself that he always made: *that's all right, that can happen – because later . . .*

Later, when he was grown up, Catavignus promised him he would be freed, and then he knew he would find her. It would be different for him, almost easy, because it was meant to happen. The right thing might tease and hesitate, but *must* come in the end.

So even now, he kept looking for and finding excuses for Catavignus' failure to save him, because the idea of Catavignus as helpless as himself was far more bearable than believing he had made a real choice to let Sulien die – and like this, *like this*.

He retreated, the steel cross suddenly bright on the inside of his eyes and lowered himself shuddering to the floor. He laid his cheek on the cool metal bench, and fitted his palm to his hurt shoulder. The ache there would have been easy to bear, but it was the last hurt he could undo, so he warmed it away. He said his sister's name once or twice.

Early that summer, Tancorix had left school for good. She had scarcely been to London in two years – when she had not been at school in Narbo, she had been in Rome with her mother, being introduced to people and trying to learn to be charming. But now she was seventeen and a half, and her parents, who otherwise did not see much of each other, had agreed to collaborate, briefly, to bring their daughter to general notice; and to begin to put out gentle feelers for a possible husband for her. Both Tancorix and her mother returned to Britain.

Boxes and trunks of their possessions arrived before they did, making Sulien oddly uneasy. He dreaded the return of noise and shrill anguish, whirling and bouncing round the house after two years of peace. When the day came, Catavignus, almost equally apprehensive, gave him the afternoon free, and he loitered in the park with his friends as long as he could, putting off his return to the invaded house.

Some of his friends were the sons and daughters of free men, but none were slaves. If he had been more self-conscious about his strange status this might have been impossible, but he simply expected friendship and attention, and got them. He spent some of the day wandering aimlessly under the trees chatting with dark-haired Paula, resting in the friendly warmth of their uncomplicated attraction to each other. Sometimes they kissed, because, they said, there was nothing else to do, and sometimes they lay on the grass in the sun together and Sulien would drape an experimental arm over her side, onto her breast or hip. Then she would wriggle away. He was pretty sure that she would stop wriggling away if he put his mind to it, but he had not quite decided whether he wanted to. Things were quite pleasant as they were.

Eventually the afternoon grew colder, and Paula said she had better go home. Sulien delayed her a little while, but she went and there was nothing else to do in the cooling park. So at last he went back to the house and found Tancorix in the living room, lying curled in a shaft of late sunlight, like a golden Persian cat.

He could not have said she was unrecognisable. Indeed, it was startling to see here and there, in certain curves and correspondences of feature, unmistakable traces of the ugly child she had been. But everything about her had suddenly, or so it seemed, resolved itself into order; and grace lay over her once raw features like a delicate and glittering veil. Her large mouth, very slightly reddened, no longer looked formless and sullen, but rich and sensual in the calm oval face.

Her eyebrows had been plucked into fine bows. Her hair, clean and primrose-bright, fell from a kind of intricate crown of little plaits and curls, down into long spirals and helices of pale gold which lay gleaming on the sky-blue fabric of her dress, and on the warm skin of her rounded neck and breasts. When she stood up the dress, embroidered simply with ivy leaves at the sleeves and hem, would fall demurely to mid-calf, but now it lay in careless folds over her knees, displaying smooth legs crossed at the ankle. She was slimmer than she had been, but not thin; her body had a softness and pliancy and firmness, and a depth of colour that made the usual language for female beauty more than usually appropriate: fruit and roses, but also expensive materials, like silk, like velvet.

If the light had been very harsh you would have seen the faint scattering of poignant little round scars on her cheeks and forehead, where the angry spots had once been. Even then, she would have been beautiful.

She had not seen him yet – she was looking expressionlessly at a little book in her lap, her eyelids lowered. Sulien stood for a second in the doorway, stopped dead at the sight of her. He was delighted, and not only because of the little darts of pleasure and urgency she had set loose in his body. It would have been ridiculous to say 'Well done!', but he almost wanted to, he would have liked to congratulate her on the wonderful good fortune of coming to look like that. She sat there like proof of his faith in the benevolence of things.

Then he stepped a little further into the room, and she looked up, so that he saw the always-startling blue of her unchanged eyes.

'But you're so tall!' she said. She jumped up and came closer, so that he could have touched her. The top of her head barely reached his shoulder.

'It's terrible!' she was smiling. 'When did you get like that? And I'm such a dwarf. No one would ever think I was older than you.'

It was true, and not only because he was tall. At fourteen

he had briefly looked pitifully gangling and loose-strung, like a terribly stretched little boy, but he did not look that way any more. His body tapered neatly from shoulder to narrow hips, and he had been told he was handsome often enough to have to believe it.

'You wouldn't want to be tall,' he said. 'I knock everything over. My feet stick out of my bed. My legs don't fit under desks.'

In fact, he loved being tall.

'It's good to see you,' he said.

'You needn't sound so surprised,' she answered, and they laughed.

'I like your hair,' he said, almost as another girl might have done, but not quite innocently.

She plucked at a long coil of it. 'Well, it took me forever to get it like this. It makes your arms hurt, doing all these plaits yourself. But mother says she'll get me a girl for that sort of thing.'

And then she glanced away, biting her lip, and Sulien realised she thought that by mentioning the buying of slaves, she had insulted him. He felt the prickle of incredulity and distaste he always felt when reminded that he was supposed to be a slave. But it passed quickly – the important thing was that she cared about offending him.

'Where's Catavignus and . . .' he felt embarrassed about using her mother's name, which was Prisca.

Tancorix sighed elaborately and glanced up at the ceiling. 'Deciding what's to be done with me. Disposing of me. There's this boy *already* . . .'

Then they heard two pairs of feet on the stairs, and flew apart instinctively, without knowing why they should do so.

He did not eat with the family that night, and accepted this as only to be expected.

The next day whenever he saw Tancorix she would smile at him furtively from behind her parents' backs. Already they felt like conspirators. In the surgery her face floated between him and his patients.

He caught a brief glimpse of the family that evening, before Catavignus took his daughter out into the city. Prisca had a hand on her daughter's shoulder, and her handsome face was lined with barely contained impatience. She sighed a lot. Catavignus kept looking at Tancorix with a mild and puzzled frown, as if he could not think who she was and what she was doing there. Tancorix's face was a patient, pleasant blank, which would have been unthinkable a few years before. But she saw him through the crack of the surgery door and her lips twitched.

He ate alone again and went back into the surgery. He spent some time pointlessly checking the arrangement of the little bright instruments in their trays. Then he settled himself on the patient's couch and read. He couldn't understand what he was doing. They had made no arrangement, but he was sure somehow Tancorix would come and find him there, sooner or later.

Much later he heard the three of them return, and felt the house stir and clatter and then settle into silence again. Still he waited. And then the door handle turned stealthily and Tancorix stepped self-consciously into the surgery. They both laughed, and hushed each other. They came closer together and their eyes met for an embarrassingly long time. They laughed again, mock-guiltily. He knew the laughter was an acknowledgement of something, and thought about kissing her, but he hesitated and asked her, politely and boringly, if she'd had a good evening.

'Theatre. So *boring*,' said Tancorix, wincing. 'I suppose you can't blame the plays for being boring, when all the audience is looking at is each other.' She was dressed for being looked at, in white. She hopped daintily onto the patient's couch and then bounced off again saying, 'Urgh. Ill people. How *can* you?'

In the end they both sat down on the floor, like children, and again embarrassed themselves by looking at each other. He asked, 'Are you glad you've left school?'

Tancorix's face grew still. Then she said softly, 'Yes. Oh, yes. I hated it.'

'Why?'

She frowned, and went on slowly. 'You remember me, when I was younger. I was bound to have a bad time, wasn't I? Of course lately . . .' she paused again and looked down modestly at her lovely body. 'Since I began to see I could look all right, lots of the girls suddenly wanted to be nice to me . . . people who . . . never used to leave me alone.' Her voice tightened to a stop. But she shook the sudden strain out of her face and smiled brightly.

'What do you want to do now?' said Sulien.

'Well, that's a silly question. What's the good of wanting to do anything, there's nothing I could do. I know what I *will* do, though: be paraded around the theatre and the Games, and then get married to some rich boring man. Get divorced later, I hope.'

She stretched, exquisitely, and lay back on the carpet looking up at him. 'Oh, *so boring*, the whole rest of my life is going to be *so boring*.' She said this gently, humorously. 'I think I would rather be a vestal virgin and have nothing to do with anything.' Then she lowered her eyelids and said blandly, as if not to him: 'Except I'm not really qualified, of course.'

He was shocked and fascinated, and could not think what he could politely say. She opened her eyes suddenly to see how he was taking it, and they smiled at each other. She said softly, 'If I could just have *one thing*, one thing that wasn't boring before . . .'

So he leant over and kissed her.

Her lips parted swiftly, her quick little tongue whetting the line of his teeth. He shivered. Her fingers went up and met in his hair, pulling down. He laid a tentative hand on her waist, suddenly uncertain, and she dragged it impatiently upwards onto her breast, rucking up her white dress as she did so. He felt her bare thigh under his clothed body, and her startled heart, unexpectedly violent under his fingers. She was not after all, perfectly self-assured.

At length their hot faces parted a little, his head bowed against hers, their soft hair mingling, and they laughed again, very quietly, at the fact they were lying on the surgery floor, at everything. That night they crept back to their separate rooms and stayed there, but not the next.

Sulien hovered, apprehensive, on the landing outside Tancorix's door. It was childishly exciting, prowling around in the dark house. Tancorix came and placed her hands resolutely on either side of his thin waist, and blind with kissing, struggling awkwardly out of their clothes, they stumbled backwards together into the shadowy room and the soft bed. They were inept and bungling with each other, but their clumsiness struck them as funny, and throughout their blundering love-making they kept having to smother each other's laughter. Sulien, afraid of looking – and being – artless and ignorant, was actually relieved to find that despite her advantage in age and the revelation of the night before, she seemed scarcely more skilful than he was. Although he had a small store of contraceptives from the surgery, which Catavignus had tactfully begun leaving in his way six months before, he had not needed them until now. He was afraid she would notice or guess that this was new to him, but she said nothing.

They fell heavily asleep, warm and entangled, her bright hair spilling over his chest. But it seemed almost at once that he woke to her shaking him and her frantic whisper in his ear: 'Get out, quick, get out!'

Sulien opened his eyes reluctantly. 'What's wrong? What time is it?'

Tancorix was scarcely awake herself. She looked up dimly at the dawnless sky and dropped back on the pillow, sighing. 'Sorry. I thought it was later. We shouldn't have gone to sleep. Suppose my parents . . . oh . . .' She hid her face against him and groaned. He stroked her hopefully, but she didn't look up.

'Do you wish . . . we hadn't?' he asked, after a while.

She grinned up at him through her hair. 'No. But it's *really bad*, isn't it? We really *shouldn't*.'

'I don't think it's bad,' he said cautiously.

'Don't you understand?' She pulled herself up to look

43

down at him curiously and then laughed. 'No, you don't, do you, poor innocent thing,' she kissed him on the forehead as if she were a great deal older than him. He made a face, insulted, but she didn't seem to notice. 'I'll be married in a year or two, probably. It's bad enough that I've slept with anybody, you must see that. But . . . a slave . . .' Her smile had vanished and she hesitated before going on. 'Did you know that if they found out a free woman had a slave for her lover they used to kill them both? Then later, they used to just take the woman's freedom away instead. That's still the law. I don't think they actually enforce it much these days, but it doesn't make any difference. Of course men can do whatever they want; but if you're a girl it's the worst thing you can do. If anyone knew . . . no one would touch me. They'd think I was . . . *disgusting*.'

Sulien got silently out of the bed and began an un-dignified hunt for his clothes. Tancorix was pulling her nightdress on. 'It's just the way it is,' she remarked flatly, 'It's not my fault.'

'No,' he said dully.

She leant across the bed and reached out to touch his arm. 'Tell you what,' she said, flirtatious again now, 'tomorrow night we won't go to sleep.'

And though he crept back to his room trying to shake free of what she'd said, he was back at her door the next night, and in those secret, quickening hours, it was easy to forget there was any threat, any danger at all. As the month drew on they grew more confident, cleverer with each other, and it was no longer laughter they had to stifle.

But one night they met too early, and perhaps they were not cautious enough with the juddering bed, or their own soft cries – though they thought they were being as quiet as they always were. But whether it was because of the sound, or suspicion, or some other errand that was instantly forgotten, Prisca suddenly opened the door and brought the light crashing in on them.

Light, and screaming. He would not have thought embarrassment could be so total and so appalling. It was like boiling water all over them, their skin scorched. They slithered apart and out of the bed, clutching at the sheets and their strayed clothes for cover as Prisca advanced. She aimed a floundering swipe at Sulien and stumbled as it didn't connect, and as he backed away she clawed out for Tancorix. The room was lurid with incoherent noise – Prisca's outraged yelling and their own stuttering appeals for her to stop.

What he mainly remembered was Tancorix's mouth opening and how all her new beauty puckered and trembled, like a curtain before an open window.

Prisca caught Tancorix confusedly by the hair and hit her across the face, and the blanket dropped from Tancorix's fingers, revealing her again. Tancorix crouched, sobbing, scrabbling for the cloth, but Prisca, grabbing blindly at hair and bare skin, pulled her up and dragged her from the room. The door slammed shut.

Sulien stood there helplessly, naked and horrified, and quite failed to imagine what would happen next because he truly believed that nothing could be any worse. So the moment in which he might possibly have dashed out of the room and the house was lost, for a minute later he heard a scrape on the floor outside, and when it occurred to him to try the door he found it wouldn't open – Prisca had wedged something under the door handle.

He got dressed quickly, the feel of clothes on his shamed skin a very slight comfort. He could hear a continued babble of raised voices coming up from the floorboards, and more doors slamming. Then for a long while nothing happened, and time went from moving in bright dreadful jumps to a dead calm, in which it began almost to seem that he might stay locked in Tancorix's pretty, little-girl bedroom forever.

Then he heard a thudding on the stairs – two people, both too heavy to be Catavignus or Prisca, approaching the room. And as the chest outside the door was pushed aside, and the two uniformed vigiles rushed at him, Sulien began to realise how things were not standing still, they were accelerating relentlessly into the blank and incomprehensible future.

Their hold on him was as tight as if he'd been fighting like a maniac. He wasn't, although he tried instinctively to hang back. His arms were pinioned, and struggling was quite obviously useless, even if he hadn't been too stunned. But as they forced him forward they kept jerking him off his feet, so that it was almost as hard to co-operate as to resist. 'What—?' he kept saying. They dragged him painfully down the stairs, and there were Catavignus and Prisca in the hall. Catavignus was standing hunched in the surgery doorway, his head bowed, and at the sight of him Sulien's shocked passivity disappeared and he began a useless pitching and wrenching towards him. 'What—?' he was still saying, as if he had a stammer. He thought he could hear Tancorix crying somewhere, but he couldn't see her.

Prisca, answering him but not looking at him, stated emptily: 'He raped my daughter.'

'Rape?' said Sulien stupidly. Catavignus straightened a little, but did not lift his eyes.

'Does she say so?' Sulien said into a room that might as well have been empty. And as he said it, Sulien had a sudden jolting vision of Tancorix, twelve years old and wild with fury and despair. Could she . . .

'Catavignus,' he cried, really desperate now, but still sure that Catavignus must make some move, must *try*, at least. 'Catavignus, you know I never would, you *know*—'

And at last Catavignus looked up, and *surely – surely*, Sulien thought, imploring. But Catavignus just glanced at him with eyes full of inert misery, and looked away at once, and as the vigiles wrestled Sulien out of the house he was sure he had been right about one thing only: Catavignus did know. He knew, and neither then nor later when Sulien was sentenced, did he do anything.

So Sulien had been owned all his life and never felt it, but if he had been anything other than a slave there would have been no lie and no arrest; and if he had been, as he had unconsciously considered himself, a Roman citizen, there would have been no question of crucifying him, no matter what he had done.

The hatch in the door opened again. The half-hours were still tearing on obscenely. Sulien did not look up to see the brief slice of a human face, and scarcely heard the guard walk away. A little later there was a metallic thud some-where outside. Someone in one of the other cells began screaming and swearing.

A minute or two passed with amazing numb swiftness, and then there was a little noise, a click that was not the sound of the hatch opening. Sulien felt the muscles in his shoulders, already knotted, tighten even further, because it was a key, a key turning in the lock, so all the time must have gone and they were ready to take him out to the cross.

And yet the boat was still moving . . .

Then the door opened and closed softly, and in the little cell was a thin girl with long wet hair, whose white face turned to him and seemed to flicker through layers of strangeness, until the features of his sister swam up to the surface from seven years' depth.

Una was so tired now that her body felt like a heap of rusting machinery, and yet, as she huddled behind the gas case on the rear deck, she had to keep every sense stretched wide. When the cohort officers boarded the boat she had to stretch a finger of her mind out to rest on each one of them, ready to tap them gently away whenever they came too close to her meagre hiding place. Even once the officers were settled in the cockpit, there was still everyone else on the river to worry about; merchants and deckhands on the other barges, and, as the morning wore on, more and more people passing to and fro on the banks of the river. And all the time every exhausted shred of her was trying to pull her down into indifference; she almost thought she didn't care what happened to Sulien or herself if only she could lie down on the deck and let her eyes shut and her flagging brain go slack. But still she sat, upright and aching, as the boat toiled along. At least she was no longer shivering much. The morning had brought a glaze of warmth to her chilled skin, though beneath it the night's cold seemed to have pooled in her flesh and bones.

At last the boat crawled out of London, and drew up alongside the huge black square of the prison ship. Una felt the boat shudder and stop, then shift a little in the brown water as a gangplank was fitted to it. Then she heard the clanking steps of the nine prisoners as they were herded down onto the ferry, and there was her brother. She hadn't moved from behind the box, so she couldn't see him; but there he was, there he was, unmistakable, like the right tune after a silence of seven years.

Una found that for all her long-held certainty that she would find him again, she was quite unprepared for this. Harsh and unfamiliar tears rose in her hot eyes, and a maundering little voice in her mind began crooning weepily *'seven years, seven years'*, on and on to itself. She was never like this. Just sometimes from an unremembered nightmare she would wake to find her cheeks wet; otherwise she hadn't cried in years. Disconcerted, she struck angrily at her eyes and scowled the resisting moisture down. But the tremor of feeling seemed to shake a little temporary strength into her, and as the boat turned and pushed back towards London she found she could think again.

They were checking the prisoners every half hour. That was bad, she had not thought of that. Still, half an hour – if the escape went unnoticed that long they might get some way. Outside London the river was calmer, so she stood cautiously, feeling her joints creak a protest as if they had aged fifty years in the night, and she crept around the bridge and looked into the cockpit. She was just slightly more confident now – the noise of the engine was almost enough to cover her light steps without the little pressure of her will on the officers' minds.

There were four of them and all had heavy guns at their sides. And behind them, on the cockpit wall, was a little key cabinet with an electronic lock. She bit her lip, hesitating. Then with a brief spasm of effort she plucked the combination from the memory of the nearest officer, and then fled back to the stern of the boat. She could see no way of getting the key except by stepping into a little space with four armed men.

She felt a weak final stirring of panic, but really she was too tired and had come too far to pay much attention to it. But she could not act yet; she had to wait until the ferry was close to her run-down wharf.

Beneath her in the cells, she could feel the steady swell of the prisoners' terror. She tried to push it back or reduce it at least to an homogenous murmur; but she could not help picking out the distinct cadence of Sulien's gradual drift from baffled disbelief into horror; and there was a particular little echo of pain when his memory of herself struck her, and she saw how it prompted a rush of despair. It was terrible to wait, with the crosses always getting closer.

Then the old walls of London closed them in, and again the river was loud with barges and tugs. Through the riot of traffic, all the wharfs looked much alike. She watched, and sometimes her exhaustion stole up on her and her concentration would falter, and she would slip with it into a kind of passive emptiness. And then she would start back into alertness, afraid the ferry had already gone too far.

But there – she thought she recognised the particular red of a warehouse roof. The empty wharf was just ahead. In a minute or two it would be behind them. Now.

She stood, and then dropped back just in time as one of the officers left the cockpit to check the prisoners. That was good – one less to deal with. How long would he be? Three minutes, perhaps?

She ducked along the deck round to the cockpit, scraping together her last lees of energy to urge every pair of eyes around her to look anywhere but at the prison ferry. She knew she would have to keep that up while at the same time doing something immeasurably more difficult, with no strength left to spend and the fourth officer about to clatter up onto the deck.

Kneeling beside the cockpit door, she poured herself in like smoke, hung in the air, made them breathe her into their blood and brains. Spread between the three of them she felt dangerously thin and half-dissolved, and outside the metal door her body felt dark and alien, like an arm lain on and gone numb in the night.

It was the opposite of what she had done to the man in the military station: instead of trying to turn their thinking a particular way she was trying to disperse all thought, to lull them down, through the usual flotsam of trivia and casual wishes into an abstraction so deep not even a stranger's step behind them would break it. She found she was helped by the rhythmic thrum of the engine, and the patterns of the water ahead. She heard the low hum of conversation ebb and stop. But she could not seem to draw them into the state she wanted without half entering it herself; she was split between gentle lassitude and her own desperate wakefulness. But she was so tired, she felt any second she might lose the balance and fall free of them, back into herself, happily half-asleep.

Outside on the deck her body raised a heavy arm and pulled at the door handle. It was like aiming your movements by looking through a mirror. Her clumsy fingers misjudged, closed on nothing and dropped. She tried again, pulling a little of herself back into her own skull. The handle turned. She saw the officer steering the boat lift his head a little and froze, still gripping the handle. But he turned back to watch the river again, and she felt the little spark of wakefulness die out.

She opened the door and stepped softly in. Part of her was, with the youngest soldier, vaguely intent upon the taste and density of the thumbnail he was probing between his teeth. No one stirred. She threaded her body through the narrow space behind the soldiers' seats, and reached out with a sleepwalker's laziness to the key cabinet. The steersman was unknowingly watching the ridges of the water split and join in perfect diamonds. She tapped in the combination, wincing at the tiny sounds it made. Again she felt a threatening stir of awareness from a man beside her, and stopped dead, trembling. Again the motion faded. She took the bundle of keys, closed the cupboard and, still slowly, still gently, drifted out of the cockpit.

The guard was coming up the steps. The door opened just as Una, thrown violently back to herself again, dashed past to the stern, in full sight and unprotected. A bargeman saw someone run along the length of the low grey boat, but as he turned to look more closely his interest somehow seeped away, and a minute later he forgot it.

The second the guard was inside the cockpit, Una shot through the door and down the steps. When she reached the bottom something happened to her sight and the floor at once darkened and diminished while swinging slowly upwards to strike her knees and slap the keys from her hands. It was a second before she understood that her legs had folded under her. She scrambled up, furious with herself, groping for the bunch of keys. Had anyone heard her fall? Yes, but only the prisoners. The air was naked now with fear. Someone, not Sulien, had begun screaming and sobbing, a horrible sound. But she folded her lips and pushed the din back as far as she could. Some of the prisoners were praying, which interested her a little.

She went forward. Both the keys and cells were numbered, and she could have found her way to Sulien blindfold.

She began speaking at once. 'We've got twenty-five minutes,' she said crisply, subduing the new shock of the sight of him: height and strange, familiar face, and stopping short the old images of him, all crowding up to have the faded colours of remembered hair and eye judged against him and corrected. *Seven years*. There was no time for all that.

'Twenty-five minutes,' she was saying. 'You can swim, can't you? We must go *now*.' But he had hardly heard her. 'It can't be you,' he said, barely a whisper, barely a breath, as if a real sound would prove it was not she, she was not there at all. He wanted to hug her to make sure, but somehow could not. He placed his hands cautiously on her arms, which seemed to shrink back a little, but were real enough.

She had known he would be dazed, she was herself really, and she had known or hoped that this would happen. Still, she could feel the precious seconds of her plan wasting and she wanted to shake him. 'Sulien, *now*,' she said.

He followed her out of the cell. If he hadn't been able to believe in pending death, this rescue was no more credible: both futures hung blurred, for the moment almost meaningless.

But when they were halfway along the passage the imagined cross put sharp, unreal points through Sulien's feet and wrists again, and stopped him short. The sobs from behind one of the doors had disintegrated into a long hopeless burbling.

'Wait,' he said. 'Unlock all the doors.'

She looked down at the keys in her hand and – he was appalled to see – hesitated.

'I don't want them to die!' she snapped, although he had not spoken. 'I can't get them all away, can I? Not eleven people, it's been hard enough . . .' She broke off and started again in a controlled undertone. 'I've planned it all. To save *you*, you see. I won't do anything to risk it now.'

There was a moan from the locked door beside them. A shudder went through her, and he saw how ill and tired she looked. Her lips were as white as the rest of her face. The river had left a silty tidemark round her neck and there was something strange on her skin – the watery remains of thick make-up over yellowing bruises on the left side of her face, still ringing her ruthless eye.

He said gently, cautiously, 'But the vigiles will look for us. If they've got more people to find, they won't concentrate on us, will they? Doesn't that give us a better chance?'

She stood expressionless for a second, then abruptly slammed open the hatch in the nearest cell door and threw the keys inside. '*There. Now*,' she insisted through her teeth.

They ran up the steps and Una flung open the door. As the daylight hit them, for all her haste, Una stopped and staggered a little. Sulien too was unnerved by the noise and chaos of the river. There were so many people, so much light – how had she thought she could help him? It was impossible. Any second they would be caught, shot – he could not understand why it had not happened already. Better for him to be shot escaping than crucified, but that would mean Una uselessly dead, too. But somehow no one looked their way as Una led him to the rear of the boat. She was gasping with effort, but he didn't know why.

The wharf was just behind them. Una tried to explain where to swim, but it was too difficult, she had no concentration left to talk with. She pointed dumbly, climbed over the gunwale and dropped, too quickly, into the water.

The water forced itself through her lips and fizzed up thickly past her as the surface closed a foot above her head. She came up floundering and spitting. Sulien was already beside her, pulling smoothly away, looking back anxiously.

'Go on,' she managed. Her head felt huge and ponderous, her neck too thin and frail to keep it out of the water. At least the passing boats kept screening them from the banks, but still there were so many people to hide from – twelve, thirteen, seventeen . . .

A barge reared like a cliff – above, towards her; and Sulien was a long way ahead now. She strove forward, splashing. What she was doing was hardly swimming now, just a slow, clumsy grasping and kicking. She seemed scarcely to move in the water, there was no time – she would never get clear of the barge before it mowed her down into the water. She struggled back, choking – back towards the prison ferry and its guns, just as the barge drove between them. The wake rolled her under the surface again, as on the other side and unseen, Sulien was sliced beyond her power to hide him. Sulien looked back and saw the huge and rusting wall cut Una out of sight, and hung, treading water, willing the boat to pass by, not knowing what to do nor realising how unprotected he was. Una pushed brokenly up into the air

53

again, her aching eyes and mind vainly casting about for Sulien.

And as the barge passed, the first shout sounded from the ferry. Then a snarl of gunfire roared overhead and smashed the water behind them; and Una knew she must have failed. 'There then,' she thought, a distant, indifferent little murmur. 'They're firing at us. After all it was impossible.' And then the bitter-smelling water fought down her uselessly jerking limbs, and clasped itself peacefully above her head.

[IV]

THE ORPHEUS MOSAIC

The villa on the hill was beautiful, but Leo and Clodia had let it go. Half the farmland that had once belonged to the estate had been sold off, and there were nettles and ground-elder growing in what was left. The garden was still lovely, but almost by accident – Clodia had planted a voracious amber rose which had sprung up everywhere, swallowing the asphodels and marigolds. Inside, the colours were begin-ning to flatten on the frescoes on the wall; there were little grey scars in the pretty face of the Orpheus on the study floor, where mosaic tiles had come away to show the con-crete underneath. There were too few servants to see to all these things.

Varius and Gemella were in the colonnade. It was noon, and Varius, absentmindedly, was undoing Gemella's brown hair from its loose knot, as she lay against him on the bench. 'What have you done?' she complained vaguely, when it was too late. He was moderately vain of his own hair, constricted into plaited stripes from brow to the base of the skull, but only of that; clothes, even expensive ones, tended to look sprawling and careless on bones that were long, flattish and square-cut, as if his body was a frame of hinges and planks. His face also was long and angular, with early lines around the eyes and mouth. He was, by descent, Egypto-Nubian, though his family had lived in Rome for close to a century. He and Gemella were twenty-seven and twenty-five years old, and had been married almost two years. They had spent the morning going through Leo's papers. Varius was the executor of Leo's will now. He had been Leo's private secretary.

As she thought Gemella kept pulling at her lower lip, making her narrow pink face look ugly. Varius put his fingers over hers to stop her. She said, 'What are we going to do?' And when he did not answer at first, 'If we hadn't tried, and something happened . . .'

'I know,' he replied quietly. 'We wouldn't forgive ourselves.'

'Well. When are we going to tell him?'

'Can't get him here yet. They wouldn't let him go, or at the least they'd wonder what was going on.'

'But it must be soon.'

Varius hesitated. 'Yes. But as for telling him . . . If we put him through that and it turned out we were wrong – did you see him at the funeral? He's going around sleepwalking, the poor kid. It's too much.'

Gemella grimaced. 'Well, I'm dreading doing it,' she admitted.

'It can't be necessary yet.'

But after a moment she shook her head. 'How old is he, sixteen? We can't keep an eye on him without his knowing why, not for any length of time.'

Varius nodded, but he sighed. 'He won't believe it any more than Leo did. Maybe that's the only sane way to react.' He rubbed at the place between his eyebrows.

Gemella pulled herself up firmly and kissed his mouth, his cheek, the corner of his eye. 'If we're wrong, that's good. But I think we can't be. And you don't think we are, I know that.'

'No,' said Varius, then, 'I hate them, and we don't even really know who they are.'

'They could have left Clodia alone,' she said bitterly. Varius stroked her back. Her eyes were still a little flushed from the morning. It was through Clodia that he and Gemella had come to meet. She and Clodia had been related: second cousins. Gemella remembered, at the age of seven, being in total awe of Clodia on her wedding day, not just of her beauty but because of something more intimidating, a kind of golden solidity, an invulnerable look. She had remained intimidating, but not wholly invulnerable. Gemella could remember also how embarrassingly and drolly withering about Leo she had grown during the last four years or so. Listening once, Varius had been both amused and dismayed enough to ask Gemella, 'You don't talk about me like that, do you?'

'No, they wanted her gone, too,' said Varius now, stroking her back, because in a way it was a compliment to Clodia, and a comfort, to think this was more than just bad luck.

They waited two weeks, and then Varius wrote to the palace.

'His true character and achievements,' wrote Marcus, 'have been obscured by so many layers of prejudice that we may never be able to peel them all away. We can show, however, that the charge that he murdered his way into power rests on no firmer evidence than the word of his successors, who had reasons of their own for painting Nasennius as a villain.'

He stopped. In the weeks since the funeral he had begun to see a kind of seasick rhythm in grief. There were memories that came on like hot blades, rasping the tears out of him. But much of the time everything felt only slow and boring and slightly damp; great flabby slabs of time in which nothing happened and there was nothing to do or feel except oddly exhausted, or more accurately, lazy. He spent vacant hours staring blankly at the fountains in the palace garden or floating in the darkness of the bath suite, shrinking from the effort even of writing a letter or reading a book. But at other times came unpredictable surges of black, angry, shivering energy which would turn into panic and horror if he didn't find something to do. When this happened he worked, partly because there was nothing else to do and partly so that he would not have to see his family.

Now he was writing a defence of Nasennius, who had been a disastrously corrupt and unpopular Emperor in the twenty-sixth century. His successors were the Novii. Marcus found it perversely satisfying to call his own ancestors liars.

He was not sure if he believed what he was writing or not. The exercises alarmed him a little for the same reason that he liked them – that they made everyone seem almost equally defensible, or equally vulnerable to attack. But he was growing bored. Writing declamations was good oratory practice and good history revision, but it seemed a pity to say that Nasennius was not a murderer when it was so much more fun if he was. He had already written half a speech trying to show that Vespasian had not been a sober statesman, but a monster of cruelty and greed. But he had not seen his tutor since his parents' deaths. There was no one left to make him finish anything.

Now the lethargy came on again and he let the cavernous room grow dark while he sat with his pen in his hand, hating the brocade curtains and, involuntarily, going over his funeral speech again with embarrassment and a cold ache. He wished now he had not let so many people hear him say those things. Was it in any way true to say that his parents loved each other? He'd spent years of his childhood alternately hoping and fearing that they were on the point of divorce. If the ambition and grudging mutual respect between them were enough to keep them together, wasn't it superfluous and wishful thinking to imagine that some unrecognisable form of love must be involved as well? He could see now that divorce had not really been a possibility. Of course his mother could never have had much influence without Leo, but Leo too must have had, in this one matter, enough self-knowledge to realise he could not do without Clodia, who could always judge what he should do next.

Things had been better in the last year and a half, since they had decided they were essentially business partners; at least, that was what he believed they must have decided; they told him nothing, but they seemed at once friendlier with each other and less close. He was sure Leo had gone on sleeping with other women, as he always had, something which had once caused fights like magnetic storms on the surface of the sun, capable of going on for years.

But they loved each other in public, he thought suddenly. Holding hands and smiling – it wasn't just something they forced themselves to do; when a certain number of people could see them they truly relaxed, they were happy.

He only became aware of himself again as someone turned on the light. A tall slave entered noiselessly and tried to help him change for supper. Marcus recoiled a little. 'No. Thank you. No, I will do it myself,' he said. They performed a kind of dance across the room as the slave advanced quietly and Marcus backed away. Marcus had to say 'No,' and 'Thank you' an embarrassing number of times as the slave did not seem to believe him and stayed a long time, uttering mild protests, his eyes fixed meekly on the floor as he shuffled implacably forward. Marcus felt unreasonably trapped. It was not that he had never been waited on. At home there were servants who cooked his meals and drove him from place to place, but they were servants. This was different, this was disgusting.

At dinner it was just as bad. The slaves hovered about the glittering table like solicitous bluebottles. Marcus could feel their eyes as he ate, trying to anticipate what he might want. He watched Drusus, lying on the couch opposite him, direct them with barely a word or gesture. There was a gracefulness about it, as if the slaves were notes of music that Drusus was composing. Marcus was thirsty, but he hated asking the slaves for anything. He hated looking at them and he hated hearing their light footsteps fluttering behind him. He thought it was odd that guilt could be so close to hostility, as if he were at the slaves' mercy and not the other way round. It would be such an ordinary thing to get up and fetch a water jug himself, but it would have astonished everyone, so he did not do it. He had a very clear memory of his parents, coming home from a long visit to the palace. His mother had flung herself into a chair and said 'Oh, let's never go *there* again.' And she had laughed, but looked sad. Marcus gritted his teeth until the image of her retreated a little and he thought, I must get home.

It was not only the bustling slaves that made the palace oppressive. It was the kindness of his family. His cousin Makaria, who he knew very well disliked him along with all adolescent boys, had taken to patting him awkwardly on the shoulder whenever she saw him, and to giving him little presents. He could see she could not think of a thing to say to him and he couldn't tell her not to try. Perhaps things should have been easier with his uncle, who had loved Leo, but they were not. They tired themselves trying not to let their separate griefs collide. Marcus hated seeing the strain on his uncle's face intensify whenever they looked at each other. Faustus kept drawing him into dismal little conversations. It was like trying to make a fire by striking two clods of earth together.

Tulliola, reclining beside Faustus, was a restful presence by comparison. She at least was the same as ever. Tulliola fascinated Marcus without attracting him at all, although she was easily the most beautiful woman he knew, with her liquid eyes and gentle mouth. It was rather that she made him want to go up behind her and make a loud noise, to see if she would do anything. He had never seen her surprised. She held her long ivory neck achingly upright under the weight of her turret of dark hair. Whenever she stood or walked, her elaborately perfect posture and the heavy steeple of hair made her seem tall, which she was not. She glided imperviously about the palace like an iceberg or a mechanical swan.

Faustus' hand was resting loosely on her hip and without seeming to ignore him she looked quite placidly unconscious of it. She was only twenty-eight, five years younger than Makaria, and there had been some disapproval in Rome when Faustus had married her. But Tulliola was too correct, lovely and inert to be unpopular for long.

Now Marcus saw Faustus look at him, search painfully

for a topic and say, 'What do you think of this Terranova business, Marcus?'

Marcus said distantly that he thought it would be a pity if there was a war.

'Well, we all think that,' said Faustus, clumsily soothing. 'You needn't worry too much, nothing's going to happen right away.'

Drusus looked up with a kind of eagerness or alarm. 'Doesn't it have to?'

'There won't be a war of Rome's making,' said Faustus, still looking at Marcus, and attempting to reassure him.

'But it is not a war of Rome's making,' protested Drusus.

Passively, Marcus let the conversation drift away from him. But he pictured the Terranovan Wall, almost mathematically at first: a line, quivering as it worked through the mountains in the West, then breaking into what it was meant to be, a neat diagonal from the head of the Camian Peninsula to Misinipeia Bay in the North. Then he saw it as a real object, but very far off, as if from space.

Faustus thought regretfully that talking shop at supper was a bad idea; he had only raised the possible war in the hope that Marcus might be interested in it. He found himself feeling as bored with it now as if it already been going on for years.

Drusus, however, was knowledgeable and keen. He was saying, 'We've got to at least raise the presence on the Wall.'

'We may very well do that,' said Faustus.

Slowly Marcus let himself draw closer to the image of the Wall; remembering now the endless grey cliff rising above the quiet grass, the square watchtowers, built under two generations of Novians. He had been there once; visiting the troops with his parents where the Wall became a wide bridge, standing on arches over the Emissourita. But that was before Nionia had strung the squads of soldiers all along the Wall's length.

'Nionia would regret it if she pushes any further; it's up to them,' concluded Faustus, looking at Marcus once more and worrying about him.

'Yes, Uncle,' said Marcus. And yet, belatedly, he felt the faintest flicker of interest. He waited for it to die out and instead heard himself saying, rather too loudly. 'No, that can't be true.'

Drusus' eyebrows twitched upwards and Makaria, who had been watching Tulliola from under her sleepy eyelids with an expression of obvious and unconscious discontent, turned to look at him. He writhed a little. He said, 'I'm sorry. I meant – surely Rome cannot be powerless.'

'Indeed not!' exclaimed Drusus.

'We can't be going to have a war by accident, can we?'

Drusus looked startled for a moment and then weary and long-suffering. 'Not by accident; as a result of Nionia deliberately flouting her obligations.'

'That treaty's a hundred and seventy years old. And they haven't attacked us.'

'Yes,' said Drusus, patiently. 'They have.'

Marcus shrank uncomfortably again but muttered, 'Yes, but *we've*—'

' "We've"?' asked Drusus.

Nionia claimed that the Samurae troops were necessary to protect her people – from all kinds of things; rape, kidnap and enslavement; they even said the Roman soldiers from the Wall roamed inwards murdering people as a kind of sport. Marcus hesitated. He didn't believe most of these things – but the kidnapping might happen perhaps, sometimes – doubtless not as often as Nionia said. But he could see what the response would be if he suggested there was any truth in the stories at all, though surely everyone knew that until now the Wall had always been porous for Romans. Nionians were not supposed to approach it, or touch it.

He went on tentatively, 'No – but those skirmishes – I think it must be impossible to know how they start. I mean, they're not trying to invade.'

'It's a little more complicated than that,' said Faustus mildly.

'Yes,' said Marcus again, obediently.

'We can't allow a standing army on our doorstep,' said Drusus.

'We've got one on theirs,' commented Marcus.

'Ours is a legal force; they accepted it under Mixigana; it's a bit late for them to complain about it now.'

Nionia held that far from breaking the Mixigana treaty they were reaffirming it; they were strengthening the border that Rome had deliberately set out to weaken.

'But surely we couldn't expect the war to stay in Terranova. And if it came to a war between Empires, if India flared up at the same time – and with the weapons we both have now—'

'They're not as stupid as that,' said Drusus.

'That would mean the whole world,' said Marcus.

'We would still win.'

'It wouldn't come to that,' said Faustus. 'There are the people to think of. How are they supposed to feel with free Romans living right next door? It isn't right for a country to be split in two like that. It always should have been Roman. It's what the Terranovans want.'

'Only some of them, I thought,' said Marcus.

'Roman citizens have been killed,' said Drusus. 'Would you just let that happen?' He said it quite without apparent malice, but Marcus could remember Drusus smiling quizzically, while he was left to look stupid, or stupidly young, even when he had been a little boy; and he felt the dim glow of interest shoot up suddenly into a steady, angry flame.

'Couldn't the territory be shared?' he asked, without quite knowing he was going to.

Makaria looked up and snorted and said, 'Well, no one would be happy that way.'

'You think Nionia would just let it go?' said Drusus.

'Have they been asked?' said Marcus, and a tiny pause hung over the table. He pushed into it. 'In any case, they wouldn't be giving up anything, and nor would we; or at least, anything lost would be more than compensated for. You would have to take the Wall down; there wouldn't be a

63

border at all. They would have access to the south, Roman facilities would be there if they wanted them—'

'In Cynoto they already say we're trying to colonise them by stealth,' said Faustus, but yet there was a kind of interest in his face now.

'But that's because it's so tense there; I think this would change that. We influenced each other in the past; they wouldn't have become an Empire without contact with us. We still use their silk. I can't believe relations have to be like this. The people could have joint citizenship—'

'But how could that possibly work? Who would run everything?'

'I don't know,' said Marcus, raising himself up on the couch, thinking rapidly now. 'There would have to be some kind of a council there – with Romans and Nionians. We'd have to work it out with them.'

'I think you pay them a great compliment, to have such faith in them' said Drusus. 'I just wish things were as simple as they look to you – don't you, Uncle?'

Marcus felt cheated. He lowered his head and said broodingly, 'Of course, a big war would solve the slave problem.'

It was true that there was a problem. There hadn't been a major war for a generation, and with fewer children being born into slavery, the slave population was shrinking. Already there was talk of making it harder to free them. But there was a ripple of dismay around the table. He saw that he should not have said it. Even Tulliola looked a little concerned, although most likely she was only reflecting what she saw in Faustus' face.

Makaria said, 'Oh, you can't really think that.'

'Come on, Marcus,' said Drusus. 'Don't be cynical for the sake of it, only theatre types go on like that.'

Faustus' fleshy face looked young and hurt. He began to say, 'Marcus, you mustn't believe that of me,' but he stopped and asked forlornly, 'Is that what Leo thought?' And Marcus saw that he had won somehow after all, but Faustus looked so unhappy that he still wished he hadn't said it. Later he would wonder if it made any difference to what followed.

Now he froze for a second and then murmured diplomatically, 'I don't know.'

Faustus sighed. 'Well, I can see you've been thinking a great deal about this.'

'No, not really,' said Marcus, truthfully.

Drusus said lightly, after a pause, 'Anyway, the Nionians are no good as slaves; they always kill themselves, just like Romans.' And he laughed.

Tulliola had not spoken all through the discussion of Terranova. Now she patted Faustus' hand in her gentle, torpid way, and appeared not to notice as he pushed his thick fingers between her slender ones. She said, 'Oh Marcus, we heard today that Varius would like you to go home. But, of course, it's far too soon.'

Marcus, still feeling guilty about Faustus, tried not to look too eager. He said, 'Did he say why? Is anything wrong?'

Faustus said heavily, 'It sounds like a fuss about nothing. He says he has some concerns about Leo's will. Tulliola's right, it's too soon. You won't want to think about such things.'

'I have to think about such things now,' said Marcus guardedly. 'I can't leave everything to Varius, it wouldn't be fair.' He thought this was true, but he didn't like his voice as he said it: it sounded pious and pallidly dutiful and he grimaced at himself a little, and wanted all the more to get home. He thought Varius and Gemella were almost the only people he felt like seeing.

The morning before he left, Makaria came trudging into his room, where he was trying to sort his own books from those he'd borrowed from Faustus' library, and uneasily watching the tall slave pack his clothes away. Makaria made the embarrassed half-smile he had grown used to seeing since his parents died.

'Look Marcus, I got you these. You like them don't you?'

'Thank you. Yes,' he said. He did not have to look to

know it was a little wicker box of honey nougat. Makaria had first brought these particular sweets back from Greece when Marcus was seven or so. He had loved the soft little cubes, and so Makaria had given them to him indefatigably ever since, every time she came to Rome or on any occasion when gift-giving was expected, until even the scent of them came to disgust him. He usually gave them to his friends, or the servants, or sometimes left them in his room going hard until the housekeeper threw them away.

'To say goodbye,' she said. 'I'm going home too.'

She meant her vineyard on Siphnos, where she lived most of the time in stubborn, voluntary exile. Makaria's love of Greece had begun during a visit to Athens as a little girl, and had hardened through her teens and twenties as she'd seen in it a way of irritating her father. She'd adopted the Greek version of her formal name, Novia Faustina, and took to wresting conversations about art or history around to praise Greece at Rome's expense. Faustus' remarriage had been the last straw. It was an open secret that Makaria did not consider Italy big enough for herself and Tulliola.

'When will you come back?' he asked, putting the sweets on the desk and glad to divert attention away from them.

'Maybe never. Rome is squalid. Civilisation is essentially Greek.'

This was something she said quite often. His parents used to laugh at it. He smiled.

Then with no warning at all, Makaria leaned forward, speaking urgently and fast, 'Look Marcus. I liked you when you were little. I'll probably like you again in a few years. I can't really stand you now but you mustn't take it personally – I just think boys your age make a room look so awful, you never seem to know what to do with your hands and you always have stupid expressions on your faces and your necks stick out and you can never stand up straight. But I am *so sorry*, and if you ever decide you just hate it too much here—'

But she got no further, for Tulliola tapped gently on the

door before entering as smoothly as a drift of smoke. Makaria looked disgusted and tramped out without a word.

'Dear Makaria,' said Tulliola patiently, to no one in particular. 'How is the packing, Marcus? Your uncle wants to say goodbye.'

The car that drove up to the steps to carry him home to Tusculum reminded him of the one his parents had taken into Gaul, obviously that of a rich person, but still smaller and plainer than most of the garlanded hulks of the Imperial fleet. Marcus stared at it carefully. All right, he was going to have to think of the crash now, he would allow a controlled amount of pain; it was only a car. The resemblance between the vehicles wasn't really that much: this car was decorated with scrolls of nickel-plated leaves surrounding little star-shaped crests of inlaid mother-of-pearl; the motifs on his parents' car had been Sinoan chrysanthemums. In short, clenched snatches Marcus saw the metal crumpled, the glass smashed, managed to stop short of picturing his parents' bodies flung forward inside it. It would have been very quick, he had been assured, and certainly they had both been dead before any help could come: but the swerve, the jump, the downwards speed – surely they must have had time had to see what was happening and hope they would survive.

The Praetorian guard who sat with the chauffeur wanted him to keep the curtains inside shut, for security, but Marcus refused dully, and watched Rome glowing through the window, the different shades of marble and glass pulsing with soft colour like many plaits of clean hair: russet, frost-white, flesh-pink, gold. The lights that scoured the sky at night had not yet been lit.

Trying to steer the pain away now he had let it go a certain distance, he looked fiercely over his defence of Nasennius again, made himself think, with painful slowness, that next there would have to be a sketch of what Nasennius was like, what he had done before he had become Emperor. But he couldn't focus on it, he couldn't imagine being interested. Instead he opened the box of sweets in case he had suddenly grown to like them again. He smelt almond and honey and remembered the powdery texture on the tongue. He made a face and decided he would give them to the chauffeur when they arrived, but as the car approached the villa and he saw Varius and Gemella looking down from the balcony, he forgot and took them with him into the quiet villa.

He looked, with love, at his fading house. The light fell squarely from the opening in the roof to the shallow pool set into the floor. Beyond the bright shaft the walls were shadowy, darkness and familiarity disguising the flaws of the wall paintings. He had thought that coming back to his parents' home might bring a new jolt of grief, but the colourless feeling was the same everywhere.

The butler passed to fetch his things from the car, and Varius and Gemella came into the hall to meet him. Gemella kissed his cheek. As she stepped back Marcus saw a tense glance run between them, and suppressed a little twitch of disappointment. He had hoped they would be immune to the unease he knew he carried about with him. He told them about Makaria's outburst. 'I only look stupid at the palace because I'm bored,' he said. 'And my neck doesn't stick out.'

They laughed, but nervously. He saw that after that furtive meeting of eyes they avoided looking at each other. They reminded him a little of his parents after a fight, and he was sorry, because Varius and Gemella had never seemed to fight. He had assumed they had not been married long enough.

He went through into the study, where Leo's papers were splayed out on the desk and black chests under the marble busts of his grandfather and great-uncles. He thought bleakly that he ought to have a bust made for his father, although he didn't like the idea of such a thing looking at him.

The butler followed him in and said, 'A present from your cousin, Sir?' and Marcus realised he was still holding the wicker box of nougat.

'Yes,' he said, 'shall I throw them away?'

'That's a waste,' said the butler reprovingly. 'Your guests might like them. Let me put them on a plate.'

'All right. Or you can have them if you like.' He put the box into the butler's hands and did not wait to see what he decided to do with them. He went to his bedroom and threw himself down on the blue bedspread.

Later he went to the Lararium at the centre of the house, and in memory of his parents, and because he had been away from home almost a month, he knelt before the little silver images of the dancing youths, the veiled goddess of the hearth, poured out a little wine and set it before them. For a moment he felt a minor comfort in the ritual, almost the feeling of a benign force watching over the house. Then he noticed an empty socket where a tiny jewel should have been on one of the dancer's sleeves, and at once, and decisively, the fragile meaning emptied out of the figures and he was certain it would never come back. Little dolls, he thought with sudden contempt: pretending to feed little dolls. Why does anyone do anything so childish? He remained kneeling for a while, staring at the dancers with dislike and pity because they kept on joyfully springing, not realising they'd been seen through.

At supper they talked of ordinary things, and yet the feeling of subdued unease kept resurfacing, and it spread from Varius and Gemella to Marcus. Although they stopped themselves from exchanging glances, still Marcus felt that the others were somehow assessing everything he said; especially when the conversation turned to more serious things, like the Academy in Athens, which Marcus meant to attend the following year. He began to think it was more than the atmosphere of loss, and more than a fight, that was troubling them. He wondered if there was something very wrong with the will – perhaps his parents had left debts? He could not imagine caring much.

Later he heard them talking in the study, in voices lowered to such a pitch as made him sure they were talking about him. He could bear it no longer and pushed open the lattice door. They were sitting together on the ebony bench, and their faces turned to him guiltily as he entered. The papers had been tidied away and Makaria's sweets were heaped on an enamelled glass plate.

'Varius, what is it?' he asked. 'You can't really think I haven't noticed.'

There was a pause. 'Have I been disinherited?' he said, smiling, trying to reassure them.

Gemella said clearly, prompting. 'Varius.'

Varius seemed to steel himself in some way. 'There's nothing about the will, Marcus. It's something else.'

Marcus felt the whole room, including himself, grow very still.

'Don't be angry,' appealed Gemella. 'We thought it might be hard for you to come back without some reason like that, something no one could object to.'

'Oh yes?' Marcus said, hearing a sharp note in his voice that reminded him unpleasantly of his father at his worst, 'and what was wrong with the real reason? And what is that, exactly?'

'There are things we have to tell you.'

'Evidently,' said Marcus, in the same tone. He sat down facing them.

'Marcus, I am sorry,' said Gemella. 'It isn't about your father's will, but it is about inheritances. But there's something I need to ask you. Do you want to be Emperor?'

Marcus glanced at the door and began to draw patterns on the table with his finger.

'Do you?' Gemella insisted.

Marcus watched his fingers. 'No,' he answered shortly.

Varius and Gemella looked at each other. 'That's bad,' Gemella said. 'Because we hope you will be. We have to hope that, now.'

Marcus got up abruptly and turned towards the door, saying confusedly, 'I'm sorry; I don't want to think about—'

'You have to,' Varius said. Marcus remembered what he had said to Faustus, and stopped. He walked back to his seat and sat down, slowly.

70

'Did you mean what you just said?' Varius asked. 'Because I thought all Novians wanted power, except perhaps your Uncle Lucius.'

'I know,' said Marcus distantly. He looked at the bust of his grandfather, at the large soft eyelids over the white eyes. He said to it, 'It's a bad thing.'

'Why do you say that?' inquired Varius. 'It's the family profession, after all.' And he smiled, but Marcus saw how intently he and Gemella were watching him now. Gemella had her fists clenched in her lap.

'If I ever speak to my uncle about something I think should happen, he tells me "it isn't that simple",' he said slowly. 'Or Drusus says it. It's not that I don't believe them. But then how do I know I'd ever do the things I think I would? Perhaps it would always seem too difficult. Maybe if I . . . maybe anyone who . . . gets into that position—' He felt oddly reluctant to use the word Emperor and mean himself. 'Maybe you find you don't care about anything so much as staying there. My father . . .' He paused, for the idea of his father was suddenly exhausting. '. . . You know how much he wanted to do. But maybe my uncle was like that once, I don't know.'

'No, I don't think he was,' said Varius.

'Perhaps not,' conceded Marcus, 'but that's not the only thing. Just wanting it. That can be bad enough. My father thought he would be Emperor. And he was so popular. So he . . . thought he could treat people however he liked. And it was true, he could. He did. Even you, sometimes, didn't he?' he said to Varius, and then glanced at Gemella. 'And you must know about that, mustn't you? The way he used to treat my mother. And all those other women. I'm not sure if she knew I knew.' He looked down at his hands again. 'He was right about a lot of things,' he said, 'but I – I don't think I liked him very much.'

'Marcus,' said Gemella quietly, 'are you saying you don't want to be Emperor, or do you mean that you do but you're ashamed of it?'

She had kept her eyes on his as she spoke. He dropped his

now, and he wrote the word No, in imaginary ink, on the table with his finger.

'Yes,' he said, almost in a whisper. He heard them both let out a breath that was almost a sigh.

Varius asked, 'And do you think you could do it?'

Marcus lowered his head even further. 'Yes,' he said again. 'I don't know why.'

'What would you do?'

'I don't think there has to be a war in Terranova,' Marcus said. 'And of course I agree with my parents – about slavery.'

They did sigh this time, and Gemella sat back in her chair; but it was hard to tell if they were relieved or sorry.

Varius said, deliberately, almost murmuring. 'You said your uncle says things aren't that simple. It's true. I want to know – have you thought what would happen to Rome without slavery? Look at what's happening to your house. Paying the servants means it costs a little more to run everything, doesn't it – and that nothing runs quite so well. And your parents were very wealthy, and they chose this – they liked doing without slaves running about every-where. And it's just a house. But the slaves grow the food and mine the fuel; they also put roads through mountains. Some of the jobs they do are so dangerous that perhaps no one would do them at all if they had a choice. There are extremely wealthy people now who would find they had almost nothing left if you took the slaves away. Money would drain out of Rome in all directions without anything new to show for it. We couldn't keep the kind of pace ahead of Nionia and Sina that we do now. In the end, there might be just a lot of broken little countries where the Empire used to be.'

He and Gemella watched Marcus again.

'Is this what you wanted to tell me?' asked Marcus, indignant.

'No,' said Varius, his long face growing more tense, 'but I wanted to be sure you knew.'

Marcus made an impatient gesture. 'Well, I'd find out

what I could do to prevent all that, or at least control it. But if it comes to it, it doesn't make any difference to what we should do. I couldn't think well of myself if that stopped me.' And he stood up. 'I was glad to get out of the palace,' he said, 'so thank you. But I think you should tell me now why I'm here.'

The purposeful expression seemed to have gone from Varius' face. 'The slave clinic your father was working on—'

'No,' said Marcus. 'Whatever that is, tell me later. What is it? Why don't you want to say? Why do you both look so miserable?'

Gemella said, 'We think your parents were murdered.'

Marcus felt as if every nerve underwent a separate hammer-tap of shock and hummed with it, like dulcimer strings. He said, '*How?*' and hearing the question shook his head in disbelief at himself. 'No,' he said firmly. 'Why would you ever think that? It was the road – it was the car—'

But he felt a great shake uncoil through him and dropped back into his chair, although he wanted nothing so much as to get out of the room.

Gemella's fingers tightened a little on the back of Varius' hand. 'If we're right, you are also vulnerable.'

'But you are not right,' said Marcus harshly.

'Marcus,' said Varius with sudden fierceness, 'Even if we are wrong, after what happened to your parents we can't risk not telling you what we think. You must see that.'

Marcus set his jaw. 'Fine, tell me.'

'All right,' Gemella said. 'The first thing was something I heard. It was a few months ago when the Emperor was ill – do you remember?' Marcus gave the briefest of nods. In the spring his uncle had been frightened by pains in his chest.

At the same time, there had been a reception at the Tusculum villa. Somehow Gemella had ended up organising most of it, and both the weeks leading up to it and the event itself had been exhausting – there had been so much to do, and it was always on the point of being cancelled:

with Faustus' health in question, was it right for it to take place? Gemella had barely sat down during the six hours it had lasted, and she spent most of the following day languidly recovering. Late in the morning, she was at the baths, in the laconicum, almost asleep in the steam. She lazed: she could not learn to like working for frantic hours under the constant threat of disaster, as Varius really seemed to.

Before marrying Varius she had rarely seen Clodia more than once a year, but since then she had found herself pulled in closer – by her own growing interest, by Clodia's endlessly persuasive appeals for assistance. She and Varius were soon working almost in parallel, Gemella spending as much time with Clodia as with him. Clodia needed many of the same things done for her that Leo did – someone to edit speeches, arrange meetings, someone with whom to discuss plans. Also, Gemella guessed, Clodia liked to feel she had private allies, specifically hers rather than Leo's.

Varius and Gemella enjoyed competing amiably over who was the more exploited. Leo's charm was strong but less unremitting than Clodia's, it was more likely to break into fits of temper; Varius was more consistently overworked. 'But you don't have to help pick dresses,' Gemella said (Clodia needed to look glamorous and yet wifely), 'and you get paid.'

She was paid after a fashion – in presents and treats (theatre tickets, a Sinoan carved statue too large for their little flat) and in ideas and talk – all of which she was glad to have, even if it was only the ideas, the feeling that she was involved, that she would have chosen. She would have changed her life only in details, she told herself – though a strange uncertain feeling overtook her when she thought this. She was becoming good at indignation on behalf of various people: slaves, and other women – Clodia, for example; it was unjust that Clodia had to work in disguise, as an accessory of Leo's. Discontent for herself was alien and frightening, it didn't feel natural to her. But sometimes it seemed feeble to be content with her life when Varius was the only part of it that she had deliberately chosen.

In the laconicum, a rush of cold air shook a warm rain of condensation from the ceiling as the women entered, but they settled on the far side of the room, and when she looked she could see no more of them than a kind of shadow in the steam, barely even distinguishable as two people. They, probably, had not seen her at all: there was a pillar obscuring her as well as the curtains of steam, and she had not moved. She closed her eyes again.

'What if it's more serious than we're being told?'

Gemella sighed gently and tried to ignore the small fretful voice, but it was shrill, not precisely loud but too piercing for the peace of the laconicum to survive it.

'Oh, Plancina, it won't be. Do stop it.'

But the high little voice went on. It seemed nothing the other woman said could quiet it. Gemella had been in there too long, really, already; only a last clutch of laziness still held her; she was getting too irritated to enjoy the warmth any more.

Plancina whimpered, 'Even if you're right now, it'll happen sooner or later. And then that'll be the end of us. You know all these ridiculous things Leo wants to do, don't you? Why doesn't he care about us, don't we matter as much as slaves? I know we're going to lose everything; we'll be out on the streets and there's nothing anyone can do.'

'*I wouldn't say that.*'

Gemella had been interested enough by the discovery that Leo was the source of Plancina's distress to lie still a moment longer, but as the complaint went on she had just raised her head, tensed her muscles to get up. At this she froze like that, completely alert now, listening acutely.

Afterwards it would be hard to explain to Varius, as it was hard to explain to Marcus now, why the tone was so arresting. It seemed even Plancina hadn't noticed it, she was distracted by her own tears: 'Of course there isn't. Why won't you face facts?'

'*Look*, Plancina,' exploded the second woman fiercely. Yet here there was a pause, as if she was debating whether or not to go any further. Finally she said, 'All I know is this: I'm not worried. And nor is my husband. In fact, he's buying the slave market at Comum.'

Marcus felt as if a cold feather had brushed over his skin, but he muttered, 'My uncle might live another twenty years, it was only angina. The doctors said it wasn't very serious. Maybe she knew that, or guessed it.'

'Varius said that when I told him,' said Gemella. 'And Clodia.' She had gone home – Clodia had sent her a large wall-hanging as a thank you – still convinced she had heard something significant and alarming, but by the next day she could not really think why, certainly no one else seemed to think it meant anything.

'I only remembered it the week before your parents left for Gaul,' Varius said. 'If your father were still alive he should have met Flavius Gabinius this week – you know who he is?'

'Of course,' said Marcus. Gabinius owned the construction conglomerate that was building the vast suspension bridge across the Persian Gulf. He had made himself one of the richest men in Rome.

'I was supposed to organise the meeting,' said Varius. 'We were trying to persuade Gabinius to put money into the slave clinic idea, or do the building work for free. It shouldn't have been too difficult. When everyone knows you're going to be Emperor, you usually get what you want, even if it's a lot.'

'Well?' said Marcus. He remembered the clinic project. His parents had meant to set up a system of free healthcare for slaves, so that their owners would have no reason to abandon them when they became sick. They had put as much of their own money into it as they could afford, but Leo had wanted the companies which relied most heavily on slavery to pay the most.

'Suddenly it *was* difficult. They'd never liked the idea, but they'd gone along with it. But gradually they became . . .' He grimaced with remembered frustration, '. . . *passively* unhelpful. I wanted Gabinius to meet Leo at the site some time this week, but I couldn't get them to talk to me any more, much less to agree to a date. And no one I could talk to seemed to take us very seriously any more.'

'So he didn't want to give my parents any money,' said Marcus, 'that doesn't mean anything.'

'No,' admitted Varius, 'but that's not what made me remember what Gemella said. One day, I don't know how – I did catch Gabinius on the longdictor. He couldn't wait to get rid of me, but I gave him a date this week, and he agreed to it. He told me he was writing it into his diary as we spoke, and then turned the longdictor off. And then . . .' Varius sighed, 'I would never have known if Leo hadn't been so difficult. He'd decided to visit your uncle that day and hadn't told me, so I had to put the meeting back. I was annoyed after the time I'd had getting Gabinius to fix a day in the first place. This time when I tried to reach Gabinius I only got an assistant – but I think he must have been new; he seemed much more impressed by Leo's name than anyone at that office had been for a long time. So I believed him when he told me Gabinius wasn't there. He went and looked at Gabinius' diary for me – which I don't think he should have done – and he came back sounding confused, and said, there must be a mistake, Gabinius hadn't written anything about seeing Leo anywhere.'

Marcus was silent.

'Of course I thought, well, that's nothing,' Varius continued, 'but I remembered what Gemella had said. It didn't feel like nothing. It felt as if Gabinius didn't think it was worth planning anything with Leo any more. And as if he had a reason for it. So of course I told Leo everything and he said "Poor Gabinius. I forget to write things down all the time, I hope that doesn't make me a murderer." I said, "If it was you, I wouldn't think anything of it." He only laughed about it. He told me I was so obsessed with paperwork I'd gone unhinged. I thought maybe he was right. In any case I had nothing more to tell him – nothing about what would happen, or when.'

'What about my mother?' asked Marcus in a small voice. 'What did she think?'

'Yes, I told her, too. She said I should tell her if anything else came up. But she didn't believe it either. I'm sorry, Marcus, I wish . . .'

Marcus said mechanically, 'No, what happened, it doesn't mean you were right.'

Varius nodded, but he said, 'There's one other thing about Gabinius. He's owned the slave market at Comum for three months now. His wife is called Helvia; she must have been the woman that Gemella heard with Plancina in the baths.'

'Still,' said Marcus with an effort. 'My parents had body-guards; they had . . .' he stopped. 'And even – even if you were right, why did you lie about it? If you really believe this you should tell my uncle.'

'Because we didn't know who might see the letter,' said Gemella. 'It's not easy to get to your uncle. And Marcus, listen – if there was such a plot, and if it was to work, it couldn't begin or end with Gabinius. They could have people in the Praetorians, or the vigiles, we don't know. But to do this, if they were going to know enough about your parents, members of the Senate must have been involved. And members of the court.'

'*What?*' said Marcus, icy and furious again. 'Do you mean my family – my cousins? *Who?*' He remembered what he had written about Nasennius the day before, Nasennius who was hundreds of years dead . . .

'We don't know! We don't know anything except what we've told you. I know it isn't much. But we had to get you out of the palace, and we have to protect you now, for Rome's sake; not just yours.'

'I don't need protecting,' said Marcus coldly.

There was a drab, wretched silence. Varius stood up and began to say, 'We won't talk about it any more tonight—'

But then Gemella felt her breath grate in her throat, and the blood scalding in her face and eyes. She tried to say

78

'Varius,' but the air was too hard and, as she made a move to rise and reach for him, blackness, hot and loud, boiled in across the lights and smashed itself against her head and heart, leaving her only a second of desperation to fight and plead with it.

Marcus and Varius heard Gemella give a horrible, throttled gasp and choke, and as they turned to her in horror saw her slip from her seat to fall drumming and thrashing on the Orpheus mosaic.

It was quick, although it did not seem so. Marcus went and knelt uselessly as her side, and then moved back as Varius tried to still her jerking body, to hold her, frantically repeating her name as she convulsed and hammered against his arms and breast. He said, 'Get someone, get help,' and then went back to begging, 'Gemella, please, Gemella.'

Marcus nodded dumbly and stumbled towards the door meaning to call the servants. But before he reached it, Gemella flung her head back hard against Varius and then the juddering tautness dissolved out of her body, and she lay back meekly in his arms. Marcus and Varius heard nothing in the room except their own fast breath.

The awful quiet froze Marcus for a second, but then he made for the door again, still trying to hope that something might be done. Varius said in an unrecognisable serrated voice, 'Stay where you are.' Slowly Marcus turned back and saw his terrible face, flat, creased, yellow-grey.

As Marcus watched, Varius looked up at the plate of nougat on the table, and then turned over his Gemella's hand to find the smudge of sugar from the sweet she had lifted to her mouth.

Tears welled up in Marcus' eyes. 'Oh, no,' he whispered. 'Oh, Varius . . .'

Varius scarcely remembered that Marcus was in the room. He was clutching Gemella and dotting small fierce kisses on her hair and flushed face. Marcus felt he had no right to see these things and looked away.

At length he said, 'I should – call someone?'

Varius seemed not to hear. 'Where did you get those?' he

said in the same alien voice, as if speech was something he had never properly learned, as if it had to be forced past vocal cords that were not designed for it.

'Makaria.' Marcus could barely hear himself: it was not just that the name came out so quietly – nothing they had said seemed to have any weight on his mind.

Varius shook his head as if trying to clear a ringing out of it. He drew a sharp effortful breath and said, 'Don't call. Long as possible. Don't tell anyone. No one knows. You see? You go *now*, tonight. After this they will be sure and – get it right.'

What Marcus wanted was to get his parents – in any case he didn't know why he was standing there, it couldn't be right. So he said stuttering, escaping into the hall, 'I'm getting some help—'

'Don't,' he heard Varius tell him, but as far as Marcus even noticed that, he thought, it's the shock, he doesn't know what he's saying. He crossed the peaceful dark of the atrium; the longdictor hung coolly in its recess – then, as he lifted the headset, Varius plunged in a lurching run after him, almost shouting, 'I said *don't*,' and Marcus flinched at the loose blow that struck the longdictor away from his head. Varius commanded violently, 'Don't touch it. Don't do *anything*.'

Marcus stepped back from him in confusion, there was a long strange instant for Varius where he could not seem to move his eyes from the fallen longdictor, rocking for a moment or two on the cold floor. At the same time he felt the fractional chill along his arms and across his breast where Gemella's warm body had lain. He went speechlessly away from Marcus back towards her. Marcus thought he heard him say her name as the door swung shut behind him, then silence.

Marcus dithered hopelessly within an orbit of a few feet. He felt so stunned into obedience that he could barely move from the place where Varius had left him; when he too looked at the longdictor on the ground, he could not even pick it up to put it back on its hook. So long it seemed – so long that at last he began to pace about more widely, abortive little journeys one way and another, but never got out of the hall. Often he crept silently back to the door of the study, and even whispered, 'Varius,' but could not bring himself to say it aloud, much less to open the door, though he had no faith that the right thing was simply to wait there. He, someone, should be doing something for Varius, perhaps saying something.

He could not keep from heading to the foot of the stairs, looking up them with miserable longing. Why couldn't he just go up into his mother's room? Even in the shock and grief she would feel, she would be able to talk to Varius.

And – he saw the crash again – the light remembered weight of the box of sweets in his hand. But the thoughts kept scudding away from him, like waterdrops flicked onto a hob. When it occurred to him the servants might have heard Varius shout, he hoped they had and wished they would come downstairs. But it seemed no one had heard, no one came.

From within the shut room at last, Varius said, 'Marcus. Are you there?'

Tentatively, Marcus nudged open the door. Varius was rising to his feet with Gemella in his arms.

He muttered indistinctly to Marcus, 'Shouldn't have spent all this time in here.'

Already Varius couldn't remember very much of the half hour or more that had elapsed, couldn't, in fact, seem to remember it even while it was going on. He had a kind of general impression that he had just been sitting there, since it first happened, holding Gemella but not quite looking at her, doing nothing, for only a few minutes or seconds. When, of course, it was a matter of fact that he had already been out of the room once. And that since coming back he had felt for a pulse, and tried to make her breathe again, although he knew – he had already *acted* on the knowledge that she was dead.

Still, throughout it the goading fact that he was going to have to make himself care what would happen to Marcus, went like a thin saw, like the sound of a gnat in a bedroom, whining out the length of time that was really going on – quite a lot of time, whatever it felt like, more time than was allowed.

He looked at Marcus, hovering guiltily in the doorway, and got himself to say abruptly, 'You're going to have to get away from here now, do you understand?' and Marcus nodded as though he'd been expecting Varius to say something like this, although in fact the words just fizzed away from him as everything else seemed to.

Varius walked forward and found as he did so that there were patches of quiet and orderliness between breaths, in which nothing seemed to have happened and nothing needed to be done; but that every new slice of air carried into him the clean smell of Gemella's skin and laid down a new layer of sharpness and weight. A few steps behind and miles away, Marcus followed him automatically. They went up the stairs and into the guest room Varius and Gemella had shared, and Varius laid her down very slowly on the bed. When she was out of his arms again and he began to straighten up unburdened, then he could see more clearly how utterly still she was, and what had happened to her face. He discovered that tears were in his eyes for the first time, blinked with mild surprise, and then was startled that dry sobs were grinding up through his body with the inevitability of a choking fit, gripping so fiercely that he had to grope his way quickly through the bedroom to the small bathroom beside it and be sick there. He stared at the wet marble of the basin for a moment of empty wonder, then came back.

'Varius,' whispered Marcus, shivering with guilt and horror. 'It's my fault, I'm so sorry.' He went to Varius, who was standing over the bed again and laid a hand, clumsily and inadequately on his arm.

Involuntarily, Varius twitched away. 'Come on, out, out of here,' he said incoherently. For a moment he paused, and turned Gemella's head gently on the pillow so that her brown hair fell sideways, hiding her twisted features and blue lips. Then he shoved and hurried Marcus from the room. They stared at each other.

'It is no good saying that,' said Varius a little more clearly. He had closed the door behind them quietly and was now standing against it like a sentry, as if he thought Marcus would suddenly try and charge past into the room where Gemella lay.

'If I'd thrown them away – if I'd just – eaten them,' and for the moment Marcus felt so sick with shame that he really wished he had.

Varius winced angrily. 'Shut up,' he said harshly. 'Do you think I want to hear that? It's not your fault. Are you pretending it is? How do you think that helps?' He shook Marcus as he began to speak. As when he'd knocked the longdictor aside, there was a slight relief in these acts of minor violence. He had to control himself. He wiped his damp face, beginning with another sharp effort, 'Did you listen to what I said? Because I meant now. Before people know about this. You realise after this they will be sure and – get it right.' But just talking to Marcus felt like trying to focus through thick cataracts. He sat down against the door and said helplessly, 'I can't think – we have to think of what to do and I can't think.'

Marcus ran down the stairs and through the house into the kitchen where there was still half a jug of wine from supper resting on the counter. Unsteadily, he poured a glass. He spilt a lot of it as he went upstairs again; thinking now about what Varius had said about leaving, and remembering that his face had been shown on longvision all over the world only two weeks ago. In spite of the poison that had just missed him the thought that it couldn't be done was a comforting one; and although he didn't know what good his presence would do Varius, Marcus didn't want to leave him. He took the wine up to Varius, who looked at him and the glass, observed clinically that he was very young, very distressed, and reminded himself how recently Marcus' parents had died. He thought pity for him, if he did not precisely feel it. He took the wine, said, with faint irony, 'Thank you,' sipped it emptily, put it down and forgot it was there.

At last he asked, 'Did the servants wake up?'

'No, I don't think so,' said Marcus.

Varius nodded. 'Good. Go and get ready.'

Marcus said gently, 'Varius, I can't.'

'Then they'll kill you,' answered Varius, still lifelessly.

'No, but – how could I try and hide anywhere when everyone knows what I look like?'

'Yes,' Varius agreed. 'You should change the way you look.'

'But, look. Even if I could do that, there's nowhere I could go.'

'No, there is somewhere. Hardly anyone knows about it. Maybe somewhere else would be better, but it's hidden – it's all I can think of. It's in the Pyrenees.'

Marcus shook his head numbly.

'It's where slaves go,' Varius went on. 'If they escape, and if they can find the way.'

'What?' said Marcus, incredulous and dazed. 'What – like Spartacus?'

Varius let his head rest against the door. His eyes were shut. 'They're not any kind of army, it's just a place to go. I think sometimes they learn Mandarin or Nionian and Delir sends them out of the Empire to teach Latin, or – I don't know. I've never been there.'

'Delir?' asked Marcus. The name sounded outlandish and exotic, un-Roman.

'I think he's Persian. He used to . . .' Varius broke off. He knew Delir had been a merchant; he even remembered, in outline, the circumstances in which he'd gone into hiding. He felt a kind of resentment of these facts for being still in his mind after what had happened; he only wanted to know the bare essentials of anything. The impatience seemed to loose a false, hectic energy that began to pump through him and would not last. Marcus noticed it happening, recognised it. Varius hurried on, muttering quickly, 'Anyway, it's his place. Your parents gave him money; your father

84

went there once. So I think he'd help you. I think they try to help everyone. Come on. There isn't time to talk about him. You have to decide if you're going there.'

Marcus said, and really it was only because, feeling as weak and guilty as he still did, he would have agreed in the end to whatever Varius wanted, 'If I can get there then I will.'

In his bedroom, Marcus flung open the chest where his clothes were folded, and knew as he did it that it was pointless. His clothes had always been given away, still almost new, whenever the first threads began to work free or the fresh colours to pulse out. He needed something old and cheap, and looking at what he was wearing, he realised for the first time how good, how obviously expensive his clothes were. He was dressed in a narrow ribbed-wool tunic over cotton trousers – all black and charcoal grey for mourning; of course he could not go in that – but they were plain and, apart from the colour they had seemed quite ordinary to him, but they weren't, now he looked; they fitted too well, the texture had some matte quality he couldn't have named; even the price of the thin black leather belt he wore over the tunic could probably have bought a whole outfit of synthetic-fibred clothes. But he did not really know what things cost. He felt a lonely pang of inadequacy and gave up for the time being on his clothes. He looked at himself for a moment in the mirror, rubbed his hands across his famous face. For a long time he could not move because he could not think where there were any scissors.

After a while he turned on the light in his mother's room and crept in unwillingly. Since her death it had grown a pure, foreign look and he felt ashamed of being there. But after some searching he found a gold-lacquer sewing box, a gift she had scarcely ever used. As he had hoped, slotted into a groove inside the lid was a pair of tiny ivory-handled scissors meant for cutting embroidery silks. He took them to the bath suite where he began to cut off all his thick hair. The scissors were dainty and finicking in his impatient hands and it was a surprisingly long, difficult business.

The blades were too small to carve through much at a time and he had to chop and slice ineptly at the back of his head, finding the stray tufts by touch. The soft hair fell prickling into his clothes, around his neck. When it was cut as short and even as he could get it, he scraped off what was left with a razor. It struck him that the hair should not be found, and he washed as much of it as he could down the large drain in the floor of the bath. The blond hair circled in the stream of water, darkening as it vanished.

Later he looked at his reflection again, but only briefly. With his hair gone the bones of his face seemed different – harder, and more prominent. He thought he looked at once brutal and defenceless, and did not like the sight of himself. He kept passing a hand over his cold scalp.

Varius passed in the doorway, nodded at what he had done and said hollowly, 'Perhaps – your hands.'

Marcus bit his nails down to the pad of flesh, and scoured away any smoothness there had been with detergent and a pumice stone. The skin stung and bled a little. He clenched his fists around his thumbs, trying to press the soreness out. Varius said, 'That's good.'

Varius was trembling again; he had had to go into his bedroom to fetch some of his own clothes and money, and had seen Gemella lying on the bed in her pink dress. He said, 'This is all the money I can find. You can't go to banks.'

There wasn't very much. They were a rich family, but there was no reason to keep cash in the house. Varius handed it to Marcus saying, 'Take something you can sell, jewellery or something.'

They searched through the dining room, the study, Clodia's room again. With everything he picked up and weighed in his hand, Marcus felt more treacherous and humiliated, as if the house were slowly recoiling from him, disowning him. He tried to take small things, things the servants would not miss, nor could be worth startling amounts of money: a bronze statuette from the dining room, a little silver vase; and from his mother's jewellery box, a sardonyx comb and brooch, a rather ugly bracelet studded with carnelians, and a heavy rope of jade beads. He could not remember his mother wearing these things, and hoped she had not been very fond of them. He swept everything into a pack his father had carried years ago, in the army. Varius made him add bread, water, and a knife from the kitchen, a razor, a blanket.

The clothes Varius had given him were scarcely better for the purpose than any of his own, but at least no one could have seen him in them before. Marcus stabbed a few inconsequential holes into them with the scissors.

At the end of the last hour in his house, Varius showed him a mark he'd drawn over a patch of the Eastern Pyrenees fifty miles or so from Tarba, on a page torn from an atlas, and said, 'I don't know where it is myself; you're not supposed to know. It's called Holzarta. There's a village called Athabia here. Go to it and wait. I hope they'll find you.'

Marcus nodded, but he pressed his sore fingers to his face, because Athabia was nine hundred miles away. By magnetway or air he might have reached it in a day, but Varius had already ruled out going anywhere near public transport. 'Obviously you've got to do without identity papers,' he'd said. 'And even if it was safe for you, it wouldn't be for them. You mustn't lead the vigiles to them.'

'But I won't stay there forever,' Marcus said, although he could barely imagine getting there at all.

'No. No,' said Varius, with strained emphasis. But when Marcus tried to ask how he could come back, he snapped, 'I don't know – something will change. It can't always be like this.'

Before they left Varius – beginning to think of what he must do when Marcus was gone – retrieved the sweet box from the rubbish and, flinching, took the plate of nougat from the study. But he could not bear to enter Gemella's room and left the sweets on the table by Marcus' bed.

They took the butler's keys from the pantry and let themselves into the garage at the rear of the villa. Marcus lay hidden on the floor of Varius' car as it rolled softly away from the unlit house. They had talked of heading south to Neapolis, where Marcus could have crossed the Mediterranean to Massilia, but they could think of no sure way of getting aboard a ship without papers. Instead, they would thread along the web of roads around Rome, towards the Pertinacian Way and the electric freight route running along the spine of Italy and splitting beneath the Alps.

When the gates opened to let Varius through, the guard asked him, 'Everything all right?'

'I've got to go home and get some work done,' blurted Varius, with difficulty. He thought afterwards that he should have added some detail, complained in a companionable way about how they both had to work all night, but all he could manage at the time was to mumble, 'See you in the morning.'

He drove out. He didn't think he needed to worry about any of the villa guards; they were supplied by the Praetorians, but they'd all worked there for years. He muttered half to himself, 'I can't see anyone watching – they might have gone. It's so late.' And then, 'Wait – no.'

He thought he had seen a shadow stir among the tamarisk shrubs near the villa's gates, though if he had not been so primed to watch for it he could not have been sure. And he did not speak again for the rest of the journey in the dark, except when Marcus asked, 'Varius, what will happen to you?' and Varius realised with mild wonder that this had not occurred to him, and answered, 'Nothing.'

For three hours, Marcus looked up at the long stripe of the tram cable and steady throb of streetlamps vibrate across the black square of the window; and Varius clung bitterly to the road like a lost climber to a final rope. They both could almost have forgotten that the steady succession of lights and the soft hiss of the road would ever stop or change. But after three hours, Varius turned down a slip road to the first cargo-tram assembly point along the Pertinacian Way.

Varius slid the car to the side of the road to rest tilted, two wheels on the rough-grassed slope. In silence, they scrambled down the hillside to the cargo trams. The air overhead was tangled with thick tram cables. By the bays where the tram units slowly ranged themselves into convoys for Lusitania, Gaul and Rhaetia, coupling themselves to the lines above, a few drivers, white-faced and tired, milled and drifted like deep-sea fish under the pale lights. They would sleep through most of the journey as the cables drew them through Europe.

It was an ugly, desolate place. Marcus and Varius waited, crouched in the grass, until the men returned to their cabs. As they watched, a long chain of tarpaulin-covered carts rolled up to the Gaul convoy and hooked into place with the rest. Varius looked up at the insignia on the tram cab and gave a stifled cry that was almost a laugh and dashed forward. He whispered breathlessly, 'Gabinius. This is his. Look, he can get you as far as Tarba. You can be with Delir the day after tomorrow. You should remember Gabinius in your prayers. I will.'

He looked almost mad.

'How do you know it's going that far?' asked Marcus anxiously. Varius had already begun to work feverishly on the tarpaulin, tugging loose the cord that held it down over the load of marble.

'It must be,' said Varius impatiently, glancing back warily as another string of tram units approached. The convoy would unravel from the back, the last trams peeling off first towards the closer towns. Gabinius' marble seemed to be at the right point in the convoy's sequence, and Varius knew that one of his construction businesses was responsible for the new governor's house at Tarba. Hastily, Varius helped Marcus climb up under the tarpaulin among the slabs, thrust Leo's bag in after him, and began to tie the canvas down again.

Through the shrinking gap, Marcus looked up at Varius' haggard face and began, 'Varius—' but Varius would not let him get any further. He said shortly, 'Don't tell anyone except Delir who you are and don't come back until you hear from me. Stay awake and cut yourself out when it stops.' And under the tarpaulin the faint light vanished as he pulled the last flap of canvas down and fixed the loops of cord on the side. Varius dodged back up the slope. As he ran Marcus' age occurred to him again, and so did the fondness that he, Varius, usually felt for him. He regretted distantly that he had not been able to say anything kinder, more reassuring, but he was sure any exchange of sympathy would have been fatal to what had to be done; there wasn't enough of himself left to spare on it. He sat tensely in the car, watching with sand-dry eyes as the cargo trams began to move. When the convoy was gone the unreality of the night seemed to roll through and past him in a great clawed wave, until he could scarcely think how he had come there, or how he could drive back towards Rome when all he could see was Gemella on the patterned floor, on the bed. He slumped back in the seat, and had no idea how long it was until he could move.

The next morning Marcus heard a whisking sound as the tram detached from the cable and felt a pull of changing gravity as it slowed. A little warm light was filtering through the canvas above him, and he realised that despite Varius' warning he had slept and the confused miles he had walked in the cold had been dreams. Yet he felt that he had not been asleep long and though he tried to think he was wrong, he could not shake off the idea that the sparse light had an early look about it.

He pushed the blanket away. The space under the tarpaulin had gone from freezing to sweatily hot, and marble dust was smarting in the scratches on his hands. He felt for the knife in his pack, cut a gash in the canvas, set his eye to it and saw nothing but white-blue sky and unlit streetlamps, and later, trees, as the tram left the highway.

Presently the tram stopped and Marcus heard the driver's feet outside on gravel. Marcus waited, beating his fingers unconsciously on the marble. He already had the feeling of something not right.

The footsteps passed, and Marcus began to pull and hack

at the hole he'd made in the tarpaulin, hauled himself out and dropped clumsily into the daylight, onto the gravel. He got to his feet, went forward, shaking his head, blinking, brushing the dust off Varius' clothes.

He was on the edge of a scraped-out building site, where the brick skeleton of something stood among scaffolding. Marcus stood and looked at it.

A builder glanced up at him from the base of the scaffolding, raised a fist and shouted 'Hey! Hey!' Marcus ran up the gravel path until it vanished among high laurels. His heart was kicking against his ribs but he felt a brief spur of elation. He was quite sure the builder had not recognised him.

Something was still wrong, and he still couldn't place what it was. He slogged up the path and came to a quiet lane between steep green hedges; but he could hear a busy road somewhere to his right and turned towards it. It was a while before he reached ground high enough to be sure of what was bothering him: if there were mountains anywhere nearby, he couldn't see them.

His sense of direction, indeed his sense of everything, had been so shaken about in the last twenty-four hours that he could still believe he'd made a mistake. He kept along towards the noisy road, clenching and unclenching his stinging hands; but when he reached it the signposts he saw stopped him dead. He was not in Tarba or near it. The road was for Nemausus, and the valley in the Pyrenees was more than three hundred miles away.

[v]

WHITE AND SILVER

Sulien, flinching, heard the crackle of the bullets in the air and, like Una, assumed the soldiers were shooting at them and the escape was as good as over. The barge was still between them, and in the final second before it slid away he was certain that already Una had been shot. He waited, horrified, kicking at the complacent water with dreadful impatience, as the barge peeled past. He saw only a vanishing wrinkling on the surface where Una had been, and then, a moment later, a dark curve of her floating dress, and the veining of her hair in the water. At once he began ploughing back towards her, with no time to think what he was doing, though he expected a second flight of bullets to stop him before he ever reached her.

So he did not see what was happening on the prison ferry, nor why, though more shots rang in the air, they never struck him.

The prisoners had stormed the cockpit. As the first prisoner, a heavy man, tore open the door, the nearest guard had time to draw his gun and shoot him in the chest. But the large body fell forward, briefly pinioning the soldiers, and as it did the others piled in behind. There was a confused second in which, in that packed and narrow space, the soldiers' guns were as good as useless. A second bullet shattered the window as a grim, cramped fight for the weapons began. No one on the river noticed Una dropping underwater or Sulien's breathless race back towards her; for now all attention was on the ferry. There was an alarmed whooping of horns from the nearby boats as the uncontrolled ferry veered through the water, crumpling a small tug against the embankment and hurtling into the thick river traffic. Rudders and propellers groaned in the water as pilots strained to wrestle their boats out of its path.

The soldier who struggled backwards through the cockpit's second door was called Laeca. He was twenty-four, far from his parents in Pergamum, and minutes before he'd been pensively chewing his thumbnail. Now, his gun smashed from his hand, he fled across the deck and plunged overboard into the river. But he'd barely swum a stroke before a stooped and scraggy figure came out of the cockpit, onto the deck, delighted by the new weapon in his hand. It was the man who'd been crying in his cell. He fired into the water and kept firing for the pleasure of it, even when Laeca had stopped moving in the reddened water.

Sulien heard the roar of noise, but only the shots meant anything to him and he never looked above the patch of water which held Una. She slipped out of sight again just before he reached her. He splashed forward and stirred about frantically, clutched only acrid water, ducked under the green surface. His blind hands met nothing, nothing. After an age a floating wisp of something brushed softly against his fingertips. He caught at it, felt a weight, and grappled her up out of the water by her hair and heavy clothes.

It was like a fight. He forced her through the water, shoving, tugging, while she hung deadweight and limp, and seemed always dragging down, falling away from him. It was a while before he saw that it would be easier to hold her out of the water if he turned onto his back. Even then it was hard; he was no better than an adequate swimmer, and he had to go in stops and desperate starts, because he still had to dodge the charging boats; and all the time he almost fancied that she was deliberately pulling out of his arms, as though she wanted to be down in the softness on the river bed.

But at last his feet bumped and slid on the weedy steps at the wharfside; and as he stood, his sodden clothes sagging around him, he saw that after all there was no wound on Una's body. He found the artery at her neck, and under his hand, as if all the time he'd known it was there, he felt the dutiful pulse. She wasn't breathing, but he knew that she would. He even grinned as he lifted her up onto the concrete, because he knew that the water would break out of her mouth, and that she would open her eyes; and it did, she did.

Una wheezed and shivered. The water felt hot and acidic as it bubbled endlessly up her throat. She wanted to say that they must get away from the water's edge, but she couldn't get a word between the ugly rasping sounds her breathing made. She looked towards the river with bleary eyes, and it was only then they saw the ferry.

It was grazed and battered now, but still it sped on. They saw it turn in a sudden violent curve, and drive a brutal, erratic course back the way it had come. On the deck, the prisoner who'd cried looked down at the bodies at his feet, and, after a while, hauled the nearest corpse upright, and with an effort, levered it over the rail and let it plunge into the water.

On the wharf, Una and Sulien watched with weary astonishment. Then Sulien hoisted Una to her feet and staggered with her towards the warehouse. As he held her up he could feel how her cold bones ached with weakness, felt the burning in her lungs subside enough for her to say 'Not there – the shed.' They lurched across the yard. 'Not inside,' said Una, hoarsely. She didn't think she could stand the dark and clutter, and the smell in the air.

He helped her round behind the shed, out of sight of the river, and they both slid to the ground, panting, leaning back against the shed's rough wall, loving the dry ground beneath them. Una remembered the rest of her plan and thought, almost luxuriously, but I will never be able to move. It would be so pleasant if nothing more could be expected of her.

Then Sulien said slowly, 'Una, *thank you*, thank you *so much*,' and folded her into his arms and hugged her. Una closed her arms loosely against his back and looked at the wall over his shoulder, vaguely saddened. She didn't like to be touched, not even the most casual brush of arm against arm if it could reasonably be avoided. But now she realised she had hoped that once away from the house in the Lupanarian District, she would be different. And it *was* different. She felt only mild claustrophobia, not disgust. Perhaps it was a start.

He let her go and she noticed that he looked paler than before. Then she had to lean forward, choking again, as the last dregs of water rose up from her lungs. But when she had her breath again she realised that she was no longer trembling, and though she was still riddled with tiredness, she knew she could stand and walk. And she realised what he must have done.

'You did that, didn't you?' she said.

'Couldn't do very much,' he said. 'You need food and sleep and clean water.' He had shut his eyes.

'I didn't ask you to,' said Una, tight-lipped.

He opened his eyes and stared at her. 'I had to, didn't I? You weren't going anywhere like that.'

'I'd have been all right,' said Una unreasonably, 'and now *you're* tired. And you didn't tell me.'

'Did you want to be ill?' said Sulien, beginning to be irritated now, 'because you'd have been much worse later. There were all kinds of things in that water. And you got me off that boat – I had to.'

She knew she was being stupid. She wasn't sure why she felt so affronted, unless it was the idea of someone else in control of her, however briefly and for however good a reason. And she had not even noticed it happen.

'Well, you ought to have told me,' she said, trying clumsily to sound a little friendlier.

'All right,' said Sulien, still a little annoyed.

'Anyway, thank you,' said Una awkwardly.

Sulien looked at her curiously. 'How did you get me off the boat?' And then he looked down at his soaking prison uniform and asked 'What are we going to do?'

Una got up, looked around warily, and went into the shed. Sulien heard her clanking around in there and a minute later she dragged out a battered black travelling bag. She pulled it open, and inside Sulien saw clothes and scraggy towels, all neatly folded.

'I couldn't get you any shoes,' she was saying. 'I hope it won't matter. We'll go to Dubris and through the tunnel. I don't know Gaul. I don't know where we'll go. Just as far away as we can. Travelling will be harder after today.'

'But you can't get through without citizenship papers,' said Sulien.

Una opened a pocket on the bag's side and said shortly, 'These are the only things I've stolen.' She sounded angry again, although not with him. She handed him a slim sheaf of blue citizenship documents folded into a plastic wallet. Sulien pulled the papers out and looked down at a list of colourless facts and the picture of an unremarkable face. 'That's you,' said Una, briskly pulling a heap of clothes out of the bag and tossing them at him. But the man in the picture was nine years older than Sulien, and, beyond a very vague similarity in colouring, looked nothing like him.

'They won't notice,' she said. Sulien was about to say that of course they would, and then remembered how no one on the river had seen them as they jumped from the boat. 'Yes,' she said wearily, answering the thought, 'I'll make sure they don't.' She had a little pack of yellow freed person's documents for herself, but she didn't show them to him.

Sulien was as disconcerted as she had been a moment before, but there was no time to think about it. They changed hurriedly inside the shed. The clothes were cheap and drab, and Sulien's were rather too small. Una had been wearing a short and incongruously skimpy green summer dress, printed with pale scattered stars, but the outfit she put on now was shapeless enough to swallow anyone shorter than she; a long, dress-like blouse over the loose Sinoan trousers women had lately begun to wear. Everything was a wan grey which seemed to suck away what little colour there was in her pale hair and skin.

Una wrapped up her sodden dress in a towel and packed it away, but told Sulien to weight down his uniform with broken bricks before sinking it in the Thames. He had scarcely begun before she took the suit from him and did it herself, complaining that he was too slow and not thorough enough, the cloth might float free; and then perhaps the vigiles would know at what point they had escaped the boat, and perhaps after all someone would remember seeing them. Then she took out the packets of money, and hesitated before she gave one of them to Sulien. She knew the safest thing would be to share them out evenly, but she couldn't rid herself of the fear that Sulien would lose everything she had so painfully saved. She could picture him doing it, clouds of money puffing like smoke signals from his pockets while he wandered innocently on. He knew nothing about the things she knew, she thought, nothing about planning and keeping things secret. 'Be careful with it,' she said, with a wary look at him. Then she knotted up her hair, hoping to make its wetness less noticeable.

Sulien felt mildly exasperated. She was a year younger than him and she was treating him like a burdensome child. But the money was hers and he was surprised that there was so much of it; especially since she claimed she had stolen nothing except the papers. When he asked she only said, 'It's mine, that's all.'

Before they set out, Una took a little pot of thick foundation out of the bag. He was surprised at first, because everything else she had packed was so rigorously practical, and then saw what it was for as she began, without the aid of a mirror, to rub it into the bruised side of her face. She had no other cosmetics and it gave her face a waxy, blinded look.

He said, 'Those bruises. I think I could . . .'

She said, 'They don't hurt any more.'

'But anyone can see you're a slave. A free girl wouldn't have bruises like that.' She scowled a little, and showed the make-up on her fingertips. 'And it looks weird, that stuff.

Noticeable,' he added cunningly, because really it was just that the sight of them troubled him – he kept wanting to touch the side of his own face.

She knew this time why she didn't want him to do anything, although again it made no real sense: it was that if you had been hit, there should be bruises – or how would you trust your memory? But that was ridiculous, so she turned her face to him reluctantly, shutting her eye, twitching slightly as he laid his fingers on her eyelid and cheekbone.

'I can't make anything vanish,' he said. 'I can't make anything not have happened. They won't show so much now, and tomorrow they'll be gone. That's all.'

He saw the pooled blood under the skin, he urged it away into the tissue, and Una felt the bruised places glow and fade. It felt like tiny weights on the muscle of her face, lightening.

They ventured out from the wharf and into London. To Sulien the city felt suddenly foreign. Every familiar sound and colour seemed unlikely and wrong, every face faintly bizarre. Even now he was not paranoid, he did not find the crowd on London Bridge actually sinister, or fancy that people were watching him when they were not. No, but he felt, and *was*, so separate from everyone else who flowed over the bridge, who were not looking at him menacingly but were unthinkingly trusting him to be like themselves, wrongly. It was lonely.

He could see Una's features trying to work into nonchalant calm, and saw that she was used to this, to slipping through streets and feeling cut away from everyone in them. But for all that he thought he managed a little better than she did, because at least he knew how it felt to walk through London quite at ease, and Una didn't. She did not really look ordinary. Her shadowy clothes were too neutral; the casual expression did not fit on her stern face. Her shoulders were raised a little and she kept clenching her jaw.

From the bridge they saw the empty steel crosses, and a

cohort boat speeding away down river, armed soldiers on the deck.

They said little as they walked through the city, both because the tiredness was coming back now, and because they could think of nothing ordinary to say. They spoke only when Sulien thanked Una, but that was often. He thanked her as they set out, and when they were past the crosses, which Una thought very thoughtless, and again when they reached the white and glittering Novius Faustus magnetway station. Una had never been inside it before, and she was staggered by the space and beauty of it, at the columns shining like vast icicles beneath the snowy ceiling, and the rows of smooth trains lying ahead like silvery necklaces in a jewellery box. Then, high above, she saw a little team of slaves, slung dizzyingly between the columns in a corner. They were polishing the milky walls.

Sulien insisted on buying food before they went any further. Una went to queue for the tickets, feeling suddenly bereft and surprised at it. Oh, we shouldn't have separated, she thought, smiling her pretty smile as she paid the clerk. He won't come back, he'll do something stupid. Something will happen.

But nothing did. Sulien came back with what seemed to her ridiculous quantities of food, and thanked her again. Una, assessing the future, thought coldly that what she wanted from him was not thanks but an apology. But without expecting to, she beamed at him, and he had already become used to her face being either blank or frowning, and was surprised.

Before they went out to the glossy trains Sulien took out the citizenship papers she had given him and whispered to her, 'What if they've been reported stolen?'

'I only took them a week ago,' she said. 'He won't have needed them since then. Why should he notice they've gone?'

'What about yours?'

'They aren't exactly stolen,' said Una.

But she was worried about it. She thought Sulien might

99

pass for a man in his early twenties to someone who was not thinking or looking very hard, but though she always thought of herself as older than she really was, the freed person's papers had belonged to a woman of thirty-one, and no one could believe she was that. There was no reason she should not be capable of making sure no one looked hard at either her face or the papers, and yet she was more afraid as they stepped towards the inspectors than she'd been in the cockpit, or at any point before. There was so much to be lost now.

But as Sulien held out the papers and tickets he heard Una take a sharp, effortful breath, and saw that as she'd said, the inspector glanced only at the colour and shape of the documents, not at the detail; and they walked past and onto the train for Gaul. Almost the instant it began to move, Una slid down the green leather seat, and fell heavily asleep.

But the train plunged along so fast that London and the countryside beyond it rattled away in an unsettling blur. Half an hour later it stopped at Dubris, jolting Una awake, and then fled on, dipped briefly under the sea like a needle under cloth, and came up in Arras and then curved away south into Gaul. Their tickets were the most expensive Una thought they could afford, and for Lemovices, which neither of them knew anything about.

Una went to sleep again and Sulien looked back out of the window. As they pushed south he watched the flat fields swell and brighten and turn cool blue with lavender under the hot blue sky. He was not quite tired enough to sleep. He ate some of the bread and spiced sausage he had bought, and wished Una would wake up. But he felt sorry for wishing it when he looked at her; asleep the tense look was gone, and she looked pretty and so much gentler than she really was. He thought, that's really her, I was always right. He thought, I should be hanging up by the Thames now; although not dead yet, no, most likely not yet dead. He smiled because it hadn't happened, but he shivered at the same time, and again he clenched his hand around his wrist, kneading the flesh with his thumb. He didn't know that he would do this unconsciously, whenever he was nervous, for the rest of his life.

At length the train stopped at Aurelianum and Una woke up thinking I've been asleep, I've made an awful mistake, they've killed him. Then she saw the moving blue out of the window, and Sulien pushing the bag of food towards her across the little table. She smiled at him incredulously. He was really there. He thanked her again. She snapped, 'Oh, stop it,' and smiled some more.

He spread out the food on the table; the sausage and bread, a bottle of water, a little pot of rabbit cooked with lovage, cheese. She ate slowly, feeling at first that she was still too tired to be hungry, but her appetite began to come back as she ate, and the food was good.

He waited until she had finished. He wasn't sure what to ask first. 'You did something to those soldiers,' he began cautiously, 'and the people on the river, and that inspector.'

'Hardly anything,' she said, 'only something they might have done themselves. Just . . . just *distracted* them, just for a minute.'

'Can you tell everything I'm thinking?'

She paused. She had never explained this to anyone before. 'No. Not unless I – no.'

'Not unless? Then you can?'

'No, really. It would be too difficult. There's too *much*.' She broke off, concentrating. 'No. I'm not saying this clearly.' She paused again. 'There's feeling. I see that. Always. Unless . . .' and she closed her eyes frowning. 'I can . . . pull back from it. There. Now it's just me in here.' She opened her eyes again and sighed.

'Do you actually see something? Like colour?'

'No.' She tried to think of another way of putting it. The words for what she meant weren't there. 'No, I could say hear or . . . or sometimes I think it's like temperature in the air. But it isn't really like any of those things.

'And just beyond that,' she stretched out her fingers as if trying to touch something delicate and receding, 'there's . . . there's the shape of . . . like hearing a conversation but not quite catching the words, you could still tell what kind of conversation it was.'

'You mean people thinking.'

'Yes, but not really the thoughts, not unless I try. Think about thinking: it isn't like reciting a speech. Half the time it's just *jabber*. That's easy, that almost – floats off, but the more complicated – the more I want to see, it gets harder and harder, and I *hate it*, I couldn't keep it up.'

He began to feel slightly reassured, then remembered how she'd seemed to answer thoughts he hadn't spoken. 'But when we were in the shed?'

'That was as much the way you stopped talking as anything else. As much the way you looked. Sometimes I can see things without trying, if it's very . . . sharp, or if the person can't think about anything else, and I think some people are more . . . more transparent, I don't know. But that's really all anyone does, isn't it? Pretty much anyone can do that.'

'And you promise you won't do any more than that, not to me . . .'

She lowered her eyes a little and said levelly. 'I have done. On the boat, before you even knew I was there.'

He bristled slightly. 'Why did you? I don't want you to again, ever.'

'I had to,' she said quietly, still not looking at him. 'I wanted to know if I was right. You see, if I hadn't been . . . You see . . .' her voice dropped to a breath. 'I was sure you hadn't – raped that girl . . .'

They were silent.

'All right,' he said at last with an effort, 'I suppose you did have to.' And then, almost unwillingly. 'If I had – what would you have done?'

'I don't know,' she said. Her hands were clenched in her lap. She raised them suddenly and scrubbed them fiercely at her face. 'I don't know. I hate to think of it.'

'How did you even know about me?'

'It was in a news sheet. Just a little piece. Just your name,' she said tersely, and then suddenly she was almost hissing at him, 'And *why did you do such a stupid thing!* I *always* meant to find you, for *years* I've planned and . . . But we would have just slipped away, it shouldn't be like this. What's going to happen? They'll always be looking for you. We'll always be hiding, there's *nowhere we can go*, is there?'

'But I never thought this would happen,' he stammered, taken aback. Guiltily he remembered Tancorix telling him that they were doing the worst possible thing.

'You should have thought,' she said bitterly. 'You must have seen what a risk it was. And just for *that*. Were you *in love* with her?' She sounded disgusted.

'No,' he said weakly, 'I don't think so.'

'Then *why*—?' She broke off, shaking.

Sulien could hardly reply that Tancorix had been very attractive. 'I'm – I'm sorry,' he said helplessly. She nodded tightly, not trusting herself to speak. He said, 'I always meant to find you, too, you know. We looked for you. Where were you, all that time?'

Her mouth opened a little and trembled. Her breath seemed to stick in her throat. She said, barely audibly, 'You looked for me?'

'Of course.' He didn't know why she should look so stricken. 'I made Catavignus promise he'd . . . he'd buy you. We knew you were in a factory somewhere, and then working in someone's house – but he never found you so I always said I would, once I was grown up and freed. I *knew* I'd see you again, Una.'

'He was going to free you?' She looked more and more appalled. 'And he would have – he looked for me, just for you?'

It was painful to think of Catavignus. He said, 'He was . . . always kind until – I don't know what to think about him now. Oh, what is it?' Una had put up her fingers too late to blot the tear that dropped between them.

'I knew where you were,' she whispered. 'You mean I only had to go *in*?'

Sulien frowned, not understanding.

'I knew when Catavignus bought you,' she faltered. 'Everyone did, you were famous for a little while.'

'But you couldn't have got there—?' he began.

'Yes, I did!' she said. 'Once, I got away from the – from the house, and I went and – stood outside.'

He was speechless. He reached a hand out towards hers, but she jerked away so violently he withdrew it. He said softly, 'Why didn't you go in?'

'They would have sent me back, it would have spoiled everything,' Una wailed. 'I was *twelve*. And then they would have known who I was and the – the people that owned me would never have trusted me again and it would have been harder later. I shouldn't even have gone there in the first place, that's what I thought. Because I always meant that we should run away and we couldn't do it then, I hadn't got the money and we were too *young*. I didn't *know*.'

He would have put his arm round her but she was huddled away from him against the window. He said, 'You couldn't have seen—?'

She shook her head. 'I couldn't do as much then. I *did* look – I'm sure there was nothing about that.'

'No,' he said sadly, 'If you were twelve then we must have given up by then.'

She made a spasmodic effort and controlled her face. She said, sneering dully, 'It doesn't matter. I didn't know. I didn't want a nice man to *buy me*, and *look after me* anyway. Look.'

She flicked the yellow freed woman's paper across the table. Sulien opened it and felt something like a scrape along the skin, even in the long second before he understood that that name was his mother's name, that face her face. Yes, that was what she had looked like. He had forgotten so much.

And it was no use waiting for some stronger feeling about her, there just wasn't one. He said to the picture, 'Poor thing.' He folded it up gently and tucked it into his pocket.

He could at least protect her picture from Una. Because he could see that Una despised her.

'That family I worked for,' Una said carefully, 'they sold me on because one day I realised they couldn't make me do anything. Do you understand? I thought, they can do what they like *to* me, but still those stairs or whatever won't get cleaned, not by me, unless I decide to do it. They said, you have to, but I didn't have to. So I decided I wouldn't. They were so angry with me. But I was almost . . . pleased.'

He could see what she meant but there was something chilling about it. He might not have her gift, but he knew she meant they had punished her, badly, and she had chosen that they should for the sake of a gesture, for nothing. He couldn't imagine thinking like that, couldn't really imagine not wanting to be liked.

'So they sold me and I was just the same and it was pretty bad. So then later I thought, it was good to know that, but it wouldn't help, and if I carried on like that someone might even kill me one day. I made people so angry. So instead I tried very hard to be, to pretend to be *good*,' sneering again. 'And by then, I think it started when I was about eleven, I could tell what people thought of me and what they wanted from me, so it was easier. So they trusted me, I made them *like* me.'

'I suppose I did that,' said Sulien thinking uncomfortably of how he'd extracted promises from Catavignus. But surely he had never calculated so.

'Yes,' said Una, and softened just a little. 'So they used to let me out more and more to buy things, or take things to be cleaned, things like that. They knew I'd come back. So for longer and longer times. And I went back, I went to *her*.'

'Was she all right?' he asked.

Una looked at him and wondered and said to herself again the word 'innocent'. For some reason she thought of the immaculate white and silver of the Novius Faustus station they had left, where dirt could never settle.

'Yes, she wasn't ill or anything. She was the same as she always was. Don't you remember?'

'No. I don't remember anything much about that time, just you. That's why I'm sorry for her.'

She sighed and thought, well, it's good that he's like that; I can't want him to be unkind or unhappy, can I?

'We were freed,' she said. 'We were freed for about ten minutes in our father's will. All of us. That's why she had the paper. But she was so *weak*, she didn't know how to do anything except be a slave, she couldn't do anything anyone would pay for and she was just scared. She liked belonging to someone. She wanted that new family – do you realise that they were our cousins? She wanted them to keep her so badly that when they wouldn't keep us too she sold us to Rufius. Or let them sell us, I'm not sure. Now do you—?'

But she stopped short, after all she could not demand that he stop pitying that poor frightened woman.

'And she was just the same,' she said. 'I told her where I was and what it was like and I said, come on, we'll go. We'll get Sulien. We'll go somewhere and we'll be fine. But she didn't *want to*. She kept telling me I should go back, it would get better or it couldn't be as bad as I thought it was. And in the end, we were shouting at each other – and I said at least give me your papers, you won't need them, you'll never leave here. She only did it because she was so used to doing what she was told. But then the new people – her owners, they came back and she *told* them, after I trusted her she *told* them where I came from and they took me back and . . .'

She touched her face, but the bruises were all but invisible now.

'Anyway, it took so long to make them trust me again,' she said. 'So that's why I didn't go in, when I went to Catavignus' house.'

She looked out at the lavender fields and thought of white – a snowflake, glittering and turning, and spreading like a gentle blizzard, a soundless explosion.

'She was ever so young,' said Sulien gently, touching the pocket which held the paper. 'I never thought of that. She must have been . . . fifteen when I was born.'

She nodded just slightly.

'Una, why did you keep saying "they"?' he said. 'Who do you mean? Where were you when we couldn't find you? And how did you get all that money?'

'It doesn't matter now, does it?' said Una.

They settled into uncomfortable silence and this time he was relieved when she fell asleep again. He pictured the map of the world and Rome stretching across it like a relaxing cat, from Persia to the west of Terranova. Latin was the only language they knew, and she was right, there wasn't an inch of earth they could be safe in.

But there were olive trees and oleanders on the slopes that rushed past the window, and though the air in the train was mechanically cooled, already his skin could almost feel the golden heat outside, and he might have been dead and was not. He couldn't have been unhappy.

[VI]

SIBYLLINA

It was good. Buying food was always risky and alarming, and what with that and walking, his bones seemed to be wearing through his flesh amazingly fast. Every day he felt a little less substantial. His chest was corrugated, when he folded his arms he could feel the jagged points of his elbows, like flints against his palms. Through the meagre-looking skin and the hard crop of darkish stubble on his head, he could see the shape of his skull quite clearly now. There was also fainter, blonder stubble on his jaw. He thought he had better shave his head again. He had left his chin alone for a while, but it was plainly no good expecting much of a beard. His eyelids were swollen a little, and showed small river-systems of purple veins above the lashes. There were bruise-purple smears under the eyes, too, like thumbprints. He had not slept very well for the last thirteen nights.

He did not look much, then, like the picture on the news stand, or on the large screen over the racing arena, or everywhere. Or the one he held in his hands. He looked at his thin reflection in the car window with satisfaction, and thought it seemed quite likely he was no such person. It was good.

He could never have thought that there would be quite so many pictures, or that people would be so fascinated. He had trudged into Nemausus that first day, and everywhere had been quite anonymous and harmless. Despite the miles ahead of him he had begun to feel a deep, sly pleasure. For the first time in his life he had wandered past shops and market stalls and no one had looked at him.

Then in the afternoon the story broke, and it had seemed to set a tremor going that had still not settled down. He began to hear his own name everywhere and kept having to force himself not to turn in response. He had seen people poring over his picture with their hands to their mouths. Worst of all, two young women had come running out of a tavern looking wild-eyed and crashed into him. As he stumbled away one of them, a curly-haired girl, caught his arm and exclaimed, 'Hey – do you know, Marcus Novius's been abducted? Leo's kid!'

'No, he's run off!' corrected the other. 'Isn't it awful? Just after that crash!' They had looked almost jubilant. He didn't know what he had said or how he'd seemed to them.

That night he hadn't dared to look for a room and had huddled sleeplessly on a bench near the temple of Diana. The next morning, he and everyone got up to find that five hundred thousand sesterces had been offered to anyone who could find him.

The one encouraging thing about the news sheets was that they let him know that there had been sightings of him everywhere; back in Italy, and in Hierosolyma, and several Roman Terranovans thought they had seen him in Caesarea Incarum. He often wondered what the people had really seen, or how many people there were in the world who looked so much like him.

He turned away from the car, and into a side street. He kept his shoulders hunched and his face lowered, almost always. Standing secretively in a doorway, he tore the picture of Marcus Novius into strips, twisted them, put them into his mouth and chewed until they were pliable and soft with saliva. Then he poked them into his cheeks, above his teeth, and under his upper lip. After some experiments, he'd worked out this way of adjusting his face in a hostel one night at the end of the first week, when the longing to look different was almost all he could think about. He'd found that anything in the lower jaw looked obvious and deformed, but filling out the space beneath his cheekbones just distorted the line of his mouth a little, and made his top lip curl under slightly so that it looked narrower. He was surprised to find it did not affect his voice when he spoke. He couldn't be sure how much difference it made to the risk of detection in the long term, but at least it made him feel a little better. Sometimes, rather to his disgust, he found the snug pressure against his gums almost comforting. It would have been intolerable to keep the wet paper in place for any length of time, but it was good for whenever he had to go and talk to someone, as he did now.

Marcus had been a very little boy when he had begun to wonder what it would be like to be mad, and how he could tell a normal thought from a crooked one. Now, almost worse than the constant, watchful dread, was the fact that such dread was quite obviously not normal. To pretend you weren't yourself, to walk along staring at the pavement hoping no one could get a clear look at your face, to believe you had been chased away from your country by murderers – surely mad people thought and did things like that. More, everyone kept saying or hinting that Marcus – the real Rome-Marcus and not this provisional and itinerant person – had gone mad, or broken down in some way. He read meaningful phrases, like 'devastated by his parents' death'; and the longvisions he saw in shops seemed always to be playing footage of the funeral, of that distant Marcus struggling with Lucius and then crying. There were other things written, anxious things about how Marcus Novius must be brought home and helped, how afraid his family were for his health. Showing Uncle Lucius was as close as the news sheets had got to bringing up the Novian Curse, but Marcus was sure they meant people to think of it. And though he flipped through countless images of that face which no longer quite matched his own, he never found anything about Varius or Gemella's death. Sometimes it seemed ridiculously arrogant to trust his own memory when every outside thing cried out that he was wrong, the things he thought had happened had not, and there were no enemies to hide from. But then he remembered Gemella's body jolting on the floor, and was shocked that he could doubt anything he had learnt that awful night and he fretted all the more about Varius. And he realised that whoever in the palace was issuing instructions to the press had been clever; they had not only encouraged everyone to look out for him, but they had made sure that anything he said if caught would not be believed. Even if he had wanted to, he could not get anyone to help or hide him now.

But sometimes even these thoughts seemed both self-aggrandising and paranoid: mad.

It was just growing dark, and he had been in Tolosa a few hours. He had not slept in a bed for the last three nights, because of the way it cut through his money, and because he had been out among fields between towns, and also because of the thing that had happened the last time. But now he was feeling a little more daring again, and besides the desire for sleep and a lockable door was growing over-powering. Already he had found a musty little inn on the outskirts of town, had been inside and looked longingly at the flat narrow bed in the tilt-floored room he had been shown. He spoke warily with the landlady: he was called Pollio, he had been an apprentice glassworker in Ruthena but had fallen out with his boss, he didn't want to go home to his parents because they would be angry – did she know of any jobs going in Tolosa?

While walking, he had worked out all kinds of other details about Pollio, more than he was ever likely to need. It was something to think about. Now he had to stop him-self from pouring them all out uselessly. As he talked he felt surreptitiously in his pockets and realised the notes he had left were smaller and thinner than he had thought – if he wanted the room he would have to go and sell some-thing. He asked the landlady to keep the bed for him, and walked back into Tolosa, which was flat and confusing, like the pieces of a broken pink plate.

Now, the wads of paper securely in place, he stood for a moment outside a shop whose window glittered darkly with rings and glass beads. It seemed like the right kind of place. He didn't know how much the things in his pack were worth; perhaps if he sold everything he could buy an electric birota and reach the Pyrenees in three days instead of another two weeks. He was frustrated with the progress he was making. But he would not show everything at once, he would be careful. He checked his gaunt face in the window once more, to make sure it had not changed back into that other boy's in the last few minutes. He took a breath and went inside.

He hesitated. A news sheet lay open on the glass counter, and the shopkeeper was glancing between it and a young woman and her mother, who were trying on rings. The women drew a little closer together as he entered, and the shopkeeper shot him a pained look. This was reassuring in one way, but he didn't really like it. He shuffled apologetically, tried to make himself look smaller. He unslung his backpack, slowly and obviously so they wouldn't think he was about to pull a knife out of it, and felt inside for the cool beads.

The girl was talking. 'It's a shame, I always liked him best. But I don't think I want him to be Emperor if he's going to vanish every time something happens.'

'I dare say he won't do it again,' said the mother absently, scrutinising the blue stone on her finger, wondering if you could tell it was only coloured glass, and if it mattered.

Marcus turned away, freezing over a little. He might have left, but the shopkeeper was still eyeing him suspiciously and now he leant over the counter and said roughly:

'Did you want something?' But then his eyes caught the jade beads between Marcus' fingers.

'Oh, they're lovely,' sighed the girl.

'Yes, well,' said the woman, looking critically at Marcus' shorn head and scuffed clothes.

'Mother, we couldn't . . . ?' the girl wheedled, without much hope, still gazing lovingly at the cool rounds of green.

'How much money do you think I'm spending on you? You're getting one little ring.'

'I couldn't just try them on? *Please*.'

'No. Anyway, you don't know where they come from.' The older woman frowned at Marcus, and added meaningfully, 'Or whose they are.'

'Quite right,' said the shopkeeper, but he looked at the beads almost as hungrily as the girl had. 'What are you doing with those?'

'My mother,' said Marcus, as he'd meant to. 'She's lost her job. Do you want these? She's always had them. She can't bear to do it herself.'

The woman gave a sceptical little cough, slid the blue ring off her finger and folded her arms. She looked censoriously from Marcus to the shopkeeper. The girl made an apologetic grimace, shot one more melancholy glance at the jade and turned back to the little heap of jewellery on the counter by the shopkeeper's news sheet.

'We don't buy junk from people who just walk in off the street,' the man claimed self-consciously. 'Try the flea market.'

Marcus shrugged and was about to turn away when some eyebrow-work from the shopkeeper stopped him.

Then the girl remarked vaguely, 'I don't see how he could be in Lacota. I think people only say it to get attention.'

'Oh, I'm sure they thought they saw something,' the woman said, relaxing a little now and turning the rings over again. 'There are plenty of boys with blond hair.'

'I suppose,' the girl said. She looked wistfully at the jade again as it vanished into Marcus' bag, and then up at his face.

'You know, you look like him,' she said, and the others looked at him for a moment – a musing, assessing look.

This had happened once before. In a hostel, in the last town, he'd found himself in a room with a pair of tourists, brothers from Mona a few years older than he was. He'd spent most of the time with them shamming sleep, trying to avoid talking to them, but he didn't want to seem unusually cagey either, and in the morning the brothers had talked so loudly that to pretend to be asleep would have looked ridiculous. They'd chatted about the places they'd seen in Gaul, about how much warmer it was than on Mona – and suddenly the older boy said cheerfully: 'Hey Pollio, you're not Marcus Novius are you? You've got exactly the same nose.'

For a second he couldn't speak.

'No he hasn't,' snorted the younger boy, saving him. 'And Marcus Novius isn't that scraggy-looking. No offence, Pollio.'

'I wish,' Marcus managed. All the moisture seemed to have gone from his mouth and throat. 'I wouldn't run away. Think of all that money.' He'd wondered if he looked as pale as he felt.

So now, although he felt as if he'd taken a step and the firm-looking ground had crumbled under his weight, he was a little better prepared. He smiled at the girl.

'My mum always says that. Thought it was only her.'

She smiled back and her mother nudged her warningly. She was a pretty girl; the beads would have suited her. He willed his heart to slow down, his hands not to shake.

The shopkeeper came around the counter and pushed him towards the door, but as he did so he muttered in Marcus' ear, 'I mean it about the flea market, go to my brother-in-law, Petrus. The stall with the red vases. He's not so fussy about where things come from.'

He watched Marcus for a while as he walked away, and when the women had finally settled on a garnet and an amethyst ring and left, he went to the longdictor in the back room.

Marcus did not know where the flea market was, and at first he walked only to calm his breath and pulse. The ropes of soggy paper were beginning to annoy him now. He put his fingers into his mouth to pull them out and found that the padding above his front teeth had slipped down just a little. It might perhaps have been visible while he spoke – and then what the girl had said . . . Stop it, stop it. He thought of the bed, the locked door, and the money. He threw the clotted paper away.

He could not bring himself to ask for directions, but he

found the flea market without much difficulty. He passed the dark dome of a temple, rearing somewhere from the city's flat bed, behind the plane trees and chimneys; and then, hesitating between turnings in a little paprika-coloured square, he saw there were figures thronging busily in a glow of electric light far off on the left. He went towards them and found that the street funnelled seam-lessly into the market: first were disconsolate-looking men and women sitting among goods laid out on trays or bits of fabric on the ground: matches, and watches, and cheap leather and silver jewellery. Further on there was a rough roof of plastic and corrugated iron cobbled together over racks of brightly coloured clothes and tables of second-hand books in the street. It was a kind of rough tongue sticking out from the arched mouth of a huge sunburn-red building, which hummed like a beehive.

Inside the path split and writhed confusingly among racks of carpets, tubs of red and yellow spices, heaps of fruit, more clothes and rolls of glittering synthetic fabrics. Presumably the market was really a simple grid of passages, but it felt like a chaotic warren. There was a hot, pleasantly complicated scent in the air, of salt and burnt sugar; of roasting nuts, ginger, and onions, and meat frying. Marcus could hardly move for people.

He did not particularly mean to look for the stall with red vases; but the first few jewellery places that the crowd carried him past were plainly not right: more silver charms on leather thongs. Then he came across a wider stall, glow-ing with light reflecting off jewellery and gilt paint, rather like a smaller and more jumbled version of the shop he'd left earlier. There were amber droplets hanging on silver chains and from the hooks of earrings, spider-shaped brooches and – he saw as he struggled free of the crowd into it – imitation Egyptian statuettes and a family of large meaty-red vases, shaped like fat globules, and made of marble or something that looked like it.

There was a man sitting square in the centre of the stall on a wooden chair, with his legs spread out. He was squat and heavy, and he would have looked out of place among so many glimmering things had there not been such a strong air of ownership about him. He stood up as Marcus entered and gave him a searching look. A younger man who'd been vaguely dusting one of the cat figurines copied. Marcus remembered that he'd taken out the wads of paper and backed away a little. His face felt naked.

'You were at Gaurus' shop, were you? The boy with the jade.'

'Yes,' said Marcus huskily, and cleared his throat. 'It's my mother's.' He pulled the necklace out again. The sardonyx comb came up with it, its silver teeth caught in the green thread. He disentangled it furtively, nudged the comb down inside. It struck him that perhaps the necklace was more important than he'd thought, perhaps it was an Imperial heirloom and people knew it, were watching for it. But surely there had been nothing about it in the news sheets, and in any case it was too late now.

'Oh,' said Petrus, smiling easily and nodded. He reached out and took the necklace, poured it back and forth between his hands like a liquid. 'Your mother's. Very pretty. Very finely carved. Your mother must be quite a lady.' And he looked at Marcus again, slowly. Marcus would have liked to cover his face with his hands, make a mask of his fingers.

'Not really,' he said, cursing himself. Why had he told that much truth? The beads could just as well have been a sister's, a grandmother's.

'Well, I think she must have been. I think so. Did she give you anything else? Would you like to sit down here and talk about it?'

'No.' His muscles had tensed, were begging him to run out of the stall.

'Well,' said Petrus carelessly, 'twenty sesterces, if you like.'

'I know it's worth more than that,' said Marcus indignantly.

'Perhaps. No one's going to buy it for much more,' said the man mildly. 'Not with you looking like that. Not worth the risk. Of course, if you have anything else from this mother?'

But Marcus hardly heard him. He'd seen another news sheet lying on the floor by the ceramic cats, a crinkled image of his own smiling face. He could not bear the calm, knowing scrutiny of Petrus and the silent assistant a second longer. He snatched the necklace back from the man's fingers, muttered, 'It doesn't matter,' and dived out into the swarm of shoppers.

He stumbled along, impatient at the slow drift; found that his face was cold and damp, wiped at it. He bumped against someone, apologised inarticulately, and looked instinctively backwards over his shoulder. Behind him, kept back by a few layers of people, was Petrus, moving as purposefully as the crowd permitted. As he saw Marcus look at him he began to push through even faster, calmly elbowing his way.

Marcus stood paralysed for a moment, seeing with awful sharpness the news sheet's dead monochrome face. The ranks ahead, shuffling gently, looked impenetrable. Then he began to move, dodging and shoving, searching with gritted teeth for breaks in the crowd as if for hand-holds on a cliff face. It was like those nightmares of pursuit and ponderous, lead-footed flight. The two of them toiled breathlessly, gallingly slowly, along a stretch of lane either might have covered in a second or so if it had been clear of people.

Then a gang of boys ahead of Marcus swung off suddenly towards a food counter on the right. This made progress even more sluggish for a moment, but they left a wavering empty space in the lane, allowing Marcus to break briefly into a real run before the other shoppers flowed back like water to fill the gap. He forced his way forward, and found with a start of delight that instead of a stall beside him was the opening of another passageway. He turned the corner, waded on as fast as the crowd would let him. For the moment, Petrus was left behind and Marcus was hidden.

Ahead the rows of stalls were much like all the others –

except one was hardly a stall at all but a narrow cubicle of draped green material, patterned and dramatic-looking at first glance. Outside was a boy and he was saying something, but Marcus noticed nothing about him. He saw only a curtained space and lunged inside it.

For a second he stood quite still, panting, in the sudden dark and stillness. Then he spun round and peered out into the market through the frayed overlap of the curtains. He saw a moving scrum of clothes and skin, separated from him only by the thin cloth, but he could not see Petrus.

He stepped back again, beginning to breathe a little more slowly. He was between two trailing layers of scratchy sateen and here on the inside, the green pattern of the fabric was a churning mass of lines of colour, like a nest of snakes. He was vaguely reminded of somewhere, and realised with incredulity that it was the great green Imperial office, with its garden fresco of vines and ivy – and he was even amused that he could see any likeness between a palace room and this shabby little place.

Only now did an indifferent corner of his brain remark to him that the boy had been droning wearily 'Sibyllina. The wandering oracle. Come on. Sibyllina,' and that outside had been a painted sign fixed to the curtain door, which said 'Fortune Telling'.

The cloth stirred and he stepped back as the boy followed him inside, chirping politely, 'She'll be ready in a minute. She's just tired now. It's five sesterces to start with, but she might see more, you know, if you felt like being generous.'

Marcus looked up unseeingly at a sunburnt triangular face under a lot of upright brown hair and slammed the cash into the boy's hands. It was a lot for something he didn't want, but he handed it over as a tax on staying hidden.

It occurred to him to look for the fortune-teller – but not yet to remember the Sybil Drusus had visited once at Delphi, or to wonder if he himself had any belief in such things. He could still hear his blood banging in his ears. He saw that the cubicle was divided in half by a second pair of curtains, which were not really curtains at all but long mismatched swatches of unhemmed material from one of the haberdashery stalls, tied roughly to overhead hooks meant for hanging up racks. From beyond the sea-coloured cloth, a tired voice called out, 'All right. Come in.'

The boy nodded at him encouragingly and then folded up his spidery limbs to sit hunched on a low stool, trying wearily to read a magazine in the flakes of light that fell between the curtains. Obediently, Marcus pushed through the blue-green shrouds of cloth.

The fortune-teller's cubicle was dim, but not really dark enough to warrant the two old-fashioned oil-lamps on her table. Sibyllina was sitting with her face cupped in her hands; long, double-jointed fingers delicately stroking and probing the skin above her temples. Her straight hair hung forward, and it was the soft brown of a hare's fur, so pale as to be almost no colour at all. Her hair and her fingers hid all but a sliver of her face; and below a broad forehead he could see only the nose, fine and narrow-boned, very slightly hooked, and the sharp central curve of pale lips. There was another length of bright green material, draped like a shawl over her hair and her limp green dress; a cheap and half-hearted attempt at mystery.

Very suddenly she took her hands away and turned up a face as thin and young as his was, with round hard cheek-bones and dark stains of kohl over eyes that were black and shocking with recognition. She burst into incredulous laughter. She knew who he was.

[VII]

THROUGH SMOKE

Una laughed.

The dark cell of greenish artificial silk and the things within it – the chipped oil lamps, the little gummy lumps of sharp-smelling incense – were a kind of fragile protective case, like that of a caddis-worm, that Una and Sulien had only recently constructed. In a village outside Vesuna, she had stalked self-consciously up to a woman outside a bakery and barked, 'Tell your fortune?' in such a way that she was almost certain to be rebuffed, as to her relief she was.

Sulien and she had walked out of Lemovices, and the air was so warm and the green such a different green from that of the dirty Thames or the London parks. She had never been outside a city before. For a little while, neither of them had been able to imagine a future life, at least not one made up of minutes and days. They could only think of warm fields, glowing and empty. It was like the spreading whiteness she'd taught herself to picture, but not cold.

Like Marcus, they had searched the news sheets for themselves, or rather for Sulien. His name and picture were duly printed but Sulien saw no reason why anyone should take particular notice of it. It was not a good picture, quite small, and crammed in a row of nine.

But there were only five pictures the next day, and they were stretched a little bigger so as to fill the page. They learnt that three of the escaping prisoners had been shot in the Thames marshes, and one had been found drowned. The others were either on the run or floating out to sea on the river. 'There, it's all right,' said Sulien. 'They'll think I've drowned, and they don't know anything about you.'

He'd stopped, and she said for him, 'They're dead, those men, and all the soldiers.'

Una thought the row of pictures would go on shrinking, until there was only Sulien.

Sulien was at first annoyed because Una put him in charge of food and then made every other decision herself; and later he was annoyed with himself for getting used to it. Sometimes he would remember and start a quarrel, but she always won and it was simply true that she was better than he would have been at planning, and stretching their money out, and thinking up names and histories for them.

She liked to pretend that their parents were somewhere else in the village or town; visiting the temple while they did the shopping, waiting for them round the corner. That first night she got them a room in Lemovices, complaining woefully about double-booking in another inn. Then she stamped sulkily across the hall to wave so persuasively at the imaginary parents she said had dropped them off, that Sulien himself was almost convinced. They trailed upstairs and Una kept whining noisily, 'Why can't *we* stay in the other place?' Sulien was impressed.

'That was easy,' said Una dismissively, but smiling.

And it was easy for her to think of reasons why a brother and sister as young as they were, and with British accents, might be staying in a town for a night or two with parents that no one ever saw, but after that people began to wonder. Then Una would feel someone wondering if they were slaves and if anyone should be told, or worse, trying to think where they had seen Sulien's face before, and it felt like a spider dropped suddenly on her skin. She would go and start packing at once. Sulien stopped even bothering to ask why.

Una had thought they could hide in the countryside because there was hardly anyone there. After a week she thought she had been utterly stupid. They needed crowds of people to vanish into, to cover up the space where their parents should have been. So after that they kept to the towns and cities when they could, where everything was more expensive, and they went on drifting south and west, never staying anywhere for longer than a week. They had half an idea that they might cross into Spain, even through the Gadesian tunnel and Roman Africa, out of the Empire. But it was hard to see how they could afford such a journey, even if they could have imagined what would become of them so far from anywhere they knew.

Una guarded Sulien, hoarded him grimly in one drab hostel room after another. Wearily, he tolerated the fact that she did not really trust him to go anywhere unsupervised. He promised himself it would blow over eventually; people would forget about him, wouldn't they? Eventually they would stop moving, he would get some kind of job. But as for medicine. If he cured anyone in any remarkable way, excitement about him would soon enough be matched up with the missing criminals from the Thames. So in a way he forgot about it. He did not ask himself if he ever expected to do it again. It would have to be all right (he could ignore the slight lurching, groundless feeling he had when he repeated this to himself). Sometimes though it did strike him, more than it ever had at Catavignus' house, that to do anything else for any length of time would be impossible, that he just couldn't, that it almost seemed strange to him that people who were not doctors of some kind could cope.

Most of the time he was simply either scared or bored.

Somehow it took him a long time to realise that Una never really told him anything about the years they'd been separated. She talked instead about the time before, in their father's home, and at Rufius'. She remembered the time Sulien had knocked her down the stairs better than he did; and she tried to remind him of certain things: she could describe the house, and Rufius' eating-house in detail, room by room, so that the distribution of staircases and the colours of paint sprang nervingly into Sulien's mind, vivid but distressing because he still couldn't tell if they were real memories or things he was making up. She told him also about an attempt to run away from the eating house he had apparently made when he was nine. Una had refused to go, being certain that it wouldn't work and that the punishment would be dire, and had said so, so dismissively, that it hurt; he'd stormed off without her. He'd got further than she expected, she admitted, wandering around London lost until the vigiles picked him up the same night. 'You hardly got fed for days, he beat you – do you really not remember?' she exclaimed incredulously, and Sulien marvelled blankly, for he did not, it just wasn't there. About everything that had happened to her later she said, peacefully, 'Well, I got moved around a bit, you know that. It doesn't matter.'

She couldn't explain that all the time the only real thing, the only thing that really had to do with her, had been the slow collection of money and detail, the diligent *honing* of the knowledge that one day she would discard everything else flatly. She knew she was not capable of such baffling feats of forgetfulness as Sulien, but she would keep faith with herself; it would be a breach of faith if it, if that – she would not even give it a description like that bad time – if all that was anything less than done with.

At last, and uneasily, when Sulien finally noticed how consistent and deliberate the gap seemed to be, he stopped asking, because that was what she seemed to want. But she wanted him to forget about it, gradually and naturally, and he wouldn't. Sometimes he looked at her, thinking about it, it was so clear on his face that anyone would have seen it. Sometimes she felt as harried as if he'd been asking her all the time.

Una's stash of money began to contract. It was appalling to her how one had to keep buying food, had to keep finding places to sleep. There was no end to it.

They could never afford more privacy from one another than a curtain between their beds. One night, Sulien thought he heard a smothered gasping as if she were trying to cry stealthily on the other side of it, but when he spoke to her she neither stopped nor answered, so he sat uncertainly before pushing back the curtain. She was curled tightly on her side as if clamped against the bed, weeping with clenched teeth, the tears screwing themselves out from beneath her shut eyelids, stifled, resentful of themselves, even though she was asleep.

In the dream Una discovered her flesh was spongy and putrid, and had to be pulled off. She did not seem to mind this much at first, and worked confidently; it was like carving a chicken. As she had expected there was no pain, nor any blood. But no one would leave her alone to do it properly; they gouged and stripped without thinking what they were doing, all at once, all over her, it was impossible to do it cleanly under these conditions. Their hands and hers filled with a horrible slithery mess of cold clumps; and she cried then, because it was so squalid, and because it seemed suddenly that there had been no need for this after all, where had she got such an idea? She was going to be disgustingly mutilated for no reason. And realising this did nothing to make the others stop voraciously tugging wet, deep handfuls away, from everywhere. She needed to put on some clothes, something long and loose over the wreck, but there weren't any; rough lolling ribbons of flesh hung from the arm bones she held out to stop them, so messy, slopping and quivering.

Sulien said, 'Una,' but she cried on and did not wake. He was about to touch her shoulder but abruptly, she opened her eyes with a convulsive disconcerted twitch, as if he had already done so, as if his looking at her made a noise. She glared at him blankly for a second, not unrecognising but caught and unnerved and almost angry. Then she cleared her throat and turned onto her back, arranging herself neatly, legs crossed at the ankle, her arms by her sides. She had seemed to stop crying instantaneously.

'Sorry, was I making a noise? Did I wake you up?' she asked, a little breathlessly, but otherwise composed. She wiped her face and looked at her palm with raised eyebrows, as if the wetness there surprised her.

'No,' said Sulien quietly.

They felt oppressed with responsibility for each other.

124

Una wanted to lie and think of nothing but white, but Sulien was sitting on his bed staring at her, alarmed and pitying, and yet exasperated with her too, because he felt forbidden to ask what was wrong, and it was unfair, she must know he was supposed to.

Una sighed with a long-suffering effort, as if she had been asked to get out of bed and start a dull day's work. 'I dreamt we got caught, I suppose,' she remarked, trying in a way to be kind.

'We got caught? And what happened?' he asked, tentatively, against the prohibition.

'Oh, I can't really remember,' Una said wearily. 'Go to sleep.'

He did not go to sleep for a while, but with the linen curtain between them she could pretend he was not there, and the shiver of mingled relief and horror could flow at last through her unharmed flesh. She made the whiteness start but expanded it slowly, driving the command ahead of it, all through her: I'm not, I'm not going to have that happen again. She was determined this would be obeyed and it was, or she became better at ignoring or forgetting, as if in her sleep she were more like Sulien. At any rate there were no more such nights.

Then they were buffeted along for three exhausting days of near-misses, so that he did not think much about what happened, though somehow it seemed worse when people began to recognise him; and Una was always tense and cross, and sometimes when she muttered bitterly that it was no good, the cities weren't any better, he couldn't think of anything to say. On the third afternoon he asked, 'You'd be better off without me, wouldn't you?' Having said it he felt ashamed for sounding so maudlin, but he couldn't help hoping it might prompt her to be a little friendlier.

'No,' she said. 'Because it's me, too. It wouldn't be so strange if you were just a boy by yourself. But everyone thinks, I wouldn't let a girl that age go wandering around the country, where's her mother? And anyway—'

She stopped, and did not say, anyway I wouldn't want

to be without you, but she patted his hand carefully, then with some effort laid her arm lightly and briefly round his shoulders.

'Why don't we just say our parents are dead?' he said, and quailed slightly, because she was already looking at him witheringly.

'Because that would be *stupid*. How would that explain what we're doing here? If we were free, why wouldn't we be with an aunt or our grandparents or something? And everyone would want to know all about it and how it happened and say how sorry they were. And nobody's parents are *both* dead.'

'Marcus Novius' are,' he said.

She knew who he was.

Later she wondered exactly how. She could have rifled through him and pulled him out like the lining of a pocket, but she had not done that; there had been no time and anyway she didn't want to. She had sat there in the half-dark for almost ten hours, stroking the fibres of lives into patterns, knotting them off always with money and excitement and love and love and love until she was sick of it. Sometimes, maliciously, she would have liked to prophesy disasters, but that was no way to make money.

And there she was sitting with her fingers trying to comb other people out of her brain. There was a shape behind the curtain, and something – nerves clattering . . .

She had groaned a little to herself. Someone was coming to be soothed. She would have to think up something especially nice. And then – then! Marcus Novius pushed the curtain back and she was quite sure before she could lift her hands away from her face or open her eyes. How could he ever have got so far? He couldn't have been anyone else.

How could a thought, an eddy of tension and panic, come with a name attached like the tag on the collar of a dog?

Leo's son had stepped back, was feeling for the gap in the curtains though his horrified eyes hadn't left her face. She

126

wasn't sure why she wanted to stop him, or why she found his presence quite so funny. Abruptly, she shut her eyes.

As suddenly as she had looked up at him, the girl's darkened eyelids dropped like shutters over the unnervingly certain eyes, and expression fell so swiftly off her face that he almost thought it hadn't been there at all.

'Sit down,' she said in a throaty, affected voice. 'There is incense on the table, light it. The god will show me your fortune in the smoke.'

The voice, the tawdriness of it reassured him just a little. She hadn't opened her eyes and there was no laughter now around the small curved mouth. It could have been only his own fear of Petrus that he'd seen in the hidden brown-black irises. Still, she was disconcerting. She turned her blank face to follow him as he walked to the chair, as if she could see through her eyelids. He did as she said. The incense lit and a sharp scent of rose and strawberry sprang up, abrasively sweet and scratching the back of the throat; but quickly the perfume faded and soon the smoke smelt only of smoke. The white thread of it lifted and broke, curling off in scrolls like the spiral of petals in the centre of a rose, opening rippling chains of pale, crocus throats, looking like flowers, even if it did not smell of them.

On the other side of it Una cautiously opened her eyes. She felt the corners of her mouth twitch up a little and flattened them out.

They would never have dared to rent the stall, they would have carried on along the back roads of Aquitania, and she would have kept shutting Sulien up in boarding-house rooms, if Marcus Novius hadn't wiped the escape from the Thames off the pages of the news sheets and out of people's thoughts.

Almost at once, they began to feel safer. They talked more openly about how they were going to live because it no longer seemed so hopeless. Una told Sulien that she'd wondered if she could make money telling fortunes, and had even tried it.

'Like the oracles,' said Sulien, interested.

'Yes, a bit like that,' said Una, trying to suppress a little flinch of the face, but Sulien saw it and guessed that she did not know about the Pythia at Delphi, and they both flushed. He kept being furtively astonished that someone who thought so clearly and ruthlessly could know so little, with odd islands of filched facts sprinkled across a great confused gulf. She hadn't known that any of Terranova was Nionian, or even where Nionia was. She assumed the Novii had always been Emperors of Rome. She could read and write, but slowly and furiously, a mind that was used to going fast having to drill laboriously through the letters as if through bricks.

And she found it mortifying. Sometimes she would hiss passionately, 'All right, *tell* me something, *tell* me what the answer is. Do you think I like being stupid?'

'You're not stupid,' said Sulien. She went on glaring at him unhappily until he said impatiently, 'You know you're not. You couldn't think everyone else was stupid otherwise.'

And he did try to tell her things, but looking at her tense, expectant face, all his own knowledge seemed to fly apart into unconnected bits, except for anatomy. She wanted to know what the Senate was for. He told her about the valves of the heart.

So now, after a pause, he said, 'But you don't know the future, do you?'

'No. Well, if someone were trying to make a decision, I might know what it would be. If really they'd made it already. Maybe that would be enough. But I tried, I went up to someone. It was no good.'

'Maybe if you looked more like a fortune-teller.'

'What does a fortune-teller look like?' asked Una.

They decided a fortune-teller wore a lot of eye make-up and usually had something hanging over her head. Sulien helped her practise, and suggested the incense: 'You need something to look at. If you stare at people like that they'll just want to get away from you.'

Una's stories changed in character, became more highly coloured and dramatic. They said, as Sulien had wanted to, that they were orphans, or that they were running away from cruel but aristocratic parents. Sibyllina didn't seem to need a convincing past, or even any past at all. Sooty eyes and an enigmatic manner were enough.

And it worked. The stashes of money began to swell again. After a week, when they came to Tolosa, they had enough to venture on getting more. So they rented the stall in the flea market, which although it made them more conspicuous in one way, was also a dark place for Sulien to hide in.

Sulien made Una pick out fabric for the curtains and at first she was impatient and indecisive. 'I don't know,' she said, nervously fingering the sparkling rolls of cloth. 'It doesn't matter, does it?'

'Yes it does. Come on,' he said. 'You've got to know more about decorating. You're a girl.'

Una frowned, but said, 'Maybe it should all be green.'

And they both began to enjoy plotting the paraphernalia of the stall. They tied up the emerald cloth, bickered mildly over who would paint the sign. They were so relieved that at last they had something in common; planning how things should look, and how people would react. They were like two children putting on a play.

But once inside the green curtains, they scarcely saw sunlight all day long. Sulien had something to do; sometimes he even enjoyed it, waylaying passersby and coaxing and flirting with them till they were beguiled into the cubicle. But even when people smiled back and gave him their money, it wasn't enough. He could not altogether avoid thinking about Catavignus, and Tancorix, and most of all that there was something better he should have been doing: taking apart fevers, mending things.

Once he said to Una, 'Why do you think we can do these things?' and she said, 'Why would there be a reason?'

And although Una soon found that she did not have to look very deeply or speak very accurately to earn the money, still the job itself left her feeling tired and smirched. While waiting for customers she sat straining her eyes, painstakingly copying out pages from books from the tarpaulin-covered stalls outside in her babyish handwriting. That way she couldn't fall off the train of words and spend long useless minutes trying to get back on.

But she hated going so slowly and she hated not knowing what things meant and every time she found out something new a huge new gorge of ignorance seemed to open up beyond it. It did not occur to her that this was itself a sign of progress. And she thought wearily to herself, 'What does it matter if you never know anything?'

Across the smoke, Marcus Novius' scared eyes were slate-blue, a cold colour.

'All right,' he said, licking his dry lips. 'Do you see anything?'

'A woman,' intoned Una, inventing. People often liked to hear such things, and she would say nothing too true, she would not frighten him – not yet.

For less than a second he thought perhaps she meant Gemella or Makaria, but then she added, 'Yes, a young woman, and love,' and he sat back in his chair, feeling relieved and foolish for taking her that seriously.

'There's no woman like that,' he said, and then added absurdly, 'Not just now.'

'Then why do I *see* her?' insisted the fortune-teller, apparently speaking to the vining smoke.

'I can't help you there,' said Marcus, sneering a little now, beginning to relax, and Una decided she would not let him do that. 'You are travelling,' she said, looking at him sternly, trying to steady the little shake of laughter in her voice. 'You are not what you pretend to be. You have been lying.'

She saw with satisfaction that he had turned white, and his hands were gripping each other painfully. 'No – I haven't,' he protested weakly. As clearly as he did she saw the bed in the little inn, and felt how primed his muscles were to carry him there.

She allowed her eyes go wide and unfocused, her voice to sink again. 'Is it the woman – are you lying to her? You must not do that. There is a chance for happiness.'

'Oh,' said Marcus shakily, hardly knowing whether it was relief or fright now that was hollowing out a chilly space in his chest. He rose, not quite steadily. 'Oh, all right, thanks. Is that everything?'

'No,' said Una wickedly. 'You should not be so frightened.'

He looked at her, alarmed, but she looked back as Sibyllina, vacant-eyed and inscrutable under her kohl. He fumbled his way out through the curtains and she was almost sorry. It had been a good game.

Sulien heard her laughing as the strange boy hurried out into the market, and realised with a brush of sadness what an unfamiliar sound it was. He went in to find her tamping out the incense, still smiling incredulously. 'That was quick,' he said. 'What's funny?'

Una's smile spread slyly. 'Do you know who that was?' she asked.

Outside, the curtain dropped back into place behind Marcus, and at once the minutes he'd spent on the other side of it began to seem clouded and dreamlike, not really part of his day. He didn't know what to make of the shadowy girl, and put her out of his mind. He burrowed on through the flea market, thoughtlessly following an arbitrary sequence of turns, and wondering bleakly if he could persuade the landlady to accept the sardonyx comb in place of payment for the room. He couldn't face trying another stall or shop now.

After a while he surfaced and saw a yellowish semi-circle of night sky, at the end of a passageway. He slipped out into the dark street, which seemed cold after the thick heat inside. He traipsed along it in the same tired abstraction that had brought him through the market, and then stopped, realising there were no peddlers crouched at the edges of this street, and that he was not quite sure where he was. He sighed and turned, searching the skyline for the dome of the temple, and as he did something latched onto him, dragging at his backpack and his sleeve, pulling the cloth tight round his neck. He was tugged backwards, collided briefly with someone's unseen body, and was then thrown sideways and scraped his palms against a wall as he tried to right himself.

The day seemed to have wrung out of Marcus all the fear that he was capable of. For a moment he felt simply exasperated, and then lit up and explosive. He flung out a wild, unfocused fist, and it thudded surprisingly against a damp mouth and the base of a nose. He felt almost happy. He drove a tighter, better punch into the man's ribs, and heard a gasp, but as he tried to pull back to strike again his arm was seized and twisted, and at the same time the second man – it was only now that he really noticed that there were two of them – brought a blow crashing hotly into the side of his face, so that his head swung round on his neck and the soft skin inside his cheek burst bloodily over his teeth. Pain held off for a second, and then went hurtling noisily through his head. Marcus slackened, dazed. His right arm was still trapped, and the backpack had slipped down his left onto the elbow, weighing it down. The two of them – yes, Petrus and the young man from the market – took hold of him together, slammed him back against the wall. Marcus' head cleared a little and he kicked viciously and blindly at shins, and only went still when he felt the pulse of his throat, suddenly tangible and constricted, pushing against something's sharp point.

For a crazy second he thought Petrus and his assistant were agents of the court or of Gabinius, sent to kill him, and he was just wondering how that was possible when Petrus detached the loosened backpack from his arm and began feeling inside it. Marcus stared, and all at once imagined the smooth studs and curves of the jewellery under the man's fingers. So stupid! He gave a silly, mad-sounding laugh, and felt the knife jump against his neck with his breath.

'Stop that,' growled the young man, while Petrus gave a

low, pleased whistle at the jewellery, the statuette and the little vase.

'Not quite frank with us, were you?' he rasped into Marcus' face, and then reached down to pull the few notes out of his pockets. Marcus looked up at the yellow-black sky, and laughed again, until Petrus' fist ploughed upwards into his stomach, and they let him drop to his hands and knees on the ground.

After a while, when the air had come back and he had spat out most of the metal-tasting blood onto the reddish street, he rose clutching his stomach and walked painfully after them. He hoped they might have dropped his bag somewhere, and that he could at least salvage the blanket and the map; but there was nothing.

Sulien said, 'Why did you let him go?'

'How was I going to stop him?' demanded Una.

'You could have called me!'

Una pulled the green shawl off her hair. 'But what for? You know we can't do anything about it.'

'Why not?' he said. And her eyes widened a little in realisation before he went on: 'If they want him back that badly, they should give us what we want, shouldn't they? Like a pardon for me. Like not being slaves any more.'

She looked just fleetingly impressed, which he was pleased to see, but then she said coldly, 'You mean, after everything I've done to hide us—'

'So we don't have to hide any more. It's not such a risk.'

'It *is* such a risk!' cried Una. 'It's everything, it's us both dead! You can't *trust* them!'

'What – the vigiles?' he said. 'We could if they had to do what we said—'

'No. *Romans. Any of them*,' said Una starkly. 'Look at what happened to you. They wanted to kill you in the worst way they could think of. And that doesn't tell you anything about them.'

He looked bewildered. 'That was bad – that was just a bad thing. It doesn't mean—'

'Yes it does,' said Una.

Sulien sat down opposite her in the chair Marcus had left. 'But it's just what we need. It would fix everything.' He lowered his eyes, clasping his hand round his wrist and murmured, 'It's medicine. I don't want to do anything else, I *really* don't, if I can't—'

'What, you want to get killed?' she demanded angrily.

'No,' he was startled that she should say such a thing. He didn't know how he would have finished the sentence. 'But I think you hate it more than I do, moving all the time. And I've been trying not to – but it's awful if you think of it going on forever, isn't it?'

She sighed and put her face into her hands again, weakening for a moment. 'I know.'

Sulien waited for a moment. 'Did he seem – you know, mad, like everyone says?'

Una remembered the barrage of dread. 'Pretty much.'

'Well,' he said, encouraged, 'you could hide somewhere while I talked to them. And then even if anything went wrong, you'd be all right.'

'Have some sense,' said Una sneering again, almost with relief because she *knew* this was wrong. 'Do you think they'll just promise you freedom and a pardon without knowing who it's for? And even if they did, we couldn't hold them to it. Why should they keep it?'

'Well, why shouldn't they? It wouldn't hurt them.'

'There were those four Roman soldiers killed. And it doesn't matter why! There isn't any safe way of doing it. You're talking about just putting ourselves in their hands and hoping for the best! But they're Romans, they can do what they want!'

'You can't really say that,' said Sulien suddenly. 'As if we weren't Roman.'

She looked revolted. 'They don't *crucify* Romans. And they don't . . .'

He didn't speak for a moment because he thought she might be going to say something about all the time they'd been apart, but she didn't.

'But it isn't as though there's an actual difference. What else are we?'

'British. Celts. Nothing – we're not part of anything,' she said, uncertainly.

'Well, we're not citizens, but our father was. Our mother's father was, too. At least, if you went back far enough there must have been Romans somewhere.'

'What does that matter? It's what's done to *us*.'

'All right, and what if we were freed, what would we be then?'

She looked across at him, almost frightened. 'Not Roman. I never would be.'

'If you had children, they would,' pressed Sulien.

Una winced unhappily and said, 'But I don't think I will have children. And no one's going to make us any freer than this.'

'Oh, *all right*,' said Sulien, irked by the miserable little sentence. And yet still it seemed to him so silly – so unnatural, almost – to give up such a chance. And he half-forgot that he had just given in, and said, 'We'll always know we could have done it. And when we're still here or somewhere just like it in twenty years, we'll know we didn't have to be.'

'I suppose we'll get used to it,' said poor Una, thinking of the boring fortunes and the concrete-brick sentences in her books. But then she narrowed her eyes warily and asked, 'Sulien . . . ?'

He said, 'All right. You stay here and I'll go and call someone.'

Una sprang up, appalled. 'I said you couldn't do that!'

'No, it's all right. I won't tell them about you. But when I've got the money you'll be all right too, even if I have to pay your owners off. And you've got the stall if anything does happen, but I don't think it will.' For he could not persuade himself he could be taken back and crucified; he could not shake the feeling that fate had produced poor mad Marcus Novius exactly so that Una and Sulien could be rewarded for sending him home.

'*No!*' Then she almost laughed with fierce relief and said, 'You don't even mean it, you're trying to scare me into going with you.'

Sulien saw that until she said this, it had possibly been true. He glowered. 'No, I will go. Look, it's because of me we have to keep hiding, I just think I should do something about it.'

'Yes, and it's because of me you're not dead! And it was *hard work*! The least you can do is not go and *die*!'

'But I won't,' he said.

'Yes, you will!' she accused him. 'You'll do it all wrong. You don't know how to make people do things.'

And she was quite sure of that, sure, now she thought of it, that if there was any chance of successfully reporting Marcus Novius it depended on her doing it.

There was what he had said about children, too. She believed what she had said – she couldn't have children because she knew she could never bear to be married. But Sulien would want friends and girls and yes, to get married one day. And he was educated and male and, even as things were, if they could last long enough without being caught, he could have these things. But she thought she could tell her own future, and it was the rest of her life between these curtains, on her own. It was not as if she did not want the open air, and money to bolster her up and soften the resisting books. And at least this way, it would all be done with.

When he tried again to go without her, she said, 'It would be better if I talked to them. They don't know about me.'

There was a taverna a few streets away which had long-dictors set into the maroon arm-rests of the couches. Una sat hunched away from the warm room and stared at Sulien, as she dialled in the code and whispered into the mouthpiece. 'I know where he is and I want to talk to someone about the reward.'

'All right,' said a bored voice in her ear. 'Where do you think you've seen him?'

'I have seen him. But I don't want to tell you where he is

yet, I want to talk about the reward. The money isn't enough. We want some other things too.'

The line went dead. Una gaped with outrage.

Now they had begun, Sulien was growing uneasy. As they entered the taverna Una had ceased reproaching him for stupidity and had seemed somehow to take over all his own intent; so that he began to feel as she had; that they were gambling with everything they had. He said, 'Oh, if they won't even listen to you . . .'

But she was already stabbing in the code again: 'They damn well will listen.'

This time it was a woman that answered. Una began commandingly, 'I just spoke to someone else and he turned me off. That was stupid. I know where Marcus Novius is but I'm not going to tell you until someone can guarantee me a pardon for – for something.' But as she went on talking her nerve began to falter and she started stammering a little. Sulien heard the high notes of a stream of questions burring out of the longdictor and Una said, 'No, it's for – someone that didn't do anything wrong. Tell me if you'll do that and I'll tell you who. And I want to be sure that we won't be returned to – or, or, or we won't be sold—'

Una would never have risked going to talk to the vigiles face to face, but now she wished she were not using a longdictor either. The operator might be hundreds of miles away, Una could tell nothing about her except what the unimpressed, competent voice told her. The woman said, 'Am I to take it you are fugitive slaves? Where are you?'

Una made a furious face at the longdictor and hissed, '*Yes.* I can't tell you where we are until you promise that—' but she began to wonder fearfully if they could trace the call anyway.

'Come on,' said the operator flatly, far away in Rome. 'It's all very well demanding all these things when we've got no reason to believe you've even seen him.'

Una deliberated miserably and chose a detail she thought she could afford to stake. 'He's shaved off his hair. He's thinner. That's why he's got this far.'

The operator went quiet, and Una looked whitely at Sulien, as the woman called her supervisor and some unheard conversation went on. Then there was a sudden transition to a brusque male voice that unsettled Una even further:

'Look, tell us where you are because we'll find you anyway. We're not going to haggle with criminals and slaves.'

'So you won't get him back,' said Una.

'Well, there's only the one deal on offer. We can't add to it.'

'Why can't you? If you can give all that money.' Sulien had seen her expression loosen briefly with panic, but she was at least in reasonable control of her voice again now and the disdainful note in it reassured them both. Una thought if what the officer said was true there would have been no reason to say it. He was only trying to frighten her. She went on imperiously, 'Then freedom and a pardon in place of some of the money. I don't know. A quarter, we would accept three quarters—'

'Tell them we don't want the money,' suggested Sulien helpfully.

'Shut up. Don't be stupid,' Una snapped.

So she went on trying to work hints of concession out of him in exchange for little splinters of information, and she began to think she might be winning a little, the officer started softening, or seeming to. If she had been in the room with him she would have known at once. But it was hard, for she had really only one thing to trade with; and once she said where Marcus was, she knew she'd lose all the power she had, and as long as she didn't, they had no reason to promise her anything. And so for a long time there was stalemate, just as she'd feared, and she knew that finally, prevaricate as she would, she would have to be the one to break it. Finally, if she wanted anything from the vigiles, she could do nothing but trust them.

And so at last she gave in, and muttered wretchedly, 'Tolosa. He was in the flea market.'

She listened for a while, then turned off the longdictor and laid the set down on the plump arm-rest. The waiter came over with the bill for it.

'Well, what?' asked Sulien, when the waiter had gone. He was fidgeting with the longdictor cords. For several minutes now he had been thinking that Marcus Novius might have got out of Tolosa, that if the vigiles came he and Una might have nothing to hand over but themselves.

'He said, Tolosa was a big place,' said Una. 'He said, they'd send out the troops for him and if we brought him to them – or if we were there when they found him – but they only said maybe. But I suppose it doesn't make any difference, even if they'd promised.'

She could not see how they could go out now and meet the vigiles. So now they could hide, or better leave Tolosa at once. But then it might be true that they would be found anyway. She murmured, 'What do you want to do?'

Sulien kneaded the skin of his wrist, but he said, 'Look for him.'

Marcus had hobbled back across the river Garumna, and wandered automatically towards the inn. He couldn't stop his tongue from probing the ragged places inside his cheek in a fascinated way. The bloody taste was still spread thinly through his mouth.

He stopped long before he reached the inn, because of course that was no good. He sat down in the doorway of a darkened shoe shop and pulled himself back into the shadows. He was still trembling a little from the fight. All right, all right, he thought. What are you going to do? You must steal some money or a birota or a car and get to Tarba. And when you are there perhaps someone can tell you how to find Delir. You can pretend to be an escaped slave.

He had no idea how to steal anything and he could not imagine getting away with it. An indulgent, fatherly voice in his mind answered him, 'Don't be stupid. You've done as much as you can. Now just go and tell someone who you are.'

He just sat there, pressing the swelling flesh on the side of his face.

And the vigiles were already searching the flea market, and Una and Sulien were getting closer.

Una didn't know exactly where Marcus' inn was, but she'd felt the direction in which he'd wanted to move, over the brown river, towards where the ground began to tilt up just a little, for almost the only time in this flat town. They went slowly, shuttling back and forth across the lattice of streets, Sulien walking restlessly ahead while Una faltered along with her eyes half-shut, running her mind's hands across the walls, over the rough road.

They carried on this way for an hour, and Sulien thought impatiently that there was no reason that they should find Marcus. And yet he felt a sneaking relief, too, because there'd been a headlong feeling growing, of plunging forward, of not being able to stop. And then he said, 'There's an inn up ahead, maybe it's that one.' Una replied dreamily. 'No, he's not there. He's here . . . he's just here . . .' and she pointed, without even following the movement of her hand with her own eyes.

He was perplexed for a second, because she was pointing at a blank wall. Then he understood and they hurried up the street and turned towards the one that ran parallel to it. Una caught at his arm to stop him going any further and said, 'There.'

At first he could not see anything, and then the bars of shadow in a doorway moved, rearranged themselves into legs, stretching out along the step, crossing at the ankle. Marcus laid his thin-covered bones out slowly on the hard tiles, turned awkwardly onto his side and shut his eyes.

Una whispered in a strained little voice: 'All right. I'll go and tell them.'

'What if he goes anywhere?' said Sulien.

'Follow him. Stop him.'

She set her teeth and went and asked to use the long-dictor in the inn. Sulien stood watching the other boy trying to go to sleep, and mentally stacked the things he needed between them: a place, friends, and the use of medicine again. The low, bubbling guilt was so creeping and insidious he hardly realised what it was at first, but it wouldn't go away. He thought, well he can go back to sleeping on feather-beds as soon as the vigiles come. The thought helped, but not as much as he would have liked.

Una wasn't long. She said with forced lightness, 'Well, it's done, they're coming.'

Marcus fell quickly into a kind of stupor, but he didn't expect to get any sleep on the doorstep. After a few minutes, his eyelids flickered up as someone moved at the head of the street. He looked, dully, and saw a narrow silhouette run softly up to join someone standing at the corner, against the wall, and it struck him that he must have seen them there before, because he was sure that they had been watching him for a while.

For a moment he just lay and looked at them curiously. Then it came to him from something about the heights of the outlined shapes and the movement of the girl's long hair, that he recognised them. Without thinking about it, simply kindled up by irritation, he swung himself upright and strode towards them.

They darted back around the corner as they saw him move – a shocked little scramble. He scoffed to himself to see them do it. He marched along the street and found them, hovering uncertainly together. Yes, they were the same, and plainly brother and sister now he saw them together, both tall and with the same wide foreheads and small mouths, although the boy's hair was not pale and his eyes not so close to black.

'You're from the flea market, aren't you?' he said coldly, lifting his arms a little to show how his bag was gone. 'Leave me alone. I've got nothing left.'

They didn't answer but looked back at him blankly; and they shifted fractionally as they stood, an almost imperceptible closing of ranks. And he saw how the soft, empty expression had gone from the fortune-teller's face, and beneath it was – had always been – a hard, untrusting intelligence. He had been right in the first place, she knew who he was. They both did.

He whispered, 'Who have you told?'

The boy said, 'It's for your own good.'

And the fortune-teller moved just as Marcus did. He made to dash past them but the girl stepped straight into his path as precisely as if they had rehearsed this together; passively let him knock into her. He pushed her aside more easily than he expected because as yet she made no attempt to hold onto him, but as she fell back, more heavily than he had meant, the boy dived at him. Marcus had never had to fight before that night, and this was the second time. He was tired and hurt, but though he lurched a little under the weight, he stayed on his feet, shoving back and slamming his fist against the boy's chest. As he did it he realised how they were trying not to hurt him, that they even had a kind of squeamishness about touching him.

But for all that, they were in absolute earnest, and as he forced the boy back and wrenched away, the girl kicked out from the ground at his ankles, felling him. She crawled grimly over and tried to weigh him down, her sharp knees on his thighs, her hands pressing fastidiously and reluctantly on his shoulders; so that just very briefly her light hair trailed on his neck and between the sheets of it he looked up at her clear desperate face.

Her brother, standing over him, asked ridiculously, 'Are you all right?'

Marcus rolled the girl off, she was not heavy, but she clung onto his arm with impersonal relentlessness; and the boy had dropped now and was trying to snare Marcus' legs with his own, trying to be gentle about holding down his arms. It was awful not to be able to get up. Marcus gasped, 'Let me *go*,' and heaved briefly upwards, but they hung, hung from his clothes and limbs, every time he detached a hand it clamped down again at once.

They did not let him go of course, though they glanced at

him nervously. The boy said 'How long?' and the girl answered, 'I don't know – five minutes?'

Marcus knew what that must mean. He jerked and thrashed and said, 'You don't understand what'll happen.'

'They'll take you home, Highness,' said the boy soothingly.

'Highness!' the girl spat, disgusted.

Marcus said, 'They want to *kill* me,' and lashed and kicked out frantically, managed to fling the girl from his arm, kicked free of the boy and struggled up into a worn-out, shambolic run. He got halfway along the street and realised how bad things were: they had only to slow him down, only to cope with whatever he could do for five minutes. They closed on him again almost at once, but he was speaking as they did so: 'Whatever they've promised you, I swear, you *will* have it, whenever this is over you can come to me and I *will* give it to you—'

The girl snarled, 'Well, we need it now.'

'No, you don't understand, *please*,' said Marcus. He was still trying to force his way between them but he wondered distantly if he could try harder to hurt them, if, say, he could strike the boy's head back against the wall, get him down and stamp on him. And he knew he couldn't. He tried to speak more calmly. 'They'll kill me if they find me, please, just *think* it might be true—'

An uncertain quiver flicked across the girl's face and was gone. She said, jeering, 'Oh, do you think you know anything – anything about having to hide? Just go home and live in a palace because this is all the chance we've got, just let us *have* it. It's the only worthwhile thing you'll ever do. Do you want us to feel sorry for you?'

Marcus said quite levelly, 'No. I want you to let go of me.'

The boy said softly, ignoring his sister's grimace, 'Highness. If they find us without you we really are finished. They'd pin me up by a road somewhere and you can take days dying that way; and I don't know what they'd do to my sister. You see – for us it's really real.'

'It's real for me,' Marcus said, pushing forward again,

frantically scanning the darkness for approaching head-lights.

The boy said to her, 'That isn't true, is it? They won't kill him.'

'*No*,' she said fiercely, but swallowed and added, 'He – thinks it is. He just thinks it is.'

'All right,' said Marcus. He stopped struggling suddenly and stared at them icily. 'Suppose I am wrong, or mad, and I just think it; still I'll be Emperor one day and I'll find you. And whatever you get from doing this, I'll take it from you.'

It was a nonsensical threat – he knew if he were caught now he would never be Emperor or anything else, but it made them hesitate for a moment. He tried to lunge through their arms again but that woke them up; they wrestled him, gripped.

The boy muttered, 'You wouldn't find us—'

Marcus pushed against them mechanically. But he was thinking of what the boy had said before, when he had been too desperate almost to hear it: being pinned up meant crucifixion. Roman citizens could not be crucified, and yet Marcus thought the boy and his sister seemed quite Roman.

Again, abruptly, he stopped moving and looked at them. This time he tried to speak gently. 'Are you slaves? Is that it? You've run away because you're slaves – and that's why?'

The boy nodded slowly. His sister's face had twisted a little at the word.

'Then you don't have to do this, because there is some-thing I can do for you now,' Marcus breathed. 'Then I can take you somewhere safe. I promise it's safe and it's meant for slaves who get away, but *please*, they're coming – *please*—'

They glanced at each other, but the girl said savagely, 'Hiding somewhere isn't free. And we don't owe you any-thing.'

'No,' said Marcus, almost hopelessly. 'But you *can't*.'

Brother and sister looked at each other, the boy said urgently, '*Una*.' And the girl nodded very slightly, and she stepped right in front of Marcus and stared at him; stared so fixedly that all her face seemed pinched up around that look. Then very gradually her black eyelids drooped, and far more strongly than before he had the impression that she could look through them. Very slowly, very cautiously, she let go of his arm, as one lifts a hand from a coin balanced painstakingly on its rim. And yet it took him a moment to realise that she was no longer touching him, because although her face was only an inch from his, it felt as if she were closer even than that. And still, although no one was holding him now, he didn't move. He stared back at the girl's still face, and though he didn't know what her scrutiny meant, he was sure that it was the last chance he had and that it was no good fighting them any more. He didn't move even when the lights of a vehicle rose somewhere ahead of them.

And she didn't say anything, she didn't say, 'Yes, he's telling the truth.' She just opened her eyes and took a shaky breath, and then she stepped back from him and gestured to her brother, and the two of them ran off down the street.

Marcus went after them.

[VIII]

DOMUS AUREA

Varius drove home through the swelling light on the grey road. It was only a change in colour: having decided that he could not yet think in an orderly way about what to do next, he knew he must not think about the beginning of the first day that Gemella would not see. He was afraid he would crash the car. He tried not to allow the possible thought that followed that one – that it would not matter; he tried to be only a thing that drove. He drove silently through multi-coloured Rome and reached Marcus' villa just after six. He got out of the warm car and saw how precisely the gravel lay and the leaves pointed. There was no vagueness or softness in things.

Already the servants were up, and the butler had come out onto the steps at the sound of the car. No one, then, had yet found what lay on Varius' bed. The butler looked at Varius curiously as he entered. Varius made some acknowledging movement of the face, but could not speak to the man. He went upstairs.

He shut himself in the room. He hadn't slept, and so there had been no point at which he could have forgotten or doubted that he would come back and she would be dead. And yet he had expected somehow – what? That either something would have happened to show him what he should do and how things would be, or else that there would be no change at all and she would be still warm as she had been when he'd left her there alone. He approached the bed slowly and laid his fingers on her hair, which was at any rate the same as ever, tough and crinkly and alive. He did not dare to stroke it back from her face. But he saw the flat white colour of her neck and bare arms. He touched her hand, and it was no colder than the wood of the bedframe, or any object would have been; and without lifting it he felt the resistance of the flesh, rigid as if the joints had never been meant to move.

He drew back from her – it – he opened the door and called out, 'Someone come, someone help.' Then he went down the stairs and said the same thing. He didn't go back into the room or look at her again.

When the doctor came, and afterwards the vigiles, he did not know where to be and went into Marcus' room where the yellow-white squares of nougat lay sugar-dusted and placid on the enamel plate. He could not believe such soft little things had done so much. And yet as he looked at them, and his heart like a fist behind his bones began to clench jerkily and unclench, he thought after all they did look lethal, plump and obvious and brazen. It took him a while to wrestle the current of anger around to where it belonged, away from Marcus and Gemella and himself, all of whom, he felt, ought to have seen and guessed.

Soon everyone would know that Marcus was missing. Now he must start to think again. The things that anyone would have had to do came to him suddenly and relentlessly – he would have to tell Gemella's parents, and his own. By difficult degrees he made himself put that aside. He could hear the movement of the vigiles in the house, below and around him. He reviewed what was clear to him; that Gemella's killers surely would not have acted so boldly unless the vigiles were at least partly under their control. Unless he could find something to say to the vigiles now, it would become obvious at once that he must have helped Marcus to escape. Sooner or later that would happen anyway, and when it did, one way or another he would be powerless to help Marcus or himself. But he might have a few days in which to work to damage them, and to make it possible for Marcus to come back to Rome.

He reached out and flicked two of the sweets into the

wicker box in which they had been presented, touching them lightly as possible but briefly feeling the powdered sponginess of the nougat against his fingertip. He felt sick. Swiftly, he took off his coat and draped it casually over the bed. He hid the box among its folds, before there was a soft knock on the door and the vigile centurion came in.

He was tall and sturdily built enough, with a squarish face handsome in outline, although it was so painfully brightly coloured that the firmness of the features seemed to be dissolving like cheese under fierce heat. His skin was baked to a vivid and permanent pink and smeared with orange freckles, jarring with the dark red of his uniform. The eyebrows and lashes were molten ginger traces, almost transparent.

He had entered cautiously and respectfully, but his scorched face altered as he looked into the room. He said, 'I thought young Leo had come home?'

'Yes. I don't know,' said Varius, 'I came in here to tell him.'

'I didn't see him downstairs.'

'He must be,' whispered Varius.

The centurion squinted with concern, and stepped outside to mutter something to one of his legionaries. He came in again and introduced himself belatedly as Cleomenes. He took off his helmet to reveal orangey hair, ruthlessly cropped. He studied Varius and said 'I'm so sorry.'

Varius gave a sick, stretch-lipped grin, finding that again he couldn't talk.

Cleomenes gave a discreet, understanding little nod and waited for a little while before asking, 'Can you help us understand how this happened?'

Varius wanted overwhelmingly to go to sleep. He was being distracted by what was not quite an hallucination but the insistent impression of a small boy crouching on the floor a few feet to his left, just outside his field of vision. He kept having to look to re-establish that the boy was only a kind of glitch – the visual ghost of the low table that stood the same height in the same place. Talking was difficult.

But lying about Gemella was worse, horrible, he felt that really he should not even be capable of it. Trying to build up to it he said, 'I've only been here an hour.'

And Cleomenes said mildly, 'But the servants say you were here last night.'

It was, of course, what the centurion was bound to say. But at once all Varius' exhaustion scattered. For an odd, bitter moment, he wanted to laugh, because he could not believe he had been so stupid. Here he had been, knowing that Gemella's killers would come after him, and that he must come up with some account of the last eight hours to fend them off. Yet he had never thought how those hours could look. But what had happened, on the face of it? His wife was dead, already he had not told the truth about it, he had been behaving very strangely. If Gabinius and the rest – whoever they were – wanted to have him put out of their way, they would have an excellent excuse.

It was just that it was unconscionable enough that Gemella was dead. Even now, knowing how naïve it was, and cursing himself as an idiot, he found it difficult to imagine that anyone could think he might have killed her.

All this hit him in a second. At once he wanted to explain the whole thing – so much, that in his shock, his mouth opened a little to start a sentence that never got beyond a breath. He stared at Cleomenes' fluorescent, courteous face and wished fervently he could tell what was happening behind it, and what would happen if he did tell the truth. The centurion was scrutinising him openly, both with what looked like pity and with obvious scepticism. Varius wondered how the two things could go together – how anyone could feel sorry for someone he thought was a murderer.

But on the other hand, perhaps Cleomenes knew that he was innocent, which would be the worst thing of all. He tried to steady himself. Really none of this made any difference. Although that was a thought so unreal as to be barely comprehensible.

He said as resolutely as he could, 'Yes, but I went home, just after eleven.'

'And your wife was alive then? Forgive me.'

'Of course,' said Varius, hearing how his real distress was helping him a little, how it made sense of the hesitancy in his voice. It seemed disgusting that Gemella's death should give him any kind of advantage, but he could have done nothing about it if he'd wanted to. He swallowed, and went on, 'She was just about to go to bed.'

'But you had to go home in the middle of the night?' Cleomenes did not sound quite so sympathetic now.

Haltingly, Varius explained about the slave clinic. He had worked on it with Leo for so long that it had not been hard to arrange the details into a story that sounded plausible enough, although he knew it could not hold for long.

'We thought we had raised the money to purchase the site and – but since Leo and Clodia Aurelia died everything – of course Leo's share of the money belongs to Marcus Novius now, and I couldn't go forward without his consent. I thought it seemed too early to press him about it.'

Cleomenes nodded again, but his mouth was puckered irritably on one side.

'But early yesterday one of our sponsors tried to pull out. I persuaded them to wait until I'd talked to Marcus. That's why he came home.' That, at least, would more or less agree with his vague letter to Faustus. 'And he hoped the clinic could be a memorial, you see – so I went home and – I've been working all night, transferring everything into Marcus' name. And writing up a new proposal for the sponsor. It had to be ready this morning or we'll lose the site.' He stopped talking with relief.

'And even then you couldn't go to bed!' Cleomenes exclaimed.

'No. I had to talk Marcus through what I'd done. And then I had to go to the sponsor this morning. I told you.'

'What sponsors are these?'

Varius named a longvision company that made comedies, with whom he had genuinely had some trouble; although nothing so serious as he'd claimed.

'And did you leave the papers in the car?'

'No, they're in the study with the others,' said Varius.

'You understand we'll have to check.'

'Yes.'

He hoped there were enough files about to keep the vigiles occupied for a while. He was a little afraid that later he might need Leo's papers, but there was no helping that. He was trying to think whether any of the servants had seen him go up the stairs without entering the study, and came unawares too close to the memory of what had happened in that room. He heard the gasp, screwed his eyes shut uselessly against the sight of her falling.

Cleomenes was watching him closely. Varius said thickly, 'Can I go home?'

'In a minute,' said Cleomenes.

'But there's nothing I can tell you.' He still hadn't opened his eyes.

'You can't think of anyone who would have wanted to hurt her?'

'No one that would poison her,' muttered Varius, still trying to prise himself out of the night before, still busy with Gemella's body turning motionless against his own. He blinked, glanced at the table again.

Cleomenes' eyes narrowed slowly. They were a light, flat brown, the only near-colourless thing in his face. He said, 'Do you think it was poison then, Caius Varius?'

Varius began to stammer but then one of Cleomenes' legionaries came in and said, 'He isn't here sir, and no one's seen him since last night.'

Cleomenes' bright eyebrows sprang upright, but he hovered for a moment indecisively, still looking at Varius before at last growling. 'All right. You won't go anywhere we can't find you.' He paused again, added gruffly, 'And let one of my men drive you home. Anyone can see you're in no state,' and charged out of the room.

Varius stood. Then moving in jerks he turned and picked up his coat, holding the box cradled carefully inside the cloth. He followed the legionary down the stairs and then some time later he realised he was standing in the lift on the ground floor of the slim block of flats where he had lived with Gemella, with almost no sense of the car journey in between. He was not even sure how long he had been waiting in an unmoving lift. He felt for Makaria's sweets: they were still there.

He spiralled doggedly up around the stairwell, walked ruthlessly into their flat, which was pleasantly decorated but tiny, because everything was so expensive in Rome. He turned all the lights on, forbade himself to pay any attention to any of Gemella's things, even to let his eyes settle on anything for very long. He would not allow himself any delay in calling her parents. He dealt as gently and swiftly as he could, steeled himself to say several times that he did not know what had happened, as Gemella's father began almost crossly to ask questions, and then stopped suddenly. Things were worse with his own mother, who after her first exclamation of distress said fiercely, 'I'm coming. I'll be there in an hour.' Even after the long and costly process of asking – ultimately begging – her not to come, he succeeded only in deferring her a few days. He turned off the long-dictor and wondered if he should have found some way of preparing her for what might happen to him next. But then perhaps nothing – nothing further – would happen; he had not given up yet.

It was true that he sometimes worked at home, that sometimes he would sit up all night if that was what it took. Impatient Leo, who thought in hot blood, demanded things suddenly and grew suddenly bored, had made this intense thoroughness necessary while failing completely to understand it, never seeing how anyone could so enjoy the detail of an idea.

In his desk Varius still had copies and drafts of the correspondences surrounding some of Leo's and Clodia's official visits, the first plans and reports on the slave clinic. Almost everything was older than the files in Leo's study, and Varius thought probably it would all be useless, but he took everything out anyway and began to sort through rapidly and meticulously, and then, at once it seemed, he woke up in his clothes, sprawled amid the paperwork wreckage on his bed, with no memory of having lain down there.

Faustus moved through Drusus' high-walled house, shedding his retinue like a snakeskin. He looked out across the garden and saw the whitish tufts of Lucius' hair moving unevenly as his brother stumbled around with his nurse. A tottering old man, his brother who was six years younger than he was! But that was because of the curse, it didn't reflect on him. This was one of the many reasons for not visiting Lucius more often. But poor Lucius! He touched his own hair nervously – he had never been vain like Leo, was fatalistic about letting his handsome body grow fat, but suddenly he wanted to look at himself. He glanced at Tulliola instead, who was almost as smooth and glossy as a mirror, and she smiled at him. He wished he could take hold of her, so that she would anchor him down among smooth and young things, but for the moment he was slightly afraid of Makaria, who wanted to be back on Salamis, playing about with her ridiculous vineyard. But he had ordered her to come with him to see Lucius. The three Novian brothers could never be together again. Makaria could at least postpone running off again from Rome, with no purpose except to upset her father.

And so Makaria had been being dreadful to Tulliola since breakfast. Tulliola, always so tactful, had said almost nothing.

'I think you might give him a kind word,' said Faustus.

'Well, I can't,' said Makaria flatly. 'It would be hypocritical. He is such an embarrassment. And I always think he has a shifty expression.'

'Oh, that is unfair,' Tulliola said softly, almost as serenely as usual. She looked just perceptibly relieved when Makaria ignored her.

'I don't know why I've got to be here.'

'He's the only brother I have left. You are such a heartless young woman,' complained Faustus, and then, to punish her for being like this all morning, 'although not so young now.'

'Yes,' said Makaria, although it was not clear what part she was agreeing with. After a while she remarked thoughtfully, 'That must make *you* very old indeed.'

Why had he got such a cruel daughter? She had had this calm instinct for saying the most wounding thing possible since she was twelve years old.

'No one has any right to talk to me like that. I am the Emperor. I am your father. You are a disgrace.'

Makaria said mournfully, 'I wish I was at home.'

'You *are* at home,' Faustus told her sternly. 'You can spare a morning.'

'You don't know that I can't spare a morning. But you *should* know, you should know how quickly things can go wrong. And it isn't a morning, it's weeks—'

'Your uncle's funeral—!'

'It's weeks, and perhaps the whole crop is diseased and I'm not there to do anything about it—'

'All that is nonsense. I don't know why you waste your time with all that.'

'I have to do something.'

'Yes,' exclaimed Faustus, 'you should get married.'

'I'm too old,' said Makaria wearily, 'as you just said.'

'I didn't. You're the Emperor's daughter; you can't be too old.'

'I've always been too old,' muttered Makaria bleakly, to the air. More loudly she said, 'I don't see that it matters what I say to him. He doesn't know who I am. I don't think he'd know who I was even if he wasn't mad.'

At this Drusus appeared and looked silently murderous. Faustus said loudly, 'Let me apologise for her.' Drusus only shrugged.

Faustus set off across the grass towards Lucius. He looked back over his shoulder at Makaria and Tulliola standing for a moment woodenly side by side. They both held themselves very straight, otherwise he thought they might have been different species. Tulliola was so fluidly graceful;

Makaria looked like a surly soldier. She was not ugly – no, she had the Novian features, straight and autocratic except for the sleepy eyelids, the full and slightly crooked mouth. But she made them look so sullen, she made no effort with herself beyond what was necessary to look tidy and not actually dowdy. Faustus wished he had got her married when she was too young and malleable to make a fuss about it – although it was true that if there had been such a time, he couldn't remember it now. For years he had dithered about it, and the hinted promise of Makaria's hand had been so useful with difficult governors, or senators from whom he needed to extract money. By the time he realised something really should be done about Makaria, she was twenty-four and had set into intransigence and it was too late. He sometimes wondered regretfully what a male Makaria would be like.

Drusus was hanging around beside them and Makaria was saying something – probably apologising, thankfully, because Drusus smiled narrowly at her.

'Lucius, you know it's Titus, don't you?' said Faustus briskly.

Actually it was true that Lucius seemed to look shifty, although it must be really that he was frightened. Having looked at Faustus once he seemed unwilling to do it again. He wrung his hands and eventually said, 'Yes,' but Faustus did not believe him.

Lucius' nurse Ulpia, an attractive, squirrel-like woman about Makaria's age patted his shoulder and said, 'Come on, Lucius Novius, it's your brother.'

'Leo!' murmured Lucius. Faustus flinched.

'You know perfectly well it isn't Leo, Lucius. You know what happened to Leo. You must know that, come on.'

Lucius cowered a little. Drusus came striding over with Tulliola and Makaria, and said moodily, 'We shouldn't have had him come to the funeral, Uncle, I'm sure he was better before then. Weren't you, Dad?'

Lucius nodded vaguely, sat down and began busily pulling the grass up by the roots.

'Oh, dear!' said Ulpia, with a kind of optimistic disappointment.

'Do you have to do that?' asked Drusus quietly, with sharp, muted frustration. Lucius looked up at him quickly, and to Faustus' surprise, stopped. 'How's Yanisen, Uncle?' Drusus asked casually, as if Lucius was not there. Yanisen, the Terranovan governor, was in Rome to discuss plans to reinforce the great Wall along the Roman–Nionian border, something Faustus was in two minds about.

'Oh, same as ever. He's a pest,' said Faustus, equally casually, hoping Drusus would not pursue the subject.

'You see, it's inefficiency,' said Drusus eagerly. 'There's no reason he shouldn't manage perfectly well on what's available. He just wants you to throw money at him, he doesn't think about changing anything.'

'Ah, well,' said Faustus, for once trying to sound old and genial and absent-minded. He knew the young man would like to govern Terranova himself. But Drusus had scarcely spent a month outside Rome in all his life. Having left Lucius hidden in the family's most secluded villa, he ranged about from house to house, in and out of the palace, but always seemed unable to do without Rome for long. He had once helped to run the People's Games and seemed to think running a country was the next logical step. Faustus thought that Drusus looked pale and strained, and possibly not very well. The old worry stirred, so old and usual as hardly to be worth bothering with except for the fact of Lucius' presence – that someone else in the family would go mad.

Perhaps Drusus had only been to too many parties, or was in love.

Makaria after all said nicely enough, 'How are you, Uncle Lucius?' with her hands clasped in front of her like a good little girl. After her grumbling, Faustus did indeed think her hypocritical. Lucius barked an abrupt laugh at her and repeated, 'How? How?' Drusus gave an involuntary sigh of irritation and moved away, towards the house, where

Tulliola was still tactfully hanging back in the garden doorway.

'I mean, *are you well*?' persisted Makaria, with elaborate patience.

'Oh, go inside and leave him alone,' commanded Faustus. Makaria was too relieved to protest and obediently went away. 'Oh, Lucius,' pleaded Faustus, quavering a little, when she had gone. 'Can't you say something sensible? Leo's dead. It's me.'

And Lucius muttered suddenly, 'Yes, I know, Titus.'

'Lucius!' Faustus breathed.

Then someone – Glycon, his private secretary, burst out into the garden with Makaria and Tulliola in his wake. 'Sir, Sir, I'm afraid I must speak with you.'

'Oh, what is it?' growled Faustus, turning irritably.

Makaria said, 'Daddy, Marcus is missing. And there's some woman in his house who's dead. And no one knows what's happened.'

'There's a woman who's dead!' echoed Lucius, whispering through his dirty fingers, more scared than ever. Faustus had stood blinking, feeling almost as if he had known it already; thinking desolately somehow, 'Of course.' They were all to be picked off. Then he saw how white and taut-faced his family had turned, how despite the currents of resentment between them, they had drawn instinctively closer together with brief, frightened fellow-feeling, and he snorted, rallying, pulling his chest up. He wouldn't stand about stunned like that. He marched between them to talk to Glycon.

'Is there a ransom, anything like that?'

'No,' faltered Glycon, 'Lady Novia's right. We don't even know he was abducted, Sir.'

'Well, what else would have happened?' Glycon miserably avoided his eyes. 'That was a serious question,' Faustus said tersely.

'I don't know, I'm sorry.'

'Well, that is a pitiful thing to say. Someone has to tell me everything they do know. Lucius . . .' He paused, and laid a hand briefly on his brother's shoulder. Lucius looked back at him unreadably, with clouded eyes, gnawing at his fingertips. Faustus grunted wearily again and strode off towards the house, feeling with a faint satisfaction the others beginning to bob along instinctively after him. 'What are the vigiles doing?'

In the car, Makaria said suddenly, 'If there isn't a ransom, surely there should be one. I mean, there should be a reward.'

'Of course there should,' retorted Faustus mechanically, although he had not yet thought of it. He was running through what he must do that afternoon: cancel the governor, talk with his advisors, someone must make some sort of statement for the press . . .

Makaria closed her eyes with visible forbearance, but presently she said hesitantly, almost unwillingly it seemed, 'I suppose . . . they do think he's alive . . . ?'

'You know exactly as much as I do,' said Faustus, feeling that this should not be the case. 'And don't be insensitive.'

'I'm not, Daddy. I just think we should be prepared.'

'Makaria dear, that's morbid,' said Tulliola wisely. 'No one would have any reason to kill him, he's only valuable alive. There's no question but that we'll soon have him back.' She slid her hand into Faustus' and said, 'I hate to think of it, though! He must be terrified.'

'Well . . .' said Makaria, too preoccupied even to sneer at Tulliola, 'That's assuming it is a kidnapping. And if we don't hear any kind of demands soon then it can't be, can it? It seems strange to me about this woman. I didn't necessarily mean anyone had killed him.'

She took a breath to go on talking but her courage seemed to fail her. Drusus said flatly, 'You might as well say it. You think perhaps it's happened to him. Like my father.'

'I said don't talk about such dreadful things!' thundered Faustus, but then added nervously, 'And Lucius was never violent – never a danger to anyone, never hurt himself—'

'Yes, and Marcus was perfectly well three days ago,' said Tulliola.

'It can be very sudden,' murmured Faustus sadly.

Everyone fell silent again, until Tulliola, with a gallant effort at normality asked, 'How are you travelling, Makaria, will you want a car?'

Makaria stared at her. 'I can't possibly leave now, can I?' she said.

Varius woke up holding his breath, reminding, testing himself, making sure of what had happened before it could come to him by itself. There must not be any moment of confusion or laziness or thinking it had been a nightmare – nothing like that. He stared grimly at the wall for a moment and got up. He tried to straighten the crumpled papers, realising that he did not know what time it was and even thought he might have slept right through until the next morning. He turned on the longvision that hung on the wall and Marcus' face appeared at once. And it had just gone half-past three. Varius blinked, making himself think about Marcus' journey. So almost twelve hours had passed since he'd watched the tram convoy begin to move. Marcus should have reached Tarba by now – would he rest there or continue south at once? He seemed, in Varius' imagination, painfully exposed, and he wished now he'd given him more detailed advice. But plainly Marcus had not been found; even if his instructions had been flawed, they hadn't failed yet.

Then instead of Marcus' face there was Tulliola, holding her long neck stretched straight under the high stack of dark hair, seated demurely against some luxurious and yet nondescript palace background. Varius was a little surprised, because she rarely spoke in public. 'My husband has asked me to say a few words,' she began, rather stilted, without really attempting to conceal the fact that she was reading her lines. Almost as soon as she opened her mouth Varius saw why she had been chosen. Even when she was distressed there was something so decorous about her, the emergency seemed tamed simply by her presence, serious rather than shocking, something to be overcome. And she held the crisis at one remove from the family; she was not herself a Novian.

Of course Gemella was not mentioned.

'I'm sure you will appreciate how anxious we are to have Marcus back at home,' Tulliola finished. 'The Emperor is glad to offer five hundred thousand sesterces for information leading to his return. Of course, this is a very distressing time for our family and for the Roman nation, especially coming as it does, so cruelly soon after the deaths of Leo and Clodia. But the Emperor will take comfort from our prayers, from the excellent work of the vigiles, and from the steadfastness and support of the people. Thank you all.'

Varius went and washed perfunctorily. He was, in passing, cross with himself for having fallen asleep, but he did not really believe he would find anything else in Leo's files. While he worked he had thought of all sorts of things: of tricking or breaking his way into Gabinius' office and finding something somehow connected to the court; eavesdropping at the palace. It all seemed ridiculous now he was not so tired. He took Makaria's sweets and the sheaf of papers, and caught a tram across Rome to the Palatine.

The palace building had scarcely kept one shape for a century at a time, but since the Blandians it had been called the Golden House. Faustus had replaced the square, squat turrets at each corner with high, supple-looking oval spires made up of fishlike scales of honey-coloured glass, and capped with gold leaf and bright blue tiles, and wherever the framework showed was more gilt, and bronze plating. Between the towers, the great flat, yellowish stone box Nasennius had built was almost the same, although Faustus had slung a low functionless dome over it like a blue lamp, and here and there added more sheets of gold and blue glass. Nasennius' picture had once frowned nervously out of the stained glass roundlets in the rows of arched windows. The Novii, piously, had replaced these with bright images of smiling gods in azure sky, although the gods all had decidedly Novian faces. Varius did not look up at them. He was so used to the palace he scarcely saw it any more, although today the sight of it seemed to thicken the film of disgust that hung over things.

Varius passed the smaller, older buildings that huddled around the palace, skirted the Circus Maximus, and turned around the Golden House to the staff entrance, showed his pass to the Praetorian on the gate. He decided not to bother with Leo's deserted office in the south-west tower – there would be nothing there, Leo had never been very interested in it. Instead he set off through the first-floor corridors, where the civil servants slogged endlessly back and forth between the towers, and entered Faustus' outer office at the heart of the Golden House. The room was huge, gilt-touched and white, murmuring faintly with the machinery that sucked the heat out of the room; for a great square of light from the enormous new windows lay across the many desks. Outside, Rome was muggy and dull, but from the newest parts of the palace it always looked sunlit, both through the blue and the gold glass.

And the pale room was, more than ever, clattering with activity, but still Varius' arrival caused a tremor of consternation. This was not unexpected. He ignored the pang of self-consciousness, ignored the ranks of startled aides. At the far end of the room Glycon's wide desk stood like a barricade between the room and the shut and guarded door to the Emperor's private official rooms. Varius strode towards it.

Glycon stood up as he saw him coming. He said, 'Varius. Surely you shouldn't be here.'

'Why not?' demanded Varius dangerously.

Glycon had a frail-looking, intelligent face, an apologetic, heron-like body, thin fair hair that had retreated high above his temples but fell from there down to his eyebrows, quite long and limp. Varius didn't know him well – certainly not well enough to trust him now – but whenever he'd dealt with him, had always found him frustrating. Glycon was definitely neither stupid nor incompetent, but he was profoundly cautious, profoundly unobjectionable; decisions that approached him seemed to slow and dissipate until they scarcely happened at all. In this way he never got anything wrong.

Now Glycon deliberated quietly for a moment, but before he could speak Varius went on, 'Has the Emperor met the vigiles yet?'

'I really think you should be at home.'

'Has he?'

'No. But you don't look well.'

'I am well.' He gestured at the Praetorian standing stolidly against the Emperor's door. 'Is he in there?'

Glycon began to look apprehensive. 'What do you want, Varius? We're trying to keep the world going in here and today of all days—'

'I have to see him today.'

Glycon stared at him, pained. 'That's impossible.'

'No, it isn't,' said Varius stubbornly. But no, no, Glycon would never help him if he went on like this. He said, with effort, 'I'm sorry, Glycon, I know I'm not behaving well.'

'I quite understand,' said Glycon softly. 'But Varius, even on an ordinary day, you know there's nothing I could do for you, every hour he has is taken. Everyone wants to see him. We're cancelling everything. Today even the Sinoan ambassador and the governor of Terranova won't get to see him, and we still can't free up enough time. And you . . . !' He hesitated a little and then murmured, not unkindly, 'I'm not sure it's appropriate that he should see you, I regret to say.'

'Yes, I do know,' said Varius. 'I understood all that before I came. So you must see I would not try if it were not crucial that I see him.'

'You can leave a message with me,' offered Glycon.

'I can't. I'm sorry. It has to be in person.'

Glycon sucked his bottom lip thoughtfully under his teeth. 'Well, what is it about?'

Varius hesitated again, trying to measure each word, feeling the weight of each one. 'I know how inconvenient this is. I know I'm putting you in a difficult position and I'm sorry. I'm sorry that's there's nothing else I can tell you. I need to say something to the Emperor, but it can only be to him.'

Glycon gave a little 'Ah!' of consternation and looked, dismayed, at the wall as if for sympathy. Varius could not help his voice rising a little. 'Glycon, you know I've never done anything like this before. Please just tell him and let him make the decision, that's all.'

Glycon made a helpless, exasperated gesture, and for a second it seemed as though he might do or say anything at all. But then, it appeared almost at random, he turned silently and the guard stepped aside as he passed through the Emperor's door.

Varius exhaled with a sudden return of fatigue. He sat down at Glycon's desk and began to flick nervously through Leo's papers. He could at least show how rapidly and unaccountably Gabinius had lost interest in the slave clinic. And Faustus would surely have to recognise Makaria's sweets, would surely see how unlikely it was that he would have used them to kill his wife. But what could he say? He rehearsed to himself: Majesty, I don't accuse anyone except Gabinius. I don't know where the poison came from. Just please have the Praetorians investigate, please don't trust the vigiles.

He sat there almost in a trance, and at last Glycon returned and shrugged faintly and said, 'Well, you can go in.'

Faustus sat and signed, over and over: some tedious letters of delegation, an edict extending the pension rights of the dependants of veterans which ought to be popular, a death warrant. At the same time he was listening to Agelastus, a junior aide, telling him about the response to Tulliola's broadcast. He was used to working on two things at once in this way, but today it was harder to keep checking what he was putting his name to; he was not even skimming properly. He forgot also to keep half an eye on his pen. He disliked his signature. He had always disliked his signature. He had once worried that it looked babyish, then merely inelegant, but the worst was now, when he was afraid unless he concentrated and did not permit the letters to wiggle, that it looked senile. He was only sixty-one, it was ridiculous. But no, today his name really did dodder and shake. Well, he was shaken. But still everything was getting done – no one could say he was going to pieces.

And Drusus was trying to be helpful but he was distracting, standing over Faustus, looking glitter-eyed and feverish with over-excitement and interrupting Agelastus all the time. But he did not send the young man away – he would not normally have liked having the whole family in the office with him, but of course they wanted to be kept informed, and today it felt better knowing where everyone was.

'There have been sightings in London, in Tomis, in Palmyra—'

'How could they have got him that far?' asked Faustus, signing.

Drusus grinned. 'They probably didn't,' he said, before Agelastus could open his mouth. 'There's a cluster in Perusia that's the best so far, isn't there? Someone saw him boarding a train. There, Uncle, that's hardly any distance. They'll have him back this afternoon.'

'But if he was getting on a train he must have left of his own accord,' said Makaria, who was sitting opposite Tulliola on one of the dark green couches ranked below the Emperor's desk.

Faustus grimaced miserably. 'Well, I don't think he'd do that. What about separatists, or someone like that?'

'Yes, Sir, we've had four groups claiming responsibility,' said Agelastus.

Drusus' grin had faded. 'One says they've executed him,' he said quietly. Faustus sunk his face into his hands.

'But they'd say anything, they're just mad people,' Makaria objected.

'She's right, there's no reason to believe it,' said Tulliola. Faustus was glowering at the word 'mad'.

'There's no reason to believe any of it, that only makes it

worse,' said Faustus. But he lifted his face to look at Tulliola. 'You did very well,' he said, repressing, in Makaria's presence, the endearment that rose to his lips, hoping she could see by looking at him that he meant it.

She smiled back and shook her head. 'I didn't do anything. Anyone can read lines.'

'Still, it has to be the right person.' Faustus handed the letters to Agelastus and looked blank. 'What am I doing now?' he asked the room at large. But then Glycon entered and murmured confidentially to Faustus that Varius was insisting on seeing him at once.

The family fell briefly silent, incredulous. Glycon raised his hands in a little flurry of deprecation.

'I have no intention of trying to persuade you, Sir; he's refused to tell me anything and he seems very agitated. I only thought you should know that he's claiming it's important.'

'*Why* did you think he should know?' demanded Makaria.

'It's your finance meeting, Sir,' added Agelastus, peering at the diary.

'Tell him to go away. Who is Varius?' asked Faustus bullishly, not troubling to examine the faint familiarity of the name.

'Didn't he write to you? He's that hanger-on of Leo's,' said Makaria.

And Faustus almost found a face for the name Varius: he was an Egyptian or Numidian or something like that, one of these people who seemed irritatingly young for his job . . .

'Oh—' Faustus suddenly lowered himself back into his chair. 'Varius. Wasn't he out there in Tusculum? Looking after Leo's things. He must have been the last person who saw Marcus – mustn't he?' His hands had begun to quiver with a helplessness he hadn't felt until now.

Agelastus urged, 'Sir, there's no time.'

'Yes, I know who Varius is,' remarked Tulliola, calmly sad. 'The dead lady, that was his wife.'

Makaria and Faustus winced identically, looking for a moment comically alike.

'Ah,' said Faustus heavily, his hand at his forehead again. But a part of him felt a little more comfortable. At least it was almost, almost clear what should be done.

'What's wrong?' asked Tulliola, alarmed.

'It's completely unsuitable,' said Makaria. 'Daddy, you can't be associated with someone like that.'

'I know,' Faustus groaned. 'But what if there is something?'

'Then he should talk to the vigiles,' said Drusus. 'It isn't your job.'

Faustus looked up to see how Tulliola was glancing between the three of them, momentarily shut out, and felt sorry. 'I don't understand,' she said, 'Someone like what?'

'Someone in that position,' corrected Faustus wearily.

Makaria regarded Tulliola almost pityingly. 'All right, someone in that position. At best he's in shock and he doesn't know what he's doing. You said he didn't seem stable, didn't you, Glycon?'

'That's right, Madam.'

'Well, the Emperor doesn't have the spare time to waste on that. But it's probably worse than that: the fact is he probably killed this woman.'

Faustus gave a low, sad growl of agreement but Tulliola stared. For once she really seemed shocked. 'How can you say that—?'

Makaria gave a hard laugh. 'Well, that's what happens, isn't it? Women *get* killed by their husbands.' Tulliola recoiled. 'Maybe he thinks Daddy can protect him. Or maybe he's responsible for whatever's happened to Marcus – he might be in with one of these groups. Leo just wasn't careful about his people.'

'I just feel—' Faustus began. But then he got up, setting his body decisively again. 'No, the vigiles must know something about him. If they think he's all right we can always have him back. When is the city Prefect coming?'

Makaria was still frowning. 'Why aren't the vigiles

interviewing him right now? Besides, people shouldn't be wandering in here off the streets, Glycon, why did nobody stop him?'

'I'll tell him to go now, Madam,' promised Glycon, both relieved and embarrassed.

'I think we should have the vigiles come,' pressed Makaria.

'No,' said Tulliola.

Again the family paused, startled, although this time Makaria also looked outraged. Although he had been agreeing with everything his daughter had been saying, Faustus felt rather pleased. He could not resist saying, 'You're right, dear, Makaria was getting a little carried away with herself.'

'Of course Makaria is right to be cautious,' said Tulliola carefully, so patient with Makaria always, and under such provocation; Faustus wanted to hug her and give her a prize. 'But I can't feel right assuming so much about someone just because something happened to him – after all, it's no wonder he's distressed, is it, Glycon? Anyone would be. And Titus, of course you should hear what the city Prefect says about Varius, and you shouldn't miss your meeting. But I could talk to him.' She glanced down diffidently. 'If that would be any help.'

Faustus pondered. 'Well, if you can be bothered,' he said.

'If he doesn't have anything to say, it doesn't matter about my time being wasted,' said Tulliola brightly.

'We are already late, Sir,' mentioned Agelastus pointedly. 'I don't think the finance meeting can be cancelled.'

'Of course it can't,' snapped Faustus, and was emboldened enough to kiss Tulliola in front of Makaria before he took the private passageway out of the Emperor's office, leaving his wife behind.

Makaria followed him with Drusus, but she muttered darkly, 'Well, it's better than one of us doing it.'

After the clean and hyperactive brightness of the outer room, Faustus' office seemed sumptuously old-fashioned. A flat garden in fresco spanned the walls, wilder than any palace garden could have been, with coils of honeysuckle and pink clematis, dark grapes and – because the artist had not felt constrained by season, or perhaps because it was meant to be a garden in Elysium or on Olympus – dots of white blossom on some of the trees. Huge as it was, the room seemed dim and quiet with leaves and the painted shadows of leaves, varied like malachite. Varius, his eyes trained on the Emperor's great walnut desk, thought for a second that the office was empty. But there was Tulliola, standing like a white reflection of the soft goddess among the orange trees painted behind her on the wall.

He stood quite still and shook with frustration and anger. She came forward smiling, her hand held out. He watched her come and said before she reached him, 'I won't trouble you. I'll go.'

She said, 'Please don't, Varius, I know you're disappointed.'

He had to take her hand, the box and the papers wedged awkwardly under one arm. It was the second time that day he had touched skin; he felt again the null chill and stiffness, overlapping somehow with Tulliola's warm fingers. His voice came out cramped and mangled. 'It's kind of you to see me. But the only purpose I had in coming here was to see the Emperor. Only the Emperor, alone. I was stupid to try it.'

Except what else was he going to do, there could be no plan that didn't end in telling Faustus everything, unless he just went home and waited for the vigiles to come and arrest him.

Tulliola protested, 'No, not stupid, of course not. But he was bound to turn you down the first time. He has more than ever to do today, I'm sure Glycon told you, but it's not only that – he doesn't know what he should do. He doesn't know what will help. And besides—' she hesitated, plainly doubting that she should say any more, and as she began again her voice dropped and her skin reddened a little. 'It's a kind of instinct. Everyone here is so – so used to things being done a certain way, you see? And he – my husband –

he's afraid of seeming . . . you know. Impulsive, erratic. All the more today, of course.'

'I know, Lady Tullia,' said Varius, although he had hardly considered it so. In fact he was surprised that she could apparently be bothered with understanding Faustus; he and Gemella had sometimes wondered how she could bear having traded herself (as they supposed she must have) to someone more than twice her age, and could only think she must be so tranquil as hardly to notice it.

She'd been looking uncomfortably at the dense carpet, but she raised her eyes now, smiling again. 'That always sounds as though it must mean someone else. Tulliola's good enough.'

He nodded, but didn't use the name. He said, 'All the same—'

'All the same,' she interrupted him, very certain, 'if it really is important, if it's about Marcus, then he will see you, Varius, I'm sure of it.'

He didn't answer her at once. At length he muttered, 'I've already said it was important.'

'And about Marcus? It must be, because you were there, weren't you? Please, Varius, what happened to him?'

He swallowed. 'No, I wasn't there.'

'Oh,' said Tulliola, confused and disappointed. 'I thought . . .' she went to one of the green couches and sat down. 'Well, I shouldn't assume – and, of course, it must be terrible for you to talk about. I'm sorry. I haven't said. Of course there's nothing I can say – about Gemella. But I wish there was.'

No one else so far had used Gemella's name. He said formally, 'Thank you.' She sat seeming to listen to him while he didn't say anything. After a time he moved a little further into the room. He ventured, 'If you think he'll listen to you – please, tell him whatever it takes.'

She nodded, but she began twisting one of her rings nervously round and round. 'But then I have to trust you that it really is worth it – that all these awful things people are saying aren't true—?'

'I didn't kill her,' he said angrily, and saw at once that he should have been more careful. She had flinched, lowered her chin into her hand.

She said, barely audibly, 'I don't know what to do.'

'I've told you.'

She made a helpless gesture. 'You haven't told me anything. I can see you don't trust me; I haven't even asked why and I won't, but he won't listen unless I have something to tell him – Makaria—' she stopped. She went on cautiously, 'No one would *let* him listen.'

'No,' he said, 'No one can be there when you tell him.'

She sprang up again and put a hand on his sleeve. 'But tell him what? That you can help them find Marcus, what? At least, you'd tell me if it wasn't that, wouldn't you – you wouldn't let us think that you could bring him back when really perhaps he's dead? And even if he's not – what will happen to him? Please.'

He said nothing. She said begging, 'Can I say that, at least? Can I say that you know he's alive?'

They stood there, silent, staring at each other interminably. Then he looked away and gave the briefest jerk of the head, barely a nod at all.

She sighed. 'You really won't tell me any more than that? I do want him back, you know. I hate seeing everyone like this – I hate guessing what Faustus feels about it—'

He whispered, 'Please, will you go to the Emperor now?'

So she said, 'All right. I'll tell him.'

Across the door to the private corridor the flat convolvulus grew uninterrupted. Tulliola went to it and stood considering. 'Perhaps if you wait in Leo's office? I could bring him to you there and in the meantime you'll be left alone—'

Varius never answered, because then the disguised hinges turned among the petals and the opening door cut a slice out of the fake trees. Makaria was there.

Varius' arm tightened on the box of sweets; they felt hidden by the papers but he dared not look, feared that if he made a move to conceal them he would draw Makaria's eyes. For she looked Varius up and down and smiled stiffly, but even before she said a thing, on instinct and from the way Tulliola stepped back in dismay, he was as good as sure that here was an end to it.

Levelly, Makaria asked, 'Well, have you learned anything?'

Tulliola continued to retreat from her. 'I think Varius should see your father,' she said, certainly defiant, but weakly so.

Makaria took her breath in through her teeth and nodded sourly, 'I thought that might happen. And why do you think this?' Tulliola remained unhappily mute. Makaria turned to Varius. 'Come on then. What do you want to tell my father?'

'There's nothing I can say to you, Madam,' said Varius dully, but looking at Tulliola, willing her also to say nothing, thinking, she has no way of knowing why she shouldn't speak.

'That hardly seems fair. Then why can you tell Lady Tullia?'

Tulliola burst out, 'He's barely said anything, Makaria, I just think—'

'He hasn't told you anything?' said Makaria in disbelief. 'Then why on earth should Daddy see him? Didn't you hear all he had to do?'

'Yes, I think this is the most important thing he has to do.'

'I don't think that's your decision.'

'Then nor is it yours. I am his wife,' said Tulliola, blazing briefly, her smooth face strange and hard with anger.

'Yes,' replied Makaria. 'And you have known him, what, is it four years now? I've known him thirty-three and when he is as anxious and as unhappy as this I can see it. And I will not have him disturbed or his hopes raised unless someone gives me a very good reason. Not on your *whim*, Tullia.'

Varius said again, hoping for nothing now except to leave the painted room, 'I'll go.'

'I think you should,' agreed Makaria.

Tulliola cried, 'Varius knows about Marcus, he says he knows he's alive.'

Stopped dead, the room silent, Varius looked back, too far off now to be angry or afraid, only coldly interested to see how Makaria would react. She said, in a changed voice, 'Do you?' and in a voice changed again, to Tulliola, 'Then he should tell the vigiles, that's his duty.'

Tulliola said wretchedly, 'Varius, I'm sorry.'

But as Varius turned again, unsurprised, Makaria saw the sweetbox under his arm. She asked sharply, 'What are you doing with those?'

And now he was right and here was an end to it, he felt more than anything excited, or at least he couldn't have given it a better name. Nor did he yet name his next decision, although he could already almost feel it coming, whistling, exhilaratingly fast.

Tulliola called out again, 'I'm sorry, Varius,' as he began to move, out of the leafy room, past the guard who had no reason yet to stop him. The whiteness and noise of the outer office dazzled him as he advanced across it, vaguely heard Glycon or someone say his name, but kept going, out into the cool and sunlit corridors. He had enough presence of mind left to go to Leo's office and bury the Gabinius papers among the files, although he did not think it would make much difference if they were found on him. He was almost sure he had given himself away irretrievably, the details hardly mattered. But at least he had done no worse than that: Marcus was perhaps safe already, and no one knew where.

Outside, at the arched gate of the Palatine, he saw a little troop of men coming to meet him, with the red-headed centurion in front calling out 'Caius Varius, I have orders for your arrest—' Or something like that, Varius was not listening.

Calmly he turned his back on Cleomenes. And he looked up at the bright palace and thought, as his fingers scrabbled clumsily on the sugary interior of the wicker box, After all, I am a Roman. And he thought of Gemella in the garden, as he pressed the poisoned honey cube between his teeth.

THE BLUE ROAD

Crouching on the damp cemetery grass, Una and Sulien were watching Marcus, lying asleep under their patterned curtains. They were still on the edge of Tolosa, deep into the graveyard outside, for the dead were not allowed in Roman cities. But out in these fields, strung between the roads that left Tolosa, there was such a great crop of them: urns, boxes and pyramids, all the jumbled houses of the dead pressing wistfully against the city like a shanty town made of marble.

Sulien knew how long the other boy had stayed awake, shifting frequently and twisting in the thin bolt of fabric, because he had lain quietly waiting himself until he was sure Marcus was asleep before he let his own eyes shut. He was hardly sure what he was watching for, or why he kept himself awake, unless there was something infectious about Marcus' reticent distrust.

Not that Sulien thought of using the name 'Marcus' by itself. He had stopped calling the other boy Highness, because Una had said, 'Don't call him *that*,' and because it was obviously an insane word to use while they were winding haphazardly through the hushed streets, hiding together behind a skip. But Sulien didn't know what to call him instead. They'd been stuck waiting alone together between tombs while Una went back to the flea market, and Sulien had tried out all the possibilities: Novius, Faustus, Leo – the names felt odd to use, too famous actually to function as names. And the boy had said nothing about it, just as he hadn't said, 'You don't have to call me Highness'. He seemed to have no preference or not to notice, he just sat blank-faced and polite, with his back pressed warily against the mausoleum wall. Sulien kept advising himself to leave him alone, he could see how wrung out Marcus was. Still, the boy seemed to assume a, what, not quite superiority, whatever Una might think – but certainly a distance. It irritated Sulien, he couldn't accept it. And he was curious.

'Did you go to school?' he asked.

There was a tired pause, and the remote voice replied, 'When I was younger. Afterwards I had tutors.'

'But did people treat you just like anyone – could they ever forget who you were?'

'I don't know. How could I tell?'

'I suppose you can't. It must be really weird.'

Marcus pallidly agreed that it was.

'But good when you meet girls?' suggested Sulien almost hopelessly, and was not surprised when Marcus only murmured something inaudible and fell silent.

Marcus didn't recognise Sulien's face or name, but he had remembered the rows of pictures he'd seen on longvision in the weeks after his parents' funeral, and he knew Sulien must be one of the criminals who'd escaped in London. He sat against the stone trying gently to think of what the men had done: murder, rape, maybe some more trivial things, he didn't know – he hadn't been paying much attention to anything back then.

After a while, Sulien guessed, correctly, at this part of what was wrong. He budged a little closer to Marcus and asked softly, 'Novius—? Leo—? Do you want to know why they were going to execute me?'

'You don't have to tell me; it doesn't matter,' said the boy quietly.

'It does,' said Sulien, stung, 'because that's why I was going to explain – they lied – I didn't do anything wrong.'

'All right,' agreed Marcus Novius Faustus Leo, too readily. Sulien felt the kind of affronted disbelief he had felt always back in London whenever anything reminded him he was a slave. He scowled in the dark, and did not bother explaining about Tancorix and Catavignus. By the time Una came back, with their clothes and curtains and money and books, he had given up calling Marcus anything except 'You', as she did.

In another moment Una would have gone and woken Sulien: should have done it already, really: it was plain that they must talk about what they'd done while he, the other one, the Roman was still asleep. But she felt a chilly kind of pleasure in being, for the moment, almost alone. She scrubbed her palms back and forth on a wet clump of grass and wiped the collected dew over her face. There were some toiletries, little bottles of hairwash and oils, in the black travelling bag with Sibyllina's make-up, but they weren't much use here. She located her little mirror among their tumbled things, checked that there were no grey drifts of kohl left anywhere beneath her eyes, and went stalking about in the pale dark for a little while, combing her hair, liking the fresh cold of the moisture drying on her skin, and liking the white mist, and the way the flotsam look of the cemetery reminded her of her safe places, back in London. Statues and boasting little boxes: all crying out that money had been spent, all nonsense! And yet she didn't feel in the mood to be pitiless to the graveyard this morning, the jumbled sarcophagi were at least more lively, she decided, than if everything had matched or balanced.

She came padding back – passing occasional posies of softening flowers and the cindery remains of food offerings – to the oblong of ground where Sulien and Marcus Novius lay, sheltered on three sides by tombs. Sulien slept as only the very tall can sleep; loose and flat, all that height endearing because laid low; more thoroughly unconscious, or so you would think, than women or more moderately constructed men can manage to be; dangling further into stillness and dark like the longest plumblines or the chains of anchors. No, she would wait and think some more before she woke Sulien.

Counting money in her head, she crept over to Leo's son, and sat longer than she knew, glowering at him meditatively, remembering that giant face peering sightlessly down at her from high above Julian Square. What could they do with that face? There was a thin ingrained coating of dirt on the skin, and a gathering bruise now on one cheek. She touched the corresponding place, where similar marks had been, on her own face, trying to think, would it help, did it work as an incomplete dark mask to hide him – or did it only underline that familiar eye, advertise the presence of those familiar bones? For the longer she watched him, the more transparent the changes in him seemed, the grime and thinness and the cropped hair – they were nothing at all, scarcely more than the mist in the air, had no one else seen those features spread hugely over city screens, couldn't anyone else see what was in front of them; how, she thought again, had he ever got so far? And they knew about the hair and the worn flesh, she herself had stripped off the meagre camouflage he had come with, and now she was stuck with him. Unless perhaps no one would remember what she'd said, the market had been full of vigiles, but would they not think it was only a hoax? They had seen only three brief figures running away.

Her mouth tightened with dislike: that awful speech he had made about loving Rome.

Above them poked a mausoleum's miniature tower: a shrill and hysterical little white chimney-thing, a cone on a ring of columns around a statue on a cube, like a child's stack of fancy blocks. When it was light enough, to practise, she read the inscription on the base:

The fates stole you from your life and from me, Aelius, my husband. I, Fadilla built this great tomb for you; I set this tower above it; I placed your statue within it: everyone shall see what eminence you held in Tolosa. And I shall always lie beside you, just as in life the same house kept us safe, so the same tomb shall hold our bones.

Una raced through, unmoved, impatient to find out how fast she could go, snarled herself up a little in the middle, and flushed, cross and disappointed. But it scarcely counted, did it, it needn't have happened if she hadn't been rushing. She recited it breathlessly to herself – but maybe she was just as slow as before, she couldn't tell. She sighed and grinned rudely at the tomb. Fadilla had made it sound much better than it was, but still it was such a Roman thing, smug and overweening and doing no good. Within the columns, Aelius' statue looked bland and sprightly. There was nothing to show whether Fadilla really lay beside him.

Una looked again at Marcus and thought after all perhaps she knew how he could go unrecognised, and it was almost because his face was everywhere, it seemed so improbable that any Novian could be here in a cemetery or anywhere else, he was too famous to occupy so little space, should have been larger and less specific, spread out perhaps into more than one body. And his face should have lacked detail, there should not be these little things – say the suddenness with which the thick lashes shaded from dark to pale blond: there was nothing famous about that.

Sulien groaned and woke, and saw Una was already sitting hunched in an angular bundle, her arms crossed over her knees, her chin resting on one bony wrist, studying Marcus' unprotected face. She said, 'Shh.'

Sulien got up slowly, rubbing his neck, feeling that his body had set to the shape of the ground like biscuit on a baking tray. That was Marcus Novius' fault too in a way; all the week before he and Una had slept in the flea market, but only Una, fairly certain of her anonymity, could go back there now.

She whispered, 'He's got nothing, you know. We'll have to feed him, everything. Our money wasn't ever meant to go three ways.'

Sulien nodded gloomily. Really, it was stupid thinking it was Marcus' fault, it was his. At least Una hadn't said so yet. 'When we're still here in twenty years, we'll know we

178

didn't have to be,' he'd said. It didn't seem such a risk any more. It was just as easy to believe that they might peacefully have forgotten ever seeing a Novian in the flesh.

He joined Una in scrutinising Marcus Novius, who was frowning in his sleep.

'I suppose he does look a bit different from all the pictures,' he said, 'but still . . .'

'I bought him a hat,' said Una broodingly.

'Did you?' he was amused that she had already begun trying to solve Marcus.

'It wasn't expensive,' she said, faintly defensive, 'I got it when I went back to the market. Because of what I told them about his hair. But it won't help much, will it?'

Sulien looked, trying to think that it would, but could not imagine any hat adequate to the problem of the quietly autocratic face.

'Bag over his head would be better,' he said irritably. Una turned her face to him, thoughtful and interested. 'What?' he asked her.

'Yesterday . . .' she could not help her lip curling just a little, 'I thought you'd be asking for his autograph next.'

Sulien made a face, annoyed. 'Well, I was trying, I tried talking to him, but he just . . . assumed . . .' he said. But he glanced uneasily at Marcus, noted the bruise and swelling, and felt his usual sorriness for any injury. 'Oh, he's all right. And I suppose, you *would* be like that, if you were – you know. Him. I didn't realise how much difference it would make, that's all.' He shook his head. 'It doesn't matter. What about this place he's going to?'

'Oh,' said Una, 'he hardly even knows where it is.'

'*What?*' said Sulien, too loudly.

'He'll wake up,' she warned, and they shifted a little. 'It's south somewhere,' she went on, in an undertone. 'There's a place called Athabia, but that's not actually it. I don't know – people have to find it even though it's secret, don't they?'

'You could find it then?'

She considered. 'As well as he could, yes.'

Sulien drew her further away from Marcus. 'Then why don't we go on our own? Or go somewhere else? Of course we couldn't let him get killed, if that was really going to happen, we couldn't get *paid* for it – but we didn't, did we? He can do whatever he would have done. He isn't any worse off than he was before.'

'We are, though,' whispered Una, fiercely. 'They're looking for escaped slaves in Tolosa now, maybe they'll work out one of them's you. I thought of all that. Of course he's nothing to do with us, he doesn't want us with him any more than we want him. He didn't even ask us to help him, really, it's just that's what it comes to. But he promised he'd get us freed. And the money. If we stay with him perhaps we can make him keep to it.'

Sulien sighed, a little chilled by her vehemence, disappointed at the prospect of Marcus' continued company; but also, as they both turned again to look at Leo's son lying at the foot of the sepulchre, he remembered how he'd watched Marcus stretching out on the doorstep the night before, nothing to do with anyone; and felt the same uncertain, hovering pity.

'Does someone really want to kill him?' he asked, and when she nodded, 'Who?'

'He doesn't know.'

'He doesn't seem to know anything much,' he said. 'What is he like, really?'

'He . . .' began Una, and found that she didn't want to answer, she didn't want to remember or think about it, sensible question though it was. She thought anyway sometimes that perhaps no one was like anything, that there were just heaps of strange components that might be arranged one way or another when you happened to look at them without it meaning much. But was Sulien like that, and was she?

Marcus was afraid of scattering apart, was trying wearily, fervently, not to let himself drift.

So she hesitated, because she could not think how to say

even this much, and she could not think any more about him without a sort of shiver and drawing back.

She said, 'He's awake.'

Marcus hadn't opened his eyes. He'd woken to the instant knowledge that they were nearby and talking about him, and he'd tried to hear what they were saying. He lifted his head, unnerved, to catch them standing over him and falling abruptly silent. The boy turned away, even mustering an apologetic smile, but the girl, Una, stared back at him, warlike and unembarrassed. She said, 'You will do what you said? Freedom and the money; everything we would have got anyway. You still promise that?'

'Yes,' he said. He wanted to just go back to sleep. The girl nodded.

'Well, what do you think?' she asked her brother quietly. He, Sulinus or whatever the strange name was, glanced at Marcus and said, 'You still think he'll do it, then?'

She grimaced, bowed her head and admitted softly, 'He doesn't really think it'll ever come to that, but if it does, yes.'

They looked at each other, and at him, pensive and complicit.

'All right, then,' the boy said.

The girl went and rummaged among their scattered belongings, and presently strode over to Marcus and held something out to him at the full length of her bony arm.

She'd changed out of the green dress and the clothes she was wearing now were grey and shroudlike, and her hot-coloured eyes were bare of the dark cosmetic. There was no trace of Sibyllina's makeshift glamour left; she looked as pale and dingy as they all did, except he thought somehow sharper and more lucid among the vapoury graves, tense and conspicuous and vengeful. He took the crumpled thing, bewildered, and she turned wordlessly and immediately and began efficiently packing up the things from the flea market.

He was holding a knitted hat made of dark, bluish wool.

Una had also bought bread and fruit and they began eating in near-silence, except every now and then Sulien – he seemed almost unable to help it – began some cheerful, frail little exchange which never got far.

The usual part of Marcus that stepped back watched dispassionately said, 'Come on, talk to them, ask where they came from, you'll be stuck with them for a while yet.' But he looked at the relentlessly chatty boy and his hostile sister and he couldn't do it. The want for Rome, for everything that had begun vanishing six weeks ago with his parents – it seemed to have swollen even while he slept like the skin on his bruised cheek. It had never been this bad or this physical before, it was like a cold bottleful of the mist in the air, suspended somewhere between his lungs, chilling his whole body, sapping all the concentration he had.

But it was not only that. It was true, he didn't want them with him. Of course they were not like the fluttering palace slaves, but knowing what they were, thinking how he must seem to them, he felt the same kind of embarrassment and nervous, guilty distaste. He couldn't, for the moment, do anything for them. And if he began uncovering what had brought them here, what the boy had done and why, what next, what could he say to them? The girl especially was the problem, she seemed already to be obscurely blaming him for something, and if, as it must be, it was for being free and rich and a Novian, what was he going to do about it? He was going to have to depend on their money. It was humiliating. He did want slavery finished. He didn't want this kind of standing accusation to exist.

Still, he had to plan something, so at last he said, 'I had a map, but it was in the bag that was stolen. I – we should get a new one in the next town.'

'Yes, I'll buy one,' said Una. 'But not in Tolosa.'

'Thank you,' said Marcus. He coloured slightly without feeling it happen. 'But then we'll have to get to the next town without it. Do you know Tolosa well?'

'We'd only been there a week,' said Sulien.

'Well, there's a road that goes most of the way. I remember it starts out along the river. We shouldn't need the map to find that.'

'Listen,' said Una, more loudly than she'd spoken before, leaning forward on her hands. 'I don't mean only that, I'll get the map because it's our money. Even if you had money on you, you couldn't use it. You can't go near anyone, not now. I don't think we should go by the main roads, or into towns. I think we should only move in the dark. No one should ever get to see you. Or Sulien.'

He was taken aback. 'You want to walk along the smallest roads in the dark?' he asked.

'I don't *want* to do any of it,' she said. 'But if we're going to, then that's the only way it would work.'

'But half the time we'd be headed the wrong way. You don't realise how far it is. It would take forever. I should have been there by now anyway – I've been on foot too long already.'

'We can't afford anything else,' said Una.

'No,' said Marcus, thinking regretfully of the things Petrus had stolen from him. 'But I got a cargo tram as far as Nemausus.'

'No,' she said quietly. 'No, definitely not. If we're walking and someone sees us at least we can run.'

'They'll have longer to find us though,' protested Marcus. He felt slightly incredulous, even though he saw the sense of what she meant.

'If we're out in the open and everyone can see us, they won't need time, will they?'

'I've got this far.' He was irritated by now. 'You only recognised me because—' he stopped. He didn't know what she had done.

'But the vigiles know what you look like now,' said Una. 'I told them.'

Marcus sat cold and speechless. She'd told him this with an easy, informative calm, and was looking at him wide-eyed and reasonable, a little like Sibyllina again after all, apparently interested to see how he'd take it.

Una, in fact, was tense, frightened of what she'd done, and also calculating: here was the first moment of clash, and she wasn't going to lose. But she wanted it to be over with quickly.

Sulien saw them glaring at each other, the invisible collision going on clear enough. He said swiftly, to Marcus, 'Look, of course we wanted everything we told you about, but we did think you'd be better at home. Everything says that.'

Marcus knew this was true. And even if it had not been, even if he'd a right to blame them, he knew he couldn't afford to quarrel with them. He was furious and there was nothing to be done or said about it. He looked down, at his hands, away from the girl. 'I know,' he said, his voice strained, 'Well, it's done now.' What a useless thing to say, he thought bitterly.

'All you're trying to do is be safe, isn't it?' asked Una severely. 'So it doesn't matter how far it is or how long it takes to get there. As long as you're not dead you're doing all you're supposed to do. So there isn't any point doing anything stupid.'

'It wasn't stupid, I didn't know what you'd done,' Marcus snapped, feeling an unreasonable hot smarting of outrage which he couldn't stop to understand. It was only some time later that he realised it was probably the first time anyone his own age – certainly any girl – had ever called him stupid.

'The vigiles might not believe us now,' Sulien said, tired, appeasing. 'You could still be in Caesarea Incarum, or Tomis or wherever.'

'Can't assume that,' Marcus muttered.

'No, exactly,' agreed the girl, quite peaceable now that – it was obvious – she'd won.

'We can't stay here all day though,' said Sulien. 'People'll come.'

Before they left, Marcus stood for a moment as Una had, reading the inscription on Aelius' tomb:

And I shall always lie beside you, just as in life the same house kept us safe, so the same tomb shall hold our bones.

He thought of his parents, still lying waxy and perfect in the crypt outside Rome. He realised he had scarcely had time to believe that they had been murdered, that someone was really to blame for this; and that even now he was too busy missing them – both of them – with sudden and awful intensity to feel properly angry about it. He thought, and the chauffeur, they killed the poor chauffeur, too.

Then he reminded himself, with a jolt of guilt, of Gemella, and of Varius.

He turned and saw that the girl was watching him again, curiously, although this time she dropped her gaze at once and didn't meet his eyes.

He remembered the hat she'd given him. He put it on and pulled it as low as it would go, down to the nape of his neck and over his forehead, so even his eyebrows were hidden.

The girl murmured quietly, surprising him, 'Your hair could be any colour. It does make a difference.'

'Good,' he said, without expression. He was looking at the mist. It was a bad thing, it meant it was perhaps going to be autumn in earnest now.

He was sure it had looked simple on the map, but it was harder than he had thought to find the river or the right way. They pushed through the cemetery, out past a line of fir trees, towards the long sad roar they could hear beyond it. And they found there was no help for it, they had to comb through a bristling knot of sliproads and junctions, burring with cars, the air thick and harmful with fumes. At the heart of the tangle they saw the river at last, but it was so cut about with strips of motorway and industrial estate that they could not get at it or keep it in sight. Even if they could have got away from the roads, they would have been lost without the signs for Tarba and Lorda – or more lost than they already were. When they could they trod along swathes of brown grass, among thistles and teazles. But sometimes there was nothing but a thin streak of road to walk on, and sometimes they would have to dodge across a loop of road while the cars shot boneshakingly past, doubly frightening because of the speed and the pairs of eyes inside them. His hat jammed down over his eyebrows, Marcus studied the asphalt ahead of him more resolutely than ever. It was so plain that no one should be walking out here. It was two hours before they finally hit the straight highway lying like a bone across the Garumna flood plain.

Una stood with clenched fists on one of the triangular ridges of earth that flanked the road and gestured briefly at the waste. 'Look, this is why it's got to be dark. We've got to get off this road. There must be thousands of slaves here – everywhere. Making things.'

The river was a brief smear, far off behind high fences and powdery cones of gravel and shale. The plain was desolately flat, under an endless blemished skin of paper mills, gravel works, slaughterhouses, slave quarters, and huge factories where they built the engines of magnetic trains. It was strange to think of hundreds of people working nearby, for they could see no one moving anywhere. Una went on, 'I hope everyone's going too fast to think – but it's bad being seen near slave places.' She glanced briefly at Marcus and added, 'So you can stop playing with that hat. Doesn't even matter much about you out here. They can only see the back of your head anyway.'

Marcus did not look back at her. In the last hours as he'd walked, kept humiliatingly between them like a captive, he'd grown again too heavy with homesickness and grief to feel either reassured or needled by what she said. At length he made an effort and asked listlessly, 'Did you work somewhere like this?'

'Yes. Lots of places,' said Una, shortly and neutrally, and they did not speak again.

But there was still nowhere to go from the road. At least, on the other side of the low banks, they were shielded from the cars, but that meant they were exposed on the left to the factories. They kept on, Una gritting her teeth, watching for anyone looking at them, trying to feel for little flying fish-hooks of curiosity, trying to stay ready to wriggle free; but it was all too fast, she couldn't get a purchase on a mind before it was gone. She looked away from the road, concentrating instead on scanning the grey porridge of yards and buildings, hoping she still had her London instinct for finding derelict places. She was relieved to turn off and buy what she could in a concrete-stranded shop, even though it meant smiling and talking to the shop assistant. It felt better being where people were expected to be. It was so easy to pretend she had parents waiting for her in the car park as not even to be really necessary – no one even looked at her oddly as she calmly picked food from the shelves, a map from a stack by the door. She came out, perkily clutching shopping bags, trotting cheerfully towards the little acacia trees behind the parked cars, where Marcus and Sulien were hiding, and before she reached them rain had begun falling. It started off thin and devious, scarcely looking like anything much but chilling and slowing them nonetheless, so that they grew impatient and were almost glad when after an hour or so it thickened enough to soak them honestly.

They stumbled at last through the scrubby remains of broom bushes, towards an empty cement works, and slumped inside a garage there, shivering, waiting for it to be dark. They were exhausted and had walked no more than perhaps seven miles. They studied the map in the poor light, Una frowning with embarrassment and annoyance, for it took a little while for her to get the hang of the net of different-coloured threads, to really believe that the thick red band could really mean the huge road they had just left. Eventually she leaned forward and tentatively traced a wavering line, pleated up and down along what Marcus knew were byroads, and tracks, and footpaths that would creep right up the mountains. He unfolded the line mentally, and sighed at the length of it.

It was a bad day, and the days and nights that followed

were not much better. By the next sunrise the factories had begun to thin out, and they could keep to the riverside, walking among fields of beans and wheat. Round hills simmered up abruptly in the east, although on the other side of the road. And as the dawn came on they saw pale prints of distant clouds that seemed suddenly to change and become shadows on the snow of white mountains, looking as transparent as tracing paper. They stared in silence, briefly exhilarated. Una had never seen mountains before, except sometimes in pictures in news sheets, or on posters advertising holidays.

But they remained pale, fragile, far-off shapes in the sky, and seemed never to get any closer. Along the road, and in the west, the land continued relentlessly flat – better for walking, of course, but it strengthened the sense that they were not really moving, that the road was merely repeating itself like a conveyor belt under their feet. Marcus' excitement at the sight of the mountains had evaporated rapidly, and his silent depression weighed them all down. Una and Sulien found they could scarcely talk even to each other. Sulien kept wondering if he should do something about Marcus' bruised face, and through the first nights kept noticing how the other boy walked a little awkwardly, one arm sometimes pressed lightly against his stomach. Sulien had occasionally almost wished that some injured person would turn up whom he would *have* to help, he was so sick of his own uselessness. But Marcus was so unapproachably sunk in himself that Sulien couldn't think how he could explain what he could do, or how he could even step close enough; and when he thought of their non-conversation in the graveyard he didn't want to. And since the bruises were not serious, in the end he let them vanish by themselves.

It kept raining. The side road they'd been following had turned back to the motorway and at night the mud drove them onto it after all, trusting the dark and the cobalt lights to reduce them to blue, underwater shadows. The night air was definitely cooling now and Marcus saw that Una's nocturnal plan at least gave them the warmth of the day to sleep in, although that left the problems of damp clothes and damp earth, and the daylight.

More, although they fretted about what the night drivers might guess from their plodding silhouettes or from the glimpse of a sea-lit face, and though they sometimes saw slaves working in the distance in the fields, no one had seen him close up for four days and four nights now. And he had seen no one, no faces except these two. One evening he surfaced enough for it to strike him as strange that he knew almost nothing about them, and had scarcely been conscious of looking at anything other than asphalt or mud or his own feet, and yet still their faces had worn into him: so that he almost thought he could have drawn them both from memory, was quite sure he could meet them again in a year or two years or five years and recognise them.

It was clear, though, that they couldn't go on this way. Their clothes and blankets were all too thin anyway, and by now everything was drunk and clammy with mud and rainwater. Everything Marcus was wearing was Sulien's – the trousers Una had bought for him in London, and a blue tar-fibre tunic with a swirl of red flame printed on it, which Una had always thought too bright and noticeable anyway. Una had on a long-sleeved, red-brown dress and her grey Sinoan blouse together, but was bare-legged underneath because the loose trousers sucked up the spray from the road and then flapped wetly and icily against her skin. There were no other possible changes. They had tried rinsing out the worst of the muck in the Garumna, but then they could not get the clothes dry again. Una had bought a gas-filled stovelighter at the motorway shop, congratulating herself for thinking how they could light fires: but they had never managed to do more than singe damp heaps of twigs, passing the lighter impatiently back and forth, irritating each other.

They were talking about new clothes on the fifth night, a

few miles before Lugdunum Convenarum as they trudged away from the chilly farm building in which they'd spent the day. Marcus explained quietly to Una, 'You do understand – when I'm in Rome again, I'll reimburse you.' His wan voice was formal and unintentionally patronising. Sometimes he thought that, as the days passed and no one found them, that Una must have been right to keep to the dark; but not always, and not now. He still thought that they – he – could have risked climbing onto a cargo tram again, and have been there by now, perhaps.

'Yes, five hundred thousand sesterces,' Una reminded him sharply. 'I think that should cover it.' And she added softly, out of general pessimism, 'If you ever do get home.' She meant that for all they knew Rome might never be safe for him; but she saw Marcus interpreting this, with a kind of internal flinch, as 'if you stay alive,' and was exasperated, and did not explain.

'He's right, though,' said Sulien. 'We'll get ill.'

'I know!' cried Una, feeling besieged. 'But I've got to get clean before I do anything – it'll look weird enough when I go and buy clothes for two boys on my own – but if I'm like this – I just couldn't be anything except a slave.'

'I could do it,' said Sulien, 'I could just say I was on holiday. And that I'd got muddy walking, which is true.'

Marcus, tramping ahead, was startled by the little pocket of silence and shock that opened up at his back. He turned to see Una had stopped abruptly, her face soft with dismay. She whispered, 'No, they might see you. You might not come back.'

'Nor might you. It's the same for us both,' he told her.

'No. You wouldn't know what they thought of you. I wouldn't be there to tell you,' said Una.

'Oh, it would be a *shop*, not a military station,' exclaimed Sulien.

Una was silent for a moment. 'I really don't want you to,' she offered finally, in a little voice.

Sulien sighed and answered, 'Well, I don't want you to either.'

Una murmured again, 'I've just got to get clean,' and Marcus didn't know why he was watching them, why he was curious, if he was surprised.

Then Sulien said, 'Why is everything stopping?'

It was true. It was a couple of hours after midnight, and apart from the endless, mindless coursing of the cargo trams the blue road had been almost empty; but ahead a tailback was beginning to grow.

'Accident,' said Marcus, as beside them a tram convoy creaked and halted. But Una had stopped too, and was peering along the row of tail-lights into the dark.

'Off the road – get off the road!' she cried suddenly, in a hoarse voice.

They scrambled over the rough-grassed bank and crouched there. Sulien felt his feet slither and a great cold blotch of mud seeping up his trouser leg against his shin.

'What is it?' he whispered. 'Can you see something?'

Una was pressed against the ridge, still craning over the top of it. 'I'm not sure – thought there was someone,' she shook her head. 'Anyway, the tram drivers have got more time to notice us if they're not moving.'

'Oh, if that's all,' began Marcus impatiently, thinking she needn't have made them plunge into the cold mud like this; they needed only to stay on the far side of the ridge, away from the lights. He made to rise and at once the girl hissed '*No,*' and her hand closed fiercely on his arm, wrenching downwards, and instead of snatching away it stayed there, gripping almost painfully, holding him in place. Lying suddenly beside her in the long brown grass, he followed her gaze along the standing traffic, and he saw there were moving spots of electric lanterns swinging down the still line of vehicles, drawing closer, swaying towards each car and each tram unit in turn.

Una breathed, 'It isn't an accident. It's a road block. It's the vigiles.'

Marcus could just make out a kind of flapping going on at the cover of one of the trams. The officers were checking inside.

'Got to get away from the road,' said Sulien.

'Wait . . . wait . . .' Una murmured.

'Why?' demanded Sulien. The yellow lights were drawing closer, they could see the uniformed figures that held the lanterns quite clearly now.

'I want to see . . .' she whispered. She was staring fixedly at a section of the convoy, but she seemed dangerously high on the ridge, her head and shoulders exposed, surely.

'Una,' warned Sulien.

'They won't see me,' she said softly. Her hand was still, unconsciously, biting into Marcus' arm, and he could feel that not only her fingers but her whole body was stone-like with tension.

Three tram carriers ahead now, the vigiles were unhooking a tarpaulin, poking about underneath it, and presently there was some shouting, and slowly they lifted something out, something long and heavy, that twisted suddenly, and kicked, and tried to pull free.

'Ah,' sighed Una, dropping at last down the little slope, letting go. The thrashing shape had gone slack now, the officers were carrying it away back along the queue. Marcus thought it must be a man from the size, but it was hard to tell.

'Who is it?' he whispered, 'What will they do to him?'

'Oh,' she said, 'They won't kill him or anything. But I don't think he's going anywhere nice. You're not the only one to think of travelling that way.'

The rain crawled more coldly, more insect-like on Marcus' flesh and he shivered.

'He wasn't – he wasn't what they were looking for?' He stopped, wondering why he should expect her to know when she had seen nothing more than he had, and then remembered how she had recognised him in Tolosa. And he wondered if she had known this would happen; but that could not be right, or surely she would never have gone near the road.

She shook her head grimly. 'No. Why would they bother? I think they did believe us. Or at least, they think you're in Gaul. But why? There've been all those sightings, everywhere . . .'

Marcus shuddered again, thinking of the boys in the hostel, the girl and her mother in the jewellery shop. He said, 'There have been other people who noticed me. But I was sure they didn't know – I thought I stopped them.'

Una nodded. 'They probably didn't know. They probably thought – just in case, once you'd gone. There's no harm in calling, is there? Not for most people. And it's a lot of money.'

Marcus felt he ought to say something, that she had been right, but she was already moving away from the bank, into the dark field beside the road.

Sulien turned to look back at the road. The lamps were coming back again. 'That slave,' he said, 'Maybe he was going to the same place we are.'

Una didn't know, there had been no time to find out. The idea at once excited and frightened them; if it was true, it made it easier to believe that they were heading for a real place. But it followed that they had just seen how quickly and easily they might fail.

They turned left, away from the lamps and the motorway's constant blue glow, towards the black hills. They had an electric lantern of their own, but it was a long time of lurching through the dark before they dared to turn it on. Once Una tripped and fell full length on the soggy earth. She got up unhurt, but with her Sinoan blouse so choked with mud that she took it off to tremble in the wet air. After a while she was scarcely any worse off than the others, for the rain flogged them till their teeth chattered.

They padded on blindly, until, almost by accident, they found their feet scraping on solid asphalt again. They switched on the lamp at last, and they were on a thin silent road, and in the round of light they realised they had no idea what road it was, or how far they'd come in the wet dark. They kept along it only because they couldn't bear the mushy fields any more, and because they thought that it at least led away from the motorway. They crept through a lightless village, and beyond it their lamp touched the pale square of a road sign. They were going south, towards a town with an odd name; Wolf Step, and beyond it a pass into Tarraconensis.

'Well,' said Sulien, 'that's where we'll buy the clothes.'

Una said nothing, rubbing her cold arms with her numb hands, and thought wretchedly that the more desperately they needed things – food, as well as clothes – the harder it would be to get them. She avoided looking at herself or the others in the lamplight, but she could feel her hair sopping like bands of kelp on her head and neck, the long streaks of dirt from when she'd fallen on her legs and arms and the hem of her dress.

The road rose and fell for a while, but then brought them down again into a place as flat as the lake that must once have been there, although the hills were all around them now, and were growing more pointed. And just ahead, quite close, were mountains, not like the ghostly patterns on the sky they'd seen in the west from the motorway, but long heaps, looking at once smooth and bony under the hide of trees, like knees and elbows and shoulders.

Before dawn Marcus saw what looked like a wet slick – something rounded but glossy and liquid-looking, gleaming sleekly at the base of a hill. A slanted lake, he could almost have thought, almost tired enough not to think of anything. But then as they got closer and the light grew the white thing organised itself into chains of glass hemispheres, like a huge cluster of pale frogspawn, or great milk bubbles among the fields; and he saw that they were industrial greenhouses, standing in swollen rows, forcing warmth and colour into yellow lilies and tropical orchids. Around them were acres of low tunnels of white netting, standing over apple trees.

Sulien had already had the same thought. 'It'll be warm there,' he said thankfully, and immediately he swung over the roadside fence towards the glasshouses.

Una lagged behind a moment, almost too greedy for heat not to care, but she said hesitantly, 'People will come.'

Marcus turned back. 'No, I don't think so. I think those things work almost by themselves.'

'But someone has to come and get the flowers?'

'Not often,' said Marcus. Una was staring covetously at the glasshouses, her hands anxiously twisted. He went on quietly, 'And look how big they are – we can hide. We can sleep in shifts. It'll be all right.'

The pale domes glowed faintly across the valley, and when they came up close, they could see the lamps strung inside, feeding the plants light. The first greenhouses were carpeted with low trays of cyclamen and flame nettles, and the great structures above them looked outlandish; so much light and vaulted space for the benefit of such little things. Una bit her lip. Inside they would be visible a mile away.

'No, not here,' said Marcus, and they continued along the quiet lines of glass until they came to a huge upturned bowl that was clouded from within, as if with human breath; and they could see the fierce, saturated green of tropical plants, and smears of orange and yellow and pink, rising high in the mist.

Sulien saw a warped frame around a sheet of glass and began prising at it, but although the pane wobbled promisingly it would not come loose, and eventually Una scowled, wrapped her grey blouse around her hand and put her fist through it.

And she stepped inside, her feet crunching on spilt earth and broken glass. 'Oh,' she said softly, 'It *is* warm.'

The heat rose from beneath the floor, glowed from the lamps, through the scented moisture in the air. Below the lamps ran a grid of slender pipes, studded with nozzles, and as Una drifted, quietened and fascinated, down a bank of orchids, between bromeliads and plump-leaved ferns, these sizzled suddenly to life, sighing out fine circles of tepid water, dousing her. She gasped a little and murmured, 'How are we going to get *dry*,' but in the velvety air the wet was not unpleasant, and she found with faint surprise that she could not bring herself to worry about it; the warmth was hypnotic after so many cold days. She smiled.

Marcus and Sulien followed her into the lacy air, and Sulien thought what a strange place this was, so sterile in one way, the brittle glass lit up so the plants would never think it was night or winter, all these bright things fixed in such tidy stripes, picked and packed as near identical as could be. And yet it was also such a human place, curved and blood-warm, and as they entered into the pulse of spray, he looked up at the network of pipes and thought of veins.

He touched a featherlike leaf and said, 'What are they for?'

Behind, Marcus said, 'Private bath-houses, things like that, I think.' He was crouching, trying to fix one of the curtains across the empty frame, thinking, there must be thermometers, if the temperature drops perhaps there will be an alarm or something, and someone will come. And, as he was surprised that he was so sure of what the two slaves looked like, he was surprised that he could wonder why Una hadn't thought of this, that he knew this was the way that she thought. He rose and picked his way forward between the plants in time to see Una sink down – the slowness and softness of the movement seeming remarkable and unlikely – and stretch out lovingly on the heated floor, her eyes shut. He thought for a moment that she looked like a different person, the hard, spiky body relaxed, her hands lying loose and curled, her damp hair spread out, a brief sensuousness resting with the water droplets on the flushed skin, on the usually blank or glaring face.

It was there only a second. She let her breath out sleepily and then jerked upright, sharp and uncompromising again. She was looking shrewdly up at the pipes. 'Can we get more water out of those? We should wash everything.' She scrambled up and ducked through the next stripe of foliage, setting out into the crop.

Una wove along carefully, still enjoying the warmth but in an absent way now, not dreamy any longer, often glancing up at the web of tubes above, intent on the water. Somewhere at her nerves' end was a faint quiver of anxiety or alertness, to do with Leo's son – but it was scarcely anything, scarcely a second's worth. She crossed the round glasshouse and found that a passageway led through into the next dome.

In the second greenhouse the air was cooler and drier, and ahead of her was a wonderful thing. This was where they grew water lilies. A great oblong pond, no more than a foot deep, was set into the concrete floor. It was lined prosaically with sheets of sheer plastic, and the yellow reflections of the lights rocked and unstitched themselves, between the round leaves, and between the fat pink and white and tawny flowers.

Una's reverie almost came back, although it was still tinged somehow with nervousness. She paced forward silently, set down her bag, and dipped her hand into the pool: the water was about the same temperature as that puffing over the tropical plants, not really warm, but bearable, far better than the rain and river water she'd been drenched in for days. She rubbed her face, then pulled off her clagged and filthy shoes and wiped and poked at them with her wet hands, hoping to make them look at least ordinarily shabby if not actually clean. Then, although the job was not finished, she slid her muddy legs into the water, between the globular flowers, and the plastic tubs on the bottom that held their roots. Then she pulled back and ran splashily, barefoot, towards the warm chamber. She called out warily, 'There's water in here, but don't come in for a minute.'

Marcus, who had wandered through the damp ferns, to the edge of the circular floor, turned and saw her wet footprints on the concrete as she spattered away again. He pulled off the woollen hat and breathed in the haze. Carved out under his skin, the hollow place was still there, but it ached more warmly for now.

Una found the little bottles in her bag and crouched self-consciously, wishing she were somewhere far away and dark, afraid of the glass and the electric lamps. She felt, as she sometimes did before and in the first moments of nakedness, an impersonal dislike of her own body. She was not exactly hostile to her flesh, nor did she compare it to anyone else's – she just wished sometimes that she could do without it. She sighed quickly and yanked the brown dress over her head, whisked herself out of her underclothes and slipped, almost in the same movement, down into the pond.

She sat huddled for a moment, shivering a little, trying to persuade her body that the heat of the tropic room was still there, that she would go back to it soon. She began washing briskly, and gradually, as the grime lifted off her, the chill faded, and she extended herself slowly, nudging the flower-pots out of the way with her feet. Her limbs floated, feeling for the moment subtle, light, almost hidden under the sheet of water lilies. She pulled her head under the water to wash her hair, and for a moment she opened her eyes to look at the pinkish undersides of the leaves, and as she did so she remembered the Thames and thought with cold clarity, I almost drowned, I did drown a little bit. And as long as the thought lasted she lay there quite still, holding her breath, her eyes open.

She didn't stay in the water long. She pulled herself out and climbed hastily into her London dress. She would have liked to get rid of this garment, which, apart from everything it made her remember, was turning baggy and colourless, and the stitching on one of the shoulder straps was starting to come apart. But she needed something to wear while she washed everything else. She dipped the brown dress, the grey Sinoan clothes in among the flowers, watched them unfurl and darken, and tried using some hair-wash on the stained mud.

Between the two chambers, Marcus Novius Faustus Leo called, 'Is it all right now?'

'Yes,' said Una, but she shifted protectively to one side of the pond, pulling the drifting clothes around with her.

Marcus came in slowly, and looked at the expanse of

lilies. He said, almost to himself, 'They have these in Rome, in the palace gardens.'

'They must be really expensive,' commented Una, a faint note of blame or warning in her voice.

'I don't know,' he admitted.

He knelt on the far side of the pond and dropped Varius' draggled clothes into the water. He worked at them in silence for a minute or so.

'You won't have washed your own clothes before,' Una stated with a certain satisfaction, watching him.

'Not before all this, no.'

Presently she threw the bottle of hair-wash over to him.

'It's not very good but it's better than nothing.'

He was looking down at his hands as they chafed the wet cloth, concentrating on this, for some reason, as if it was complicated and difficult. The water rolled, a small wave from further out skating quietly towards him; he lifted his eyes and saw that Una had caused it; she had stepped into the water to retrieve her own clothes, and was standing calf-deep among the leaves and round flowers, in her short damp dress.

They looked each other briefly in the eye, and away, equally aware that she had just been naked. While they had each occupied one edge of the pool, while her legs were folded under her on the ground, it had not been so obvious.

Firmly, Una carried on with what she was doing; here was no threat, no reason to retreat or even to want to. She began to wring out the Sinoan trousers. She reached up and succeeded in suspending them from the lights, and began tweaking them carefully, so that they would not dry crumpled. The leaves lapped against her legs.

She said, practically, 'I can't get my shoes clean. But do you think this is enough? Would you guess?'

She had invited him to look at her again, she realised, but never mind.

He shook his head, and meant it, but they both knew it didn't count for much; he didn't really know how a free but poorish girl should look. He applied some of the hair-wash, and went on stirring the clothes.

'My cousin Drusus went to the Sybil at Delphi once,' he found himself beginning. 'I don't know what she said to him, but it was about his future. But you . . . you don't know what's going to happen, if we'll get to the mountains.'

'No,' she said, hanging up the brown dress.

'But you are like that, you are a—' he didn't know what to call her. 'You know . . . something.'

She shrugged and stepped out of the water. 'You, that's all,' she said lightly, strained.

'Or anyone.' She went back to busily wiping the mud off her shoes, waiting for him to feel, as Sulien had, invaded, angry. Nothing seemed to happen. 'Oh,' he said blankly. She glanced at him quickly – his eyebrows had gone up, although he was startled rather than incredulous.

'I wish I could do that,' he said finally.

She saw with shock – he was more interested than anything. She didn't answer.

'But you don't know everything about me.' It wasn't really a question.

She shook her head. She said, uncertainly, 'There was what was there just then, in the street, when we were trying to hold on to you. I was looking to see why you thought someone wanted to kill you, and if it seemed like it might be true . . . but I couldn't – find that – without being – or, knowing—' She broke off. Again she didn't know how to say this, and she wanted to stop trying, this was making her think too much of what it had been like, that night in Tolosa. 'Not everything you ever thought, or that ever happened to you, *you* don't know all that.'

He nodded, trying to imagine what it would be like, almost thinking for a moment that he could, but it was too strange, he couldn't hold an idea of it. Suddenly, a voice that seemed almost not to be his began. 'Did you see—?' and stopped, stuck in the middle of a question he was afraid to finish, although it was obvious now that this was what he had been asking from the start. 'Anything – wrong,' he

went on, forcing himself, 'Anything like the beginning of?'
And this time he couldn't get any further. He looked across
at her, touched his forehead.

His head was bare and the steam had already carried away
some of the dirt on his skin, she could even see that his
sandy hair had grown a little, now it was visible. He should
have shown up more patently than ever, as the huge prince
on the London screen – but whoever thought any of the
Novii could look like this: so raw with entreaty that she
was disconcerted? Some floating part of her whispered, you
knew he was afraid of that, you knew how it felt. She
silenced it, alarmed, and said, hedging, 'But I don't know
what that would be like.'

'No, you must,' he insisted, his voice was hoarse, almost
a cry. And he was sure of it, she must know something. He
couldn't tell anything from looking at her, the ruthless look
wasn't there, but her face was so blank, so well-armoured.

But then it altered. 'No,' she murmured, 'no, I didn't see
anything like that.'

'Oh,' breathed Marcus, his eyes closing of their own
accord. For a moment, as the tension trembled out of him,
he felt almost as shattered as if she'd said the opposite: he
was unstrung with relief, sick with it. Then that passed and
he was just wiped out and happy. He grinned shakily at her.

'I did think you were a bit – screwed up, anyway, at first,'
she continued quietly, 'because you were so afraid someone
wanted to kill you, and there didn't seem any reason. But
not later.'

Marcus' face darkened as he felt that the fear he'd grown
up with was after all not gone, that here was the shadow of
it returning. 'But even if it's not there now, it could still
come.'

'Well,' said Una, 'Yes.' Her shoes were as clean as she
could get them. She rinsed her hands and got to her feet. She
added shortly, 'But it could come to anybody.'

He said 'This is the truth, isn't it? You're not just—?'

'Trying to make you feel better?' she said dryly, and
almost smiled. 'I wouldn't do that.'

When she was gone he stripped and washed quickly in the pond, uneasy under her hanging clothes. After a while Sulien called out to him that he had found fruit growing in the tropical chamber, although not much of it was ripe.

[x]

WOLF STEP

It felt like summer again, except when the wind blew; but Wolf Step was pressed between mountains like a bookmark between pages, and when they reached it, in the late afternoon, the new sunlight skimmed above the roofs without touching them, and a wide dove-grey shadow spread coolly across the narrow dove-grey town.

And it seemed like a long time since they had seen much of anything in the sun, even each other. Stealing along from the greenhouses, they blinked at the daylight, and were afraid on the roads; exposed enough by the light to be stared at once by a farmer standing among yellow cows in a green field.

But they could see in colour again. Una had not known what a shock it would be, or realised how the flat look of things in blue or yellow light had come to seem normal. Now the warm mountains looked like piles of coins and amber. She had never been anywhere like this, never seen anything like the ten huge birds, scythe-shaped, rust coloured, flinging themselves at the ground and sky and each other, over a field of cut corn.

She and Sulien stood underneath them, faces upturned.

'Killing things,' murmured Sulien. And for him the knowledge made the birds slightly chilling; beautiful as they were, and they were furious with each other too – they were trying to frighten each other away.

'Well, they have to,' she said.

A little amused that they should be so astonished, Marcus said clumsily, 'They're only buzzards.'

Una rounded on him, feeling her ignorance jabbed at, and snapped, 'Well there aren't any in Britain, or in London anyway. Not everyone gets paraded all over the place like you; I didn't know birds got that big.' She turned away and repeated softly to herself, 'buzzard,' to fix the name, and to calm the sudden smarting of all these things that plainly everyone should know, and she didn't.

Marcus both saw what he'd done and thought she was ridiculously touchy. Sulien hadn't seemed to mind particularly.

And ahead, under the coppery peaks, the colours gave out again and Wolf Step was all soft monochrome. They walked towards it in irritable silence.

Just outside the town a tram cable joined the road abruptly, almost out of nowhere. A short convoy thundered past them, raising the pale grey dust that lay everywhere and went hammering through Wolf Step. They hadn't understood how important the pass into Hispania must be. Something about the feel of the dust, as a cloud of it rolled over them, seemed familiar to Marcus: then he saw patches of the town's grey stone rising in crags between the trees, and knew it was marble, and there must be a quarry somewhere nearby.

The convoy made Una worry about finding somewhere to hide Marcus, but it turned out to be quite easy. Just after the tramline appeared a little gravel track sloped away from the road towards the water. It was the same river they had followed all this way, they had scarcely noticed the blue thread on the map under the red and yellow lines, turning south almost where they had turned. The real Garumna had never been blue, of course; and here it had become a strange, whitish, pearly green, and ran very fast, and looked very cold.

By the river, at the bottom of the slope, the track led, pointlessly, to a large building that had possibly once been a barn. Someone was still using it as a woodshed, perhaps; the messy heaps of logs and planks inside looked quite new, but it was hard to believe anyone went there often, for the shed itself was almost farcically wrecked: the square door hanging from the frame at a lackadaisical tilt, a big, exact hole punched through the tiled roof, ivy coating the walls inside.

Thrown on top of the fuel, mysteriously, were three or four children's school desks. Outside, Una slung down her bag and got out her make-up. 'Well, it's all right, and there are the trees behind. If anyone does come, you can hide.'

'Can I?' jeered Marcus wearily. 'But I thought I'd write my name on my head and stand out here shouting Hail Caesar.'

Una glanced at him covertly around the kohl brush, knew he was resenting her for resenting him, and went on poking the black paste onto her eyelids. She meant not to answer at all, for what was the point? But she found herself saying with false mildness, 'You'd have done as good as that before now, if we hadn't been there to stop you.'

Marcus remembered her pulling him to the ground by the road block and shut his eyes with mingled shame and anger. He had not properly thanked her, but he could hardly do it now. It would come out wrong. More obscurely, he was disappointed with her and furious with himself for reverting to this half-concealed wrangling so quickly. And things were worse than before – they had never attacked each other so openly until now. How could it have happened over some birds? By the pond, in the greenhouse, he had started to think that after all they could talk to each other, that it wasn't hopeless; and she had told him . . . but when he started to think of that his head seemed to flood with confusion and he wished she'd hurry up and leave so that he could get clear again.

He found that in the midst of all this he was watching her apply the kohl with a kind of fascination; he couldn't remember seeing a woman putting on make-up before. She was absorbed now, painting deftly but so quickly and ferociously that he was afraid for the soft skin. He watched her winking at herself, one eye closed and soft and passive, growing dark under the brush; the other still pale, open, concentrating.

He thought, at least when she's gone at least I'm going to ask Sulien why we keep doing everything she says. Then he saw that evidently this was not altogether true, as Sulien was gathering together the wads of cash from Una's bag.

'You're both going?'

'There isn't enough money,' said Sulien. 'At least, not for food as well. So Una's going to do the fortune-telling.'

They had taken some apples and tropical fruit with them from the glasshouses and the orchards around them, but they had only a hard fist-sized lump of bread left. Marcus felt again – and worse than ever – mortification at costing the two slaves so much in money and in danger, at being a responsibility they had to put up with. He said thickly, 'I'm sorry.'

Sulien shrugged. Spending the extra money on Marcus was a nuisance, but it was just part of the way things were now, impersonal, like the long rain. Marcus' continued and obvious shame about it was getting wearing.

Una said, 'I wish you'd stay here though.'

'I know,' said Sulien.

Una sighed, hung the green shawl around her neck and the two of them started up the track.

Especially in the first days on the road from Tolosa, the slaves' company had made Marcus feel only more bitterly lonely than he had before, and he had longed to be on his own again so steadily that it needed no thinking about. Now, at first the quiet of nobody there seemed as good as clean water; so much better than the silence made by no one talking. He let the stupid mood that Una had somehow got him into drift and subside. After a while a little dark lizard flecked with white spots came out, and Marcus watched it until it vanished into the grass again.

But the peace turned dull more quickly than he expected. He had nothing to do. He had put one of the children's desks straight and had been sitting on it awkwardly in the shadows; but as the shade deepened and grew colder, and no one came to find him, there seemed no reason to stay there, so he got up and paced around the grassy yard in front of the shed. He found he wanted to start moving again for moving's sake, not out of the usual fear of wasted time and being caught. He knew this dead time must seem longer than it was, so he didn't know how long it was before he decided he would walk to the head of the track, just in case he could see the others coming back.

Una and Sulien walked up to the road and into the shaded town, as another fleet of trams rolled past, looming and incongruous on the little high street. For Wolf Step was just a sliver of a place, scarcely more than three streets lying side by side along the river banks. It would hardly have deserved to be called a town, except that it looked busier than the village they'd crossed during the night. Beyond a bridge leading to a quiet row of ash-coloured houses, the high street opened into a cramped forum, no bigger than a London back garden. Further on, as they'd hoped, they could see that the street was lined with shops. Across the river, high up on the crag, stood a little temple with a white Minerva perched outside it, looking severely down on Wolf Step, sharp against the pale grey.

Una eyed the forum as they passed it and whispered to Sulien, 'Well, that's where I'll be, but we'll find a clothes shop first.'

The river forced the streets into a gentle S-shape, and in the hollow of the second curve they found what they were looking for; a shop selling boots and clothes and sleeping bags for the mountains. They peered cautiously around the door. The shop was bare of customers.

'It'll be fine,' said Sulien. 'I'll come straight back and find you. You can buy the food on your own if you like.'

'All right,' she said, smiling unhappily. She draped the shawl over her head and went back to the forum alone.

She hovered nervously at the corner of the forum that met the street, studying it. There was a tiny basilica, which seemed to be shut for the day, but there were still people about. They were mostly tram drivers, she thought, shaking the cramp out of their legs, and watching the dirty public longvision fixed precariously to the larger of the two scruffy cauponae that framed the far corner of the forum.

Someone had wiped a half-hearted smear in the dust on the screen. It was playing a patriotic film, and probably a patriotic song, too, for here were some excited, overdressed children opening and shutting their mouths like triumphant fish while they showered a beaming Faustus with rose petals; but there was no sound in this slow little place. In silence Faustus was crowned, Faustus waved at crowds of delirious Romans, Faustus married Tulliola. It was all very cheerful. Here was Faustus smiling with Leo and Clodia, as if they were still alive.

Una sighed and set her teeth. She could hardly expect her customers to come to her, as they had in the flea market, she would have to pick out each one and do almost all the work before she even knew she was going to be paid for it.

She crept a little further into the forum, around the basilica, and fixed her eyes on a man who was just paying the bill at one of the plastic tables outside the caupona. When he stood up she marched over and plucked, with distaste, at his sleeve.

'Would you like to hear your fortune, Sir?' she asked, in Sibyllina's voice. She felt, briefly, uncomfortable. Several of the men were looking at her with varying degrees of interest, someone – the caupona landlord – was examining her legs, assessing her slenderness under the brown dress. But he disappeared with the bill into the caupona and she felt better. After all it helped if Sibyllina was attractive – what else was the black eye make-up for?

The tram driver she'd picked, though, was not paying much attention to her. 'Get out of it,' he said roughly, pulling his arm away, as she'd expected. Una retreated a little and then said casually, 'Perhaps I could have told you whether Momus really wants to sack you, and what Dora meant when she said that about Sicily.' And she turned away, smiling tersely to herself, quite sure that he'd follow her.

She led him to the steps of the basilica and asked for three sesterces. She sat with him there and recited the usual things. 'She's tired of living in Lugdunum, but it doesn't mean she's tired of *you*.' After fifteen minutes, she said she couldn't see any more without more money. She knew he would refuse, but it was just as well to be rid of him and move onto someone else. She folded the notes up very small and thought, I'll just do that four, five more times.

Once or twice she misjudged and sat working for minutes at someone who then wouldn't listen and charged past her, but soon she had six sesterces, and then twelve, and she began to relax enough to grow bored. Although she kept talking softly and fluently, she couldn't stop her eyes from wandering to the glowing longvision over the yellow-painted caupona. The film was over now and the screen showed lists of economic figures, floating and vanishing over a background of vaguely soothing ripples. She had not the first idea what they were for, but sometimes between customers she stared at them as if she could force the numbers into making sense by will alone.

The numbers twinkled and faded, and the screen went dark for a moment. Stop daydreaming, Una told herself, and got to work again.

She had been concentrating diligently on the trouble a woman from one of the shops was having with her stepchildren, when a sudden change in the brightness of the screen, the knowledge that a still white square had appeared tempted her to glance back at the longvision; and she saw that the white square was a shot of a drawing, and there was a frame of ordinary longvision footage beside it. Two pictures, and the pictures were of Marcus. One was a still from the recording of the funeral, but the other was a competent sketch of him without his hair.

The little forum seemed to swing and clang disastrously around her. Una lost what she was saying, opened her mouth as silently as the singing children, stammered out at last in a thin, unsteady voice, 'No, your husband isn't being fair.' But on the screen, text crawled along a blue ribbon beneath the two faces, and said that while the call that had described Marcus Novius might have been a criminal joke (it appealed to the consciences of the runaway slaves to come forward again if it were not) the public should be aware that Marcus Novius might look different. Viewers should also search their cellars and outbuildings, just in case.

Una smiled at her customer and tried to gather herself. This was only what she had thought might happen, this was exactly why she had stuck to the dark all this time, why Marcus was waiting by the river's edge. Perhaps this was the first time the drawing had been shown, she tried to think. But no, she was sure it was not – that plump woman, crossing the forum, had just glanced up at it with a kind of internal nod of recognition. Everyone in Wolf Step must be walking around with that picture in their heads, and walking out of the town perhaps, and down the gravel track. And it was daylight now. She and Sulien would go back and—

She cut short the little spool of panic, impatient with herself. Well, she thought firmly, or made herself think: suppose the worst is true, suppose we went down to the shed again and they'd got him, yes, if we knew he'd be killed, well – go on, say it – then it was better that we weren't there. We'd have lost the money, but we'd have lost the risk too.

She could hold this thought, cold and glazed in her head, but somehow the conviction went on creeping up and down her arms and legs that it would be her fault, she was the one that had told the vigiles. She'd have killed him.

The woman was earnestly telling her something so that Una had not had to speak for a moment, thankfully, and she was just promising herself that she need only get this over with and then go. And then, prompted by the mention of fugitive slaves, the longvision reminded her casually that three of the London criminals were still loose, and here was what they looked like.

She hadn't seen Sulien in over an hour. It was unendurable. Una was on her feet, feeling as sick and half-drowned as she had ever felt on the Thames, muttering indistinctly, 'That's all, I can't stay, I'm sorry.'

'Oh, no, please,' protested Una's customer, looking hurt and abandoned, sorrowfully blocking her path.

'You can have the money back. I'm sorry,' said Una. She felt for the money in her pocket and tried rapidly to separate the notes, and she could even see, with a distant scorn at herself, what would happen, but she could not stop it: her fingers were shaking, the money was bound to drop to her feet. A few notes began to flutter away as she grabbed for the main bundle, and Una would have left them there, but the woman had stooped instinctively to help and reached out for them, so that Una could not move forward without tripping over her. And someone else – the landlord again, had joined in obligingly now, gathering up the fallen notes, saying something reassuring. By the time Una had stepped around her, the woman had risen and was thrusting the money back at her, pawing beseechingly at her hand. Una felt ready to scream.

'No, I don't want it. You were going to tell me what I should do,' pleaded the woman. The landlord had taken hold of Una's wrist to put the money back into her palm.

'You should – I don't know. You should stop trying so hard to make Lavinia like you. You should pray to Juno. You have to decide for yourself. I can't see any more, I'm sorry.'

The woman turned away at last, disappointed – but something else was wrong. Una felt as if something were sliding inexorably up her sleeves, down her collar, up under the hem of her dress—

The man from the caupona hadn't let go of her wrist.

He said, 'You're a bit flustered, aren't you? Better spend some of that on an orange juice or something.'

Just as when the money fell, she could see what would happen, and she couldn't see how to stop it.

He was no taller than she was, with fluffy sparse hair, and he'd kept his friendly eyes on her face as she spoke even though he was considering her hidden breasts. And yet the scrutiny wasn't only sexual, it was almost as if he had put her on a pair of scales, was belting a tape measure around her waist. For these things had happened to her, sometimes, in the London markets.

She said, insanely brightly, 'Oh, that'd be nice, but I'm late.' She thought desperately that if she hid what she knew, if she didn't show that she was frightened, perhaps she could keep him uncertain, perhaps that would be enough.

She withdrew her wrist successfully, gentle and smiling so that he would not have any reason to stop her, but at once he had a sympathetic hand on her shoulder.

'Look, it's free to you. I'll put it in a plastic cup and you can drink it as you go. Your master won't mind that, will he? Where is he, anyway?'

She knew it would be better if she admitted to being a slave, convinced him that she did indeed have a master waiting for her – but then how could she explain the money she'd been earning, alone and unsupervised, and in such a manner?

'What?' her voice came out almost as a croak, although she was trying to sound at once amused and indignant. 'You mean my dad.'

'Your dad?' he repeated, his voice a little lower, but otherwise as light and conversational as ever.

And she knew he was quite certain now, and nothing she could say would make any difference, and there was nothing to do but try to run.

His warm hand was ready to clench down on her left shoulder; his other hand would be ready if she tried to dart past him to the right. Una said softly, 'Yes, my dad,' and then whipped unexpectedly backwards, so that he had to lunge forwards after her, his loose fingers closing, too late, on air.

Una felt a kind of painful triumphant sob scratching at her chest, as he staggered, briefly off balance, empty-handed. But behind her was only the caupona, she was letting him herd her like a sheep. Except that she was in a pen already, there was no way out of the forum that didn't mean dodging past him. Before he could steady himself she rushed sideways, but there was no room; she smashed in among the tables, so that she fell almost into the seat of a white plastic chair while the others skidded hollowly around on the concrete. Una cried out in fury, clawed upright and started to push her way through the skittering things. A slim, dark-haired young man, perhaps nineteen, was sitting against the caupona wall and watching uncertainly, a little shocked, a little embarrassed. Una said to him despairingly, 'Why don't you *help* me?'

Behind her the landlord grunted, 'It's all right, Tuccius,' a bit out of breath now, but still benign and sensible. And of course the little start she'd had was finished, his hand closed, crunchingly tight around her arm, gripped the other as it flailed and punched, plucked her out of the disordered furniture, hugged her against his solid body. Una spat something incoherent, 'I'll *kill* you,' and jerked her knee upwards, but it only glanced harmlessly across his thigh as he swivelled her round, clutched, and lifted her off her feet. Her arms were wedged against his chest, her body stretched taut, and why, why, raged Una, did she have to be so light and feeble? She had not even hurt him. She would have liked a knife sticking out at every joint, barbed wire for tendons, a ridge of nails down her spine, so that holding her so he would have already gouged and killed himself.

Tuccius nodded uncomfortably, and wandered away.

The landlord said, damply in her ear, 'You see, we get a lot of runaways through here, I don't know why it is. You get to be able to spot them.'

'I'm not a slave,' Una tried to shout, choking. She stamped backwards at his knees, and felt such a pang of pleasure at doing some damage, however useless, that she scarcely cared as he did something she was quite used to, turned her wrist over and drew it up her back.

'Now, come on, lovely,' he said regretfully. 'Now, if anyone else caught you saying that, you might even be executed, and I think that would be such a waste.'

Inside, the caupona had a kind of flimsy sea-side look, painted white and sky blue. Somewhere music was playing; a soprano swooping babyishly over breathless flutes; a love song. A tram driver was poking vaguely at the harpasta table as if he was about to begin a game. At the counter, a second was drinking mulsom wine from a little chalky glass, and serving him was a woman with puffed hair dyed a strange, orange-streaked purple, which must have been meant to be auburn. They looked at Una, lashing, swearing, screaming in the landlord's arms with a kind of indifferent interest. The men were ready to help bind Una's hands with electrical tape, to get her through the little door at the back of the room, if necessary. They had seen this happen before.

Despite what he'd said to Una, Sulien was apprehensive about entering the empty shop, but he walked straight in and started examining the waterproof jackets, reminding himself that he knew how to do this, he didn't have to make such an effort to seem normal, the way Una did. She had dinned into him some story of brothers and holidays, and made him more nervous in doing so; but he was soon sure that there was nothing to worry about – at least, that the shopkeeper was not going to take one look at his face and call the vigiles. There was only a bored young woman leaning sleepily against the counter, who was, at first, completely uninterested in him.

The shop felt sleepy, too. The lights were dull and the clothes on the walls were all earth and wood coloured, or sometimes, at the most, a muted grey-blue. Sulien found them vaguely depressing; and the more so when he discovered how expensive they were. He tediously gathered some of the cheapest things he could, and then gave up for a while, disheartened, and turned instead to the racks of brown and yellow boots, all solid and stolid-looking like root vegetables. Sulien began lifting these and turning them over. It was going to be harder than he had expected to stretch the money around everything.

Roused by having to tell him the prices of things so often, and now it was clear he was going to buy a number of things, the shop assistant sighed wearily, trooped across and looked despondently at the boots he'd chosen.

'Those,' she said heavily, 'aren't any good.'

Sulien looked at them, a little bewildered. 'They must be some good,' he said, 'Or what are they for?'

'Times when it isn't raining. I don't know what they're for. Water will go straight through them, anyway, you want something like these.' She tapped a pair which proved to be fifteen sesterces more expensive than those he'd picked up. She seemed very sure and Sulien wondered briefly if he should wait until Una had earned some more money; but he was afraid of the time it would take, and he remembered that even the cheap town shoes he'd picked up in Tolosa weren't as disastrous as that.

It felt strange talking to the shop assistant, and he realised how long it was since he'd spoken to anyone except Una and Marcus. He was incredulous. He wondered what kind of people they would find hiding in Holzarta, and found that when he tried to imagine he couldn't even get started, he had no picture of it at all. He felt suddenly dejected. He thought, this isn't how I want to live.

Once he'd decided to disbelieve her, the assistant seemed to feel personally hurt, and Sulien even thought she might be lying when it turned out that there were no boots of that type and price which were small enough for Una. In fact, it seemed at first that there was nothing of the right size in the shop. At last, the girl produced a pair from a back room with an air of moral victory. The boots were apparently very sophisticated, and cost twice what he wanted to pay.

Sulien ended up losing twenty minutes wandering in a frustrated circle around Wolf Step looking for a second shop which didn't seem to exist. He came back exasperated, haggled with the assistant over Una's boots, and bored himself almost to madness trying to decide what he could afford with the remaining money. Finally, the young woman wrapped everything up in thick paper and Sulien emerged onto the high street again, sick by now of the little grey town. Outside it was darker than he had realised, and he wondered for a moment what Marcus had found to do all this time.

At least it was not far. It was somehow embarrassing carrying so many parcels: they were not heavy, but they were annoyingly bulky, and he kept having to stop to rearrange them. At first Sulien could not see Una in the forum, and thought she must have walked up the road to wait with Marcus by the river. It was the scraping and rocking of the plastic furniture that made him glance over at the yellow-fronted caupona, where he saw a man heading towards the door with someone in his arms, a woman, a girl, but he was forcing, dragging her . . .

Of course he knew it was Una. But she was hidden by the man's body and for just an instant, he saw what the few others in the forum saw; a man punishing a slave.

Sulien flung the parcels down and sprinted towards them. For the moment he was more indignant than frightened for Una, for he did not expect much difficulty in making the stranger let go of her. The few skirmishes that had sometimes happened on Catavignus' street and in the park had never been very long or very violent, and Sulien felt only aversion for them anyway, but they had been enough to give him a reasonable confidence in his tall body. He had already seen that the other man was shorter, older and only averagely sturdy, and Sulien expected, without really thinking about it, to be able to scare him without having to fight much at all. But the landlord had Una inside before Sulien could reach them, and as he closed the last couple of yards and dragged open the clattering door, it struck him that if the man wanted to sell Una, if he had done this before, then there might be a knife or a gun.

Inside, under the wistful song there was a terrible, quiet, hoarse shrieking which sounded nothing like Una's voice, barely even like language although he heard dimly that it was repeating thickly, 'I'll *kill* you, I'll *kill* you.' Una was crushed flat against the glass-topped harpasta table, and her face looked nothing like her either, flushed, the eyes mad and fixed and tearless, the lips pulled stiffly away from the teeth as the awful voice ground its way through them. But as Sulien hurtled towards her the voice gasped and stopped and with a kind of spasm the face untwisted enough to show a glimpse of his sister.

He couldn't see a weapon, but he saw the tape the landlord and the purple-haired woman were using to fix her wrists together, and how many people there were in the room. For all that, they were not expecting him, and for a moment the two tram drivers were alarmed or nonplussed enough to just stand awkwardly as he lunged past. One of them even said, 'What do you think you're doing?' as Sulien seized the landlord's shoulders and wrenched him away from Una. Una slid off the harpasta table, dragging her trussed wrists out of the purple-haired woman's hands and stood free and recognisable for a second. Sulien swung the landlord round to face him and punched him so that he toppled against the blue-panelled wall.

But then the other two pulled him back, and as Sulien fought to keep his arms free, the man rose a little blearily and went to help his wife, who was towing Una away, towards the shiny blue door at the back of the room and Una cried out again, a hopeless, furious screech, as they flung her through and locked it. Sulien could hear her kicking or throwing herself against the wood on the other side.

Sulien hit and kicked because he had to. But as the door shut, all the bright clarity went out of the fight and a kind of sickness spread over it, staining even the pointless blows he made connect. The heavier of the two tram drivers, the one he'd been concentrating on the hardest, punched at his face and Sulien was surprised that he had time and strength to see and block this; because he felt he'd grown slow and enfeebled. But as he pushed the fist aside, the man's question returned and hovered, the tone changed. What did he think he was doing? Did he really expect to incapacitate three men so totally that they would let him cross the room, take the key from the landlord's pocket, unlock and open the door, then walk out again past them, with Una, untouched? And there was the woman too, she'd cowered away now behind the counter but he thought she was looking for something back there, perhaps only for the first heavy thing that came to hand, perhaps the gun he'd been worried about from the start.

He could hear the sounds of the fight now, too; a conversation all vowels and spit. And now the landlord was free to join in. Hardly knowing why, Sulien wrenched forward to meet him, and as he moved the smaller man, who'd been trying fruitlessly to get Sulien's arms behind his back, hooked a foot around Sulien's, jabbing at his back at the same time. And the sharp edge of the glass-topped table flew fascinatingly towards Sulien, slowly enough for him to begin an imaginary conversation with Catavignus about the likely injuries it would cause. He was interested in the angle and the speed and was asking, with compassionate professional concern, 'Will he fracture his skull?' as the hard thing struck.

But nothing broke except his skin and time. Worms of light, rather lovely things, crawled or flew about delightedly in the air. Sulien discovered dreamily that he was lying relaxed on the cool floor, although he seemed never to have fallen there; it was just where he had turned up. He closed one eye as a thick pendulum of blood lowered tremulously across it, stared calmly at the scuffed table legs with the other. He would have gone back to sleep if they would have left him alone; but there was all this fidgeting going on;

they were taping his wrists. He could not seem to care or do anything about it. Through a lazy smog of warm pain he thought perhaps it was for the best. They would put him with Una. And later they would get away somehow, if they could talk about it together they'd be able to think what to do, it was bound to be all right one way or another.

Then he heard what had never stopped: the thudding against wood, the voice. And a clear place seemed to gather within the brume, feeling no bigger than a large coin, but within it he could think, get up. Go on, stupid boy. The voice had possibly just called out desperately, *Sulien*.

He tried to lift his head and the flying lights roared back, and the bolus of pain in his skull churned and swivelled sickly, and for a second the clear space was swamped in it completely. His head dropped the inch or so it had risen, and it was a moment before he could find his way back to try and sort it out.

Usually he would have put his hand to the hurt place, it was harder when he couldn't touch – and he felt doubled up on himself, it was like trying to use a damaged pair of pliers to fix themselves. But still lying there passively, he tried to make sense of what had happened to his head, he found the pain and the haze and said to them, with difficulty, stop, go out, go away.

It had only just begun to work, but abruptly he tore his arms away from the gummy tape and the hands that were working at him, and queasily hoisted himself up. It felt like performing a great clumsy vault over a dizzying wall. But for a second they were too surprised to hold him down. They stared up at him, comically shocked as Sulien stood and lurched, looked across the four of them at the locked door. And he backed away and ran, out into the forum, a long tail of black tape fluttering from one wrist.

He pelted as far as the bridge and had to stop, he felt so sick. He leant against the low wall and clutched it while his head pulsed and reeled. He didn't remember being hit in the stomach but he found he was close to retching. Well, of course, he thought impatiently. Quite normal. Concussion.

He raised his hands cautiously to his forehead, breathed out shakily and tried again the vertiginous work of thinking his way, both from inside and outside the bone, or so it felt, to the bruised tip of his own brain, searching out and quieting the swollen fibres.

Blood was still coursing extravagantly down his face. Sulien wiped it off as best he could, wincing, and smeared his red palms unthinkingly on his clothes. He felt with his fingers for the wet cut at the centre of the mess and pressed it. There, he was all right, it was no worse than an ordinary headache now.

No one seemed to have come after him. He had not even thought of that until now. It probably seemed too much like hard work. He ripped the tape off his skin and threw it away.

Already, as he'd run jarringly across the asphalt, he'd been moaning silently, No, no of course not, against the gathering accusation that he'd just left her, he was pathetic, treacherous. Now the pain was cleared away the charges flooded clamouring into the space, redoubled, multiplying. He'd been right in the first place, it would have been better to stay where he was. He couldn't remember if she'd really shouted his name or not, and he hoped he had imagined it now, for it seemed to have prompted him to run away rather than to help her. He looked back and could see ranks of soldiers on the longvision above the caupona. He'd come scarcely any distance at all. Una was no more than two hundred yards away, there were only two thin walls keeping her out of sight. She would be all right, because he was going back for her, but she didn't know that yet, she thought she was finished. And if they did what he supposed they wanted, if one of those men smuggled her out to Spain or somewhere – he couldn't bear to think of it and yet in horrible involuntary starts and recoils he couldn't help it.

But really he knew enough already from the dreadful possessed look on Una's face. It was almost beside the point to wonder what would happen to her. He'd seen it starting. She would disobey until somebody killed her, she'd jump off a roof. He wanted to think that he still didn't know her well enough to be sure of this, but hadn't she as good as told him she was capable of it, on the train, that first day?

No, of course not, none of it was going to happen, he was going to stop them. The way of doing it must be there already, it was just waiting for him to find out what it was.

But apart from some incoherent thoughts of killing them all somehow, he wasn't planning anything, he was weeping with horror and guilt. He'd thought of them pushing her through the blue door and said aloud, 'Oh, poor thing,' and the very sound of the words made it worse. The dirty oblong tracks of glue on his wrist, the slight stinging where the tape had pulled hair away, made him remember the cross, and everything she'd done. He sobbed and despised and bullied himself until he managed at least a provisional stop.

If there were two of them, he began, thinking uncertainly of Leo's son. But Una was not really Marcus' business, he would not want to risk being taken for another slave, or recognised. And even if Sulien were that sure of him, and he was not, they would still be outnumbered and going by what had happened in Tolosa, he thought the other boy was probably a worse fighter than he was himself. And with that he forgot Marcus' existence altogether.

What else? There might be a door at the back of the caupona, he could – break it down? No, but pick the lock, perhaps. Oh, with what? How?

He kept annoying himself by circling back to the idea of simply trampling his way over the caupona people, killing them. It was like checking the same place over and over for something he'd lost. And this was just a stupid rant of an idea, he didn't have a weapon, and he couldn't kill anyone, certainly not four people, no matter what they'd done.

He didn't have a weapon, but if he had, if he went back and threatened – no, not just threatened, was really ready to do it, kill them, all of them if it came to it – Actually, there was a knife in one of the bags, Una had bought it on the motorway, they'd used it for bread. It wasn't very sharp, but if you had made up your mind what to do with it, if you pushed hard enough, it wouldn't have to be.

Sulien never thought of himself, at ten, pressing the kitchen knife against his own flesh, nudging the pan of boiling liquid over Rufius' arm. But it was as if he'd found a seam of cold running right through the centre of him, joining him up like a line of stitches over a cut; and though it went counter to everything he thought he knew about himself, he was aware suddenly that he could do it, he could probably do it quite coolly, if he had to. But he knew also that he couldn't ever be the same afterwards, however necessary and justifiable it was; whatever anyone else might think, he wouldn't forgive himself.

Well, that made no difference.

He started up the road towards the little track, and turned back again after a few paces, not because he'd changed his mind but because he was afraid to leave the bridge; they might move Una while he was away. He repeated this caged little motion a few times before he could bring himself to go.

Behind the door was a cold stairwell almost choked with stacks of the plastic chairs. Snarling and gasping, Una kicked at a tower of them until they fell, wheeled and hurled herself as helplessly as a wave against the door, and did it again and again because it was something to hit, not because it was a way out.

She'd felt a kind of shudder of hope as Sulien charged into the caupona, but as the men closed on him she'd known the only question was whether this would happen to them both. And when they first flung her in among the chairs she couldn't help wanting it to, they shouldn't separate, not after five weeks, not after seven years.

Then outside the thuds and scraping of the fighting grew suddenly quiet. Something had happened to Sulien, he didn't seem to be there. Cold breathed across the furious heat. Sulien, she whispered, and shut her eyes to look for him. It was probably the only thing in the world she could have concentrated on. They'd really hurt him, he was hardly conscious. She shuddered again and muttered emptily to him. Go on, Sulien, get up. She kicked urgently at the wood again, groaning and not hearing it. Get *up*.

When he was gone it was hard to remember he'd ever been there. Soon she began breathlessly whirling and battering again among the fallen chairs. She thought with a kind of murderous glee that if she broke her bones she would be worth less money, that would disappoint everybody.

Every now and then she could get her breath slow enough to think, well, I've done this, I know this, when somebody buys me I'll be good and nice until they trust me, so then I'll get away, I can do it. But she wailed to herself, even if this was true she'd be lost in Spain or Africa, she'd have no money, no way of finding Sulien ever again. And in any case, as her skin burned with rage and her heart whirred and stuttered so hard that it seemed it might blow out like a fuse, she knew she couldn't wait and plan and stay passive in that way again. She could hardly think how she'd done it before.

She was frightened of herself. There was no way of stopping, ever. She tried to think of whiteness but it didn't work, she couldn't begin even the first turning spark of it, she couldn't breathe.

Marcus had been up and down to the road several times now. He wished he had something to read. He still thought that probably the slaves had not been gone an unreasonably long time, it was just that he was going crazy for something to do. He sat on the desk and rocked it restlessly back and forth, and all of a sudden remembered that he had sometimes seen Una with a book in the mornings before he fell asleep. He wished he'd thought of it before – and yet he hesitated before looking for it, she wasn't there to say he

223

could, he had no right to go rummaging through her things. But they'd been together a week, all their belongings were mixed up anyway, and he'd seen the entire contents of the bags disgorged what seemed like dozens of times. So, tentatively he unzipped the bag, and was glad to find that the book was wedged obviously down one side. He drew it out and at once a fold of paper dropped out of it. Marcus bent to pick it up, meaning, conscientiously, not to look at it because it seemed to be a letter. But the few words he couldn't help seeing as he stooped were enough to tell him it was not, because he recognised them:

O you my native land, the home of gods.

For whatever reason, she was copying out the book. He turned over the crumpled sheet of paper and read:

You are the bravest warriors we have,
But all your strength will win us nothing good.
If still you'll follow me in chasing death,
Daring the last extreme, then understand
That all the gods who held our empire up
Have fled their shrines like traitors. We're alone.
The city that you'd save is burning down.
Well then, let's die. We'll pour into the fight
Defeated; without hope; and unafraid.

Their courage mixed with madness by these words . . .

It was one of the passages he'd had to learn by heart. He didn't know what he had expected, but it was not this. He could see it was a lesson of some kind. She was trying to begin something – not learning to read exactly – but learning how to read a book? He stared at it, somehow touched; and impressed too, for with all the obsolete words and endless names of cities and heroes she'd chosen a madly ambitious place to start. But he thought he could guess why. It was because Virgil was supposed to be the best, the

224

pinnacle, something you had to know if you were going to know anything at all. They'd spent endless hours on it at school. It was funny to be reading it now, sitting on a child's desk.

He found he could have told the bit of paper was Una's even if he had never seen the book in her hand; even though so much about it surprised him. The careful letters were pressed rigorously into the paper, but they were round and childish, and wherever she'd made a mistake she'd penned a neat box filled with fierce black hatching over it and obliterated it utterly. In the margins she'd drawn things, sometimes what seemed to be enlarged copies of the printed letters in the book, whether they were for practice or for play he couldn't tell: L, U; drawn with clear slow lines, flaunting obsessively faultless serifs; and sometimes birds and trees and faces.

He sat reading the familiar words for a while, but there wasn't much light left, and in the shadow he soon had to strain to get through the lines. He put the piece of paper back in place and tucked the book away, wondering if she'd know he'd borrowed it, and if she'd flare up again. He hoped not, because he wanted to ask her what she thought of it, and if he'd guessed right. He could hardly imagine reading it for the first time.

He wished that she, that they, would come back.

He stood up and started up the track again, but instead of hovering at the edge of the road as he had done before, he simply went on walking, down towards Wolf Step. He hesitated when he realised what he was doing, but only for a moment. It was almost dark, the hat was pulled down low on his head, and it was hard to believe that such a quiet little place could be dangerous. And yet even though he felt that, as he walked there was an odd sense of urgency growing; it seemed important to go and look for them.

So he found Sulien, walking alone out of the town, but in the act of turning to look back at it. 'Hey,' said Marcus, 'Where's Una?' and then was shocked by Sulien's blotched and glossy face.

Vaguely, Sulien noticed Marcus had blanched slightly at all the blood. Evidently he looked dramatic. Some idiotic fragment of him felt rather pleased. 'Hello,' he said.

Marcus stammered in alarm, 'What happened to you? That looks bad. Shouldn't you sit down or— or—'

'It's all right,' said Sulien absently, still with the twitchy blandness of suppressed hysteria. 'Can you do something for me?'

'But all that blood,' protested Marcus.

'Look, it's fine,' said Sulien impatiently. 'Lot of blood vessels on the scalp. I was going to be a doctor. I've made it better anyway.' Marcus saw with confusion that indeed, despite all the blood around it, the cut looked older than it should have done. He was startled, too, by the revelation about being a doctor, but Sulien was still talking. He said, 'Can you go and watch that caupona in case they take Una out?'

Marcus didn't understand, but far more than the blood on Sulien's face, the distracted, feverish look there told him how wrong things were. It was like the look Varius had, after Gemella died. He would have guessed the vigiles had arrested Una, but in that case he couldn't think why she should be in a caupona.

'What happened?' he asked again, in a low voice. 'Why's she in there?'

'I think they're smugglers or – black market,' said Sulien, not very clearly, feeling a dangerous renewal of shame and panic as he began telling what had happened. 'Some of the tram drivers are in on it. They must have guessed she was a slave, so they took her. I've got to go back.'

On a kind of reflex of patrician outrage, Marcus said, hearing how ludicrous it sounded, 'It wasn't even dark! You can't just grab people off the *streets*!'

'Why don't you go and tell them that?' shouted Sulien, suddenly furious, tears threatening his eyes again. Marcus was quiet. Sulien went on less roughly, 'Yes you can. You can if you think no one cares, or that no one can do anything about it. And I can't call the vigiles, can I?'

There was silence for a moment. 'Then what are you going to do?' asked Marcus.

Sulien glanced at Marcus, who was standing fixedly, with clouded eyes, and not looking at him. As far as he could tell Marcus was simply scandalised by the lawlessness of what had happened, perhaps a little dismayed for Una's sake, too. Sulien didn't care about that. But he was afraid of saying what he meant to do. Exposed to air it would look either too ridiculous or too dreadful for him to go through with it. 'Never mind,' he answered shortly, moving past, up the road, and then was amazed when Marcus suddenly said firmly, '*No*, Sulien, what are you going to do?' and he found he'd stopped obediently in his tracks. He hesitated, opened his mouth. 'I'm going to get the breadknife,' he said. 'And after that I'm not sure.'

Marcus did not respond at first, and whatever authority had been in his voice had disappeared, he was just standing uselessly, the distant look back on his face. Sulien didn't know why he'd stopped and turned away again, and this time Marcus asked, 'Did you get the clothes?'

For a second Sulien was speechless. Then he said in disbelief, 'The *clothes*?' and spinning round he would have hit Marcus, but when he looked at him he was too disgusted even to do it. He pushed at him instead, and spat out with more contempt than he'd ever thought he'd feel for anyone, 'I dropped them in the forum. I don't know if they're still there. Go and look if you want them.'

Marcus said 'No, I need you to do it. At least, if you think you can without being caught.'

And again, Sulien's fists clenched with revulsion, but Marcus had sounded neither thoughtless nor defensive, and the half-abstracted expression wasn't there any more either. He'd looked and sounded intent, resolved on something. 'Why?' Sulien said hoarsely.

And Marcus said, 'It won't work if they see me like this before we go there.'

Sulien blinked, and when he spoke his voice wavered

somewhere between scorn and thin, dubious hope. 'Why do you want to come? What do you think you can do?'

'What you said. Tell them they can't,' said Marcus.

The clothes Sulien had bought were clean, and they had the crisp seams of garments that have never been worn. But that was all, they were plain and heavy, and though they'd cost more than he could easily afford, Sulien doubted their newness could disguise their comparative cheapness. He said 'Look. You haven't thought. Even if they don't recognise you, you're with us and you're our age, and we're both trying to get her back – they'll just think you're another slave.'

Marcus didn't answer for a moment because he was concentrating, concentrating on stripping away and undoing the huddled layers of the creeping, substitute person he'd learnt how to be since leaving Rome. He said, at last, softly, 'No, they won't.'

Sulien sighed with anxiety, and stuck the knife in his pocket, in case. He rubbed his face. The blood was setting now into a hard granular mass over one eyebrow, and caking stickily on his forehead and cheek; but he did nothing to wash it off and nor did he change out of the red-streaked clothes. At least there would be a contrast between the two of them. They'd agreed also that Sulien would carry one of the bags, while Marcus walked unencumbered.

But as they approached the dark forum he began to notice the change that was coming over Marcus. His shoulders lowered and straightened, and his head lifted so that Sulien realised for the first time how hunched he'd always been, and that the difference in their heights was less than he'd thought. But that was the least of it. Upright as his spine now held itself, there seemed to be no effort or tension in it, as if there were no reason for effort or tension ever to exist.

Then above them the screen blinked and showed what neither of them had so far seen, the two bright squares, the still from the funeral, Marcus' new face held in pencil lines.

Sulien and Marcus stopped and looked at each other helplessly. It was hard to know what to say. Eventually Sulien muttered, 'I didn't know.' He thought perhaps he should tell Marcus that it was all right, that he didn't have to help, but he couldn't bring himself to do it; the first part at least was so plainly untrue. Nor could he ask or beg that Marcus just carry on as if nothing had happened. And so he didn't want to see Marcus making up his mind and looked away from him with a kind of embarrassment, tried to believe again in what he could do with the knife, alone.

Marcus wished Sulien hadn't said even that much. He couldn't quite answer, 'It doesn't make any difference,' he didn't want to acknowledge the pictures; he didn't want to make the decision again. He was aware, impersonally, that he had to, that he was doing so, but he managed, deliberately, to avoid noticing it. He couldn't even let himself think what was true, that Una had stopped him from stumbling into the roadblock, that she'd started reading a book and hadn't finished it yet, and that he couldn't possibly go back now. He just lowered his eyes from the screen and pretended it wasn't there.

Sulien heard him say, 'I'm sorry,' and thought resignedly, well then. Marcus carried on apologetically, 'But you have to go first, you have to be the one to open the door.'

Disbelieving, Sulien could only mumble, 'Thank you,' but as he stepped forward, the tone of Marcus' voice began to worry him. It was apprehensive, diffident; it didn't match the confident stance.

To walk casually through that particular door felt against all reason. And to his overwrought gaze the little tables looked alarmingly packed now, with drivers and locals starting the evening's drinking. Some looked up at Sulien's bloody face with distaste. The landlord, who – Sulien was satisfied to see – had a black eye starting, stared at him incredulously and one of the tram drivers from the fight rose from his seat; but Sulien realised with a start of distress that the other man, the one who'd tripped him was missing, and he could hear no sound from Una. He thought, oh, if they've already gone—

And Marcus was trying to gather up the right state of mind again, and he thought, Drusus, Drusus at the centre of the orbiting slaves, looking at me across the table so that I was sure I was wrong. And though at the time he'd felt only awkward and frustrated, he knew how Drusus did it, it was like owning a piece of machinery and knowing how to make it work; even if he'd never used it – or not deliberately.

Sulien glanced back to see Marcus moving into the electric light, and was startled by how whitely furious he looked, and yet the anger was only a kind of varnish over something else that seemed to go much deeper; and was a calm, total confidence in having a right to be there, or anywhere. Before he even spoke Marcus ran an unhurried glance around the caupona and it seemed to shrink around him; and the stains on the tabletops and the cobwebby rolls of dust in the corners became suddenly visible, as if he'd planted them there.

He turned the same cold look on the landlord, making him smaller and more threadbare than he had been before; and said, very quietly and yet very audibly, 'I want to know what you're doing with my slave.'

The landlord shifted doubtfully under the look, but returned a version of it, which took in how young Marcus was. He repeated uncertainly, 'Your slave?'

'I think so,' replied Marcus curtly.

The landlord shrugged and said, 'Someone's made a mistake. And you're a bit young to have slaves of your own, aren't you?'

A woman at one of the tables tittered nervously and the disdain and fury on Marcus' face intensified, and he snapped, 'I don't think my age gives you a right to my property. I would like her back, now, please.'

The man held up his hands, looking bewildered and put upon. 'But you're not making sense. We haven't got anyone of yours.'

Marcus visibly lost patience with the landlord and turned to his plum-haired wife. 'Open that door,' he ordered her, and to Sulien's surprise she made a little fitful movement to do as he said.

'Hey,' said the landlord, stepping between them and the door, stopping his wife with a look, 'hold on. You've got a nerve marching in here and talking about property. This is mine. Either sit down and order something or get out.'

Trying to be ready, Sulien put the bag down and felt for the knife, but Marcus murmured to him, 'You don't need to do that, not yet,' in a voice that was both that of the supercilious aristocrat and the reserved and anxious boy who'd walked with them from Tolosa.

The landlord carried on, 'Who do you think you are – who are you?' And, though he'd begun bullishly enough, his voice lowered nervously as he finished. And he looked at Marcus oddly, still hostile, but probing and baffled.

Marcus was afraid that in another second the landlord would realise what it was about him that was familiar, but he didn't want to answer too quickly, he made himself stare back coldly, frowning, as if it was a slight to be asked his name, as if it was beneath him to give it. 'I'm Quintus Cornelius Lartius,' he said at last, cobbling together the names of two boys from school, senators' sons.

Oh, come on, thought Sulien, senators couldn't pass through a place this size without everyone knowing, how are you going to explain that? And indeed the landlord stared and said, 'I hadn't heard there was anyone called Cornelius in town.'

But Marcus just shrugged and answered caustically, 'We shan't be again,' and Sulien realised that Marcus didn't have to think of an explanation because he simply wasn't going to explain. He went on, 'And if my slave isn't here, where is she? And how do you explain this?' And in one terse move-ment, he reached across, took hold of Sulien's chin and gave his head a sharp jerk to one side, displaying the mess of blood on his face. Sulien felt his head chime with renewed pain and shock, for Marcus had done this with such indifferent confidence, almost without looking at him. He might have been indicating a scratch on the paintwork of a car.

The man was beginning to look seriously uncomfortable now. Some of the customers were gaping at them unashamedly, but the occupants of at least one table had left the caupona in embarrassment. The landlord protested, 'He just charged in like a maniac – no one hit him anyway, he fell over and hit his head. And look what he did to my eye.'

'You were stealing something and he was trying to stop you. You can't expect much sympathy. And now look at him, we've lost the evening's work from him as well as the girl.'

It was hard enough for Sulien to stand there silently, pretending to be obedient or even inanimate, still incredulous at being touched like that, not knowing whether Una was still behind the blue door or not. At this he couldn't help the recoiling prickle that crept over him, the wintry arrogance in Marcus' face and voice had now reached such a pitch. He didn't know why he should feel like this when he understood and was grateful for what Marcus was doing. But of course this, the inarticulate, walled-in anger was not really about Marcus – nor even, which surprised him, solely about the man who'd done this to them. And at last he thought reluctantly; because this is what I'm supposed to be, this is how people are meant to talk about me. And not only me, not only here. Everywhere.

And though he tried to remember how he'd behaved in Rufius' kitchen, he didn't really know how to be a slave. He didn't know whether he should even speak, but he couldn't bear it any longer and said, 'Shall I check she's still there? Sir,' he added awkwardly.

Marcus glanced at him, apparently in vague surprise and displeasure that he had spoken to him, but nodded.

The landlord stood solidly in his way, but as Sulien approached he flinched indecisively, and although he would not move aside he plainly didn't quite dare to stop Sulien shouldering past either. Sulien ran and tapped on the door and whispered to it, 'Una, Una, you're still there, aren't you? Una.'

There was a horrible nothing for a moment, but then a ragged scrap of a voice said, 'What are you doing? What's going on?'

Una had at last worn herself out and dropped into a bruised stupor on the tiled floor. Now she pulled herself up by the door handle and had to keep holding it to stay on her feet. She was too exhausted and desperate to make sense of what was happening on the other side of the door, there were too many people, she didn't know what Marcus was doing.

'There. That's her,' said Marcus.

'Well,' muttered the landlord feebly.

Marcus ignored him. 'Now open that door at once.'

'Wait, wait a minute,' said the landlord stubbornly, 'If she's yours – you ought to have papers – proof—'

'You're the one who ought to have proof. I've had enough of this,' said Marcus quietly. 'I suppose the vigiles have turned a blind eye to you for a while, but they won't any more, my father can make sure of that.' He gestured at Sulien again, with just the smallest necessary movement of his hand. 'Run and call them,' he said, and thought, he's between us – he only has to stop us getting out. And he hoped the older man couldn't tell he was holding his breath.

But instead the landlord gave a wide and fragile grin and crumbled completely. 'Now,' he said, 'now, you're over-reacting a touch. Sir. I just meant – you should be more careful, perhaps, letting them run about like that – it's only a mistake, isn't it?'

He actually patted Sulien affectionately on the shoulder as he prodded him aside to get at the door. He unlocked it and looked discreetly away from Una as she stumbled out, as if her bound arms would be less noticeable if he couldn't see them himself. Marcus thought, as Sulien had, that Una barely looked human, her face bloodless, the eyes dilated and staring. But he only glimpsed it for a second, for almost at once she was in Sulien's arms, and he was telling her, 'You're all right, you're all right.'

While Sulien was undoing the black tape, the landlord was still babbling, 'I swear, if she'd said who you were – but she was out by herself – she told me she wasn't a slave at all.'

'Yes,' said Marcus unrelentingly, 'she's a deceitful girl. I would have thought that was our problem and not yours. Or did you think you were kidnapping a free citizen?'

The landlord grinned hopefully again. 'No harm done,' he ventured.

'You've injured my slave and cost my family time and money,' said Marcus, rather wearily now. But to his amazement, the landlord went around the counter opened the till with hands that trembled slightly, and counted out forty sesterces. 'My apologies,' he said faintly, pushing the notes across.

Marcus felt he could not keep this up much longer, but he paused for the right length of time, examined the money as if he thought it might be dirty, and at last picked it up in silence.

'A drink – if you'd like a drink, free—' the man said, groping blindly for bottles. Marcus shook his head impassively and said, 'I've been here quite long enough,' which, he thought, was almost the only truthful thing he had said in this place.

He turned away and behind him Una and Sulien followed, unsteadily, past the watching customers. Sulien had had his arm around Una's shoulders but he had to let go and stop to pick up the bag by the counter.

Marcus felt less capable, more vulnerable, now his back was to his audience. He could hear the landlord and a few of the customers moving to the doorway to watch as he walked away, and forced himself not to look back. But outside the door he slowed to fall in beside Una and Sulien. Una's hands were free now, but Marcus thought at first that she must be hurt, that she seemed to be limping; but once he was close to her he realised that she was just so stiff with shaking she could hardly hold herself upright or move forward. He was shaking himself now it was over, they all were. He reached out to take her arm to steady her, hoping that to the onlookers behind the gesture would look domineering and possessive. She started with shock so violently that he was startled in turn, but then, without turning her head to look at him, she reached tentatively across her body and took hold of his fingertips, and prised at them. He loosened his grip, thinking she didn't want him to touch her, but she didn't let go, and he realised she was trying to steer him to the right, the wrong way, down through Wolf Step towards the Spanish pass.

'Why that way? What is it?' he asked her in an undertone.

'Because they'll know, they'll guess! They don't believe it yet, but they're going to!' Una breathed, her voice high and strange, a muted wail. Her hand fell away loosely from his and she didn't speak again. He was struck that she could even think at all at such a time. Involuntarily he looked back at the watching gang standing in the caupona door, and saw above them what they still could not, his own face. He turned again at once, chilled, and they veered together slowly across the forum, down the main street.

As soon as they were out of sight of the caupona, Sulien dropped the bag again and pulled Una towards him, and after a second she raised her arms stiffly and clutched back. They stood there rigidly together, unmoving, completely silent until Sulien said through his teeth, 'They didn't hurt you. They didn't—?' and Una shook her head, speechlessly. Marcus was about to move away a little, and was quite unprepared for Sulien to reach out roughly and crush him against them both, so fiercely that Marcus almost lost his balance. He could feel Una, still trembling, between them. Taken aback, Marcus patted them lightly, realising that except for his family, almost everyone in Rome had always been cautious about touching him, would only do so slowly in order to give him plenty of warning, as if he were very fragile, or very aggressive, or contagious.

Una detached herself gently, turned to Marcus and

rasped, 'Thank you' with a kind of terse sincerity. They passed quickly through the grey street until they came to another bridge, and walked along under the balconies of pale houses on the other side of the river, beneath the Minerva temple. They had to use the first bridge, across the forum from the caupona, to get back onto the road that led to the woodshed where their other bags and the clothes for Una and Sulien were hidden. But it really was dark by now and the landlord had retreated inside, and if he was calling to tell the vigiles that Marcus Novius was in Wolf Step, they hadn't arrived yet.

Despite what had happened they had to stop at the one shop in a shut-up village a little way to the west of Wolf Step, for bread and a few packets of rice; but they couldn't have walked very far that night or waited for morning. A few hours later they'd left the half-hearted path which had begun as a patched crumbling road, and thrown themselves down under the dark pines on the mountain. The steep earth was surprisingly soft and puffy with bulges of moss, over the powdery black soil. It was the first time since leaving the cemetery that they'd had to sleep completely in the open; they had always been able to find empty farm or factory buildings until now. They had passed a water-bottling plant at the mountain's foot, which at least told them that they could drink safely from the streams, but since then there had been nothing, nor any lights for miles, nor any sound of a road.

Una and Sulien had never been so far from these things, and Marcus had barely come close to this remoteness. He'd ridden through the emptiness out near the Great Ravine in Terranova, but in a cavalcade, with his parents, and body-guards ahead, and servants and assistants in the cars behind.

At least they had sleeping bags now, and a little saucepan to cook the rice, and unbelievably they'd got a fire going.

'Wolf Step,' said Sulien. 'So there must have been wolves up here. Do you know if there still are?'

'There aren't many anywhere,' said Marcus, 'and they

236

only attack people in winter when there's nothing to eat.'

'What about people in autumn who've helpfully packaged themselves up in bags and gone to sleep?'

'I think we'll be all right,' said Marcus.

'Hmm,' said Sulien, and tried to howl mutedly, like a wolf some way off but getting closer. Marcus laughed. Sulien asked, clumsily, 'Should we call you Quintus Cornelius Thing, while we're on our way?'

Marcus had never noticed that Una and Sulien didn't have a name for him. He felt ashamed. 'Oh,' he said, 'no. If Una's right then the caupona people might tell the vigiles I was calling myself that. Una,' he added, 'are you all right?'

For it had been a long time since Una had spoken, and she had not opened her book. She was lying silently on her back, motionless, open-eyed.

'Yes,' she said distantly, but didn't move.

'You must have called yourself something, before you met us,' persisted Sulien.

'Yes,' agreed Marcus, strained, not quite understanding what he wanted to say, 'But I don't – want to do that again. I'm sick of it. You can't call me Novius or – or any of the other names, because they're too . . . But Marcus is all right. Almost everyone is called Marcus.'

'Not if anyone can see your face,' murmured Una, expressionlessly. But then at last she turned her head and said, still in a monotone, 'But there's no one out here, so it doesn't matter.'

In which case, Marcus thought, they could almost as well have called him by one of his more formal, more dangerous names. But he did not say so. He found it was a relief to think of someone using his first name again. They were quiet for a while, and then Una said in the dark. 'Tell us about what you'll do when you're Emperor.'

Marcus hesitated. 'I might never be Emperor,' he said, 'My uncle can choose anyone he likes. It was going to be my father. He would have made me Caesar, I suppose, I . . .' It was hard to think of this now. He had never entirely liked the thought of his father as Emperor, somehow, and his own future had seemed more unreal then than it did now, when it was far less certain. 'And now . . . it doesn't have to be me, it could be Drusus. He's older.'

He remembered suddenly what the girl in the jewellery shop had said, that she didn't want him to be Emperor because he'd run away. He wondered if his uncle thought the same thing.

Sulien said, 'Then it has to be Drusus. Doesn't it? Who tried to kill you.'

Marcus was silent. He said quietly at last, 'Of course, I've thought of that.' And he couldn't go on for a moment. He said painfully, 'He's my cousin. Perhaps they want him to be Emperor, the people who – who killed my parents. Maybe they just want anyone who's not my father or me. He might not know anything about it.'

He looked at Una again, but couldn't see her face clearly, only the points of reflection at her eyes. 'Don't you know what I'll do, if it ever happens?'

She took a breath as if to speak, but didn't, and Sulien said, 'What are you talking about?'

'Slavery, I think,' said Marcus, still watching Una, 'People weren't supposed to know, although they did. My father said he would abolish it. So I thought that would have happened by the time I was Emperor. I never really planned to do anything, it was so far away. But now it isn't. Now there's no one else to do it.'

'So you would, because of your father,' stated Una, ambiguously.

'It wasn't his idea,' said Marcus bitterly. 'It was my mother's. Though you wouldn't have known. I think he forgot it himself.'

'You *have* to do it,' said Sulien, and he turned to Una demanding, 'Did you know? Why didn't you say anything?'

'I didn't know till now,' she said in a low voice,

'You must have done, or you wouldn't have asked him,' said Sulien stubbornly.

Una paused, and when she spoke it was to Marcus. 'No.

238

There was something, and I didn't know what. I didn't think it meant very much.'

'What?' Marcus said, startled and indignant. 'It means *a lot*. It's why all this is happening. I've always thought – I mean I always *knew* slavery was wrong, I *always* wanted it stopped.'

'I knew you wished there weren't any slaves, because they embarrassed you. Because we were there with you and you wished we weren't.'

Marcus flushed. 'That's not fair.'

Una rose on her elbow. 'Are you angry because I knew you felt like that about us? Of course I did. So did Sulien. By the way you spoke, by looking at you. Anyone would have done.'

'Why does it matter?' said Sulien. 'I don't care why he does it or if it means anything to him. I never heard of anyone who even thought this. I don't care if he thinks it's wrong or stupid, or if he hates us, so long as he does it anyway.'

Una said softly, '*You* never thought of it before. You never minded . . . anything.'

Sulien frowned. 'No,' he admitted more quietly, 'No, I didn't mind. I just wanted it to go away. For me. But now it's different.'

Marcus said, 'I will. I will stop it.' And though this, ultimately, was what had driven him all this way, promising it to real slaves felt harder than he would have thought.

They fell into silence again as the fire glowed and turned to flakes, and Sulien examined the endless day and turned away from it, and willed himself rapidly asleep. But he dreamt he had an eye disease, a new kind of glaucoma. It meant he couldn't see anything he tried to look at closely, because it dissolved and became invisible. He could see a room, his hand around the glass of water he held, and later, round the knife, but not the knife or the glass, he had to do everything by touch. The water spilt everywhere, he cut himself. He could see the frame and the glass of a mirror, but at the centre of it his reflection faded too rapidly for him to see what was wrong. He thought something had happened to his face.

Marcus had forgotten the money the landlord had given him. He thought of it now with surprise, it was hard to believe it really existed, but he felt for it stealthily, and it was still there.

It would get him to Holzarta, alone, if he wanted it to. Marcus stared in the darkness. It had been such a fact of things, that he had to travel with the slaves, that it was strange to realise that the reason for it was gone. It was not only that he didn't need their money. He wasn't in their debt any more, after what had happened in the caupona, not so long as he made sure that they could find their own way. Even though he'd been able to help them this time, they were probably more in danger with him than without. And he would leave them an address so they would know how to claim the five hundred thousand; in case they didn't follow, and he didn't see them again. He could even leave half the money he had now, as an instalment against what they'd spent on him.

But they would not understand, perhaps. They might not believe they would get the reward in the end. Perhaps it was still an underhand thing to do. And if anything did happen to them, he wouldn't know. He'd get home at last, and go to Athens to study, and all this time would seem bizarre and fantastic; but he'd wait to pay out the money, and the claim on it would never come.

'Marcus,' whispered Una, an unmoving dark shape beyond the feathery remains of the fire. Somehow it made him catch his breath, perhaps only because he had thought she was asleep. But of course, it was the first time she'd used his first name, or any name for him at all.

'What?' he asked.

'We won't mind. You don't have to worry about us. If you want, we won't go after you.'

He could only just hear her, and she'd spoken so lightly that he didn't mind that she knew what he'd been thinking, and only briefly searched the words for an implicit instruction to leave. He wished he could see her, but though he strained his eyes he could make out only an outline in the dark. He hadn't asked her yet about the copied pages of the book. And he remembered now how bored he'd been, sitting on the desk, waiting for them both to come back.

He sat up and reached out, the roll of notes in his fingertips.

'He gave it to me because he thought you belonged to me,' he said. 'But it was compensation for what he did to both of you.'

She didn't take it, or speak for a second. 'You look after it, anyway,' she murmured at last.

'All right,' said Marcus, and after a moment he put the money into one of his shoes, which lay beside him; it seemed more neutral than sleeping with it close to his skin. And he pressed his face against the new padded cloth, and fell asleep more rapidly than he had in weeks.

But Una lay and watched the sharp and unfamiliar sky through the black pine needles. The man would have shut the caupona for the night, and later, when his wife was asleep – but she couldn't think of it, she began a shred of white to wipe it out, she could do it now.

But she still couldn't sleep, because she was too aware of Marcus, lying on the other side of the ashes. She didn't know how she should feel about him now. No, she knew, she should feel grateful, and she did, more than grateful. She was overwhelmed by what he'd done, she would never have thought him capable of it. But he had not only been acting as somebody else, an arrogant young nobleman, he'd been acting as himself as well. 'Yes, she's a deceitful girl.' How could she not draw back from someone who knew, instinctively, how to say such things, how to look at everything in a room as if it was his, or as if it had been offered to him and he was turning it down? Marcus was Roman to the tips of his fingers. And he had done this for her, and was afraid of going mad. She knew too many stupid little things about him.

She'd started the conversation about slavery, painfully, as a kind of reparation, as an approach to what she couldn't quite say. She could have known more precisely what Marcus meant to do. And now she could almost see that this was exactly why she had not wanted to, it was exactly so she would not have to feel this way. It was so that she could go on thinking of him clearly. She thought confusedly that she wished he'd decided to leave just now, that she wished she'd never met him.

And that wasn't true, or right, none of this was. She felt it was ridiculous to feel this way. She felt as if she were betraying something.

[XI]

I AM A ROMAN CITIZEN

Someone knocked against the back of his head. Varius tried to force the lump of poison down whole, and the centurion gripped his throat, clawed determinedly at his face, prising apart his gritted teeth. Varius choked, biting and twisting away, dragging down. Cleomenes sighed and cursed at his hurt fingers, struck him again with businesslike competence, wrenched. And the piece of nougat was ripped out at last, wet and a little bloody; Cleomenes' blood, Varius thought, although at least one of his own teeth seemed to have broken.

But it did not matter; he could feel that it was happening anyway. He gasped, 'You're too late,' for the air did not want to enter his lungs any more, his blood strained its way from his tightened heart, everything doubled and retreated. He kept thinking, is this it, is it this, come on, faster. And he lay on the turning ground and waited, until he couldn't think any more, and he wasn't there.

Later, he kept blindly trying to finish whatever the task was, but he couldn't remember; he had the panicked feeling of an appointment missed, something crucial not done. He'd been moving darkly, he'd heard the road and the engine, and all the time coming back and finding the way out again for a while; and he knew he was ill, too, because of the smell, stale sweat layered with bleach, and the lacklustre, comprehensive pain.

It was dirtily hot. Someone had been shouting for a long time, in a breathless, unpunctuated flow:

'Bastard complacent liars it's a deliberate deception it's

criminal it's in the water supply they infiltrated the post service too I am a Roman citizen it's an abuse of my rights you are all uneducated it's theft it's staring you in the face it's not even human either it is human or it isn't!'

Feet went past towards the voice, which abruptly stopped.

He was under a lank blue blanket on a rattly institutional bed, to which he was tethered. A prison hospital, then. He felt flat and bored and disgusted. Without thinking yet in terms of another attempt, or taking much interest in his immobilised body, it seemed unreasonable that he should have to be there, in the bed, in his skin. He shut his eyes, which were still not quite right, as if that would be enough.

Cleomenes, who was standing patiently by the door, said, 'That was a stupid thing to do.'

Varius didn't know why anyone should say something so fatuous and ignored him.

'Varius. The longvision company never asked you for another proposal. You hid the poison from us. You never went home. Where did you take Marcus Novius?'

'Why couldn't you leave me alone?' muttered Varius. 'Would it make so much difference?'

'Yes. It isn't justice,' said Cleomenes, unhesitatingly. Varius snorted a little, scornfully. Cleomenes added, 'And you *will* help us find Marcus Novius.'

'Well, maybe you will find him,' said Varius, 'but no, I won't help you, because I don't know where he is.'

But he glanced apprehensively around the little cell, at the door, at an innocuous-looking cabinet, and at the red centurion in his blood-coloured uniform. He vaguely flexed his tied limbs, tensing. The hot air was sour and sharp where it hissed over the broken corner of his tooth; where the fence of bone had been too weak to keep the poison in. He was afraid that Cleomenes, or someone, would find a way of chiselling or gouging the knowledge out, through the same channel. He did not know how far he could trust himself. Filtered into his education had been inspiring stories, possibly designed for boys, about feats of Roman courage. They included terrible things done to Romans by barbarians, terrible things that were invariably withstood. The choice was always the betrayal of Rome and no one, apparently, in the stories, ever made it, no matter what was done to them. There was one in particular that Varius, aged thirteen, had wished he hadn't read or been told, it wouldn't leave him for weeks. It involved eyelids being slit and sewn back, the victim left in the white sun, refusing, still, to commit whatever ill-defined treachery was demanded. Varius had been at first massively relieved to realise that the story was probably not true; but later he had thought that if the thing – doing that to somebody's eyes – had been imagined, it had probably happened somewhere, or would one day. He'd thought – perhaps he was wrong – but he'd thought, there were too many people in the world to believe that none of them, in the right circumstances, would ever be capable of doing that. The part not to believe was the part about heroic endurance; or at least, he thought that if anyone ever held out successfully, it was to do with chance, a fluke, down to time running out somehow, or to things the interrogator was not prepared to do.

He should never have to worry about this, of course, not in Rome. That was part of the point of those stories – citizens should never be tortured, never. But he didn't believe that he could simply deny knowing anything and then expect to be left alone.

'Were you getting rid of his body, Varius? Or did he get away from you?'

Varius lay silently trying to interest himself in the blue weave of the blanket, but he was faintly startled by this. He frowned.

'Your wife,' Cleomenes began again, wearily. Varius listened warily. For now the thought of Gemella was as the fading pain had been, saturating everything but vague, part of the background. 'Had you found out something, or did you just suspect? Did you think it was with young Leo?'

Varius actually laughed and blurted out, 'You *really* think I killed Gemella?'

245

Cleomenes snorted this time. 'We know you were there when she died. You didn't call for help, for a doctor. You moved her body and you vanished for seven hours. Yes, I think you killed her.'

'Good,' said Varius, and Cleomenes' forehead crumpled with freckly confusion. He no longer looked looming and sinister to Varius, he seemed almost funny and endearingly stupid. 'But then you won't be working on this for very long.'

'What are you talking about?'

'I don't think I'll see you again. I think I'll miss you.' Cleomenes opened his mouth, puzzled and irritated, but Varius didn't let him start, 'Why didn't I get rid of *her* body, Cleomenes? It was poison, so I must have planned it. Making plans, making plans work is my *job*. You seem to think I'm unemployable. If I'd had time to think about it, all the time I was finding out how to buy poison, why would I leave her there and then *come back?*' His amusement, if that was what it had been, dried up suddenly. 'And I would never have done it,' he whispered.

'Because you loved her?' asked Cleomenes sombrely. Involuntarily, Varius snarled, and strained briefly against the straps, unexpectedly incensed, the knowledge that Gemella was dead suddenly vivid again. It was as if the centurion had violated something. Cleomenes carried on, 'You see, I can believe you about that, and not believe everything else. Perhaps you thought it was for her own good somehow, perhaps you thought she'd be happy. I've met people like that. And no, they weren't always stupid. I don't know what you thought you were doing afterwards. I don't expect things to make that kind of sense, not any more.'

'Well, then,' said Varius, eventually, laboriously. 'Then the public should know. There should be a trial, shouldn't there?'

'I shouldn't worry about that,' said Cleomenes grimly.

'Yes, you should worry about that,' said Varius, quietly now. 'Please.' And then he added, 'Goodbye.' Cleomenes hadn't shown any signs of leaving but after that Varius just looked dully at the blanket or at the white ceiling, and did not answer anything the centurion said, and pretended neither of them was there.

Finally, giving up, turning back in the doorway, Cleomenes growled at him, 'In the end we'll find out where you drove. You know we will. You won't be able to carry on like this.'

'Cleomenes,' murmured Varius slowly, still not looking at him. 'The sweets were a present to Marcus from Lady Makaria.'

Cleomenes hesitated just for a second, and then scowled in disgust and banged out of the door, which, needlessly, was locked behind him. Varius thought he shouldn't have said anything, it wouldn't make Cleomenes do anything except perhaps tell one of his colleagues, and now they, the conspirators, would know how much Varius had guessed about them. He was afraid Cleomenes was right; he wouldn't be able to carry on like this.

But he must, he was not to let himself off by thinking that, whatever was coming.

His body was getting better remarkably quickly. He didn't need to be told, the next morning, that there was no longer anything much wrong with him. He ached unclearly still, but his heart, his breathing, his eyes were all right again. He didn't understand how something could be so deadly and yet lose its power so fast.

It was a long time before he said another word to anyone. As he had expected, others in red uniforms came to see him, but Cleomenes did not return. Varius decided he would not speak even to the orderlies who brought him food or let him, occasionally, out of the bed. It was the nearest thing to a strategy he could think of. He tried, as he'd tried driving back into Rome, only the day before, to be there as little as possible. He thought if he could convince himself that he was a thing, a stone, incapable of knowledge or speech, the vigiles might be persuaded, too, and give up.

But at the same time he tried to analyse what was happening, what the nurses and doctors and guards and soldiers did, in case there was any advantage to be gained that way. But sometimes he thought that this was a trap, that he might go to pieces trying to work out what had a purpose and what was only routine. For example, although he was well now, he was not at first moved from the hospital cell, or allowed to get out of bed except sometimes to go to the bathroom. He had to stay in the sweaty night-shirt he had been given. He was fairly certain that some of this was done deliberately, to make him feel powerless, and knowing that helped him just fractionally. But why did they keep him there? So he would be unnerved by the medical smell, by the shouting – because it was a convenient place to mutilate someone? Or because there was nowhere else ready? Having decided not to speak, he couldn't ask.

Nothing so bad as he'd feared had happened yet; the vigile officers hit him, and sometimes held the pillow down over his face. They shouted, where was Marcus Novius? But it was only a noise that happened when they were in the room. He didn't answer them because he was working at the belief that they were also things, things that just happened to be in violent motion: there could no more be a conversation with them than there could be between a fall of hail and the ground it struck. It was only whenever they went away that he let himself think of them as people and judge them as excitable and unimaginative. They might possibly kill him by mistake; they hurt him, but in a dull repetitive way, that did not interfere with pretending not to be there.

Then the guards led him out through the hospital wing, up resounding metal steps, into the prison. The physical relief of being able to get up and move was there for a moment, and then lost in the dread – that this must be the beginning of it, something much worse was going to happen. They put him into an ordinary, yellow, windowless cell, with a latrine, and went away. Varius paced about, his muscles enjoying the movement despite his battered flesh, thinking he might as well get some pleasure out of this

248

minor freedom while it was still possible, listening for sounds in the corridor, and waiting. No one came in, nothing happened.

This went on for a long time. The lights never went off, so he didn't know how many days. He was at first absolutely certain that the endless light and the silence and the waiting were calculated to cut and work loose the strands of him that still held the location of Holzarta in place. Later, he wondered if they could possibly have forgotten about him, and suspected immediately that he was meant to think this. And yet what were they *doing* all this time? One day – one night – after a while it occurred to him that maybe they no longer came to ask him where Marcus was because they knew, they'd found him, and now they were just keeping Varius out of the way until it was expedient to kill him, too.

Food still arrived, silently. He didn't eat very much and he considered ceasing to eat altogether. But that would take far too long, enough time for it to become obvious what he was doing, and then he would be stopped and things would change. He was afraid of botching it again and waking up to find that things had, again, got worse; he was afraid of doing anything to draw attention to himself.

No minute, no hour of nothing happening was a guarantee of the next minute, or hour.

Sometimes despite this and the light, he slept, and didn't know how long he slept, he thought it was not much, although in fact he was sometimes unconscious for eighteen hours at a time. Then later, for no obvious reason, for long, blank, exhausting periods it would become impossible. Until now he'd avoided thinking directly about Gemella, not only because it was too painful but because he felt it was dangerous to do anything so human; but as time went on he couldn't help it. Some of the time he believed that if he talked to her she could hear him, that they were not really separated – what little distance there was between them would soon be closed. And at those times the light and the silence became peaceful, easier to bear. But

249

then the other times would be worse. Better not to do this. He tried to devise memory games whenever he felt his thoughts begin to hop and splutter manically like an out-of-control piston; although the games sometimes risked veering off into the sort of insane, unstoppable monologues they were designed to prevent. But it was impossible to keep up the studied, semi-conscious apathy he'd managed in hospital. In a fractured way he felt a little more like himself – although that could not last if this went on much longer – and he was appallingly worried about his parents. Would they have been told anything at all, did they know what he'd tried to do to himself, would his mother have come down to Rome and found only a locked flat? He hated the idea that they would have been told he'd murdered Gemella. They wouldn't believe it, he told himself firmly, but sometimes he thought wretchedly that they might, there might seem to be no other explanation, they might have to.

He thought – it was part of the bounding nonsense-thought – that he almost wished the vigiles would hurry up and come back, even beat him again, he was so *bored*. And what he'd said had come true, he did miss Cleomenes in a way, it would have been a relief to see almost anyone.

Then, one night – or what he called one night because he had been asleep – the door unlocked and woke him up. He seemed to feel the key turn all over his body, icy, switching him into wakefulness. Four of the prison guards entered and again his body clenched with grim anticipation and he thought, here it comes. He sat stiffly against the wall and neither resisted nor co-operated as they cuffed his hands and ankles. Behind them were a couple of other men, who looked like guards or vigile legionaries or something of that sort, but were wearing a blue uniform he did not immediately recognise; it was rather fancier than the usual guards' clothes, like a private livery. He couldn't decide if this seemed any more ominous than anything else.

He reminded himself not to speak, although the temptation to ask what was happening was almost overwhelming this time. They had got him down to the ground floor before he thought – Oh – the *stairs*. A missed chance. Well, not really, because the men would never have let him do it. He stifled a strange twinge of painful laughter, because the idea of somehow spurting up out of their hands like a rebellious fish they had caught, and diving with a whoop down the stairwell onto the concrete struck him as funny.

He assumed at first that he was being taken somewhere else in the prison, but instead they made him shuffle like an invalid down into a yard where a glossy van was waiting. Not a prison van. It was blazing daylight and Varius was just blinking and marvelling at this when one of the men in livery placed some kind of rough bag over his head. Varius decided immediately that this had no function except to frighten him; and, for a moment, more clearly than fear, he felt a kind of petty annoyance –· something like, for heaven's *sake*. Even if he could see where he was going what could he possibly do about it?

As far as he could tell after that, it was the prison guards who helped get him into the van, but he thought it was the others who drove him away. In the back, under the coarse hood, Varius smiled tightly at a minuscule victory; for exactly as they covered his eyes he realised that there was something familiar about the blue uniforms. He'd been trying to think what military or civil cohort they could be attached to, but he'd been right to notice the extravagance of the livery; he was almost sure they were part of a troop of private bodyguards, and so he thought he could guess where he was going, even if they meant it to be a surprise, even if knowing offered no comfort at all.

With no warning another vehicle, a car, would erupt too fast from a junction, the driver of the van would have an instant to see it coming but no time, nothing to be done; he, Varius, would know nothing until it hit, and then it would punch the van sideways, fling it cartwheeling off the road. He would hear the windows burst, the helpless cries of fear and pain, for everyone in the van would be equal now in powerlessness, as·they were lifted out of their seats, turned over, smashed against the walls and windows and each other; he would feel the spray of glass fragments rain down on the hood. He wouldn't be completely unhurt after such an impact – it would be unrealistic to expect that – perhaps as he flew, fell, he would feel a wrist break, a crack knocked into his ribs. Then he would be lying still, in the crook of the wall and ceiling, and around him there would be silence, or groaning in the silence, but no sound of anyone moving. He would struggle out of the hood and be startled to find that the guards were unconscious or trapped or dead. Of course he would hardly believe it. Disbelieving, then, expecting them to revive and stop him, he would search the guards for the keys. Find them. One of the men would look at him, unrecognising, moaning for help. Varius would look away. The chains would slow him down, so would whatever minor injuries he'd received. Unlock the shackles. Climb out of the glass-fringed shell, walk calmly away in the bright sunlight.

The van kept moving, smoothly.

It was the first time he had pictured an escape in which he remained alive. Varius was alarmed by how suddenly and intensely he saw it all, how it played brightly inside the darkness of the hood, as if he wasn't the one making it up. He *must not* do this. He reminded himself about being a thing. He was allowed to observe what was happening, but nothing more was allowed, he must not imagine or wish for anything at all. It would make it worse, when it started.

They were somewhere quiet, and even through the hood he had the impression of sunny space. He could hear birdsong, and then a distorted, echoing shriek which shook him badly for a second, until it occurred to him that it might be the cry of a peacock, bouncing off high invisible garden walls. Yes, this all seemed that he was right. The door they pulled him through seemed narrow by the way they moved – a servants' entrance, he thought. But he knew that these furtive seizures of detail were only like one of the memory games, a way of distracting himself from what was surely about to happen, at the top of these stairs, at the end of this corridor, through this door.

He heard a sighing sound like waves, and couldn't understand it. He tripped and staggered. He was inside, and yet the floor beneath him seemed to be sloped. The fetters wouldn't let him get his balance back and he toppled over onto all fours, making an instinctive, bitter little noise at the unnecessary humiliation of it. He felt soft carpet under his hands and rose as quickly as he could, fumbling awkwardly. Someone helped, steadied him. He couldn't help a useless, defensive twitch at the touch, but he had developed a kind of superstition about showing any emotion, so he tried to stifle his astonishment when the bag was lifted over his head and he saw where he was.

He was standing in a broad aisle between the plump and somnolent seats of a lavish entertainment suite. The aisle slanted, like a beach to the sea, down to a deep oval stage, where girls would dance, perhaps; for a section of the stage could be drawn back from the little orchestra pit below it. Beyond this a curved screen rose and filled even part of the ceiling in an enormous domed recess, for watching long-vision or recorded screenshows, or to act as scenery for the stage; and there were special lamps, too, which could have thrown seemingly solid figures of light among the dancers, gods and centaurs. But for now the screen was only a moving fresco, where a crystalline lagoon spread away from the stage up to a sugary blue sky, where gaudy birds sometimes flew.

Around him the seats were not cramped together, as they would have been in a public theatre, but spaced between little rosewood drinks cabinets, where glass boxes of marzipan and crystallised ginger stood among the vases of wine and liqueurs. The waves he'd heard breathed and whispered from great speakers built into the walls. There was something like this in the palace, he believed, but he had never seen it, and it seemed the least likely place in the world to be standing with his hands and feet chained, with one broken tooth, expecting to be tortured.

He'd guessed he was going to Gabinius' house. But he had not expected this, and he had not expected Gabinius in person.

'Varius,' said Gabinius, almost as if they were meeting at last to discuss sponsorship of the slave clinic, his voice amiably crisp – and yet deliberately modulated with something else – kindness, regret.

He knew Gabinius by sight, of course, and would have done even if they had never spoken – Gabinius was, if not exactly famous, then certainly well known, and he was physically startling. Varius even knew somehow that as a twelve-year-old Gabinius had been accidentally knocked out wrestling at school and for some reason had lost every hair on his body as a result, and no hair had ever grown again. Lashless, beardless, his bare pink skin looked oddly delicate and exceptionally clean. His large eyes were grey and very shiny, and should have been blue to match the babylike face. And he was monstrously big, so big as to confuse the sense of proportion, six foot six at least, with great blocks and slabs of fat packed tightly under the skin: over what should have been, and never had been, an athlete's frame. He was taut and pyramidal and permanent-looking; beside him Faustus' style of fat would have looked loose and shambolic. Varius looked at him with mute, hot-eyed hatred, and dragged his feet slowly away to sit on the edge of one of the yielding chairs, staring straight ahead at the wavelets.

Gabinius moved surprisingly fast for such a monument of flesh. At once he was in the chair beside Varius, leaning forward sincerely across the bottles and vases. 'Varius,' he said, compassionately, urgently. 'Are you badly hurt? If you're still in pain I can get someone in here right away. Listen, that was nothing to do with me, and I'm sorry for it. I want you to understand that I don't see any need for anything like that. I don't like it. Truly. And nothing is going to happen to you here. Do you understand? Do you believe me?'

Varius said nothing, but Gabinius seemed to relax all the

254

same. He settled back comfortably and looked serenely at the electric sky. Presently he said conversationally, 'I think you should go somewhere like that. That is a real place, you know, except for those birds, I think they put those in. Somewhere, you know, unspoiled. Because what you need is a *rest*. I can tell; you don't think you can ever feel better now, but you're wrong. One day you will.'

Varius felt a kind of nauseous incredulity that Gabinius should speak to him like this. It was surely obvious that he could not be allowed to survive, he knew that. He didn't understand what Gabinius was trying to do.

When he didn't answer Gabinius said quickly in a different voice, no less friendly but lower and more acute. 'Come on, Varius. I know you can talk. It really won't make any difference.' But after another pause, Gabinius went on cheerfully as if he was simply keeping up his side of the conversation: 'One of those thugs broke your tooth, didn't he? Horrible. But you can get that fixed, these days. My son – he's nine – he came off a swing and got both of the front ones, right across the middle. But you'd never know now.'

He inserted a bead of vanilla cream thoughtfully into his mouth and got up, strolled purposefully towards the screen and inspected it, then turned back to look at Varius. He said decisively. 'So you understand. You can afford all these things. Within reason, you can afford anything you want.'

He waited calmly. After a moment he said, 'You can say whatever you like.'

Varius had been watching him involuntarily, first in confusion and then in disbelief. Now again he'd made a small sound, of disgust this time.

'What was that?' asked Gabinius. 'What did you want to say just then?'

Varius whispered, 'Do you think that will work—?'

'What?'

'After what you've *done*, do you think you can just offer me money and I'll help you?'

'No!' said Gabinius. 'No, I don't think that for a minute. I'm not offering you money. I have already given you money. There are a million sesterces in your account now, and they are going to be there whatever happens and whatever you do. I've said what I think you should do with it, because you look just worn out, but if you don't like it, you can give it away. Spend it on that clinic if you want.'

Varius shook his head and silenced himself again. But he was trembling with anger he hadn't felt since talking to Cleomenes in the hospital, trembling with the desire to harm Gabinius. He even looked at the objects on the nearest cabinet, wondering if he could use any of them as weapons. No, it was stupid, what did he think the chains were for? Just be quiet, he urged himself, don't be here.

Still, it was impossible, even now he remembered and tried, to think of Gabinius as a thing.

Gabinius said sorrowfully, sitting beside him again, 'Yes, I know. How old are you? Very young. No one your age should be thinking the way you are.' Varius, who without any special reason for it had never, even as a child, considered himself young, felt a distant bewilderment at this. Gabinius continued, 'I think I can guess what you've got into your head. I think it's that either you'll get another chance to do what you tried outside the Golden House, and you'll be successful; or that in one way or another one of those guards or one of the vigiles, or someone of mine even though I've told you otherwise, will do it for you. And maybe we'd give out that you'd done it yourself. Or that perhaps you'll get your way and there'll be a trial, and of course if there was a trial you would be executed.'

Varius' skin crept a little at how accurate this was, but he shrugged. Gabinius looked pained. 'You see, that's what I find really upsetting. You don't even mind, do you? Because this terrible thing happened to you and now you don't think you've got anything left. And it's not true, it's not true at all.'

Varius staggered forward out of the chair and limped stubbornly up the slope to get as far from Gabinius as the shackles and the silent bodyguards standing discreetly in the doorway would allow. Gabinius, quite unperturbed, barely paused for breath. 'I could understand your position more if I was the one who wanted to change something, if I wanted to pull everything apart, but I don't; you want to do that. I just like things the way they are. And are things really *so bad* that it's worth throwing your life away, putting your parents through that? Where did this come from, anyway? Did Leo and Clodia . . . I don't know – *indoctrinate* you? Or does your family have any – any *connection*, any history with slavery? Would you know? I know people usually like to cover it up.'

At the top of the aisle, at the mention of his parents, a spasm of fear made Varius stop. He turned slowly, when he was sure it couldn't be seen on his face. 'No,' he said.

'No? Mine has. Not so far back. My grandfather.' Of course Varius had known this already; everyone knew about Gabinius' origins. 'He was in the palace to start with, he just washed the kitchen floors. And now—' Gabinius revolved gently, indicating the room, and the fact that it was his. 'I'm not – I *won't* be ashamed of him, either. He was a wonderful man. I'm the first one of my family who can stand for the Senate. And I'm going to. This, *this – only* in the Empire can that happen. Varius, the only places in the world where there isn't slavery of some kind are the places where everyone, to all intents and purposes, is a slave. We're the only ones who give them the chance to work their way out of it.'

'Not for much longer,' said Varius. 'There are too few of them.'

'Well,' said Gabinius, 'Then only the best and the cleverest will get there, people like my grandfather, people who just don't stop. I think that's a good thing. Otherwise everyone gets you know, flabby,' he looked down at his own body, grinned good-humouredly, and amended, 'Lazy.'

Varius said, 'I don't think we're ever going to convince each other.'

Gabinius sighed. 'You're probably right there. But I do hope I can stop you behaving in such a self-destructive way. Because ultimately, it's selfish. You know that, really. I've said it already, but how are your parents going to feel? When you're dead, and you're not only dead but you're a murderer, and you're a traitor.'

'Tell me how yours feel about you,' snarled Varius, unguardedly. And as he'd done so many times before, he promised himself that of course his parents wouldn't believe it.

Gabinius only nodded acquiescently and said, 'I'm not a traitor. Leo was. It's a pity he ever met that woman, I know it wasn't only that, but . . . I'm a Roman citizen, I just want to keep Rome safe, he didn't. And I want a safe world for my children to grow up in, I think that's natural. And – I should have made it clear earlier, but I thought you already realised the attempt came from the palace – I wasn't involved in what happened to your wife. Varius. Please. I wouldn't have let that happen. That was done badly, of course – or we wouldn't be here. And whatever you may think, I'm sorry, and I wish you would just let me do what I can to make things better for you.'

He was following Varius up the ramp. Varius backed away from him again, and, even though he knew it was futile, said to the nearest blue-liveried bodyguard, 'Take me back to the prison.'

'You know he won't. And since you asked about my parents, well, sadly they've both passed away, and even at my age you don't stop missing them. But at least that's the way it's meant to be, no one's children are supposed to go first, and that is the point I've been trying to make. I've told you: the money is going to be there whatever happens and whatever you do, even if you're not alive to spend it, although what a waste that would be. It would come to light eventually. You were Leo's executor, weren't you? I think it would probably turn out that a similar sum was missing from his estate. And that would be why you killed them: Marcus Novius first, and then your wife, because they'd found out what you were doing. Your parents will spend the rest of their lives looking back on the whole of yours, and they'll think that they never saw it, they never noticed the terrible thing they must have done to you, to make you turn out like that.'

Varius had flinched profoundly, tugging the chain tight between his fists. But he said, having almost to cough the words out: 'I don't care – how you make it sound plausible; I've had to give up on my reputation already.'

'Really? Have you? You can think like that? But no, you don't have to; because you're hoping Novius will come back one day. You wouldn't be there to know about it, of course, but that's what you're counting on. But your parents aren't exactly young – they had you pretty late in life, didn't they – your mother, I think, had problems carrying a child? Three miscarriages before you? So no brothers or sisters. Oof!' Gabinius blew his cheeks out, shaking his head. 'Well, how she'll feel . . . it's just . . . unimaginable.' There was a remote control in his hand; Varius hadn't seen him pick it up, didn't know where it came from. 'So you must remember that they might not live long enough to see your name cleared.'

The sleepy gasping of the waves continued a second after the sky and the turquoise sea turned black. It was startling how convincing the lurid illusion of space had been; the room seemed suddenly dark, claustrophobic. The new sound was a confused thudding and creak of shoes, an occasional mutter, the slightly quickened breath of the unseen man who held the lens. The new image filled only the central portion of the expanse, and was first an untidy bedroom, then stairs, then a somehow desolate living room. There was no sign of his small cross mother, his slow father interminably listening to the news, but then, of course, as things were, they would not be doing such ordinary things.

He had almost known, since he had begun to believe that nothing, for the time being, was to happen to him physically, since Gabinius had first spoken of his parents, that this must be what he was here to see; but still it struck like the loudest possible noise, the brightest light, erupting against sleep. The fetters tripped him up again, he sat down suddenly on the ramp, he couldn't think of anything to say that wasn't a plea.

Unmoving, Gabinius said, 'They're not there just now. They're here in Rome, looking for you. They don't want to tell each other that they're both afraid you've done something stupid, which of course, you did.'

Varius closed his eyes, breathed, 'Please, don't.'

Gabinius turned and, a little clumsily, for it was an effort for such a big man, lowered himself to sit on his heels. 'Stop me,' he said, quietly, patiently.

'No.'

There was no sound. Then, 'Varius,' Gabinius appealed softly. Varius' teeth ground, a kind of slow cry expelling itself through them. He could not say 'no,' again, but he said nothing else. It was hardly at all the thought of the slaves that stopped him; he knew, in an academic way, that it was very important to him, almost more important than anything – but it was just too hard now; he couldn't see the usual never-ending cruelty, or abstract, preventable deaths as clearly as those dismal pictures of his parents' home. But Marcus was so young; and Varius was responsible for him, somebody had to be, Leo and Clodia weren't there. He pressed his shut eyes against his fists until it hurt, as if he could push through into the throbbing dark.

Gabinius sighed heavily and stood up. Varius could only see the darkness, but he felt the slowness of the movement, heard the weariness of the other man's breath. 'Varius,' Gabinius said. 'Look.'

He knew he would somehow be made to, but he would not do it.

Gabinius repeated dully, with what at least sounded like reluctance, 'No brothers and sisters. Horrible. At least, your wife's parents haven't been through that.'

Varius' hands fell slackly away from his face, his head rose of its own accord. He'd pressed so hard that it was almost a minute before the thickness cleared from his eyes. But there was a bleariness on the screen too – this time they were recording through leaves, crouched, possibly, in a suburban garden. The lens moved, searched for a clear space. There was a street – not a street he recognised, though he could guess, roughly, where it must be. There was a figure, that flickered a little, pulled out of shot, and steadied; walking slowly along the far side of the street, arms folded, perhaps heading home from school.

Rosa was surprisingly lanky and knobbly, but then he could never remember that she was thirteen, fourteen now – she was fixed in his head at eleven. It made it worse somehow that he wasn't, in truth, especially fond of her. All the first year, every time he'd gone to Gemella's house, she hadn't seemed willing to let them out of her sight; she was at once brashly aggrieved and fascinated by him. She kept trying to get hold of him alone so she could hiss inquisitorial things like, 'Are you in love with Gemella?' and, then, cantankerously, as if she were Gemella's father rather than her sister, '*What are your intentions?*'

But she looked bleakly adult now, and it was not so much the added height as the empty way she was trudging along, and her expression, which, with a shudder of focus, had suddenly become visible.

He couldn't feel shocked this time, all that seemed to be over with.

Gabinius muttered, 'Once the news gets out about you, and what you've done, and they've had a little while to think about that; then your parents would be first. This—' Rosa had outpaced the lens, but it met her again later, outside her house, staring forlornly at the door before going in. 'This would happen later. Gemella's family would know you were responsible for their daughter's death, like everyone else. And you will be. They just won't know which one.' Varius' body jerked as if a brief current had been fed through it, although he was hardly aware of it. He looked helplessly at Gabinius' large face hanging between him and the screen. 'Listen, before I say anything else, I'm going to tell you that we'll be careful when we find Marcus Novius, nothing like a car crash, we'll use something different from the poison in Lady Makaria's sweets. I promise you, he won't know anything about it. He won't be hurt. But her . . . it has to be completely clear to you what to do. So the point here is that one day they wouldn't find her, and then one day they would, but she wouldn't be easy to recognise, she'd be . . . burnt, maybe, or cut to bits. And they'd know . . . that it had taken a long time.'

Varius moaned, not after all beyond shock. Gabinius shook his head, almost remorsefully, 'It's all right. It's not going to happen, is it? I'm not doing this for fun. I just want to be sure.'

Frantically, Varius clutched at what he scarcely thought was a real suggestion of weakness. He got up, breathless and jingling. 'You don't want to.'

'Of course not,' said Gabinius, apparently, for the first time, a little offended. He mumbled, 'Leo was one thing—' and stopped. And Varius, who had spoken almost at random, began gabbling on a dreadful surge of hope.

'You don't have to. Marcus isn't even seventeen. You said that – *I* was too young – you said you had a little boy. Marcus is sixteen. You don't have to. Who made you think you did?' He heard with sick wonder the bizarre gentleness that had come into his own voice, as if he were talking to a hurt child. He even dragged against the chain to lay a consoling hand on Gabinius' arm. 'Of *course* Leo was different. It was just – it was just like in a war, wasn't it? To protect Rome. I *do* understand. He was a threat he – he knew he was making himself vulnerable. But Marcus – and *she*—' he couldn't look at Rosa again. 'They're *children*. You don't want to.'

Gabinius murmured sadly, 'It wasn't my idea. And I wish it was different.' He turned to look fiercely at Varius, while Rosa jolted backwards out of the house, along the street, quivered and began dolefully walking again. 'But what about *my* children? What about their inheritance?' He nodded again at the opulent room and said, 'That's what all this is for. It's not for me. How is this supposed to last, if things turn out the way you want?'

Varius still pleaded, 'No, you would always remember, you couldn't—'

Gabinius, who had never until now even raised his voice, roared at him, 'I need to know I don't have to! You need to know that I would! Shall we start? Shall we start with your parents, so you know this isn't a *joke*? Do you want someone pouring acid over that girl? From now on, I don't blame myself at all! *You've* forced my hand!'

He wiped his face.

Varius sagged emptily. Gabinius gripped his shoulders. 'Now. Where did you send him?'

Varius whispered, 'I don't know.'

Gabinius shouted again, savagely, 'Don't be so fucking stupid!'

'No,' said Varius, almost too quietly to be heard. 'No, no one is supposed to know. It's a slave's refuge.' It was a long while before he could say any more. It was as if his body wanted to keep him quiet, as if it remembered the poison and was willing now, far too late, to shut down. 'It's in the Pyrenees. I told Marcus to go to a village called Athabia. I thought someone there would find him and show him the way. That's what the slaves do. I don't know where it is.'

'Slaves?' repeated Gabinius with the quick blankness of something recognised. He frowned. 'But not the east Pyrenees? Somewhere called Wolf Step – heading into Spain?'

Varius stared at him, shattered and uncomprehending. 'If you lie, it will be worse,' said Gabinius, doubtfully.

Varius just shook his head.

Gabinius sighed again, and changed his hold on Varius' shoulder, guided him quite tenderly into one of the chairs. Varius let him do it, dropped back against the velvety seat, like a smashed body in a smashed car.

'All right,' said Gabinius. He picked up the remote control, and the glittering sea flooded back, a white sail drifting slowly across it, and the waves began forgetfully droning. He rubbed Varius' shoulder comfortingly. 'All right. The second it's over, you go home. You'll go right home and see your poor mother. Look, don't look like that, don't feel that way. It's not your fault. You couldn't do anything else. The whole thing's a shame. These are bad times to live in. That's all there is to it.'

[XII]

DAMA

Dama dreamed his teeth were falling out. It began with one of the molars, back in the upper jaw. He felt it shift, swing back and forth in the hurt crater of the gum, and then the sharp root snagging on the pulpy flesh, on the grains of his taste buds as he rolled it forward across his tongue. He spat it out into his hand, which should have told him it was a dream, and he thought, well, I can do without one tooth.

Then another went. Then they began to fall in twos and threes, and sometimes they splintered as they came loose, and dropped in separate wet shards, crunchily, like bitten nuts or boiled sweets. He shook and gasped with terror, and that made the teeth come out all the faster. He stumbled away from the half-finished tower and ran along the broken stones, panting and weeping, bits of enamel scattering from his mouth.

He woke up slick-skinned with sweat and, after the initial relief of pressing his sound jaws together, he was annoyed. He could not understand why it had been so overpoweringly horrible, or why, if he had to have night-mares, they should be about teeth. It was undignified. There were much worse things.

He got up at once. He prayed for a little while, just in his head, without any external sign of it. For the most part, he tried to make it wordless; he felt, without knowing why, that it wasn't right to be too specific, to ask for anything, even to say anything. But he couldn't suppress a kind of mutter at the base of it. God. Show me what to do. Give me something to do. At some point, probably not for an hour or two, Lal would turn up to help him clean his teeth, to clip some of the hair from his face. He knew she didn't like doing it, although he didn't think anyone made her. He didn't like it either, but someone had to help him. After all this time he ought to be, he *would* be used to it, he would face it.

Lal had walked fourteen miles – into the village and back – to get her hair cut short, the way some girls these days wore it in Rome. Delir was angry with her for taking the risk over something so silly. Dama was not sure if he felt, as he did, exasperation that she should want anything from Rome, that you couldn't just pick out the things you liked from an evil place and leave the rest. Poor little Lal, though, she was bored too. It wasn't her fault.

He suppressed the knowledge that there was not really anything for him to do today, or rather, that nothing was urgent. He could watch the monitors, even though it was not his turn, but sitting passively looking for something that even now, would probably not come, didn't feel like doing anything.

In the beginning he had explained how to do things, how to level the slope, how to sink piles and lay the beams, about the distribution of loads, how to run the generator. Now, although there was plenty of work in keeping everything going – he couldn't be the one to do it.

He would go and check all the exit routes, and make sure none of the wires had come loose.

He probably had bad dreams because of the spiral-wings, even though he'd been the only one who was not really frightened. Last night again they'd heard the grinding hum come close, and then turn in the air and fade, so that the ear expected it to vanish and kept trying to persuade the distant throb that it *was* vanishing, although really it had reached a steadiness, and then it gradually grew again. Everyone was terrified. He and Delir kept repeating that they could not be seen. They had turned everything off, although even that was more for comfort than for necessity.

He went outside, although Lal begged him not to. They

might have special glasses, she said, they can see in the dark. Not through rock and trees and round corners, though, he said.

What bothered him was the fact that every second, from the noise, from the circle it seemed to be describing over him, he expected the aircraft to come into sight, he was sure of it, he kept thinking, it's just up there. He stood, urging them into sight, but the burr of the wings grew louder and louder, and he could not even see the lights.

Come on. Here I am.

They first heard the rasp in the morning sky, for they'd given up walking by night because the woods felt so richly empty, they'd almost ceased wanting to arrive. And it was barely a sound to begin with, but a sudden, simultaneous drop in their own voices, a chill as they heard how loudly they had been talking. They could barely look at each other to see if the sound was real before the air was full of it; an accelerating growl, throbbing closer.

They could only stand still as it came on: a silver bee gnawing through the air. It rose from behind them and – the young trees around them seemed so sparse and transparent – it was suddenly terribly visible; they could see, in detail, the pallid sheen of it changing as it moved, even the fine joins of the panelling on the underside. They felt their hair stir, their clothes flap, in the cold, churned air. It drilled over them, ahead, westwards.

Una broke away from the tree they'd pressed against, and ran a few agitated steps after the craft as though she'd wanted to catch it, wheeled and looked at Marcus, crying, 'It's what happened in Wolf Step! I knew they were going to recognise you. Those bastards, I hate them.' She felt hot, shivery. It was not fair, they should think Marcus was in Spain if they had to think he was anywhere, she shouldn't have to feel as if it was her fault.

'Una. They didn't even slow down. They didn't see anything,' said Sulien, going after her.

For the first day or two out of Wolf Step, Una had been so

267

silent, brooding and striding blankly along, but then, quite suddenly, she seemed to wake up out of it. And since then they'd been bothering less about how far they should walk in a day, they'd been talking more and more noisily. Una and Sulien knew who Varius was, Marcus had heard everything about Tancorix and the escape from London, and didn't remember that he'd thought of disbelieving it. Una had even told them something, a reassuringly childlike thing, about the years alone in London; that when she was eleven, she had collected dead flies from a window ledge and inserted them neatly into cakes she was supposed to be packaging. Once again, they were all dressed about the same. It seemed as though anecdotes about dead flies in a factory were no different from Marcus' stories about watching the divine Emperor get drunk.

But still Una thought, this is only because we are *here*, and there isn't any background. It's only for as long as this lasts.

'Stop trying to calm me down, we've got to think what they're doing! They could land over there – no, they couldn't land, but they can lower people down.'

Marcus was looking west after the spira. He said, with seeming calm interest, 'It's a Daedalus, the army use that model, not the vigiles.'

'What? What does it matter? They're all after you, aren't they?' demanded Una, but, in the same breath, 'Do you know how many people it holds?'

'About ten, I think.' She nodded, slightly reassured by the number, as she would have been by almost any reliable piece of information. 'But I meant they might not be looking for anything. It could just be a military exercise.'

'You *know*—' Una began with fierce impatience. She stopped, watching him. 'You know it isn't an exercise,' she finished softly.

He didn't answer at first, considering, feeling her look at him; he had to admit: 'Well, all right. They're looking for us. But I've been in one. Sulien's right, they didn't see us.

I'm not surprised they didn't. They might have done if we were moving, but we weren't.'

She went on looking at him, until he said, 'All right, I thought they were going to kill us. But it's not rational,' and she almost laughed.

And the peace of the woods settled back for a while. But the afternoon of that day they heard the machines again, sweeping south towards Spain, and again, faintly, the night before they reached Athabia, when at first they could not tell where the spiral-wings were. Then they saw a pair of lights far off, going back and forth in the dark, over and around the village itself.

Wolf Step had seemed tiny, but Athabia was barely there at all. They could have walked a circle round it in less than five minutes. The small white houses had shutters painted dark red or green, and one or two had little ornamental spikes standing on the apices of the black-tiled roofs; otherwise there was nothing very remarkable about them. They were spread about a loose, wavering loop of cobbled street, which turned around the plain stump of a fountain and then drifted off almost into nothing. Only one vague road led away from the village, down among sharp green slopes, on which they could see no other buildings, and not even a column of striding pylons. There were sheep on the nearest bare flank where the cloth of beech forest parted to show grass, that was all. Even in the centre of Athabia, there seemed to be no one about.

They didn't want to make themselves visible, but if they did not, nothing would happen. Outside, among wet trees, they hesitated about what to do with the bags, hiding them in the end, so that they would not look so obviously like travellers, and so they could run. 'Well,' said Marcus, when there was nothing left to do but go. They walked fatalistically along the street towards the little fountain.

There was a slow seep of rain. There was no public longvision anywhere. The single white shop seemed to be a caupona of sorts as well: through the open door they glimpsed a few old men, sitting morosely inside, with glasses in their hands, beside a shelf of canned and potted food, and bottles of hair oil and pens.

'I can't understand them,' announced Una suddenly. She looked rather frightened.

'What do you mean?'

'I – the feelings and pictures and things are the same – but all the words – it isn't Latin, I don't know what it is.' Of course there were Sinoans and Nionians in London, but she had never been surrounded by another language before, and she was distressed by how much it alarmed her. Having always thought, I am not really Roman, she had never considered how she was, naturally, utterly dependent on Latin, for it was so omnipresent that it was easy to forget it was a language at all, that it did not simply spring, inevitably, out of everything.

'We're in the middle of the Empire – why aren't they talking Latin?'

Sulien and Marcus heard it too now, a child and a young man in overalls arguing about something near a garage. It sounded extraordinary to them, long clattering chains of syllables spiked with Zs and Xs; for a second Sulien was reminded of what little Catavignus had taught him of Greek, but the next he thought it was no more like Greek than like Latin, there was no reference point at all. Then after a few seconds they realised that they'd heard Latin words as well, or versions of them, not recognisable at first and rather startling among the rest; car, engine.

'How much difference does it make?' Sulien asked her. 'If they were going to report us, could you tell?'

'Ah . . .' Una turned uncertainly, looking from the garage to the shop. 'I don't know. Yes, maybe, but—' She might have thought it would be a relief, not having to understand so much, but it was not, she felt as if she had tinnitus, and if she just waited and concentrated, it would clear.

'You know that shop?' said Sulien, 'I don't think they had any news sheets there. If they don't speak Latin, maybe they haven't even heard about Marcus. Anyway, it's got to make it harder to tell anyone.'

'They might speak Latin. They just don't think in it.'

'Oh, I never thought of that,' said Marcus suddenly. 'In the Pyrenees there *is* a different language. They're – something – Vascones.'

This did not add much to what was obvious. 'Can you understand it?' said Sulien.

'No. I just heard of it, I can't even remember when. It's Aquitanian. But I don't think they call it that. It's older than Latin.'

They stood foolishly about near the fountain.

'They teach languages, at this place?' said Una, after a while in which nothing had continued to happen.

'Varius said so,' said Marcus. 'Mandarin and Nionian.'

The thought of Varius made him grimace with guilt. The last six days – at least, the days before they'd first heard the spiral-wings – had been so much easier, he'd even been happy. But the better things were, and the further he was from Rome, the more he worried that he should never have left it. It had become an insidious, repetitive mumble that was most audible in the quiet nights and got to him on the point of sleep. He should not have let Varius decide everything. He should have thought more clearly about what might happen.

'None of us have to go to Sina,' said Sulien. 'When this is over we'll be able to live wherever we like.'

They looked up again. Still there was nothing in the grey sky.

'Yes, but we might as well do something,' said Una.

Sulien turned to Marcus. 'Would you learn Mandarin and Nionian for fun?'

'Er,' muttered Marcus, embarrassed. 'I know them already.' They stared at him. 'That is, I kind of know them. I was better at Greek, but Greek's only good for writing.'

'Mandarin and Nionian and Greek,' wondered Una.

'Well, I had to,' Marcus said. Then he smiled and added, 'And I can say, "Thank you, it's an honour to be here," in Quetsua and Navaho.'

'Say it,' commanded Una, abruptly.

'No.'

Say it, *say* it, urged Una and Sulien, laughing now.

But the mechanic was looking at them over the bared innards of an ancient car, so they stopped.

'We should be quiet,' muttered Una, 'and we can't use your name around other people, even now.'

'No,' said Marcus, regretfully. 'I got quite used to being Pollio—'

'No, it can't be anything you've used before.'

'I know. I'm just so sick of fake names.'

But Una had retreated slightly, turned to look casually out across the mountain. 'The mechanic knows something about us,' she said.

Marcus looked at her quickly. 'Does he recognise me?'

'No. No, I'm almost sure he doesn't. But I think he knows we're slaves.'

'Well,' said Sulien, 'maybe that's how it works.'

'He's coming,' warned Marcus. The mechanic had pushed the engine back into place and was walking briskly towards them. They moved a little closer to one another.

The mechanic stood and looked at them. He was about thirty, with the compact sturdiness of a pony, with straight, horselike, tan-brown hair, 'Latin?' he queried.

Una nodded hesitantly.

'Ahh—' he growled, but to himself, not them. He was frowning impatiently as he rummaged, visibly, for the next word. 'Lost?'

'Not exactly,' said Una.

'You wait there, I think,' said the man positively. 'Someone comes looking for you, you see?'

They could not think of an answer. He smiled at them encouragingly. 'Romans. No one here cares a lot, you understand what I mean?'

They did not, or not altogether. He tried again, 'Here we are very—' but he ran out of Latin words again and clapped his cupped hands together once or twice, perhaps trying to say, tightly-knit, inward-looking; and he left them alone.

272

'I think he's going to tell someone,' Una murmured, when he was gone.

'He can't be going to call the vigiles,' said Marcus. 'Why would he tell us someone was coming? He wouldn't talk to us at all.'

Una shook her head in frustrated uncertainty.

'I don't think that's what's wrong,' continued Marcus hesitantly, after a pause. 'But there's something else.'

'What?'

'Varius. The spiras were *here* last night. They weren't just searching around, they were focusing *here*. I don't think it can be because of what happened in Wolf Step. They should have thought we were going into Spain. I'm sure they did think that at first. But it could be Varius. But it'd take a lot to make him do that. I don't even want to think—' He broke off and gritted his teeth, because it was literally unthinkable.

'He could have told someone he trusted and he might have been wrong about them,' said Sulien, quietly.

Marcus gave him a quick, grateful look; nothing like this had occurred to him. 'But in any case, it looks as though they know where we are.'

'Do you mean you think we should go?' said Una.

'Do you, if that's what's happened?'

Una hesitated. 'Possibly.'

'No,' said Sulien then, to them both, 'We've come all this way. And we can't give up and go somewhere else, because there isn't anywhere else. Look, I think if the vigiles find us here, then it would happen anywhere and we might as well get it over with. It's still the best chance we've got.'

After a while they were almost too bored to worry any longer. The rain dripped with desolate persistence. Sulien and Marcus wanted to buy something in the shop, more to pass the time than because they were hungry, but were put off by the risk and the language barrier. But after two hours Sulien was sick of it and bought some biscuits by pointing and smiling. They ate them drearily, slumped on the ground, by now, against the fountain.

Then someone who had circled around from behind them said, in clear, unaccented Latin, 'I know who you are.'

Marcus looked up in instinctive alarm, but the young man standing over them went on, after just a second's hesitation as he summoned the name: 'Sulien.'

Sulien got to his feet in slow shock. As long ago as their arrival in Tolosa he had begun to feel almost convinced that no one was really bothered about the fugitives from the prison boat any more. Una's intense wariness about him had come to seem – half the time at least – less like a rational fear than a neurosis, sometimes trying and sometimes endearing, that had to be humoured, for her sake, not for his. And even when he saw that the man who knew his name was plainly not a vigile legionary or any kind of soldier, the shock did not disappear. It was as if the stranger carried it about with him, or wore it. It was not just the fierceness of the expression, for that was not hostile, in fact he did not have to be Una to see that the man had recognised him with glad, excited interest. But Sulien looked at him with a physical feeling of something awfully, pitifully wrong.

Marcus noticed that both Una and Sulien had blenched a little, that Sulien had lifted one of his own wrists and was holding it protectively to his body, not so much as if it were injured but as if it were a talisman or a treasure.

It was true that nothing about Dama looked quite right. He was shorter than either Marcus or Sulien, with a dense, stocky body, but something about the way he held himself, and about the roundness of the head on the wide shoulders, was wrong for the muscular set of the torso. Yet not very long ago he had been an angelically beautiful little boy, and, at certain turns of light or of expression, residual flashes of sharp beauty would shake free, as from an obscure and partial halo. His curly hair was the colour the woman in the Wolf Step caupona must have been aiming for – a glossy, copper-beech-tree auburn. But instead of lengthening out of themselves into adult good looks, the delicate small features had stayed almost the same; and the little nose looked stranded, the outlines were too soft, the cheeks too blank and formless around the cherubic red mouth, over the small sharp chin with its unloved and unintentional-looking scrubby beard. The neat russet freckles were strange beside the few lines, which were still shallow, for Dama was only about twenty, but the more visible for the surrounding freshness: plainly adult marks scored, as if with a compass-point, into the clear flesh of the forehead and around the eyelids. The eyes were large, round, long-lashed, the irises flat round panels of bright, pale aquamarine, completely without flecks or streaks, within precise rings of darker blue, like two kinds of mineral inlaid together, or like enamel applied to the eyeball.

The expression, helplessly single-minded as a thrown stone, belonged on a much older, harder, and more aquiline face. It was familiar to Sulien from somewhere, but he did not realise at first that it was like the expression Una sometimes had.

Una felt the same shock, and she could not quite tell what it was or where it came from. Latin was plainly Dama's first language, but he was almost as hard to pierce or translate as the Vascones were; more difficult even, because it wasn't only the words that were enclosed from her. It was strange, because it was not an inscrutable face, and it wasn't as if there was nothing there. But there was a kind of resistance; when – and she began at once – she tried to feel for the grain of the thoughts, she was somehow turned back on herself, as if she'd run up against a sphere or a mirror. Perhaps it was because of the frustrating incomprehensibility of the Vascones, that she felt somehow provoked, or fascinated.

Dama asked Sulien eagerly, 'How did that happen? How did you get away?' but he checked the excitement he felt and shook his head to stop Sulien answering him. He stared at them all. 'You picked a bad time to come,' he said, nodding grimly at the empty sky. 'You must have heard those spiras. Someone's said something.'

They were silent, Marcus nodded uneasily.

'It's difficult. There's a balance. We're no good if no one knows about us. But if too many people talk, we're done. Before you left, or on the way, did you tell *anyone else* where you were going?'

'No,' answered Una.

'Do you have *anything* to tell me about this?' He cast another unforgiving glance towards the sky.

She hesitated, not wanting to speak. 'Something happened on the way. Some people guessed we were slaves. They might have called the vigiles.'

'When was this?'

'About a week ago.'

Dama nodded slowly. 'A week . . . And you are all slaves?'

'Yes,' said Marcus.

'No, not any more,' said Una.

Dama grinned and was transfigured with delighted accordance, a vivid-faced child after all. 'No. Good answer. Of course you're not,' he agreed emphatically. He surveyed the resemblance between Una and Sulien, and then examined Marcus, sharply but without, as far as Una could tell, the least ghost of an idea that he looked familiar. 'You're brother and sister. But you – you weren't on the prison boat?'

'No, Gnaeus was the valet where I worked; he got out with me,' said Una calmly. Marcus realised with a kind of embarrassed amusement that he felt vaguely gratified by this. Una continued. 'He's how I heard about this place.'

Dama turned zealous azure attention onto Marcus, 'How did you know about us?'

'I met someone in Sina,' said Marcus.

'One of ours?'

'No, I think he just knew someone who knew someone. It was a while ago,' said Marcus with deliberate vagueness.

'I hope he was damn careful talking about it.'

'He was,' Marcus promised him. 'I was working for someone different back then. But I told Una when I ended up in

London, because things weren't good there. And then there was what happened to Sulien.'

Dama looked him up and down, and then jerked his head at Una, summoning her a short distance across the cobbles.

'It was definitely that way round?' he asked her quietly, '*He* told *you*?'

'Yes.' Of course this was true.

'And you're completely sure about him?'

'Yes,' she said.

Sulien couldn't understand why she, at least, couldn't see what was wrong, no, why anyone couldn't.

Dama came back and asked with unnerving simplicity, 'Are you spies?'

Marcus' eyebrows went up. 'No. But does anyone ever say yes?'

Dama smiled again, but coldly this time. 'No one's ever been a spy,' he said mildly. 'Doesn't hurt to just ask. You can't tell if someone's lying if you don't make them lie.'

It was Marcus he continued to examine, keenly. Sulien, thinking he should draw Dama's attention away from him, made an effort to quell the mounting feeling of nausea. 'You don't think we're lying, do you? We've come all this way.'

'No. Because I know you were a slave. And if you are, Una must be too,' He looked at her and added gravely and courteously, 'I mean, you were once. And you both back up Gnaeus. So.' But he paused, frowning and troubled, trying to understand the feeling that he *was* being lied to. And yet he believed they weren't a threat, they were telling the truth on everything that seemed important.

He turned to Sulien, who was leaning against the fountain, watching the moving water. 'But they're after you, then. They've never been as close as this. They'd given up trying to find us, years ago.'

'I'm sorry,' said Sulien, feeling indeed overcome with regret, as if he'd forgotten that he was not the one the spiral-wings were searching for.

Dama looked at him sadly and compassionately. 'It's all right. You need our help. We planned for something like this. They won't find us. Come on, then.'

He started off. Una went after him at once asking, 'What if you got here and it was the vigiles waiting for you, and they just grabbed you?'

'Like I said. It's never been this bad. They've never known where to look. But if I went out here and didn't come back, that'd be a good warning there was something wrong.' He paused and murmured, 'And it wouldn't do them any good, having me.'

'You can't know that, surely,' said Marcus, attacked again by the idea of Varius in such a situation.

Dama didn't answer.

Sulien felt dizzy, sick.

'What about the villagers, though?' Una asked.

'There aren't many that could help them if they wanted to. It's pretty much just Palben. And he knows what he's doing. Even if he showed them the way we'd see them coming. You'll see.'

Una turned to Sulien now, questioning. He smiled weakly at her, but he wanted not so much to reassure her as to tell her silently – *his hands*.

Her lips parted slightly with dismay. She must have understood.

A little later Dama told them cheerfully that if they had been spies, if they'd been carrying any kind of tracking device, it wouldn't have worked; he carried a machine that blocked signals around it; there were more at the camp. He jerked his head downwards, to indicate the device, a block-shaped bulge in his breast pocket of his thick jacket.

At the gesture, Una glanced at Sulien, who nodded palely. It would have been more natural to tap the device with a finger, but Dama's hands never moved from his sides. And yet he was perhaps the most alarmingly energetic person Sulien had ever seen. Despite the miles he'd walked already he could barely keep still, pacing about impatiently while they collected their bags, and once when they paused to rest.

He led them down the blade of a hill, into the forest again, among tree trunks either slim and white, or coated in bristles of grey-green fur. He guided them for some time in what they gradually realised was a chain of swift, confident circles, through the densest glut of the woods where they could see virtually nothing of the shape of the mountains around them, and where there was no path.

He no longer seemed worried about Marcus, and returned to what proved to be intense curiosity about Sulien and Una, and the escape from the Thames. Marcus could not understand why Una and Sulien were so subdued when Dama listened with such greedy eagerness, growing, as the story came out, excited almost to the point of mania. But even Marcus had noticed by now how Dama's arms hung slackly within his thick sleeves, like knotted ropes, or pennants on a windless day. They were not absolutely inert, apparently, for once or twice he lifted his left hand a little, to push a supple branch out of his way. But the movement was halting, stilted; the wrist seemed almost to creak as it rose, not even reaching the level of the elbow. It looked unnatural, like the contracting of an electrified dead thing.

He kept avidly asking questions: 'I wondered if any of the Thames people might make it here. Only you and those other two left now. You don't know what happened to them? You didn't plan it together? *How did you get out?*'

'My sister,' said Sulien shortly.

Dama, glittering with mingled confusion and awe, regarded Una. 'Are you the one who killed the guards?'

'No!' said Sulien, before Una could speak, recoiling at the sudden memory of another thing he had not had to think of for a while: the body of the soldier, pivoting on the handrail as the thin slave heaved him up, diving impassively into the thick Thames. 'No, we were off the boat by then.'

'But if the guards were alive – how did you open the cells?'

Una told him how she'd swum out to the ferry, but tried to be unclear about how she'd hidden, how she'd got hold of the key. She could not face explaining, she felt equally unnerved by the force of his curiosity, and by the locked doors behind his animation, and by what she now understood must have happened to him.

Dama frowned. 'Why didn't they see you?'

Sulien put in quickly, 'We were lucky.'

Dama stopped moving for a moment and sighed. 'How close did you get?' he asked, quietly now, 'to the crosses?'

Then the trees lashed. Somehow they did not even hear it coming until it was upon them: a spiral-wing that broke out of nowhere and lunged down, grinding so low, so close, that above them a shielding layer of leaves was stripped away in an instant.

At once Una, Sulien and Marcus flinched still, but Dama simply lowered himself to the ground and sat leaning back against a tree, looking upward almost appreciatively. Una watched him; as the sound went on and the spira roamed about, his lips moved softly: he was talking, softly and contemptuously, she realised, to the pilot of the aircraft: 'Idiot. No, wrong way, oh, completely wrong. Have to do better than that. What do you think we are?'

It passed. He rose with a stunted shrug, and remarked with seemingly impartial scorn, 'You'd think they'd learn. They'll need people on the ground if they want to have a hope.' And he led quickly on, not noticing how this unnerved them, asking Sulien, 'So, what had you done?'

'I didn't,' said Sulien.

Dama's face twitched with unmistakable, involuntary disappointment; more, a kind of contempt. Then it altered. 'Oh,' he said, 'the rape.'

'It wasn't rape,' muttered Sulien. That sounded too feeble to stand alone so he added unwillingly, 'It was – almost every night for six weeks.'

Dama absorbed this. 'Bitch!' he exclaimed, after a moment. Sulien shook his head reflexively. Whatever else, Tancorix had surely made no serious effort to save his life, and yet he'd managed so far to avoid thinking much about whether she was a bitch or not, and he didn't want to begin now; he didn't want to think of any of this. After two hours or so they met a river, vitreous and bulging over sleek stones, splitting the mountain into sharp, curved slices like oyster shells. The way into the gorge seemed to be blocked, for a fall of stones had surged down to the water. But Dama skittered up the landslide, surprisingly agile, at one point hooking himself along by nothing but the two smallest fingers of one hand, more often keeping his balance by hurling the weight of his upper body violently back and forth, leaping on before the stones could shift beneath him, his face fiercely happy with effort. They climbed up after him and watched him bounce down to the ground. He stopped and looked up at the trees. 'Wave if you like,' he said. 'They can see you.'

They looked, feeling apprehensive, but could not see the surveillance cameras fixed among the branches. There were pressure pads, too, Dama said, attached to wires beneath the soil, which would set off alarms if anyone found their way, unguided, into the gorge. There was the faintest of paths visible now, scarcely thicker than what deer or badgers might leave, but it let them cut precariously across the hard green flanks of the wet gorge.

'You have longvision, then?' Sulien asked.

'Have to,' said Dama. 'Not that it's a very good one.'

'We haven't seen a longvision in ages,' mentioned Una, carefully offhand. 'Have they found Marcus Novius yet?' She was afraid that turning the conversation this way was dangerous, but she felt they had to know how deep Dama's apparent lack of knowledge about Marcus went, and whether the others in the gorge might share it.

'Oh,' said Dama disgustedly, 'not you too.'

'What?'

'Who cares if they've found him? It's stupid – it's *hysteria*, people getting *obsessed* about someone they've never met. Even here! And yes, it's on longvision all the time. As if one spoilt kid losing the plot was the most important thing in the world. I never watch it. I go out when it comes on.' He sighed and added. 'No, they haven't found him. I don't even want to know that much, but you can't help it. That's not what the longvision's for. It's in case there's ever anything about us, or our people. And so we can know about people like *you*,' he went on warmly, evidently getting over his irritation. 'When things happen – like slaves taking over a prison ferry!' He seemed almost to have forgotten that Una and Sulien had not been involved in that.

Marcus and Una glanced at one another. They knew what to be ready for. Marcus adjusted his hat.

'We get news sheets too, sometimes, from Palben, he's the mechanic you met, he's good. In fact, we get most things through him, food, and equipment – and – and painkillers. The other Vascones just don't really bother to notice us. You see, that's what we needed, when we started this place – it's amazing, isn't it, to be as close as this to Rome, and the people aren't Romans!'

Dama enjoyed explaining all this, evidently – about the alarm system, and that the rockfall was not natural, that the Holzartaeans had built it as a first line of defence. He grinned with undisguised satisfaction at their surprise that the camp was evidently so much more sophisticated and well protected than they had expected.

But Sulien wondered if the others had noticed what was far less obvious than the ruined arms, although it was growing worse the longer they went on walking; a stiffness in the motion of the feet, the roll from heel to toe not smooth but jerky and paddle-like.

Dama said, 'We're here.'

Again they could see nothing. They could almost have thought the camp, the cameras, all of it, only existed in his head. They had come to a right-twisting bend in the gorge and within the turn the slope fell away from beneath them, bell-shaped, obscured with trees and bracken, and then dropped off in a sheer cliff, down to the invisible river.

'There!' said Dama proudly, 'You can't see it, can you?'

He galloped, crablike, down to the edge of the cliff, so precipitously that Sulien could not see how the atrophied arms could hold him back, how his feet could be flexible enough to stop him from rushing over the edge, but he braked somehow, shoving his feet against roots and pitching his weight backwards, and stood waiting for them to follow.

'Look.'

Projecting out of the cliff, invisible until you were almost on top of it, was a girder and beneath it was slung a kind of steel basket which could be raised and lowered from within by a system of pulleys.

Dama stood motionlessly. Finally he said, glowering, 'There are ladders, but I can't use them. Even the lift, I—. You have to help me. I can't get down by myself.'

Sulien asked at last, 'How did you survive?'

Dama stopped as if shot. He stared at Sulien, stiff, eyes accusatory blue-painted pellets, the freckles like a small explosion of shrapnel scars in skin that had turned opaquely white, nothing childlike left.

Very slowly some of the colour came back. 'Oh,' he said, 'You worked for a doctor.'

'I didn't just work for him; he trained me,' said Sulien. 'And there are . . . some things I can do.' He paused, and went on tentatively, 'Let me see.'

Dama seemed to contract. 'No.'

Sulien was reluctant to say, I can help you, because he was afraid that he could not, he could picture the dead nerves lying like cinders, just barely holding their original shape, ready to fall away at a touch. 'Is one hand worse than the other?'

'Shut *up*.' Dama made a little rocking movement; he would have liked to have shoved Sulien back. 'It doesn't matter what it's like. It's never going to get any better. Don't be curious about it. I, I have to accept that this is how it is, forever. Be glad you don't know. I just don't want people *looking* at it.'

Sulien felt ashamed to push further after this, but also

283

that he had to, it was like a command. 'I understand that, but, I—'

This time he must have said something about helping. 'Leave it, *please*,' said Dama, in a low voice, genuinely pleading.

'No, I can't. I'm sorry. Please let me see.'

Dama turned away, paced bitterly and finally muttered abruptly to Marcus and Una, 'Can you go away?'

They retreated a little way along the cliff and Dama turned to Sulien, but shuffled restlessly, and did not look at him.

'How long ago did it happen?' asked Sulien.

'Too long ago for anyone to do anything,' insisted Dama, but then added breathlessly, 'Can you?'

'Perhaps, I don't know.'

'Oh,' whispered Dama unsteadily, 'don't say that.'

Sulien thought he would have to help Dama to get his arms bare, but he said impatiently, 'I can do it.' He plucked angrily and laboriously at his waist, and Sulien saw that the heavy jacket he wore had been altered so that Dama could get it on and off without help. It fastened, in modified Sinoan style, low on the sides, with large pegs pushed loosely through thick loops of wool. Dama picked out the pegs with his two mobile fingers, clumsier, with embarrassment and defiance, than he might normally have been, nudged the cloth with his chin and teeth over the shoulders and shrugged his way, flushing, out of the sleeves. Underneath he wore only a hemmed strip of linen, as a kind of vest. It did not join at the sides and so could be put on by slotting the head through the hole in the centre, without the use of the arms.

The arms dangled, bones in sheaths of skin, and the furrowed hands were grey-skinned and clawlike below the sunflower-shaped scars buttoning each wrist.

Dama did not look at them. He said harshly, 'Can't all be as lucky as you.'

'Or as you,' said Sulien gently and carefully, trying to

make it clear that he knew how great the difference was. 'You're alive.'

Dama screwed his face up irritably. 'Yes, yes, *yes*. Don't think I'm not grateful. Delir – he didn't think, he just – did it.' He paused and said firmly, as an absolute truth, 'I can't ever pay him back.'

Sulien handled the right arm gently and professionally, trying to imply, by a certain tone of voice and businesslike economy of touch – and trying to feel – that he had seen other things just as bad as this. But it was not true, there was nothing as bad as the vandalism done to the intricacy of the ligaments and nerves, the deliberate wreckage left behind.

The two of them kept talking, not only because of Sulien's horrified curiosity, but to keep Dama's mind away from the possibility that something could be done to help.

'Delir saved you? How?'

Dama said flatly, without expression, a recitation of facts. 'It was on the Appian Road. I was on the end of the line. There was an accident further along the road. The soldiers went to deal with it. Delir saw me. He was a merchant going into Rome. I was very young. That's how all this started. He just – he and his friends tried to smash up the bottom of the cross, you know, where the levers are, and they broke the mechanism somehow and got it down. And they lifted me off it and took me away and hid me. Delir had a friend who was a doctor. He had a lot of friends. They got the joints back together. They gave me pills, for pain and stuff.'

The thick nerve that fed the thumb and the first two fingers had been split completely; beyond the macerated patch where the spike had shot through there was nothing left of it but shrunken rags. There was a little life left in the last two fingers, as he had already seen, but the hand was half-full with a thick fuzz of old pain; thin, rigid rods of pain lay alongside the bones of the arms, coiled in the shoulder, under the crooked bindings of tendons and the dying muscle.

'Just pills?' Sulien tried to keep the horror out of his voice.

'Strong pills. They couldn't take me to a hospital,' said Dama. 'They couldn't say I got like this falling downstairs, could they?'

Sulien nodded. 'How long were you up there?' he murmured.

Dama lowered his eyes, allowing himself to see his wrecked flesh. 'Six or seven hours perhaps,' he muttered. Sulien had to swallow and pause in his inspection for a second, but Dama went on, 'I can't remember any of it.'

Sulien only said truthfully, 'Yes, that sometimes happens, after the worst things,' but he could have sighed with relief and gratitude – to Dama for telling him, to the universe and the circuits of the brain for intervening to save Dama to this small extent at least, for offering the next best thing to this hideousness not having happened.

'I know,' Dama said vaguely.

Sulien asked, not, 'What had you done?' but, 'Why did they do it to you?'

Dama looked at the peaked horizon. He announced blankly, 'I killed three people.'

Sulien glanced up from the hand he was examining as a slow, estranged itch crept over his skin. Dama looked back at him, a cold, far-off, forgiving look. Sulien's intact hands had lifted very slightly on his own and Dama thought calmly, now you're wondering what they did. He did not think Sulien would ask him any more, although for the moment Dama felt quite remote and friendly towards him, and would not have minded.

Sulien indeed shrank from the thought of the ravaged hands whole and engaged in killing. And the invisible knife in the dream came back to him first, and then the memory of the real one, the idea of killing the people in Wolf Step; a clear spiteful flash, as if there was a risk he might still find himself doing it. He willed it all out of his head. He told himself that for the moment nothing mattered as much as the demolished arms, not to him. And he thought he'd

found something. Both arms seemed at first equally devastated, the ligaments ripped, the hands dead, but in fact the
left wrist must have been fastened slightly crookedly, or
pulled tauter than the other had been. For the spike had
scraped bone, but somehow slid past the thick nerve, snagging and crushing it, but not severing it altogether. It too
was clogged up with fibrous scar tissue now, but beyond
the mess the blood still flowed and the nerve branched
smoothly into the fingers. Dama's weight, swinging over
to the right, had slowly stretched and torn at the knot of
nerves in the shoulder. But the brutal tension on the right
arm had eased the strain on the other enough to keep the
nerves from shredding apart, stretched and twisted out of
shape as they were. As the cells had tried to heal themselves little buds had formed on the pale nerve-sheaths,
damming them up so that barely a flicker could get past to
work the muscles or carry feeling back up the arm to the
brain, but they were alive. It was too easy for Sulien to
imagine they were under his own skin.

He'd placed a finger lightly over the scar, his other hand
on the shoulder. Dama's thumb, and then his index and
middle fingers, jerked, as if he was beckoning.

Dama jolted in turn with shock. 'How did you do that?'
he demanded. He stared fiercely at his fingers, willing them
to move again. 'I still can't feel anything. How did you do
that?'

'I don't know,' said Sulien, concentrating on the scar on
the nerve.

'They haven't moved since – for four years,' choked
Dama. 'It was a – is it a miracle? But I still can't feel
anything—'

'What?' said Sulien abstractedly. 'You can't move them
because there's a block here – and here – it would take a
while, and I *can't promise you*, but maybe I could clear that
away. You might get some feeling and some movement
back.'

Dama's face was appallingly radiant and desperate. 'And
the right hand—?'

'No,' interrupted Sulien quickly. 'At least, not the fingers, I'm sorry. The nerves here—'

'You could do something about that?'

'No,' repeated Sulien unhappily, 'Not where they've been severed. Nerves heal worse than anything else. It's been too long.'

Dama went on looking at him the same way, wide-eyed, hope and disappointment not distinguishable. He nodded.

'I'll do everything I can,' promised Sulien, feeling that for the moment he wanted to think about almost anything else.

Dama screwed his face up again, in an ambiguous, ardent scowl. He said, 'Thank you.'

From a distance, Marcus and Una could see Dama furiously struggling his way back into his jacket. By now Una had explained what had happened to him. Marcus said, 'Do you think it still hurts?'

Una nodded dumbly. They both felt they wanted to make some violent movement, to thrash their arms about, but they were afraid Dama would see them.

'If I could stop that happening—' began Marcus, and then stopped, grimacing. 'I was thinking of the boy who was crucified in the story. I was thinking if I stopped it, maybe that would lift the Novian curse. That's not why I should do a thing like that, is it?'

'No,' said Una, with instinctive severity, but then added, 'That wouldn't be the only reason why you'd do it. You can't help thinking of something like that. It doesn't make it selfish.'

They tried to look down into the gorge, but still they could see nothing but leaves.

'How long are you – are we going to be here?' asked Una suddenly. 'How would you know that it was safe to go home?'

'I suppose my uncle and everyone would have found out who killed my parents; they would announce it on long-vision,' said Marcus doubtfully, 'Or Varius . . . I suppose Varius would have to come here.'

'But how long do you think that would take?' Of course he had no answer for that. 'Well, what I mean is, when do you decide you'll never hear? And what would you do then?'

Marcus said quietly, 'Then I'd have to go back anyway.'

Una frowned in annoyance and distress. 'But you can't do that.'

'I can't stay away forever. I'd have to go to my uncle. As long as I could make him believe me, I'd be all right.'

'That's just stupid,' she said with the certainty that could sometimes be so crushing. 'That's just what they'll be afraid you'll do. They'll be ready for that.' He didn't reply. Una went on talking rationally, but unusually fast. 'Of course – after a few years, say four years, or two years – that would be one thing. They'll stop worrying about you in the end, it would be easier to get past them. And you'd be older, you'd look different. I can see that *then* – That is what you're thinking, isn't it – that you'd wait two years?'

She knew it was not.

'Well,' he said, 'maybe I won't have to wait, maybe to-morrow—' he broke off, and looked at her for a moment in silence, thinking that in the right light her eyes were almost a blackish red, and that perhaps no one would have thought that could be a beautiful colour. He did not want to say that tomorrow he might find he could go home, because he found he did not want it to be true; but that brought him back to the start of the thing, the guilt: he should not have left Varius, he should not have left Rome.

He said to her with inept heartiness, 'And then, you'd come and see me, you and Sulien? You should see Rome, anyway—'

'Yes,' she said compliantly, because for now he wanted her to. But she thought that she couldn't go to Rome, it would never work that way.

Dama called them. Sulien was still pale and quiet, he muttered to Marcus how they had to help Dama with the lift. Dama stumbled tense and tight-lipped between them, while they half-lifted him down into the steel basket. Like one of the bags, thought Sulien sickly as they threw those in after him.

Dama pointed out a handle that he could not turn, and looked at it ferociously for a moment trembling with frustration and excitement. Una worked it quietly and the cables moved, the lift rocked and began to drop them in slow jerks down the face of the gorge. And after the fourth or the fifth downward jolt they realised suddenly that behind the wet ivy there was no longer wet rock, but wooden planking, and they heard feet run past on some unseen but level, man-made floor, and then, very faintly, some crackly music playing, and beyond it the low hum of a generator.

Shelved against the face of the gorge like a flight of steps, and as tidy and methodical as an office block, were rows of weatherboarded cabins, thirty perhaps in all, supported here and there by steel frames or blocks of concrete, and at the lowest level standing out over the water on stilts, connected by narrow walkways and ladders shallow enough for Dama to climb. The cabins were invisible from above because they were roofed with grass and bracken, and even small trees; and they were still hard to see from dead in front, because of the bindweed and ivy that coated them, and because in places the cabins themselves were painted dark green or the grey of the rock around them. Further up, another of the huts rather stretched the limits of camouflage, for there was a curving, meandering pattern of zigzagging petals around the door and the boxy windows, with a cautious flight of swallows between them, so that it looked almost like a child's play-house, except that the lines had a clarity that was adult, or nearly so, and somehow their precision gave the strong impression of someone with almost nothing else to do. But on one of the lowest walls, someone had lately scrawled a forceful row of Sinoan characters in defiant red.

'WE'RE DOWN HERE!' translated Marcus, hesitantly. Nearby, in Latin painted in a different yellow hand, spiky and neat and not quite fitting for graffiti, was 'ALL ROADS LEAD *FROM* ROME'.

On the far side of the river was another line of older huts, aerials sprouting among the brambles that capped the roofs.

Before the lift had even touched its bed on the reinforced edge of the river, the zigzag door burst open, a girl in a wine-coloured embroidered dress – a city dress, quite wrong for the mountains – ran out, looked at them, and cried fervently, 'Oh, *good!*'

'Lal,' explained Dama inadequately. Sulien waved. Lal was already hurrying along the walkway to get down to them. Then Delir appeared behind her and Dama bounded out of the lift towards him, wanting to tell about Sulien, that soon his arms would be better and everything would be different.

Somehow, having come so far, they had vaguely expected some kind of colossus; someone imposing and charged up with conscious destiny as Leo had been, or at least large and visibly important like Faustus, or even Gabinius. But Delir was a little man, with little hands and feet, a confident small face and a vigorous way of walking, which he had cultivated early on to try and counteract his shortness. But as he came nearer, Una could see that this liveliness was, at least in some measure, fraudulent. His fine black hair was pushed backwards, and it was growing thin and coarse and showed the scalp beneath it. From any distance, with his daintiness of shape and his large, visible smile, he would look youthful and jaunty, and even close up, by sheer will, he could somehow force the same impression. His dark eyes, wide open, seemed almost aware of their own alert brightness, to be manufacturing it deliberately. He even had a sprightly way of wearing the creases on his skin, that said, look, these lines don't really count, they have been caused by smiling. But if his manner slipped for a moment, as it did now, you would see how deep the lines were, and that it was impossible to judge whether he was closer to forty or sixty. When he was alone, even in the sparse seconds between one thing to be done and the next, between one person going out and someone else coming in, his eyes would fall shut, he would lean against anything, the table or a wall, almost comatose, before hoisting himself together and bouncing out again. And now the smile with which he had appeared was vanishing in sad astonishment, and these things were more visible.

Una tried to get something in about Marcus being Gnaeus, a valet from London, but Dama was already speaking loudly and eagerly.

'You remember what happened in London, Delir, the prisoners who took over the boat – well, they were there – and *listen—*'

But Delir plainly was not listening. He brushed past Lal and Dama to gaze dumbfounded at Marcus. 'Oh, God,' he whispered, 'Leo.'

Dama's face crinkled as he looked, with a second's innocent puzzlement, from Delir to Marcus, and then he gave a kind of raw, hiccupping, half-mad laugh. 'Oh, of course. You're Marcus Novius. You said you were a slave, and you're the Emperor's nephew. What in hell are you doing here?'

He took a wavering step towards Marcus, and it was suddenly obvious that he wanted to attack him, but he stopped short about a foot from Marcus as if he had run into a wall, curling his fingers into parodies of fists, lifting his crippled arms the little way they would go. He looked at his hands with a stifled cry of fury, and since he could do nothing else he spat full in Marcus' face. Marcus could do nothing but recoil and stare, wiping his face. Dama shouted, 'You're going to wreck everything! *Do you know how long this took to build?* You brought *them* here, didn't you!' He jerked his head wildly at the sky since his arms would not allow the violent gesture he wanted.

'Dama,' cautioned Delir sternly, but Dama was beyond hearing.

'This isn't *yours!* This isn't *for you!* Why did you ever come here? Get out! Leave us alone!'

THE MAP OF THE WORLD

'Dama,' said Delir firmly, 'That is *enough*.'

Little as he was he had grasped Dama's shoulder fiercely, dragging him backwards a step. Imposed onto Dama's immobile fury, the movement looked almost shocking. Dama trembled with a kind of dumb white heat, and, under the authority of Delir's glare which, for him and at this point, was clearly absolute, he whispered, 'I'm sorry.'

He had said this to Delir. He looked at Marcus as if he might repeat the same thing, but did not.

Lal had risen onto her toes with apparent exhilaration, and now gave an impatient, delighted hop. She said sensibly, though rather more loudly than either Delir or Dama had spoken, 'What if anyone heard all of that?'

And other people had begun to emerge, a Sinoan woman out of the opposite hut with the aerials, three or four men in their twenties or early thirties. Delir nodded at the woman and said, 'We had better go inside.'

As they went with him, not into the cabin with the curlicues, but the one below it, they realised with anxiety that the woman was following them. Inside the hut was very neat, and in a cramped way, almost obsessively comfortable. There were cushioned chairs, and books ranked along a desk and standing in towers on the floor. The shape of Delir's bed was just visible through the plain curtain that divided the room. A map of the world, in three separate sections, took up most of the largest wall, apparently for decoration rather than for use, for it was a beautiful thing, and untouched by pins or the marking of pens.

The woman was perhaps forty, with black hair cropped, slim but not as delicate as Marcus expected Sinoan people to be; she was an inch or so taller than Delir and sculptured-looking, the bones comparatively raw. For Una she wasn't as unreadable as Dama or the Vascones, but nor was she quite transparent; there was a kind of rapid shuttling between languages, words snapping with hasty efficiency back and forward to be translated.

She asked, her Latin perfect but slightly flat-toned, 'What is it, Delir?'

'I'm not altogether sure,' said Delir, and as Marcus shifted restlessly in the seat he'd reluctantly taken, 'It's all right. I don't know why you've come here, but Ziye is quite safe, I promise.'

In the beginning, and even now sometimes, the idea of Holzarta, and then the solidity of it as the cabins went up and stayed up, had fired Delir with excitement and pride. Now from time to time he examined the whole place, and counted the people who had been there, people who might have lived in tatters, or have died, and he thought these are *good* acts, the person that did this is a *good* person. And then instead of pride he felt a kind of prickling, embarrassed anxiety, as if he had somehow given a false impression and made a fool of himself. He *knew* he was not – he just did not *feel* like a good man – or a bad one either, he had never worried about himself in that way. But surely he was not the kind of person who was supposed to be doing this. He liked *things*, and he could not stop missing them. In truth he also liked money, and the healthy currents of it, he had been good at that. Now, if Palben had not provided jars of wine fairly frequently he thought he would not have been able to continue. He might scold Lal about the haircut, and for painting patterns on the hut, and he might worry vaguely about her ancient fashion magazines, but it wasn't fair, he was the one she got it from.

It was because of Lal that now when he looked at the two youths he could not help feeling menaced. The one whose name he did not yet know had dropped with a tired sigh into a chair that was too low for him (not a problem Delir ever had), casting long legs about untidily, then, with sudden self-consciousness, drawing them in so that his knees poked up awkwardly above the level of the seat. Delir could still be amused at his own feeling of doom as he noted the height, the tously brown hair, and what he thought of vaguely as a kind of pointiness about the cheeks; also when he considered Marcus Novius' straight features and glamorous status, and even found himself unworthily resenting the poor boy's aura of tragedy. He was glad that at least there was a young girl with them, sitting stiffly with clasped hands and a blank face, maybe she would be good for Lal. There was a regrettable uniformity about the slaves that made it to Holzarta – they were almost always young men. This had not troubled Delir in any personal way when Lal was thirteen, but it had become much more significant now she was a year older. At the moment she was just managing not to caper with drama and curiosity. It was all very well, all this about virtue (now he felt ashamed for calling it so), but it surely was not a good or virtuous thing to bring up your little girl to be a forger. He had not meant to. It was just that false papers were a necessary part of what they did, and Lal had turned out to be so good with the brushes and tweezers and sheets of plastic.

How had it all happened? Not by accident: if, at the start, on the Appian Road, seeing the young boy on the cross and deciding suddenly that it could not and must not be borne, if he hadn't known quite what he was getting himself into, he had certainly known that he was changing everything. And afterwards, of course, there had been many stages at which he could have stopped. And possibly he did match his idea of what being good should feel like to this extent – that he was completely sure those stages were past, and that he would never stop now as long as there was any need for such a place. And this was although when he was alone, leaning shut-eyed and saturated with gravity against anything, sitting on the floor even, he said always, and sometimes aloud, 'I can't, I *can't*—' Only four years ago, he had almost never been tired, not in this way. It was not that he could not get enough sleep. Of course he was sensible enough to tell himself that no one could do everything, but it was the stories he heard that wore him out, and the endlessness of it, that there was more damage even in this little place, than he could ever put right – there was Dama – let alone everywhere else, on the beautiful map of the world.

Marcus, thinking that Dama seemed to be lurking malevolently behind him, and still doubtful about Ziye and Lal, told Delir indistinctly that he'd had to get out of Rome, someone had tried to kill him, and had killed a woman called Gemella instead.

Delir said, 'I'm sorry. I should never have used your name. It was the shock. I met with Clodia and Leo – when was it? Three months ago.'

'I didn't know,' said Marcus, feeling for the first time a faint hurt that it had been Varius who had told him about Delir, that his parents hadn't trusted him. He added baldly, 'They were murdered, too.'

'I knew it,' exclaimed the woman called Ziye, with the most animation she had so far shown. On learning who Marcus was she had widened her eyes slightly in surprise and interest, but remained quite composed. She had scars, too, shallower, more numerous and more chaotic than Dama's, and yet not scars that could have been caused by any one accident, nor even (for surely she must have been a slave) by simple beating. There were vertical nicks on her chin and at the corner of one eye that must have been done with some sort of blade, a messier, three-cornered mark on her cheek, a splashy crescent on her jaw, where, Sulien judged, she had collided with something blunt and jagged, more than once. But he was sure the wounds had been cleaned and stitched up carefully afterwards, for everything had healed well, without any hard ridges or stretching. Her strong arms were bare from the elbow and showed a few similar blemishes. Unlike Dama, with his long heavy sleeves, she had done nothing to cover her injuries, her tufty hair even seemed calculated to display what hanging locks might almost have concealed. And indeed the scars had not spoiled the handsome austerity of her face, only given it a rather startling cast.

'So did I. Didn't I tell you!' burst out Lal.

Ziye had caught Sulien furtively studying the violent patterns on her skin and stared at him, untroubled, but with raised eyebrows so that he writhed and wanted to explain about his medical training. He began looking at Lal instead, in a series of curvetting, unsatisfying glances thrown in loops around her head: skimming at the upper part of the face – away at the wall – at the lips – at Delir, to show that all this was only in the course of looking around. But it was impossible to get a decent impression this way and he almost wished she would shut her eyes for a while so he could put together what he had seen: skin at once strong brown and pink; black hair in short bright wings (he didn't notice how new the dark blades of it were, although he liked what was the effect of it, the exultant way in which she held her head), black eyebrows large but exact and satiny, her eyes apparently not brown but sandy green. She was not much shorter than her father, but still little, and all the liveliness she had inherited from him was still real. Just as she finished speaking Sulien finally made a mistake and looked at her directly, but, at least, discovered that he was right in suspecting that she was also looking at him. He smiled, and made Lal give a small gulp of startled laughter.

'Yes, we wondered. But I thought it was a kind of – wishful thinking,' said Delir regretfully, having glanced uneasily at Lal. 'I hope you understand. If people like that have to die, one wants not to believe in accidents, it's easier to think at least it meant something—'

'Well, it did,' said Marcus, bleakly.

'Yes, of course, I believe you. And I suppose you have been coming here all this time.' He glanced at Dama and reminded him softly, 'Everyone here had to find somewhere safe.'

'And now it isn't safe. And not everyone has the whole

Empire after them,' said Dama, very quietly, not trusting himself.

'Everyone had someone looking. Especially you and me. And they won't find us with those wings.'

'It is *not the same*. All right, they can't see us. But if it's that *important*, of course they can do it, they can do anything they want. They just have to flood the place with soldiers.'

'They would do that if they wanted to take him home,' said Ziye, 'But that is not how you would kill someone in secret.'

'Calm down, Dama,' urged Delir softly.

Already, Dama was truly trying to do this. But he couldn't stand still: he kept prowling around, to the door and back, in a restive little oval. When Palben had signalled that afternoon about the new slaves he had been so happy, so grateful for something worth doing. And now he couldn't stop his pulse rushing with fury and hope and curiosity, he couldn't calm down. 'There must have been somewhere else you could have gone,' he ventured to Marcus at last, almost apologetically, more quietly even than before.

Delir gave him a complicated look that involved exasperation and compassion and guilt. 'You know we can be out of here before anyone gets close.'

'And *leave* everything?' said Dama, anguished, for he was the one that had planned everything, who had lain awake at night cutting every plank in his head, so the others could dig the real earth and place the real beams.

'I don't see why it should come to that,' Delir assured him smoothly, 'But you're right, we should be very prepared, even more than usual. You were checking the routes out, this morning? Had you finished?'

It was as obvious to Dama as to everybody else that Delir, out of kindness, was offering him a good reason to go away and clear his head. Silent for a moment, Dama sighed to himself, struggling with the odd sourness of gratitude. 'No, I hadn't finished. All right,' he said, and smiled patiently and unconvincingly at Delir. He looked uncertainly at Marcus and said to Una and Sulien, 'I will see you.'

When he was gone Una asked in a small voice, 'Are you sure he won't tell anyone?'

'Yes,' said Delir simply and positively.

'It's just, when we first saw Marcus, we called the vigiles and tried to make a deal. Not just the money, freedom too. I thought someone here might try the same.'

'Not Dama,' insisted Delir. 'And no one else who lives here permanently. But—' He stopped.

'No, *no* one would!' protested Lal.

'I hope not. I think not,' said Delir. 'And it would be difficult to do from here anyway. But once people are away, the risk is then, I think.'

'I want to tell everyone,' said Marcus abruptly, strained. He knew Una wouldn't like this, and he said to her, 'If everyone knew, they wouldn't tell. Because Gabinius and – whoever else, I think they might want to kill anyone who told them about me, wouldn't they?' He turned to Sulien, thinking of what he'd said in Wolf Step, about the amateur slavers. 'Especially if it was an escaped slave, because – they could. Because there wouldn't be anyone left who could complain.'

He wanted his name back, and somehow he badly wanted Una to agree with this, but she said, 'Varius said not to tell anyone except Delir.'

'Varius didn't know how long it would take to get here, or that I'd meet *you*. Six people know already, beside everyone who saw me on the way.'

'It's too many people,' said Una quietly.

'I think it would be better if you tried to just blend in,' agreed Delir.

'But who do you think would tell, who would do that?' Lal harped on, upset. 'Not just to him, but *you*, and all of us? Who are you talking about?'

'Nobody. But with everyone who comes through here, with all the things that happened to them, we can't be sure of what they'd do. I suppose you know how they keep showing your picture? I could restrict use of the longvision – it's dangerous anyway.'

'Oh, someone would work it out if you did that,' scoffed Lal, 'if he says "No, honest, I'm just a slave who happens to look like Marcus Novius," but suddenly no one's allowed to watch longvision! If everything stays normal, it might be all right. And besides if you stopped the longvision everyone would go mad.'

'It's true,' Ziye told Delir. Sulien noticed Lal make an odd little face at this – not exactly bad-humoured, but certainly sardonic.

'Well,' said Delir, 'you've watched the reports as much as anyone, would you have guessed who he was without being told?'

Marcus sat feeling unhappily like an exhibit or an article of evidence, as Ziye looked at him. She shrugged. 'I don't think so. No, I wouldn't have thought about it.'

'I would,' remarked Lal perversely, compounding the growing sense of irritation she had wakened in Una. Una wanted someone to say something reassuring to Marcus; but she could not do it herself, there were too many people there and anyway she couldn't think of anything.

Luckily Delir seemed to feel the same obligation. 'Don't worry. Usually we move people at certain times, when we know that sympathetic people, freed men with farms and so on, even guards working at the ports, are ready to help them. The next shift needn't be for a while.'

Sulien said, 'Yes, and it won't be only you saying you were a slave, there'll be Una and me, too. We'll say you were there in London.'

Marcus nodded. He supposed he must have thought that his reluctance to reach Holzarta would vanish once he was there, as reluctance to, say, go to a party often does. But Dama had put paid to that, at least for the time being. He did not know where he wanted to be.

'And you must not leave the gorge alone,' Delir told him, finally.

Lal announced that she would show them where to sleep

and also that Una ought to share with her. Una smiled prettily and a fraction too long.

Outside, alone as she had wanted to be with Novius and the slaves, and as was not unusual for her, Lal felt her buoyancy suddenly deflate. Oh, they don't like me, she thought despondently. She had been talking too much and doing everything too much, she always did. Thinking this did not make her behave any differently; if anything she talked all the more loudly and hyperbolically and tried even harder to be funny, disliking it, but not knowing what else to do. 'It isn't as appalling as you might think,' she said, far too archly, of the intermittent hot water, and the lavatories that could have smelt worse.

She felt depressed about her clothes. Her mulberry dress probably looked stupid with the thick boots she had to wear, and Delir certainly told her she looked silly, or at least aggravatingly intent on doing nothing useful, when she went tiptoeing around the mud in her little glittery slippers, even though it was he who had somehow got them for her, as a birthday present. And despite having lived in the gorge for almost four years, she did not really have anything else to wear. The clothes she wore to dig up turnips were no different from her thin, brightly coloured dresses, except that they were so wretchedly old and out-grown that she did not care about them any more. She could not conquer her belief that anything with long sleeves must be adequate for bad weather, whatever it was made of. This meant that when she did not look tattily over-dressed she looked almost more poverty-stricken than any of the escaped slaves, and was often cold. She put on the fancy shoes before supper anyway, and then felt hotly conscious of them until her feet were under the table and they were, thankfully, invisible.

Una, Sulien and Marcus found that nothing much was expected of them the first evening. There was a curfew and a blackout, because of the spies in the air, and so they ate very early; in the largest of the huts, at the bottom of the gorge, where they could hear the river purring outside wooden walls papered with business-like notices of evacuation procedures. There were also a few paintings by children, old and rather distressing, showing multicoloured figures smiling orangely as they crept from dark houses, and hid on blue trains.

There were sometimes as many as a hundred people in the gorge; at present there were thirty-nine. Everyone seemed almost aggressively pleased to see them, but in an impersonal way; it was because of the spiral-wings, they wanted to prove they were undefeated. They sat on long benches among what seemed, especially to Una, to be an indistinct mass of youngish men, all at at least five years older than they were. Lactus, Calvus, Celer – Lal boisterously introduced everyone in such a way as it was impossible to see where the names attached; and told Una and Marcus, knowingly and accurately, 'I suppose it's been just the three of you for weeks and now you're spooked by there being so many people. Everyone is at first.'

And it did not always wear off. There was haggard Pyrrha, who had been there four months and still sat or stood like the stump of a cut tree, as though struck into a paralysis of fear and desolation by whatever her dead gaze met; a wall, the food in front of her. She could not finish anything, not even eating or plaiting her long frayed hair which splayed dryly over her scraggy shoulders. She was worse now even than usual, and had been for days, because she did not believe Delir when he said the soldiers would not find them. Delir was generally good at unravelling such knots of horror and shock, but so far no amount of talking to her or sitting silently with her or finding her gentle things to do had noticeably helped. She hardly spoke except to her little peaky daughter, Iris, who had to keep bossing or cajoling her to make her get up or sit down or show any sign of life. Pyrrha only ate at all because Iris prodded and prompted her and said ghastly, parodically grandmotherly things, like 'Come on, I want to see a nice clean plate!' and Pyrrha, will-lessly, lifted the heavy spoon to her mouth. Iris was nine, and preternaturally adult and competent. She washed and tidied things robotically without needing to be told, apparently disturbed by nothing, and seemed to view Pyrrha almost indifferently, as a challenge to which she had to keep rising with ever more heroic patience. You would think the little girl must have chivvied her mother up and down mountains, all the way from Rhaetia; it was hard to see how such a human shred as Pyrrha could have brought herself so far, much less had any strength to see to anyone else. But she had.

'No, no,' explained Lal, monologuing helplessly on, and grinning encouragingly at Pyrrha, 'She was amazing, she just grabbed Iris one day and ran off, and she got half the way in her master's car and she hadn't even driven before. Iris told me about it. It's actually only *now* that's she's like this, I think it's because—' Delir made despairing faces at her until she stopped, although Pyrrha was as apathetic as ever, and Iris only nodded at them coolly.

Una felt a gnawing miserable anger at the sight of them, as well as kind of garbled envy, that Pyrrha had grabbed her daughter and run off, that she'd had the resolve to do that at least, even if she'd never have enough left to do anything else.

Sulien felt a disproportionate pang of unhappiness when he looked at Pyrrha and Iris, and yet did not think directly of his own mother. Yet he was not spooked by the many people in the room, in fact, he felt braced by the embattled cheerfulness and simply relieved that a large group of people was still possible, and life was not all creeping about in secretive twos and threes.

And though Pyrrha was the worst, there were several others who wore, in milder forms, the same stunned look; an angry trace of it hovered over the face of the man beside Sulien, an occasional warp in the expression of reticent confidence that would have been natural to him. He was a year or two past thirty, with soft dark hair, possibly called Calvus – no, Tobias. It turned out he was the one who had written, 'All roads lead *from* Rome', on the outside wall, and seemed now faintly embarrassed about it. 'Childish,' he muttered.

As a slave Tobias had begun by reading endlessly to an illiterate owner who had once been a slave himself, and later performed jobs that should really have been paid for, accounts, or simply acting as a kind of human appointment book. Now he passed people out of the gorge able to read the false papers Lal had made for them, and to write their new false names.

'Oh, I won't stay, I'm sure, not forever,' he said, 'But I don't know where else to be, you know? At least here I know people. When I got out I wanted to *do* something, I wanted to knock doors down and walk into slave quarters and just say, "Well, let's go." I couldn't do that. But if they get out on their own, I can help them *stay* out.'

Sulien looked at Tobias and then off into space, struck by this. He thought of Dama's arms and the dull horrified feeling lifted very slightly. If he helped Dama, and there were bound to be others – it need not be only a sad atoning patching-up; you could see it, he thought confusedly, as *for* something. And afterwards, if, when he and Una were free . . . ? Then, with a calm bright revelatory shock, for it was so obvious, he remembered Leo's and Clodia's clinic. He was excited. But he could not ask Marcus about the slave clinic, because of course Marcus was supposed to be Gnaeus, and to know nothing about it.

Lal had hesitated for a moment about where to sit. She felt pushy and that she ought to leave the strangers alone, felt also that this would be neglectful, and dropped into place next to Una, opposite Sulien and Marcus. Partly because Delir had been making faces she leant across the table and whispered, 'Did you guess about Ziye and my father!'

'No, what, really?' Sulien glanced about. Ziye and Delir were seated at different tables, at different ends of the room. Delir, all deliberative gravity of the earlier conversation apparently gone, was blithely arguing or explaining something, both hands in the air. Ziye was eating quietly with a kind of solid, self-contained stateliness. Neither, so far as he could tell, had so much as glanced at the other.

'They truly think that if they sit apart like that, I won't know,' said Lal.

'Are you sure?' As he was meant to, Sulien felt strongly the unlikelihood of such a pairing, and was not quite sure how he could express it without being rude about one or both of them. 'She's . . . taller than him,' he tried lamely.

'It's not just that. *She can kill people with her bare hands*,' hissed Lal, and then concluded rather sadly, 'Only she doesn't know.'

'*How – why* did she kill people?'

'Well it wasn't as if she wanted to kill people, of course, she had to. She was a gladiatrix, and being Sinoan and fighting like that, and not needing weapons – I mean, she had them sometimes – that was her gimmick. And she got to hate it. And the more she got to hate it the worse she was at doing it, and she knew that sooner or later she wouldn't be good enough and someone would kill her. And of course I can see all that, I can see why you'd hate it, but I wish she'd tell people how you do it, all the same, I mean, it would be a good thing to know. Like Pyrrha, look, maybe if she knew how to kill people, that is, not necessarily kill them, just hurt them, then perhaps she wouldn't be so petrified. It's not as if you'd go around murdering everyone you saw. You'd just know you could. But she won't, Ziye won't.'

Tobias had fallen silent, trying to look politely deaf, and yet was evidently not surprised by any of this. Una and Marcus looked anxiously at each other, not impressed by Lal's powers of secrecy. But Lal referred to Marcus naturally as Gnaeus, and listened credulously to what she knew to be partly lies, when Tobias asked them where they came from and how they had escaped. In fact after a while Sulien realised with surprise that, for the moment, the risk was not Lal at all, but Marcus and Una themselves. Una and Sulien had begun explaining truthfully about London, and how they had been separated. Lal was listening with gratifying absorption but Sulien felt himself drawing inexorably closer to having to tell about the cross, and why he had been heading there, and felt all the bright realisation of a minute ago sinking into an uneasy, contaminated feeling. He did not want to watch Tobias, or Delir, or Lal deciding to believe him – or not.

He muttered that Una had known where he was, and had stolen papers, and he stopped talking. No one had apparently recognised him as Dama had – of course, no one else was as preoccupied with stories about crucifixion, but he knew it would come out, really it would be better to tell it now, but he could not bring himself to do it.

So Una took over, and started explaining how Gnaeus had arrived in the household and had told her about Holzarta. She glossed over the crucifixion as well, although she left a space for it; she said she and Gnaeus had separated while she went to find Sulien, and then met again at Dubris. Marcus, who had been sitting in dejected quiet, began list-lessly concurring with what she said, then adding an occa-sional detail about working in Sina, and suddenly Lal and Sulien noticed with alarm that they were enjoying it far too much. Tobias had asked, of their time as slaves in an implied London home, 'It was bad then?'

'It's always bad, isn't it?' said Una quietly, but then where elaboration, or refusal to speak further should have been, she looked at Marcus and added, 'Wasn't it?'

'Yes, we were – beaten a lot,' said Marcus hurriedly, confounded.

'It was worse for you,' returned Una courteously. 'He noticed you more.'

'Well. They worked you harder. You had to deal with worse things. His bedsheets.'

'He sweated,' hazarded Una.

'Oh, worse than that,' said Marcus recklessly, 'Scratch-ing himself day and night.' Una, shuddering, nodded at the memory of the fictional sheets. Marcus carried on, 'Anyway, I hadn't properly made my mind up to go—'

'You were scared,' Una taunted gently.

'Of course,' said Marcus, 'but then I realised Una was

306

planning something and it seemed—' He deliberated and said softly, 'It seemed like a sign.'

'It was awful when Gnaeus found out. I thought he was a creep. Yes sir, no sir. You seemed so *smug*. Anyway, I wouldn't have thought—'

'What about you?' Marcus was leaning forward now, 'You always made that face – like that, blank – as if butter wouldn't melt in your mouth, as if you weren't even there.' He'd sketched the face he meant, in the air, his fingers unconscious inches from her skin.

'Well, you *did* tell on me, at least once, when the key first went missing – or someone did.'

'I would never have done such a thing,' protested Marcus, with dignity. 'He was a real bastard.'

'Of course he was.'

They were grinning at each other. It was in danger of becoming too obviously a game. For Una was not simply grafting Marcus onto her real past, this wasn't the house in the Lupanarian district. The imaginary household was hellish, of course, which was why they had had to leave it. But they had made it together, like a treehouse, and no real person lived in it but them.

Lal nudged Una quietly under the table, and Una lowered her eyes, suddenly aghast, more so in fact, it seemed to Lal, than was at all necessary.

Una had suddenly remembered that same voice, saying convincingly, 'Yes, she's a deceitful girl.'

Lal and Sulien began talking talking resolutely and nervously about Dama, for he was not there, and not, apparently, because of what had happened by the lift.

Lal said, 'He doesn't let anyone see him eat, I suppose he must have to hunch over to do it – I don't know.'

'Where is he, then?' asked Una, a little shakily.

Dama ate alone, in the monitor room, hating his clumsy hands, watching the screens for murderous shadows, fervently, waiting. But there were no spiral-wings in the air that night, no spies on the paths.

Later, when Lal and Una were inside the patterned hut,

Lal said brightly, 'Right!' as if introducing some new phase of exciting but testing activity, and then said nothing else for a while. Occasionally five people had slept in Lal's hut, but often Holzarta was empty enough for her to have it to herself. The inner walls were planked levelly and the year before, Lal had painted large pictures on them, all of long women in long dresses, spaced at caryatid-like intervals, doing nothing, just standing or perhaps striding, their arms held in angular gestures. They were almost no more than fashion-plate fantasies – and yet they had a kind of stretched, flat elegance like that of Egyptian paintings, with the ceiling resting on their ornamented heads, their long pointed feet weightlessly skimming the floor, and their long secretive eyes.

Blue and crimson as they were, they looked a little ghostly in the near dark. Una and Lal had the electric lantern on only long enough to make up Una's bed, which, when Una dropped flat upon it, felt astonishing; she could not stop her spine and hips and shoulders pressing sceptically against the sheets for the slope and stones that must surely be there within the deceptive padding, like lumps in batter.

She admired Lal's paintings, truthfully though without much feeling to spare on it, and muttered something dutiful about the forging equipment on the desk. Still she slightly adjusted her opinion of the other girl's silliness, for whatever was done with the little brushes and cotton wads would be detailed and difficult. But then again, Lal was brimming over with what seemed to Una absurd curiosity about Sulien.

She would really have been interested in the forging another time, but now she could not relax enough, despite the safe, obliterating softness of the bed.

Lal studied Una's long pale hair in the half-light and shook her head a little to feel her own hair settle pleasantly against her cheeks and neck like many soft paintbrushes, while feeling a minor grief for the amputated black plait lying, slightly creepily, on the desk among her stamps and bottles of ink and solvent, as if she might one day reattach it. 'And it looked so pretty long,' Delir had said sadly, when he had finished hectoring her for going into Athabia at all. 'Oh, it did *not*,' said Lal. 'It had gone all ratty.' She had a faintly proprietary urge to restyle Una and said, 'What straight hair you have, can I try something with it?'

'No,' said Una instinctively.

'All right. I know how you feel, when my hair was long Poppaca and Flora – oh, they've gone now, months ago – they were always twiddling it and it was really annoying. I think when hair gets to a certain length people just can't leave it alone. But now mine's gone I still want something to play with.'

She looked hopefully at Una, while thinking, there's no reason why we should get on, it's like people expecting you to make friends with other six-year-olds just because you happen to be six, and here I am doing it to myself, how *pathetic*.

'Well. I don't normally do anything with it. Just put it up sometimes,' said Una, making a distracted effort to give, at least, a polite imitation of this sort of talk.

'You and Sulien,' said Lal, succumbing to curiosity about him. 'It's odd, you can see you're brother and sister, but it doesn't *feel* as if you look alike, even though really you do. Were you really apart for seven years, or did you only say that because of covering up about Marcus? Because that's awful; it's amazing that you could find him after all that time.'

'I always meant to,' said Una. 'He tried to find me too, only I didn't know.'

'Oh,' said Lal, pleased by the rightness of the reunion, sad for some ghostly Una and Sulien still alone and separate in London. Presently, and more slyly she said, 'And Marcus? Tell me how you really met.'

Una closed her eyes, trapped and nervous and sick. She did not want to talk about Marcus. She told about the flea market in Tolosa. Lal, to Una's temporary relief, got side-tracked by the fortune-telling for a while, amiably intrigued

309

without seeming entirely to believe Una, but she came back to Marcus in the end.

'You know, I think he looks better with his hair messed up,' reflected Lal. 'Better than in the pictures anyway. But it's a pity he has to be blond, none of the other Novii are, are they? Just Clodia Aurelia, and I don't think I like blond hair on men.'

'He's not that blond,' said Una vaguely.

'Oh, well, anyone can see that *you* like it,' Lal teased. 'And to think you nearly got him killed – it's a good thing he doesn't hold grudges, isn't it? Has he kissed you yet?'

'Oh, no,' murmured Una helplessly. She went miserably limp on the bed. As Marcus looked at her, as they smiled at each other across the table – and then, when Lal startled her out of the unaccountably stupid game they'd been playing – she'd seen everything that had seemed light and supple set like rock and encase them, in a shape or pattern; too *much*. Surely it was not just a question of her not seeing it before, although each fine thread of him that had settled on her one by one, little strands of tension and fascination and amusement – they were so harmless in themselves, scarcely anything.

And Lal could somehow see the whole thing at a glance and saw no reason why she should not just say so.

'Oh, no,' echoed Lal, downcast and contrite. 'I'm sorry.' She waited, but Una just lay looking wretched, so at last she invited, very gently, 'So, don't you want him to, then? – don't you feel—?'

'No,' said Una, 'No, it's no good.' And *now* what am I going to do, she wanted to wail, but would not.

'It's all right, you don't have to,' said Lal reasonably, despite being wrung with pity for Marcus. She waited again and asked, 'But why – why not?'

'*Because*—' Una didn't know why she should feel so compelled to give an account of herself to friendly Lal, who was gossipy and so *young*, Una thought, almost forgetting she was only a year older herself. But she did feel it, she felt in the wrong, guilty at least of negligence, and she wouldn't be able to explain it to Marcus.

Her voice had come out as a moan; she checked it and started again, raising herself authoritatively on her elbows. 'Because, look,' she said steadily, 'what would be the point? If things were normal for him we couldn't even meet, and if we did, we couldn't talk to each other. If he were in Rome, he wouldn't feel like this. And Rome is his *real life* and this isn't; this isn't even him. When he gets back there he'll start to be – someone else. It only seems as if we know each other. We don't.'

'Well, I suppose my father and Ziye wouldn't have got together, if they weren't cooped up here.' But Lal did not press this. She did not exactly disapprove of Ziye and Delir's affair, but she did feel there was something a little ridiculous about it.

'But they're staying here,' said Una. 'He's not.' She was silent again, and at last finished bleakly, 'And anyway I just don't, I just can't.'

Lal's impulse was to hug or at least to pat Una, but it struck her that she might not like being touched, not by a stranger anyway, people who came to Holzarta were sometimes like that. And she thought, oh that's what it is, that's why, poor Una.

On the whole, Una felt all the more weakened at Lal's boundless sympathy for Marcus and herself, it was as if they were both the homeless victims of a famine or an earthquake. And yet, to her surprise, she was a little soothed too. 'It's all right, you don't have to,' had been a good thing to say.

Marcus, she was sure, hadn't seen it yet, he hadn't realised how much he wanted from her. 'I suppose,' she said painfully, 'I won't see so much of him anyway, not now we're here.'

Lal did not think this was a very good plan, but could think of nothing else to suggest and so only murmured a lulling assent. Una changed silently into the old nightdress she'd been given, and instead of lying awake worrying about

Marcus, she rolled her clean body over on the soft bed and dropped into willed dreamlessness as suddenly as if she'd found a switch to turn, a trapdoor to fall through.

The next day Una met Dama on the walkway, no longer pale and furious but seemingly delighted with her and with everything else. He told her, 'I saw your brother, and my arm – *already* it's different, how is it possible?'

At the top of each arm below the shoulder, where the muscle had once swelled and now was only a slack string, there was an oval of flesh that had felt as if it simply was not there. He realised now it was one of the few things about his injuries he had come to take for granted, sometimes noticing unfelt and meaningless bruises where he'd knocked against something, without wasting bitterness on them. Now the numb place on the left arm was hazily full of raw shivery feeling, like pins and needles or the fading of nettle-stings. The cloth of his sleeve where it touched seemed to sweep across the grain of the skin, making it fizz, miraculously heavy and abrasive and sore; it was wonderful.

He said, 'Sulien told me about you. You can help us, too. You were meant to come here, I think, both of you.'

'We wouldn't have done if it wasn't for Marcus,' said Una, and suppressed a new flaring of anxiety at his name. She had not seen him yet, she had thought at first that it couldn't begin to seem strange to him so early; but it was beginning to feel strange to her. They had had no choice about seeing each other, before.

Or no, that was not true – all the time in the woods.

Dama seemed to hesitate. 'Well,' he said uncertainly, 'well, yesterday I – I shouldn't have done that – but—' impulsively, he brushed his hooked fingers against her hand. 'I'll show you something.'

It turned out he was taking her to Delir's cabin, which was empty.

'Is this all right?' said Una.

'Yes, yes. It's as much an office as—' He left the sentence

unfinished because it felt like a waste of time; he wanted to explain why he'd brought her here. 'Look.'

'What?'

'The map, a Roman map. Can you see how it's distorted?'

Una looked at the oceans and at Dama, baffled and embarrassed. The three panels of the map were hung at graceful intervals of six inches or so, so that the lines of the land-masses had to reach pitifully towards one another across the wall, and made her imagine the sea pouring away into pale space. Surely that couldn't be what Dama meant, but what else was there?

Dama explained quickly, 'Think of the world and then skinning – peeling it. The shape of the skin couldn't be flat like that, could it? So you can't make a globe into a rectangle without distortion.'

'I didn't know,' said Una, with a kind of angry humbleness, stiffening slightly. She thought, anyone could have worked that out; there's so much I don't know even to *think* about.

Dama glanced at her. 'Why should you know?' he asked, gently impatient. 'Who would have told you? When would you have had time or a reason to think about it? Now, look how they've done it. They've made Europe – and Italy – and *Rome*—' he gave a short gasp of laughter, '*twice* the size they're meant to be. And they've *shrunk* everything else. Everything to the South anyway – Africa's much longer than that. You see? They have from here . . . to here . . .' Here he clenched his teeth in frustration; for he could not point properly, he had to move closer so that his face was inches from the oblong world and step from one edge to the other, fiercely tilting his head at the Empire's limits. 'But even that's not enough, they have to make it look like more. I don't know why Delir—'

Why Delir has such a thing, he would have said, but he stopped himself. After a moment he added, trying to indicate the Pyrenees on the map, 'And we are here, and this isn't theirs.'

'Did you ever see Leo?' asked Una. Dama sighed slightly

and nodded. 'Then, didn't you know . . . you must know what he would have done?'

Dama frowned, thinking. 'I know he talked about abolishing slavery,' he muttered at last. 'When, though? And I saw him. He was part of *that*, whatever he said.' He jutted his chin again at the map. 'I could tell he expected everyone to treat him like – like *God*. Women especially, and slaves. And because he expected it they did. But why should we—' he broke off and amended oddly. 'Not just worship. *Gratitude.*'

Una would have expected him to say, 'Not just gratitude, worship,' but she felt a chime of recognition, remembering with confused guilt what Marcus had done for her in Wolf Step; *how* he had done it. She said, 'But no one else has even tried to make slavery stop. And Marcus—'

Dama interrupted, 'Why do we have to wait for someone like that?'

'It doesn't matter what he was like, at least, what he would have done matters more. And now there's Marcus. You asked why he came here. He had to. *That's* why.'

'But *we* could make it happen,' said Dama eagerly. 'There are so many of us. Remember what you said to me yesterday when I asked if you were slaves? Why do we behave as if we're *weak* when we needn't be, when we *are not*. That *must* be what you want.'

The pure-coloured eyes were fixed on her and made her look back at him: Una said, 'Of course it is.'

'Good,' whispered Dama. 'I knew it.'

They stared together at the map, with the same indignant excitement.

Dama murmured, 'Maybe they will even call him a god, Leo, now he's dead. Like they think they can shrink continents, they think they can make a thing true by saying it. All those cheap gods. Either there's one, or there's nothing at all. Nothing else makes any sense.'

[XIV]

MURDER

The spiras had not come back. If they had known about the village, what was happening now, what were they doing? Marcus needed to think about something else, something that was not the threat against them, or Varius, or Una.

He noticed that he never saw Una alone. There were plenty of reasons for it; though he was not as busy as she seemed to be, there were tasks enough to keep them apart. Cooking, washing, the vegetable plot, the monitors – they did the same things, but almost never at the same time, except when there were so many people around that they could talk only briefly and in lies. He was not to leave the gorge, and so he could not, as she did sometimes, go out to help herd the surreptitious sheep on one of the near hills. And then sometimes she was with Tobias – although why? he thought. She might need time to practise, but she didn't need to be taught how to read.

There was the matter of the Sinoan lessons, too. On the first morning he had gone to Ziye and said in Mandarin, 'Perhaps I could help with the lessons. Only very basic things of course.'

Ziye had smiled at the use of her language, but answered, 'Your accent is nice. Better not to show it, I think. Better not to seem too educated.'

'A slave could have learned something. I said I'd been in Sina, as a valet.'

'All right,' said Ziye, switching back into Latin. 'Help me with the teaching. Perhaps you will be more patient.'

Una came at first and worked so tenaciously at the

pictographs that even if he had had nothing to do himself, they could have talked about nothing but Sinoan. Of course she did. In fact, he liked the sight of her predatory look as she concentrated, occasionally catching her lip in her teeth, because he could have predicted it. But then one day she was not there. She came once more and then never again.

They still met sometimes at meals. 'What happened to learning Mandarin for fun?' he asked her.

'Oh, well,' said Una. 'There's so much else to do. And I don't even know how Latin works properly yet.'

'Come on. You can speak it,' he objected. 'You can read and write.'

'Not well enough. And it's like Sulien said; we're not going to Sina.'

This conversation nagged at the edge of Marcus' mind for days. It was not *right* for her, as the dogged expression in the Sinoan classes was right. You're not like that, he told the spectre of her that went with him everywhere now, whether he liked it or not, starting arguments with him while he taught Iris the syllables that meant 'My name is Iris,' hanging against him as unobtrusive and persistent as the touch of clothes. When had she ever been so casual about something she couldn't do? And to be suddenly as certain as Sulien that there would never be any need to go to Sina – she'd never before seemed happy to count on the money and freedom Marcus had promised: why had that changed *now*, when they were, they might be, under siege? And so sometimes he did wonder doubtfully if she could be avoiding him deliberately. Why shouldn't I get bored of Mandarin like anyone else? the ghost-Una demanded. He had a certain idea of her – there was no reason she should do anything to match it.

Sometimes – and there seemed to be no motive of work or study for it – she was with Dama.

Every day he expected it to come to an end, he *had* to see her. But he felt it like a slow, acid impatience, it ate away imperceptibly, married itself to the unfolding feeling that everything was wrong, he shouldn't be there. He couldn't see what had happened, until the morning he heard her clattering above and past him on the high walkway, as he was about to enter Ziye's hut. As he turned and saw her she stopped in mid-stride as if she'd run to the end of an unfelt tether, and looked down. An oddly stricken look.

'Delir heard from Palben; there's a new slave in the village. I'm going too,' she said, and then ran on.

'Please be careful,' he called after her.

He saw Dama was already waiting for her in the lift.

Delir, coming to the door to watch Una and Dama rise out of sight, smiled at Marcus without noticing the boy's expression as he ducked away into Ziye's cabin. He, Delir, could feel coming on the sense of guilty release he felt whenever Dama was out of the gorge. He didn't want anything to do with the feeling. He loved Dama, because of Holzarta, because someone *had to*. And yet he was like a moving bloodstain – like what he was, the evidence of a crime. But Delir couldn't understand why he felt as if it were his own crime, as if he'd murdered Dama or had been the one to mutilate him, not as if he'd saved his life.

Delir had not thought of anything except what he was doing, that day on the Appian Road. But he believed that the religion that he did not think of for days at a time, lying stored in his nerves, had insidiously manoeuvred him into saving Dama, and into everything that had followed. And he also believed that he would have done it all anyway. When he noticed the contradiction it didn't bother him.

But, charging up the slope, battering foolishly at the foot of the cross, shouting, 'Come on! Idiots!' at his startled colleagues, he hadn't thought of what Dama would do afterwards. There was no time at first, and then, in the early desperate weeks while they had to keep moving the boy from one friend's house to another, Delir leaning hard on poor Polybius (whatever had happened to him?) to keep up the drugs that stopped the wounds from putrefying, when it had seemed likely that all Delir had done was give Dama the chance to die half out of his mind on a cushion of opiates. When the holes had finally begun to close up and it turned out that Dama would live as the parting gift of the remarkable physical strength that had been ripped out of him, Delir, still not knowing how long the pain would last, began to realise that there was nowhere on earth for Dama to go, no slot to which he could be returned even if he could have crawled back towards it, across the impossible distance he'd been flung from normal life. At this point he could not move his arms at all without agony, or walk. And yet it was not only those hours on the cross, which thank God he could not remember, there were the years before that. By now Delir knew what Dama had done.

Delir had never had any interest in converting anyone, but Dama would have latched onto anything and Delir's religious inheritance was the first thing handy. Delir remembered how fiercely babies clutch at a finger however lightly it is brushed against their palm; how touched (like all parents) he and his wife had been by that in Lal, because it seemed so trusting. Watching Dama trying to get through the seconds without screaming, he thought of the reflex as a wired-in, despairing stubbornness, a permanent fear and readiness for being abandoned above a fatal drop. It had nothing to do with trust. And he felt the same urgency as Dama, there had to be a rope, a branch to hang from, *some* comfort, *something*. He had not seen his own religion in that light before, it was just there, like an inherited house; but he felt he could, hypocritically, have pushed Dama towards anything that would promise to help, even if he himself had believed in nothing at all.

He still couldn't see what else he could have done. But somehow he did not like to think of it. The same uneasiness contaminated the memory of the whole rescue, and felt something like regret. He couldn't approach this feeling without being appalled. There could be no sense in which it would have been better to let Dama die like that. Could there really be any part of him that thought that arms that would not rise above a certain point made a person unfit to live? The idea was so disgusting that he shied away from it into paralysis and so could never get near the truth; which was that he felt as if pulling down the crucifix had been a promise that hadn't been and couldn't be properly fulfilled. And Dama's gratitude stretched on endlessly anyway, neither of them could ever get out of it. Delir thought, sometimes, he must as good as hate me. He knew Dama would do more or less anything he said, and he had not in fact done anything to discourage that, because if he felt that someone had to care for Dama, he felt also that someone had to keep him under control.

He felt as answerable for Dama as if he'd made him, or resurrected him in a ham-fisted hurry and set him on his injured feet, botched and unfinished, and said, well then, get on with it.

Dama would be away for most of the day perhaps. Delir sighed as the guilt about him intensified before the relief won out. Still, he had to decide what he was going to do.

That morning he'd asked Dama casually, 'Do you happen to know why they were going to execute that boy?' Instinctively, he had avoided the word 'crucify' and Dama, in fact, had noticed the suppressing impulse both with affection and impatience. Oh, just *say* it, he thought, what harm do you think that will do?

But, with complete confidence in Sulien's innocence, he answered Delir's question.

Sulien, in fact, had something of the same feeling about Dama. There was no surgery that could have done anything for him, no knife could have found the numerous little lesions without lacerating the stretched nerves even further, before it ever came to trying to unpick the snags and scars. Standing over Dama each morning in silence, trying to correct and start again and accelerate what the body had already tried to do, Sulien felt far more acutely than usual the physician's desire to prevaricate, not to raise hopes, not to be pinned down. But sensation was bubbling hotly back into Dama's clawed fingers and slowly loosening them. He could extend both arms further than before, and

319

even raise the left hand to the level of his face for a few trembling, elated seconds at a time.

But soon there would be nothing more Sulien could do. The muscles would grow in strength with time and exercise, but Dama was right-handed, and the right thumb and first fingers still curled stiffly and would not move, as if simply perpetually cold. For now at least, Dama was so ecstatic at every new advance that he seemed less bothered about this than Sulien was, although Sulien worried that he didn't fully understand that the hand would not improve. But though Sulien was exhausted after these sessions, while he worked he was excited, caught up in it.

Afterwards he would go and lie on Lal's floor on the pretext of looking for Una.

'Do you like it here?' he asked.

'It's good in summer. There are beautiful places. There can be thousands of flowers. It's a pity you weren't here then . . .' Oh, God, she thought, cringing, suddenly hearing these sentences as dripping with over-eager charm.

'And what we do here is *good*, of course I want to do it. I like forging,' she said hurriedly, feeling on safer ground here, not seeing the danger of babbling until it was too late. 'It's *artistic*. It was more interesting to begin with really, although more boring, too, I spent weeks just staining paper blue and yellow – and you have to throw so much away. But I have a lot of the right paper now. And then you have to think about things like how will the colours age? I needed this particular red, and I made it, but after a few months it changes to pink. And obviously that's no good. Of course it's better if you start with a real one rather than making one from scratch, because of the numbers apart from anything else, none of mine would stand up if anyone went and looked them up properly. And these days we have some real ones – the Vascones sold us some since they hardly use them. But it's a bit mechanical just changing the pictures.'

'Show me.'

'All right,' she said briskly.

She sat down at her desk and showed him how she could wipe out a name or date, leaving the paper intact for a new one, and the stamps she'd chiselled out. She felt a morbid dread of knocking over a bottle of solvent, making a mess, ruining her materials and giving herself away. And so she worked more slowly and cautiously than she usually would have done, unsmiling, without looking at him through the whole process. The effect, briefly, was mildly unfriendly. She was trying to counteract what she thought she had done by saying she wished he'd been there to see the flowers. She thought, looking at herself as if from outside, she would have known at once how such a person felt, that she was pitifully, embarrassingly transparent.

In fact there were moments when Sulien was pleasurably confident about Lal, generally when she was not there or at the beginning of conversations. But not all the time. Feeling both ashamed and justified, he had asked Una if Lal liked him.

'I'm sure you'll find out,' said Una, infuriatingly.

'Yes, but does she?'

'Are you blind?' said Una, who felt with mingled amusement and annoyance that she had to either leave them alone whenever Sulien came round or sit there as an involuntary chaperone. She thought, unreasonably it seemed to Sulien, that it would be unfair to tell him anything else. Still, on the whole he was encouraged. But he thought at such moments as this, taking them at face value, that Lal must be changing her mind about him. He didn't understand how nervous she was because what was there to be nervous about?

'That's brilliant,' he said, when she handed him a blue document, less than half-finished, but in the details already indistinguishable from the real thing. 'Could you make money like that? That would be even better.'

Lal grinned, amused out of the worry about the bottles.

'It wouldn't be a good return on the time it would take. And there wouldn't be anywhere much to spend it. My father used to travel everywhere once, I went with him

321

sometimes. But now, when I would *appreciate* it, I'm not even supposed to go into the village. I wish I could see theatres and – and *shops* and things. Is there anything wrong with that, do you think?'

'Why should there be?'

'Dama thinks there is. Especially Rome. I think he thinks you can't go there, almost that you can't even think about it, without,' she frowned, considering, 'without its rubbing off on you. Without condoning what it does. Maybe you can't. But have you ever been there? I wish I could, for a week or a day even, just to see what it's like. There must be things going on . . .'

Sulien lifted the half-finished paper she'd made. 'You could make yourself one of these and go.'

'On my own?' she said.

He could have said, 'With me,' but it would have been too much. He could have told her about London, too, she would have liked to hear about the parks and the races, perhaps. But not just yet, he thought again. He was relieved that she hadn't asked.

'No, I can't. But look, I have made papers,' she said, pulling them out of a drawer. He scrambled closer to look, kneeling on the floor beside her chair. The picture was hers but not the name. 'They took my father's citizenship when this all started, when they knew he'd rescued Dama and he disappeared. We're not really anything now.'

He considered and rejected things to say: You're in good company; Nor are we; or It doesn't matter. Not only out of opportunism, he laid his hand on her knee, lightly enough to be interpreted as entirely or mostly consoling, if necessary.

Lal began, out of her helpless inability to leave silences unfilled, because they were staring at each other and not talking, 'And no one stays here – of course there's Ziye and Tobias and – but there's no one I can—'

She felt ashamed of such plaintiveness. She found before she could finish whatever idiotic thing it was she was saying, that his face was rising up towards hers. She put her hand on his shoulder, she was not sure for what. She had to droop her head over his to kiss him.

On the day Una went with Dama to meet the new slave, Sulien had decided, not exactly that he would certainly tell Lal about Tancorix and the cross, but that he would not avoid another opening to do so.

Marcus knew, Una knew. Otherwise they did not tell anyone but nor did they make any special effort to be secretive. They simply walked out past the huts, up the hill, heading for the blind spots of the cameras. But almost at once it began raining so uproariously that they turned back, and Lal said, 'That's another thing about this place.' The trees rattled, the slight path cascaded over their feet. They were cold and at serious risk of falling over, and exaggerated both these things, hanging onto each other as they staggered through the brown water.

They were talking, to begin with, about Marcus; Lal had asked vaguely if he was all right.

'I don't know. No, maybe he's not. He's worried about his friend Varius.'

'Of course he isn't only worried about his friend, it's to do with your sister, too,' remarked Lal.

'What?' said Sulien.

'Nothing!' she cried. Afterwards she had to realise guiltily that she had spoken, yes, spontaneously, yes, because it was hard to stop herself, but also out of amoral curiosity to see if he already knew.

'But what—?'

'No, it was something stupid that I thought that I'm completely wrong about! No, it doesn't matter! Let's talk about – yes, tell me properly about how you came here, you've never done that.'

And this sidetracked Sulien more effectively than she could have hoped. He began undecidedly, 'Well, really we met Marcus in Tolosa—'

'I know, Una told me. Before that. What's London like?'

'Dirty – and beautiful.'

'Would you go back?'

Sulien foresaw a kind of ambling guided tour of amusing impressions of London, leading with awful gradualness toward Catavignus' house; the boat on the Thames. He said abruptly, sounding strangled, 'I don't know – I was going to be – crucified.'

'Oh,' she said, horrified. After a second of shocked staring she caught at his wrist in the protective way he did himself, then, fast, lifted it to her mouth and kissed it, on the inside, at the twist of veins. Somehow this flicked through Sulien more sharply than any of their kisses on the lips so far, any of them until this next one. He pulled at her unclearly, their feet skidded together, they rocked, off balance, not caring. She kissed him back, just as eagerly at first, and didn't break away until the proper time, but after a moment he felt her change position against him, her arms round his neck hanging there mechanically, her body not exactly either stiff or slack but somehow apprehensive. They came apart.

'Why?' she asked cautiously.

'Right,' said Sulien, steeling himself. He had not practised this but he had determined that if it came to telling he would do it as quickly and starkly as possible. 'All right. The man I worked for had a daughter. In the summer she finished school and came home. And we started sleeping together.' This was one of the difficult junctions in the story. He was certain he had done nothing wrong; perhaps he had been stupid; but the whole time was now so garish with embarrassment and horror that it was hard to keep the two things distinct. He flushed but got past it successfully. He could not allow her to form any picture of the lights coming on and the screaming. 'Her parents found out. One of them, the girl, or her mother, one of them said—' this was the second hard part, and it was worse; he had to break off, look away from her and mutter very quickly. 'One of them said I forced her. That was why.'

'Oh,' said Lal again. She felt young and foolish. 'That's terrible,' she added.

'Do you believe me?'

324

'Of course,' she said at once. He felt that she *would* say that, he had his arms round her still, a kind of skewed face-saving politeness would drive her to it. Still, he could see that she was telling the truth; she did believe him. But it was belief, or faith, or trust; and if he'd said, 'Do you *know for certain* that I'm not guilty of this?' there would have been a longer pause before she said, politely, yes.

The rain did not strike until Una and Dama were almost at the village. The walk had gone quickly because they were talking all the time, in an animated, unfocused way, about the possibility of war with Nionia, about the ways things should be changed.

And he told her about the sect, explaining discontentedly, 'Delir thinks it'll die out altogether in the end – but he must know it *can't*, how can it if it's true?'

'Why would it die out?'

'Because it doesn't accept new people, at least, it's not meant to. You're supposed to be born into it. From *both* parents. But it could hardly have been like that to begin with. I think it's because of Rome. A price for being left alone, you see. To control it. It's similar for the Jews. It's almost like a quarantine. There were other sects that disappeared. There were other prophets. Mani. Jesus. Rome knows what it's doing, it goes for things that challenge it, and this does; stupid little gods don't worry them.'

'Sulien told me Zoroastrians worship fire, but . . .'

'No. But fire is a symbol. If there was a temple here, there should be a flame kept burning all the time. That's all. Well, they do the same in Rome. For Vesta.' He was smiling a little, scornfully.

'What would you be doing it for?'

Dama hesitated, and muttered slowly in a soft, rhythmic voice, so she knew it was a quotation from scripture: ' "Lord of lords, king of kings, watchful, eternal, creator of the universe, giver of daily bread." '

After a silence she asked tentatively, 'But if they don't accept new people, you . . . you wouldn't be meant to . . . ?'

'No. But no one can really help what they come to believe,' said Dama.

They saw the new slave sitting huddled inside the caupona, leaning against the window and fearfully watching the old men as they drank. Una rapped on the glass, making him jump and stare palely at them before creeping out.

He was mild and thin and in pain. His hands shook, he coughed harshly and whispered, 'Are you really from Holzarta? I don't know how I got here – I don't know how I had the nerve.'

'What's your name?'

'Tasius.' He wheezed, pressing his ribs, a scraping, inward sound, '*haaah*,' like pebbles sucking down a beach. 'I came from— *haaah*—' the effortful sound again, 'from Sicily.' He gave a sickly, watery-eyed smile. 'No point— getting out— was there— it's done for me anyway— it's getting worse—'

'You'll be fine,' said Dama brusquely. 'We've got someone who can sort you out. What did you do in Sicily?'

'The— sulphur mines. Ten years I think. It was the dust— *haaah*— you breathe it in— and you can't ever breathe it out. Getting worse all this year. I thought at least I'd find out – if that was it, or if I had any chance. But the dust— *haaah*— it's still in there, it feels like— it goes on getting worse— even in the open air.'

'You're going to be fine,' repeated Dama, who was rigid with vicarious rage.

At first Una saw only that Tasius was indeed nervous, which was natural. Then that he was very aware of something in his bag, something sewn into his clothes. Then that his nervousness was both less and more than it should have been, he had come all this way, he said, but there was no real relief in him; and nor was he exactly afraid – of them, or of the Vascones, or that the vigiles were after him, or of his illness. What he felt was something she recognised. He was watching for any sign that he was not producing the right impression in them; he was doing everything he could to be convincing.

'Bless you for saying so,' he whispered.

'Are you a spy?' said Dama suddenly, as he had before.

'What?' panted Tasius. 'No. Why, why do you think there are spies coming?'

But the thing, coin-sized on the back of his neck, stitched under his collar, was a tracking device. There was a bundle of thin poisoned needles disguised in the padding of his bag. There was nothing wrong with his lungs.

Una stood still, not lifting her eyes from him; she would not shiver. But the little instrument under his collar must be mouthing to someone, something; perhaps as little as a mile away, perhaps less. The black brick of wires that Dama carried should have gagged it; but they'd come so close to Marcus. She had a precise vision – *his* vision – of darkness, Marcus asleep, one of those needles calmly entering his skin. She whitened it out. Whatever else, that was not going to happen.

'Is it close?' said frail Tasius, pressing his side.

'No,' said Una. 'No, it's a long way.' If Dama had been Sulien, or Marcus or anyone else, she would have known without looking if he had understood this. And she didn't know, and she must not look.

'But you came—?'

'Oh, not from there!' she tried to smile at the notion. 'Can't *walk* from there!'

For a moment she was not sure how she was going to explain this, but then Dama said, his voice only slightly tightened, 'We've been in Osaskia for a while, we just come past the pick-up points every now and then.'

He had seen that Una needed help; of course she didn't know the names of nearby villages. But he did not dare say more. He was not a practised liar, and he was furious.

Una was desperate to talk to him alone. 'You'd better not stand in the rain,' she advised Tasius kindly, hastily. 'We've got to talk to a few people. Have you eaten anything?'

There was not much he could do except let her hustle him benevolently back into the caupona, and have Dama speak Euskara to the landlady to get him some bread and soup. She drew Dama rapidly out of the door, and they walked in silence until they reached the fountain at the centre of the village.

Una did not realise until Dama began to speak just how angry he was, and it was strange for her, to walk along beside such kettle-like rage and not feel it.

'Bastard,' he said through his teeth. 'Scum. How dare he think up something like that. How dare he come here and pretend he's had his whole life wrecked. God, he must think he's so clever, breathing like that and everything. He must have practised. Think, he said it because he knows *those things happen*, and he doesn't care.' He swallowed, cross with himself now for ranting, though it was hard to stop, he was so disgusted. 'Does he have weapons?'

'Yes.'

'A gun?'

'I don't think so.'

'That's something,' said Dama. But then, flatly, 'That'll mean he doesn't need one. They'd send someone who knew what he was doing. They'll have got him out of the army, he'll be trained. Does that seem right?'

Una nodded.

'Then he'll be all right with a knife, or nothing at all.'

He paced crookedly to the fountain and back. He said curtly, 'I've got a knife with me, too.'

Una said nothing.

'We'll get him into the woods. He won't be expecting it, at least. I don't see that we've got any choice.'

Una muttered, 'You can't do it. Your arms.'

'No,' said Dama at once. 'I'm sorry.' He turned away again, testing his arms, looking at the numb fingers of his right hand with a revival of hatred unfelt since Sulien had come to the gorge. 'I'm sorry,' he said again, softly. 'I don't want you to have to do it, either. I don't *want* you anywhere near him.'

Una did not altogether understand the strength of her own reluctance. Shut in the stairwell in the Wolf Step caupona she'd been frightened by what she could have done if her hands were free, at the feeling that she'd been right all along about herself, she would stop at nothing. And she could still feel it, touch-and-recoil, as if she'd carelessly put her hand on a lit stove. But now she just stood, staring at Dama, calm but immobilised, cut away.

Perhaps she still felt a kind of pity for the fictionally dying man. For it was not merely that she did not want to do it herself, she did not want it done at all.

Then at last she said clearly, 'He hasn't done anything yet.'

Dama gave a little restless sigh. 'Would you rather let him do something?'

'Of course not.'

'Una. It's hard, but you don't have to feel guilty about him. He's the one who should do that. He's forced our hand, he didn't have to come here. It's reasonable that we should defend ourselves.'

'Marcus,' said Una with the same detached dullness. 'It's Marcus he's come for.'

If the image of the sharp point approaching Marcus had been real; if Tasius had come anywhere near making it come true; and she'd been there to see it and there was, beyond doubt, nothing else to do – that would be another thing. She'd thought; he was so close – but still it was a closeness measured in miles, not inches, not in the reaching out of a hand.

Dama made an impatient sound again. 'Well,' he said, 'it comes to the same thing. Anyway, he's something that should not be in the world. You, you better than me, you know what he's like.'

'Yes.'

'Then,' said Dama again, 'we don't have any choice, do we?'

'Yes.'

Although she had, at the moment of saying this, no clear idea what else to do. They stood wordlessly again. What she didn't want to kill was the warm body eating and drinking in the caupona, now, now, now, innocent between history and intention, innocent even of the mind inside it.

She saw Palben's garage and said impulsively, 'We could borrow Palben's car.'

'Why? Can you even drive?'

She shook her head, humiliated 'What about you?'

'I could before,' he said bitterly.

'And now?'

He was silent, experimentally stretching his arms forward, pulling them back.

'Even if I could—' he began slowly.

'We could get him away. We could take him as far as we can and just leave him somewhere, what could he do then?'

Dama said, 'Even if I could, is it likely? If someone had to drive, why would Delir send someone whose arms hardly work?'

'But when I met you, *I* didn't see what was wrong at first, and now you're so much better,' pleaded Una. 'He doesn't have to notice.'

'No . . .' murmured Dama, suddenly oddly abstracted. 'He might not.' But he frowned. 'It means getting into a box with a killer.'

'I know,' said Una. 'But he's here. That much we don't have a choice about.'

Part of it was simply fear for her.

Just get this over with, Marcus kept telling himself. He was in Ziye's cabin, holding up flashcards. Just don't think about it for now. But even if he didn't, what would happen later?

She didn't know what was out there, anything could happen. He didn't want to think at all, he wanted to go after her. Well, you *could*, he thought. Why don't you? And every sensible warning that answered back seemed both cowardly and stupidly irrelevant. He realised for the first time that lately when he thought in conversations, as he often did, the other voice was no longer any version of his own, or of one of his parents, as it had been. It was not that he was always sure what she would have said, it was just that everything sounded and looked and felt like her. Of course the voice had to be Una's too.

Ziye was terrorising sullen Tiro, who had not looked at the sheets of symbols she'd written out for him between one lesson and the next. When she'd said that she was not patient, Marcus hadn't believed her. She was always so self-possessed. Then he'd been shocked by the glacial rages she could work herself up into, and the state of absolute petrifaction to which her victims were reduced. Tiro, twenty-five and hulkingly large, shifted hunch-shouldered, and stared, white-lipped, at the floor.

'Go on. Tell me what the problem is!' hissed Ziye. 'Why have you come here? Can't you speak even your own language?' She stood and waited for answers. Turning rhetorical questions into apparently real ones was one of her ways of extending pain.

But Marcus knew by now that he'd been right about her in the first place. After twenty years in arenas it was hardly surprising that she'd learnt how to fake anger, even sadism; while all quick spontaneous fury had been worn out of her. Now, if it was at all possible, she would scare Tiro into possessing saleable skills, for his own good. And she was careful. Even though she was not so compassionate of Pyrrha's catatonic horror as Delir was, she never turned her corrosive tactics onto such brittle people.

Pyrrha came because Iris led her in by the hand, put the papers in front of her and sometimes succeeded in getting her to copy out a pictograph, mimic a sound. But Iris was alone today, Pyrrha was ill.

Mother. Teacher. Cat. Dog. Marcus was in loose charge of the children. The flashcards were for Iris; the three others, Crispin and Felix and Marina, were children of Marinus and Helena, who looked after the camp's food. They had lived there so long that though they were younger than Iris they were far ahead of her, and Marcus had them laboriously translating a story involving a dog, a cat, a mother and a teacher.

'What's the point,' muttered Tiro finally. 'I can't teach

331

Latin, I can't teach anything. I don't know Sina. How could I do anything there?'

'*How indeed* could you do anything there if you make no effort . . . ?' recommended Ziye, for his own good.

Marcus had been dealing the flashcards mechanically. They grated on him somehow. He tried to concentrate, seriously, on Iris' education. Everything that distracted from Una irritated him and everything that distracted was necessary. He went back and forth, helplessly, deafeningly, like the clapper of a bell.

He put the cards down and said abruptly, '*Shi* can mean teacher or corpse or louse.'

This was probably not a very useful thing to tell Iris. She was nine. He was doing an unconscious impression of one of his tutors. 'Or poetry, or wet,' he went on.

'Why?'

'Because it used to have different tones for different meanings, like other words you've learned, like *ma*, but now all the meanings take the level tone: *shi*.'

'Why doesn't it do the tones now?'

'I don't know,' said Marcus untruthfully. He was already drifting away from compound words to watch Una run past on the walkway towards Dama – and further back, the first time he'd seen her. He said with an effort, 'Now you have to add another word, like *zhang*—'

'What are you doing here, Marcus Novius Faustus?' asked Iris.

Marcus surfaced slowly through layer upon turbulent layer of Una to look at Iris in disbelief. She had spoken quietly enough not to be heard under Ziye's crisp tirade and was staring at him coolly.

He was just not prepared, he was caught short. Worse, disastrously even, he felt blood heating his face. He tried to remember how this was done. He smiled. 'You think I look like Marcus Novius, do you?'

Iris gazed at him seriously. 'Very, *very* like,' she said.

'Well. It almost seems a shame I'm not,' tried Marcus. 'It

332

would be more exciting. I've never even been to Rome, I'm afraid.'

Iris screwed up her little face, considering this, and dismissed it. 'I saw you on longvision. People are very worried about you,' she said reprovingly. 'I don't think you should be here. I think you ought to go home.'

He didn't see how to decide between trying to persuade her not to tell anyone and pressing on with pretending she was wrong.

'I haven't got anywhere else to go, Iris,' he said firmly. 'Just like you.'

Tasius' laboured, well-acted, agonised breaths set their teeth on edge. Una felt she could almost have given up the whole thing, cried out, 'Look, we know you're a spy, now what are you going to do?' just to get him to stop. He made her chest hurt, she had to stifle little involuntary copycat coughs.

He was lying crumpled beside her on the seat, his eyes shut, but she knew he was watching them furtively from under his pale lashes, glancing often at the mountains as they moved past. Sometimes his head even fell weakly against her shoulder. She tried to keep her body relaxed, not to suck in her breath.

Dama was rawly aware of how close Tasius was to Una. He eased the car out of the village, feeling at once the *weight* of it, the pull on the muscles of his arms. To make the machine move at all was more than he could have hoped for, and he felt both fierce, thankful pleasure at it and something else. He could not grasp the right lever properly, he could move it only by leaning the heel of his hand down hard upon it and tugging back. He should not be like this, he should not have to be glad about such small things.

They crawled away from Athabia down the potholed track, curved through the woods, then up the bare mountain into the thin snow.

'Somehow I got the idea it was nearer,' rasped Tasius.

The first quiver ran up Dama's right arm. Casually he lifted his hand from the control stick, flexed it gingerly, put it back.

'It's safer like this,' said Dama shortly.

'Tell us how you escaped,' exclaimed Una, to keep him busy.

'Too— *haaah*— tired. Sorry,' Tasius whispered.

On the further side of the mountains the wrinkled snow faded, the beeches gave way to dry pines. They drove on into the rain shadow, where there was a faint warmth in the air and the land changed fast. Here it was emptier even than the lopsided peaks around Athabia, or seemed so because they could see further, across endless regular dunes of brownish trees, miles of them, silent. The puny road sank among them as if into an old bed. Yet as the car sloped down it they saw how the layers of earth had been twisted and buckled and broken off as the mountains formed, and now pointed upwards rhythmically like many razor-sharp walls marking out line after paranoid line of territory, like harsh hands poised to clap.

Tasius tensed slightly. 'We're going into Spain?'

'Yes,' said Dama, tight-lipped.

Did Tasius (the name felt truthful to Una – and after all, why not use his real name? How could anyone from Holzarta possibly recognise it?) – did he guess that they knew? Not precisely, not yet. But something felt wrong to him. Perhaps it was only that the journey was so much longer than he'd expected; but he had been a good soldier, he neither dismissed the feeling nor let it goad him up into panic; he examined it. Una could feel him replaying the meeting in Athabia, assessing what he'd said, if anything there could be a plausible reason for their suspecting him. He thought about the sulphur mines of Sicily – could he have said something about them that a real slave would recognise as impossible? Surely not. He had said so little, and in any case he knew what he was talking about, he'd done research.

He thought, with such sudden sharpness that Una needed

334

no effort to see it and had to turn her face to the window to hide the flicker of horror there – how could they survive out here so far from anything? The soil looked so dry, too – how could they farm?

Dama's arms were shaking hard now, not the loose fitful quakes of cold or fear, but a kind of deep, sustained *rattling*, like cables in a high wind. The tendons contracted in protest, creaking, pain hardened in his elbows and shoulders. There is a way of bargaining with pain involving breathing, long breaths in and out working like besieged diplomats, conceding ground to pain in return for a slowing of the onslaught; or at the least, distracting. Dama knew all about this, but he could not do it freely, he forced himself not to breathe too deeply, not to make a sound, except sometimes under the cover of Tasius' false choked breaths. At least that was one good thing about the awful noise the man kept making.

Una was as conscious of all these things as Dama was of the assassin sprawling beside her. It seemed to make no difference now that she couldn't tell in any immediate way what Dama thought or felt, she knew all the same.

Tasius sighed, and delivered a long explosion of guttural coughing, letting Dama take a deep gulp of the palliative air. Then he got up to move awkwardly from beside Una towards the seat opposite her. She watched powerless, as for a second he loomed, stooping, over Dama and surely could and *must see* how white he had turned, his juddering arms. Sitting motionless behind Tasius she hurled all the force she could find against him, to push his attention any other way. He was too alert, too awake, all she could do was make him think the harder about the lack of water.

Hearing the movement Dama clenched his teeth and locked his arms into a moment of steadiness that burned in clear hard lines from spine to fingertip, also thinking, you don't see, you *will not* notice. And Tasius only lay down and stretched himself out, his long, vein-streaked hands resting lightly on his chest, loosening every muscle carefully, so as to quell his own nervousness, so as to think.

There could be springs, they could dig wells, he reasoned, the place wasn't a desert. Certainly it was easy, out here, to see why it had been impossible to find them. Yet he merely allowed these ideas as a line of argument, which he tacked dispassionately onto his doubts without cancelling them out.

He would think out clearly what was the worst that could happen, and how he would react; when he had done that he would feel better. If for any reason he couldn't do what he came for today, he must at least find out, for certain, exactly where the camp was. So if this were some kind of a trap, he would—

Una stared out at the brown ridges. How could she keep him from thinking if he would not talk? She would have to talk instead, but why should he listen, how could she make him?

She said conversationally, sounding almost like Lal: 'It's funny your turning up just now, we've had all kinds of people turning up lately. You'll hear some amazing stories when we get there.'

Good, that had his attention. He said languidly, 'Really? Who?'

'Yes, a mother who ran away with her little girl. She drove her master's car a hundred miles without ever having driven before; isn't that incredible?'

'Astonishing,' he murmured dutifully, shutting his eyes again.

'Who else was there . . . let me think . . .' but if she carried on this way, and did not describe Marcus, he would wonder why not, he might guess. 'Well, you'll see, we're nearly there,' she finished miserably.

A brief interruption, nothing more. He was thinking about the circumstances in which, with a stone or empty air held in his fist, he would jab at the back of her neck, breaking it.

'That's good,' he said sleepily.

He opened his eyes dimly and smiled up at her with an invalid's patience, scrutinising her. He didn't find her attractive, there was not enough colour in her, her mouth was too small, she was too young; but all the same she was good-looking in a sparse way, she might still turn out quite nicely in a few years. If she got herself killed it would be a pity. He thought of himself almost as an accident, a missing step, a blind corner; not malevolent, just something that might happen to her, through her own carelessness and bad luck. He didn't want to hurt her – or either of them, in fact, but especially not her. He felt that it was wrong to hurt or kill women in the same way he felt it was bad luck to break a mirror. You might as well try to avoid breaking mirrors, but if despite your best efforts one drops out of your hand, if, for some odd reason, it was ever necessary to do it on purpose – well then. And she would be the second- or at most third-to-last person he ever killed, because once this was over, he wouldn't ever need to again, he would retire and do no harm to anyone.

But he would prefer, then, to concentrate on the young man. If anything were to go wrong he would almost certainly have to kill at least one of them, if only because they had come so far now, it might be difficult to keep them both under control until he could get back, and plainly he couldn't let them go and warn the rest. He had no weapons except the needles, which he could not get at quickly. That was in case they'd wanted to search him. (The thought heartened him – surely they couldn't suspect anything, or they would have done that.) But if they produced anything, he'd have it off them before they knew where they were. Otherwise, there were plenty of stones around. What he would do was this: get hold of one of them, use their knife if one had turned up, otherwise make it clear that his hands were enough, make them tell him how to get to Leo's son. Each of them might possibly be mad enough to let him kill them rather than do this, but perhaps not so mad as to sacrifice the other. He needed to work out which one was more likely to choose a death they wouldn't see over one in front of them. Girls are supposed to be more tender-hearted, but the man had seemed the more emotional, and might

337

feel more of a responsibility. The only thing was that if he was holding the girl, and then he had to kill the young man, there would come an awkward moment when he needed somehow to switch them round.

He decided he would hurt her enough to slow her down, throw her to one side, then when the boy moved after her, dig a knee into his back, use his stone or else drop him, kick him in the temple once, which, if he did it properly, should be enough. Then he'd just use the car to take the girl back to his base; even if the young man hadn't told the truth already, they'd get it out of her later.

He relaxed. There was nothing to worry about now.

And there was no way Una could tell Dama about any of this.

At last Dama saw through watering eyes, high up in the dun-coloured rock the long gashes he'd been waiting and (as his muscles and tendons screamed in blind rage) praying for: the first visible sign of a cave system, so much further along the road, it seemed, than he'd remembered from four years before.

'We're here,' he gasped, letting his hands drop singing and pounding into his lap. 'Look, the caves.'

For another moment Una sat still, anguished, because she could see now that it was impossible to simply open the door, wait for Tasius to get out and then speed away. He would make sure he stayed close to them, and besides, his fake infirmity would make it far more natural for him to *follow* her. And Dama's state couldn't really be concealed any longer, if Tasius looked at him closely he'd see in a minute that he was in pain, that there was something about his arms. She thought, if what they'd told Tasius had been true, someone would have had to take the car back to Athabia.

She stepped briskly out of the car and held the door open as Tasius climbed out beside her. There was less than a second when she thought she might risk diving back inside, but Tasius, just in case, had another coughing fit and swayed, leaning first against the door, blocking it, and then against her, resting his weight on her shoulder, smiling, whispering, 'sorry,' between stifled breaths. Una made some compassionate noise, and moved away from the door. She said quickly to Dama, 'Well, see you next week.' She turned her back before she could even see his start of horror and strode off the road, down into the scrub.

Despite the many stones and roots underfoot she walked a few paces with her eyes screwed shut. *Sulien*, she thought, and also, *Marcus*.

Tasius limped after her, coughing.

Sulien and Lal staggered soaking back to the cabins, not silent, since they would both have found that intolerable, but talking in a strained, fast way about nothing, exclaiming often at the violent rain, searching the trees for something to tell the other to look at. Lal kissed him uncertainly and fled into her room to stare at her hieroglyphic women, whose long eyes seemed to her suddenly taunting with knowledge that she lacked, even though she had painted them herself. She had not been sleeping with anyone and then nearly getting killed for it – just not sleeping with anyone, more to the point.

And Sulien had not long been inside his own cabin when Delir came and peered in the doorway.

Oh *no*, thought Sulien, imagining, accurately as it turned out, how this would go.

Delir raised himself unconsciously onto his toes and bobbed as Lal did, partly to look taller, partly to look comical. He was intensely uncomfortable.

'It is horrible here sometimes, isn't it?' he asked, and then thinking that this might sound as if the people were horrible, 'I mean, how anyone would live in this rain who did not have to. But, you see, we needed to find somewhere with a population we could trust, and the Vascones . . .' Also like Lal, he sometimes babbled when he was nervous.

Sulien stared in silent, anticipatory agony. He felt he ought to bring this to a head at once and ask directly, have you heard about what happened in London, but out of some residual hope that Delir had really come to complain about the weather, he couldn't.

Delir heard himself beginning the history of how and why he had chosen the gorge in the Pyrenees, and having more ability than Lal did to stop himself at these times, he said, 'I have to talk to you.'

'Yes?'

'About Lal?'

'Yes.'

'I think it has been very hard on her, living here. Very unfair. For a long time she has been hoping, I think, that someone would come, closer to her age. So she could have friends. And here you are. And Marcus. And your sister. And you – I don't know what you do for Dama – I don't know if I think it's *possible*, even, but he is better, I can see that. That's a very good thing. Thank you.'

'That's all right.'

'But Lal.'

There was silence. This time Sulien could bear it no longer and said generously, 'You know what I was supposed to have done?'

Delir actually smiled at him thankfully. 'Yes, that is part of it.'

'I didn't.' How many times in his life was he going to have to say this? Delir did not answer, moved his head sorrowfully in what might have been a nod.

'You know what they do,' suggested Sulien in a small voice. 'They were citizens. They could say what they liked.'

'I know. I'm sorry. Look, I believe you *almost* completely, *this* much—' he held up his hands, fingers upright, and then folded down the thumb. Nine out of ten. 'Perhaps I would completely if it was not for Lal, or if Lal were someone else. That is not fair and you must be angry, but she is my *daughter*. And – I am sorry – but I suppose it is true at least that you seduced this other girl?'

The word 'seduce' sounded lividly ridiculous to both of them. Sulien couldn't work out what to do with it, whether

340

to confirm it or how to correct it. They looked anywhere but at each other.

'And Lal is *fourteen*.'

'I, we haven't, we weren't going to,' mumbled Sulien wretchedly. This was probably more true than not. He had thought about it, of course, but as an unfocused set of desires, not an immediate plan of action.

The word 'forbid' was not right here. This went on for some time, and it emerged slowly that Delir was tentatively, shamefacedly asking not that he should not see Lal again, nor even exactly that he should not see her alone; only that it should not be often, and, obviously, that Sulien should keep his hands off her.

Left alone, Sulien felt more miserable anger with Catavignus and Tancorix and Prisca than he ever had before, which, he thought, was insane, as though they'd had more right to have him tortured to death than to keep trespassing on his unintended life. Good as he had always been at making the past drain out of him, it seemed unnatural to him that it should keep coming back. It was, it should be all over – except for these occasional deep tremors of remembered fear – and the nightmares he'd had once or twice, since meeting Dama.

There would have been more comfort in being angry with Delir, but he was not.

He tried to find Marcus, but he was still in the Mandarin class.

Later, when he was back in the dark little hut, truanting gloomily from washing sheets, Lal whirled in, illuminated with passion and rage, all hesitancy surged away in sheer fury, and she hurled herself on him, kissing him violently and yelling, 'Are you going to let him do that! What right has he?'

He couldn't think of this as counting under his mumbled promise to Delir: he couldn't have backed away from her or held her off. The best he could manage was a gradual blurred retreat, kissing from her lips to her cheek to her hair, away.

'What else can I do?' he said quietly. 'If it wasn't for him, I wouldn't have anywhere to go.'

'Did he say that to you?!' Indignation was an easier feeling than sudden and horrible uncertainty; she shouldn't have charged in there without thinking, making herself so clear. Her face glowed. She thought, after all, perhaps he doesn't mind very much.

'No.'

And Sulien wanted to say, or rather could barely stop himself from saying, it was almost a physical need – 'It's just for a while, it won't always be like this.' But why should it not? He could be pardoned, Marcus could have him made a freed man, and it would make no difference, Delir would always wonder if he might have been guilty, and other people would, too, people would always find out. But *something* will happen, he thought stubbornly, clasping Lal, even while he recognised this as nothing but the force of mental habit.

Delir approached, treading as heavily as such a small man could to give them warning, and said, 'Lal.'

'Oh, haven't you done enough!' cried Lal, spinning to face him, and breaking into mortified tears.

'Please Lal, I only want to be sure that you're safe.'

'But I'm *not* safe, I live *here!*' and Delir flinched at the truth of this. 'If I've got to be here, why can't you let me do it in my own way! And you are a hypocrite! I didn't like thinking of you with Ziye, but I never said anything because you were *happy!*'

Delir was appalled. 'Ziye? You know about Ziye?' he said, croaking.

But then they heard more shouting coming from outside, breathless shrieking sobs, someone calling Delir's name.

Looking back, Tasius could no longer see the road above the stone pines, but he listened for the car beginning to move. It did, with a mild whirr of electricity and heated air. Una led him forward, cramped with dread, wishing she could be certain of what Dama was doing. Tasius would be forced to walk slowly as long as he thought his persona held, and at first she thought she might take advantage of this, that she might leave him behind, hide, and skirt ducking around him through the trees. But that way she would have doubled the distance she had to run; and he would be, as he was now, between her and the way back. He would find her before she could fight through so much scrub. No, somehow she must get him in front of her.

'Are you up to this?' she said, turning and smiling concern at him. 'Are you sure you can walk?'

'Yes,' he panted, but after his little display by the car he couldn't very well risk a sudden return of vigour; he had to let her hang back for him, hold a branch out of the way so that he could pass. That had him a step ahead of her a second; but again he staggered, wheezed, steadying himself against her, anchoring her. His limp arm, heavy for all its leanness, brought shrilling back all her revulsion at being touched. She fought down the convulsive jump her shoulders wanted to make. They were at least side by side.

She snapped off the end of the twig she'd pulled aside, thrust the broken tip into her pocket, sharp end first, pressed down.

'Not far,' she promised him. But if they went much further it would be obvious that she did not know these dry hills.

She dropped the twig and began idly patting her clothes, then feeling in her pockets, gradually quickening her breath, frowning, silently begging not just him but the whole world, this *must* look believable, *please*—

'Oh, no,' she said.

'What's wrong?'

'There's a hole in my pocket – look,' she said, and showed him the tear she'd made. 'Oh, *no*. I knew it was starting – but I forgot about it, I'm so stupid! Can you see a key this big, with a black fob? Oh, *please*—' They both stared at the ground. 'I know I had it when I got out of the car, oh, I must have done. You didn't see it on the seat, did you?'

'No.' Tasius studied her, undecided. 'There's a key?'

'We blocked all the ground-level entrances to the caves and built gates,' said Una distractedly, going through the charade of searching her pockets again. 'It *wasn't* in the car, it can't be, it must be just here, it must just have fallen—'

'Won't they— *haaah*— let us in without it?'

'Yes, they'd find us eventually – but it might not be until tonight – it might be tomorrow morning – oh, it's *got* to be here!'

Tasius stooped, frowning at the dust. Certainly it could be a trick, but if it were not, if there were a real key and he ruined his cover over such a stupid little thing—

'Careful,' breathed Una, 'it's so dusty, it might get buried.'

She was afraid to say 'don't move'. She tried not to seem eager to move away from him; she made a great show of searching the ground right at his feet, even circling him so that he was, once more, between her and the road. And then she began tentatively to retrace her steps, almost crawling, patting and fingering the sandy earth.

A stone, fist-sized, lay ahead of her hand as it scraped and shook. Sharp-cornered at this side, bulbous and fat on the other; she seemed to see it with extraordinary slow clarity, as if she would always remember it. She picked it up, not knowing what she could do with it, only with a kind of satisfaction at stealing from his thoughts.

This way she moved perhaps twenty feet from him, no more, before she heard silence where the next rasped breath should have been.

The car ought to have been out of earshot by now, but on a sudden dusty breeze Tasius had heard not the sound of turning wheels but the quiet buzz of a running motor. At the same instant he thought, if they were so cautious as to have their pick-up point forty miles from the camp, why would they choose a cave-system in full view of the road?

At once he was closing the little distance between them. Una spurted forward off her heels, a disordered, top-heavy dive into the undergrowth, clawing, burrowing like a snake, rocks and spines snagging her clothes, bloodily plucking the skin from her hands. Then she lay still, gathered in a tight coil at the base of a clump of dry broom, buried there. She heard him slow a little as he waded after her. He knew, within a few metres, where she must be, but he could not see her. It did not matter, she could not move any further without giving herself away, she'd given him more time, she'd trapped herself.

Una shot up through the whipping twigs, fist aloft, and shouted triumphantly, 'Found it,' causing just a faint, instinctive spasm of confusion and self-doubt as she hurled her stone at him. He was so close that she did not miss, as she had expected to, having had no time to judge and no confidence in her strength or aim anyway; but it struck the arm he had to throw up to protect his head, and slid off. It no more than bruised him, but he couldn't help sidestepping and stumbling a little as he did so on that unsteady ground; taking his eyes off her as he turned his face out of the stone's flight.

She didn't even see this. She ran loping and hurdling through the shrubs, threw herself at the crumbling slope up to the road, and here she would be slowest, here he would almost certainly catch up with her; and it was true, he was at the base of the short rise as she was halfway up it, stretching after her. She felt him snatch at her foot, and if he could only get a hold firm enough to turn and snap the ankle – but he could not, she was lifting away as his fingertips touched her and his own feet were sliding in the sand as he tried to push himself up the extra inch that would let him clutch with his long hand's full strength. She staggered up, and again he grabbed for her, and there was a second where they might have toppled together back down the slope; but she had the hard road under her and he did not, and she tore away, ahead, as he pulled himself onto the roadside.

The door of the car was flung up. Dama had turned round, driven fifty yards or so up the road and then, when he hoped they could no longer see him, gently reversed it back into place. Una heard him shouting in desperation, not hearing himself, 'Get *in*, get *in*, oh God!' as Tasius came for her, as if she might otherwise not have known to do this. Una crashed in through the door, grabbing at the seat, at him. Tasius called, 'Stop, stop now or I *will* kill you both,' and he had hold of her at last now, as Dama shoved at the controls with another crick of pain, and the car veered clumsily up the road, Una's legs still hanging out into air, trailing Tasius skidding through the little stones. For the first time Una gave a breathless scream, for Tasius still hung from her, hauling, to pull himself in, to drag her out. Dama flailed out sideways, his useless right hand brushing against Una's body but powerless to grip and hang onto her; but he crooked his arm somehow around her head, her shoulder, and squeezed clumsily, crying out as her weight, the weight of both of them, wrenched at the trembling muscles. Una reached up, not only to cling on now but to push blindly, as hard as she could, against the controls. The jab of speed nearly sent the car flying off the road, but it ripped at Tasius, flicked him half onto his side, and dropped him winded in the dust. The car hurtled up the road, lurching, the open door banging and rocking on the roof.

The sun was going down. Tasius got to his feet. He kicked in fury and sent a little spray of sharp pebbles into the quiet air. He stood in a hundred miles of nothing.

Dama drove fifteen miles, speechless and damp-skinned with pain. At last he said, his voice scarcely recognisable, 'Can he call for help?'

'No, he only had the tracking device.'

Dama let go of the controls with a gasp and the car jolted to a stop. He hunched protectively over his arms, folding them loosely, cradling them, breathing hard.

'Oh, I'm sorry,' whispered Una. 'Sulien ought to be here.'

'It's all right. It's good really, I never thought I'd be able to drive again, or do anything.' But he lay back in his seat as Tasius had, eyes shut, face twisted, panting.

'Perhaps I could drive back. I've watched. You could tell me what to do.'

He smiled wearily at her. 'I can't let you smash Palben's

346

car. It'll be better in a minute – we'll just sit here for a little while—' then he opened his eyes, frowning. 'The car. I never thought of it. He could identify it. We'll have to tell Palben to change it or something, or they'll go after him.' He sighed. 'You see, he might have to walk for a few days – but we haven't got rid of him.'

'I know,' said Una, guiltily silent for a moment. 'But he doesn't know where the camp is. It could be anywhere. I couldn't – we didn't *have* to.'

'We had a right,' said Dama, as he had before.

'But anyway, he was ready for something like that. He would have stopped me, he'd have killed you.'

'But that was because he had time to think,' said Dama, but he smiled at her again. 'You're mad,' he said. 'Walking off with him like that. Who did you do it for?'

Una looked away, guardedly. 'It didn't really make any difference, I wasn't any safer before.'

'With me,' he said. 'No, I couldn't help you much.'

'You did,' she said softly. 'You know you did.'

He closed his eyes again. His sleeves had worked up, showing the round scars on his wrists.

She asked, 'What did you do when you were a slave?'

Dama did not open his eyes. 'Like you, lots of things,' he murmured. 'The first thing: when I was little I used to sing, if you can believe that. I had one of those voices, very clear. It wouldn't be anything special now. Anyway, so I sang at parties and that. On my own, in little choirs . . . it's so long ago. The last thing: building. Laying magnet lines, once. An office block . . . very high . . .' He looked at her, sidelong. 'I suppose Sulien told you what I did?'

He had. She didn't know what to say.

'It's all right. I don't mind telling you. But it wasn't any kind of accident or mistake, if that's what you're hoping, I wasn't set up like Sulien. I wasn't even defending myself. It didn't do anyone any good. This, *this* would have been different.' He twisted his neck to look back along the empty road. And then he stopped deliberately, his lips folded and said firmly, 'It was wrong, it was *evil*, whatever

347

the circumstances it was still – I know now, I'm sorry for it now.' But he had barely finished saying this when he burst out resentfully, 'God, I was punished for it enough, though, wasn't I, *before* as well as after! What about *them*? At least it was quick.'

Una said warily, 'You must have had a reason?'

'*Yes*,' said Dama bitterly, then, again with the air of forcibly correcting himself, 'At least, I thought so. Like I said, we were building this tower. And there was this kid.' He paused and said wonderingly, 'He was older than I was, *I* was a kid. Anyway. We'd got very, very behind, everything had gone wrong – the weather, and some legal business – and materials that hadn't turned up – so, the walls should have been going on and the frame wasn't even finished. Twelve-hour days. Fourteen-hour days. It was very hot. Maybe better than being very cold . . . but it was stupid, it was obviously *not sustainable*. People were falling apart.'

'You were—? Is that why?'

Dama shook his head vaguely. 'I was losing weight I suppose. But I didn't get ill. I almost never . . . But other people. The person I'm talking about. I think he had dysentery. Something like that. It wasn't even as though he was my best friend or anything, he hadn't been there that long. If it wasn't for what happened I might not remember his name, I can't remember some of the others and it seems bad, because at the time – you know when you work with people and you can't get away from them, but they're like the only people in the world, and so you – you love them.'

Una felt compelled to say painfully, 'No,' and opened her mouth, but stopped before the word was out, rubbed a hand across her face. 'I don't know. But it wasn't like that in London. I always meant to get out and so I only thought about that, do you understand—? I couldn't— concentrate— on anyone except Sulien, and the people I worked for. They trusted me better that way.' There was a moment of silence. She repeated, 'Do you understand?'

Dama muttered, almost sneering, 'Well. Your way worked better.' Then he looked at her and said quickly,

'No. Of course I understand. So, look. I was *reasonable*. I said, excuse me, perhaps you haven't noticed but Niceros can't carry on like that. No, I'm not talking about me, yes I know we're in trouble with the client. "Oh, this is exactly the problem, no wonder we can't get the thing off the ground when you're all skiving." But he said finally, "Well, we'll see." I knew that wouldn't be any good. And I could have hit him or tried to kill him even then. Because anyone with a pair of eyes could tell that Niceros was going to die. But I did think just *perhaps* the supervisor might do something; it was better than nothing. And then the engineer and the client came and walked round the site and stood on the scaffolding, going, "Oh, this is terrible, what the hell is going on here, why have you let it get like this?" to the supervisor. So they put it up to *eighteen-hour days*.'

He stared at her for a second, indignant as if this had only just happened, appealing for agreement. She nodded. 'But because they were there I said again, to the engineer this time, you have got to leave out Niceros. And the engineer said, unfortunately we can't spare anyone at this stage. The client didn't say anything but for God's sake, he must have had some idea, and anyway it was his building. They had their chance.'

He stopped again, but said nothing to amend this.

'I didn't expect it to be the way it happened, though. I thought one morning they just won't be able to make him get up, and they'll see how bad it is, and then he'll be dead a few hours after that. But instead we were putting in a cross-brace. I didn't even notice he was standing anywhere that dangerous. And I didn't hear anything. When I looked round he just wasn't there. When I looked over the edge I couldn't see him on the ground because of the angle, so . . . he must have just fainted I think, but . . . even though there wasn't anywhere he could have gone, even though there wasn't any time, because I hadn't heard a scream or seen him fall I kept sort of thinking that . . .' he shook his head again, frowning. 'But really . . . I already knew I was going to kill them. It's strange how I knew . . . it's strange how I *made* it happen.'

It was as if she had been expecting those exact words. Physically she relaxed, leaning back more passively against the seat, as if giving into an anaesthetic or some other inevitable, coercive thing. 'What do you mean?'

'I wanted the supervisor to leave the hydraulic wrench somewhere I could get it,' said Dama. 'I just thought about him doing that and wherever he went I was *telling him to* and *making him do it*, and I could see where I wanted him to put it and I just, I *knew he would*.'

With every word his voice was quieter and more emphatic. He was no longer looking at her and his face and body barely moved. 'I needed it for the lift in which they had to come up the scaffolding. We'd put up the beams of the roof. Finally, you could see the shape we were making. They had come back, the engineer and the client, and they were on the top level, saying at least it felt like a tower now. And the wrench was the only thing I could have used, and I had it. While they were on the other side, I picked it up and walked round to the lift. No one stopped me. I knew they wouldn't. I climbed over into the lift and went— *shrrr— shrrr—*' He'd lifted his better hand, and made a kind of whirring sound, so engrossed in the memory now that it almost didn't occur to him that she couldn't hear and see the eight huge nuts spinning loose of their bolts, as he did. 'I took four of the bolts right out and left the others just resting in the nut. I had to stand in the basket while I did it. It still bore my weight. But not the three of them, when they got in.'

That fall had not been silent, like Niceros': there had been the creak as the bolts held the basket in place a second longer, and then, the screams of the men inside it, the deaths themselves indeed quick – even all the time in the air beside the floorless structure, so many unfinished stories to pass on the way down – he knew it was merciful. The men themselves might not have thought so, but they had no point of comparison. He sighed, surfacing from it. 'There,' he said.

'And then—' possibly she wanted the story to go on past the killing so that she could defer deciding how to react to it. 'How did they find out it was you, who told them?'

Dama's face had been set and rigid. Now he blinked with the mild, innocent bewilderment that made him look about ten years old, and said, 'I did.'

Una stared at him unable to speak. She hardly knew what she felt. At last she whispered, 'Didn't you know what would happen?'

'Yes. Of course I wasn't thinking of that when I killed them, I was only thinking of what I was doing. But I had to. The contractors said they would have it done to every tenth one of us, unless . . .' He shook his head dismissively. 'Anyway, I can't remember the actual event. Just woke up like this one day, at some little house in Napolis.'

Una said, not reading his mind in any way she recognised, but with a kind of leap of intuitive certainty that was quite foreign to her, 'That's not true, is it? You remember.'

Dama felt a shock like a soft breath on the blood of the heart.

'How do you know?' he gasped helplessly. 'You told me you couldn't see what I was thinking.'

'Sometimes,' said Una hesitantly, '*you* seem to know things about *me*.'

Dama shook his head – there was something more urgent than how she knew. She was sitting on his right and so it had to be his worse hand that he laid on hers, still trembling with fading pain. 'You *can't tell* Delir. You can't tell anyone, it might get back to him.'

'No, all right, I promise,'

'No one knows that,' he told her, relaxing a little.

But they could not look away from one another.

Presently Dama said as a kind of afterthought, 'It's true there's some time I can't remember; but it was later, because of the drugs and being so ill. That's why it was easy to say I'd forgotten everything.'

After a few more minutes they started moving again, stopping often, Una sometimes leaning across to steady his arms.

When the Sinoan lesson was over Marcus went across the river into the hut with the monitors, and offered to watch instead of Tobias.

Half an hour earlier Iris had shrugged, murmured, 'All right then,' and meekly gone back to studying the different forms of '*shi*'. He was afraid that she didn't believe him, that she simply considered that they had agreed to disagree, but to keep pressing would have removed any doubt.

But it was hard to concentrate even on this. Come back, he urged Una silently, staring at the many screens, trying to force the specks of light to form her image. You must be all right. Come back, come back.

And she was there, she was not hurt (he could not yet see the bruises and fine scratches on her hands and face), although where was the new slave? He had been right to worry, something must have happened, he thought he could tell that from the way she walked, the way she looked at Dama.

She was alone with Dama, and for a second he had the impression that they were holding hands, although they were not, they were walking close together, that was all. But still, while the relief that she was safe did not go away, he felt a hot, unmistakable clamping of jealousy that, in itself, might almost have been enough to answer the question that had calmly presented itself that morning when he saw her rushing away from him.

It was, 'Are you in love with Una?' although, as it was her voice, it should really have been, 'Are you in love with me?'

But already he knew; he could not understand, now, how he could ever not have known. The first time, when she lifted her hands away from her face – then when she'd tried to pin him down, the touch of her, and her face, above him, and they'd looked at each other in desperation through her hair. And later, in the graveyard, *lit up*, he'd thought or felt – and he hadn't known what it meant, how was that possible?

And she knew! – he thought, with a second reverberating shock – that was why he could hardly ever find her. She couldn't feel the same for him or anything like it – except now he remembered times when he could almost have thought— He felt suddenly that he should not be watching her, but he moved his eyes only when she vanished from one screen to another.

Then he heard the noise outside, someone crying and calling for Delir on the other side of the water.

It was another twenty minutes before Una and Dama arrived back at the huts, and by then the place was in chaos. It was a while before they could understand what had happened; which was that Iris had told her mother that Gnaeus was Marcus Novius Faustus. Pyrrha was beside herself with terror – the spiral-wings really were after them, they would not stop until they found them – and now everyone knew.

[XV]

COLD CEDARS

The conversation in the entertainment suite seemed stuck to Varius. Even apart from the central fact of it – that Marcus would die and it would be because of him – he couldn't get certain phrases of it out of his head, or peel away the strange, horrible rapport that had somehow arisen between them. He felt it ought to be impossible for them to understand each other at all, he wanted Gabinius to be so far away from him and so utterly separate as to be beyond sense. But Gabinius had not only uncovered facts he had no right to, like his mother's miscarriages, like his behaviour after Gemella's death, but could apparently put these things together until he had a model of Varius that was far more like him than it should have been. And it went the other way, too. Varius found he now understood certain things about Gabinius even though he had no wish to do so. For example, when, after Gabinius had finished with him, someone abruptly emptied a sedative into his arm, he knew it was not merely to keep him out of harm's way for future use; Gabinius had truly meant it as an act of kindness. And he could hardly help taking it so, he was so grateful to be flicked out of consciousness.

And in the same way he was certain that when it happened he would see Gabinius in person again, it would be Gabinius who told him.

He was living in a nice little white room somewhere high in the house. There were things to keep him occupied – books, and music. He touched neither. When he wasn't

354

drugged into warm indifference or sleep he sat staring out of the window, which would neither open nor break, at cold cedar trees.

He remembered what Gabinius had said about killing Marcus. 'He won't know anything about it.' Of course, of *course* he had to hope that was true, and that it would be quick. But out of a kind of misshapen selfishness he *wanted* Marcus to know he had betrayed him, because the idea of Marcus thinking, right up until the end, that Varius had sent him away to safety, and was still protecting him, was insupportable.

What would he do if Gabinius really let him go? They could make sure that he never got near Faustus again, or any other important person. There would always be the threat against Rosa and his parents, and against anyone else he tried to tell. Anyway he'd reached the stage now where he could hardly see the point. There would be no one left to save.

Sometimes he thought in a weary dutiful way that no, that was not good enough – perhaps he could write down what had happened, make many copies, send them – some-where – leave them to be read by – someone – but he couldn't think about it thoroughly, suspected he would never be able to.

And then – he hadn't expected to survive before, but now if he tried to imagine existence much beyond this, any ordinary thing he might do, his mind seemed to knock into a wall and have to retreat, baffled. It was like trying to imagine infinity, it just couldn't be done. He no longer thought of suicide as a stoic retreat or scarcely even as an act at all, it was only that nothing else seemed credible. But everything Gabinius had said about his parents had built them up into a deadlocking obstacle as flat and inevitable as the necessity of being dead. Sometimes he felt as if there ought to be some way of explaining to them, making them see that it was really for the best. But he still knew that that would never be possible. But he still couldn't think of anything else.

Gabinius should have had nothing to do with such a feeling.

For now he had no opportunity. He was never alone. The blue-liveried bodyguards were always there, mostly discreetly silent although one, youngish and fair-haired, tried from time to time to cheer him up. Varius never spoke to him, not now out of any stubborn decision to be silent, but because he just couldn't, he had no energy left for it.

But there were two other things that made him wait. First, there was the feeling that he should be there to hear that Marcus was dead, he ought to witness it, since he'd made it possible. But also he thought sometimes of Tulliola and Cleomenes, and after all found himself hoping that perhaps they could do something – perhaps they could stop it. He did not believe that anything like that would happen. But it was enough, when he could think clearly, to keep him in a state of dreary, sick suspense while he waited.

So when Gabinius came in, grave and arms folded, all his brisk affability missing and began, almost exactly as Varius had imagined it, 'I wanted to be the one to tell you,' he felt a watery expectant chill in his bones, but also something close to relief.

'I told you I'd send you home and I can't. We haven't found him.'

Varius forgot for a moment to think of Rosa or his parents and felt a quick shoot of unsteadying delight, so unexpected and so violent against the ground of featureless despair, that everything seemed bright and wavering and unreal. But then he remembered, and said in dread, 'You can't do anything. There's nothing else. I told you the truth.'

'I know you did,' said Gabinius soothingly. 'Don't worry about that. We've spoken with someone from the camp. Someone has come forward.'

'One of the slaves?'

'Yes.'

Varius sat down by the window. He was sickened. Then he thought dully, what right did he have to feel any such

356

thing, after what he'd done? He rested his head against his hand, on the window sill, looking out at the dark trees.

Gabinius said. 'You'd think that would be it. But it seems – or so we're told – that we can't get at him. That they can see you coming and just disappear. That they're already considering doing this. And apparently this slave can't or won't do it for us. So we've got a bit of a problem. Do you see?'

Varius felt a second unreasoning outsurge of elation, based on nothing more than Gabinius having a problem.

'You know, I really wish you'd never got involved in any of this. Not that it's your fault. We should have been more careful. I thought we had been. Because you're just wrong-headed, you've obviously got a lot of good qualities. I don't think of you the same way as Leo.'

'Yes, I know,' said Varius, irritably.

'Well. So what – from my point of view – needs to happen, for this to be over with quickly, is for him to be away from these people. On his own.'

Gabinius seemed to want him to guess what he meant without having to say it. After a moment he remarked, 'And he owes *you* a lot.'

And Varius realised slowly why Gabinius was so gloomy. He'd come, in effect, to say 'I'm very sorry, but you will probably have to be killed after all,' almost, Varius thought, as he might have said to an employee, 'You know what a bad year it's been, I'm afraid you can't stay on.' The idea made him laugh, and Gabinius looked pained and confused.

Afterwards Varius was aware of his blood speeding through him, a tense knot twisting in the muscles of his side. He'd been so stupefied with hopelessness for so long that his excitement now felt unnatural, almost dangerous, as if he'd suddenly doubled in height and couldn't get used to it, couldn't move without knocking against walls and breaking things.

Don't be an idiot, Marcus, he begged, stay where you are.

He couldn't really think that there was much hope for Marcus in this, how could there be, when they'd closed in

357

on him this far, and when no one could be trusted, not Varius himself, not the slaves?

But things were no longer funnelling away, inescapably, as they had been; nothing was certain. He could no longer spend hours staring emptily at the cedars, he had to keep standing up and striding purposelessly around, he even opened one of the books for the first time, although he could hardly focus on the words.

That evening, in the Golden House, Faustus was alone, slumped in his midnight-blue drawing room, a jar of wine at his elbow, not wanting even Tulliola's company, not yet noticing that the music he had been listening to had stopped.

'Why can't you all go to hell?' he said, by way of greeting, as the door opened.

But it was Makaria, face creased, eyes pink, a few sheets of thin paper in her hand.

'Daddy. Daddy, it's so horrible, I'm sorry, but you have to read this . . .'

Faustus pulled himself heavily upright. 'Have they found him, then?'

For he guessed at once that she must be going to say that Marcus was dead, because in general if she cried she never let him see it. After all these weeks and false shots of hope, he no longer believed what would have been the most promising thing; that Marcus had been kidnapped. He had been told that Varius was being questioned about the woman's death (she'd been strangled, apparently), and he thought the most he could hope for was that the sight of the killing had somehow triggered the Novian curse and someone who was not Marcus and never would be again was roaming in terror around the Empire.

'No, but it was that man, it's Varius.'

And what she handed him was a confession. Varius admitted that Marcus had discovered that he was embezzling from Leo's estate. Gemella had caught him shortly after he'd murdered Marcus and started screaming, panicking him. He'd never intended to kill her, and when she was dead he hadn't been able to believe it; that was why he'd left her there, in the Tusculum villa, half hoping that she was only stunned, and that when he came back she'd be all right.

Then he had driven erratically around Rome and up into Latium, where he'd thrown Marcus' body into the Tiber. Since it had not so far been found, it probably never would be now.

'But those people that saw him—' began Faustus instinctively, though his eyes were already beginning to blur.

Makaria simply shook her head; she was now sobbing so hard that she couldn't speak. He drew her into his arms and she clung to him as she had not done for years, twenty years in fact, since he'd divorced her mother, when she was thirteen.

[XVI]

BLACK STANDARDS

After the drive back through the snow, into the rain, and then the long walk through the wet beech trees, Una and Dama were so worn and breathless and shivering, and yet also so caught up in a kind of tattered exhilaration, that they had scarcely considered what they would say about Tasius. Una helped Dama, wincing, into the lift and they both fell silent as their feet touched the metal and they swung above the small height, uncomfortable, remembering.

And then the lift sank them into confused clamour and they forgot to think of it.

'Is *what* true? Someone tell me – is *what* true?' somebody was repeating urgently. A child's voice took up the same question.

'All right, but she's got a point, hasn't she? You should have told us to begin with, at least then we'd have had a choice. You shouldn't have lied.'

'Did you know? Who else knew?'

For all the noise, Marcus was the first thing Una saw, perhaps because so many other people were looking at him now. He was standing on the bridge with a small but growing knot of people jostling around him; and yet not touching him, they left him at least a foot of free space while they elbowed one another, as if he were poisonous.

Marcus looked shabby and pale and strained, and yet he seemed different to Una. She was reminded again of his face on the London screen; without any of the patrician haughtiness he'd assumed in Wolf Step returning to him, it seemed that now so many people knew who he was, a kind of imperial aura was becoming visible, and growing, fed by so much attention, like the silk of a balloon over its flame, like heat-haze, rising impersonally, whether Marcus liked it or not. He held himself differently, accepting the space around him as a given. He looked older than he really was.

Sulien was there with him, though, the only person inside the superstitious gap around Marcus, also trying to reassure everyone. But he kept glancing helplessly up at Lal, who was standing on the next level, looking down in horror. They could not stop passing the same look back and forth between them, reaffirming something that was mostly powerlessness. Lal had been crying but then startled out of it, and because of that she looked out of place there, where no one else in tears would stop for a while yet.

'It was the only place he could go,' Sulien was telling someone, Tiro.

Marcus said more quietly, 'The spiras haven't been back.'

And he looked at Una, almost in the same moment as she first looked at him, and she felt intensely visible, as if she had been the one everyone was staring at and not him, visible to the point of vanishing like someone standing in a too-bright light, in too much sun. Her pulse banged guiltily, as if she had been caught happily stealing some unimportant thing, something she'd been sure of getting away with.

She thought again, please don't. It's too much, I can't.

He said to her, across Tiro, Calvus, Tobias, certain of being heard despite the shouting and crying between them, 'You're all right.'

Tiro looked instinctively to see who Marcus was talking to, then went on insisting, 'But no one was looking *at all* before. No one really cared. Now! It's only a matter of time!'

In the centre of the scrum Delir was trying to quieten Pyrrha by standing very still and talking so softly that they could not hear from this distance what he was saying. But Pyrrha's jumping, contorted face seemed all liquid, she was scrambling back and forth in frantic indecision, beating at the air in front of Delir as if she would almost, if she could have brought herself to dare, have hit or shaken him, and pulling at a resigned Iris, and trying to gather together a small but chaotic bundle of clothes that had fallen out of her arms. She was making a bubbling, gulping sound that could only slowly be made out as, 'What are we going to do – we can't stay here – why did I come – why did I come – why aren't you doing anything?'

Una realised that she had never before even heard her speak.

One of Iris' small dresses, dropped onto the walkway, had blown down to the fast river's edge, soaking fast on the wet green stone. Iris, who had been staring at her shrieking mother with detached misery, the only dry-eyed child there, now made a weary, tidying move to retrieve it.

'Don't go near the water!' screeched Pyrrha, and when Iris jadedly ignored her, she yanked her daughter away by the arm, so suddenly that Iris was jerked off her feet. Pyrrha clubbed at her untidily with her free hand, spilling the last of the clothes. 'Listen to me! You have to listen to me, *I'm your mother*—'

Una flinched, reminded again of her own mother, wanting not to see them, not ever to be in the same place as they were.

At the same time Sulien, seeing Una's scratches, the battered look of both of them, pushed towards them. 'What happened?'

'I . . .' stammered Una, feeling very tired by now, beginning to see that she should have had some false answer ready, but she hadn't been prepared for all this, she felt that all the quickness of thought had been shocked and rattled out of her.

Tiro, twitchy with newly wakened paranoia, turned to them belligerently. 'Weren't you picking someone up?'

'There wasn't anyone,' said Una.

Tiro hesitated. 'Why were you so long, then?' he said, and drew increased suspicion from his own words. 'Dama. What's going on?'

Dama, still white, still nursing his arms against his body, muttered, 'There wasn't a slave, there was a spy; but don't worry, we got rid of him.'

'They were *in the village*?' For all his distrust, Tiro's voice was loud with appalled incredulity.

Sulien and Marcus had moved at once towards her in concern; and then felt how alarm was rolling out from Tiro almost palpably, like shock from a rupture in the earth. Pyrrha sank down, crouching, shivering, clutching Iris who stood woodenly in her gaunt arms. Pyrrha pressed her head against Iris, as much to be sheltered by her as to protect or comfort her, wailing, 'We should have stayed where we were – I should have put up with it – *it'll be so much worse when they find us.*'

Tobias said quietly, rationally, more to himself than to Marcus or Delir, not wanting to associate himself with the panic, 'I don't understand. Why couldn't this be dealt with in Rome?'

Delir gave up on Pyrrha, looked around and called out decisively, 'Who was watching the screens?'

'I was,' Marcus said.

'Then go back to it,' said Delir. 'Please go back to it, Marcus,' he added resolutely, causing a new, milder throb of shock and making Pyrrha moan again; but after a moment the rest grew quieter, dazed.

Marcus hesitated, feeling that he wanted to be there if they were going to talk about him, wanting also to be the one to explain.

'There should never be a moment when no one is watching the screens,' said Delir firmly.

Marcus said to Una, 'Later you have to tell me what happened,' and he turned unwillingly back towards the monitor hut. Instinctively, the people in his way – Calvus and Helena – fell aside, clearing a path.

'Good,' said Delir. 'No one can come here without us knowing, as is always true. Now. Come with me.'

The mess cabin was the largest room they had. Delir, dwarfed and hidden by the throng, bobbed on tiptoe for a second and considered the long table. No, that would be too high. He hopped with consciously absurd sparrow-likeness to stand on a chair, teetered half-deliberately, to be sure he had everyone's attention, then turned and then began speaking and ceased to be comic at once.

'Yes, that's Marcus Novius Faustus. He came here because he had to. I think I would have to help anyone in fear of being murdered, especially someone that young, for his own sake. But it isn't only for his own sake. If there are any of you who don't know that Leo came here, and why, it was because he meant to put a stop to slavery when he became Emperor. And then there would be no need for a place like this.' He said this emphatically but as levelly as everything else; only Una, Ziye and Lal knew about the leap of wistfulness that accompanied the words, not that Lal, leaning bleakly against the wall furthest from him, felt very sympathetic just now.

She looked across at Sulien, on the other side, with Una and Dama. Sulien, yet again, shot her an unhappy look and Lal, even while turning the same look back, was irritated by it this time.

Delir continued, 'Because we could live anywhere, and we wouldn't have to think up lies about ourselves.' He'd given speeches before; he deliberately said 'we' instead of 'you,' although he was aware their history was not his – but after all, he'd lost his citizenship, he was a criminal. 'It's already true that no one has any right over us, not *truly*, but everyone in the world should *know* that it's true. And that was why Leo and his wife were killed. It was not an accident. The same thing will happen to Marcus Novius if he is found, and for the same reason. Everyone knows how hard the vigiles are looking for him, and that they've offered money. But if anyone, here or anywhere else, helps them to find him, that's what it means: Marcus' death.' And it was deliberately, too, that he used only Marcus' first name here, as for someone intimate or for a child, and such an ordinary name, too, bare of its dazzling appendages. 'Marcus' death, and no certainty for us, ever. We are hiding now, *as we always have done*, so that soon we never need to again.'

Tobias, near the front, mentioned as gently as before, 'You could have told us this from the beginning. You could have trusted us.'

Delir couldn't say what was closest to the truth; I might have trusted *you*, Tobias, but no, I couldn't possibly trust everyone.

'Tobias,' he appealed, smiling. 'Look at poor Pyrrha.'

Pyrrha was sitting at the table with her head in her hands, still lamenting softly, Iris patting her with nurselike duty.

'She's had good reason to be scared in the past. Of course this is frightening news. I did not want anyone to be frightened. But I still say that we are not going to be found. Even if they find the gorge, and however close they are that won't be easy, still they won't find us here. And only the people are important, not the place.'

Dama drew his breath in over his teeth, scowling, but he said nothing, no, he would think it disloyal. Delir thought, and later I will have to talk to him, too.

Tobias had nodded dubiously, doubtless aware that the question had merely been dodged. Delir bounced off his chair saying, 'Now come here Pyrrha, I will get you a glass of wine, and you will tell me how I can convince you not to worry.'

But it didn't work, or not much – it never did with Pyrrha. Even Iris' patience with her seemed to have been worn out for the time being, and while Delir tried to comfort her mother she sighed with tired exasperation and walked away.

Una and Sulien, pushing to get out of the cabin, for Una was almost as besieged now as Marcus had been, almost tripped over her. They stopped, arrested by the look of unchildlike exhaustion on Iris' face.

'It's my fault,' she remarked flatly. 'I should never have told her. I shouldn't ever tell her anything. But she was just sitting there and not saying anything again, you know, and she wouldn't get dressed. I was just trying to get her talking.

I thought it was interesting. But everything makes her more frightened, everything, I should have remembered that.'

Iris alone was less painful than Pyrrha-and-Iris together. 'You didn't know that anyone wanted to kill Marcus,' said Sulien.

Iris shook her head heavily. But Tiro was asking Una, 'How did you know the man was a spy?' and she answered vaguely, 'Sometimes I just do know things like that about people.' Pyrrha already was calling out plaintively for her daughter, and Delir had moved on, there were other people to be pacified.

'Oh well,' said Iris, resignedly, setting her small shoulders, going back to work.

Later Delir found Marcus on the other side of the gorge, in the little monitor hut. Ziye came with him, and although they were not touching – and indeed it seemed possible that they might be in the midst of a postponed argument – it was for the first time quite obvious that they were a couple. Marcus didn't know what had prompted this lapse of secrecy and was surprised.

'We will do the next watch,' Ziye said.

'Is everything . . . all right?'

'I hope so. Yes.' Ziye's usual crispness had a slight edge to it, not directed at him.

Delir blinked at Marcus wearily. 'Ziye believes we should evacuate immediately.'

'I think everyone would be easier to manage if they had something definite to do,' said Ziye quietly. 'You're too tired to keep calming people down one at a time. And it is true. The village is too close.'

'I am so sorry about this,' said Marcus.

'No, no.' Delir sat down and stared at the screens where nothing was moving except rain. 'I don't want to wish anyone dead,' he said softly, 'but I wish you would become Emperor soon.'

Outside, Marcus stood alone at the base of the gorge. Below him the river was white in the darkness, talking angrily as it moved. He thought he could feel the camp around him crouching, huddled, like something wounded and hissing. He went back to his cabin and commiserated with Sulien, who was sprawling on his bed in a state of incredulous, half-amused despair.

Sulien told him everything, and then asked suddenly, 'Is anything going on with you and Una?'

Marcus felt persecuted. 'No,' he said.

'Well. Is there going to be? Are you going to try anything?'

Marcus hesitated. 'Do you want me not to?' he said at last.

'Huh,' said Sulien bitterly. 'Yes, maybe I should forbid you. Might feel better if I took it out on somebody. Yes. Stay away from my sister, you pervert, I don't want you corrupting her.' He felt briefly, faintly unjust to Delir, who had not said anything like this, but it was a relief all the same. He grinned sourly. He'd at least got an unhappy laugh out of Marcus. He added, 'And if she so much as looks at you I'm going to disown her and make you sorry you were ever born. No, of course not,' he went on, quietly. 'Only. Is it a good idea? I mean; if you do anything, be careful.'

'Of course I would,' muttered Marcus.

'I know. Well, you'd better. But I meant, be careful of yourself, too.' He was silent before going on. He thought, seven years and I don't know where she was. 'Because . . . I think you'd be better off with someone who . . . I don't think it's very easy for her to like anyone. Not now, anyway, not like that.'

Marcus came perilously close to asking, 'What about Dama?', and couldn't think of anything else to say.

'Come on,' urged Sulien, 'count yourself lucky. At least you *can* find someone else.' And Marcus still couldn't answer, he couldn't have told Sulien or anyone else that he found this unimaginable. He made a vaguely demurring face. Sulien persisted, 'It can't be that difficult. Don't you remember what I said in Tolosa? Once you *can* say it without getting killed, surely you just say, "Hello, darling, I'm the heir to the Empire." But what am *I* going to do?

367

What's to stop this happening with all girls, *every* girl, for the rest of my life?'

They were dumbfounded with pessimism. Eventually Marcus said, 'Do you think there's absolutely no way we can get drunk?'

The next morning there were the usual things to do, Sinoan lessons, preparing the food. And it was as Marcus had known it would be, he could feel people tensing and going quiet, everything rippled around him like water round a boat. Sulien said, 'Just carry on the same as before. They'll get used to it; we did.'

But all that day Delir had to send small search parties out into the woods to look for Pyrrha, who'd fled weeping and crumbling towards the Spanish mountains, dragging Iris with her. It was not until nightfall that Ziye came back leading Iris by the hand, for once in floods of tears, inconsolable. She'd been on her way back to the camp, looking for help, but she couldn't clearly describe the way she'd come, and it was another four hours before Tobias and Tiro carried Pyrrha home, having found her lying like a white length of rubbish – a plastic bag, an old dress – soaked on the cold earth. She'd scratched at her wrists, no more, with thorned twigs, and had chilled rather than bled into unconsciousness. Even when she'd been warmed up and Sulien had established that there was nothing badly wrong with her, she lay shivering in bed and made no sound except sometimes a kind of mummering, or the chattering of her teeth. Iris holed up beside her in a nest of blankets, and for three days wouldn't move, or let anyone except Sulien into the room.

Marcus was carrying a crate of plates away from the mess room to be washed, when Delir called out from his room, 'Don't bother with that now, Marcus, come in here.'

Marcus left the crate near the door. To his surprise, Una was there, standing near the third panel of the map, Sina rising behind her. Her hands were in anxious knots.

Delir said, 'I thought we should know what we have to worry about.'

He hadn't altogether believed in what he knew of Una's fortune-telling, for so he still thought of it, until Dama had described the encounter with Tasius. Even now he felt a slight distaste about it, though he could see that he must make use of it.

'Una, can you tell if anyone is thinking of telling the vigiles that Marcus is here?'

And he was sure he wasn't naïve, he didn't expect that it wouldn't have crossed anyone's mind and he thought he was prepared for whatever she might say; but he was shocked when she whispered, 'Almost everyone.'

Una had the conspicuous, vanishing feeling again. She moved forward, agitated.

'It isn't like it sounds. They can't help it. It's just – impulses; it comes into people's heads and they think – oh, I could be rich. Then they think "No, no, that's awful." ' She bit her lip and muttered, 'But sometimes they think of it again.'

'All right.' Delir had dropped back in his chair, appalled, reassessing quickly. 'All right. Is anyone considering it, *seriously*?'

'Maybe Marinus. Maybe Tiro. I'm only going by how often they've thought of it, but I don't know – I can't be near everyone all the time; even if I could it's too many people to be certain. Of course I'll try, though.'

'I'll talk to Marinus and Tiro.' Delir sat forward resolutely, and both Una and Marcus were struck by how firmly he believed that a total, sacrificial offering of attention could fix almost anything.

But Marcus said, involuntarily, 'And Dama?'

He wished at once that he had not spoken, it seemed the most humiliating way of betraying his jealousy. Una had lowered her eyes and her face was at its blankest. But Marcus hadn't forgotten the powerless hatred with which Dama had spat at him.

Delir, on the other hand, was shaken, angry.

'Never, never in a hundred years. Don't you know he designed everything here? It's all he has. And the hatred he has for Rome – it's excessive, it's *wrong*, but how could it let him even talk to them, let alone take their money?'

And Una whispered, 'Marcus, he would have killed that spy if he could.'

But she answered herself: for Holzarta, for Delir, not for Marcus. And it came to all three of them at once, that if you could bargain for the freedom of two people, why not for forty, why not, at least, that an illicit settlement in the mountains should be overlooked. After so many failures, it must be a feasible arrangement. And the thought knocked through one more barrier towards the possibility that anyone might do it.

Delir turned to Una, appealing, all his hesitancy about her ability dissolving in the strength of the desire to have this refuted. 'But you would know?'

'No,' she admitted quietly. She tried to explain the resistance she seemed to hit whenever she tried to read Dama.

Delir said, 'Still. I know him. It's quite impossible.' It was the kind of thing he usually tried to avoid saying.

Una hung around uneasily outside, as Marcus picked up the crate again. They were both very conscious that they were alone together. It had been so long, they felt, although the time could have been nothing at all if they had been friends living in a city. There was a moment before either could talk. Una saw it would be possible to smile and slip away from him when he took the plates to the kitchen, but twisted with compunction and unhappiness at the thought of doing it. She had missed him, but she couldn't think, I've missed you. What she felt grew every second closer to panic, melted relentlessly through her like a hot iron through cheap fabric, until there was almost nothing else left; so that she couldn't name what was wrong with her, she felt like an animal scared out of knowing which way to move, with only enough wit to hate itself for being like this.

Marcus said stiltedly, 'Are you still reading the book, the Virgil?'

'It's propaganda.'

'You must have known that pretty early on.' Impatiently.

'I can't be happy liking it. Every time I come close, every time I start to think it's meant *for me to read*, it stops me – it wants me to admire something that I . . .' How was she even saying these things?

'But do you mean – without wanting to – you *do* like it?' Someone had asked him something like this once, he couldn't, for the time being, remember who.

'Yes, I – I want to know how it ends.'

'He never finished it. When he was dying he told his friends to burn it, because it wasn't perfect.'

They were down by the water now. Marcus was hardly more at ease than she was, thinking, this is no good, Sulien was right, you knew that from the beginning. It was strange that he could feel this, and that any further proof of it would be unbearable; and yet be so gripped by a reckless desire for certainty and, even more consumingly, the need for her not to go away. He headed past the cabins, upstream, without saying anything, but it was plain he wanted her to come with him.

Una murmured weakly, 'I should be here—' The water was too loud, he hadn't heard her. She called, 'I should stay here, in case anyone thinks of giving you away—'

'You must get so sick of doing that. Just a little while away from it.'

So she went with him. The one clear thing she could have said to herself was that she didn't want to disappoint him, she felt there ought to be some gradual and imperceptible way of doing it.

They walked to where the cliffs were sharpest, where the water shouted out of the high rock, white, strident.

She felt as if she really had vanished now, as if her habit

of imagining whiteness – snow, or white light – had sped out of control and swallowed her.

He'd taken her hand, which was cool with spray from the river. He blurted, 'Una, I don't care that they're looking for me. I'm glad I had to leave Rome, I'm glad it went wrong – because I would never have met you.' He wasn't sure how loudly he'd spoken, whether she could even hear him.

And now he touched her face, making every move with the same tentative caution with which, in Rome, people had occasionally touched him: giving her plenty of time to move away. She did not move away. She even, when he kissed her, let her cold lips part very slightly, but with a kind of pale obedience that he felt, and that appalled him. Otherwise she just stood there in his arms, and it was like kissing a statue; she was as unresponsive and also, it seemed, as incapable of fending for herself, of resisting.

He drew back and found that she was almost in tears, something he'd never seen before. She said, 'I'm sorry, I—' and couldn't get another word out. She tried to bring up the corners of her mouth, and failed.

He had seen her frightened before, but never so defence-less, never so enfeebled, everything he was in love with unravelled. How had he done this to her? It was impossible not to feel as if he'd been lumbering and brutal, and at the same time, knowing he hadn't been, angry with her for making him feel so. He thought incredulously, exasperated, why should you be so scared of *me*?

This new, frail, unrecognisable person needed com-forting, so he said gently, trying to make it true, 'It's all right.' And much less honestly, 'It doesn't matter.'

She gave a little, despairing nod. At risk of making it worse he put his arm round her, pulling her against him in a companionable way; he might have kissed her forehead or something, but he couldn't somehow, it felt fraudulent.

'Do you want me to leave you alone?'

She made the helpless little half-smile again.

When he'd gone she sat hunched up on the stone, staring

through the hot lenses of water in her eyes, at the distorted river. For a long time the tears were quite steady, they did not fall, they would not go away.

Marcus walked back. The anger with her protected him for a minute or two. Why had she let him kiss her if she found it so unbearable?

It lasted almost no time at all. Though he still couldn't think out or explain what she'd felt, instead he seemed almost to *remember* it: powerless because you were afraid of being powerless, with no choice because you couldn't remember that you had a choice. Had he ever felt that? No, it was only that for the moment she seemed more real to him than he did, he couldn't remember what he himself was supposed to be like.

And she was afraid of hurting him, too, he recognised, although of course she had done that anyway.

Because there was no holding it off now, he was completely used up in a sort of obsessive, pulsing *pleading* with her, to call after him, for this not to be true. It seemed abject, pathetic. He also thought, I've wrecked everything, although he knew that this, or something so like this as to make no difference, would have happened eventually, whatever he had done. He wanted to go back to where he'd left her, not to do or say anything, just because he felt he was walking the wrong way, as if against a current.

Tobias must have seen him coming back on the monitors (and kissing Una too? He blushed, but couldn't remember the distribution of the cameras), for he appeared suddenly from the bramble-roofed hut, looking nervous, bemused.

'Novius—', he said the name with a sort of disbelieving self-consciousness, as if it were a bizarre quotation. Marcus shook his head – please not now. Tobias grimaced urgently. 'Something's happened. I've just seen it, there's something on the longvision—'

He wasn't the one doing the watch, then, for the long-vision and security screens were in neighbouring huts, not together. Tobias sometimes let his students watch the longvision, making them spell the words they heard. He had to have been looking out for Marcus. He said, 'It's about you – I don't know what to make of it.'

He was making diffident but urgent gestures at the door of the longvision hut. Marcus felt weary apprehension, and did as Tobias wanted, went up the steps and through the door, looked at the scratchy little longvision in the corner. Tiro was there, too, with Celer, and Marinus, and his wife. They turned shocked faces to him, then back to the screen.

'—of treason against the Emperor and the State.'

The whole screen was filled, in silence, with some picture of himself that he did not recognise; presumably it could not be older than a year or two, but he seemed to look about twelve, and very blond, the sun apparently in his eyes. Slow music gradually growing louder, and himself again, standing at the podium, just finishing his funeral speech. They had caught the one moment when he had, quite by accident, given the right look: a direct, solemn, outward stare, seeming to meet the viewers' eyes – in this case, his own. Before he could be seen trudging gracelessly down the steps, the papers in hand, other pictures, other scraps of footage took over, himself with his parents, waving.

Helena said, 'It's finished.'

Tobias murmured, 'Wait a minute. They're playing it over and over again.'

Indeed, a dark subtitle had appeared. 'A special announcement. There will be no ordinary sessions today.'

An unmoving picture of the Golden House. Black standards outside, black pennants hanging from the upper rows of windows.

Someone said, 'The palace asks for the following message to be given to the Roman people. "The Emperor has been told that the vigiles no longer expect to find Marcus Novius Faustus Leo alive. This is too painful a time for any of the Imperial family to speak in person at present."'

That was all the palace apparently wanted to say. It vanished and a sober information official arrived tactfully with the explanation. 'It is understood that a confession has been made, and that Caius Varius, a former aide to the Emperor's brother, will face trial very shortly for Marcus Novius' murder; and for the murder of his wife, Gemella Paulina, whose death was not made public until this time, and for treason against the Emperor and the State.'

A picture of Varius had appeared in the corner of the screen, and remained there as the spokesman talked; Varius startled against some blurred brick background, head just turning towards the lens. Even though he'd been woken up a little by whatever had surprised him, and there were no bruises or cuts visible on his face, even in such a small picture, Marcus could see how he looked shattered, dismantled, half-dead. There was a slackness about the eyelids, the muscles of the face. Anyone who knew him would have seen it.

Marcus put out an arm and leaned slowly and deliberately against the wall.

Then the sequences of himself came in again, and the music grieving over him.

'It's not really going to be like this all day, is it?' said Helena, disgustedly, as the cycle began again.

But Marinus whistled, 'Well, what the hell are they doing?' and Tiro said, 'Do you know that man?'

Marcus shook his head, not denying, shaking the question away. Then he said clearly, 'No, I don't really know him, he worked for my father. It must be a mistake, or something – I don't understand it.'

'Where are you going?'

'To tell Delir.'

He didn't notice whatever else they said to him. He told himself, you must decide *now*, right now, before anyone else can find out and stop you. He did not yet let this form itself as, before Una comes back. He went across the bridge, thinking and thinking, yet hardly aware that he was doing so; just as if, though he knew he was shocked, though the guilt and fear for Varius writhed and capered – moaning at him that however worried he'd been until now it had not been enough – it was of no interest.

He'd meant to go to his own and Sulien's room, just to stand still out of sight and think, but there was no need. He went past Delir's cabin, he'd never had any intention of going in.

Lal was listlessly drawing up the next week's rota, or had been doing so. She got up, and absolutely without purpose, except perhaps with the idea of looking sluttish and worrying Delir, applied stale gold make-up, which Flora had left behind when she went, elaborately to one eye, and could not get the other eye to match. Hot tears bubbled without warning from beneath the mismatched gold daubings. She began rubbing the make-up off and lost interest in that, too, and sat down again at her desk with eyelids still smeared, and examined her rota. It was good at least to have a task that let her stay lurking inside, where she was safe from the risk and hope of running into Sulien, and the grating irrelevance of everything else. But this was a dangerous job, too, because Sulien's name loomed and burned out of the lists. Deciding his actions, putting him in one slot or another, was both satisfying and painful. She was fair, she tried not to make his life either easier or more difficult than anyone else's, although she wanted to do both (because why couldn't you have put up more of a *fight*, she thought, touching his name again with her finger).

For a moment when the knock came at the door she thought it must be Sulien, simply because she couldn't think of anyone else, and rubbed in quick horror at her soiled eyes. When Marcus came in she was briefly flattened with disappointment, but in the same moment, saw the fraught, tense look of him and was, despite herself, interested enough to be slightly consoled. She thought shrewdly, something has happened with Una; but didn't expect him to say so urgently, 'Can you help me?'

Lal frowned, re-evaluating. She was sure she was right about Una, and this did not fit.

'I need you to make me some papers. You can do that, can't you, quickly?'

'What?'

'And I have to borrow enough money to get back to Rome.'

'*What?*'

'I have to go back and stop them.' His fingers were tapping a breathless, tachycardiac rhythm on the wall. 'They're saying Varius killed Gemella, that he killed *me*. They'll execute him.'

'Who's Varius?'

Marcus sighed and explained it impatiently, feeling himself start to shake now with frustration and alarm.

'I don't know what's been happening to him, all this time. It's *enough*. I've got to go now or I know Delir will stop me.'

'No,' said Lal decisively. 'I'm going to stop you.'

'You don't understand—'

'Yes I do, *you* don't. I'm not going to help you, because this is what they're trying to make you do. Surely. They're trying to get you on your own so they can kill you.'

'I know.'

After a second or two she gave an irritable little flick of the head, twitching away what he'd said.

'Marcus, everyone thinks you're already dead, they've explained you away *already*, they can do it so *easily* now!'

'I won't go the way they expect.'

'You don't *know* which way they expect! Oh, God!' Lal jumped to her feet, suddenly alive to how serious this was. 'They wouldn't *do* this unless they knew where we are – they're just waiting for you to come out!'

'You can help me there, too. They know we go to Athabia, so I won't go there, we can work it out—'

'*No, we can't!*'

Again there was a moment of silent impasse, in which they could do nothing but stare, turn away from each other and stare back again, faces twisted both with exasperation and appeal: you *must* change your mind.

'Lal. Listen to me. It's easier for *me too*,' said Marcus finally, with strained patience. 'No one will help them now. If I'm already dead, why should anyone call the vigiles if they see someone that looks like me? If you give me the papers I can go where I want.'

'It doesn't matter about the papers, you wouldn't even get to use them,' said Lal wearily.

'I will, I've got to.' He turned his head sharply, teeth clenched, flinching, as if to dodge something that had been thrown at him. He'd remembered Gemella, slipping down onto the mosaic floor. 'Gemella and Varius were married. She's dead, already someone's died because of me.'

'You can't blame yourself for that.'

'I don't! I didn't know it was going to happen, I didn't have any way of stopping it! But after *this*— !'

Lal sighed this time, violently, emptying herself of breath. She sat down on her bed, pushing her face into her hands. 'Well. Maybe you always will feel guilty. Perhaps you should. Perhaps you'll have to . . .' she could hardly be heard, she wished that there was someone else to say this, '. . . you'll have to accept that. Because there are more important things than how you feel.'

She looked up at him apprehensively, afraid he'd be disgusted with her, that maybe any decent person would be. He shivered, but said nothing, seeing, unwillingly, how hard it had been for her to say. He cleared his throat but could only mutter, 'But Varius . . .'

She said more quietly than before, 'He sent you to us? To keep you safe?'

'Yes.'

'What would he tell you to do?'

He hesitated. Reluctantly he said, 'Yes, I think he'd tell me to stay,' and was quiet, they both were, neither of them moved. Then he said, just as softly, 'And so would Delir, and so are you, even though Dama was right, I *have* brought the vigiles this close, I *am* risking everyone here. So why? Why is everyone doing so much for me?'

'Because we want you to be Emperor,' answered Lal.

'*Yes*. And if I let this happen, *how can I be?* If I don't even try? If I just keep letting other people protect me and I don't do anything for them?'

'But you will. When it's time, you will.'

'How will it ever be time? Who's going to make it time? I'm not the heir, not yet. If my uncle thinks I'm dead, he'll have to name someone else anyway.' He thought, with sudden compassion, poor Uncle Titus! My father and now me! 'And he was ill in the spring; or maybe they'd kill him, too. Then everything Varius did to help me, and everything Delir has done, and Una and Sulien—'

He shouldn't have mentioned them. He felt a hideous pull of anticipatory loss as he realised for the first time that he was trying to leave without even seeing or speaking to them first, without saying goodbye, that he was going to put hundreds of miles between himself and Una. Lal saw it, saw him falter.

But he still said, 'Then there'd be no good in ever going back. Drusus would be Emperor, I never could be. And why should I be? I let Varius send me here, I've hidden. What have I done that shows I should be Emperor? And Varius was the only person who knew what was going on. If he dies, and I'm just *waiting* here, why should anything change in Rome? I have to be there. I've got to go home.'

And Lal could not quite understand why she could say nothing to this. It was not exactly that she was certain he was right, but all her arguments seemed weak before she could get them started; it didn't seem to matter, even to herself, what she thought. And she couldn't any longer believe that she didn't have to persuade him, that she could just refuse to help him, she could tell her father. Instead she tried, with final cunning, 'What about Una?'

He'd been looking straight at her. Now he lowered his eyes, suddenly inarticulate, losing all the clarity with which he'd been speaking. He hadn't known that Lal knew this. He mumbled, 'Explain it to her. Say goodbye.'

'That's all?'

He smiled crookedly. 'She knows everything else.' He thought and added, 'Say, everything we agreed about the money and their freedom still stands.' He was dismayed by how cold this sounded, how far it was from what he meant.

He tried again: 'Say, afterwards, I want to see them both, they should come to Rome. Tell Sulien that, too.'

But he could not seem to imagine this happening. He said it and knew he'd never see either of them, never see Una again.

If anyone, Una especially, had tried to stop him then, he would at least have hesitated, and that must have meant giving way in the end. Delir could certainly make it impossible for him to leave, physically impossible even, if all else failed.

But Lal shut her eyes and found herself saying, 'I'll tell them. Stand over there.' She hung a sheet over the door to make a plain background for his face.

She had blank templates ready, but the time it took her to take and clip out the picture, stick it down, write in a new name, place and date of birth, stamp it, seemed terrible to Marcus. How long had it been since he'd left Una by the waterfall? It must already be half an hour.

'Gnaeus Nemetorius Carius all right for you?'

'Yes, yes.'

And it was long past noon, there were not many hours left before dark. A map at least had been easy to get hold of quickly, for they were everywhere, everyone was supposed to be familiar with the hills around the gorge, to memorise the escape routes marked out. He studied it and the emptiness that protected the camp made him sigh now. In the north was a little town called Iluro, only seventeen miles away, where he could have caught a train to Tarba, and from there towards Rome. With regret he decided that anyone looking at the same area would predict such a route. Better to go the wrong way, into Spain. But that way there was nothing within thirty or thirty-five miles. He calculated grimly: on the way from Nemausus he'd sometimes walked as much as twenty miles in a day, but as he failed to sleep and his flesh waned and ached, he'd usually failed to keep up the pace the next day. And in the woods, on the way from Wolf Step, they'd allowed themselves to go no faster or further than was easy. But this time, if he threw all the strength he could into walking, walked in the light and the dark, saved nothing at all for the following day, because there was no need – he *would* make it in a day, *less* than a day, he decided severely, setting his body, warning it. There was another station at Panticosa, a tiny spa town, Lal said; he picked it because it seemed a perverse place to head for, so far south and east. He was not sure what he'd have to do then, whether he could go straight back through Gaul or if he'd have to ride to Pompaelo or Caesaraugusta first, but he hoped it would make little difference. He thought he could be in Rome early the morning after tomorrow, though it was so hard to believe, it felt so far.

There was still the money. Lal had almost nothing of her own and he'd need – two hundred, three hundred sesterces?

'It's all right, my father has a little safe, I can open it,' said Lal.

'I'll give it back.'

'Yes.'

'There's enough?'

'Yes.'

'But enough so that you can spare it – the camp'll be all right without it?'

'Don't *worry*, not about *that*, anyway.'

Marcus nodded, unhappy, but it wasn't fair to show hesitancy about this, it was as if he was trying to prompt Lal to share accountability for the theft with him, to encourage him to go.

Lal marched robustly round to Delir's room, hoping he wouldn't be there, but at the door she heard voices, and paused.

'I hate thinking of anyone waiting in Athabia and no one coming for them.'

'We can leave word with Palben, he would tell them which way to go.'

Ziye was there, then.

'But if they're in no state to go any further? Think of Pyrrha, or Chilo, do you remember?'

Lal glowered a little and went in anyway. Delir smiled

with surprise and hope, it had been days since she'd come near him voluntarily. But Lal said stonily – in fact out of a kind of compassion for him – she couldn't act friendly now and then have him find out it had been a trick: 'Iris says Pyrrha's started talking again. She's asking for you.'

Delir got up at once.

'Delir,' said Ziye, 'It can wait a minute—'

'No, no, it can't. Are you coming, Lal?'

'I am still doing the rota,' Lal told him coolly.

Delir looked at her sorrowfully. Oh, you awful, self-pitying little man, thought Lal clearly, vacillating between annoyance and sympathy. She was worried that Ziye might not follow Delir, but she smiled warily at Lal and slipped out after him at once. Afraid of being left alone with me!, realised Lal, startled and pleased at the idea.

She pulled back the curtain that screened Delir's bed; the strongbox was underneath.

While Lal was gone Marcus fidgeted with his identification papers and the map, seething with impatience and anxiety by now. If Delir was still there how could she get the money? And if he was not, someone would tell him about the longvision, and Varius. He tried to write a letter for Delir but he could not get any further than 'I'm sorry. Thank you.'

He glanced at himself in Lal's mirror. His hair was still shorter than it had been in Rome, but it wasn't stubble, it looked ordinary. He thought he was taller but it was hard to be sure, maybe it was just wishful thinking. He pushed uncertainly at the flesh of his jaw, thinking the shape of his face seemed somehow different, too. He was beginning to be glad of these changes, if they were really there; but he thought, with a shiver of incredulity – soon I'll *want* people to recognise me, soon they'll have to.

Lal came back and handed him the sheaf of money in silence. He said finally, 'Can you change with whoever's doing the watch? Or they'll see me leave. Try and keep it quiet as long as you can.'

Lal groaned faintly. 'I am in such trouble, you're getting me into such trouble . . . !'

Marcus squeezed her hand. 'I won't forget.'

She gave him a little kiss on the cheek. And he went outside. He wouldn't see her again, he wouldn't see Delir again – he shook himself. Why should he think this way? He didn't intend to get killed. Why shouldn't he come back, afterwards?

He needed his coat, a change of clothes. As he packed he realised he had nothing of his own to take with him. The clothes were those Sulien had bought for him in Wolf Step, and he shoved them into Sulien's pack. (He thought there had been another bag, but he couldn't find it.) What little else there was belonged to Varius, or were remnants left in the camp by men or boys he'd never meet, who – the thought brushed against him strangely, even in his hurry – were doing real things, moving in real places, unless they were dead.

He snatched up his coat and found under it the blue-grey hat Una had given him. He'd been stuffing things into the bag in an agony of haste, but he stared at it quietly, attentively, as if he'd forgotten what he was doing, as if it were a work of art. He did not put it on. He folded it gently and unnecessarily, and put it in the pocket of the bag.

Settling down in front of the grey screens Lal saw him walk quickly past the lift to one of the nearer ladders, climb up onto the path and away from it, into the beech forest, followed him through it.

But at the top of the hill, out of her sight, Marcus stopped. Below, ahead of him lay a great bare stretch of ribbed cold grass, flecked with thin sheep. He stood on the edge of it, and bit his lip. He could see himself as if from a distance, a moving, coloured point, tiny but plainly the only human on the mountainside. Anyone in the air, anyone even looking out from the valley or the next ridge, would see him as soon as he stepped away from the trees. And if he toiled down through the woods, looking for another way southeast, how long would that take?

The scale of the empty land around him had encouraged him at first. But he felt paralysed by it now. He thought, idiot. It was further than he'd let himself think, of course it was, he couldn't walk a straight line through the mountains.

And he'd been allowing Una's name to beat along in his head to the rhythm of his feet, growing louder and fiercer the further he went from her. He was starting to think how *wrong* it was, not only that he wouldn't see her again but that *that* should be the last way he saw her, after a failed kiss, and her so meek and speechless as if she were someone else completely. And what was she doing now, what would she do and how would she feel when she realised he'd gone?

He'd just been standing there, he hadn't been watching, listening! Suddenly he could imagine someone coming up silently behind him, saw it so intensely that it was as if he was the killer and not himself. He turned. He could see nothing.

He couldn't consider going back. Move, move, he urged himself, and couldn't.

And two miles to the north, the little group of men knew where he was. They had let him travel far enough to be sure he was out of sight of the camp's cameras, out of earshot, beyond help. They knew when Marcus travelled east from the gorge, when he turned south, they knew when he stopped. They began to move.

[XVII]

THORNS

Una thought, I have to pick some point at which to go back. Pick now, because I'm never going to want to, it's no good waiting for it to feel right, it won't.

She picked now, over and over again, before she got up competently and walked back along the gorge towards the cabins, her face, she thought, made straight like a bed. Since the motionless tears would not submit to glaring and sink back into her eyes, she had to skim them out, fastidiously, one at a time. They had been fixed there so long that it hardly felt like crying, she could think of it almost as an act of neatness, as simply discarding something. She wiped and blotted her cheeks thoroughly, like a cat.

She also felt, I've ruined everything. She couldn't think of any way of reassuring herself, of promising herself that if she only did this, it would be all right. She couldn't think even of what to want next, a way of being with Marcus, of living in the camp that she should aim for. She only wanted it not to be now.

She didn't want to face anyone, and yet she felt that she didn't want to be alone any longer either. Perhaps she could find Sulien and help with whatever he was doing, without explaining herself. With mild surprise she found herself thinking of Lal, too – she could go and sit among the mural women and take over the rota and let Lal talk to her about Sulien. But Lal could hook things out of people, she *liked* to do so – she was too dangerous.

Of course she could hook things out of people herself, but it was so different. And for Marcus' sake what she should do now was go touring round the camp probing and listening. She could at least do that, although she didn't want to know what anyone felt.

Just outside the huts, leaning forward against the slope, she found Dama, dragging fiercely on a string he'd looped around a young branch, rotating his arms out from the elbow, again and again. The right end of the string was twisted between his fingers and round his wrist; he couldn't hold it.

She wished she knew if he'd seen Marcus, walking back, but otherwise it was good to see someone without having to breathe air thick with what they felt. She was confident that she could say, amiably, 'Hello, what are you doing?' without any quiver in her voice or face.

'Sulien said I should do this, or something like this, nearly all the time. My shoulders, the muscles here. It *is* helping.'

But he'd stopped, and he shook the string off his fingers with a look of disgust.

'It must look ridiculous, pulling a tree about.'

'Of course not.'

But he did not start again; he began walking beside her. He said, 'Are you all right? Are you unhappy?'

She hadn't been warned, she wasn't braced against unexpected sympathy. Pinned between the two questions, she said, 'No!'

'No? I think you are.' He wanted her to let him console her and yet he was not certain how to do it, and afraid of making her say something about Marcus that he would not wish to hear.

'I'm fine!' but she saw this was not enough, she could feel now that, if nothing else, the effort of looking normal was showing. 'I'm – tired.'

Dama smiled rather stiffly. 'All right, you are fine, I don't look ridiculous.'

'You *don't*,' she said, with a kind of impatient gasp that he should think such a thing; it seemed to unsteady her further. 'Why should you?'

Dama murmured tentatively, 'Is it that . . . you used to know that you should get out, you should save Sulien, you should get here, and now . . . ?'

Una sighed, beginning to relax into a kind of sad trance, and feeling a tired relief that he had not mentioned Marcus. She did not trouble so much about controlling her voice. 'I do – yes, I wonder what I should do.' And it was true, the distress about Marcus seemed to overbrim out of its right place, to permeate through everything. Since he'd left her she'd kept finding herself thinking, what am I going to *do*, what am I *for*?

'You could stay here and help us.' She nodded patiently. He said, 'It isn't enough.'

'Oh, it is—' she thought he must have been offended by the look on her face.

'I feel like that.'

They walked on in silence before she whispered, 'How did you know I did?'

'I think we are similar in some ways.'

'Yes,' she said, still dazed.

'But you mustn't think you're going to waste your life, *I* know you never would. Neither of us will, when there's so much work, so much to work *against*: Rome, slavery.'

She said unhappily, 'That's for Marcus to do.'

'No, it's for everyone to do. You feel that, you know it.'

'Yes, because everyone who does nothing is part of it,' she said, surprising herself, warmed through for a second.

Dama, as at the moment when she'd said she wasn't a slave any more, was delighted, his face, for a moment, illuminated. But Una said, wearily again, 'Yes, I feel like that, but I don't know what we're supposed to do about it, I can't—'

They had reached the huts. To Una they looked somehow flattened, hollow, missing something, as if she was seeing them out of only one eye. It seemed natural.

'If your Novius—' Dama heard the rough edge in his own voice and knew this was a mistake; he began again quickly, 'If it does happen, everything will change and we have to be ready. To help. To make sure no one gets in the way, or stops it. If it doesn't – if it doesn't then – then we have to be ready again.'

'He isn't mine,' she said, speaking a little coldly for the first time.

Delir was stumping crossly along a walkway on the right, with Ziye, who called across to them, 'Have you seen Lal? Or Pyrrha?'

Una shook her head. 'Oh, *that woman*,' said Delir, with rare sourness and indeed, self-pity. 'If she's gone berserk again I swear so will I, I will bloody well go mad and see how *she* likes it.'

But Una didn't move, and scarcely noticed as Delir and Ziye hurried down the ladders and across the bridge, darting past her. The sense of cold, of *lack*, was worse now and more urgent. It was as if she had forgotten a warning, or walked into a familiar room where the shadows had changed because one of the lights had stopped working.

Dama was troubled. 'What is it, is it what I said?'

'No,' she said, but distractedly, and stood another second, allowing the feeling room to move now, urging it on, for soon she would see what it was. She turned in a slow, automatic circle. 'He isn't supposed to leave the gorge, he—'

She did what she had never done before and ran up to the hut Marcus shared with Sulien, threw open the door. Following her, Dama demanded, 'What are you doing?'

Una stared at the disordered room. She had not a clear enough idea of what it should be like. Except that Marcus was not in it, it betrayed nothing. She could see clothes she thought were Marcus', jumbled together with Sulien's; their belongings were too few and too indistinct from one another for the absence of any of them to show starkly that someone had vanished.

She did not think to look for the wool hat, even now she had no idea how much power she'd bestowed on the little thing.

She dragged out a protesting drawer in a fever, there must

after all be some evidence. She could not *find* Marcus, and she was the more certain with every breath that she would not find him; and suppose it was not that he had left the gorge, suppose Tiro or Marinus or someone else had really been willing to murder him and she hadn't seen it?

Dama stood, watching her intently, with a sort of hurt, stern vigilance. 'He's gone somewhere?'

'His *coat*,' cried Una suddenly. 'And Sulien still had our bags, they're not here! *Marcus*.' She put both her hands to her face, but for a moment felt angry, trembling relief. If he had left the gorge freely then he had stupidly endangered himself; but still Pyrrha had come to no harm in the woods, or rather, the only harm had been caused by Pyrrha herself. And they had found Pyrrha pretty easily.

He wouldn't go off because of her, in a *sulk*? The idea was frightening and embarrassing, but at the same time it provoked the scorn that had always strengthened her, like the heat of a strong drink. It was possible to see the whole thing as ridiculous.

'Delir had better know,' said Dama blandly.

Strangely, this had not occurred to her yet, her only instinct had been to tell Sulien.

But Sulien and Delir were both already coming out of the longvision room. In the laundry Helena had told Sulien that the news people seemed to think Marcus Novius had been murdered ages ago, and there wasn't going to be anything else on all day; and Delir had gone in looking for Lal and had seen the small bewildered audience watching the mournful cycle on the screen.

As Una and Dama approached they heard Delir asking Tobias angrily, 'Why didn't anyone come and tell me?'

'I thought you had been told already, I thought you were talking about it with Marcus Novius.'

'Marcus has already *seen* this?'

She didn't understand yet why they were already agitated, but she felt the cold creep back; she thought, this is worse, this is much worse.

'He's gone,' Dama told them abruptly.

Sulien and Delir turned to him with the faintly affronted, reproachful look of people who have no time yet to take in what they have heard. Sulien said, 'What, Marcus? What do you mean?'

The broadcast was clearly an attempt to account for Marcus' permanent disappearance, but Sulien and Delir had seen it as the prelude to some kind of new assault; it was not at once obvious to them that the aim was to goad Marcus into the open.

At the same time Una whispered, 'What is it? About Varius—?'

She was about to rush between them into the longvision hut and see what they'd seen. But something stopped her, someone nearby, on fire or tied up in knots with guilt, knowledge, dread. Lal, as obvious now as if she had been in full sight.

Una flew up the steps into the monitor hut.

Lal, crouched in the glow of the screens, had drawn back against the far wall as if she expected to be physically attacked. She'd gone on staring at the top right screens after Marcus had disappeared, keeping Marcus' secret out of a deadly indecision, sometimes jigging or drumming her feet as the uncertainty over what she had done mounted to a physical pain. She could hear the noise outside, and feet rushing towards her door, and she cowered a little more closely as Una surged in like a personification of revenge: staring, white-faced and accusing; but Lal said quietly, without waiting to be questioned, 'Yes, he's gone back to Rome for Varius. He told me to explain to you.'

The others had poured in behind Una, and Lal braced herself for some kind of outburst, from Delir at least if not Una, but no one spoke, and Una continued to stare tensely at her, but without recognition now, only because it was the last thing she'd been doing.

'Lal!' exclaimed Delir, baffled. 'What are you talking about?'

Una was not conscious of how Dama was watching her face for any sign of how much this would mean to her. She stated calmly, 'Then they're just outside. They wanted to pull him out of here, and they have.'

Then there was a short time in which she seemed to have no business in the room; weakness rolled abruptly through her, and the growing racket of shocked voices, Lal and Delir and Ziye and Sulien, swept on without her taking any part in it. The wall had tapped suddenly against her shoulders and the back of her head, she couldn't do anything but stand there, lax. She and Dama were the only people quiet in the room.

'You've been sitting here, keeping this a secret? Lal! Don't you realise that they must know exactly where we are, don't you think that is important enough to tell me?'

Ziye muttered, 'Well, this is it, there can't be any question of staying here, now,' and Tobias began swearing unobtrusively and viciously to himself.

'I *had* to.' But now Marcus was gone, Lal couldn't seem to remember what he'd said to her, why she'd done what he wanted. 'I had to help him.'

'You wanted to help him but you let him go out like that, could you really not think what you were doing?' Something struck him and he gasped. 'You even came in and *lied* to me, didn't you – why?'

'So you'd go away and I could take some of your money for him,' offered Lal baldly, feeling a self-flagellating need for forthrightness now.

She held out Marcus' note but Delir barely noticed it, beginning, 'You are *stealing*?' and Sulien, stung by how wretched Lal looked, moved between them saying, 'Delir, stop it, it's not her fault. Marcus must have known what he was doing.'

Lal was touched but not comforted; for she looked up at Sulien quickly and saw how horrified he was beginning to be. He'd taken the sheet of paper from her and the four words on it looked so weakly final that he had to start to believe in what had happened.

She said, obstinately, to try out the plausibility of the words as much as anything, 'He thought he could get through; he was going southeast, it isn't obvious – he *could*.'

But Delir looked at Lal and Sulien together with a bitter air of putting two and two together that he'd never shown until now. 'Oh! Was *that* why, is this your idea of getting even with me?'

'No!' Lal shrieked, starting up, enraged into counter-attack for the first time, looking around as if for something to throw at him. 'It's got nothing to do with it, how can you *say* that! What about Varius, anyway?'

She had made Delir pause unhappily. 'We can't – solve everything, we cannot protect everyone,' he said.

Una began to hear what was being said again; she looked up, at Sulien, not at Dama. Sulien said to her, hurt, holding the sheet of paper, 'You can't just disappear like that – he came all that way with us. I'd have thought he'd at least say something.' Una shook her head, 'No. We wouldn't have let him go.'

Lal broke away from Delir's continuing outrage to say to them beseechingly, 'He didn't want to. He said goodbye, and you should find him in Rome, afterwards.'

The word 'afterwards' shook Una forwards. She cried, 'Oh, he's so stupid. They'll kill him. Why am I saying they *will* do it, how long has it been? They've had time already.'

Again all speech stopped. Lal took in a breath divided raggedly into three, like three steps, as if she was going to speak or cry, but only shrank back again.

Sulien too felt a self-rebuking start at standing still for what had really been barely a minute; he said firmly, 'No. We can catch him up. Lal. Which way is it?' Lal began mumbling, but Una seized her wrist abruptly and insisted, '*Show* me.' And Lal let herself be dragged; they would have fled stumbling out at once.

'Was *that* him?'

Dama, expressionless, had just been about to let them past, Sulien had almost cannoned into him. Now the four of them, Lal hanging desolately from Una's arm, froze at the door in an awkward huddle.

Tobias had tapped one of the lower screens. 'I saw someone on the perimeter.' Una rushed to look, but could only see bland trees.

'What? No.' Lal turned shakily back to the monitors and blinked at them. She pointed at the opposite corner. 'No, he was here. He was going towards Panticosa, it's in Spain.' It only occurred to her now that she'd begun obediently pouring out Marcus' route without even thinking, when Marcus would have wanted her to keep quiet. It appalled her; she seemed to be behaving as if she thought Marcus couldn't succeed – and in that case it was a terrible thing that she'd done.

'Are you sure? Someone coming in?' Delir stared at the featureless screen, hesitating. 'Lal, you must at least have *watched*?'

'I couldn't concentrate,' confessed Lal, almost sobbing.

'No,' said Tobias, quite calmly now. 'He was moving outwards, or we'd see him now.'

'Maybe he decided to go a different way, maybe he was coming back . . . ?'

'We *can't just stand here*,' raged Una, agonisingly aware of the seconds now.

And now they did as she said, they spilled from the hut and across the gorge, up out of the camp. There was no formal division into search parties. Tobias led down the gorge towards the village and the shadow he'd seen on the screen; and Delir, struggling up the way Lal had pointed, said crossly as she scrambled after him, '*No*, for God's sake, go back and be safe.' But Lal cried, 'I *can't*,' and when Delir had left her behind she ran after the others, Tobias and Ziye and Una. She expected that Ziye would at least attempt to send her back, but Ziye instead gave her a curious look, neither angry nor compassionate but amicably business-like, and thereafter seemed too intent on running and scanning the trees to notice her.

Una hardly knew why she had chosen to go that way, unless it was that the figure Tobias had seen at least meant something definite and alive to run towards. She thought, they wouldn't leave his body, I'd never know what they did to him, it would, it *will* be months before we could be certain he was dead.

But at the same time she found a quiet, optimistic homily running on with her like something Sulien might have said: There cannot be that many of them. It's one thing to have all the vigiles searching for him, but how many people could you actually trust to *do* the thing; assassinate one of the Novii and keep quiet about it? You would have to choose carefully. Perhaps they are getting desperate. And in so much forest over so many mountains, anything less than knowing precisely where to look can't be enough, you might be half a mile away from your target, half *that*, and still not find them. He could, he *could* get past.

They climbed over the artificial landslide that shielded the entrance to the gorge, hesitated and began to fan out, along the river, up the hillside, but before many minutes had passed Una and Lal, picking breathlessly up into the woods, heard Tobias shout. They both stopped, winded for a moment with hope. Lal, forgetting not to touch Una, clutched her hand. But Una didn't mind, having no time or presence of mind to think of it, as they sped and staggered down into the valley; also finding how tension could be earthed through a grip on another set of fingers.

They met Ziye at the bottom of the hill, just as Una felt a lurch of disappointment; for ahead of Tobias there was someone who was not Marcus, two people, two people who began to run, tottering, as they realised they had been seen.

But it was hopeless, for the second she saw them move, Ziye bounded forward after them. She felt her body to be out of form, past it; but the others saw her break into an astonishing, beautiful, lupine sprint, and as she raced terrifyingly ahead, Lal, even in her misery, could not help feeling a spark of excitement that finally they would see something of what she could do. They did not, or not exactly. Instead of unleashing any intricate blizzard of hands and feet, Ziye simply sprang, beautifully, and brought Pyrrha down to the ground with such ferocious animal litheness that neither woman seemed human; the lank creature in Ziye's grasp looked so like prey, a rabbit or sparrow, or any panicky dun-coloured thing; and they would hardly have been surprised to see Ziye open her throat quickly with claws or teeth.

Of course, she simply held Pyrrha easily against the ground, fixed.

At first Lal couldn't understand why; she thought that perhaps Pyrrha was just running away in panic again. Pyrrha at once began to keen and sob, and Iris, yelping in wrath and anguish, began beating at Ziye's back and head with her little fists, and then with a stick after Ziye batted her efficiently away the first time. Tobias had stood stunned for a moment but then dashed forward to scoop her away. Iris dangled in his arms, spitting, kicking.

'Iris, Iris,' mourned Pyrrha.

Iris had been squirming and scratching Tobias, but as Lal and Una approached wanly, and she saw how outnumbered they were, she seemed suddenly to lose interest and hung so limply that Tobias gradually let her slip down onto the ground. She wandered over and looked dispassionately at her mother without making any further attempt to help her, and could be seen visibly detaching herself from anything that might happen now. She went and leaned wearily against a tree.

'Una,' said Ziye, through her teeth, 'tell me if I'm right.'

Una reeled forwards, feeling like a ghost, a slight thickening of the damp cold air, her hand still resting numbly in Lal's. She stared at Pyrrha, and whispered, 'You *sold* him.'

'No, no I didn't, they were going to get him anyway!' wailed Pyrrha. 'They were going to *find* us, they'd have taken Iris, this way it's better. Oh let go, let me go!'

'What about Marcus, and Delir, and all of us who *helped* you?' hissed Ziye, disgusted.

And Una demanded, though her voice still had no strength in it, 'What arrangement did you make? What are they going to do?'

But after that they could get no sense out of Pyrrha, who as so often was conscious of nothing but terror and persecution. She would only moan, 'For *Iris*, for *Iris*, to *look after* her, I'm no good, I'm never going to be any good, I can't do anything, what else was I supposed to do?'

Iris, vaguely occupied with picking the bark off a twig, remarked, 'You might as well let us go. It doesn't make any difference now.'

She was so quietly certain that Una, shuddering, felt the hopeful chirping little monologue begin to gutter out.

'Don't *talk* to them,' begged Pyrrha. Iris ignored her.

'It was that day when you ran off,' Una said, still on her breath. 'You went to the village.' For a moment she could not think how she hadn't seen it, and then, as she saw how Iris watched her in trepidation, she saw bitterly, because they were never there. Because they hid from me. How did they know to do that? There was a pause while she struggled to remember, but then the answer came: I told Tiro how I knew about Tasius, and Iris was there. That's what all that show of being ill and keeping everyone out was for!

And she had never wanted to be near Iris and Pyrrha.

'Not like that, not at once, it was *so awful*,' whimpered Iris, piteously. 'You know how scared she was. I didn't want to go with her but I *had* to. And then she didn't know where to go, and – I said we should go back and I *left* her because I thought that would make her follow me. But she didn't so I had to go back for her and she'd done that with her wrists. Although – with *sticks*, it's pathetic.' She looked with familiar contempt at Pyrrha. 'And we were there for hours and hours. And it was so cold.' She shivered.

'Oh, we've got to go, why won't you let us go, they're waiting for us,' complained Pyrrha.

'And I *kept* saying, we have to go back, we can't go anywhere. We haven't got any money. And in the end I thought, of course there's a way we could get some.'

Tobias was more shocked by this than anything that had happened so far. 'It was *your* idea? A child!' and to Pyrrha,

'And you'd commit murder because your little girl told you to!'

'It *wasn't* murder, it was bound to happen anyway,' whined Pyrrha, while Iris sighed, 'I *don't know*, I can't remember, it was so cold and horrible! I don't think I said it. Maybe we thought of it at the same time. The thing was . . .' She looked at Pyrrha again, wistfully this time. 'It was like when we escaped, she was *better*. She knew what she was doing. She said off we go then, we'll go to Athabia. She was like that until we started getting back and then she started . . . *worrying*, again,' she said euphemistically, and shrugged. 'But, well, so we went to the village. We said – *she* said, she knew where – where he was.' She didn't want to use any of Marcus' names.

Pyrrha was snivelling more quietly now, she said in a hurt, appealing voice, as if she hoped she could win them round, 'And they wanted *me* to kill – to – they thought *I* could do it, and of course I couldn't, I wouldn't do that!' She gazed at them, eyes round with wronged entreaty. 'Then – they just asked me to wait and meet them and take something back for them, and that's all I did, really that's all.'

'Take what?' grunted Ziye, making Pyrrha begin to weep and shake her head again; and Una could almost see what it must have been, but she couldn't find the will to force it into sight before Iris spoke, she shrank almost from hearing it.

'A thing to put on him, or on his bag, so that when he moved they could see where he was,' said Iris dully. 'A tracking thing. They said to do it this morning.' She looked up at them and said, trying to smile, with a brief return of her inane, grandmotherly, clucking self. 'So – there we are! There's no good arguing about it now!'

A hot, useless fountain of urgency boiled up through Lal, because she could see herself, stepping into her father's room and instead of robbing him saying, 'Help me, Marcus is trying to leave the camp,' and it looked so possible and clear that she felt she should still be able to do it. Great gouts of tears coursed out of her, soundlessly. She let go of Una to bury her face in her hands, because she was afraid of Una now, of everyone who would understand, rightly, that she had done this, but Una especially – and Sulien.

And Una closed her eyes, with a blunt, certain feeling of striking hard ground at last. She said loudly, 'How long has it been?'

'I – I don't know,' whispered Lal.

'But more than an hour.'

It was impossible that the assassins should have waited so long to intercept him.

Una nodded, also mocked by the need to change what had only just happened – so little time since they'd been standing together by the white trunk of water! But what she felt was how cold and distant and impossible it was. So she did not exactly think, if only I had done that, but she wanted to remove herself from the memory and insert someone else, someone who would shake her head when Marcus said, 'Do you want me to leave you alone?' and could kiss him properly or at least say something, presumably, afterwards.

She almost thought that instead of that, she could just have hung onto him, not bothered with any show of affection, just weighed him down, as she had done in the street that first night.

Her skin seemed to sting where he'd touched it.

Ziye hauled Pyrrha onto her feet, with such a grim look of intent on her scarred face that Iris gave a little cry of protest and Pyrrha was shocked into apprehensive quiet, and stuttered softly, 'What are you going to do to me?' Ziye said slowly, 'I'll say this to you because you have a child, otherwise I wouldn't waste another second on you. Ask yourself whether they'd leave you alive, knowing what you know.' And with that she released Pyrrha with a shove and spat, 'Now, go where you want, only be sure it's away from me.' She turned her back and left Pyrrha standing, trembling, mute.

Lal breathed in soft, disbelieving agony, 'It isn't them.

They don't know what they're doing, I did. I could have stopped him so easily. Oh, Una, I'm so sorry.'

Una stared at her heavily. Ziye said, 'You couldn't have known.'

But Lal could not allow this, she shook her head, desolate. It was no defence. She murmured, 'But I should have done, and it doesn't matter – I knew enough to know I shouldn't do it.' For she remembered all the *true* things she had said: this is what they're trying to make you do, they can do it so easily now, there are more important things than how you feel – why had she suddenly abandoned them? She thought, only because it had seemed right, and she could produce no reason for it.

Then Una said to her, in a high tired voice but deliberately, one block of words at a time, '*He* decided. Not you. And for him it *was* right. But it was right for us to try and bring him back—' She stopped, hearing the past tense growing relentlessly towards Marcus, but it hadn't reached him yet; she hadn't said '*he* was'. She stared at Lal, pulled at her hand, fabricating a burst of irrational hope.

'No, we still don't know. We can look for him. Come on, we can still try.'

Tasius was carrying the little portable screen, on which the spark that was Marcus Novius had begun fleeing south once more, as if he felt them coming.

Tasius never usually felt any desire to kill anyone, just a useful sense of his own capacity to do it, the knowledge that he had already been as much changed by doing it as he could be; it held nothing new for him. But this was new: this time, although he knew he was thinking about extinguishing only a young boy – a child almost, whom he had never met and who had never injured him – he wanted ferociously to be the one to do it. Quickly, expertly, as he'd planned. He wanted to prove what he knew, that he was subtler and *better* than either of the two other men with him now, Ennius and Ramio, that he had been the right choice in the first place. He was even a little scared by how fierce the feeling was, how he wanted to obliterate the girl and the odd-looking young man, too, to *punish* them, even though they were nothing to do with the task in hand.

He could not put it aside, he was kept itching with rage by the fact that what he was doing now, following a point of light on a screen, required next to no skill at all. And he was infuriated by Ennius and Ramio, because he did not rate them. He felt that they were too informal; they talked too much. It seemed to him that they wasted time on stupid little bragging jeers. (It did not occur to him that he had not noticed this about them until the jeers were aimed at him.)

Were they even good shots? Well – he was being un-reasonable – of course they would be, good enough, no doubt. They were ex-Praetorian and ex-army like himself, or so he had judged, without asking them. They would not fail, certainly. But he would be far from surprised if they shattered the boy's shoulder before striking his head. Admittedly it made no difference to the outcome, but he had taken seriously the instruction that the boy was to feel as little as possible, and took it seriously still, despite the alarming intensity of the urge to pinch him out of life. If he could not be the one to take the shot, he would rather have been in one of the other groups and missed it altogether.

Of course this was not the army, he had no rank exactly – so he had not been demoted. But he knew his status had plummeted. Ennius and Ramio, and the others, treated him with scorn that was incidental but not hidden. He felt permanently constricted with humiliation. He wished he'd lied, when he'd finally trampled, exhausted and furious, back to the little base in the woods, ten miles northeast of Athabia. He could have said that the slaves' technology was better or their searches more thorough than either he had expected or than seemed to be true. He wished Dama and Una really had found his needles. But he was so tormented with frustration that he could not do anything but explain what had really happened, that he had done everything right and yet the girl had known.

They assumed he was lying as it was, that really he must

400

have done something so blindingly stupid that even these cornered wretches could not help but rumble him, and then had not even had the competence to get the location of the camp out of one of them. It was sheer luck that an informer had come forward so quickly afterwards. Today Ramio had said, handing him the tracker, 'Think you can handle that?'

He did not know what effect, if any, this would have on his payment. They would still have to be sure he would be silent. He had been, for a day or two, unpleasantly conscious that there was another way of ensuring that – but with the start of this operation he had ceased worrying seriously in that way. He just could not wait to see the back of these people, he was sick of the whole thing.

'Straight ahead, heading south again,' he said neutrally.

'What is he *doing*?' muttered Ennius to himself, not requiring an answer, for Marcus had moved in an agitated little knot, and until a minute ago had been heading north again towards the trees. Tasius said nothing although the question exasperated him. He found Marcus' erratic progress quite natural. Cretin, he thought to Ennius; he doesn't know which way is safest. He is afraid. He wants to go back.

And he could not avoid an illicit, heartening thought: the plan might be that he merely guide Ennius and Ramio into sight of Marcus Novius and let them take it from there. Nevertheless, he was armed, too, and indeed the quick emphasis of a gunshot would suit this mood better than the stealth of the poisoned needles he'd carried into Athabia. Something might still change. He might still have his chance.

They reached the peak and crouched, looking down the bare green slope towards Marcus.

There were still some hours before sunset, but the low grey sky allowed only a little shadowy light in among the trees. Sulien found he had left Delir and Dama behind. He paused for a second, deciding it was probably better if they spread out, and then trying to make certain that he was going the right way. He went pushing on, beginning to think for the first time what he'd do if he found Marcus, how he could make him come back. He'd been jolting single-mindedly through the trees as if Marcus must immediately see he'd made a mistake the second Sulien appeared and told him so. Or as if he'd simply got lost and needed to be picked up.

He began rehearsing, with real and intensifying anger, arguing Marcus through the millions of people, Varius included, who couldn't be helped if Marcus got himself killed. But he was just concluding, least logically and, he sensed, most persuasively, 'There has to be some other way to save Varius, come back and I'll help you,' when, on the very edge of visibility, which was not much of a distance through the beeches, he saw a shape, closing the spaces between the bars of the trees, human, moving.

Thank heaven he did not immediately call out 'Marcus'. For it was a small group of men – three or four – he couldn't see them clearly – stealing resolutely along. Sulien froze, then stepped loudly and belatedly, or so it felt, behind a tree trunk too slim to hide him perfectly; and in imagination went through a detailed, instantaneous process of being seen, caught, questioned, shot – before in another moment he'd lost sight of them.

He couldn't understand why they were all in a single group, instead of combing the woods separately, why they weren't looking around; if they'd been as absorbed in watching their surroundings as he was himself they surely must have seen him. And yet there had been a confidence about the way they moved; they had certainly been focused on something. Were they following Marcus then? He wondered uncertainly if they'd been trained to track people by following broken twigs and crushed leaves, as he'd heard that Terranovan and African hunters could, or had been able to once.

He didn't know what to do. If they were heading for Marcus, how could Sulien get to him first? He wondered if there was any way of distracting them – looking through the woods they could easily mistake him for Marcus – and leading them away from wherever they were going. But he remembered what Una had told him of the spy chasing her through the scrub, towards the car, and knew he was too close, with nowhere safe to head for, no means of shaking them. It could only end one way, and almost immediately.

He was afraid too that Delir and Dama would stumble into them as he so nearly had himself. But if he went back to warn them he'd lose the assassins altogether, and they would never know what had happened.

Hardly knowing why, he found he was simply creeping after them, shuddering at the noises he made in the undergrowth, and at the thought, really I can't stop them from doing anything. He tried to think, or wish, suppose they did it wrong, suppose he was only injured, then I could . . .

And like Varius in Rome – although he could not know that – he had the sense that if all he could do was watch, then he should at least do that. He'd forgotten his indignation with Marcus, he felt too sick with the forlorn, powerless feeling that he couldn't bear to see him die.

Ennius was gazing downwards through binoculars, Ramio had his gun ready on his shoulder, both were still quite composed. Tasius was the only one to feel the clutching of anxiety in his stomach.

'This isn't right,' he muttered, hating having to say this.

The others must assume that Marcus was hidden down in the crease of the valley.

They glanced at him, more disdainful than questioning, as he had known they would be. He cleared his throat, trying to keep both anger and confused horror off his face now. 'He should be visible now.'

'Are you holding that thing upside down?' demanded Ramio.

'Four hundred yards,' Tasius told him quietly, professionally, 'And straight ahead.'

Ramio grabbed the screen out of his hands, stared at it with slow bafflement. He said dubiously, 'Is the scale right?'

But Tasius ignored him as certainty, appalling and hilarious broke over him. He snatched the machine back and broke out of the cover of the trees, careering down the stark grass. A small drift of gaunt, mad-eyed sheep bolted in an alarmed eddy as he approached, and then slowed to a forgetful trot. Tasius stood and laughed at them, dizzy. One had fled from him awkwardly, hobbled by something; a long thin thorny sprig, snagged in the fleece of its side, dotted with ripped wool, and dragging behind it on the ground. And there was something else, a greyish loop of twisted fabric, caught on the prongs of the branch. Tasius wanted to slam the screen he held down on the ground, and yet at the same time he felt a kind of shaken amusement – satisfaction, almost – that he knew would soon fade into real apprehension and fear. He could hear Ennius and Ramio angrily blundering after him. But they couldn't blame him this time.

He didn't need to check again to be sure the animal was moving as the point on the screen moved; and the transmitter must be bundled up in the knotted shirt.

Running uphill, Una felt a pain like sharp teeth locked in her side, her head filling and pounding, and she kept running to keep it so, it would have been deadly even to slow down enough to catch her breath. She could almost remember this from the week she'd had to plan saving Sulien from the cross, the night she'd escaped. Once she'd decided that she *would not let* them kill him, at least, that *nothing* she could do would be spared, then the terror for Sulien could be held off, or almost. But now she felt that in another moment this ruthless state was going to fail her, because it was a cheat, a lie. In London she'd known what was going to happen and when, she'd known until the moment she heard the shots that she hadn't failed yet, he was still alive.

Still, she could not keep up with Ziye, who was out of sight. Lal struggled on beside Una, panting, still weeping – and then, just above the camp, Ziye was there, standing still waiting for them, with Delir and Dama and Sulien. Lal sobbed again at the sight of them, feeling after the renewed pang of guilt that she'd expected, a terrible surmising fear at the subdued way they were all standing there together.

To Una they seemed only as uncertain as before and she demanded, breathlessly, 'You haven't found him. Why have you come back? We have to keep on.'

Dama said, 'You mustn't go any further that way. It's too dangerous.'

'*No*, it was Pyrrha, they're tracking him, you don't understand,' gasped Una, about to break between them.

Sulien caught her gently and said, 'No, listen. How were they tracking him?'

Delir was calmer now, and more hopeful, but now the urgency was gone it had left him undisguised; he'd lost the illusionary extra inches in height, the alert way of wearing his face, he was worn out. He said, 'Sulien thinks that they haven't found him yet. They may have lost him somehow.'

'They *haven't* found him,' said Sulien stubbornly, and tried to explain what he'd seen.

Watching from the ridge he'd seemed to have a kind of double vision; he began to guess from the jerky, agitated movements of the men down on the slope that something had happened that they did not expect, but he was somehow as slow to believe it as he would have been to accept a disaster; his eyes tried to convince him that what he had dreaded had really happened, tried to make a dead body out of the flap of cloth and the long branch.

One of the men, he thought, was talking into a radio-longdictor. And then they separated, spreading across the harsh green flank, back towards the trees, down into the valley, pointing dark goggles around. It was a while after he saw Ramio entering the woods again, some distance to the west, that Sulien, lying painfully among the mulch and sharp sticks could dare to move. Then he'd started horribly at a cracking in the wood behind him, but it was Dama and Delir, edging laboriously up through the forest.

At first he didn't mention the bit of fabric they'd been pulling at, for he hadn't been close enough to see even that it was a shirt, let alone that it was Marcus'. All he could say was that he'd seen the men split up. It was hard to explain why he was so sure they'd been shocked and angered by something.

Una listened, at first horribly grudging the time, her lungs and throat seeming to bristle and thaw as her breath began to come back. She said, almost protesting, 'Perhaps they only split up – to surround him.' To her surprise, this sounded strained and unlikely. 'There's a tracking device, like the one Tasius had.'

'Pyrrha did it, and little Iris,' added Tobias quietly, arriving behind Lal, who whispered again, 'It's my fault.'

'Pyrrha!' Lal could see Delir trying to force himself to treat even this with impartial acceptance, not to be surprised, or feel betrayed.

'Marcus found it, then,' said Sulien, with quick conviction.

And as when Lal had first told what happened, no one could speak.

Una thought, still, we don't know, and if it's true, still, it's so dangerous for him, and if he makes it to Rome it will be worse. But it was real thought again, bracing her. She looked up. 'We need a car again. We can meet him at Panticosa.'

Deliberate and stern as she was, she seemed very young to Delir, and it was almost on instinct that he cautioned her gently. 'It may not be as easy as that. You couldn't be certain of finding him there.'

'If he isn't there then we'll go to Rome,' said Sulien, just as certain as Una.

Before Delir could speak again, Dama said softly, 'I can drive.'

'Can you?' Delir asked doubtfully. 'All that way?'

'I can do it,' insisted Dama, a faint edge in his voice. He said to Una, 'And I know Rome. You'll need that, if you get there.'

Lal had recovered enough to think cannily at this, oh, is *that* why?

'You know it?' Una was surprised.

'I was born there, it's where I grew up,' he said impatiently, as if they should have known this about him already. And he said to Delir, 'Or shall we say it's his business what he does? Because we could. We could say he's going his way and we'll look after ourselves, not hang around waiting for him or any of that lot. I'm happy with that. But do you want someone to go after him now? If you do, you should say so.'

He was questioning Delir with an insistence that seemed at once reverent and faintly hostile, prepared to accept anything he might say, but in the meantime almost bullying him.

'Yes,' said Delir, almost as if he was admitting to a flaw.

'Then I'll do it,' said Dama, simply.

Delir blinked at them as if he were on the point of falling asleep and said, 'You'll need money.' And looked reproachfully at Lal.

While Una gathered her clothes, identity papers, the electric lantern she noticed that Lal was grimly packing also; all the bright dresses that, in Rome, might for once look unremarkable.

Una was not sure quite what to say. She stood and watched for a moment, but Lal didn't comment on what she was doing. Una considered and thought, no, she should not come, but she felt she had no business stopping her. She said at last, 'You must say goodbye, anyway.'

'Of course,' said Lal, crossly.

Dama and Sulien were waiting outside. Lal went calmly to Sulien and said, 'I've got to go with you,' and Sulien felt a start of troubled excitement, but before he could decide how to answer Delir and Ziye came out with the envelopes of cash, and Delir was horrified at the sight of Lal with her bag on her shoulder.

He demanded, regaining some vivacity in his alarm, 'Have you gone completely mad, Lal?'

'No,' replied Lal.

'You've been behaving so childishly lately – keeping

407

these stupid secrets – and now you want to run away from home?'

He wanted to slap himself in the face in fury the second the words were out of his mouth. Everyone around him had run away from something.

Lal said steadily, 'I'm not running away. When I know what happened to Marcus, I'll come back.'

'That may be what you think,' said Delir, and spluttered slightly: 'You can't! I will not—'! for how could he say, with Una and Sulien and Dama standing so close, 'You are not doing anything so dangerous,' or 'I'm not letting you go anywhere alone with this boy,' when he did not, in fact, dislike Sulien, and sometimes felt an embarrassed guilt when he thought of what he'd said to him. He exclaimed, 'But you are not going to do anything of the kind!'

Lal regarded him patiently. There did not seem to be anything useful to be said to this.

'You have absolutely no idea what you're talking about! But I know; you're hoping this is going to turn into a sightseeing trip in Rome!'

Lal began, infuriated, 'If that's what you think—' but with huge, obvious effort cut herself short, and waited again in uncomplaining silence.

'Yes, it is!' cried Delir, feeling a palpitation of doubt, hearing that he was blustering ineffectively but ploughing on helplessly anyway. 'So you can just put that down and behave reasonably.'

Lal said, without rancour, what she knew millions of children must inevitably say to their parents, 'Unless you actually shut me up, you can't stop me.' And she stared levelly at her little father, who was much her size, and told him, not vindictively, 'And even that wouldn't be easy.'

'Oh, rubbish, Lal!'

'Well, it's perfectly true,' remarked Ziye quietly.

Delir and Lal both looked at her, startled, and in the second that Delir continued to stand there, silent, Lal moved past him, touching his arm uncertainly. 'Goodbye,' she said.

Delir stood motionless, and realised she'd gone halfway down the walkway already before he tore after her.

'Lal. All right. You can go if you want, but I wish you wouldn't. Please don't.'

Lal did a frustrated little hop. 'Oh! I'm sorry, but – oh, let's not go over it all again—'

'Listen. All right. I know you're not being stupid. You know it's dangerous. I know you think you should do it anyway. But please change your mind.'

'But I can't change my mind; *you* were the one who said I should have stopped him.'

'Well,' conceded Delir softly, gathering up her hands, 'you tried to stop him. I'm sure you tried. And he went anyway and now look how you feel. What am *I* going to do, if you won't stop now?'

Lal had to realise that she was beginning to hesitate now. She was looking at Sulien, lips and brows puckered with a kind of appeal or grief. She whispered, 'Do you want me to come?'

'Yes,' he said at once, and emphatically; but in such a way that she knew it wasn't advice.

'Oh dear,' she got out, at length, eyes prickling again. 'I think I'm not going to.'

Sulien nodded, and, because after all he was going a long way, kissed her then openly, without warning or even an apologetic look at Delir. It was a rapid, obstinate kiss, lips and teeth knocking hard against each other. Lal let go of her bag to clasp his head.

Oh, well, Delir thought, overlooking it with an inward shrug, drunk with luminous relief.

Lal said, 'Please be all right,' and Sulien whispered to her, 'I'm going to come back.' And she embraced Una quickly, and then Sulien again, and then he had to let her back unwillingly away from him to butt her head softly, crossly against Delir's shoulder.

Sulien was quiet for most of the way; but before they reached the village, he said tentatively to Una, 'I think this is right.'

409

'Of course it's right,' she said.

'But I don't only mean . . .' He paused, trying for words. 'Do you remember when you said, why would there be a reason for the things we do? I think there is a reason, or at least, there can be.'

Una finished for him, in a low voice, 'To stop people being bought and sold. We could say we're meant for that.'

Dama almost crowed, 'Yes, you should say that.' But after a silence Una asked sceptically, 'How?'

Sulien said, '*This* is a start. We are *meant* to do this.'

Dama interjected again sharply. 'By fate? By God?'

'No.' Sulien didn't care if this didn't make any sense. 'Or yes, fate, maybe, but only because we decide it, not otherwise. Not before.'

Dama frowned a little but only muttered, 'Well, maybe it doesn't make any difference.'

They walked on and Sulien frowned too, thinking, why is he doing this? He still hates Marcus. He shouldn't be with us.

Still, in Athabia he had to admit it was a good thing they had brought Dama, for Palben was unsurprisingly reluctant to part with his car, even for money, having been forced to exchange his old one in a hurry after the last time. It was not only that Dama could speak enough Euskara to conduct the conversation, he just somehow waited, ruthlessly, for Palben to give in, which at last he did.

Una watched Dama, and thought, as she had thought before, he can make things happen, he makes people do what he wants. And she was not sure if this was as strange a thing as knowing thoughts without hearing them spoken or mending cut flesh; or if it was only force of will; or if there was a difference.

The earliest Marcus might feasibly have reached Panticosa was in the first few hours of the morning. But they waited there long after that, until the end of the following day; loitering around the station, trying to look like customers for the little mineral baths, Una stealthily and nervously studying the other passengers and the occasional vigile officers. Marcus did not come.

The carriage was a hollow of dim light, enclosed in walls of speed and dark as the train cut away towns and fields like a scalpel, whistling across the slick of charged air. Marcus thought drowsily, until it stops again I must be safe, no one else can get in. His head had fallen back against the seat and he could hardly imagine lifting it; every joint and taut string of his aching body was slackening by tiny warm degrees. He felt finely scattered, strewn.

The knitted hat, still folded into a soft square, rested loosely in his hand. He had carried it so, or in the pocket of his coat, like a charm, since his paralysis on the ridge. He'd unslung his bag, looking for the map first, and then having stared at it almost blindly, he felt for the little roll of wool, thinking as he did it, how sentimental, how pitiful.

And as he took it from its pouch his fingers brushed the edges of the little slot that had been torn, no, cut, through the inside of the pocket, into the lining of the bag. In the space between the two layers of fabric something lay; a thing which he thought was a coin, and so nearly left it at that. It was the diameter of a coin, but much thicker. At first in his haste he somehow, stupidly, assumed that it was part of the bag, an obscurely necessary weight, like a ball bearing. And then he knew it was not. And then knew what it was.

His first reaction, of course, was a sheer physical compulsion to throw it away, to get away from it as quickly as possible as if from something revolting, rotting, infectious. His hand, which had even made a little spasm of repulsion at the thing resting in his palm, drew back of its own accord to do it. Then he thought – if only it would keep moving afterwards, if I could make it move.

There had been what felt like an insanely long time, exposed on the bare grass, when he thought he would never get near enough to the stupid sheep, scrambling after the damn things and flinging the shirt at them like an increasingly clumsy lasso. It could almost have been funny. All the time he was close to screaming at himself, put it *down*, put it *down*, *run!* He'd only been able to think of getting the rope of cloth with the lump of metal inside it around one of the animals' necks. It had seemed easy enough, as an idea. When he saw the trailing thorny spray, he cast the shirt at it in a kind of despair, could not believe it could catch, or, when it did, that it would stay there. He ran, fell, ran.

And thinking of the southeast arrow his progress had made, he circled down west and charged desperately through twenty rickety miles of forest towards Iluro after all. He was still trying to leave a false trail. At Iluro he'd stood in the shadows watching the bright doors of the station. Someone must surely be waiting for him by now. He hoped they still had very little idea of what he was doing but they'd had time to try and come up with something, some way of plugging his ways out. They could have the vigiles out again. Watch for a boy alone, who looks like dead Marcus Novius, trying to get to Rome.

He waited in the shadows until he'd found a group of young men going out for the night. They were a few years older than him but he'd ignored that and called out to them as if greeting old friends, and, before their surprise could show, he ran up, asked the time to get some response out of them, and then kept on relentlessly talking to them, pushed in among them when they reached the clerk, said casually 'the same', when they asked for tickets, walked to the train with them while they were still too nonplussed to tell him to go away. He found he'd bought a ticket for Aquensium, northwest and out of his way, which was good. Once on the train, and to their relief, he abandoned his new friends, got off after only a few miles at Benearnum and changed it for a ticket to Tarba. Only when he reached that had he begun to head for Italy directly.

He wished he could let Varius know what was happening, that he could say: wait, but don't wait to be killed, look, I'm at Nemausus already.

It was astonishing that one could travel so far in such a little time. The train had whirred into Tolosa, and he'd tensed because it was known that he had been there before, and because even the word was heavy with Una. But he was so tired that even the permanent thought of her pulsed with an empty, hypnotised calm, like the lines and knots of warm pain in his body. He smoothed the wool mindlessly with his thumb. He slept.

[XVIII]

THE CAVE OF HANDS

Una found she had taken to thinking over and over, copying Dama, 'Please, God.' And it was true that every fierce instinct of hers towards absolutism attracted her to the notion of one god, strung under things, through space like the laws of physics of which she was aware of knowing so little, or else a flat pure mechanic emptiness. At this stage, both possibilities seemed almost interchangeable for her; they both had an uncompromising clear finality, and she liked that. But she kept up this embryonic prayer involuntarily, even though she reflected that any power that would protect Marcus because it was asked but would otherwise let him die was no better than the squabbling brats in the Pantheon, who seemed to her like an increasingly shabby con. She tried to ask Dama about this, but he didn't answer her clearly and she thought she had perhaps offended him.

The time at Panticosa was horrible because there was nothing to do, nothing certain to wait for, not even a sign that waiting was pointless. They speculated nervously: come on, let's go; no, he might rest for so long, he might get lost, we'll wait another hour.

And when they began to drive again, although there was a relief in having made a decision, Una hated the feeling that they were only acting out a story they were telling themselves, as if they thought they could make Marcus be alive by behaving as if he was. When they left Panticosa behind it was harder to talk. Una and Sulien could not bear to comment on the arbitrariness of their departure, that Marcus might arrive perhaps minutes after they left, and much worse, that it was already too late to find Marcus anywhere alive: and they could hardly think of anything else.

Dama, especially, did not speak. He drove painfully and dourly east along the dry mountains, finally turning north back among the damp pines. They had to stop briefly every hour or so, so that he could rest his arms and Sulien could work on the gathering pain. Sulien said, 'I'm not sure you should be doing this,' and Dama rejoined curtly and truthfully, 'It's too late for that now,' then added, 'Anyway, I'm all right.' But he seemed more closed off than ever to Una; what she'd come to think of as a glossy protective carapace over his thoughts seemed to have thickened when she'd thought it was giving way. And yet even though he was silent, even when she shut her eyes, she could not have forgotten for a minute that he was in the car. That she knew he was in pain was part of it, but not all. He seemed to weigh on the fabric of things, exerting a force, a pull, the shock they'd all felt when they first saw him. It was as though his atoms were more densely packed than was normal.

They rode at last right up behind the cargo trams through the heart of Wolf Step, so that Una had to choose either to turn her head to the left and look across the forum at the yellow-fronted caupona, or stare fixedly ahead and not see it. She looked, deliberately and coldly and shuddered with a kind of thriftfulness; but afterwards she felt the restless urgency of finding Marcus was growing worse, and at the same time the memory of his disdainful voice, confidently sneering over her.

It was well past midnight. A few miles out of Wolf Step Dama said, 'We should sleep somewhere. I can't drive any more tonight.'

No no, we keep going, Una wanted to say, but nodded silently.

'I know somewhere,' he said. 'There are so many caves in the mountains and we thought of setting up around here, but it's too close to people. We couldn't trust them.'

'About right,' said Sulien, who'd also been chilled in Wolf Step.

'Still, they'll leave us alone for a night here, they think it's haunted,' said Dama, voice thick with scorn.

He drove them, wincing more openly now, through the flat green plain before Wolf Step into a clutch of hills, stopped the car suddenly. He scooped up the electric lamp awkwardly by its strap and led the others up the small, wooded hill, through the break in its side into the wide pool of dark. There were several low flat-bottomed depressions in the floor, like inverted furniture, and ribbed growths of rock hanging and standing at the back of the cave, more like swags of billowing drapery and massive bundled curtains than like stone pillars, seeming to sway and flow, as the light did; and there were new mineral fingers growing through the ceiling in nodules, and delicate spikes. The chamber was a good size, like a small house.

'It's too cold to sleep here,' said Sulien, shivering. He could see his breath in the air.

Dama ignored this. 'Look, look.' He swung the lantern around the cave, unsteadily, because his arms were shaking again.

At first, in the trembling light they saw only a dense bloody staining that looked at first like some natural deposit, spread across the pale walls in interconnected russet puffs and sprays. Then they saw that scattered through the red haze were many hollow shapes: the outlines of hands, the ruddiness burning out from the palms.

'Thousands of years old,' whispered Dama. 'This is why they think there are ghosts.'

Sulien began, interested, 'Oh, I saw something like this in a magazine once.' And then Una said, 'Their fingers.'

All the hands were mutilated, splaying stumps truncated at the first joint, beside slim whole thumbs. They were of all sizes.

Dama said in the same spellbound voice, 'There are so many. Look. Women's hands. This one is a child's, but it's whole. But all the rest cut like this. Some have some fingers left. How could they survive, afterwards, back then? They must have starved. Look. It's the right hand.' He'd held up his own right hand, as high as it would go, against one of the red-haloed prints.

Una suggested tentatively, 'Unless anyone helped them.'

'No one helped anyone,' said Dama softly, as if he'd been there and seen it.

'The fingers might not have been severed,' said Sulien in a low voice. 'They could have just curled them under, like this.' He lifted his own hand, to illustrate it. He'd been prompted by Dama's hand on the rock, the bent forefingers.

Dama gave a little stern twitch of irritation. He felt, but couldn't have explained that he felt, as though Sulien had criticised or meddled with something that was his. Coming back to these images, he had the same odd triumphant pleasure he'd felt when he first saw them, in facing them, *facing them down*. 'Why would they do that? It's punishment. Or torture. And they wanted to show what they'd done. There are more further in.'

They had not realised that the cave stretched further, through a black opening at the top of a low bulging slope. Sulien backed away from it. 'I'm not going any further.' Dama looked faintly contemptuous. 'I'm not scared of these,' said Sulien impatiently, gesturing at the handprints, 'But what about the cave, how do you know the roof won't fall in?' And though he'd have gone in readily enough if he'd seen any need, he felt himself recoil from the old darkness under the huge load of ground.

'It's fine, I told you, I've been here before,' said Dama, but really he didn't want Sulien to come with him, he wanted to talk to Una alone.

'Anyway,' said Sulien, 'it's freezing, we'd be better off staying in the car.'

'The car will get as cold as this when it's not running, so we'll make a fire. And the light won't show, in here.'

But still he did not turn back to the mouth of the cave, to look for wood, he clambered towards the receding pitch-black. He still had the lantern and it was perhaps only out of the instinct to stay with the light that Una did as he wanted and went with him.

'Una,' said Sulien, warning.

'It'll be all right,' she said.

Sulien waited for a moment in the dark, and then went back to the car to see if they'd even remembered the stove-lighter, and because the night sky seemed bright compared to the enclosed blackness, once the lantern was gone.

Dama passed Una the light, partly so that she could choose what to look at, partly because the weight was hurting too much now. They'd come to the edge of a kind of dark plain; the damp ceiling, low and jutting just above their heads, ran flat above them as far as the light showed: the walls were beyond sight; so that it was as though they were under a rock sky, on what could have been one of many wastes, one above another, or between the pages of a stone book. The damp floor was rippled with fluid ridges, that looked as if they would be as soft as the ripples in wet sand on a beach, but were not, and held their shape underfoot.

She followed Dama away from the plain down into a little dungeon or a temple, growing slender miniature colonnades of rock up from the floor; and the walls dappled even more densely with red and dark hands, patting along the swell of the stone; a fingerless silhouette framed in an arched alcove which might have held the statuette of a household god, the thumb and palm delicate, female, emerging from a black shadow, not a burst of red flame.

Una asked, 'Why do you like it here?'

'Like it?' He was startled; he had not precisely realised that he liked it; only that the place was important, and should be seen. 'I don't know. I suppose – if you've seen it, then you *know* – you *know* that . . .' He was not inarticulate, but what he felt did not come naturally in words, it had to be shoehorned forcibly into them. He said at last, 'That this is *really* what people are like. That they always have been.' The light she held hit the back of his irises so that, as the black pupils twisted and shrank, the pure colour

418

glittered more brightly even than usual, like round tiles of turquoise. The shadows, strangely, made his eager face sharper and clearer than it would look in sunlight; beautiful, and not childlike.

He said, 'It's different for you, you must have always known that anyway.'

Wasn't this indeed what she had always known? She smiled uncertainly. 'It might be easier not to.'

'It might be easier, but not better; because *once you do know it*, and you say, yes, all right, *that's* how things are – then you are – not safe from it, not physically safe – but you can do things. That other people couldn't do. You. You rescued Sulien. That shouldn't even have been possible. And you tricked that man.'

'We both did that; I was so sure he was going to see . . .' she hesitated but said, 'You didn't let him see that your arms were hurt.'

'Well, we both did it, because we knew. You can refuse to let things stop you. Even *yourself*. You can do a lot, if you can start from that.' And then he paused and said resolutely, 'Why are we doing this?'

Una had felt excited by what he was saying, she had recognised it; but now she made an apprehensive, shying little movement. 'You know. Or you wouldn't be here yourself.'

'I'm doing it because I said I would,' said Dama at once.

'No one made you say that.'

'I said I'd help, because Delir wanted it and I owe him everything. And because you were going.'

There was a little chime or a hand-clap of silence. As if there hadn't been, Una said, 'You heard what Sulien and I said. For everyone like us. That's why.'

'Yes, but this Novius isn't the only chance, no one is. There are as many chances as there are people who are prepared to find out what needs to be done and *do* it, whatever it is.'

'He's the first chance, anyway,' said Una.

Dama nodded, not so much agreeing as allowing this as a

possible position before saying, glancing away from her, 'And is that the only reason you want to help him?'

'Oh . . .' Una sighed, beginning to feel hounded, 'why are you asking? You know how long we spent with him, getting to Holzarta. Of course I have to know if he's all right.'

'You weren't with him so very long.'

'But all day, every day – you know how it is. It felt like a long time.'

'So would you say you were friends with him?'

Again Una remembered Marcus in Wolf Step, giving such a good imitation of ownership, and she thought wretchedly, how *can* I be, really? So she said, 'I don't know.'

'But – you don't love him?'

'No,' she said, as quickly as an eye blinks to protect itself.

'Good,' said Dama, just as quickly. Of course it was what he'd been wanting her to say, but somehow the word wasn't enough to rest on, he found himself saying, as if to fill it out, as if for her: 'Because, it wouldn't be any good for you, even if we find him now and make sure he's safe. However he thinks he feels about you now, what would you be with him? If you weren't an embarrassment you'd be something he'd picked up for fun, a knick-knack, a *thing* he'd got. How could his family let you be anything else? And that would be too much like what you were before, wouldn't it?'

Una didn't speak, or move. And now he knew he would have done better to say none of it. But he felt impatiently that she should *know* he hadn't meant any insult – how could he, to talk of things that had been done to her and said nothing about her? And that made him want to hurry onto something else, to the important thing: 'So, then, afterwards, what will you do?'

'I can't think about afterwards. I have to think about *this*,' she said mechanically.

'No, you have to think,' said Dama. Then, deliberately, stepping closer to her, 'Come back with me. Help me. I mean, we'll help each other. Back to Holzarta at first perhaps, but then we could go wherever we wanted, wherever needed us. It's right. It's what is supposed to happen . . .'

He took hold of her shoulder, with just his better hand at first, pulled her towards him. Una seemed to feel the weight of the hill now, over her head, all around her, not temptation really, but power, duress. But with a bulb of resisting anger in the centre of it, around which things seemed to heat and shift. It was nonsensical to stand there inertly when she didn't have to.

She lifted his hands, guided them away from her, returned them neatly to his sides, looked at him across a foot of empty space.

'No. It isn't supposed to happen.'

'All right,' he said, expressionless. They drew back from one another. After a few seconds, he said, looking down at the pierced scars on his wrists. 'Is it because of this?'

'If you really thought it was that, you wouldn't want anything to do with me.'

'Marcus Novius, then.'

'You don't know him. You shouldn't talk about him,' Una said, in a short, unexpected blaze.

'*Tell me, is that why?*'

'Yes,' retorted Una, as if impulsively signing her name to something she hadn't read.

'All right,' said Dama again. He turned away from the lamplight, his face invisible. Presently he told her methodically, 'Well. Then. I said I'd help you in Rome. So I will. But when I'm sure that's done, I'm just going to go, do you understand? Won't be any point hanging around.'

'Back to Delir?'

'Perhaps,' he said dully, and then, through his teeth, 'No. No, I don't need to go back there. And he won't be sorry, not really.'

The bright, molten-glass indignation continued but Una began to feel an alarmed unhappiness for his sake, too, to think disbelievingly, what *is* this, what are we saying to each other? 'I don't want you to do that.'

'It doesn't matter what you want, I'm afraid.'

She looked at him and only shook her head, couldn't say, I'm sorry; she left the light with him and stumbled back out into the utter dark, finding her way unthinkingly by touch and memory. For a strange moment the anger, or what she still called anger, felt like a kind of elated astonishment.

It was not what he had said about her, not what he'd reminded her of. It was the way he'd talked about Marcus, that he'd made what she knew Marcus felt about her sound like lazy acquisitiveness. Dama hadn't even realised that he'd done this.

Was that all she'd meant, saying yes like that – that she was angry? Dama hadn't thought so, and she hadn't said anything to put him right; and why anyway did she care so much about a slight to Marcus that couldn't hurt him; hadn't she only a minute before been remembering Marcus' voice and expression in the Wolf Step caupona, and telling herself they couldn't even really be friends? Wasn't it about the same – even if it was wrong – a fairly reasonable view of things?

It *was* wrong, completely wrong, and what did she care about Marcus' family, they were nothing to do with her.

No, she'd known perfectly well really, that Dama was asking her again, do you love Marcus? She hadn't thought what she was saying; it ought to be retractable; it wasn't.

You would have thought that to acknowledge a thing, to let it have the right name it must have been howling for, ought to make it quieter and more manageable. But she found, as Marcus had, that the opposite seemed to be true, that everything she'd felt for him since the first evening between the green curtains, above all now the terrible fear that she was never going to find him again, pounced greedily on the words – love and yes – and rampaged and gorged and fattened itself with monstrous, confident speed.

She shut her eyes and saw white; the white air by the waterfall, the cold kiss.

She could still remember what she'd felt then; that it was too much, that another step would wipe her out into nothing; she couldn't keep from remembering now that it was also something like that she'd felt staring at him in the

Tolosa street. And it was still too much, but that just didn't matter, it wasn't a consideration any more.

Another quick pulse of lightheaded happiness; she knew he felt the same, how amazing, how many people could know anything like that?

And then, inevitably, as if the ceiling had indeed broken in over her in a dark, crushing shower not of rock but of wet earth, she was smothered with fear and regret. She didn't want to step back into the pale scene by the water, she wanted to forget the whole thing; but she wanted to pull *him* out of it so that he was *here*, she still couldn't think how she could tell him all this, but he didn't know, he didn't, and how was he ever going to, he was dead perhaps already?

Her fingers, cautiously held a little sightless way before her, actually stretched and clutched as if she could make him be there and tangible in the dark. And the black air seemed to clutch back on her suddenly, she couldn't tell if the course she remembered through it was right or if she'd simply made it up. It was possible that she had been walking completely the wrong way. She couldn't go back to Dama for the light. She turned, and immediately wished she had not, there was no way of judging, when she tried to turn back again, which way she was facing. Dark bulged against her eyes. 'Sulien!' she cried out, panicked.

'What?' he called, a long way off, but it was enough, she hadn't made a mistake after all. She staggered towards his voice, into the first cave, where she couldn't see the handprints on the walls, or anything but the wide pale glow of the open air, where Sulien was, coming back at her shout; he'd found the lighter but no dry wood, he'd been thinking about Lal.

'What's wrong?'

Una said tersely, 'We *can't* wait here for hours and hours, surely no one's going to get any sleep anyway,' put her arms round him crossly, and began to cry.

Sulien did a kind of soothing jostling, sweeping his arm capably up and down her back, confident in sympathy as he always was. He was barely surprised. He said without needing to ask her again what the matter was, 'Of course he's going to be fine. Of course you're going to see him again.'

SAEVA URBS

There was so much city, there were so many unsuspected streets. Marcus spent the night, and the last of the money his crooked progress across Gaul had left him, in a scratchy little hostel in the Suburra, where he'd never been before.

The proprietor looked at him, blinked.

'You must always get people saying this – but you look just like—'

'Marcus Novius, yes, I know,' he said calmly. And he thought of leaning across and saying, I'll tell you what happened – but it would be too complicated, he was too tired for anything like that yet. In what was more of a cupboard than a room, he fell asleep rehearsing what he was going to say, cutting and compressing it, knowing he wouldn't have much time. He woke to find great welts on his skin, itching furiously, raised by bedbugs he'd been too exhausted to notice.

He'd continued his journey in a series of oblique feints at Rome; avoiding the great whirring Vatican Field terminus and travelling through to Ostia where he caught a tram back into the Roman suburbs. All the way he'd been asking himself how could he get to see Faustus alone without being dragged off somewhere first, and answering with increasing ruthless certainty; you *can't*. It wasn't even a question of the conspiracy being ready to stop him, although they probably would be, and would certainly take advantage afterwards; you just couldn't step straight from here into the glazed stratum where his uncle lived, close though it was.

But he knew now what he was going to do, and having decided, he'd had most of a day to wander round Rome like any tourist, limping a little from the trek the day before. Fear for himself and for Varius attacked him at abrupt, grinding intervals – having decided he could not act until the next day, it struck him suddenly that Varius might not have even that much time: they know it's gone wrong for them; they know I'm out of Holzarta and they can't *find* me – there's no need to go through with a trial now. They'll kill him and say it was suicide or an accident or another prisoner – a patriotic prisoner roused to fury by an attack on the Imperial family. It might be happening at any moment.

No, he tried to reassure himself, surely not quite this soon.

And yet for much of that day, instead of being afraid, he had a dreamlike feeling that it should be impossible for him to be here again, as if he was breaking not merely a spoken prohibition but a physical law. He saw Rome as though the scale had changed and a kind of bright depth had accumulated over it, like layers of time – far more time than the few months he'd been away. Though every sight – the glass cap of the Colosseum, the gold palace towers shining over it, the Tiber – plucked at him with an expert poignancy, nothing looked the same, everything was magnified or slanted, seen at strange angles, and teeming with fierce cars and intent people, legs chopping angrily along like blunt scissors, who did not look at him. He had known that his was the most frenetic city in the world, and yet he had never seen it on the move like this, never, at least, been carried along on its flow, alone. How could he have done? Whenever he had arrived in a place, things stopped. Now he swam through a wild-eyed crowd on the Sacred Way like a minnow, almost worrying that he might stand out by being the only person to be walking slowly, for despite everything he was fascinated. He kept needing to touch things, a pillar, a wall, he let his hand drag along the smooth balustrade of a bridge over the Tiber as he crossed, stroking it.

He had never understood as precisely as this how the

different familiar landmarks fitted together, he realised now that he'd tended to think of them almost as islands, connected not by distance but by the number of minutes it took to ride in a car from one to another: little tunnels of time. But this was how you walked from the Ostian Road, across the Aventine, to the Forum, to the foot of the Palatine. It was like suddenly understanding a mathematical equation, lucid, pleasurable.

He would never be able to do this again.

He saw Una everywhere: he should have been prepared, given the phantom-Una's ruthless power to coalesce out of trees and air, for the fact that there would be no stopping her once she had real girls and women to work on, hundreds upon hundreds of impostors who could stun him by having hair of the right length or straightness or some approximation of the pale shade – he did not even need to see these qualities together – or even to see so much, he managed to assemble her out of the most unpromising sets of features, prompted by nothing identifiable when he looked again. Even though, he thought, she was really nothing like everybody else. Still, with stupid repetitive eagerness, it flashed over him again and again, that she'd come after him, she was really here in Rome.

And he felt like his own ghost, too. He stood by the huge and bight-shaped Saepta shopping arcade, and watched the largest public longvision in the world, wrapped around the horseshoe of its outer wall. It bristled a bright spume of advertisements, then a display of house-high dancers, hectic and yet doleful, and then announced to the shoppers and tourists that the Emperor was to give an address the following day about his nephew's murder. There were black pennants out for him, all over the place; some presumably hyper-enthusiastic monarchists had even gone into mourning, which was almost the strangest sight he'd ever seen.

Marcus left the inn early to be sure of getting into the Forum, and getting a good place to stand. It was two hours before anything was due to happen, but hundreds of people were already there with the same idea in mind, and pushing as close as the Praetorians would let them get to the rostra – which was not so very close; there was a space reserved for sombre rows of aristocrats and senators. The guards and the vigiles were thickly spread, ringing the forum, perched on the roofs of the surrounding temples and glassy basilicas. They frisked Marcus rapidly and grimly and shoved him onward through the cordon along with everyone else, without looking into his face. Marcus scouted the Forum furtively, wandered over to a statue of a woman with wings, in the act of sprinting towards the rostra – Victory.

Some camera technicians roamed around vaguely. Nearby a family were quietly consuming an early picnic. The place filled steadily until Marcus could scarcely see the podium. The Emperor was very late. Marcus had forgotten that this lateness was usual and was almost dancing with impatience and nerves. He leaned against Victory's plinth, shaking a little now. Like so much else, the idea of the statue, the intent expression it should have had, reminded him a little of Una; although in reality the statue's face smiled implacably but serenely, despite its rushing limbs.

This time, because of what he was about to do, the idea pierced through what fragile resignation he'd been able to muster about Una; oh, he thought, *be here*.

Faustus was not aware that he was late. He sat with a kind of vacant relief in the centre of the short file of cars, as they glided the tiny distance down to the Forum. He forgot somehow what a short a journey it was and was irritated by how soon he had to get out again.

A corridor of black brocaded screens had been set up from the road, past the edge of the temple of Saturn, shielding the family's way to the rostra. Here Makaria stood for a little time on her own after she'd descended from the car, vacantly rearranging the dark shawl draped over her head. If Faustus did not look too closely or think what the occasion was, he could feel pleased at seeing her dressed up and looking, he thought, quite feminine, quite graceful: the veil

428

softening the outline of her stiff short hair and the military rigidness of her shoulders. But now she had drifted and stopped, unconsciously, and he could see that her face looked haggard, lost.

She had reason to look so. She had been – and he could find no way of saying so or thanking her for it – wonderful all this time. She had seen to everything, she had scarcely slept. When he ranted at a hapless speechwriter over the incompetent first draft of his address she silently made deft notes of what he wanted, and had rewritten the thing herself before he could realise and growl that it was absurd for her to attempt it. As he would have done.

Drusus was trying just as hard, but could only really offer the well-intentioned effort he was making. He was effect-ive, it was true, at getting people out of Faustus' way, and he suggested things almost continually, but then somehow he would be in the way himself. Faustus had let Drusus chair various meetings – with the press department, with a committee of senators. Drusus told the senators Faustus was too busy to see them and that they couldn't have any money, which was much what Faustus had needed done, but Drusus had not even gone through the show of listening to them, and left them all resentful and unhappy so that Faustus had had to see nearly all of them privately anyway to smooth things over, or even have Makaria do it. Drusus was at once too calm and too anxious, or calm and anxious in turn about the wrong things.

Faustus looked at him now and thought for the first time, and now you will have to be Emperor, how will you manage? Not that he could precisely say he had made a firm decision in favour of Marcus, though he supposed it had seemed fairer to Leo to let it go that way. In truth, after his brother's death, he had shrunk from thinking of the question at all. It was bad enough to know that so many other people must be thinking about it.

Drusus evidently found the little delay oppressive, while they organised themselves behind the screens, and, through some quirk of heredity, was drumming and drawing complicated patterns on the side of the car with his fingers, the way Marcus had sometimes done when nervous or impatient. Neither Leo nor Lucius had ever done that. Faustus tried to think if they could both have got it from one of his own parents, but could remember nothing.

Well, there was no good thinking about it now, it was out of his hands, unless he picked some senator and broke the family line – and poor Drusus, there was no call to do that.

Drusus went and nudged Makaria in a way presumably intended to be encouraging, and she rallied with difficulty and said briskly, 'Well. Has to be done, hasn't it?' She said this with a particular brave glance at Tulliola. For these last days Makaria had even tried hard to be pleasant to her – and it was slightly clumsy, slightly grating – and yet he had to concede that this was perhaps at least partly Tulliola's fault. Not that Tulliola had done or said anything rude, of course not – but she seemed to retreat very slightly from Makaria's attempts at friendliness; to apply an abnormally withdrawn version of her usual tranquil quiet. Probably after always being the one to make this kind of effort, Tulliola felt a little taken aback to see it in Makaria. It was understandable. She stood now holding his arm, a little wan in her black. She had paid no active part in the preparation for – whatever this was, since it was not a funeral. And he was glad of it, she seemed to know how good it was to have one person who did not talk to him about Marcus, who could pour peacefulness over him, even now.

Slowly, they walked up onto the rostra and Tulliola pressed Faustus' hand before he left her with the rest, and went forward to the podium. He looked down to where, in a square of clear space, the body ought to have been, but of course there were only more people.

He began reading at once, and after a gruffly mumbled start instinct took hold of him and he began to act Makaria's speech, to give it the pauses and rhythm it needed for effect. It would never occur to him to call this performing insincere, he had approved these words, and the more powerfully he spoke, the more convinced he was that he meant them, that they were right.

And Marcus heard the change happen, and realised he was doing almost the same thing, waiting for the right moment in the speech, the point where an applied shock would take the greatest hold.

'I have no need to repeat to you the terrible news that we first heard three days ago. I would like to say that it is a comfort to think that not only my family but the whole Roman world shares our grief and shock; and if it is too soon for that to be quite true, still I do believe it may come to be true, and I am no less anxious to thank you all for joining us in trying to accept what has happened. It is hard enough to understand how such tragedies can follow one another so quickly. It is impossible to understand the person who could take my nephew Marcus Novius from us so young, and take from him a future that would undoubtedly have been—'

Marcus shuddered with the strangeness of ever hearing such words. And he reached up for the edge of the plinth, felt a pang of sheer stage fright, dragged himself up onto the pedestal of the statue, clung to a bronze arm, a bronze flight of silk.

Faustus went on reading stubbornly for a moment without quite looking at the disorderly thin figure on the edge of his vision emerging like a worm from the ground, scaling one of the statues as if it were a climbing frame, loose-clothed limbs flailing and swinging in an offensively child-ish or acrobatic way. Some part of himself asked with terse but distant interest, now is that a stupid prank or is he going to point a gun at me? He was more conscious of his face boiling furiously with the embarrassment of having to decide whether or not to stop and wait for security to deal with it, with anger at the callousness of it.

The man or boy was shouting something that he couldn't immediately hear above his own words: 'Uncle.'

The second Marcus was above the heads of the crowd a detail of vigiles was pushing through the mass towards him, probably not even recognising him or listening to what he said; probably only out of pure instinct to get a shouting youth, a heckler, down from his perch and out of sight. Precariously, Marcus pulled himself higher, clutching at the goddess' hard outstretched wings.

'I'm Marcus Novius Faustus. Uncle, look at me.'

Faustus was slow. It was in fact the scuffing of shock from around and behind him that made him hear the words, long seconds after they had actually been spoken. He looked back before looking again at the boy on the statue and saw that Drusus had put a hand to his mouth, Makaria was shaking her head and whispering something – it *can't* be. He turned again and peered at – what? – the right age, the right colour hair – a possible resemblance that must surely mean nothing.

'When I was ten you bribed me not to tell my father you'd broken that mask he brought back from Mexica.'

Faustus did not notice his hand as it numbly swept a flutter of papers from the podium.

But Faustus was not the only one that Marcus wanted to talk to. He leaned down dangerously from the statue's shoulders, so he could stare directly into the eyes below him.

'Look. Turn the cameras this way. Romans.' How strange it was to use that word as a call, but it was working; the vigiles were finding it hard to reach him because they were no longer the only ones pressing towards the statue, the whole crowd seemed now to be closing in on him.

'Romans. Look at me because I'm proof you've been lied to. The truth is that the people who want you to think Varius is a murderer are the people who killed my parents, and killed Gemella Paulina – and they're the ones I've had to hide from all this time. Uncle, they're all around you—'

'Marcus,' cried out Faustus, as the vigiles swarmed up the plinth. He made to dash forward from the rostra, but the Praetorians held him back – and with good reason perhaps, for the crowd was in a tumult now that his own shout of recognition had fuelled up even higher. An incredulous roar

432

had gone up, almost a cheer in places; and they yelled in protest as the officers prised at Marcus, loosening his hold so that if he did not slide down the statue into their arms he must overbalance and plunge to the ground.

Once they had him down the vigiles almost lost Marcus under the feet of the crowd, so possessed were the on-lookers now with a need not only to see but to touch him, as if he might have been an hallucination or some kind of holographic trick. He was jubilantly patted, his hands grabbed at, his hair ruffled. He didn't resist it, encouraged it even, shaking the hands and writhing against the vigiles to look into face after face, saying, 'Remember Varius. Remember you saw me.'

Everyone was trying to placate Faustus.

'Sir, your safety—'

He could no longer see Marcus, he tried to track the moving centre of the uproar but he couldn't, his own guards were in the way. He shoved at them and raged. 'What in hell do you think you're doing? Can't I go where I like, I thought I was supposed to be the bloody Emperor.'

And then the surging mound of people was shut away. They were still yelling and stamping outside, but the moment the van door slammed Marcus felt changed, diminished, in the small contained space. It was as though a second before he'd been older and warm with authority and fame, and was now again chilled, powerless, young. He hoped the shiver he felt flow across him could not be seen. He stared in silence at the vigile officers who stared round-eyed back, and promised himself, they can't do it now, I've stopped them; they can't kill me. Everything had happened pretty much as he had expected.

But he hugged himself as if he were cold. All he could feel now was the physical truth that they could choose to do anything, he was alone, and shut in with them, and what-ever happened to him next he would have no more say in it. There was nothing left for him to do. He'd used it all up.

The vigiles didn't know what to do with him. They settled on calling him 'Sir', in a brusque yet cautious way

433

that might possibly be ironic, depending on how things turned out. The van drove away.

In frustrated disgust, Faustus marched abruptly away from the rostra down behind the wall of dark screens.

He barked, 'Well, what are they doing? Where are they taking him?'

For the moment no one seemed to know. The Praetorians and vigiles were preoccupied in trying to control the crowd; ripples of havoc were spreading out from the Forum, and inwards too, as people who had seen what had happened on public longvisions just outside tried to press into the Forum in helpless swells of curiosity. Several arrests had been made, more than one van had left.

Makaria had to go and lean for a minute against one of the cars, her face hidden in the crook of her arm.

Glycon was talking to the Praetorian captain. 'Is it safe for the Emperor to go back out, would that help? Sir, if you were to go back and address them—'

'I refuse to do anything until somebody gives me an explanation for all this,' snapped Faustus, folding his arms. 'You. Do you know where he's gone or not?'

The captain said hesitantly, 'They'll need to take him down to the station and they'll need to check him out – and if—' He frowned, and seemed to give up in disbelief on whatever he might have said. 'Well, if it was just a joke, perhaps they'll lock him up for a night and let him go.'

'*What on earth are you talking about?*'

Tulliola whispered breathlessly, 'But, it can't have been – we don't *know* who it was—'

Faustus stared at them all. He said slowly and ominously, 'Get Marcus *back*. I want to see him *at once*.'

And as he meant them to, everyone fell silent. Glycon said, 'Yes. Of course.'

Marcus thought they had stopped at a military station, but no one opened the doors and after a minute they began moving again.

He said, 'Where are we going?'

'Hospital.'

'All right.' He felt a little more uneasy, although this made good enough sense.

After this, almost more shyly than professionally, the vigiles began trying to make him prove he really was Marcus Novius Faustus Leo. After so long in hiding Marcus felt intensely reluctant to tell them anything, but there was no reason not to do so now. Quietly, he described rooms from the palace, from his own house, told them about the state visit to Terranova two years before. He found himself trying to behave as if he were telling the truth.

'All right then.' They had no immediate way of knowing whether he was making all this up. 'And where have you been?' Again in the laboured, aggressive-polite voice.

Marcus just couldn't face this. 'I'd rather tell my uncle about that first,' he murmured.

At the Aesculapian, of course, everyone asked him the same thing. The narrow island was connected on both sides to the city by bridges, and felt almost more guarded from the bulk of Rome by the umbrella pines around it than by the river. The Aesculapian was an elegant, polished little hospital, with a kind of well-fed, well-funded glow about its tan walls. Sick or injured people would have seemed incongruous here and indeed, though they must have been about, Marcus did not see any. He was swept upstairs into a consulting room, and then into a room like an ordinary bedroom, with three soft upright chairs and a desk, the bed seeming almost incidental. He thought he could hear a nearly continuous rasp of vehicles arriving outside. He felt hemmed in. He was finding it increasingly hard not to retreat into an uncooperative quiet, to refuse whatever was wanted of him. He would not eat or drink anything they offered. The nurses urged him to lie or at least sit down, but he stood a hovering, tense distance from everyone, arms still warily folded round his body.

The staff here seemed to find it easier to believe that he really was Marcus Novius. They were less disturbed by his

435

presence than the vigiles had been, or at least, more certain of how to behave. A nurse and doctor pored together over a few pictures of his face, of Faustus, Leo and Drusus, comparing length and breadth of features.

The pictures were not from a news sheet – where had they come from – the palace?

'Does the Emperor know I'm here?' he asked.

'I'm sure he does,' the nurse said restfully, staring disquietingly at the lower part of his face and then looking back at her pictures. She remarked, 'Faces can change so quickly at your age.'

'How long is this going to take?'

'Please won't you sit down. This is difficult if you keep pacing around.' Reluctantly, Marcus came a little closer, but stayed standing. 'It really is important that you explain where you've been.'

'I will later. I don't want to endanger the people who helped me.' He wondered if even this should not have been said.

'Why would they be in danger?'

Marcus said nothing.

These interviews went on repetitively. Between them, told to wait, and left alone, he crept out into the corridor, at first simply to establish that he hadn't been locked into the room. He came to a landing where there was a window overlooking the approach to the building. Yes, the vigiles who had driven him there were still standing outside, and there were more of them, milling about near the bridge. A Praetorian van drew up as he watched. He reminded himself that if Faustus was coming this would be necessary – *especially* if he believed what Marcus had shouted across the Forum. But it seemed unlikely he could get out, should he need to. He went back to the corridor and explored a little further. He passed the doors of other bedrooms, and saw another patient at last, an old man in a gold-embroidered dressing gown, glimpsed through a half-open door, sitting on the edge of a bed, who coughed and scowled at him. He found another window, at the side of the house. The trees hid the ground directly below him, so that he couldn't see any officers there might be. Experimentally, just to find out what was possible, he pulled at the window. It didn't open. How would he have climbed down anyway?

The nurse who'd been checking his face against the pictures saw him. Marcus started guiltily away from the window. 'Could you go back and wait in your room?'

She walked him back there. After a while, a new, perhaps more senior doctor in grey, with bristly hair stippled with badger-like black and white came in.

'Would you say you've been well, all the time you were away?' Marcus nodded. 'You don't want to tell anyone why you disappeared?'

'I've told everyone,' said Marcus.

'You believed your life was in danger?'

'Yes.'

'But not from Caius Varius?'

'*No.*' He'd been over this before.

'And Leo and Clodia Aurelia – may I offer my condolences – you said you believed they were murdered?'

'Yes.'

The man nodded impassively. 'Did you meet anyone with any serious diseases, say, anyone who might have had typhus or a consumption?'

'I think not. I know I'm not ill. I've already told someone this. Twice. Can I leave, or is the Emperor coming?'

The doctor wrote something down. 'Yes, he's coming. Have you been in any fights?'

'Yes, but that was months ago.'

'Any head injuries, while you were fighting?'

'No. That is, my face, but it's been fine for ages,' he said restlessly.

The doctor got up and Marcus instinctively backed away to keep the distance between them constant.

'I need to take your pulse,' explained the doctor patiently.

'No you don't,' insisted Marcus. 'It's been done.'

'It needs to be done again.' He advanced.

'No,' said Marcus. The distrust he'd felt since arriving

437

here had suddenly risen up into a scorching blast, and he looked at the door, but for a fatal second he was disarmed by the fact that he wasn't being rational, nothing had happened, and you just couldn't dive out of rooms or attack people simply because they made you nervous. And the doctor moved, not calm and appeasing any longer, driving his weight forward to trap Marcus against the wall to which he had retreated; and now, after it had happened, without even the impression of having seen it, Marcus knew that as the man stepped forward his hand had turned in an adjusting flick, as something that had been hidden against his wrist slid down ready to be used. Marcus pulled to the side, trying to wrench his arm free, to kick, to force the hand back – but there was no time, this was not even really a fight, it was a matter of one small action and – he felt with cold disbelief – it had happened already. The doctor let him go and vanished through the door, leaving Marcus still propped against the wall, his hand still to the place where the cold needle had driven through the fabric of his sleeve, through his skin.

Despite Faustus' insistence by the rostra, a harried hour went past. They were all almost sick with shock. The trembling loathness to believe that someone who was supposed to be dead was really alive, however much that might be wished for, was stronger and more weakening than Faustus would have thought possible. In the face of it, it was almost only sheer perversity that kept him certain that the boy was really Marcus, more even than the anecdote about that turquoise mask-thing of Leo's. Everyone looked frail and grey-faced. They decamped back to the outer office of the Golden House where both the staff and the Imperial family hung over the longdictors and dashed about in tense flights that Faustus accelerated by saying, 'I promise, I am going to start having people executed any second—'

For it seemed that either Marcus had never reached any of the vigile military stations, or that if he had someone had immediately sent him on somewhere else. It took time – perfectly normal, predictable time – to reach the right people to establish this, for they were still dealing with the disturbance in the Forum, they were elsewhere.

Makaria paused in rushing from one longdictor to another. 'Daddy, for heaven's sake, you are making it all *worse*. Even if it is him, how could the vigiles know that, what else could they do?'

'Why do you keep saying it might not be him?' He paused. 'And what was he shouting about – is anyone going to find out why what's-his-name confessed to killing him if he's alive?'

'I don't know!' Makaria darted on into the private office.

'He said someone killed Leo and Clodia,' said Faustus.

Then Tulliola, also looking as shaken as Faustus had ever seen her, called across the room. 'We've found him. Titus – it really is him.'

'I know that,' said Faustus without thinking.

'On the island, in the Aesculapian.' Foolishly and instinctively pacifying, she added, 'Apparently it's very nice there.'

'That's less than a damned mile away, why's it taken this long to find that out? And why's he in hospital? There wasn't anything wrong with him,' insisted Faustus, although in fact he had not seen Marcus very clearly, and did remember now his impression of shabbiness, of poverty.

'Well, I suppose they had to make sure there wasn't anything wrong with him,' said Tulliola weakly. 'I suppose they had to take him somewhere. But it sounds like they really think it's him.'

Faustus was at the Aesculapian within minutes.

The Praetorians withdrew to an unobtrusive distance as he hurried up the steps. He said to the brown-bearded doctor who greeted him, 'He's all right, isn't he?'

The doctor bowed, possibly trying to conceal the pause before he answered. Faustus noticed it anyway. 'He seems . . . very anxious. You had better see him before we talk any more. Of course we've done our best to establish

439

who he is, and we wouldn't waste your time if it didn't seem possible that this really is your nephew, but it's not the same as a family member—'

'I know it's Marcus.'

The doctor nodded with a regret that Faustus also registered, and showed him upstairs.

Marcus was standing stiffly in the middle of the room. He turned his face towards the door as Faustus entered, but did not look at him, just swept unfocused eyes that way once, and then looked down and to the left, not at the floor, not at anything.

He said, formally, 'Uncle.'

'Marcus,' whispered Faustus, 'what happened, where on earth have you been?'

He would have embraced him, and was not sure at first what stopped him. He did not notice consciously that Marcus had shifted, straightening his body resolutely as if he wanted to shrink away in revulsion but would not let himself. He saw, though, that Marcus was trembling, more visibly than Faustus had ever seen a person shake before, while at the same time his white face wore an expression of intricate, strained calm, maintained against some appalling internal pressure.

'In Gaul,' answered Marcus shortly. 'Can we go somewhere else?'

To Marcus' shock, the stipple-haired doctor had come back, following Faustus. He said, 'Your Majesty, I'm afraid a nurse saw him trying to climb out of the window.'

After the first few minutes, in which he had been stunned into a kind of fascinated *waiting*, and could not move, Marcus had staggered breathlessly out again, down the stairs. He looked at the passing doctors as if through a pane of thick glass; he didn't know who he could approach, how he could tell them what had happened.

Another nurse, an older woman this time, said, 'Please. There are other patients,' and then, seeing his face, 'Is there anything wrong?'

440

He whispered, 'Yes. Please, can you help me, the doctor, the man with the the grey hair—'

'Which doctor?'

'He can't be a real doctor. Listen, please, he injected me with something—'

'Yes,' she said reasonably, ignoring the not-real doctor. 'Oh, do you feel a bit strange? Never mind. I'm sure it will start to help in a minute, why don't you go back and have a lie down?'

'No, you don't understand, it wasn't medicine,' he took in his breath and told her as steadily as he could – it was surprisingly difficult to say – 'I think it was poison—'

The nurse looked at him for a moment in silence, a thoughtful, reassessing look. 'Oh,' she said kindly, 'I see. No, no one would do anything like that here. Please don't worry about that. It's all right.'

'No,' said Marcus, seeing the way she looked at him, his voice weak with hopelessness. He tried once more. 'Look – *please* – someone who shouldn't have been here, I think. He was – tall, not the one with the beard. His hair wasn't just grey, it was sort of – it was speckled.' It was hard to marshal his thoughts to come up with a description, he couldn't remember clearly enough how the man had looked.

'Well, that sounds like a lot of the doctors,' she said.

'But it wasn't, it can't have been.'

'Let's go back upstairs,' she said.

Marcus looked about in despair, for something, an escape. He could see no other way of putting it so it would sound credible, not here of all places; it was strange how he thought he had made people believe him in the Forum, but here it was as though the very light, the brickwork, sucked the plausibility out of what he said. If he resisted, if he managed to run out of the hospital, if he tried to tell anyone else, nothing would do any good. He thought, *why* has this happened, I can't understand it.

He thought, and in a minute, she'll have to believe me.

She took his temperature, which was apparently normal. He tried to think that when it got worse, when it was obvious that there was something wrong, or perhaps if Faustus arrived soon, there might still be a chance. He wanted to beg the nurse and the doctor she summoned not to leave him alone. They talked about giving him something to calm him down, but didn't seem to want to do it yet. They promised to be back soon, they withdrew.

Marcus sat, waiting again, shivering.

He thought, sorry, Varius—! and again was overcome with incredulity, if he was really – if he really was going to die now, surely it would be obvious that he'd told the truth – not that it was any comfort – they'd given themselves away, *why*? This couldn't be right, couldn't be happening. He couldn't tell if the burring, the *pouring* of his heartbeat was the first symptom of the drug or of horror at what had happened to him.

The walls, or rather the brush strokes in the cream paint, somehow drew his attention, being surprisingly obvious, casting their own shadows. Then they began to move, faintly and regularly, as if a soft wind were breathing across a pale crop, or like small fronds of tissue engaged in some organic process, like cilia in the lungs.

For a little while this seemed more or less normal, he had too much else to think about. For a kind of mental company, because waiting here alone was unbearable, he'd been dwelling on the idea of Sulien, thinking regretfully, that was *different*, we were really friends. Well – goodbye.

And then during the next throe of protest – but this doesn't make *sense*! – he thought for a second he had lost the woollen hat he'd carried all this way. But having realised that it was still in the pocket of his coat, hanging over one of the chairs, he couldn't bear to look at it; the memory of Una brought tears into his eyes. He could allow himself to think, perhaps I could stand it if I could explain to someone, but not, if I could *see you*, because he would not see her; he felt if he thought of her any more clearly he really would be finished.

Then he looked again at the walls, at first with a kind of detached interest, independent of the continuing horror. He might have felt relieved, that *that* was what it was, perhaps he wasn't about to die. But the more he looked the more the movement seemed awful, he couldn't distinguish his aversion to the little swaying tags from the fear of dying, which was getting worse, not better.

But he tried, he managed after all to rake up a little resilience. He thought, come on. As long as you know it isn't real and remember what happened, you must be all right. He concentrated sternly on the wall, on the impossibility of paint and plaster moving like that. It was like trying to levitate things by looking at them, the trembling scrim seemed to have nothing to do with him at all, there was no reason it should do anything he wanted. He shut his eyes, enduring the rocking seasickness in his head when he did so. He opened them and it was ten times worse.

The painted skin of the walls was sloughing off to show the flayed muscle underneath. The tortured hide adhered, stringily, resisting, but was ripped mercilessly away. The red flesh was *alive*, it pulsed and wept.

It was *not real*, he knew it was not real, though a dizzying, rolling plume of revulsion made him lurch; for a second he thought he might even lose consciousness. He gritted his teeth: he refused to be like this, he would not be this weak and panicky, surely he could manage something better than that. He forced himself to walk to the wall and lay his hand on it, though it was such a horrible thing to do, he could only get there by a huge, expensive outlay of will, by promising himself cool plaster under his palm if he made it.

And he *felt* the thing, warm and sticky with blood; worse, it winced at his touch and began to quiver in agony, he could hear loud dying animal breaths coming from somewhere.

Marcus started back, and had to bow his head, gasping; he felt as if he'd never get back the breath or the strength that those few steps, that touch, had taken out of him. It was not that he began to believe it was real, but it no longer seemed to matter that it was not. There was nothing he could do about it; he might always be this way. After all this time he'd found out – he thought – this is what it's like, then! He began to think that if he wasn't going to die, he'd be mad, perhaps the drug could do that, perhaps it had triggered the Novian curse – and if he had to see things like this for the rest of his life – the idea was unendurable, he'd rather it had been poison.

The floor was turning spongy and wounded, too, it was hard to stand upright, but he couldn't touch anything again after that. Still, he had never pressed so much terrible effort into anything as he did now into trying to seem – at least normal enough to be listened to. But it was because of this that he couldn't look at Faustus – he knew that if he saw this peeling or flaying happen to a human being, then he would scream, that was just a fact, no determination could change it.

'I can't talk to you with him here, can we go somewhere else?'

'What?' said Faustus.

'He's not a doctor. He must have come in one of those vans. He drugged me so you won't believe what I said. Look.' He lowered his voice but couldn't bear to step any closer to Faustus. He said, incredibly carefully, 'It seems like it's happened to me, doesn't it, the curse. That's what they're telling you.'

'No, of course not,' soothed Faustus, infinitely pitying. Marcus gave a sharp sigh of frustration.

'We haven't given him anything yet,' said the doctor, the agent, softly, 'but he does seem to feel very threatened, it's been getting worse since he arrived. He said something about poison. But then, he was saying something similar when he appeared, wasn't he?'

'Go away, get out of here,' said Marcus, quietly, but the words still sounding like the repressed shout or scream they plainly were. He swallowed, again made an exhausting effort. 'I didn't understand what it was at first, but if every-one thinks I'm – like Uncle Lucius, then it's almost as safe as if I were dead. You see?'

'I see,' said Faustus, with a gentleness that again brought powerless tears to Marcus' eyes. The walls pulsed, bled.

'Please can't we go away. Please, at least – at least, the reason I came back – Varius—'

'Yes, we'll go somewhere else. I'll find out about Varius,' Faustus promised, in the same way.

Marcus thought, that's it then, there's nothing else.

Outside the room, there was a noise, a struggling, an erratic clatter of feet. Marcus heard a nurse cry breathlessly, as if in the process of grappling with someone, 'What do you think you are doing? You can't go in there, someone get the vigiles up here!'

The other voice, unbelievably, said, 'No, you might as well give up, I *am* going in here.'

The door opened, she forced her way in.

At first he couldn't look at her because he was afraid of what he'd see if he did, but then he couldn't help himself, and though he could still see the skinned flesh flinching around her, she didn't change, her face, the red-black eyes, beautiful. He felt, of course not, I couldn't ever see her like that, no matter what happened.

Una had rushed straight at him, as if she would collide with him, touch him, but drew herself up a foot short, staring at him. Then she even glanced to the wall, as if at the bleeding tissue he knew she couldn't see. 'It's not real,' she told him.

'I know,' he said.

'But it won't last,' she murmured. She turned to Faustus and said levelly, 'I know it's hard to believe, but you have to. It's true, this is a trick; if you keep him with you it'll wear off. I *know*.'

'How can you be here?' Marcus whispered.

Faustus watched him talking to the air, and wanted to weep himself with compassion. The bristle-haired man had changed back into the vigile's uniform in which he'd arrived and left half an hour before, though Faustus could not know that. There was no one in the room but Marcus and himself.

445

Hours later, Agelastus said to him, 'We need to think about how we're going to tell the people this.'

'Later, for all the gods' sake,' breathed Faustus.

'But he was saying some very inflammatory things, I'm worried the public won't understand that he couldn't help himself. Perhaps – if they saw him like this. Only very briefly, of course.'

Faustus sacked him on the spot.

CAELIAN

Dama felt an angry shame now and refused to recognise it. He never repeated to himself what they had said to one another, never checked to see whether he had really made himself ridiculous. If he could not help the incident replaying itself hotly and venomously, he could at least compress it, draining the sound out of it as he did so, shrinking it to a kind miniaturised dumb show, Una and himself, in a remembered cave small enough to be held in the hands, miming in the unsteady light and the crushed air. In the end he would simplify it down even beyond this, to an exchange of gestures; her pushing back his hands, the movements rendered more cramped and puppet-like than they had really been.

He tried to give all of himself that would have felt disappointment – that might have *thought* about feeling it – to what he was doing, as absorbed in it now, in getting this *over*, as if Marcus was someone he loved. He drove, vengefully. He was almost glad that it hurt, he wanted driving to take more effort and dedication than, at first, it did, but then, when it indeed began to exhaust him, of course he was angry with the car, the road, his body.

They were late in finding out what had happened in the Roman Forum. When Marcus climbed the statue, the heavy black car was still on the coast road from Arelas to Nicaea, Una staring at the grey sea, and they drove on, obliviously.

Sometimes, still, white or platinum bowls of light appeared on the water's surface and seemed to blaze with their own power, as if quite separate from the thick sky;

and Una, who had barely glimpsed the sea when they left Britain, felt another start of amazement, as if this light was to do with Marcus, and with her.

And then again – a blunt remembering and guessing; looking at the sea seemed a criminally pointless thing to do, the silver fire was flatly dreadful in itself. She felt, as Dama did, like a landmine, charged up, loaded with wanting to move and do something, and she sat very still, as if even to move a wrist would risk disaster. They had been taking short breaks from time to time, but an hour inside Italy it was obvious that Dama, staring out of blurring eyes, needed more than that.

Beside Dama, where Una had sat until today, Sulien felt his own arms seem to brace and burn; the car was a box of strain. He began to insist, at first simply worried about Dama, then really beginning to think they might crash unless someone stopped him, 'Dama, stop. Come on. We didn't sleep properly last night or the night before, you've done a day's work already. Stop, *stop*.'

He was aware of Una behind him, letting her breath out slowly, wanting to disagree and stopping herself. For another half hour Dama ignored Sulien, then gave in suddenly on the outskirts of Genua and stopped at last, in a half-empty gravel car-park by a port.

'I'm all right,' he remarked, in a normal, friendly voice, and shortly afterwards went to sleep. Una gave a shivering, relieved sigh.

She and Sulien got out. 'One of us could drive, I'm sure,' announced Una.

'All right, maybe we can, but come on, something to eat first.'

She could see that this pause was inevitable, but she thought, as she had thought at every rest, suppose *this* is when we ruin it all, or *this* is, suppose he dies and we missed stopping it by exactly as much time as we spend here? Even that assumed too much, very probably there would be no issue of their doing anything. Once in Rome it was hard to see how they could find him, even if he was there.

'All right.' She smiled at him. He was very sorry for her.

They didn't know why so many shops seemed to be shut. Una thought the whole city seemed thick with little obstacles and mistakes, to be deliberately slowing them down. And at first, out of a kind of displaced solipsism, it seemed unsurprising that Marcus seemed to be about in the street, like weather or a rumour, that other people should be thinking of him.

Then – they had found a bakery at last – there was an elderly man looking morosely at the bread rolls, mulling over a phrase, 'you've been lied to', and there were the components of a scene or a narrative, neither exactly images nor words, but lumps of memory, made of bits of both; a statue, the Roman Forum, *Marcus*, these things hanging together but she had not quite made sense of them yet, and then the man was concentrating seriously on what he was going to eat and how it wasn't fair that he was going to have to make it himself. Una was enraged with him. She was about to try and claw the thought back, and then turned, forgetting him, as if Marcus might be somewhere in the shop. The mood was everywhere, piled up in the houses, too much like her own for her to have seen it at once. It was a suspense, a jitteriness that she remembered now from weeks, months ago, from the day the news broke that Marcus Novius had disappeared. Outside, a woman ran across the street to talk to her neighbour, excited but angry somehow too, as if she'd been cheated out of something, and musing at the same time – it seemed to float reedily across to Una – thin, he was looking thin.

Una felt a tantalised, thirsty clutching towards relief; but everything was all disjointed, that was part of the point of it, no one was quite certain what had happened.

And Sulien had noticed the atmosphere before she said anything. The shop seemed not to have been open long, but he could see across the counter into a back room where the men loading the bread oven and working the dough were reluctant to come out and deal with the customers, or even to fill the shelves; the boy they sent out from time to time kept hurrying back to the conversation going on in there.

Una whispered, 'I think he's alive, or he *was* – I think he was on the longvision. Everyone knows something.'

Sulien stared at her for an instant and then went and called over to the bakers, with a straightforwardness that rather shocked Una, 'We've been on the road since yesterday, have we missed something?'

In Rome, he was about to add, but they knew what he meant at once. And they were delighted, their teeth shone in brief eager crescents; it was as though Sulien's lack of awareness was a present. They elbowed forward, almost ready to fight over it.

'You don't know? Well, you know there was this ceremony today?'

'No,' confessed Sulien affably. Una felt torn, feeling instinctively that they should be more cautious than this, wanting to rip the information out of the men.

'Where have you *been*? Oh, well, it was on longvision, and someone had jumped out of the crowd—'

The baker's assistant interrupted, 'But you didn't see that at first, you just heard someone shouting.'

There was another struggle for control of the story; the head baker won it back. 'You heard this shouting and the picture swung round, there was this kid up on a platform – I mean, on a statue, and it seemed like the Emperor thought it was Marcus Novius, but—!' He put up his hands with a fierce grin, as Una and Sulien exchanged an undisguised look of troubled hope. 'No one's *said*, they haven't explained anything. I don't see how they can *do* that.'

'What do you mean? What happened then?' demanded Una, her voice loud and startling.

'It cut out. It just started playing music.'

Behind them the old man burst out with surprising, adolescent indignation, 'They're just going to pretend it didn't happen! Something's been going on and they didn't want him saying what it was. It's sickening. He said Leo and Clodia were murdered, I always thought as much.'

'Well really, it probably wasn't him,' said the boy, who hadn't spoken so far.

The others turned on him, again with a kind of delight. 'You didn't even *see* it! Why didn't the speech go on? The Emperor called him *Marcus*, for heaven's sake!'

'He could have been wrong.'

They all began talking again so heatedly that Una and Sulien could have walked out without paying if they'd wanted to. The agitated time they spent looking for a public longvison proved to be wasted; they were too far from the centre, and when they at last found a little private one in the corner of a confectioners, it turned out that whatever had happened, it had not been shown again.

Una wanted to break the screen for refusing to give up what it had known. Millions of other people had seen Marcus. Naturally, the funereal sequence of pictures of Marcus was not repeated either, though as a last resort she would even have liked to have seen that, as if they might somehow reveal something if they were studied hard enough, so that she could see his face.

As yet there had not even been the promise of an explanation. And though by now they had heard several accounts of Marcus' appearance in the Forum, the details were always different, and when they walked back to the car they still felt only passably sure of what had happened.

Una said slowly, 'Then he got there, and he was alive four hours ago. And he still – he *must* be, because how can anyone kill him after what he said? At least, that's why he did it. But then – why aren't they saying, yes, he's alive, it's a miracle?'

'I suppose it's only been four hours,' said Sulien, though the confused slowness with which the news had come out dampened the optimism he was, of course, trying to feel. Perversely, the very ease with which he could now repeat to her that they as good as knew for certain that Marcus was safe, made the words seem weak even before he framed them. 'Well, it doesn't make any difference to what we do, except we know it's worth getting to Rome. He wanted us to meet him there. If everything's fine then we'll just do that.'

Una noticed herself feeling forlornly that if Marcus had really succeeded, he would be nevertheless irretrievable, that if she saw him again it would be a matter of being led into some large room which she could not clearly imagine, where he would be waiting, where nothing could be said. And she wanted to cry out with disgust at cavilling at anything that would keep Marcus safe.

Dama was still asleep, but woke disconcertingly as they approached, without any sound being made. He blinked at them whitely, the freckles looking again like a scattering of dark little wounds against chalky skin. 'How long was I asleep? I can start driving again.'

'Forty minutes, or less than that, and you can't,' said Sulien. He began sharing out the food. Dama took it slowly, his face closing, so that Sulien remembered how he disliked letting anyone see him eat. But he could do it now almost without any sign of his injury, only holding the bread cupped rather than grasped between finger and thumb, propping his left arm at the elbow with his right, bending his head perhaps a little further forward. Still, he was silent and didn't look at either of them. His body was stiff as if barricaded against any comment, though Sulien felt like saying, more in exasperation than in kindness, no one would notice if they didn't already know, at least they wouldn't if you didn't sit there looking like that.

He told Dama what they'd heard; it was hard for Una. She and Dama seemed to have agreed tacitly to speak to each other but never exclusively, always including Sulien in whatever they said.

Dama listened and said calmly, 'Four hours is a long time. We should go.'

Sulien sighed, because Dama's arms would again go numb with pain and tiredness after only half an hour or so on the road, and the thought of being shut in with that was worse even than the danger it would cause.

'I'm going to do it,' Una said, voice taut, exaggeratedly reasonable. 'I've watched. Otherwise we're going to lose the rest of today, aren't we?'

'Oh, shit,' said Sulien, dismayed, looking at Una and Dama, unsure which one of them was more likely to kill them all and feeling that he might not be able to stop both of them.

'No. Look, how long is that? That's all the same road, and it turns there, and then it's all the same again. I've only got to keep going.'

She'd stated this to both of them, but Dama looked at her, too directly, violating the pact. He said at last, 'Show me if you can get round the car park.'

The car stuttered a little at first, then limped forward in slow yet alarming jolts. Sulien groaned. 'Shut up,' said Una, humiliated, leaning grimly forward over the control sticks, her teeth gritted. Dama said, in a measured voice, 'It's all right. You don't have to push so hard, just hold them. You can do it more loosely than that.'

Una sighed, changed her grip on the controls and pushed the car around the yard, smoothly enough this time.

'Go round once more,' said Dama. Una sighed again and again began the circuit.

'What are you doing? – No!' Sulien said, as at the same time Dama repeated, 'Go *round* once more.'

'It's *fine*,' Una said firmly, driving with severe and only slightly uneven competence out onto the road. Sulien looked helplessly ahead for whatever it was that was bound to hit them.

But Dama gazed impassively at her and at the road and said, carefully as before, 'All right, so long as I watch you, and you listen to me.'

Now that Una and Dama were side by side again, it was very obvious that something, Dama, or more impersonally, the tension between them, had a chance here to jab out, to hector and punish Una. That this did not happen, the well-hidden effort that prevented it, was almost more draining. Dama was – for Una at least – a surprisingly good teacher, he was attentive, patient; everything he told her to do or not do was well judged. And Una responded well, too, the slight shaking or bucking of the car under her hands soon stopped. She was afraid of going fast, but Dama said, 'It's more dangerous here if you go slowly. You're not going to lose control of it,' and she pulled up to the right speed, trustfully, though turning pale. They were still good at this, at sharing work. Sulien saw this, and wanted to beg them, to beg Dama, to stop it.

After four hours of this, Sulien saw, too late, that he should have prepared himself for the last mile of the Pertinacian Way into Rome, but whenever he'd managed to relax enough to think about anything but Una's driving, he'd been wondering sadly what the journey would have been like if Lal had been there, if she could have balanced out the trapped feeling Dama was making in the car.

And now the lamps and headlights began to show crosses, their shadows flattened by the blue light. It was possible to see them almost as some innocent structural thing, the uprights of a fence, miniature pylons, but they dragged at Sulien's eyes, and not only with sick compulsion but the feeling of a duty to look. Only a few, the closest to the city, wore bodies, like scarves. He thought none were alive.

Sickness made him weak. He missed Lal more, remembering how she'd kissed his wrist, and at the same time was glad she wasn't there; because it could still happen, to Dama and himself – already they'd had to stop at a control booth for an identity check, and Una had presumably held back the vigile guard's power to notice either the falseness of the papers or what a strange little group they were; but it was still there.

Una knew she would have to find somewhere soon to hand the car back to Dama, so that he could perform all the stopping and starting on smaller roads that she knew she couldn't be trusted with yet. She wished she had done it already, so she could look at Sulien. She said to him quietly, 'We'll be past them in a minute.'

Sulien couldn't answer her as he might have done if

they'd been alone, because of Dama, whose presence complicated his own feeling as well as her concern for him. He knew, without being able to look, that Dama was watching the crosses steadily, not overcome as he was, but with an *eagerness* in revulsion. He thought, how *can* you?

And as if answering, Dama turned and looked at him briefly, with an odd smile. It was a partly companionable look, as if saying, how are you taking it?, but also observing the difference between them, almost a little condescending, as at a novice, noting his own greater knowledge of what had been done to the bodies outside.

Despite the knot of nausea in his stomach, Dama felt a punitive satisfaction in driving back through the crosses to Rome, where he'd never wanted to be again, as if he'd come to burn the place down.

Queasily shutting his eyes again, Sulien thought, would I just stare at them like that if it had happened to me, is that all the difference? But of course, Dama had killed someone, more than one person, before that. And, he thought, remembering Wolf Step, but I could have done, too, you wouldn't have thought so but I could – all three of us in here could, but only Dama—

He believed he knew that Marcus couldn't – or at least, that the inability would last a long time. But if he gets to be Emperor he'll have to, not do it himself, it's true – but he'll have to have it done, he won't be able to get out of it.

He remembered also thinking, about killing, that he wouldn't be able to stay the same after it, and glanced again at Dama, though he couldn't see his face any more; he was calmly helping Una guide the car into a layby; she came and sat beside Sulien, smiled at him anxiously as Dama drove them through the suburbs.

Then Rome itself swallowed the car like a pill. Una and Sulien had thought they were used to cities, but even on its outskirts, old as it was, and though its age glowed warmly in its marble and coppery stone, Rome had a fierce vigour and newness that London didn't have, the old things

455

polished and varnished over so many times that they still glittered.

They left the car and walked to the centre, which lay under a thick tent of electric light, holding the stained dark so high above the ground that people still moved as busily beneath it as if it were not there.

Sulien felt the headiness of it in a strange groggy way. He knew Una must be thinking, all the time, Marcus was here, he is here. They had the impression of knowing the Forum so well already, from pictures and longvision, that it was startling that it should also be a real, physical place; and Una had to stare at it, wondering where Marcus had stood. But Dama led them through it all, radiating a quick contempt that extended to Sulien and Una when he caught them slowing to look up at the statues, or the towers of the Golden House. Sulien thought, beginning to be able to ease the crosses away from his mind: is it really all part of the same thing, the crosses and this – as Dama, marching ruthlessly and silently along towards the palace, was as good as shouting that it was, that every stone and pane of glass was culpable. But it was so beautiful, and ingenious and vital, it was dishonest not to at least admit that. And Sulien gazed at everything on Lal's behalf, feeling, though Delir had been unkind to accuse her of wanting to go sightseeing – it's not fair if she never gets here, she really would like it.

The Colosseum looked smaller than it did in the pictures, but still smooth and formidable.

And again they'd missed the news breaking. Una saw that though the agitation about Marcus was still there, it was subdued, half-sated, although here and there were hot patches of suspicion and discontent. She scarcely tried to translate it this time, they just sped to the nearest longvision.

The screen on the Colosseum's side would usually show only advertisements and footage from the games within, not news, but today it held the text of an announcement that had been playing periodically throughout the Empire for the last two hours.

'No circumstances could detract from the Emperor's delight at his nephew's as yet inexplicable reappearance. Nevertheless, Marcus Novius' health remains a concern, and he is likely to be receiving medical attention for some time. The implications for the Varius case are being investigated.'

This had been the most explicit statement that Faustus would agree to.

They stood, stranded, staring at it.

'His health . . . ?' muttered Una tentatively, swallowing the note of shrill alarm she could feel gathering in her throat. 'What have they done to him?'

Would they say that if he was dead, at first – and then let the truth out later?

Why would the Emperor allow such a thing, after what Marcus had said in the Forum?

Sulien read the announcement the first time with the same confused distress – what's wrong with him? And then looked more coldly at the words, as though they were symptoms.

He said, 'They mean he's mad.'

Dama frowned at the text. 'How do you know it means that?'

Sulien shook his head, 'That's how they would say it. That's what every word of it means. Look at it. "Circumstances." That's the only thing they'd want to say without really saying anything.'

'He's right,' said Una, in a low rational voice. 'What else would it be?' She reflected, and turned to Sulien. 'Could you do that – are there drugs that would have that kind of effect?'

Sulien admitted, 'Yes.'

Una nodded and was silent. After a while she remarked quietly, 'He's afraid of going mad.'

'I know,' said Sulien.

Una re-read the message carefully, thinking of Marcus with a kind of strictness, trying to resist the pull of pity and misery. She said tersely, 'Fine. Never mind. Then we've just got to find him.'

457

But they turned away from the Colosseum and Rome glowed, huge around them, hostile. Marcus need not even be within it. Una whispered, 'What happens if it goes on for too long?'

Sulien looked away, shiftily, 'I don't know what they've used, or how much. I don't think it would be anything that could kill him.'

'But can it get to a point where he couldn't be the same again?'

'I don't know!' insisted Sulien.

Her mouth contracted a little with pain at the thought of it, but she nodded. 'Well then, the Golden House.'

So they climbed the Palatine hill, up to the arched façade where of course there were so many Praetorians, in front of the palace gates and behind them, uniformed, armed. Sulien felt a sick tremor just at going so close to them.

Still, they were not the only ones pressing as close to the gates as the Praetorians would allow, looking across floodlit pines, at the Golden House. Again it was hard to believe that this was a real place, much less that anyone – any real and knowable person – could live there. Sulien tried to imagine Marcus going in and out, and could not. And if Marcus was there now, he thought, how could they ever get through all that?

Una looked at the gold structure with a sort of helplessness; there was too much of it, too many people inside.

'I don't think he's here,' she said. She was studying the Practorians. 'They would have to know, wouldn't they?'

But if he is there, she thought, I'll find out, I would get in, I will.

Dama said in disgust. 'And he could have a whole floor to himself, look at the *size* of it!'

They began walking away from the palace at once as if they had somewhere to go. But they didn't have anywhere to go. They walked down to the Forum, but felt uncovered and vulnerable there among all the smooth surfaces and all the people. They went a little further – Una and Sulien did not know where – and for a while they just sat at the bottom of a long flight of curved steps, helpless. Occasionally Una realised with an awakening of fear that someone was looking at them, not because a group of young people leaning against steps looked out of place in itself, but because they were so nearly still and silent when everything else was moving. They looked as if they were in the middle of a quarrel: she and Sulien sitting side by side, not looking at each other, her head in her hands, Dama pacing about again, but they were fixed like that, unnaturally.

'Someone knows where he is,' she said. 'A lot of people. We must be able to get near one of them.'

Finally, Sulien said, 'Where does Lucius Novius live? Could they have taken him there?'

Una looked up. 'Do they let people know where he lives?'

'I think it's on the Caelian,' said Dama.

'Could you actually find it, though?'

'I – sang over there a couple of times.' Dama flushed as if this was an absurd and embarrassing act for which he had been and was still accountable. 'Not at that house, I mean, but at parties round there. I remember people talked about him. I think I still remember which way they said it was. And it's not built-up there, there's only a few villas.'

Sulien and Una had almost no idea of the Caelian other than the name; Una had not even known that it was a hill. They did not have far to walk, and yet when they reached it the dark public gardens seemed to soak up noise and light like a soft cloth, so that it was hard to believe the Forum and the Circus were so close. A few fine, lamplit streets and footpaths cut between oaks and cypresses, but a rich peace lay everywhere, leaking out of the occasional villas inside their walled grounds.

Dama's breath quickened with tense frustration at first when he found that the contented paths all looked the same to him in the dark. He began muttering faintly to himself as he tried to force the house where he'd been taken to sing into mind. It was harder than he'd expected, it was a part of his life he found distasteful to think of.

Then they passed a drive leading up to an ornate little

villa, whose gates were carved with dolphins and sea shells. That was it, shells, thought Dama, and laughed scornfully at the house, 'Remembered it as bigger than that. Looks like a jumped-up *cake*, doesn't it?' He turned and looked east, and downhill. 'All right. Then it's this way.'

When they found Lucius' villa, before they saw the two wandering Praetorians turn ahead of them to be let into the scowling gatehouse, they guessed that they had come to the right place, not because the exterior was lavish but because it was not. What they could see of the villa looked blind and paranoid, presenting nothing outwards, as the palace did. There were only high, blank walls, lined inside with some thick rough hedge, over which they could see just the edge of the villa's roof, and a few treetops. For all that, it did not seem especially heavily guarded, and the walls could have been climbed, but they could see cameras on the roof pointing down into what was perhaps not so much a garden as a protective moat of land around the main structure.

They retreated to the north wall, and stood between trees.

Sulien said, 'What do you think?'

Una did not want to think Marcus was not there, because what else did they have? But she could feel nothing of him within the walls, at least not yet.

She muttered sadly, 'Perhaps if we go to the front again, I could at least get nearer to the Praetorians.'

They had watched the guards entering the estate from the east, and this time they would have approached along the west wall, then Una said, 'There's someone on that side – he's coming.'

They were not doing anything illegal yet, but plainly the guards should be kept from knowing that there was anyone loitering around the villa; and there was not time to run out to the further trees. Instinctively they pressed into the shadows at the base of the wall.

'Praetorian?' Dama whispered.

'Yes. Could be. Something like that, but—'

Someone trying not to be seen, sneaking along, as they were, looking for something – for them, for intruders? Una gave a sigh of reluctant effort and began sifting through him for the places to push, to say – keep on with that, think about how angry you are – the prefect, Laevinus, yes, it was a disgrace. (Plainly he was a Praetorian or a vigile officer, she didn't fully understand the distinction.) Yes, already it was hard for him to think of anything but that, the awful argument with Laevinus, his career in ruins—

She caught her breath in excitement: there was the idea of Marcus, *inside* the house.

They saw him now; a tall shadow, a man in dark clothes, not a uniform, and he came slowly, sidling, as they had been, with one eye on the lights. But so angry, why was he so angry, why didn't he know what he was trying to find?

And he was going to walk right into them. It was true that he was glumly immersed now in this argument with his boss, so much that he might pass within a few feet of them without noting the little signals from the periphery of his vision, but he was still automatically skirting the outline of the wall, as, it seemed, he'd done at least once already, and unless they moved, in which case they would walk straight across his path, he might even put out a hand to brush a branch aside and touch them.

Una was aware that Dama was tense and trembling, and was sure that it was with abhorrence as well as fear; that the probability that this was a vigile officer or a Praetorian, just the idea or the name, was enough for that.

Then the man hesitated, leaned against the wall, raising a sad hand to his face, thinking, in fact close to moaning aloud, 'What am I doing?' And unbelievably, it seemed, he walked off into the park, and Una remembered Dama's story of his certainty that his supervisor would leave the wrench for him, that he could sabotage the lift without being stopped, the strange forced luck that had made it happen.

But the man was miserable with guilt and baffled fury. Una whispered reassuringly to the others, 'Don't worry. But he's not meant to be here, and we need to talk to him.'

Sulien was almost less startled by this than by the

461

ferocity with which Dama tried to stop her, silently, making a desperate, right-handed grab for her arm, too horrified even to remember his fingers wouldn't hold.

The man started with guilty shock as he realised he'd been seen, and drew himself up in an awkward, justifying shrug. He saw a woman, no – barely more than a little girl if you looked at her face – separate herself from the dark, from another figure, two other figures who followed her reluctantly into the open.

They might not be up to anything yet, but obviously they shouldn't be there. A girl hanging around private property at night with two boys, what were their parents doing? His instinct was that he ought to move them on, and he even felt a jab of annoyance at doing the Praetorians' work for them, before he remembered why he was here and froze in embarrassed perplexity. He was, of course, loitering around in a dubious way himself, he'd even had thoughts which, in sheer incredulity, he could hardly bear to acknowledge, of lying his way in, or worse, climbing in over the wall. He didn't want to believe that he was creeping around an Imperial house like a burglar, that he'd deliberately picked dark clothes for the purpose, dug out a hat to cover his too-bright hair.

But even if none of these things had been true, he didn't know if he had any more than a citizen's right to chivvy along dodgy-looking kids. He didn't know if he had a job any more.

Cleomenes wanted to hit – not people, not even in his imagination – but objects, and was powerless to do so. For days he had found his fist swinging up, his foot drawing back, to attack walls and tables while grunts of rage gathered behind his teeth. The blows never fell. He was paralysed by the thought of sounds of violence (even against furniture) being heard through his thin walls. Of course, more practically, he might hurt himself, he might break things he could not afford to replace. He wished he were rich so as to be able to destroy his belongings in freedom.

462

But this had not been a concern during and after the disastrous (surely, it must have been disastrous) encounter with Laevinus that afternoon, when he had longed, at the least, to sweep some papers off a desk, since he appeared actually to be walking out in a fury, and would never be able to go back.

He could not do it because he believed all the time, despite the gales of indignation, that he was making a terrible mistake, a sequence of terrible mistakes. Things *could not be* as he was increasingly certain they were. What are you *doing*? he asked himself, appalled, as he restrained his fist so that it merely tapped the wall apologetically; as he deliberately ruined his career.

If he was right – if what he thought Varius had been hinting was right – then he might be in danger himself soon, already in fact, and that was so ludicrous that it as good as proved he couldn't be right. And yet here he was.

Still, he said thickly, out of discomfiture and – heaven help him – fear of witnesses, making a shooing gesture, at which the older of the boys bristled defensively, 'Go on, you've got no business here.' And this was so like what Laevinus had said to him that afternoon that he glowered at himself.

Already, and with betraying urgency, the boys were trying to obey him, the shorter one, struggling to wrestle or drag the girl away, growled at him, 'We're going, we just wanted to see the house,' but without the casual flippancy the words should have had – no, with intense, excessive hatred. They really must be in trouble.

And the girl said, 'We have got business here. We're trying to find Marcus.'

Cleomenes gaped. After a moment he fell back on simply repeating, *'Marcus?'* knowing whom she meant, but disapproving of the use of the first name alone.

'We can call him that. We know him. He was with us all that time.'

Cleomenes' face organised itself slowly into a quizzical look, but he did not speak this time.

'We thought the same as you: that he might be here. And you came because you want to know about Varius, don't you?'

'Who told you that?' he gasped, not just stunned but frightened, too; for hours now he'd been dimly afraid that his intentions, confused as they were, were known and that something was going to happen to him. Although how these stray children could have anything to do with – with *what*, with his colleagues, people he knew? He'd got it all wrong, he must have done.

Dama hissed furiously, 'We can't *deal* with him, what do you think you're doing?'

Una persisted to Cleomenes, 'When we met Marcus he'd been gone two weeks, it was in Tolosa. Did you hear about that? And you're right, everything he said in the Forum was true. Varius never tried to kill him or Gemella.'

Cleomenes said softly, 'Who?'

'In the palace. In business. The vigiles.'

Cleomenes opened his mouth a little, but said nothing, realising abstractedly that there was no question of snorting derisively, saying, rubbish. He looked at the ground.

'I want to get in,' said the girl. 'You can get us in.'

'*No*,' said Cleomenes, his own idea appalling him when it was said aloud, striding blindly away as if from a pushy beggar. Like beggars, they followed him.

'But you're right, you were right, what else did you come to do?'

The tall boy said, 'What is this, Una, who is he?' and the terrible girl dragged at his elbow, demanding, 'Why don't you say? Why don't you tell us?'

'Nothing to do with you,' said Cleomenes stubbornly.

'It's got more to do with us than with you,' she cried with an angry rawness in her voice that made him look at her, interested. 'I told you, we *know* Marcus. Didn't you come here to find out what's happening? Why are you trying to get away from us when we know all about it?'

Cleomenes stopped, took a few indecisive steps onward,

as Sulien said, 'You've got to *tell* us, anyway, is Marcus here?'

'I don't *know*,' said Cleomenes, groaning, stopping. 'I only came here because—'

'Why?'

Cleomenes cast about in the air, as though trying physically to shake them off. 'Well, I didn't really know where I could go.' He'd gone home and changed rapidly out of his uniform, finding part of his mind warning him steadily, don't stay here, get away from here quickly. And he'd gone out, taking his vigile's pass with him, and his gun.

He said, a little more distinctly, 'What I've been trying to do is talk to Varius. But they won't let anyone see him. At least not me. And even before all *this*, he'd said something like that might happen. I got moved across town. And it did happen just after I made the arrest. But he'd lied so much and he never really told me anything – but then *this* – lately! What am I *supposed* to do?'

The job, heading a squad tackling gangs in the Suburra, had not quite been a promotion, in that his rank and pay hadn't changed; but his work had never involved so much strategy before, the people around him were more interesting, and there was at once more prestige and more excitement in handling such a specific, serious task. It was understood that there was a good chance a real promotion might follow. It had been abrupt, but there'd been a change of policy higher up, that was all.

But he did not stop thinking of what Varius had said to him about Lady Makaria, and more than that, Varius' whole manner, his apparent slowness to believe that Cleomenes really suspected him, his odd laughter. Cleomenes had been told that as the case involved the Imperial family, he must not discuss it with anyone until it was resolved. He did not question this. But he was just uneasy enough to try and keep an eye on the case.

And so, although he had reported everything Varius had said, he'd taken an afternoon to go round to the Tusculum villa and found the place alive with vigiles and Praetorian guards, who did not want him there. He left them alone but afterwards he'd tracked down the butler and established that Lady Makaria had indeed given the sweets, she always did, although Varius would certainly have had plenty of time to poison them after they arrived. Cleomenes wrote this up as an addition to his original report and sent it onto his old station. He never heard anything back. This wasn't unusual, yet he kept waiting, calling over from time to time at the urging of a faint scratching of worry. All he'd heard was that Varius was still silent, the search for Marcus now was focusing more on these apparent sightings of him. When he first heard that Varius had confessed at last, he'd felt a twinge of disappointment at having missed it.

In the dark on the Caelian, he broke off, staring at the grim-faced adolescents, starting as if until now he'd been talking in his sleep.

'Who are you?' he demanded. 'What are you doing here?'

'I told you,' said Una, patiently. 'We want to find Marcus.'

'Oh yes, you met in Tolosa,' said Cleomenes, sounding jovial with near hysteria. 'Is that where he's been all this time?'

'No. Not all the time.' Dama had looked at her, she knew that his horror of the centurion hadn't abated, and she decided she would say nothing about Holzarta, nothing about slavery even, if she could help it.

Sulien asked, 'You arrested Varius – are you with the vigiles or the Praetorians?'

Cleomenes again noted the tone of voice, heard fear this time, and looked again at the other young man, who was standing a small, tense distance from them, as if he wanted to escape but was invisibly tethered. He answered, with a little huff of gloomy laughter, 'Vigiles, more or less, I shouldn't worry about it too much for the time being.'

The girl went on, rapidly but very clearly, 'We were going to claim the reward money until he told us what would happen. We know about the poisoned sweets, and how else could we?' Cleomenes jumped again with surprise. 'They killed Gemella, but of course they were meant for him. That sounds right to you, doesn't it?'

For two and a half days, Cleomenes had been trying to find someone to whom he could explain, but in the meantime, he'd acted without letting himself draw conclusions, without being able to believe his own doubts. Now in bafflement he found he was surrendering to the suppressed sequence or story of what he'd done. The whole thing seemed so preposterous and dreamlike now, he couldn't think of any reason not to.

Slowly he said, 'There wasn't anything about the poison in the confession. And I haven't been able to see the actual sweets, or my report, even. People have been – trying to stop me. Well, of course they were, I haven't been doing the job properly since I read that thing. Laevinus told me, you didn't determine cause of death, that isn't your area. But still, I *saw* her.'

Laevinus had said to him, in quite a friendly tone, 'Cleomenes, there's a good team working on it; you've got plenty of your own to do. You've got to trust other people to handle things once in a while.'

After this, Cleomenes had sat at his desk deliberating for a minute or two, and then written a note to Renatus, the city prefect, and Laevinus' immediate superior.

'I haven't really been into work as such. I tried the prison. I went to see both sets of parents. So Laevinus and Segestes and Buteo have been telling me, seriously, leave it alone. Yesterday I thought it had started sounding like – threats – oh, not exactly threats!' he corrected himself immediately, and then was silent. He muttered, 'Warnings. Yes. Threats. Anyway—'

But again it was a moment before he went on. He seemed to have assumed that once he started talking about this it would sound ridiculous, and was becoming alarmed that it did not. He said, 'And no one had told his parents anything. They didn't even know he'd been arrested; the first they heard was when it was on longvision.'

He remembered it; it appeared that in the week before the

announcement about the confession had come out, they had got to the point of quarrelling openly over whether they should think of Varius as still being alive. The father had been lying in a chair almost motionless, and barely managed to acknowledge Cleomenes' presence; the mother, on the other hand, kept jumping up and running around, shedding tears all the time while still talking furiously, as if the crying was something happening to someone else. 'Look at him. What have they done to him?' And of course she went on to say – Varius could never have done anything like that. They were so happy. And even if they hadn't been, never, never.

Of course Cleomenes had heard that sort of thing before, and he reminded himself that it was almost unimaginable that she should say anything else, and he knew also he should ignore the picture she'd shown him of Varius and Gemella together. Because Varius had struck him as nervous and volatile, he'd imagined Gemella as being much the same, he'd thought of them as yes, in love, perhaps, but probably throwing things at each other half the time. But they didn't look like that in the picture, side by side in a garden, in a conventional enough marital pose, but with a depth of relaxation between them, that made the formality look like the fleeting interruption of a warmer, more graceful movement towards each other. It meant nothing, except it showed up that Varius' mother was right, Varius did look bad in the picture on longvision, worse than when Cleomenes had last seen him.

He'd hoped Varius would have told his parents something about what had happened and what he meant to do, but he hadn't. Cleomenes talked to Gemella's family, too: and Gemella's mother had said, bleakly, 'You think you know someone,' and stared, trembling, at her knees, while her gawky younger daughter worked desolately at her homework. But her husband exclaimed, 'No, no, it must be a mistake, why would he confess to that? He spoke to me. I would have known.'

'How could you have known?' his wife said through her teeth. 'And you said he hardly explained.'

'I would have known,' Paulinus insisted.

Cleomenes went back to the station, unsure whether really he'd learned anything and knowing he would have to account somehow now for the meeting he'd missed. The station was set around a square and he saw a herd of vans, presumably returning from the ceremony in the Forum nosing in around the public entrance, and the way down to the cells. The activity didn't reach up across to his building, and he slunk miserably upstairs into his office. His secretary Antonia ducked instantly round the door to cry 'Marcus Novius was just in the Forum!' so that Cleomenes stood there blinking, saying, 'What?' before bolting after Antonia into the general office, where the longvision was.

He was luckier than Una and Sulien had been – his colleagues had been recording the broadcast. Cleomenes sat and replayed it several times to be sure he'd heard the words properly. And he simply couldn't do anything for a moment, dazzled with disbelief and fury. Right, he thought, and got up, but could not immediately think where this outrage should take him. He made a vain effort to contact Renatus, already feeling certain that there was no point bothering with Laevinus. In the end he drove over to the prison once more, almost on purpose to be doubly infuriated by being turned away again. He came back to hear, still several hours ahead of the rest of the world, about Marcus' condition, just before Laevinus called him upstairs into his office.

Laevinus' skin was pale and damp with anger. 'Can you tell me why you attempted to go over my head to Renatus? I hope you can.'

Cleomenes was already angry enough not to respond with the humiliated self-reproach that Laevinus wanted. 'Why can't I get to see Varius?'

'You don't have any business seeing Varius. You have a hundred legionaries and an important project that you're neglecting, and you've let me down, too; I am finding it seriously hard to remember why I gave you this position.'

'When is he going to be out? Because obviously we'll have to drop the whole thing now.'

'And I have given you several warnings which you've deliberately chosen to ignore—'

'But we *are* dropping it, aren't we? We don't have any serious choice.'

Laevinus regarded him sourly, but said, 'That's rather premature. He is still the only serious suspect in a murder.'

'How can he *possibly* be a suspect in a murder?'

'His wife is certainly dead. His alibi was nonsense, you established that yourself.'

'Well, it seems like we have another witness – whose very existence makes the confession look pretty *weird*, at the *least*, Sir. Who seems insistent that Varius isn't a murderer.'

'Are you trying to suggest something? Because I don't like your tone.'

Cleomenes looked at Laevinus and felt a faint unexpected chill. For the first time he took up the slightly cowed posture that the situation called for, lowering his eyes apologetically. He didn't answer.

Laevinus looked slightly appeased, and explained, 'Possibly the individuals who interrogated him went too far. He must have thought that was what we wanted to hear. It doesn't mean that the bulk of what he said wasn't true. He may very probably have intended or attempted to kill Marcus Novius, who, I'm afraid to say, is hardly coherent. He seems to think the entire world *except* Varius wants to kill him, including people who don't exist. I heard from the Praetorians. He's talking to walls and things. Tragic. Well, I'm not a doctor, but, if you think of what had happened, and being betrayed like that—'

Cleomenes had listened only to the first part of this, but he considered it carefully, as if in a moment a better, more complex meaning might flick open, as at the touch of a switch. At last he asked quietly, hoarse with disbelief, 'Eliciting a confession by torture?'

'Oh come on. Can't you hear how dramatic you sound. I never said torture.'

'Well, what else—'

Laevinus said, tapping a hand on the desk to emphasise wearily over-articulated words, as though Cleomenes were a tiresome child, 'I said, Applying. More pressure. Than with hindsight may have been advisable.'

Cleomenes thought about this too and asked reasonably, 'What does that mean?'

Laevinus said nothing for a while. Eventually he remarked, 'The individuals will be dealt with. But if it gets out that all a criminal has to do to be let off is make a false confession—'

'But he's a *citizen*, we can't – anyway, what about the sweets?'

'What about the sweets?'

'Well, they were poisoned, weren't they? He nearly managed to kill himself with them, didn't he? If he murdered her without using them, and he didn't kill anyone else, what were they for?'

Laevinus sighed again. 'I don't have any information about poison right now.'

'It's all in my report.'

'I don't have your report right now. Someone will be dealing with it. But in any case, why would an innocent man be running around with any kind of poison and try and commit suicide rather than explain himself?'

This was the question that had kept Cleomenes certain of Varius' guilt for weeks, and still he had no answer for it. Nevertheless, he was about to say, but the sweets came from the palace, we know that – but as he took a breath to do so he felt the chill again and he thought, why am I wasting time trying to convince him of something he already knows? He's *in* on it.

He stared, and for a while couldn't find anything to say. He was suddenly afraid to remind Laevinus of anything he knew. At last he said hesitantly, 'I want to see his lawyer.'

'You can do what you like in your own time,' snapped Laevinus.

'I might,' retorted Cleomenes, and found he was tramping a bellicose path out of the office, out of the building, into the street. He did not know, now or at the time, whether he had meant this as a resignation; or whether, if he had not, he should assume he'd be sacked for doing it.

He spent some time in longdictor-cauponas around Rome, trying to call the lawyer who, apparently, was to represent Varius. When Cleomenes finally reached him the lawyer seemed entirely uninterested in what he had to say. Cleomenes urged, 'But I arrested your client. And I now think I have evidence for his defence.'

'Then leave your name and address and I will contact you later.'

'Will you really?' asked Cleomenes crossly, and the lawyer turned off the longdictor.

After this all he could think of was trying to find out if Marcus Novius was really talking to people who didn't exist. He'd come to the Caelian, prompted, like Sulien, by the idea of Lucius Novius; but he had some reason to hope the idea was right. Two hours before, he'd started a chat about the day's events with a porter from one of the smaller villas, who had seen two huge and darkly ornate cars gliding down the hill from the north, late that afternoon.

He mumbled now, 'All that about Leo and Clodia – and people lying, people around the Emperor – and Varius—'

Una said firmly, 'You already know that was true.'

Cleomenes nodded and then made another cramped, flailing gesture of frustration. 'Bloody – *Varius*! Why couldn't he tell me any of this?'

'He must have had some sense,' muttered Dama, involuntarily.

'What's the matter with you?' asked Cleomenes sharply, as a real question, frowning at him. Dama shrugged and turned away, cradling his arms again. Cleomenes, giving up, said to Una, 'But he must have – he *knew* I wasn't part of it.'

472

'Even if he did, you might still have passed on what he said.'

'Well, I *did*,' whispered Cleomenes. 'What, do you think whatever happened – that made it worse?' He looked soft and helpless with horror for a moment. Then abruptly he said, 'Fine,' and went striding back towards the villa. They pursued him again. 'Wait here,' he ordered them.

'*No*,' said Sulien, pulling him back, preparing for a long argument, but Cleomenes only looked at them for a moment and said again grimly, 'Fine.'

They went after him, but Dama murmured bitterly to Una, 'This is completely wrong, having anything to do with him. That lot are worse than anything, think what they *do*.' Worse than Emperors, even, he felt, who at least didn't have much choice.

Cleomenes led them up to the gatehouse as if he were heading a charge. He pulled off his hat, held his vigile's pass overhead and shouted, 'Vigiles. Security check.'

A little door in the black gate opened and a Praetorian legionary, who looked young and vulnerable as an opened shellfish, said, 'What?'

Cleomenes pressed the pass into his hand as if it was unusually important. His higher rank only applied in a different force, but at least, he reckoned, if he'd been fired the Praetorians would be unlikely to know about it. 'In view of recent developments,' he said loudly, patronisingly, 'it seems obvious Imperial security isn't up to scratch. I'm reviewing it. Your perimeter's full of holes and you haven't got anything like enough bodies out for a start.'

The young man frowned anxiously. 'I wasn't informed.'

'What,' wondered Cleomenes, with heavy disdain, 'is the point of a random check if you know it's coming?'

'But you're not Praetorian.'

'Yes, well, Praetorian failings have clearly become entrenched, someone's got to come in and sort it out. Look, this isn't a request. Let's hurry things up a bit now, all right? I need a better look at the camera angles and I need to look at procedures inside.'

He pushed forward, but the guard stood his ground, although tentatively.

'Who are these?'

'You may well ask. Shady-looking kids climbing in and out over that wall, and no one turned a hair. Luckily for you they're Renatus' kids, they're helping me out – aren't you?'

He placed avuncular hands on Sulien and Una's shoulders, avoiding Dama by instinct. They smiled.

'Renatus?' repeated the Praetorian pallidly, so that Cleomenes felt lacerated with guilt and pity. 'That's right,' he said.

'Well,' said the guard helplessly, handing back the pass, 'All right, then.'

He led them through the gatehouse, waving assurance at the two other young Praetorians stationed there. Inside the wall the high villa stood distrustfully at the end of a drive inside its dark grounds, still plainer than an Imperial residence might have been expected to be, bunched protectively around the garden framed within it. Cleomenes looked around, making critical noises. He wished urgently he'd brought a notebook with him to use as a prop, and hoped the Praetorian was still too unnerved to notice its absence.

The guard tried instinctively and apologetically to accompany them, even to show them around, but Cleomenes snarled, 'Get back to it. I'm observing. I've observed *you* already,' and the Praetorian quailed obediently, and let him into the house.

The second they were through the door, Cleomenes crumpled against it, turning inward and knocking his forehead softly on the smooth-painted wood, agonised. 'Oh,' he whispered, 'what am I doing? That poor kid. What did I just do?'

Una and Sulien didn't know quite what to do with him. 'Come on. It's all right,' said Una briskly.

Cleomenes asked distantly, 'Did you say Tolosa?' and studied them for a second, eyes narrowed, and then with a suddenness that shocked them all, shot out a hand, jerked Dama's wrist forward, and plucked back the sleeve.

474

'Oh, hell,' he said.

Dama pulled free violently, white, staggering, hissing, 'Don't you ever – don't you *ever* touch me.'

But Cleomenes was already moaning, even with an edge of horrified amusement in his voice, 'Oh, hell. You're all slaves, aren't you – of *course* you are!' He seized Sulien by the shoulders and looked into his face. Almost gloating he cried, 'You! I know you, you escaped from something, didn't you? Oh, Jupiter! What – in *hell* – am I doing?'

He sagged again, and Sulien said, 'Look. Yes, we're all slaves, and we were safer where we were, and we still thought this was important enough to risk coming here. And it was the same for Marcus, he knew he could be killed if he came home, he did it to tell what's happened. And he's done it, he told someone at least – he told *you*.'

Cleomenes sighed, and lapsed into acquiescence. 'Yes, there's no point worrying about it now,' he said. 'But he isn't here. That wouldn't have worked if he was, not if what you say is right.'

And Una knew, with a heavy settling of disappointment, that this must be true. It wasn't only that she could not go on believing she could be in the same house as Marcus and not know it. For Marcus to have been moved in that day would surely have meant hours of work and upheaval for the guards – and – she thought of this with a confused implicated feeling – the slaves. The tension would have barely died down; she would still feel it.

For she was becoming aware of the slaves now, cleaning, and turning off lights, closing up the house.

They stood at a loss. Meanwhile Dama had had to go and lean on a little table where a vase of lilies stood, struggling to bring his breath under control. Una thought he might faint, but he'd drawn away from them, there was nothing she could say to him.

'There might be someone here who knows where he is, anyway,' she said finally. 'Someone came here today, you said.'

'What? Do you want to wander around hoping for something to turn up? Until we bump into one of the Novii?' said Cleomenes, and groaned again. 'We're all going to be arrested, and then – oh, this is all just a *joke*.'

'Well,' she said, 'why shouldn't we? They'll think we must be all right, or we wouldn't have got past the guards.'

They moved forward self-consciously, through the hall into the house. As they reached the colonnade around the garden, a girl appeared out of a nearby dining room carrying a bucket packed with cloths and cleaning fluids. As she saw them she instinctively stepped backwards, frightened, the swiftness of the moment an apology for being seen at all. Cleomenes waved his vigile's pass at her, but there was no need, she didn't dare to challenge them.

Dama, walking unsteadily, dizzy with fury and shock, gave her a long reeling look, and wanted to shake her; he couldn't separate his powerless sympathy for her from the horror he felt for this place now. He wanted to rush out of it and lie down on the cool grass. He still couldn't breathe regularly. The lilies in the vase, the very carpets seemed horrible, offensive.

Cleomenes began to feel embarrassed about the effect he'd had on Dama, but he said, 'Better to look for people than have them see us,' and began flinging open doors of salons, gleaming with polished wood and mosaics, a library, a second dining room. He surprised a butler who was apparently checking that all the furniture was placed exactly right. 'Sorry to bother you, security check,' said Cleomenes again.

The butler seemed to have no trouble believing him, for though he was older than the young Praetorian he was far more used to accepting what he was told. But he remained agitated, almost frightened, but not as the girl had been, simply of running into anyone who was not a slave. It was something else.

'I wish someone had warned me,' he said fretfully.

'That would have been quite impossible.'

'Yes, I quite understand. I just wish . . . that's all.'

476

'There's nothing to worry about,' Cleomenes promised him, slightly puzzled. 'Now, I just need to ask a few questions. You had a visit from the palace today, yes? Can you tell me which rooms were used?'

'Well, most of the Emperor's attendants waited in here and in the hall. The Emperor and Empress just went straight upstairs to see Lucius Novius. They weren't here long.'

'Right, right,' said Cleomenes. He went to the window and pretended to study it. Trying to give the air of turning to casual chat while he did so, he said, feeling rather clumsy, 'Did you . . . I suppose the staff had a few things to say about today? This Marcus Novius business. Extraordinary.'

'Oh no, at least, they may have talked to each other about it, I wouldn't have listened,' said the butler, nervously pious. 'But it's unbelievable, yes, it's all so sad.'

The conversation jolted awkwardly on a little longer. Una was already sure that the butler didn't know anything useful, but there was no way of saying so. Of course they had all met slaves like the butler before, slaves who were genuinely loyal to their masters. Sulien had been himself, of course, and even now he had to work to feel repelled by it, as he knew Dama and Una would; although Una was making herself look very demure, and Dama was hanging back in the doorway, in shadow.

'Ah well,' said Cleomenes, at last, giving up. 'I'd best get on with it.'

'I could look after the young people here for you,' suggested the butler, discontentedly. 'I could fetch them something. While you look around.'

'That's kind of you, but there's not much point, really, we'll be finished in a minute or two,' said Cleomenes, meaning it, because it seemed unlikely to him that the other slaves would have picked up anything if the butler had not.

'You won't need to disturb Lucius Novius, will you? If you do I really should see him first – or the nurse, that is.'

'Oh, I shouldn't think so,' replied Cleomenes, herding Una, Sulien and Dama out.

'You see, it's bad for him,' called the butler, and again, there was something odd there, thought Una.

In the passage again, Cleomenes said morosely, 'Come on, then, before someone twigs.'

'No, let's try Lucius Novius,' whispered Una, already striding lightly up the quiet stairs.

'Oh, we *can't*,' implored Cleomenes. 'Come back. No. Anyway, can he ever . . . talk?'

'I think so,' said Sulien, 'If he can't, he can't have us arrested, can he?'

'Poor old man,' said Cleomenes, who thought this was callous.

'Anyway, I might not need to talk to him,' said Una. Cleomenes shook his head but found himself going helplessly after them.

Windows looked down from the first landing into the herbs and rhododendrons in the garden. Everything around them was expensive and, in a dark, plain way, lush, and yet the house had a stifled, unhealthy feeling about it. Around them the walls were a heavy wine colour, painted with simple murky leaves. They padded forward on the soft plum carpet, and alarmed more slave girls hurrying up to the dark floor above them in utter silence.

But there was a light under a heavy door, and music playing, quietly.

Una said, and even if there had been no need for quietness, she would have whispered here, 'Someone's there, that must be him,' and she walked softly to the wall of the landing and leaned against it, and she said again, 'That must be him, surely, but—' and the frown that had been forming on her face untwisted slowly into an incredulous, scornful little smile, and to Cleomenes' horror, she opened the door.

They saw a little old man – for so he looked, at only fifty-five – sitting wrapped in a large gown, who turned misted eyes to look at them over his fingers; and his nurse, a pretty woman in her thirties, with soft curls of warm brown hair, who was standing in the middle of the room but had the unsteadied look of having suddenly moved – away from the chair, away from Lucius.

Ulpia gave an angry, startled cry, 'We didn't call for anything—'

'He's not mad,' said Una, flatly.

'What, who are they, tell them to go?' It was a loose, thin, crumbly voice, and the lines in the face, although they were deep and had been fixed a long time, were loose and wavering also, and had set the face into a permanent look of sly and baffled worry.

'You're not mad,' repeated Una, in disgust this time, stepping straight into the room.

Lucius blinked at them and nothing changed in his expression, none of the haze lifted within the vacant grey-green eyes, but he said, 'Aren't I? Am I not?' with a sad, scared hiccuping giggle on the fringe of his voice.

And for a moment at least, Una was not so sure. He was hard to work on, his thoughts seemed to slip and crumble as his voice did, out of meaning before they had properly formed. But she thought he let them do so; he'd allowed himself to forget how to hold them in place, and she would have thought that hardly anything could be worse; but forgetting *comforted* him. If he wasn't mad in the sense that Marcus had feared for himself, he didn't seem sane either.

'Who are you? Get out!' stammered Ulpia, and thought first of pushing between them to call for help, and then remembered the bell on the wall and stumbled towards it.

'If you do I'll tell everyone,' Una informed them. She gestured Sulien and Cleomenes and Dama into the room and shut the door.

'No, oh no,' said Lucius, as Ulpia subsided in confusion. 'What do you want, are you burglars?'

It was only then that the others began to believe what they were seeing and Cleomenes, turning instinctively to Ulpia first, said, 'Is he really not – are you—?' and Sulien demanded, 'But *why*?'

479

'You're upsetting him, get out at once,' said Ulpia miserably. Lucius writhed and hid the lower part of his face. Above his fingers his skin had turned a high red, up to the thick white hair.

'We want to see the Emperor.'

'Titus? But he isn't here,' protested Lucius plaintively.

'Call him here.'

Lucius took his hands away from his face in wonder. 'I never do that. I can't.'

Una gritted her teeth with impatient rage that this weak creature was keeping her back from Marcus. 'Then have someone else do it, I don't care!'

'No,' yelped Lucius, cowering. 'I won't give you any help. Do you want to kill my brother? I always knew something like this would happen.'

Sulien came forward and told him, 'It already has.'

The red left Lucius' skin and he lowered his hands slowly to his lap. For the first time the nebulous look cleared a little and a possibility of sense lurked sorrowfully in his face, as if – and this was odd, because Una was sure he had not – he'd thought of this before. He said quietly, 'Leo. Oh – poor Leo.'

'Not just Leo, Marcus,' pressed Sulien. 'If you got your brother here and made him listen to us, he could stop it.'

Lucius looked relieved. 'Marcus isn't dead. Did you think that? Apparently people thought he was dead, but no one told me, thank heavens, until it was all cleared up. He'll be looked after, he'll be all right.'

Una cried, 'He wouldn't need looking after, there's nothing *wrong* with him.'

Dama said hollowly, surprising the others, for it was a long time since he'd spoken, 'For a little while perhaps. They can say he jumped out of a window or drowned in the bath.'

Una shuddered. But Lucius seemed already to be forgetting what they'd said or that he'd believed it, and he shook his head. 'No, they wouldn't do that. That can't possibly be right.'

480

And Ulpia had recovered herself a little, and she said, 'Tell who you want, no one will believe you.'

She was moving for the bell again, but Cleomenes sprang across the room; took hold of her shoulders and jolted her competently away from it, and, for she was about to scream with outrage and fear, he pressed a hand regretfully over her mouth. Lucius tottered to his feet in alarm and Cleomenes said firmly to them both, 'Sorry. I don't understand *what* you're up to here, Sir—' and then scowled at hearing himself say the word and went on, 'It seems a ridiculous stupid thing whatever it is. You'd better stop it now. We need you to do something useful and no one's touching that bell until I'm sure we've agreed about that.'

'But I can't, I don't believe you and I can't – it's been *twenty years*!' said Lucius pitifully. 'You aren't going to hurt Ulpia, are you?'

'No,' said Cleomenes, 'but you've got to see this is a lot more serious than – playing a game or whatever the hell you think you're doing here.'

Lucius made a shrill laughing noise again and said shyly, gabbling, 'But you know, I don't really have to do anything – once people believe it already they just keep on without any help. I sometimes think, even if I wanted to, there's really nothing I could do about it now. I just do what I feel like – that's almost all I do, I just don't stop myself from doing things, and that's so very nearly enough.'

'But what in the gods' name *for*?' asked Cleomenes in disgusted exasperation. He'd pushed Ulpia into a chair but was still standing over her warningly.

Lucius blushed again. He whispered confidingly, 'I thought it was really going to happen. I thought I was going mad. A horrible few years. Titus was hardly in Italy and Leo was in the army; and I was supposed to go everywhere and do all these things – these festivals to run – and all these meetings, and the speeches were the worst; I couldn't sleep, for *weeks* before. I just couldn't. And Titus was going to India and I thought what if something happens to him there, or anywhere, and I have to do this all the time? And Drusilla and I should never have married, an awful mistake, they talked me into it. And Drusus was – it was driving me – I'd always been so frightened of it, we all were, my father and aunts and Titus. And Leo. But when it came to it . . . I thought . . . oh. That would be all right. Then someone else would have to . . . I'd be let off then.'

'But for God's sake,' said Una. '*No one* can be let off as much as that. You'd got no right.'

'Oh—' said Lucius, distressed, but not quite seeming to follow her, 'Titus was all right, and – and Drusus was only little and really I never saw him much.'

Sulien burst out, 'How can you even stand it? What about *people*?'

'I've got Ulpia,' said Lucius, trying to smile at her reassuringly, 'And Sorex the butler knows, but he wouldn't tell a soul. He's worth his weight in gold.' Dama sneered scathingly at this, but Lucius didn't notice and carried on. 'Sometimes . . . sometimes I have good spells. Titus . . . he never used to be lonely. I think he might be now – he did seem upset today – but I didn't know that was going to happen.' His eyes lowered with grief. 'Poor Leo,' he said again.

'But your *son*—' said Sulien, shaking his head with helpless incomprehension. 'Does Drusus Novius know?'

'Drusus . . .' Lucius' pale eyes glittered with abrupt tears. 'Oh,' he whispered. 'I ruined things for him. Yes, he – he found out.' And he glanced at Ulpia in such a way that Sulien thought with as much certainty as Una, Drusus Novius found the two of them together, and they didn't have time to move apart – that's how it happened. Why does *she* do it, though?

Lucius said, 'And it's been six years and he never gave me away. I didn't think it would matter that much for him – I never thought – and it's so dangerous, being in this family, I never asked to be – do you realise how ridiculously dangerous it is?'

Una glared with revolted contempt and Cleomenes said

with strained patience, 'That's what we're trying to do something about. Now help us.'

Lucius had fallen into a pensive silence, softly wiping tears away from his eyes. But now an odd guilty shudder went through him and drawing himself up he cried hoarsely, in an hysterical parody of Novian authority, 'No! You have no right to be here! You are to leave me alone! We're going to get the guards and Ulpia will tell them you burst in and threatened me – and it doesn't matter what you say, they won't believe you – you will all be crucified—'

They were shaken, almost as much because he was so awful and embarrassing, like a child in a tantrum, as because of the words, and because they were trapped. Cleomenes said, 'Quiet, keep quiet,' and as Lucius and Ulpia both scrambled for the bell, with what felt like appalled disbelieving slowness, he pulled out his gun, and pointed it at Lucius.

They fell still, of course, and Ulpia was crying a little now, but she whispered, 'Don't be stupid. That won't work. You won't get the Emperor over here that way. All you'll do is get yourself killed. You know that.'

'Just stay quiet,' said Cleomenes, trembling a little with near-panic at what he was doing, trying in fact only to think how they could get out. Ulpia was right, but she would call for the Praetorians or the vigiles the minute she was sure they were out of earshot. And the thought of tying up and gagging the Emperor's brother was bad enough, but worse was the fact that he could see nothing to do it with.

But Una came close, ignoring the stalemate, and looked at Lucius. She said softly, 'Did the Emperor tell you where Marcus is?'

'No,' panted Lucius, shrinking from the gun. 'Why should he tell me anything?'

Una just stared, and didn't seem to react, but Sulien started with disappointment. For a moment he too had been immobilised, staring at the gun and Cleomenes, who looked as wretched as if the weapon were aimed at him; but now it was as if a shutter had dropped across the room and lifted again: they'd perhaps lost all the ways out, and for nothing. He turned, suddenly looking for something, slapping the inside edge of the door, and it was there, a key standing out of the lock. Sulien plucked it out, calling in the same moment, 'A knife, Cleomenes, have you got a knife?' and Lucius and Ulpia blanched with dread as Dama replied, in the same low, dull voice with which he'd spoken before, 'I have.'

He dragged it out of his pocket, and it was an old, blunt, shapeless thing, with a single blade hinged on a plain lump of metal, and Una knew it must be the knife with which he'd wanted her to kill Tasius. He was holding it left-handed, forefinger and thumb circling it, but the smaller fingers doing all the work. It was hard to see that it could be much use to him. Still, she was relieved somehow to see it move into Sulien's hand, as if danger had passed, although it hadn't, it was getting worse.

The bell cord ran inside the wall, appearing where it was set into a shallow oblong alcove of its own. Sulien had to edge his way carefully through the frozen group of Cleomenes, Ulpia and Lucius to reach it, to hold it carefully steady while he sawed it through. He let go of it slowly, praying he wouldn't set the bell off, feeling Ulpia watching him and praying that he would. The ends vanished into the cavity.

'That's not going to be enough,' said Cleomenes whitely.

'It'll have to be, come *on*,' urged Sulien, dragging at Cleomenes, at Una's arm, and they backed out of the door, Cleomenes last, and Sulien flicked the key over in the lock. As they fled down the stairs – but still walking fast, not running yet – they could hear Ulpia pounding the door and calling for help, and if they could hear it, the slaves would too; and they had – as Sulien and the others followed the stairs around the central hollow of the house, they looked up at the sound of alarmed footsteps on the flight above them. They sped through the downstairs passage; and the butler had heard the noise too, and was rushing for the stairs, and as they passed him Cleomenes said in a forced, sensible voice, 'Yes, you'd better go up, sounds like there's some kind of problem – we'll get out of your way now—'

They crossed the outer garden, into the gatehouse, and the Praetorian guards started to meet them, and Dama felt a cold, expectant dilation at the heart; but then the rest could have laughed when they realised, from the guards' worried, deferential faces, that they were still only afraid of looking slack in front of the centurion. Cleomenes managed to grunt, 'You'll be hearing from us shortly,' as they pressed out.

As they did, Una clutched urgently at Sulien's arm, and he saw that a wild smile had spread across her face. She whispered, 'He lied, Sulien! I didn't want him to know that I knew, but it's a hospital or a sanctuary – I know where it is!'

Then they heard a sharp noise, a bell ringing, inside the gatehouse. Cleomenes shoved confusedly at them, saying, 'With me, run—'

Dama knew that it was when he tried to run that the residual stiffness of his feet began to count; he could do it; but he wasn't fast, and as he began to fall behind, and he knew that the gatehouse door had opened again and the Praetorians were coming, he thought lucidly – it's just nature, nothing that can't run is supposed to survive.

And then he felt a convoluted spur of humiliation as Cleomenes saw what was happening and grabbed at his shoulder, seizing a rough handful of his jacket and dragging him along by it. They broke through a formal line of trees that would have been no cover at all in daylight, for the Praetorians were shooting now – but they could not fire well in the dark, and Cleomenes hauled Dama and steered Una and Sulien, downhill, around the outer side of another house, so that it masked their flight down to the street where he'd left his car. In the bad light, Cleomenes, cursing, thought he would never manage to strike in the familiar code on the keypad, but the doors sprang open on the second furious try; they struggled in, and as the car shrieked up the quiet road, Sulien gasped, 'Where are we going?'

'I don't know,' Cleomenes answered harshly. He was forcing himself, against instinct, to slow to a sedate, unremarkable pace as he turned into a more thickly housed Caelian street. He tried to think what the Praetorians would understand of their trajectory, where the vigile cars they summoned would come from.

'Tivoli,' Una said, breathlessly, 'Marcus is in Tivoli.'

Cleomenes shook his head, as if shaking water or smoke away from it. He muttered, 'Well, we'll think about that later,' and turned south towards the Aventine, looking for people, and traffic to vanish into.

[XXI]

SANCTUARY

At least, Cleomenes thought wildly, it was all decisively cleared up now. There was no more need to worry about his job, or to wonder if there was anyone after him, or if he'd made a mistake. For the moment the only serious question was where and when to get rid of this car – for the vigiles knew it, and the Praetorians had his name. And after that, he had nowhere to go, he couldn't take the slaves home or to his brother's, and he couldn't go away from them, he was the same kind of thing as they were now, there was no help for it.

He thought Lucius had had a point after all: once catastrophes actually happened, it wasn't so bad, in a way.

They left Cleomenes' car in a dull street on the Aventine, and finally lay down on the floor and seats of Palben's car, in a great lake of vehicles around the Janiculum station. The slaves had, at least, brought blankets with them, but it was cold and cramped and miserable, and though it was long after midnight, Cleomenes was surprised by how abruptly and utterly the others seemed to plunge into sleep. The girl and her brother lay curled opposite each other on the bench seats in the back, the girl's pale hair draped like a scarf across her face, one hand holding it there, as if for warmth or for disguise, even in her sleep. And the young man with scars on his wrists was between them on the floor, unmoving. Cleomenes thought he remembered the case now, a boy who'd been rescued by a merchant for some reason; and they'd both disappeared. He was fairly sure that Dama was a murderer.

In fact, though Sulien fell onto the seat in exhaustion stored up over the last two nights, and lay quite still, at first waiting for sleep and then trying to coax it, the sound of the guns behind them had set off a shiver that kept searching through his body and wouldn't die down. He could feel sickly surprise that anyone ever lived to old age when the body was so susceptible to tearing and breaking, while, at the same time, his heartbeat's insistence that nothing could ever make it stop was keeping him awake. He shuddered at the unforgiving good sense of the thought: if we're caught the thing to do is fight, try and run away, do any stupid thing that makes them kill us there and then.

And Cleomenes was writhing and sighing continuously in the front seat. At last Sulien pulled himself up and said quietly, 'Do you think it's possible that this can work?'

'What?' mumbled Cleomenes, trying to persuade himself he was asleep.

'Getting Marcus out – and – to Faustus Augustus, I suppose.'

Cleomenes opened his mouth but was silenced by a little of knock of dismay that, yes, that was what they were going to try and do, that if he had a future at all that was what it depended on.

Sulien went on tentatively, 'Not that it exactly – matters. I know I'm still going to try and do it, I already decided that. You see, we want him to be the next Emperor, it's very important, it's worth – And anyway – I couldn't leave him like that. It's like Dama says, they'll kill him. What they've done already is bad enough. And obviously, if it doesn't work then—'

Of course he'd been going to say something about death, but he looked at Una with her hidden face, and obviously he meant her death, too, and Dama's; and he felt that to say this would be bad luck, a way of letting his guard down. And there was Cleomenes too, for whom he suddenly felt guilty and sorry.

'*You* don't have to be involved,' he said.

'I can't see that. What else can I do now? There's Varius,

he's sort of my *fault*, that needs clearing up. And anyway –
go into hiding, what – forever? I couldn't do it. That
wouldn't be any sort of life.'

Sulien thought about Lal, and he could have said, 'Yes, it
is,' to that. But he didn't, thinking, well, whoever you meet,
it's not where you'd want to meet them, and you can't
make things go as you want.

He only nodded then, and said, 'Anyway. If it doesn't
work, then I know that'll be it. I suppose that's all right, at
least, it's not, but it doesn't matter. But – but I wondered if
you thought there's any likelihood it *could* work. Because
we won't be able to talk our way in anywhere again after
this. And getting out – well, it would be like that just then,
with the guns.' He stopped and muttered, 'Although of
course that would be better than—'

Cleomenes saw that the boy had wrapped his hand
around his wrist, and could guess what the gesture meant.
Escaping slavery was a crime in itself, and he thought
Sulien had probably done worse than that; and that was as
much as Cleomenes knew about him. But it was sad that
anyone so young should be trying to talk himself into his
own death.

Cleomenes thought of Lucius again. He felt slightly
deranged himself, he would have believed anyone who told
him that he was.

'Oh well,' he found himself saying. 'Yes. Yes we've got
the Praetorians and the vigiles to worry about – but they're
only *people*. And you know – people really overestimate
how many crimes we actually *solve*, let alone prevent.
Well, you must know that yourself.' Sulien gave a kind of
sad half-laugh. 'Yes,' argued Cleomenes. 'It's – it's not
hopeless, it's not impossible.'

And it was somehow so completely necessary to reassure
the boy that he found himself believing this for the time it
took to say it, though afterwards – in fact, as he saw it was
starting to work, he thought, well, that was a whole lot of
rubbish.

Una slept for two hours almost exactly, but was hardly

aware either of sleeping or of waking up. She seemed to be thinking all the time, listing issues to herself – guards, cameras, where the car should be – and knowing that really it was all meaningless until she'd seen the Tivoli hospital. And sometimes she seemed to be there already, searching up flights of stairs and through cellars, and yet it was partly the house she'd escaped in London, though it had sprawled and put out extra dusty floors and annexes like tumours, where she hid and fled, for she was pursued constantly. Still, here was the window she'd climbed out of, and she would go in through it this time because this was the worst place for Marcus to be – and she couldn't find him – and then she did find him, and – she was interrupted before they could touch each other – she knew then that it was a dream, because she could feel that she'd only reached Marcus by the force of wanting it so much; she'd cheated the structure of the dream which intended her to go on searching endlessly.

Some time after that she shook her face free of her hair and lay staring for a while, still thinking about windows, thinking – alarms, how do they actually work? A flat sourness lay over her, after the sting of joy in the dream, as if she'd been made a fool of. For a second she'd seemed to see Marcus in perfect detail, the proportion of pale to dark blond in his eyelashes, the exact degree of asymmetry at the mouth. Her hand still thought it could feel the texture of the wood-coloured hair, even though she'd never touched it yet. Here came the first of several little gaps in her thinking where she was too trampled with love to go on. It was awful, really, being like this; had she not been better off before she ever met him, even before she'd really got used to Sulien – hadn't she been more intact in herself? But was it possible that she might become that way again – if she both failed to save Marcus and somehow survived herself? She felt a ruffling of terror at the thought, no, certainly it could not happen.

Her body began to prickle impatiently with having to lie there and wait. She tolerated it as long as she could for fear of waking the others, but at last she could no longer bear it; she couldn't think of anything useful lying in the car, she needed a building to look at.

She climbed out of the car as stealthily as she could, lowering the door softly behind her, and walked to a closed car-charging shop. She stood against each wall in turn, judging how far she could see to each side like that, and then examined its windows. She believed if she smashed them an alarm would go off, but she couldn't see anything on the glass that told her why. She felt a little better, trying to work it out.

She felt a faint premonitory chill as someone moved behind her. It was Dama, following her from the car. He said, 'Come on, come back. You're not going to be able to do this if you don't sleep,' but Una shifted anxiously and began speaking as he approached, as if she'd expected him:

'We've got to do it very soon. Really it should be now, before they can bring anything in, while they'll only have whatever security was already there.'

And though she sounded so deliberately businesslike, Dama knew she had to be thinking of how many hours Marcus had already spent locked up, drugged – that he would have to get through the rest of the night and all the next day before she could even try to help him. And she could see it must be obvious to him, it was strange that since they'd left the cave she'd been becoming again effortlessly certain of what he was thinking, although all the time she wished that she could get away from him.

In any case she felt as though longing for Marcus was leaking tactlessly out of her skin, making a kind of lurid mess in the air. She folded her arms guiltily across her body as if to cover it up, to hold some of it back.

'Nothing stopping them putting in as many guards as they like,' Dama remarked. He felt a little more relaxed now that Cleomenes was asleep and powerless.

'Yes, but I mean cameras and – that kind of thing.'

'We can't go too quickly. We've got to look at the place, it's got to be planned. It's going to be more than difficult.'

'I know, I'm already trying to.'

'Of course you are.'

She looked away and studied the window again. 'Can you cut through glass?'

'Obviously you can,' he said, with a slight grind of hostile impatience in his voice that he'd never shown before at her not knowing something.

Una flinched. She said appeasingly, 'I meant, is it easy, whatever you use to do it – can you buy it easily?'

'Yes,' he said, gently, this time, and he added, 'I know something about alarms, I put them in round Holzarta. I can guess where they'll be, at least.'

'Good. Yes. And I've kept people from seeing me before. But I can't be too far away from them, and if watching is what they've come to do – if they're concentrating on it – then it's hard. I thought – if we came in towards one of the corners.'

'They won't have the same guards on all the time, they'll have to do shifts. Maybe at the point when they change – mind you, they must have thought about that. And what about the other patients?'

And so for a while they discussed what they could, trying at least to work through what they already knew or could reasonably assume, and as they concentrated the strain between them began to wear away. Una felt, although it was not quite an easy feeling, grateful that he was there and that he'd come out to talk to her, for it was helping, talking practically like this; he was helping her think.

She said, 'It has to be very late, because it'll be easier for me; people can't think so well.'

'Can't they? What about you, now?'

'It's different. I feel fine. I did sleep, it seems to have been enough.'

'Well, it won't have been, not by tomorrow night, you know that really.'

So they went back to the car, making Sulien groan vaguely, briefly woken as the door opened and shut. And though she could hardly believe that it would be possible,

Una did fall again into a busy, nervous doze. Soft tassels of her hair hung over the edge of the seat above Dama, just hair, smooth, but in the dark quite colourless and not even beautiful. And he would have liked to touch it – not necessarily in a very sensual way, just to flick or brush his fingers against it quickly. It was only a little thing, and she would never have known, but because of that it seemed devious, and so he stayed still, just looking at it. And for a while, he felt simple tenderness for her, as if all he cared about was that she should be happy. He let himself enjoy the feeling, aware even at the time that it wasn't permanent.

It was only half an hour's drive. Una said, 'I don't think we're being followed,' but all the way Cleomenes kept anxiously checking the road behind them anyway, even though it occurred to him that he might as well believe her for consistency's sake; it was only on her word that they were going to Tivoli at all. He didn't follow this thought, though he was aware of an inward nag, pressing him to do so – come on, what's this *about*? Where does she get all this stuff from, and should I be going along with it? But it was all too bizarre and incredible: if he thought about it, he would stop, and he must not stop, it was too late.

And yet the others seemed descended into a fragile calm; Sulien could still feel a grip of sickness in his stomach, dread of what was, what might be coming – certainly still there, and within a finger's reach, but it was somehow possible not to bother with it now. He sat watching the woods appear as they drove into the Tiburtine hills, drowsily – after all, he hadn't had much sleep.

In Rome Cleomenes had hastily bought a lot of things, spreading his purchases between shops, for he felt they must look glaringly suspicious. Somehow he could not remember the legitimate uses of these things: rope, a glass cutter, wire-shears, heavy tape, a sledgehammer (although he knew really that was a stupid purchase, it might slow him down, and if he used it he'd almost certainly be heard). Thick sheets of paper, which at least looked innocent

493

enough. Screwdrivers. Chisels. Paste. He felt comforted or armoured, by equipping himself so, even though he thought he had acquired far more than was necessary. He'd bought as if he meant to re-enact every illegal entry he'd ever heard of.

And of course he still had his gun, and of course he always hoped he would not have to use it, but especially now, because he did not think any situation in which he fired it could be survived for long.

When they reached Tivoli it felt serene and forgetful, the graceful houses all shades of softly tanned flesh. They ate breakfast in the street, outside a caupona, almost peacefully, even though they couldn't eat much. It was cold, but the air was palpably clean, it made Una and Sulien notice, as they hadn't before, the bloom of dirt that hung over Rome. The town leaned against the deep pure hills, half sunk into the olive trees and cypresses. They could see why people fled here from Rome, and why the rich hid their mad here, where the lucent air and the sulphur spas might make up for the embarrassed aversion they felt.

But several studded and ornamented cars were waiting near the forum, and they saw brittle and angry people standing among their uniformed slaves; not there for a holiday or a rest. A young woman with tangled hair and a face red with helpless anger was being pushed by the slaves towards a car decorated with wrought bronze, and she was roaring, 'No, I don't want to, no, I'm not going anywhere with you. I don't like it, I don't like it!' while an older woman who might have been her mother, her hair piled in crisp gold curls, dressed in elegant burgundy, watched with her arms folded. Her face was fixed in a wince, either disgusted or wretchedly unhappy. She was plainly aware of the people in the forum staring, unashamedly entertained.

For there were no other patients now in the Galenian sanctuary; Faustus had had them all turned out. Those that couldn't be sent home immediately had spent the night in the grand inns around the spas while their families were summoned to pick them up. The families were uncertain of how furious to be, in view of how much money had been foisted upon them along with their cumbersome relatives. A few of the sanctuary staff were still tending to their former patients in the town, the rest – and more still were being brought in – were already committed to caring for Marcus, as if by sheer weight of numbers, they could cure him.

It wasn't hard, then, to find out where the Galenian was; not in fact within Tivoli itself, but four discreet miles south of it, on the slope of a wooded hill. They drove past it once, and saw sentries standing against heavy gates, and behind them a long drive leading away through oak and chestnut trees, the sanctuary still unseen.

'We can't leave the car anywhere near them. I don't see that we're going to be able to get very close,' said Cleomenes, sucking his breath unhappily through his teeth. 'And if they're really worried about it, they ought to have people around on the hill; not just on the property.'

'They won't see us,' said Una.

'All right, fine, they won't!' said Cleomenes, with a little incredulous shrug.

'What about this car, though? If they don't wonder why a car's left for hours on the road next to them and miles from anything else, then they should.' The sky had been getting darker for an hour or so, and suddenly thick rain began to fall rancorously. He sighed.

They drove around to the rear of the hill, onto an empty lane where it seemed they could have left the car undisturbed for days, but Cleomenes was still unhappy, until they found an overgrown track running off into woods, away from the sanctuary. They climbed slowly up the wet hill, gasping a little in the downpour. Una felt a scraping of anticipation as they got closer.

But she too began to worry painfully about the distance they'd come from the car. It was perhaps eight hundred yards up to the edge of the sanctuary grounds; another two hundred yards across the gardens, where the lavender and almond trees stood bleak and stark in the winter rain, to the Galenian itself, standing among them like an iceberg.

Eight or nine minutes, running, in the dark? Of course it wouldn't matter how far it was if no one knew until the next morning that they'd been there. But Cleomenes was right, there were two other men patrolling the hill – neither so close yet that she could get much sense out of them. Once though, as they looked through the fence at the sanctuary, they had to break away and hide among the trees, for there was a groundskeeper in a waterproof cape, wandering bleakly through the rain on the other side.

Hiding the ugliness of the metal fence, there was a layer of trees on the inside, too, deep enough in places to offer a few yards of cover. And on the western side Una stopped and said, 'I don't think they could see us get to that bush, and then there's that little building.' For there was a laurel, high and bulbous, and beyond that a small temple of some kind, just more than halfway to the walls of the Galenian. But there was only open space between the laurel and the temple, and beyond that nothing but low shrubs to screen them from the guards, looking sombrely down from balconies on each pale face of the sanctuary. At this distance Una could barely tell any more than what they could all see: that there was somebody there. She couldn't press against their thoughts any more than she could have spoken to them.

And Marcus too was still indiscernible.

But for now Dama was barely interested in the guards, he was studying the fence itself. 'If we cut it, that man in the cloak will find it, that's about all he's there for,' he muttered. But there was no obvious need to cut through the fence: it was simple chain link – Una had been right, there had been no time yet to bring in anything better. It was about ten feet high, and fairly sturdy, but even Dama would be able to climb it with a bit of help. 'Before now – they'd have been less worried about people coming in than people getting *out*,' he murmured, almost talking to himself. 'Don't think they'd have got any cameras in yet . . .' He knelt, looking through the holes in the fence without touching it, at the ground on the far side. 'What *I'd* do – do you remember what I told you when you came to the gorge? I'd have sensors either in the posts or just under the topsoil . . .'

He looked up into the rain, and abruptly he hurled all his weight at the fence, so that it clashed and rippled.

'What are you doing?' cried Cleomenes.

'Finding out if there's an alarm on it,' Dama said, laying his arm quickly against the fence to still it.

'And what if there is?' They couldn't hear anything from here.

'We need to hide,' said Dama, with a definite twang of satisfaction in his voice at Cleomenes' dismay. He was already galloping downhill back into the woods.

And plainly there was an alarm. They had plunged again into the brushwood, against the ground, behind the tree trunks, and then, on the edge of the garden, a guard came tramping quickly, a little way ahead of the groundskeeper, who had to skip and hurry to keep up with him. Sulien, sitting with his back against a tree, his legs, he hoped, obscured among dead leaves and wet wood, was the only one who could see them, working rapidly all the way round the fence, sometimes plucking at it with irritable, confident fingers. Sulien could hear an alert, angry mutter going on between them, but not the words through the rain.

He saw the man in Praetorian uniform peer through the mesh, and something in the look, something even more than his fear of being seen, pinched at him coldly.

And Una, trying to work on the man's impatience and irritation to hurry him on, felt the look too with the same pang. He was not like the groundskeeper or the guards at Lucius' villa, just a man doing a job, keeping out intruders. She thought he was like Tasius. He would kill Marcus the second it was possible; in the meantime he was there to keep him inside. He knew he wasn't mad.

But he passed by. Una struggled out of the brush panting, 'We've got to move. The others in the woods, I think they're coming.'

Cleomenes emerged, furious. 'Why in hell – can't you wait for them to find us in their own good time? It's all bad enough already, without you—'

But Dama ignored him, staring gleefully at the fence, his face bright and angelic. 'Throwing things at it would be better.' He'd dragged a bulky lump of rotting wood with him into the open, he tried to make Sulien take it. 'You'd better do it, I can't.'

Sulien stepped back from him. 'They're looking out for someone here—' Then Una, who had been watching Dama's face with a curious frown, said, 'Not in daylight, not if it keeps happening.' But she shook her head and hissed, '*Hurry*, further down the hill.'

But knowing they were coming, and where from, it was easy enough to avoid the watchmen closing in to check the perimeter from the outside. They struggled round to the rear of the house again, and Dama made Sulien fling the lump of wood at the fence, and this time a blast of wind carried to them a faint ringing from the house.

'It could be the weather setting it off, you see,' panted Dama, 'or something wrong in the circuit. Keep this up for a few hours, and by the time we go in they should either be ignoring it or they'll have turned it off. And even if they haven't, and they come out in the rain and check every single time, they won't be *believing* there's anybody. We can at least get to that laurel before they're down here, we know there's enough time for that now. Don't know what we're going to do after that, but—'

'Go in while it's light,' said Una, 'and wait in the garden.'

She had seen that the guards on the sanctuary balconies hadn't been the ones to respond to the alarm, which was bad. But it was true, when it was so obvious that no one could approach the house without being seen, and with the sanctuary as awake and busy as it could be with a single patient, the guards and doctors would hardly believe that anyone would attempt it.

Many things that day felt like desperate or vicious children's games, dragged out beyond sense or enjoyment. For they almost did enjoy it for a while. Sulien and Una found they were laughing at each other in a weak, fatalistic way, dodging around the fence, throwing things from their hiding places, pulling the exasperated Praetorians out into the rain. For the guards were conscientious; they kept coming, even when it was obvious they no longer thought there was any likelihood of finding anything. There must be some rule that every alarm must be checked, whatever the circumstances. Once Sulien said, with mock pity, 'Oh let's give them a rest,' and they left the fence alone for almost an hour, so that the staff thought that the problem might have fixed itself, and after that they started a hail of missiles that barely allowed the guards time to reset the alarm, though by now they were tired and sick of the rain.

But the rain was weaker than it had been. Dama said, 'I think we'd better go in before this stops. Make sure they do blame it on the weather. And it's getting dark, too.'

It wasn't late, but it was true that the light was beginning to turn grey. The others hesitated. Una thought, it's got to be ten hours before we do anything. 'All right,' she said.

They edged back to the western side of the fence. Sulien said to Dama, 'Let's get you in first.'

Cleomenes looked at Dama doubtfully. He said, trying to be sensitive about it, 'Are you sure you shouldn't wait with the car? I mean, we don't all need to go in, do we?'

Dama looked at him with a new flaring of dislike. 'I'm not leaving it to you,' was all he said. And he glanced quickly and protectively at Una and Sulien, thinking again, I'm doing this first. I'm making sure they're all right. First.

'Una and I have to go anyway,' murmured Sulien.

Dama said to him, 'All right, help me.'

Sulien braced his foot against the fence post, and again they heard the faint shrilling from the sanctuary, as Sulien pushed and lifted Dama up until he could hook his arm painfully over the top of the fence and fall awkwardly to the other side. Cleomenes was watching with obvious apprehension, thinking, that's not going to be good if it ever comes to getting out. Dama turned away, and fled to the laurel. Sulien swung himself up behind him, feeling slightly ashamed of the ease with which he could do it.

Inside the wall of leaves, the tree formed a kind of loose room, rounded and uneven, high enough for them all to stand, though uncomfortably, with branches pressing against knees and shoulders, sprouting a few blobby lower chambers at the edges.

Una entered, looked around and said crisply, 'All right. Over there can be the toilet bit, when people need it.'

The three men looked at her and away, briefly united in embarrassment.

'It's going to be ten hours,' said Una. 'We might as well have these things straight from the start.'

They heard the guard coming round along the fence once more.

'They should check here,' breathed Cleomenes.

But after so many false alarms the Praetorian and the groundskeeper stamped around the garden boundary, and Una did not even have to nudge their attention away from the laurel.

Once or twice more they set the alarm off from inside, before the rain stopped, almost for something to do. Una tried, as she'd sometimes done before, to put herself into a kind of hibernation until they could move. It was a pitifully boring time. At first, they were too cramped with anxiety to talk. Then Cleomenes and Sulien started chatting quietly, offering each question as an expression of wonder at having such a conversation in this place. Una joined in softly, to keep from glutting herself into senselessness on the thought of Marcus' closeness.

They saw lights appear and then go out in the sanctuary windows, as the sky grew dark; and then a great blaze of lemon-yellow light sprang up around the house, even lighting the laurel leaves on that side, like panes of green glass.

Cleomenes gave a sigh of real despair. 'This is *insane*. We've got no way of dealing with that, have we? What's the point of coming over the fence if this is as far as we can get?'

And Una clenched her teeth. The laurel was opposite the

right edge of the sanctuary's western face, so that if he turned that way the guard on the south wall would just have been able to see a slice of it, except that the low oval temple, lying almost on a projection from the building's corner, stood between them, the left focus of its curve just cutting through the man's line of sight, on the other side projecting beyond the sanctuary's wall, out into the front garden. Una had thought that if they came in from the temple, although they would be within view of two men instead of one, they could be on the very edge of each field of vision, which might help her. But the space between the laurel and the temple was quite open to the Praetorian on the west wall. And though she could see the shape of his thoughts more clearly now, still she fell short, she had no hold on them.

'Maybe when they change shifts,' she muttered.

'That won't be any good,' Cleomenes said. Una felt like letting out a cry of anger with him, but he was right, for a few hours later, looking through the glowing leaves she saw it happen; a guard simply came out onto the balcony and stepped into place beside his colleague, who did not turn away until the other was settled. They did not seem to speak or do anything at all to distract each other. There was no moment when the garden was not watched.

Una pressed her face into her hands and looked again across the grass to the little white temple. She said to Sulien, 'I think I could do it, if I was as near as that.'

'Stop him seeing us?' he whispered back. 'But how could you get there?' They both tried to measure the empty distance to the little shrine, and it was about forty yards; to both of them it looked like a great blank stretch, starkly bright.

Sulien looked up at the man with the gun on the sanctuary wall, and said unhappily, 'No, Una.'

But what was the good of saying that? He wouldn't stop her, and in any case, how else could they get any further, what else could they do except creep back to the fence? He could not even go with her.

'I think I can see enough to know when to do it.'

He said, with a kind of random clutching for other ideas, 'At least – can't we do something? We could distract them. We could set the alarm off again.'

'But he's not the one who moves when it goes off. He might look *harder*. And it would wake everyone up. No, I'm going to wait like I said, until they're bored and tired.' She smiled, trying to reassure him. 'I won't do it yet.'

But Sulien almost wished she'd gone at once if she was really going to, there was so much time still to imagine it happening, to keep trying and failing to come up with something better, to think, hundreds of times, no, I've got to stop this, I *mustn't* let her. They sat at the base of the tree together, and couldn't go on talking.

And it had happened, the man had been turning his eyes back and forth the garden in long quick sweeps, like a fast pendulum, but his tired attention caught vaguely on something on the other side of the garden, a shadowy lump, not human-sized, not a threat – but was it an oddly planted shrub or a bit of blown rubbish that the groundskeeper had not cleared up? One – two seconds – and she must go now, and she took a breath, whispered to Sulien, 'I'll wave across. Come one at a time.' And she did not move, her legs taut and braced, waiting to do it, but waiting for the man to look up, back across the garden, for there was nothing to stop him. The seconds in which she could have reached the temple passed, and she had wasted them. The wind blew, and the thing was tugged at and yet anchored – a plant; he looked away from it. Una gave a little hurt gasp of failure. She thought of Marcus and felt scorched, shocked that she could be such a coward. 'I could have done it – it isn't really very far,' she said hoarsely.

Sulien said in the same rough voice, 'You're right, we were exaggerating it, it's not far.' He cleared his throat. 'It'll be easier now.'

And more than an hour passed – yes, there were times when the guard's concentration lapsed, but he always kept up a kind of restlessness, he was ready to jolt out of it, and

502

yet she was so frantic not to have missed the chance alto-gether that every time he looked to the far edge of the garden she thought desperately, was this the same, was this as good?

Then they all saw him rub his face, and when he dropped his hand, sighing, he lifted his eyes a little above the garden, for the sky was clearing and a few stars showed, and he thought he saw a spiral-wing passing far off, without even noticing that he was thinking of it. For all that he must have slept in the day to be ready for this, tiredness, only for a moment, had wiped through him, that was as much as she was certain of.

She whispered, 'I think, now.'

'Go on, then,' said Sulien, sounding confident; and she knew that he didn't want to say it, that he was forcing himself; but she pretended not to. She crept out into the yellow light, slow for the first second, so as not to shake the leaves.

Don't think about anything, she thought, running, watching the pale wall. But she couldn't stop thinking, though she felt it might leach speed out of her body; the whiteness she pictured was only partial, under and around it she saw how the wall was not approaching fast enough; and she was counting the seconds of her flight, and trying to estimate if she was cheating, counting too slowly, promis-ing herself too much time; and she was flung out to check and worry at the sanctuary guard; and aware of Sulien and Dama breathlessly watching her, and always of Marcus – and the guard blinked and knew something was moving below him, something dark on his left, darting. He turned towards the temple; he raised his gun.

Una dropped in the temple's shadow, trying to leap, to fall up across the space into him as she fell onto the grass, to work more quickly and abruptly than she had ever done before, and still so far from herself, so precarious and stretched. That he had really seen someone running *must* be only one thought, there must be others. He hadn't really been able to judge the perspective – a bird, a bird, it was

503

probably just a bird – Una shoved at this idea, forced it. He looked hard at the space around the temple for a long time. Nothing, there was nothing there.

Una was aware of her heart clattering, and yet how far away from herself she was still, just as sometimes she'd had dreams of sliding helplessly off roofs, while half-awake, while she could still feel the blanket around her.

For a long time she let the guard look around, alert and cautious; she tried only to keep pressing on the idea of the bird, hoping that in a minute he would come to believe he had actually seen dark wings. Sulien and Dama were watching her in torment, as she leant sprawled against the sanctuary wall, quite still, and they looked from her up to the sanctuary balcony; they could see that the guard's head was turned this way. Finally Una felt herself sigh, down on the ground, as she began to remember and trust this way of smoothing and quieting, and drawing together the sleepy woolgathering mood she wanted. She would begin the same process on the other Praetorian on the south wall, now, while she was still alone – and it was difficult and weakening, but she knew she could do it. She turned her hand in a slow blind wave, not looking across to the laurel as she did so.

Sulien ran across at once. Una kept tightening and then slackening her clasp on the men's thoughts, creating barely perceptible breaks or blind spots, each a few seconds long, but feeling to the Praetorians like less even than that, no more definite or significant than blinking.

Dama came last, still shaking from watching her run, remembering her rush from Tasius, towards him.

They crouched against the curved wall for a while, panting, not from the run but with surprise and faintness at having reached it at all. They were safe on this side; no one could see them. They edged around slowly, and through the shadowy doors they could just see the statue of some young god within, Apollo or Bacchus, medicine and madness, Sulien thought, but they couldn't tell which. This time they went in pairs, Sulien and Una first, leaving Dama and

Cleomenes in the pool of darkness by the temple, so that Cleomenes saw in amazement that what Una had done had happened again when it looked even more hopeless; they really had flowed unprotected across the floodlit garden, in easy view, and the Praetorians had not stirred.

He was aware of Dama still mutedly loathing him, and was even sure that the young man had somehow made sure that they were left together to keep an eye on him, to protect his friends from him. Cleomenes eyed him with exasperation, and even muttered, 'What do you think I can do? Turn you in, now?' But Dama said nothing. And what, Cleomenes thought, even if he had suddenly decided to start shouting out to the Praetorians, did Dama expect to do about it?

Una and Sulien had dashed along a taut diagonal to the corner of the building, and when they were among the ornamental shrubs at its base, they dropped suddenly out of sight. To his joy Cleomenes realised that there must be a well running along the wall of the sanctuary, at least on this side, letting daylight into the windows of the basement. And that was very good, they would be quite sheltered there; from hearing perhaps as well as sight.

But as he and Dama followed, Cleomenes still told himself: this is a dream, this can't be done; but they did do it, they were at the flowerbed. They lowered themselves down the sunken wall onto a damp, sloping concrete floor.

Cleomenes went straight to the nearest window, a few yards to their left, closer to the guard on the balcony but that couldn't be helped. He peered through it; the yellow light from the garden reached in a little way into the dark room; he could not tell much about the room, but the room or corridor beyond it must be dark too; he could see no edge of light under the door.

And as he had thought, there was a fine circuit, barely visible, inside the glass, following the frame of the window. The fine wire was designed to tear if the glass was broken, setting off another alarm. He frowned slightly, for the panes were not as large as he would have liked, and the hole he hoped to make would be smaller still.

He took out the tape first, biting it off with his teeth, and applied it across the central panel of the window, pressing it down hard and reinforcing it, making a long oblong just inside the line of circuit. Una, still muffling down the guards' watchfulness, looked at him almost sleepily, unable to summon the interest she would have liked to feel. But even Dama, who could see what Cleomenes was doing, felt a guilty stirring of admiration at the grim competence with which he worked, scoring the glass with a painful, scraping sound, in yet another rectangle within the lines of tape. Cleomenes remembered exactly where to find everything, reaching for Sulien's backpack to get out the paste and paper. It was possible that some part of him had always wanted to try this.

He smeared the paste onto the rectangle of glass, but it wasn't thick enough; he reached up to grab a handful of wet earth from the flowerbed, mixing it with the glue. 'Help me with that,' he said shortly. Sulien obeyed, smearing the glutinous stuff onto the window, carefully, for he could feel the the brittleness gathering along the etched lines.

Cleomenes pressed the paper down over the muck, and then hesitated for a second, because this could easily go wrong, the blow had to be hard to break the glass along the scored lines; in spite of the tape that was supposed to hold it steady, cracks could certainly travel up through the remaining rim of glass and pierce the wire; and though the slime and paper were meant to hold the glass together and smother the sound when it smashed on the floor inside, there would be some noise. He tapped the spongy paper over the glass once, weakly, as he'd touched every wall he'd wanted to hit for the last four days. Then he knocked it through with his fist; and the rectangle of glass inside the tape fell with a wet crunching, crumpling thud, not the usual high shriek of smashed glass. It was still enough to make them all wince, and stay very still for a minute or two, waiting.

Cleomenes watched anxiously as the girl fed herself, easily enough, through the gap, and it wasn't much harder for the two boys, her brother, though he was as tall as Cleomenes, was still far slighter than him. Thicker-set, Cleomenes had to be helped in from inside, twisting awkwardly sideways, and he froze when, despite his care, his shoulder brushed slightly against the taped border of glass that still held the frail circuit. Nothing seemed to happen, and he climbed in.

The muddy glass ground and snapped underfoot. They had come through into what must be the sanctuary's infirmary. The pungent clean smell struck Sulien with an unexpected force of familiarity; he looked at the patient's couch, the little cabinets, feeling a grazing of nostalgia.

He heard a quiet, sharp sound from Una and turned to her. 'Do you know where he is?'

She nodded and said in a stiff little voice, 'Yes. But it's not, he's not—'

Now that she could dare to retreat, slowly, from the guards on the outside balconies, there was Marcus, just detectable, two floors above her and far off on the other side of the house – she could hardly believe that it had been only four days since he'd been within reach.

'How bad is it? What's it like?'

She shook her head. 'I don't know. Horrible. Almost not *him*—' and this was true, but still it wasn't quite right; for he was utterly and at once recognisable, as she had feared he might not be. But something was so wrong, he seemed further away than he really was, much further, out on a terrible, mountainous, lurching distance from everything.

'Well, we thought that,' said Sulien quietly. And no one spoke for a moment. 'I think that door's going to be locked.'

It was, but the lock was only a simple thing, intended to keep the patients from getting at anything dangerous. Cleomenes unscrewed it into a couple of pieces, only worried about the extra time it took. He muttered, 'This is the way out, and we've got to try and come back to it. They go out the way they come in, the ones that get away.'

507

Outside they patted their way along the dark walls, as though they were blind, not daring to use any lights. The corridor was complicated, turning abrupt corners and suddenly knocking them into steps. Finally it brought them to the stairs, and they came up onto the ground floor, where they could at least see; the yellow light in the garden leaking in through the unobstructed windows, across the wide empty lobby, shining on the floor of a silent dining room. They felt suddenly exposed, and retreated to the walls.

At the far end of the lobby a broad staircase rose proudly. 'He's up there,' whispered Una, almost choked with how close he was, and with this new panic. 'But there're people all round him. You can't – you can't even get close to the room, they're at the top of those stairs. They're all awake.'

'What do you mean? Where are they?' demanded Cleomenes.

Una made an inarticulate grimace and alarmed them all by running softly across the lobby and creeping up the stairs until she could peer up onto the landing. But she came back. 'There's a gallery, and glass doors and a passage with bedrooms, but they're *sitting in front of the doors*, it's all lit up behind them; you can't get past. And there are other people asleep, at the far end, I suppose they're doctors. The whole floor—'

'But no one saw you just then – you stopped them?' pressed Sulien.

'Yes – but the doors are locked. I can't *do* that, not get the key and get four of us behind them – they're *in the way*.'

Cleomenes nodded impassively. 'I thought they might do that,' he said.

Una felt absurdly that this just wasn't fair, the guards had no *right* to seal off the floor as well, they had already done as much as was reasonable.

Cleomenes said, 'What about the floor above?'

Una relaxed slightly, considering, concentrating. 'There would have been more patients. No, if we could get up there, it's empty. But those stairs—'

From here they could see the lights on the first floor.

'There'll be another way up,' said Sulien, suddenly uncomfortably conscious that there must be slaves to clean a place like this, and they would need hidden routes and boltholes; that had been managed even at Catavignus' house – but for the other slaves, not for him.

And they found it, a narrow flight twisting up from behind the dining room, but Una shook her head wildly, and pulled the others back, for there was a guard on the first-floor landing here, too, and the stairs were so thin that if they had climbed them they might have knocked right into him.

'Then the other way,' said Dama.

There was a pause before they moved, as if they were shouldering a weight. 'All right,' said Cleomenes, but he lifted his gun from his waist, as they inched along the hall, up onto the bottom steps.

There was this much helping Una: the guards hardly expected to have to strain their eyes to spot trespassers on the landing. They had already let themselves yield a little to the lateness of the night; they were sitting rather than standing; sometimes they read, sometimes they even propped their faces in their hands with their eyes shut, though they would not let themselves sleep. Una sat huddled on the fourth step, leaning her face against the banister, eyes closed. She mouthed something to Sulien and though he wasn't sure he'd understood it and didn't want to be the first to leave her, he shot up the stairs, dragging on the banister, trying to shift his weight onto it to keep the steps from creaking. He came up, right opposite the door to Marcus' corridor, and saw the guards, very close, one with bleared eyes turned down to a magazine – one seeming to look straight at Sulien, which froze him into a dreadful dithering half-second when he couldn't see the stairs to the third floor, didn't know which way to go. Right, he thought Una had been trying to say, and ducked almost blindly towards the corner of the gallery, where the next flight of stairs was narrower, darker; anticlimactic after the confident breadth of the first.

Una was last, drained from the effort; but scarcely looking at the guards, uninterested in the brief glare of light
before she reached the safe darkness on the second staircase, she didn't pause, she kept climbing.

She led the way now, pushing through another pair
of double doors, onto a black corridor where a few open
doors showed hastily stripped bedrooms. Una moved faster,
almost running, unswerving, nearly to the end of the corridor, where she flung suddenly into one of the unlit rooms.
They found her already kneeling on the floor, waiting.

'Here,' she said. Dama saw her hand, unconsciously
pressed against the carpet, almost caressing it.

And Cleomenes sliced through the fabric, slowly levered
up the floorboards, knocked through the plaster. The rooms
had high ceilings and, in the dark, they could hardly see the
floor below, and nothing else; but they could barely stop
Una from slipping straight through the hole. Cleomenes
grabbed her arms as she moved her weight out into the air.
He lowered her and she dropped crouching into the circle of
crumbled plaster on the floor.

'Marcus,' she whispered.

[XXII]

DARK

The room seemed full to the top with dark, as if with a liquid; they were in a tank of it, breathing it; they looked at each other through it. He was a shadow on the bed, she a shadow in the middle of the room; they could not see each other's faces. It was a moment before she could notice the chaos around her; what furniture there was lay turned over on the floor, the bedclothes were a dark heap near her feet; Marcus must have flung them there. Though it was so late, though he was on the bed, he hadn't been asleep. It was as if – there were moments when he thought this might be literally true – the capacity for sleep had been cut out of his head. He could almost feel the sharp-edged space where it had been. His heart still thrummed as if he'd just run a mile.

He'd raised himself on his elbow. She saw him lift his eyes slowly to the hole in the ceiling. He'd started at the noise as they broke through, and watched the plaster shower down on the floor, with alarm but somehow without surprise. Thicker, solid dark was raining through now, like black sand.

At the centre of it was a human column of dark, wavering slightly, pulling in all the light. It was impersonating Una. That had happened before, it kept happening. Already he did not know how long the creature had been there; time had pooled, spread out.

He remembered still that he'd been drugged, several times now; it had gone on for years, his whole life – longer than that – centuries. Certain things came to him with the force of revelations: he knew what had happened to time, why he seemed to be outside it: it was because it had already happened (he remembered the shock of feeling that), he was dead, this was what it was like; after all, he knew people had wanted to kill him. And besides he knew his parents were dead, and they were here. He hadn't precisely seen them, but they were close by. Sometimes he thought they were elsewhere in the sanctuary, just below this room, or beside it; sometimes he knew they were even closer, folded up in a segment of previously unsuspected space. He could hear them moving there.

Neither the belief that he was simply mad, nor the memory of the injections was incompatible with this realisation. It all seemed simultaneously likely: parallel.

'Marcus,' said Una again, and for a moment could feel the movement of springing forward gather in her body, she would press against him, kiss him; and that would be enough. But to her dismay a pang of immobility struck her; she looked up and, as she knew she would, saw Dama, hanging over the opening in the floorboards, watching.

Slowly, she stepped closer to the bed, and Marcus *drew back*, facing her patiently, but he'd jolted up, sitting tense on the bare mattress, not taking his eyes off her.

He'd seen the thing with Una's voice wade forward, creating eddies in the ankle-deep dark. The black continued to pour, little gaseous plumes rose off it where it stirred. The precipitous horror began to move through him again; it was scarcely fear of death any more, just horror without an object or an answer, unbounded, endless.

He told her, 'Go back, get out.'

Una fell back, unable to ward off a slap of hurt. She stood helplessly, and could see it all, a scorching dark travesty advancing through the room, herself; she felt the shapeless time, the flooding blackness against her skin.

She shook it off and looked anxiously at the height above them. Cleomenes and Sulien were trying to do something with the rope: if she put the table on its feet, she and Marcus could stand on it and reach up, but Marcus wouldn't be able to do that, not like this. Already it looked dangerous and implausible, even to her. And she could see no other way out; the window was barred, and with good reason; if they'd tried to take him out through it he'd have fallen at once.

She didn't dare turn on the lights.

She moved closer again, carefully, and to Marcus the approaching shadow seemed hot, smoking, like metal heated just to the point of turning red. So he flinched when the figure tentatively picked up his hands. But the fingers were cool, and she was near enough for him to see the paleness of the hair in the strained light from the window, and this really looked like Una's face.

'Please, Marcus. You saw me only four days ago, you remember that? I—' She stopped, hesitated. 'And we heard what you did, millions of people saw it. You got everything ready, it's just not finished. It still can be.'

Marcus looked at the hands holding his, with a kind of helpless suspicion. He felt as though he was about to be duped in some ridiculous way, and he was going to be taken in, even though he could see it, he was that stupid.

'I'm coming down,' said Sulien, scrambling through, into the black torrent. Marcus started again, realising there were more of them, held in reserve, in the ceiling.

But the voice— 'Sulien?' he ventured.

'Yes.' Sulien moved out of the dark spill, walked obliviously through the dense shadow on the floor. He looked at Marcus cautiously. How long would it take to wear off by itself – a day, perhaps? Marcus must have been dosed perhaps two or three times, the guards would have done it, or perhaps a new doctor; the original sanctuary staff couldn't be allowed to see Marcus spontaneously recover. He could see Marcus watching them warily, and said, 'You're all right, Marcus, really, you haven't always been like this. It's not going to last.'

Una said to him, 'Can you do something?'

'Yes,' said Sulien, still watching Marcus. 'I've got to, haven't I?' But he was anxious. He'd always worked by

513

being able to understand exactly what was wrong and he was afraid that here he would not be able to. He walked to Marcus even more slowly than Una had, even as he worried that his very care was making it worse, that he looked too stealthy, as if he was trying to catch something. He sat down on the bed, and tried to take Marcus' wrist from Una to check the pulse, and a warning spasm of memory made Marcus wrench grimly away from them, fists clenched.

'All right,' said Sulien, soothing, although for the moment at a loss. He decided he'd have to give up on touching Marcus at all, although it was so much more difficult that way. He tried to think of something else.

He began talking quietly, 'Listen. This isn't anything to do with you. It's just a compound, it would break down on its own. But I—' His voice faded. He'd found a certain low pitch and rhythm, and the words weren't only to reassure Marcus; they were like a solution, a vehicle. He began to feel that yes, this could work as a substitute for touch, he could see (or not exactly *see*) the disrupted teeming and sparking, in the star-shaped cells, in the dark. But it was so complicated; he wasn't sure what would help. And he felt already that he wasn't helping, Marcus wasn't calming down.

'What?' demanded Una, unable to stop herself. She'd been watching him in choked tension. And she noticed too late Marcus' gathering alarm, the temptation he'd felt to trust them waning as he heard them talking about him, trying to decide what to do to him.

'I'm not sure what I'm doing—' began Sulien.

Abruptly Marcus shoved Sulien away from him, so hard that he had no time to adjust for it and fell, flinching at the sound of the impact among the scattered furniture, almost before he felt the physical shock. Marcus rose unsteadily to his feet on the bed, though that too must be swallowed soon. The grainy blackness was lapping a foot deep now, and he didn't know what would happen if he touched it, otherwise he would have rushed for the door, hammered on it if it was locked. Demons or ghosts mimicking his friends— 'No,' said his own voice, loud and authoritative in the room, although he knew he hadn't spoken. 'They are not here, that's all.'

Una had turned away from Marcus in defeat, checking Sulien wasn't hurt. Sulien got up, uninjured, but feeling painfully taken aback – it was odd how it was hard to forestall that, even knowing that this wasn't Marcus' fault. He and Una looked at each other wretchedly. They were afraid that if they approached Marcus again he might cry out or attack them once more, and be heard.

Dama said to Cleomenes, 'For God's sake – go through and knock him out. We'll have to carry him.'

Marcus shuddered. He must face the possibility. However terrible. He might never have met them. If they weren't here in the room it was possible they were not – anywhere.

'Oh, you *can't*,' protested Una, stricken, feeling her eyes prickle. On an impulse of grief she caught his hand back, fiercely, forgetting to be slow and cautious. 'Marcus, I *know* you can't believe that.'

He tensed, but didn't pull his hand away. No, it was true, he felt with infinite relief, none of the jolts of comprehension had been worse than that, but he couldn't have invented Una and Sulien, or felt so much for them if he had; and there was a little comfort just in that, they existed or had existed somewhere, in an inaccessible fold of space. Una—

By now Cleomenes was sitting with his legs dangling through the gap, irresolute. He could see the sense of Dama's suggestion; whatever Sulien was trying to do didn't seem to be working. But he was afraid of doing it; it wasn't as easy as Dama seemed to think to strike a blow that would knock someone out and yet cause no lasting damage. And to do that to Marcus Novius of all people. He wasn't sure how they could lift an unconscious body up into the ceiling, in any case.

'Wait,' murmured Una. Marcus relaxed just fractionally. After all – you could look at it this way – it was better than nothing, hearing Una's and Sulien's voices – even if they weren't really here, even if the reproductions were actually malignant. He sneered at himself for stupidity, folly – but he thought he might as well just leave them alone – whatever they did, they could hardly make things worse.

Sulien stepped towards Marcus again, without modifying his pace this time; as he might have moved towards anyone. But he looked at Marcus uncertainly, and for a moment did nothing.

Una muttered. 'Go on, I think I—'

She thought, if she could help make Marcus listen to Sulien, even exert the faintest little hair's-strength tug that way – even that much might count. She gazed steadily now at the heavy black, brimming against the edge of the bed.

Sulien said, 'You're fine. The compound would break down anyway. It's breaking down now, all the time.'

Marcus and Una both looked slowly at him, across the dark swamp, and Una thought, there should be some way of helping Sulien, too.

It was extraordinary, watching Sulien working; she felt at once that she could never understand it – manoeuvring such unthinkably tiny and hidden things, and that she herself could see it more clearly than he could, because she could watch both of them; Sulien and Marcus. It would help Sulien if he could be more certain of what was wrong, and what he was doing.

She didn't want to disguise to either of them that she was there, watching. And she knew how, with great effort, to lay subtle trammels, nudge the course of an idea, but for the first time it seemed to her she might be able to do some-thing else, carry something with her, even though it meant prising up something so heavy and fixed, lugging it such a baffling distance.

She sighed as if she was going to sleep; the twist of difficulty seemed to drag her right away from herself, for a second she couldn't remember what she was trying to do, or anything.

Sulien said to Marcus, 'But I'm trying to make it go faster, because you're going to have to come with us: help me do that, it helps if you just keep listening to me.' Something about the voice made it difficult not to listen. Hesitating above, Cleomenes stared down, fascinated.

Then Sulien suppressed a little gasp. For a horrible second he'd thought he'd seen the dark in the room thicken, move and fume. And it was gone, and when the shiver of relief had passed, he knew *that* was what he had to push back.

And then, downstairs, the little flaw Cleomenes had knocked into the glass moved, twisted, crept; split the frail wire; and all through the sanctuary alarms bawled and struck. On, and on, and on.

It was as though every atom of the air rang, battering them, and for the first moment none of them could do anything except gasp, couldn't think of anything except the need to get away from that sound. It seemed to attack the whole body, not just the ears. Una could hardly hear herself saying what was certain, what was so obvious – 'They're coming—'

Dama shouted down in agony, reaching helplessly through the gap, 'Get *out* of there, come on!' And Una and Sulien dragged desperately at Marcus but they themselves were almost paralysed by noise and horror and the recent effort, and it was worse for him. For a moment of instinctive hope Sulien wondered if there might be some way of hiding; but nothing could hide the hole in the ceiling, and even as they begged, 'Marcus, please, come on,' Sulien thought despairingly, *why*, how could they get out that way now, up into the ceiling, down the stairs? And there was no time for three people to climb up through the hole even if Marcus had been able to do it without help. The guards were running down the corridor; even through the roar of the alarm, Sulien could hear them.

Cleomenes plunged down into the room, and slammed on the lights. The black blasted off the floor, out of the air. Painfully, as his pupils squeezed against the sharp light, Marcus saw Una and Sulien, shocked and indecisive, still apparently there, although the air was full of howling, as solid as the dark had been, as hard to move through. A man with red hair impossibly ploughing across it, navigating hillocks and peaks of noise like a red boat.

Cleomenes yanked Marcus off the bed by one arm and threw him aside, dragged the bed across the room, turned it onto its side, rammed it against the door, tried to wedge it there. Sulien heard the door unlock, saw it knock against the bed as it opened, and rushed at the barricade; they both shoved, groaning. Una hovered near Marcus for a moment, who was standing shakily against the window; still splintered with confusion, feeling the noise coil and crush like a snake; but seeing the same room they saw. Then she ran across to drive herself at the bed, trying to force her weight and strength to be more, gasping to Sulien, '*No*, it was working, go on; I'll hold it.'

Sulien hesitated, and darted back to Marcus, tried to pick up again the silent willing back of the fever in the nerves – but then Una cried out with effort as the door thudded, strove against the bed's edge; and he had to run to the barrier again, pushed.

Above, Dama fed the rope down through the hole – Sulien had already tied it to the bars of the window; but as he did it he knew it was no good. He couldn't help pull anyone up; they couldn't leave the door. He was poised to drop down and join them, but he hung back, he didn't know what was stopping him.

Outside, a voice said, 'Get away from the door.'

Cleomenes improvised frantically: 'No. I am armed. Draw back or I'll kill Marcus Novius now,' but Una whispered wretchedly, 'They don't care – they know, they want you to.' And the door pushed and banged again.

And she thought, and they can do it, kill all of us, Marcus too, they can say it was our fault. It is; we've given them the excuse. Oh, please don't let them. And she thought grimly: No, if you're going to do that, pray to be able to think of something. Please, help me think.

Well, she told herself, *try* to think, then.

She turned, pushing against the bed with her back and

shoulder, looking distractedly around the disordered room, at the barred window; the floor.

She ran to the centre of the room and called up:

'Dama, come down, bring everything.'

Dama hesitated. He hurled Cleomenes' equipment down, but didn't follow. Una could not wait to wonder why, she fumbled through the things, which for a moment seemed to hover meaninglessly before her eyes, losing helpless seconds to the haste and noise shaking her body; found the short blade Cleomenes had used for the carpet.

Dama said, 'Where the bed was.'

She obeyed unthinkingly, crouching by the empty corner; stabbed at the carpet, tore, gritting her teeth with effort. She saw Marcus watching her, guardedly. He muttered tentatively, 'What are you doing?' and she said, 'The ground floor – the windows aren't barred.'

But the door heaved again and there were only Cleomenes and Sulien to hold it back now. Sulien strained against it, shouted, 'Dama, *help* us!'

Dama gave a strange little unhappy breath, unheard in the noise, and didn't move. And Una screamed, 'They're going to shoot through the door, *now*, they're going to shoot through the door, *Sulien*!'

For a moment, crouching by the hole she'd torn in the carpet, she couldn't move herself, until she saw Sulien and Cleomenes throw themselves down, then she clawed out and dragged Marcus to the floor, as the new noise roared and the wood broke.

The panels of the door splintered hotly around the punched-in holes, the bullets puffed through the bed, smashed into the walls, shattering the window behind the curtains. Under their flight, Una and Marcus lay still, almost relaxed. Her arm, after the first second of pinioning him against the floor and against her, lay over him, her hand on his hair. She whispered, 'I'm sorry. We've ruined it. But – I had to come after you, I had to see you.' And put her fingertips to his face, ran them along the contour of temple and cheekbone.

519

And the door gaped wider against the bed than it ever had before. Cleomenes shot desperately into the gap, Sulien kicked against the bed from the floor, knocked the door weakly shut, rolled to press what strength he could against it from the floor. Cleomenes pulled himself up to stand, back to the wall, fired again through the door.

He stopped, panting; he hadn't heard anything, a cry to tell him he'd killed or wounded anybody. They must be conferring outside; he'd warned them back for a moment, perhaps. He felt for the only other case of ammunition in his clothes – his gun was empty.

Sulien forced himself to get up onto his knees, crushing against the door, although for the moment the pressure from the other side was gone. He knew it would come back; he thought there were at least three of them; more would come, and Cleomenes did not have that many shots to fire. Una had not yet touched the floorboards.

Marcus looked at Una, without certainty, with the waning chemical still whirring through his blood. He said to her, 'Una. Whether you're here or not. I'll go wherever you want.'

The scream of the alarm stopped. The blood seemed to cool and swill in their skulls. It was as if they had been in violent motion and could feel it almost more dizzyingly now it had ceased. The next second the men began to shout jarringly through the pierced door. Between the sounds, Marcus and Una lay as if on warm grass, in the fraction of humming silence.

A voice, appallingly close to Sulien, yelled to him, 'Get back. The gun won't help you. Reinforcements are coming. We will blow the door out; anyone near it will be killed.'

'Don't answer,' Cleomenes mouthed, though Sulien wanted to shout recklessly that the room was packed with explosives, the guards were the ones in danger. He pushed closer.

'This is your last chance, get out of the way now and I won't shoot.' And abruptly, almost before the words were finished, Sulien felt another great blow against the other side judder through him. Cleomenes, who had still been fiddling with the slide on the gun, had to fling himself awkwardly against the bed. The gap opened, slammed shut, forced open.

And Marcus seemed to see Sulien, exhausted, struggling to hold back a door that kept crashing against him. He staggered up, through the roiling echoes of noise, across the surging ground, and not really knowing what they were trying to keep out of the room or why, let his body cannon clumsily against the barricaded door, beside Sulien.

'Marcus, you stupid bastard, you idiot,' gasped Sulien, nonsensically, as they both pushed, hardly aware of talking at all.

And Una was attacking the floor again, ferociously ramming the chisel between floorboards, hissing with fury when they wouldn't move. She swung the hammer at the chisel, tore up and shoved the first board aside, stamped through the plaster beneath, pulled bitterly at the plank beside it – almost enough, not quite. She had to cry out in warning again before another burst of gunfire punctured the door, and lying across the gap, kept gouging and levering as the air thundered. Above the bed, the upper panels of the door were becoming a ragged mess, the men would be able to see in, aim properly in a minute. Cleomenes fired back again, again there was a moment of respite.

Una pulled the third floorboard loose, and Sulien called again, 'Dama, get *down*.'

'No,' Dama whispered apologetically, so that Sulien could barely hear him, 'I couldn't come down – I wouldn't be able to get up again in time—'

'What?'

Dama said more firmly, 'They don't know what's happened in here. Put the bed back where it was. Hide everything.' Una stared up at him, guilty, desolate. 'Do it now.'

At first it seemed impossible. Cleomenes drove the guards back from the door with another volley, but Sulien

521

found himself panting, 'Give it to me – you're heavier, hold the door.'

'No.'

'You're being stupid.'

Cleomenes gave a muffled snarl of vexation and did as he was told, slammed the gun into Sulien's hand and charged into place against the door. Sulien felt the weight of the pistol with alarm, as if he hadn't asked for it. He said, 'Go on.'

He backed into the room, and though he didn't believe in anything he thought stupidly to Apollo: please don't let me kill anybody. He fired through the centre of the door. He thought that none of the blasts had been so shatteringly loud, he could feel a horrible shaking building up in his body, but he could keep it still, for the moment, just—

Crouching, Cleomenes leant in against the bare wood as Una dragged the bed back, into the middle of the room, left it there. She shoved all the rest of the furniture in around them, Cleomenes grabbed at it, trying to build a blockade around himself out of flimsy chairs. Sulien shot again, repeating, 'Go on.'

And Una said, 'Come with me,' and Marcus followed her through the jagged gap, dropped blindly after her into the dark below.

'You, go on, put the bed back,' said Sulien, firing.

Cleomenes left the door, with only the gun and a few chairs to keep it closed now, drove the bed towards the wall over the hole and the wreckage, rolled under it, struggled down. Sulien was alone in the room.

He tried to fire again and found he'd emptied the thing. Dama shouted to him from above and seemed to be scuffling around up there, but Sulien didn't hear or see: he threw himself down and slid under the hanging sheets as the tattered door crashed open, sweeping through the wreckage of the furniture.

Cleomenes found Marcus, bruised and hurt, his ankle twisted by the drop, Una clutching his hand, on a doctor's office floor. 'We've got to move,' said Cleomenes hoarsely.

But they couldn't, they could only stand, staring up for Sulien. But he did not appear, and they heard shouting, violence.

Sulien lay on the ruined floor and couldn't move. The sheet barely hid him, the hole was a foot ahead. He had had no time to swivel round, and any movement now would show where the others had gone; the only way he might possibly have got through was by diving headfirst. He laid his cheek quietly against the wood, protest seeped out of him, strangely enjoying the smoothness of the inside of his eyelids, the several pulses tapping against the wood beneath him, even the splinters in his hands.

Dama had wound his right arm over and over in the rope, painfully let his lower body down through the gap, hung there, held up by the rope, propped on his chest and left arm.

He thought passionately, come on then.

He kicked and dragged, thought again of Una running from Tasius, and shouted into the empty room before him, 'Run, get out – they're coming through!'

The guard stepped cautiously into the bedroom and saw Dama, struggling up through the hole in the ceiling, and called: 'They've taken him, they're on the floor above!'

He heard them move! In the corridor – they were running for the stairs! Dama gave a breathless laugh, as the guard pulled at his legs, as he clung and fought – and in his left hand was what he had not even realised was there, the screwdriver Cleomenes had used on the floorboards. He toppled, abrupt dead weight on the man's shoulders, cast backwards out with the screwdriver, and he had no thoughts at all, no clear expectation of death but a bright, ruthless expansion of each second that meant the same thing.

He made no effort to break the momentum of his fall, it was all he had – and he drove his weight behind the thin rod in his hand as he hurtled down. With disbelieving, savage triumph he felt blood bubble up between his fingers. When they crashed against the floor, Sulien could only see Dama's hands, but the guard's head fell languidly onto its side, looked straight into Sulien's eyes, gasped and choked. He could not call out. The screwdriver was still lodged in his larynx. Dama was leaning on it, also gasping, pressing it there with all his strength. Blood scattered and burst and gulped.

Sulien watched, endlessly. Finally Dama got to his feet. He said, 'Get out, Sulien.' Instead of crawling towards the hole in the floorboards, Sulien heard him stumbling through the upturned chairs and out into the corridor.

Sulien was not even sure how Dama had known he was still there.

For a moment longer he was unable to look away. The man was – he had been – healthy. Sulien wondered how old he was. He stared back; he was still alive. Sulien thought it was even just possible that he could have saved his life.

Blood welled up from the man's mouth. And he would have killed Sulien, or his sister, or his friend, and in turn the shots Sulien had fired could easily have killed him. But the soldier had lonely minutes to go before he drowned in his own blood, and Sulien watched with pity and awful, urgent thankfulness that he hadn't been the one to do it. The trembling he'd managed to hold back broke out all through him.

Then he raised himself, feeling the man's clouding eyes follow him as pulled himself away, scrambled round and swung down through the gap.

Dama jogged, panting, into the passage and found no one there to stop him, they were already closing in on the upper floor. He laughed. He lurched along the corridor, tripped down the back stairs. He thought they had caught on and were coming down after him, but still he had burst down into the dining room before anything happened. He paused for a second, looking across the lobby, trying to work out where Una and Sulien must be. Out in the garden already, on the other side of the sanctuary; running into all that light? And where was he? He'd just come down the slaves' stairs – behind him was a kitchen, a utility room – he laughed again, a rasping painful little sound, as what to do next presented itself, easy and obvious.

He ran into the utility room, turned on the light, as there was no reason not to, and knowing what he was looking for, and where it would almost certainly be, went to the fuse box as if he'd fixed it there himself. It was high on the wall – but he climbed up onto a counter and ripped the box open, vaguely noticing the blood he left on the metal. He scrabbled at it fiercely, struck at the switches, tearing loose what wires he could. The light died – yes, and out in the garden too – but it could just be turned on again; it must be obvious why it had suddenly failed. Yes, he could hear a din of running feet overhead. Why hadn't he brought the hammer with him? He darted out into the kitchen, filled a bowl with water, ran back and dashed it into the box. The wires buzzed and spat brief flakes of blue light. Dama smiled, entranced, and pounded out into the lobby, for the basement steps, as the guards reached the top of the grand central stairs and saw him. Come on then.

They fired, but Dama careered down, tripped in the dark and fell the last few steps. He wondered distantly if he'd been felled by a bullet, if he might possibly not have noticed – but he groped to his feet, staggered fluently down the unlit corridor from memory. 'Run!' he whooped again, to the imaginary companions ahead of him, and worried that his pursuers must hear the mania in his voice. He knocked against a wall, rebounded along the basement corridor, through the open door into the infirmary. This was further than he had expected to get. He scraped up through the sharp frame of the window, clambered up the low wall of the well and ran stiffly into the dark garden.

As he expected, more bullets ripped after him – from the windows, from the well – but he almost crashed into the temple wall and found with sheer confusion that he was still unhurt. An uncertain squeezing of nausea rattled him. He wondered how long it would take them to find the dead man in Marcus' bedroom. Four now, that's four—

He dashed on, as the guns burst again. He believed they were shooting at only him, and if he had come this far with his stiff feet, Una and Sulien must have gone further, he had done it – was doing it. He ran against the fence and knew he couldn't make it over, he was surprised it had taken this long already, but he jumped and grappled, seemed, impossibly, to run *vertically*, and though the fence scratched and jabbed him, he fell down on the damp earth, in the woods on the other side, astonished.

He didn't want to move. He wanted to lie where he was. He found suddenly that he was exhausted, surely he had never felt so tired. He sobbed dryly, and made himself get up and lurch wearily down the hill. What would they do? They were coming, casting torch-beams about the wood. Dama crumpled quietly behind a fallen branch, and it was such a relief, to have to lie there, curled up, still. He gave another tearless sob into the earth – not regret, no, in fact should this not weigh against what he had done before, being self-evidently necessary, being *good?* He'd saved their lives, Sulien's— Una's—

Still the guards had not found him. He wiped his hands once more on the ground, started dully up again. The blood bothered him less than the fact that he could still feel the warmth of the other man's body, the roughness of the stubble on his neck. He'd had to touch him, for such a long time, such an intimate thing to kill someone like that, not like what he'd done to those other three . . .

He was far from safe; they would keep looking for him and he knew he would not try to get back to the car; it seemed clear enough now that he'd never meant to do that. So – no transport, just a little money from Delir, and such relentless aches in his arms and legs that he didn't feel up to walking anywhere. But he would, unless or until he was killed.

Why had it not happened sooner? It seemed wrong – disappointing – for him to die now when he felt so weak and cold and useless, when a minute before he'd been incandescent with certainty and euphoria. Why, God? He felt that there *must* be a reason, and he thought slowly, maybe I was protected, I have been saved because I'm meant for something more, something better. A little glow of peace and pride warmed him for a moment, but he was too tired to hold it, and the belief that Una would be all right now was waning too – even if they'd made it to the car he couldn't see where they could go next. But he had done everything he could.

Eventually he got up again, trudged into the dark.

Marcus ran, the repeated blows of hot pain in his loosened ankle troubling but distant; he knew he had to run anyway and he did it. But still everything was slow, even the urgency; they might have been running, climbing up this fence, running once more – for hours. The likelihood that none of this was real no longer stabbed and shouted, it just lay softly through things, acceptable. And it no longer occurred to him to question where he was. It made enough sense, an enclosed sense of its own: Una was there – they were in the woods – in the Pyrenees—

And Una bit her lip with grief. The dark had sprung suddenly, miraculously across the gardens just as they were about to run desperately into all the sharp light. They heard the shots echo from the other side, and there could only be one reason. But the bangs kept coming, and though it felt impossible to be glad of that, why would they go on firing if any of those bullets had found Dama?

But they must stop at last, and she wouldn't know why. She thought for a moment, maybe he'll be at the car – or we can drive round and look for him. But she answered herself at once, No. They had no time, but that wasn't the point. He said he'd just go, and if he wasn't dead then this was when he'd do it.

But Sulien had dropped at last through the ceiling, shaking but all right, and Marcus— He stumbled sometimes, with his hurt ankle and the continuing fickleness of the earth beneath him. She staggered with him, dragged on his hand. Her fingers felt cold and thin when she had to let go to climb the fence, alone. The unfamiliarity of it, voluntarily touching someone for so long, slowed her just slightly as she took his hand back, on the other side. But they went on running, and she forgot about the fence, and that they'd ever come apart at all.

They came to the road, ran across it. Sulien was afraid that they'd never find the car in time, he still couldn't think clearly, couldn't remember the way. But Cleomenes seemed to, they followed him to the overgrown track. The black car was still there.

'Dama,' said Sulien, unhappily, seeing it was empty – seeing Dama's hands pressing down on the screwdriver.

'Too bad. In,' Cleomenes ordered him, shoving him towards the car.

Then for Marcus everything underwent a kind of jump or quiver – and was the same afterwards, he and Una were running through the wood – but it made no sense at all. The pain heated his ankle again, less blurry this time, a real pain in a real body. The baggy seconds snapped shut. He looked down at his hand, saw what it held.

For a moment he was almost reluctant to look at her – in case his senses were still subject to elaborate tricks, even though it was somehow obvious now that they were not. But he turned his head cautiously, and she was there.

Speechlessness cut heavily down through him, as decisively as an axe splitting a log, cut through more than his voice – his breath, his power to move – it was more than speechlessness; it hurt him, it was so much.

He looked again at their joined hands and carefully let go, he'd remembered her stiffness in his arms by the river in the gorge – and she didn't need to pull him along any more.

'Get in,' she said.

He got in. She sat beside him, an inch of space between them, as the car began to move. Cleomenes backed onto the road, drove blindly away from the hill. Una and Marcus continued to stare at each other, every time he found a way to begin on what had happened – they had dug down to him from the floor above – the speechlessness struck again, chopped his thoughts away. He couldn't even ask her, how long was I drugged? *How did you get to me?* He remembered lying on the floor beside her; he was almost certain that she'd said to him, I had to see you – but how could he count on that, when he knew he'd also seen solid darkness sopping across the floor and bleeding walls? For a while it seemed possible they could go on like that indefinitely, bruised, speechless.

Then she put her lips against his, deliberately, then moved back so they could look at each other, and then kissed him again.

He kissed her; he could remember the curved precision of her small mouth from the first time, he could not understand how this could be so different. Starts of amazement interrupted the delight: How? What has happened? He pulled her closer and then slowed with doubt, not that she was there but – he wondered anxiously – does she think she *has* to do this? But her arms tightened fiercely, her mouth seized almost angrily on his. He thought she must have known what he was thinking, he didn't mind.

He pushed her back just for a second, holding her face between his palms. He whispered, laughing at her, 'You changed your mind, then?'

'Oh, shut up,' she said, as their faces came together again. They were not even alone; they had to talk; they would have to stop. But she thought his skin was warmer than other people's, steadily warm without being feverish; match flames lit on his teeth and lips, passed weightlessly into her mouth without going out. They would be visible through the skin; if she opened her eyes she would see them.

[XXIII]

MAKARIA

Marcus said with sudden panic: 'Varius. They haven't – he is alive, isn't he?'

'I hope so, Sir,' said Cleomenes, and Una and Sulien were both surprised – it seemed they had forgotten that this was a possible name for Marcus.

'What does that mean?' asked Marcus, looking at the back of Cleomenes' head with a mild shock, belatedly grasping that the red-haired man really existed.

'He was yesterday afternoon, at least, it sounded like he was. Laevinus thought they could deal with him, even with you alive.'

'Yesterday?' repeated Marcus. 'How long has it been?'

Rubbing his eyes in the front seat, Sulien said, 'All of yesterday and the night before – half the day before that, I guess. About forty hours.'

'That's all?!' Marcus fell silent again, then murmured, 'It still feels like it could have been—' He shook his head, as the memory of what had happened in the sanctuary floated clear, as he began to guess how much more they must have done. 'Sulien. I don't know what to say – I'm so glad to see you.'

Sulien saw the man with his mouth full of blood, and wanted badly to tell someone that he'd seen it, not to be the only person in the car who knew about it. He could see Una was too absorbed in Marcus to notice much. She was leaning against Marcus, his chin resting on the top of her head, their hands gripping each other as if lives depended on it. They were happier than he had ever seen either of them, and out of bewilderment and tension and guilt, they were trying not to be.

He grinned at Marcus. 'You always knock over people you're glad to see?'

'Oh—' said Marcus, remembering it, startled into embarrassed laughter. 'I didn't hurt you, did I?'

'What – you?' mocked Sulien, with a little effort. He thought, I've been awake for so long.

They were storming through the hills towards the main road. Marcus said to Cleomenes, 'You were holding the door shut. I'm sorry – I don't know who you are.'

Cleomenes explained himself shortly. 'Thank you for helping me,' said Marcus. He felt dazed again.

'Premature,' replied Cleomenes grimly. 'I'm worried they're going to cut us off at the top of the road.'

He had heard Una and Marcus kiss. In one way he was amused and pleased with himself, for he had suspected as much the night before. Still, he thought, if they both get out of this, that's going to be a problem for somebody.

'Have they had time?' asked Una. 'They've got to get up that drive, and they never saw this car.'

'They've got time to call whoever they've got in the palace, anyway. I suppose that is where we're going.'

'We can't go anywhere else,' Una said.

'They don't know that though,' said Sulien. 'In fact, they'll think we'd have to lie low. The drug wouldn't have worn off for hours yet.'

'In any case,' insisted Cleomenes, 'they are going to have people there.'

'I know,' said Marcus. 'I couldn't go there to begin with. But it's different now. My uncle knows I'm alive, everyone does. They can't say I'm anyone else and drag me off somewhere and pretend it never happened. And you're all witnesses.'

Cleomenes thought, so they kill us, too, but it was true, there was nowhere else.

Marcus whispered to Una, 'And there's you – I don't know who's part of it, but you will, they can't trick you.'

'No,' she said, 'We'll be all right,' and he smiled, because she almost never said things like that. But then another flinch of alarm came and he asked Cleomenes, 'Do you think they'd kill Varius *now*?'

Cleomenes was slow to answer. 'It would be a big risk, after all this,' he said, and did not add anything to this, though the sentence was obviously unfinished.

Marcus sighed, beginning to feel how tired he was. Una's hair was smooth under his cheek, his thumb lay under the cuff of one of her sleeves. Only at her neck and the slight wrists could he feel her skin growing warm against his. He thought again of Varius dead; he couldn't kiss Una – but it was nearly impossible not to, the worry itself wanted to be blotted out on her mouth, he wanted so much to be any-where alone with her, or just go to sleep like this, even, if nothing else was allowed.

And the sky brightened, not with dawn, which was still hours away, but with the city's own light. The Golden House stood above it at once peaceful and sleepless, shining.

'Give me my gun back,' said Cleomenes suddenly.

'It's empty,' said Sulien.

'Well. Don't tell anyone else that.' He smiled. 'Marcus Novius, do you know – is there an entrance that's less guarded?'

'Yes,' said Marcus, 'but don't go to it. Go to the front.'

Marcus was still in his nightclothes. All they could give him was the set of clothes Sulien had worn for the first couple of days out of Holzarta. The clothes felt grubby but he needed them, he remembered the caupona in Wolf Step – there were certain ways of talking that were impossible if you weren't dressed. He and Una smiled foolishly at each other, at once collusive and embarrassed, before he pulled the clothes on awkwardly, as quickly he could. Una had turned away slightly but glanced furtively back through her hair at his brief and incomplete nakedness, his arms, his back—

They stepped out of the car; they walked up to the curved

façade of the Palatine gate. There were four Praetorians watching over the metal entrance within the carved stone, six or eight more, impassive against the palace wall inside. So many hands full of guns, thought Sulien, with sad apprehension.

Marcus pulled up the tired muscles in his back and neck, yawning. He looked at the guards and thought, good, even more would have been better, and went forward to meet them. He said, 'You know who I am. Open the gates.'

They stared. It did not occur to any of them that he was anyone other than Marcus Novius, or to say so.

One of them hesitated and shouted, not to Marcus but to Cleomenes and the rest, 'Why have you brought him here? Step away from him.'

Una, Sulien and Cleomenes stood around Marcus and did not move or speak. 'You will not talk to them like that again,' said Marcus, finally.

Taken aback, the guard muttered apologetically, innocently, 'But you – Sir – you shouldn't, you're supposed to be—'

'In the sanctuary in Tivoli,' finished Marcus for him loudly, so that the man was embarrassed. 'Do you think I should be there? Do I seem to you as if I need to be?'

He stood and let himself be looked at. It was two hours before dawn. His fingers were knitted tightly between Una's; his hair was rumpled, his clothes looked what they were, meant for someone else and thrown on hastily in the dark; he was barefoot and limping on the paved ground. The man lowered his eyes. 'No,' he admitted softly.

Marcus repressed a little shake of relief.

And the answer, 'No,' altered things, it was simply obvious now that Marcus couldn't be sent back to the Galenian.

'Then open the gates,' said Marcus.

Then from the line inside a guard broke away, calling, 'Open the gates,' and his hand shifted very slightly on his gun as he did so, although more out of desperate instinct than decision. He couldn't see what to do, he had to get instructions – the one clear thing was that he must get the boy away from all these people.

He pressed the button on the wall and the gates swung apart. He said, 'Come with me, Sir, your friends can wait, just while we check them out, security—'

Una's hand tensed, but Marcus didn't need the warning. 'No. They're coming with me, through the main doors, up the main stairs. We're going to see my uncle.'

'At this time?'

The guard clenched his teeth, scared of failure and powerless. The other Praetorians were already looking at him, surprised.

'Come with me, Sir, anyway,' he said thickly.

'What do you think's going to happen to me between here and the door?' asked Marcus, looking at him, and then smiled, suddenly shrugging. 'All right,' he said peaceably. 'I'll come with you. And you two, you can come and keep an eye on my friends, if you're worried about them.' And as he gestured to two of the men, Una felt a little questioning pressure on her hands – are they all right? She nodded.

But as they reached the doors the Praetorian who'd opened the gates darted away around the corner of the palace, leaving the others dismayed and cross.

'He's going to call someone inside,' murmured Una.

'It'll be all right,' said Marcus.

And they went in. Behind the great blue windows the huge stairs poured down to the marble floor, glittering with flowers and leaves of green and blue and gold tiles. Suddenly conscious of his dirty and rumpled clothes, and not just that, of all the time he'd been away, Marcus paused for a second, confused to be there. But still, he knew where he was going.

Tentatively placing their feet on the first step, Una and Sulien had a strange, awed feeling, not entirely pleasant. They thought, so this is what the Golden House is like inside! And they saw that it was not strange to Marcus, he walked up into the great loft of gold space above them and it was so hard to believe what was obvious, that anyone they knew could have seen all this hundreds of times. They came into a long room lined with paintings and busts standing on plinths, and hung with droplets of gold lamps; and Sulien and Una looked at all the enamel and gold with helpless admiration and Una thought, I think I hate it.

A man Marcus recognised – the chief steward who managed the household, acquired the slaves – came stumbling, blinking, seeming like Marcus to have just thrust himself into his clothes. He said in a voice blurred with sleepiness, 'Sir. You must be exhausted. Shall I take you to your usual room?'

'I need to see the Emperor first.'

'Of course,' said the steward, patiently, after a moment, 'But it is so late. He'll have to be woken, it must be explained to him.'

'I can do that.'

Marcus tried to walk past but the steward danced grimly into the way.

'You really must wait. Your clothes, you haven't got any shoes on. He'll be angry at being woken. Do you even realise what time it is?' And he grabbed Marcus' arm, the grasp startling because it was plainly not allowed. He was thinking, you're only a kid, whatever else you are. I can deal with you.

At the same time, Una shouted as the guard who'd opened the gates, and another with him, lunged at them, tried to wrench Marcus away.

They knew what they were trying to do now, although they were desperate and scared – get Marcus Novius into any lockable room, as far from the Emperor as possible, keep him quiet by any means – the drug could be here in twenty minutes, that was all they needed. The others would have to be killed and smuggled out – the guards that had already seen them could be told that a group of criminals had been manipulating the poor boy for some reason. The impression that they'd seen a sane person would, must fade, they could be reprimanded, told to count themselves lucky the Emperor hadn't been informed of their stupidity . . .

But there were only three of them, there had been no time to gather any more. And their guns were as useless as Cleomenes' – although that was enough to scare back the steward – for the sound of a shot would wreck this last chance they had. But it was already wrecked: there were too many people to keep quiet, Marcus dodged and punched, and when they dragged Una aside they couldn't keep hold of her if they were to get to him, couldn't stop her shouting, 'Wake up, come *here*,' and they were all shouting then – for Faustus Augustus, for help. And Sulien stopped fighting abruptly, and instead pushed at the nearest plinth. It fell with a disastrous thud, the head rolling from it as if it had been struck off a body; and at once they could hear the palace waking up in alarm at the noise. Marcus and the others tore away and ran down the long room, and the steward, trembling on the floor by the fallen bust, realised that instead of going after them the Praetorians had fled, back towards the stairs, away from the sound.

The doors they flung open were carved of scented wood, or painted with birds and hillsides. They ran over mosaics, glowing carpets, and then, bursting out of the private apartments to meet them, in the midst of a gathering crowd of heavy-lidded attendants, Faustus was there, growling, his eyes crumpled up and his face loose with sleep.

Except for Marcus, they all stopped in sheer surprise at seeing him, that man, the Emperor, right there and nowhere else. He was tall, but he seemed not quite tall enough, he took up only so much space. And yet he looked no different really, even with his face and body battered with interrupted sleep, from all the pictures, and the sameness was somehow unsettling, too, like seeing twins. Una glanced at Marcus, because he'd had that effect once – but she couldn't remember it properly. He caught her hand again.

Faustus mumbled, 'Marcus – what are you doing here?' and then, remembering that Marcus probably couldn't explain, he repeated sadly, 'Marcus,' and glared in suspicion

536

and anger at the others, then stuttered in mystified outrage to the people around him, 'Who are these people? How did they get in?'

Marcus said quickly, 'There's nothing wrong with me now. You can see that, can't you?'

Faustus stared at him, with a kind of bewildered sagging.

'Uncle, it was all true, everything I said to you, but they drugged me at the hospital before you got there. When you talked to me, I was – seeing things, but I'm not now. I won't again, at least—' he knew he'd never forget the skin peeling off the walls, the pitching horror, 'It hasn't happened to me yet, like it hasn't happened to you.'

Faustus frowned, trying to think if this could be some trick of the disease, if Lucius had ever seemed as direct and clear as this. He'd heard of persuasive madmen, but not under the Novian curse – and that was not at all how Marcus had been in the Aesculapian.

Sulien said, 'My sister and I have been with him nearly all the time. And I'm – I'm kind of a doctor. He's not mad.'

Faustus shook his head, baffled. The boy didn't look anything like a doctor. And he was startled and affronted by the fact that a shabby girl was unapologetically holding Marcus' hand and staring curiously at Faustus himself without any display of deference, but – surely Marcus couldn't have been picking up girls in the state he'd been in before—

He breathed, 'I can't understand this—'

Cleomenes added, 'Sir, I can confirm there have been attempts to kill him. I've seen it. I'm a centurion with the vigiles, or I was a couple of days ago. I think I can say that the city prefect is part of it, and a few of my colleagues, and some men who at any rate wear Praetorian uniforms.'

'And Gabinius,' said Marcus, 'and—' he faltered, it was hard to say this, for Faustus was beginning to look weak and ill with confused horror. Marcus felt almost ashamed. 'And people here, Uncle,' he finished. 'And they killed my parents.'

Unexpectedly, loss began spilling through him, as if a

glass of it had been tipped over. Una moved closer, so that through both their sleeves he could feel her arm against his.

'I can't understand this,' repeated Faustus. These words, his voice as he said them, disgusted him; how slow and pathetic he sounded. The Emperor shouldn't say things like that; and yet he couldn't seem to pull himself together. He tried to think of better questions to ask, but could only manage: 'Who are you talking about? How – how have you got here?'

Marcus struggled, he was afraid that if he seemed too emotional Faustus would think he was mad again. He wanted to say, *they* got me here; this is Una, this is Sulien; you don't know how much they've done. And he would say all that, but there wasn't time yet. 'Please bring Varius here, right now – and don't let anyone call ahead, don't give them a chance. They might kill him, even now.'

'I need to be the one to go,' broke in Cleomenes.

'Yes,' said Marcus urgently. 'And he has to get through quickly. Please, write something threatening anyone who tries to stop him. Or harms Varius.'

Faustus made a move of the head that hardly meant anything, shuffled back into the private rooms behind the gilded doors, letting them follow.

Varius felt it was, at least, simpler being away from Gabinius; the prison was a simpler place. He'd been back there five days, and in some ways things were better for him there than they had been before. The lights went on and off at normal times; Gabinius had even sent some of the books from the house with him. Their presence bothered him; they kept him from being able to pretend that Gabinius didn't exist. Now that he was newly frantic to know what was going on, he found he was capable of boredom again too; but he didn't want to benefit, in any way, from anything Gabinius had done. So the books loured in the room, and he would glance through them feverishly, and then be angry with himself, which would then seem idiotic. He was kept alone, for which he was largely thankful; he didn't think he could face other people, especially in large numbers – except that they might have been able to tell him something. Since Gabinius had said goodbye to him no one had explained anything. He felt gnawed with suspense, fell into erratic darkened subdivisions of consciousness, rather than real sleep.

When the door opened he thought instantly, even before his eyes were open: I know it's still night. They've changed their mind, this time it's happening: a gun, a cudgel? And he started up and saw a man wearing dishevelled dark clothes, not a uniform, with red hair.

Cleomenes saw a jolt of surprise and hope lift Varius' face, freeze there and then seem to go out, leaving, apparently, only a polite interest.

'Cleomenes,' he said, formally.

'Yes. Sorry,' blurted Cleomenes.

Varius shrugged. 'Never mind.'

'Come on,' said Cleomenes, pushing the door open.

'All right.' Cleomenes could see a businesslike cast settling over him as he got up, strange on a body visibly thinned and sapped. They left the cell. 'Where are we going?'

'The palace.'

Varius slowed as he walked for a moment but didn't stop. He asked levelly, 'Does that mean Marcus is there?'

'Yes.'

Varius was silent for a while. Cleomenes expected more questions, something – but Varius only said mildly, 'Good.'

Cleomenes was confused. Varius seemed curiously unimpressed by his own release, by the whole thing. He was quiet, but didn't seem listless or inert, as if he were too shocked or weakened to take in what was happening. He walked briskly enough through the corridors of the prison to the car. When Cleomenes spoke to him he answered courteously and without hesitation, but he did not talk unprompted. Otherwise he was silent, sometimes glancing about, around the car, out of the window, with a kind of mild scepticism. For some reason Cleomenes was reminded of a teacher, which made no sense to him at the time, but later he thought, yes, it was as if Varius was a teacher going through a declamation a student had written – nodding, not uninterested, occasionally a little surprised, saying from time to time, 'Oh, you've done it like that, have you?'

Cleomenes wondered, does he think this is some kind of trap, that I'm going to kill him or something? But he knows I wasn't part of it, and even if I had been, I could just do it, I wouldn't need to lie to him first. He felt rather aggrieved.

Nothing so specific had occurred to Varius. He did not know why, now Cleomenes had said Marcus was alive, he shrank from asking any more, but there seemed no reason to think about it. He walked up the steps to the palace, moving provisionally as he was doing everything, prepared to accept it for the sake of argument.

Marcus had been sitting drowsily on a couch, and a girl lay propped beside him, asleep. There was another boy slumped in an armchair, half-asleep himself. Tulliola was there now, too, and though Faustus looked slovenly in his lush dressing gown, she had dressed fastidiously before coming out, only her dark hair hung loose of its usual tower, soft.

Marcus got to his feet at once. 'Varius.'

Varius looked at him and the breath he'd just taken stayed motionless within him for a long moment, otherwise nothing changed in his face. 'I told them where to find you,' he said.

Marcus said, 'How did they make you do that?'

But Varius looked away – not as if it was something too terrible to be spoken about, but as if he'd simply lost interest in the subject. 'It doesn't matter.'

Tulliola said, 'Of course it matters. I'm sorry, Varius. I wanted to believe it wasn't you, but I couldn't understand – I wish you'd told me more.'

Varius gave a noncommittal nod. Marcus had moved towards him but he sat down, opposite Faustus, looking composed and ready to be helpful.

'I don't know how much you've already been told,' he said.

'Everything,' interposed Marcus. He was distressed.

'Well, don't repeat it. If there's still any doubt over it I shouldn't be prompted, I suppose.' He had not turned his eyes back to Marcus and he went on, dispassionately, 'We already believed Leo and Clodia had been assassinated. My wife was killed in mistake for Marcus. The poison came from the palace, so I sent Marcus away, he will have told you where. It was all I could see to do. The following day I tried to tell you, but I was arrested.'

He stopped, folding his arms. He felt as though this ought to be enough, even though he knew it wouldn't be.

Faustus asked, wearily shoving back his hair, 'What happened after you were arrested? That confession, did they use force to get that out of you?'

Varius looked startled and slightly amused. 'What? No. That wouldn't have been necessary. I suppose they thought it was easier just to write it themselves.'

'But it would have come out that it was a forgery.'

Varius made an involuntary, scoffing little grimace. 'I don't think so. Probably I wouldn't have challenged it anyway—' and suddenly he jumped in his seat and a look of horror shook his face. His fists were clenched. He said, 'I'm going to write down these names and addresses – please, make sure they're all right. Surely there wouldn't be any point now, there hasn't been time, but—'

'What has this to do with—?'

'Will you do it?' demanded Varius.

'Yes,' said Faustus. Varius shivered and fell still. 'But why are they in danger?'

'Oh . . .' Varius shook his head dismissively, calm again though uncomfortable. 'Gabinius threatened to have them killed. I've only recently been returned to the prison. For much of the time I was in Gabinius' house.'

'Gabinius,' repeated Faustus. 'Why?' He was starting to feel better, in control again, but Varius had begun to look obviously cagey and nervous.

'So I would tell him where Marcus was,' he said unwillingly.

'And it was to prevent that that you tried to commit suicide?'

Marcus was appalled. 'What?' he whispered. 'Varius, you didn't, did you?'

Varius scowled, glanced resentfully at Faustus, and made another evasive gesture, embarrassed this time. His body seemed to close protectively on itself. 'Seemed like – it seemed – sensible,' he muttered.

'Sensible?' Marcus blinked. Shocked tears had come into his eyes. 'I'm so sorry—'

'It was political,' said Varius a little more clearly. He looked up and manufactured a flat, brief smile. 'It wasn't your fault. I told you that before. Never mind about it.' And he turned away from Marcus again. He drew himself up in the chair and asked Faustus resolutely, 'Is Lady Novia in Rome?'

'Makaria? Yes, she's about.' She was still staying in the palace, because of the memorial ceremony – she had been wonderful—

'I think she should be here, now.'

At his tone, Faustus felt the confidence he'd been gathering back drain coldly away. He whispered, pleading, 'Makaria?'

Tulliola had seen the change in his face. She said sorrowfully, 'Oh – we could leave her alone until the morning.'

Faustus seemed not to have heard her, he continued to stare at Varius, beseeching. 'Oh, no, you must be wrong, I can't bear it,' he murmured. But at once it struck him – because of *me, my* fault, and he found that the guilt was so fluent, so well prepared and certain, that he knew about hers, knew it was true because it was his fault. She had never liked – he flinched – she had even *hated* Leo, because he laughed at her – he used to tease her about getting married – or was that all? He didn't know. But it wouldn't really have been Leo, he knew, or Marcus: it was him, because of her mother, the divorce – because of him. He

542

didn't really know anything about her, plainly, the poor little— He'd never had any reason to think he knew her, even before this.

Then suddenly he shook himself, and said roughly, 'No, it can't wait. Tulliola, would you tell Alexion to go?'

Sighing, Tulliola went to the door to speak to the slave, and this time the movement woke Una, and she opened her eyes with a pang of confused anxiety for Marcus. She looked, for a bewildered moment, at the embroidered dragonflies on the cloth beneath her cheek. She had not exactly forgotten where she was, but she could hardly believe she had been asleep in the Emperor's rooms. She pulled herself up on the couch, and saw a man, haggard and yet younger than she had expected, who must be Varius, sitting reasonably across the desk from Faustus, despite the effort it took, as if he was not steeped to the bones in distrust and wariness.

Marcus had been lingering unhappily nearby, but he retreated now, sat beside her again.

Makaria came, hunched and irritable, but without the staggering, helpless look of a body under the immediate shock of wakefulness; she must have woken earlier, with all the noise. 'What's happened, are you all right, Daddy?' she began, and stopped, seeing all the people there, seeing Varius first, then Marcus. She was alone at the far end of the room, and everyone looked that way, as if the space around her was a stage. She said, 'What's wrong?'

Faustus got up heavily and went to her. 'Well, there's some very *good* news, Makaria. Marcus is all right.'

'Good,' she said, blankly.

'His mind, I mean. He shouldn't ever have been in the Galenian.'

Makaria looked quickly from Marcus to Varius. She lowered her voice confidentially as she spoke to Faustus. 'How do you know?'

'I'm fine, Makaria,' said Marcus quietly.

Makaria stared at him, and her face broke slowly into a smile. 'Marcus!' she exclaimed.

Varius had been unable to keep his eyes on her, he looked at the top of the desk and said with slow care, 'My wife was poisoned by sweets that Lady Novia gave to Marcus.'

'What— those sweets?' Makaria blinked. 'But of course she wasn't.' She frowned with dawning alarm. She said, again in a suspicious undertone, 'Daddy, why is he allowed to – what are all these people doing here?'

Varius forced himself to stand up and face her. 'I'm sorry, your Majesty. She was the one who stopped me from reaching you. And I was arrested immediately after I saw her.'

'Well—' Makaria shook her head, 'Yes, I suppose, but what about it?'

Faustus asked gently, 'Have you been in contact with Gabinius – for any reason?'

'Gabinius? He's repellent, why would I want to talk to him?' Makaria looked briefly relieved, almost cheerful, as if she felt herself on safer ground, but then it was gone. 'What are you saying? That I'd – that I tried to hurt Marcus?'

Varius said, 'And Leo, and Clodia.'

'Well, this is ludicrous,' observed Makaria, with seeming confidence, waiting for somebody to agree. But Faustus looked away and everyone else seemed to withdraw their eyes from her, one by one. Now, and quite suddenly, colour dropped out of her face and it turned stiff and old with terror. She had to clutch something or fall, and there was nothing but Faustus to clutch at: 'Daddy! You can't *possibly*, you know, you *know*—'

'Oh, I don't know, Makaria, dear . . .' Faustus murmured, almost apologising, he never called her anything like that, and he felt so sorry, so sorry for her.

Makaria reeled away from him, tottered towards Marcus. 'But none of it – Marcus, you don't really think I'd ever do anything like that? Those sweets – you *like* them – because I was worried about you, I was going to ask you to come out to Greece. And what – I had Varius arrested? I *didn't*. Of course I didn't think he should be there, I didn't stop Tullia calling—'

'Makaria,' began Tulliola, with patient compassion; but

then she could not seem to hold it; anger lit her face again, the second time Varius had seen it happen. 'If I'd realised what would happen to Varius, I'd have stopped *you*. I knew I was right about him, I was just such a coward. I should never have let myself be so scared of you.'

Makaria was gazing at Marcus and had barely looked at Tulliola. Then she turned her head slowly, as Varius nodded brusquely, confirming what Tulliola had said.

'Why are you saying that?' she asked.

'Oh, Makaria . . .' said Faustus again.

'But that isn't right – what are you trying to do?' Tulliola turned away from her sadly, but Makaria gasped. 'It's her. I don't even know what this is, but it's *her*, Daddy—'

'Oh,' said Tulliola, upset, 'don't make it worse—'

Still curled against the arm of the couch, Una sat up; she rubbed her hands across her face to scrub the tiredness out, concentrating, trying to be absolutely sure, before she got up and murmured to Marcus, 'That's true.'

Marcus flinched with surprise, forgot to look at Makaria or Tulliola for staring at her. It was pointless to say, 'Are you sure?' He knew she was.

And Varius hadn't looked at the pale girl properly before, and he was shaken to see now that she looked as certain as if she'd been there in the Imperial office, listening. 'Who are you?' he demanded. 'What do you mean?'

He saw also that Marcus believed her, and not only Marcus but the other boy too, and, strangest of all, Cleomenes.

Marcus looked at Tulliola and muttered as if dreaming, 'You could have done. I forgot. You came in after Makaria gave me the sweets. You told me to go to my uncle, you didn't come with me. You could have done it then.'

He had once wanted to see her surprised: at first it hardly seemed to show. She frowned, but her milky forehead was so pliant, like a child's, that it did not crease, her smooth dark eyebrows moved together, that was all. She gave a startled, hurt little laugh. 'Of course I couldn't, Marcus, please – I know you're upset – this is all so horrible—'

545

Varius started again, and looked wildly at Marcus, an unmasked look for the first time. He choked, 'I told her I knew you were alive.' He took a step towards Tulliola and then backed away from her, unsteady with revulsion, and anger with himself, and rage, and grief. 'That's why you were there to meet me, wasn't it? You worked so hard to get it out of me. And you told Lady Novia, I thought that was what did it— but it was *you, I* told you.'

Faustus gazed, baffled. 'Why didn't you ever tell me about this?'

'Because *Makaria*—' insisted Tulliola. 'I didn't know it was true – I trusted the vigiles, why shouldn't I? And *Makaria*—'

Varius hadn't listened to any of this: 'You *talked* about her. All that about how sorry you were – when you'd *killed* her,' and Tulliola was retreating timorously, frightened of him, towards her husband, but Faustus said slowly, 'You got up before I did – who were you talking to? And you suggested the Galenian . . .'

'Titus!'

'Why did you marry me?'

'Oh, Titus. You can't ask me that.' And indeed, he thought, it was unfair, a stupid question. Look at her, why did he think she had married him? Still, she moaned. 'After all I've *done* for you; I *love* you.'

Little twists of outrage and horror were appearing in her face. They did not make her less beautiful; it seemed that nothing could. Her eyes shone, lovely as seals' or giraffes' eyes, the lashes, heavy and soft as black feathers, glittered with tears.

Faustus looked at these things and went to Makaria, as quickly as he could, and closed his arms round her, shielding her, as if Tulliola might have sprung at her or shot her. 'Oh, my darling, I'm so sorry, please try and forgive me – I'm so sorry—'

'How could you?' stuttered Makaria, stiff in his arms, shaking.

'I'm so sorry – I'm so sorry—'

Tulliola began to shriek and cry.

Faustus did not let go of Makaria. He said into the room – he did not need to look around for someone to instruct: 'Get her away. Make sure she is well treated. But get her away from here, right now.'

It was done surprisingly quickly and ruthlessly, as if it had been done before, although they could all hear Tulliola still calling out and sobbing in the corridor, for what seemed like a long time.

Makaria drooped at last against Faustus, trying to breathe. Faustus hoped she was having to forgive him by default, for she had no strength to march coldly away, she had to let someone comfort her. He could feel betrayal and anguish infiltrating him, like the first shivers of illness, enfeebling his muscles and wrinkling his skin; he could guess, already, that he would not really get over this. But Makaria was all right, that was the main thing. Relief was the main thing. He really was relieved.

Varius crossed deliberately to the far side of the room, as far from the others as possible, fell into a chair there. He buried his face in his hands for a moment, and then lifted it, observant and collected again.

Later, mastering himself, Faustus mumbled, 'Right. Varius, we'll talk again later, but is there anything we can do for you right now?'

Varius stood up. 'Yes. I need to see my parents.'

'Of course, I'll arrange it,' said Makaria, grimly wiping her face and driving her shoulders back. 'There's a long-dictor in the blue study.'

Varius felt and suppressed a wary reluctance to go with her. As he reached the door, Marcus started after him, feeling there was something they must say, it was very important, even if he didn't know what it was. 'Varius,' he said again, pained.

Abruptly Varius turned, and dropped a hand onto Marcus' shoulder: affectionately, but also pushing him back. 'Look,' he said, his voice harsh with the need not to shake. 'I can't believe you're all right. It's wonderful; and

547

I'll want to talk to you. And thank you, because I suppose you came back because of me. I don't know how you can have managed it, I'll want you to tell me that, and yes, I suppose I'll tell you – what I've been doing. But I can't yet. Don't worry about me, I'm all right, I just can't see you yet, that's all.'

He lifted his hand and let it fall back again, a kind of pat – and went out of the room.

And later still, when Cleomenes was gone, too, Faustus thought, there's no going back to bed now, not to *that* bed, not after this. He said, 'Come on, Marcus, there's more you need to tell me. We'd better get this sorted out now,' and hurried him out.

Una and Sulien waited in the darkened morning room. The slaves came, promising bedrooms and baths, and tried to urge them away, which made them feel uncomfortable and tainted, but they didn't want to leave until Marcus came back. They tried to talk to each other, about how strange it was to be there, and of what they would do now, but they were too tired, they seemed to have been tired for weeks. Una lay back again, without knowing it, on the embroidered couch. Sulien spilled down from his chair onto the silk carpet, pillowed his head on the seat, on his folded arms.

Marcus came and kissed Una's cheek through her hair. She jerked and gave a little cry of shock as she woke, but kissed him back the next second, and they laughed. He said, half-lifting her up in his arms, 'Come on, you can't sleep the whole night there.'

'It's morning really, isn't it?' She sat up, and saw that the sky was indeed a yellow-tinged grey. 'Where's Sulien?'

'I've already found him a room. I came back for you, I wanted – we haven't been on our own.'

They went out into the passage, where the walls were painted with golden trees, and the long carpet was dyed with cinnabar and malachite.

'I don't really want to sleep in the palace, it's horrible,' she said vaguely.

'I know,' said Marcus sadly. 'I never liked it when we had to come here.'

'Didn't you?' she asked, and then, looking at him curiously, 'What's wrong?'

'Nothing's wrong. It's good, I hope.'

She understood. 'Oh,' she said quietly. 'The Emperor.'

He sighed, silently promising himself and her: it's still not for a long time. Even though his uncle had looked so much older, he would recover – it was still a very long time. 'Yes, he's changed his will.'

'And you're his heir?'

Marcus nodded. 'And you're free, of course, and Sulien. I've told him.'

Una was silent, running her fingers pensively back and forth over his, frowning. She was too tired, perhaps, to think what it meant. She was conscious of the slaves in the palace, waking in their quarters, whisking away in the corridors before they could be seen, like mice. How was she different now, what was she?

'And the reward,' added Marcus, 'But it's my uncle's money, not mine – because he promised and you did a lot more than just tell them where I was, of course. I thought you should know that, because . . .'

She nodded. 'Thank you – yes—' And they looked at each other, almost as if these things had made them sad, and they kissed again.

'And Dama?' said Una suddenly.

'Dama? I don't know – was he there? I didn't realise. I'll try.'

Una remembered – they had never been in the room together; Marcus couldn't have understood what was happening when the lights went out on the sanctuary gardens. Poor Dama – she should have thought of him more these last hours. And she all but forgot about him again now, and that they were in the palace, and everything Marcus had just told her, because they held each other again, not sadly at all now, this time she thought the warmth was like a liquid, a syrup; without meaning to she might drink it all and he would have nothing left, but she couldn't help it.

'No. Wait,' she said, drawing back. 'You're not safe, what about Drusus Novius? Is he in the palace?'

'No.'

'Well, bring him here. I'm sure she was thinking of him, and Lucius – I can see what it was now. He didn't want to have to think, but when we told him he almost knew Drusus must be part of it. That's why he wouldn't help us.'

'Uncle Lucius?'

Una had to explain. He was so incredulous that it was some time before they came back to Drusus. At last Marcus told her, 'My uncle will have the Senate approve it tomorrow. But part of it is that Drusus doesn't succeed – even if anything happens to me.'

'What, then, he suspects?'

'Not exactly. He says it's so no one can use Drusus as a figurehead – but like Uncle Lucius, I suppose: he doesn't want to find out.'

'What – and nor do you? You can't just leave it at that; it's wrong and it's too dangerous. Get him here.'

Marcus shook his head. 'I *can't*. Look, even if it's true, he can't do anything to me now. There's nothing to gain and it would be far too dangerous for him. And after tonight – and with my father dead, it's so hard on my uncle, Una, I don't think he could bear it. It seems like – there's so few of us left.'

Una muttered disapprovingly, 'This is a mistake,' but she would convince him he was wrong after she'd slept properly, it was too tiring now.

'I can't believe it about Uncle Lucius,' said Marcus again. 'I don't know what to do about it. Maybe nothing. I suppose I can't tell Uncle Titus, it would be horrible for him to find out now.' He shook his head. 'But then the curse hasn't hit for decades. I don't know if that's reassuring or not. We must be about due.'

'Well, you have to think,' said Una. 'All that has to

happen is a Novian wife passes off her boyfriend's baby as her husband's, and the curse doesn't have anywhere to go.'

'And I wouldn't be a Novian, and I shouldn't be Emperor at all.' They grinned.

'You'd probably get away with it. There still wouldn't be much competition.'

'Oh, no, no, I swear, I couldn't live with myself, I would give up the whole thing. And you and I – we would – we would go and live on an island, or something.'

'I don't know: if you're not a Novian, and I'm – well, I might be able to do better, now.'

But it hurt a little, joking like this. She thought of Ziye, and Tobias, and Dama again.

'Still,' he said softly, 'do you think there's a chance?'

'No, not really. Those pictures in the windows outside, they all look like you. Except for your hair.' She remembered it as mere stubble; she stroked it.

He opened the door of a bedroom, all coppery-gold and dusty green, the bed almost too huge to be a bed. His arms were round her and she remembered the glimpse of his back, felt at once desire and debilitating nervousness, fear of her own clothes coming off – as sometimes skin confuses heat and cold, and fingertips in hot water seem pricked with splinters of ice. 'I can't, you know – not yet, I still – it's just—'

'Shh,' he said. 'Do you think I'm complaining? I thought I was never going to see you again.'

And then they stumbled into the room, dropped one after the other onto the shimmering bedspread as if they had both been killed where they stood, and barely had time to wind themselves close together before they fell asleep in their clothes.

Gabinius said no one really needed more than six hours' sleep, and that was being generous. He had trained himself to do with less and less. He liked being awake, he thought of it almost as a sport at which he excelled. Fat though he was, he considered his body must be good for something to keep going so much longer than other people's. So when one of the slaves woke him before dawn and called him to the longdictor, of course it meant something was wrong, but it wasn't exceptional. Better, always, to do without sleep than not to know what was happening.

His home office was, of course, close to his bedroom, separated only by the length of a breakfast room, so that he did not wake his wife, and so he wasn't distracted by the thought of her being able to hear what he said.

He listened to the longdictor and stiffened with consternation and disbelief, for he had thought this was, *at last*, dealt with.

'Shut up,' he said. The man was telling him about a dead agent of his in Marcus' room, which was irrelevant for the moment; there were only two more things he needed from this conversation: 'When did this happen and how long before he's normal?'

He called Laevinus. 'I assume you know what's happened. It's that centurion, isn't it?' he said. He restrained himself, he had already raged at Laevinus, 'How could you be so incompetent? You should have known *exactly* who was going to be there, and not just if things went as planned!' It would be redundant to go over it again.

And he had said much the same things to Tulliola, but more gently, because she was so beautiful.

Laevinus' voice was tight. 'We're doing it, but you must remember he knows that. He's avoiding his house, and we found his car this afternoon on the Aventine.'

'Then go after his friends – his relatives. He must have somewhere to go, he's got twelve hours to wait, if he's thinking of proving anything.'

'We are doing it.'

Gabinius turned off the longdictor, feeling an unfamiliar waft of foreboding. Laevinus was afraid, but not afraid of him, not really.

Gabinius sometimes said, as a joke, that there was nothing, really, nothing in the whole Empire, that wouldn't be done better if he was the one to do it. And it was part of the joke that he really meant it. He meant, genially: look how conceited I am, but it's true.

He contacted Renatus and arranged that they would meet, *at once*, at the vigile headquarters, so he could see exactly what they were doing – they'd spent enough of his money. Renatus sounded reluctant, and that worried him – if the bastards thought they could wash their hands of it now . . .

Still, there was time; they'd handled him turning up in the Forum. It could still be fixed.

But he was barely dressed when he had to go to the longdictor again: Tulliola, a scared little whisper: 'He's here. I've got to go.'

'What?'

'He's got here.'

'*Already*?'

'I tried to have him stopped, of course – there wasn't time. They're bringing Varius.'

Gabinius whispered, with a kind of superstitious bewilderment: 'It hasn't even been an hour—' But he turned off the longdictor. She didn't need his help, even if he'd had a way of helping her. He was sure Varius didn't know she was involved.

He stood, his lips pursed, considering reluctantly: how much was there to gain if Varius were removed, and could it be done in time? He hesitated, and tried Renatus again, asked, with more tentativeness than was usual for him: 'About Varius. Can we reach anyone in the prison to—'

This time Renatus made no secret of wanting to get rid of him. 'Who do you think is going to do it now?' he snarled. And the line went dead. That, almost more than the words, actually shocked Gabinius.

He leaned on his desk as if he was trying to push it across the room, swearing. He had not been stupid, he had thought what he must do if such a time ever came, he always had money ready. But it was so hard to learn how to give up: optimism, instinctive and ruthless, slowed him down. He still felt that everything could be solved with energy and attention. He looked around at the house and thought, stay, go to trial, even; last it out, it's only going to be a question of money.

But no, no, he told himself. When such a time comes you have to recognise it. He laid his head down on the desk, only for the length of a breath, he could not remember ever doing that before. Of course he had been trying to protect his own empire, of course he wanted to get closer to the Senate – but the future, the future. Fury with Rome, and pity for it overwhelmed him. It would die, it would die, nobody cared about it any more.

He called the slave back. 'Pack a bag for me and have the car brought round.'

Despite everything he felt a little glum relief about Varius. He'd really hoped there might be a way of keeping him alive, and he'd felt dishonest and regretful when it had seemed impossible. He didn't want people to die unnecessarily. And it was more than that: of course he knew Varius would never precisely forgive him, but Gabinius had hoped somehow that over time, as he got older, he would at least develop more of an idea of how things actually worked. And he liked to think he was giving Varius the chance to do that.

He padded quickly to the safe in his bare feet and took everything.

He woke Helvia gently. 'I've had an urgent call, I'm going up to Comum. I'll be a couple of days.'

She stared up at him, motionless, and didn't comment. She'd guessed, he thought, she was too scared to say anything, which seemed suddenly irritating. Well, never mind. With a sudden pang of tenderness he wanted to go and say goodbye to his children, but he would not have done that if this had really been a business trip; there was no point worrying them. They would be better off without him for a while, but not forever; he would bring them out to him when he was settled. Still, he stood on the landing for a moment, looking wistfully up the stairs that led to their rooms, before he lifted his two cases and went down.

He left the chauffeur standing, bewildered, by the steps of

his house. He woke the peacocks as he drove through the gates, and they cried out. It was a long time since he'd driven anywhere himself, and perhaps he'd been slimmer then, for it felt awkward. He wasn't going to Comum of course, he pushed doggedly along towards the coast, contemplating his body with annoyance; it was going to be so hard to blend in, looking like this. Terranova, he thought, a lot of space. Perhaps even the Nionian side would be safer, he believed there were places where Roman values had taken root – enough for him to feel at home.

He stopped at Ostia and hurried to the dock. He unlocked the gate on the gangway to his pleasure boat, and carried the cases of money and clothes down onto the deck, let them fall on the plush seats in the cabin. He started the engine, it was strong, he was more used to this than driving the car. And it was a good boat, of course, he could go a long way fast.

But he'd barely begun to move in the glittering black water when a pair of vigile boats darted out and cut him off, and a team on the jetty were shouting for him to stop, to come out, they were aiming their guns at him. He cursed Laevinus and Renatus, and the others who'd abandoned him. He swore to himself in a long torrent, almost despairing and yet not quite, even now.

He turned off the engine, and sidled out slowly, his hands spread wide, but they shot him anyway. The first bullets buried themselves in the heavy armour of his flesh, so that he had time to feel terrible surprise, before two at once broke through his skull, and knocked him overboard into the sea.

[XXIV]

THE SIBYL, THE PAINTBRUSH
AND THE FIELD OF MARS

i

VARIUS

Varius walked through Rome. It was December, but today the cold air was blue and glassy, and within it the city felt strangely delicate and pure. Varius noticed everything as if it were very fine-beaten, very thin, and had even to be looked at carefully – carefully but not slowly. As he had in the flat, on the day of his arrest, he felt reluctant to let his eyes settle on anything for long. He walked partly so that later he would be tired and, with luck, would sleep, but also because he could, to show how there was nothing to stop him.

His father had gone to the flat for him to collect some of his clothes and other belongings. Varius still couldn't face it; as he could not yet face seeing Marcus, or Gemella's parents and Rosa, who would have to be involved when it finally came to packing up properly and deciding what to do with Gemella's things. But he would do it soon; he was aware that some decisions were beginning to make themselves; he could already picture certain possessions of Gemella's that he knew he would keep, at least for now; others that would go into boxes even if he didn't know yet where the boxes would go.

He had meant to tell his parents as little as possible, to spare them, and had ended by telling them all of it. His mother harried at the vague places he'd tried to leave, and when he attempted to think of actual lies his mind went blank, as though it all could have happened only one way. It didn't occur to him that this might have been a good thing. He was still irritated with himself about it; he thought he should have been more resolute and inventive. He'd been staying with his parents since arriving at their house from the palace, before dawn, to their cries of amazement and relief.

Since then his father had taken to having long, careful conversations with him about foreign policy, trying to disguise a mute, imploring look as he spoke, offering him monologues on the status of the Aztecs, questions on the direction Sina might take if there was a war, as if these things were nourishing, like baby food, like mashed-up apples or carrots. And his mother followed him about, talked to him, cooked for him, fussed about his broken tooth until he obediently went and got it fixed although he had almost stopped noticing it – never, in fact, left him alone. In a fond way he was beginning to find it tiresome; it was another reason to get out into the air. He wouldn't stay much longer.

He'd heard the afternoon following his return that Gabinius was dead.

He crossed the Field of Mars. If he wanted he could walk out of the city; he could leave the country. But when he thought of that he heard Gabinius encouraging him to take a holiday and felt disdainful and obstinate, and unable to do anything that looked like taking his advice.

And yet he would have to. He still had the money Gabinius had given him. He had assumed and hoped that someone would confiscate it, but, though the lawyers that were still scouring over everything had been surprisingly slow to believe that he hadn't embezzled it from Marcus, it seemed that it did belong to him. Well then, he would have to get rid of it, it would be impossible – sickening – to live off something gained in such a way. He didn't want anything to do with it, but still it was a fact, a duty. And the logical thing was to spend it on the slave clinic, even if he felt constricted by the fact that Gabinius had guessed he might do that – it was stupid, he'd just have to get over it. Even aside from the money, the clinic probably depended on him now if it was ever to exist, the plans had slipped so far since Leo and Clodia's deaths and his own imprisonment. Not just yet, he couldn't do it yet – but he would have to do something eventually. He knew there might be jobs for him in the Golden House; he didn't want them.

He did not feel as he wanted to about Gabinius' death. He wanted to be brutally, unrepentantly glad, and felt instead uneasy. He told himself it was because there hadn't been a trial – he remembered what Cleomenes had said when he'd come round in the prison hospital – it wasn't justice, and Gabinius would never now explain. But really he knew there was nothing else he wanted to hear Gabinius say, and in honesty he was thankful about the trial; he didn't want to go over his part in the business again. Gabinius was punished; he was dead – what more did Varius want?

He wanted not to think that he might in any way, even slightly, regret Gabinius' death just for its own sake, just because they'd had those conversations. How could that be possible when Varius knew what he'd done and been prepared to do, and had never stopped hating him? It made no sense; he would almost have preferred to believe that he was bloodthirstily angry that Gabinius hadn't suffered more.

He went up the Janiculum hill. He did not particularly want to be alive; he was, at best, more or less willing. Nevertheless, he was prepared to meet Cleomenes today and thank him for saving his life, or for his part in it, on behalf of a possible future self who might really be glad about it.

The Tiber glittered as if it were clean. Varius looked down at it for too long and cold tears dazzled in his eyes. He was afraid of all this, all this wandering around Rome and gradually doing the things he couldn't face and beginning to contemplate planning the clinic, afraid he might come to trust it all too much and forget that it would not return Gemella. He was creeping into a dead end; when he started living like a normal person again, *then* it would be the clearer that she could have been there, he'd lost her. So what was the good of it?

Nevertheless, it was early, there were still two hours before he was due to see Cleomenes. So far these walks had always been unplanned and aimless, but it occurred to him now that there was something useful he could do at the same time. He would not want to live in the flat again; he would have to start looking around for other places where he might live. He folded his arms against the cold, and walked down from the Janiculum towards Transtiberina and the Aemilian bridge, and the plane trees there.

ii

SULIEN

Palben was stolidly pleased with the money they gave him with the car, and waved off their apologies, but he seemed faintly suspicious of Marcus now. He looked uneasily at the guards that accompanied Marcus and muttered: 'You are the Emperor's – not brother, I can't remember – you are related to each other? But what were you doing here?'

Marcus tried to tell him, but he couldn't gauge how much Latin Palben actually knew and after a minute Palben frowned and gave up trying to understand. 'There has been trouble?'

'Yes.'

Palben nodded. 'I thought it.' He stepped closer to lower his voice, and jerked his head subtly towards the mountains. 'They are very quiet.'

They were worried by that, of course.

The peaks were whiter than they had been, and a little snow was flying between the bare trees. The guards were easy-going, that was why Marcus had chosen them. They weren't supposed to let Marcus out of their sight, but they did. Their presence all the way hadn't been as burdensome as Una and Sulien had expected, but Sulien thought, how

559

could you cope with that sort of thing, all the time? For the moment Una didn't care, she hardly noticed them, but it was good and strange to be away from them, in uncrowded space again.

Dama was an unsettling presence in the woods, it was as if he was a little way ahead of them, showing the way as he had the day they arrived. Una tried to hope they might find him safe in the camp, though really she did not believe there was much chance he would have come back. And if he had not, she was afraid that when Delir heard what had happened he would think Dama was dead, and then she might begin to think it herself. And if he was there, then he would see her with Marcus, and what would he feel, what could they say to each other?

Marcus muttered, 'I wish . . . Just throwing money around after making things so difficult – I wish I could be a bit more use than that.'

'Money's all right. Better than nothing,' said Una. It wasn't really Palben Marcus was thinking of. He would have liked to be able to go to Delir and say, you don't have to worry any more, you're all safe now. And he had thought it would be easy, that after everything, Faustus would have to understand that Delir wasn't, or shouldn't be, a criminal.

But Faustus had said solemnly, 'Listen, Marcus. A pardon for everything he's done is one thing. And if that was all I wouldn't hesitate – but is he likely to stop doing it?'

Marcus was dismayed.

Faustus sighed. 'Of *course* I'm not going to send anyone charging in after him. I do understand, I believe what you say about him. But I can't just give him a licence to do anything he wants, much less to whoever might happen to be with him. Some of them might not even be slaves. You just don't know what they've done – *he* may not know. And even if you could vouch for everyone who was there with you, you said new people arrive all the time . . .'

'But – he can't stop,' said Marcus quietly. 'He has to carry on. I want there to be somewhere for people to go. I want to help him.'

They were in the green Imperial office, among the painted vines and flowering trees. Faustus nodded.

'I know. And I want you to be Emperor, I wanted Leo to be. I know what you're planning to do. But I'm not going to do it, I'm not going to throw everything up in the air, I'm not . . .' He sighed and was silent for so long that Marcus almost wondered if he'd forgotten what they were talking about. 'I'm not made for it. And as long as this is an ongoing crime . . .'

But however worried and sorry they were because of this, Marcus and Una could not stop smiling at each other, dazed and weak, and almost impervious to everything.

'These poor people, you're going to make them ill,' Sulien had told them in Athabia. He was tense, they couldn't get to the gorge fast enough for him.

A week before, he had seen Tancorix.

Glycon had handled it all; he had been gentle and discreet; it was quite impossible to tell how deplorable he found the whole business. It irritated Sulien, while this process was going on, that such gentleness should be necessary, that Tancorix should have to be wooed into telling the truth. Glycon had found her living in Novomagius, in Germany, with her husband. He talked to her soothingly: she had only to say what had really happened, whatever that might have been, let him write it up, sign it. A judge would look at it, nothing would happen to her. Although normally her husband or father should supervise and represent her, that could be dispensed with, if that was what she wanted, her family need not know anything about it.

'All right,' she said, startling Glycon. 'Fine. I'll come.'

'What do you mean? There's no need for you to leave home.'

'I'll have to come and see Sulien,' she said combatively.

'No, that's not necessary at all.'

'If I can't see him I'm not doing it.'

'But we can't have a situation where it seems as if he's intimidating you.'

Tancorix was surprised. 'But he's younger than me,' she explained, childishly.

So she'd come to Rome, and Sulien met her in a judge's rooms on the Capitoline hill.

She did not look like a wife. She almost looked younger than she had when he'd last seen her, a year or so closer to her sullen, thirteen-year-old self. There seemed to be a kind of film over her skin and yellow hair, a faint pastiness and oiliness; the hair was drawn back and the comb-tracks showed in it. For a moment he thought she was getting just slightly dumpy again, too, and then saw with a sudden blow of realisation and alarm, what was still almost hidden, what anyone without a medical eye would probably have missed. 'Don't worry,' she said sourly, seeing him look, and glowering, though not at him. 'Perfectly legitimate. Not your problem.'

And yet all the fresh colour was still there, really, withheld and lurking. Already Sulien began to feel sorry for her.

And she was trembling, but she raised her head with a sort of fragile bravado. 'Well,' she said, unnecessarily loudly, 'There you are. I might as well say. I didn't – tell my parents you'd raped me. Well, it was pretty obvious what we'd been doing, wasn't it? My mother did it to punish us. Or not us so much, she said it was my father's fault because of the way he treated you. She said she'd trusted him with me, and this was what happened, because he let you do whatever you liked, because he cared about you more than me.'

At this they looked at each other, both hurt and abandoned, mirroring each other. Sulien bowed his head, patiently. He just had to get through this. When he was out of the room, when she'd signed the paper, it would go away. Tancorix continued, 'She locked me in her room after – before they arrested you. She kept locking me in places, while she set things up with Epimachus.'

'Oh,' said Sulien.

Tancorix looked exasperated. 'No. Don't just say "oh" as if that made all the difference. You can't always be so *soft* on people, Sulien. Yes, she kept locking me up, but they were going to *crucify* you. Don't you think I could have tried a bit harder?'

'Well, I don't know,' said Sulien weakly.

'My father didn't want it to happen. If I'd ganged up with him he might have done something about you. It didn't really occur to me. I kept sort of pleading, but just in the same way as I kept crying, I didn't really expect anything to come of it. I was just so *embarrassed*, I felt as though whatever happened, there was nothing I could do about it. I could have shouted out of a window and told someone. But I'd really got the idea no one could know, the world would just end – I just caved in. I didn't do anything properly. I was as bad as him.'

'Did he never even say anything?' asked Sulien, in a whisper.

'He just wanted an easy life,' said Tancorix bitterly.

'Well, he had more chances than you. And you're here now, you're different.'

Tancorix gave a startled little gasp, and rolled her eyes in apparent scorn, although they were sparking with tears. 'Well – thank you – you are completely – ridiculous, but that's very nice of you.' She gulped, and composed herself with a little shake. 'Anyway, well done for getting out, naturally I was very pleased about that.'

She'd been married with punitive speed, and as far away as possible, beyond reach of association. Epimachus was an old acquaintance of Catavignus' who'd expressed an interest months before, but Prisca had thought Novomagius too far off for Tancorix, and Epimachus too old, until that day in London.

'What's it like?' asked Sulien softly.

Tancorix sighed, and gave a sophisticated shrug. Her face assumed an arch and weary look, which briefly revealed a little more of her beauty: 'Well, obviously it's just really *boring* and I hate it. It's provincial, it's cold. There's *this*,' she glared down at her waist, 'And I feel sick all the time. Obviously it goes without *saying* that I hate my husband.'

'How old is he?'

'Forty-one.'

It was about what he'd been expecting, but still his face fell with sympathy. His eyes dropped to her waist again and he thought, so *awful*; and if he'd withheld any speck of forgiveness from her so far he would have released it now.

'Well, *exactly*,' said Tancorix, amused, and despairing. 'He doesn't know about you, of course he doesn't know there was anybody. I did the thing with red ink on the sheets. My mother told me to.'

Glycon cleared his throat. She had lowered her voice, but only as a gesture. She was still very audible.

Unabashed, Tancorix turned gracefully to Glycon. 'This idea that no one finds out – I don't know how convinced I am by that. Realistically, how public does it have to be made?'

Glycon tried to restrain his annoyance. 'But your name was never mentioned publicly anyway. And as you have already admitted that—'

But Tancorix didn't even let him finish. She scowled violently, a scowl that seemed to involve her whole body. 'I don't care, I don't care, you can tell anyone you like! I don't *care* about these people, I don't *want* to protect my marriage!'

Sulien began to feel drawn in and worried. 'Look, you don't have to do anything much—'

'I want to!' She had become luminous and alarming with excitement. 'After all, it's only a question of the truth! My husband can make up his own mind; if he doesn't like it that's *great*. And as for my parents—'

Sulien shifted uneasily from foot to foot, for some reason feeling compelled to offer prudent advice: 'I know you're not happy, but you've got to be careful—'

'No,' she said, beaming, 'that's what I'm just noticing.'

'But when you get back—'

Tancorix sighed, wonderingly, 'I'm not going back. I didn't tell anyone I was coming. I was going to say I had to visit someone in Narbo, someone from school. But I didn't, I just came, I didn't know why.'

'But what will you do?'

She laughed. 'I don't know! Have a baby! See what happens after that!'

'But I don't want things to end up worse for you.'

'For heaven's sake,' exclaimed Tancorix, marvelling. 'Don't worry about what *I'm* going to do. People must just walk all over you, all the time.'

'Not really,' said Sulien suddenly, unexpectedly finding his voice unsteady. 'At least, I don't think so. I nearly killed some people.'

The nimbus of danger and triumph around, Tancorix retreated a little. She looked at him. 'You?' she asked, quietly. 'Do you mean the soldiers on the boat? Of course I heard about that.'

'No, at least, maybe that counts too—'

'No, it doesn't.'

'Then it was just chance I didn't.'

'I bet that's not true,' she said.

'It is.' For some reason he could not stop himself. 'And it just meant someone else had to do it instead, and I don't know where he is. And still, I couldn't really have helped this man, but he was closer to me than you are and staring at me and—' unconsciously he put two fingers to the side of his throat, 'and his mouth was filling up with blood. And I don't even – care exactly, but—'

'But you obviously do.'

'Well, yes, but he would have killed us, so I don't know why – well, I do know, but—'

Tancorix shook her head, confused. 'I don't know what you're talking about. But you're not *bad*, Sulien. Anyone can see that.'

Sulien sighed, and shook his head, but smiled at her cautiously: 'Well, thanks.' What exactly was he thanking her for? 'Thanks for doing this, I mean.'

'Well, you shouldn't have to thank me.' She gazed at him,

with unmistakable wistfulness. 'It's not really to the point, but I've missed you,' she remarked.

She didn't seem to expect an answer, and that was good, because he couldn't think of anything to say to that. He found he wanted to say he'd missed her, too, to make her feel better – but he had not, how could he have done? He didn't know why he'd told her about the man Dama had killed.

He was surprised afterwards at how slow the excitement and relief had been to hit him as he realised what had just happened: it had all gone, no one could come after him now; he could tell Delir. But at the time he felt primarily anxious. He wanted to get away from Tancorix, though he was startled and confused to find himself not only pitying but liking her again. He wanted urgently to see Lal.

The loose snowflakes made their slow way down, disappearing on the fast water and the wet grass. The slight path led up from the river, so that Sulien, Una and Marcus could see nothing but trees. But as they drew closer to the camp, Una began to frown and start ahead, and when they climbed down through the wood to the first ladder she whispered something— 'Oh, no.'

'What?' demanded Sulien, And he guessed, but didn't wait for her to tell him. He pushed in front to scramble and jump down the ladder, ran up the little shelf of planking to the camp.

No one was there.

Una and Marcus were following him, and they stumbled through the wreckage cast around the bottom of the gorge, stifled with dread that they would find bodies sprawled on the floors of the huts. But they did not, although in rage or desperation Tasius and the others had broken the camp to pieces, beaten in floors looking for hidden compartments, smashed the monitors that must have warned Delir and the rest that they were coming. The splintered wood had long been soaked, weeks had passed since this had been done; it might have been only hours after they'd left the camp to follow Marcus.

Marcus and Una turned in towards each other, helplessly, away from the devastation, and then looked at Sulien, and hid their faces again. Marcus gasped, 'I shouldn't ever have come here.' And Una thought – all the *work*. She hoped fervently now that Dama hadn't seen this.

Lal's patterned door swung coldly. Sulien sprang up to it, because it occurred to him, with the desperate conviction felt in dreams, that she would have written a letter for him, and although she would have hidden it, the agents wouldn't have been looking for letters, and he would find it at once. And although she could not have said clearly, in this letter, where she had gone, she would have encoded it somehow, or not even that, he would just read it and understand how to go after her.

But even if there could have been a letter it would have perished into unrecognisable wet rags; everything was sodden with the rain that had blown unchecked through the door for weeks, and there was a dismal smell of mould rising from the damp walls. And there had plainly been no time. He was at first appalled by how little she seemed to have taken with her. All her things – and he knew she'd loved them – seemed to be scattered about and ruined. He thought with horrible speed of her defenceless in the mountains, caught, interrogated, murdered.

No – he remembered the maps, Delir's plans – there had been packs in the monitor room to be grabbed in an emergency. And in fact she'd packed another bag when she'd meant to come with them.

But a drenched cherry-coloured dress lay curled on the floor, pitifully like an animal with wet fur lying dead by a road. She had been wearing it the day Tasius came to Athabia, the day he told her about the cross and Tancorix. The dress had been just as doused in rain then, but he could remember the warmth of her within it, as they clutched at each other. And he put his hand to his wrist, not to protect it against phantom spikes, but to try and hold her kiss there, on the pulse. 'Oh, Lal,' he said, aloud.

He touched the dress but felt the stagnant weight of it

and did not lift it. He was hurt even worse by the chips and slivers of glass that lay near the upturned desk – her forging things, wrecked. He bent over them, grieving; this was where he'd knelt before kissing her for the first time. He wanted something of hers to take with him, and in the end he found a paintbrush and a little ink bottle, intact on the floor, and picked them up delicately. But he let them lie in the palm of his hand for a while, and just stared at them.

Outside, Marcus and Una did find a kind of goodbye, a sign: above the other graffiti Tobias had written 'That Way', and ringed it with fierce arrows pointing in every direction, like the rays of a sun.

iii
DRUSUS

Faustus considered it out of the question for Tulliola to wait for her trial in an ordinary prison, so she was in a tiny, beautiful villa in the Campania, but heavily shut up there; she was not even allowed into the garden. The villa belonged to Faustus and Drusus knew why he had it: between his divorce and his second marriage he used to take women there. Tulliola might have been here with him herself, swimming with him, perhaps, in the little willow-fringed lake. Drusus scowled at the idea. He thought it was disgusting to send her there now.

She was sitting by the window, and the heavy curtains were outlined in squares of light. He didn't know why she'd got them shut; was that part of her incarceration, had Faustus been as cruel as that? Or perhaps she didn't want to be seen, did she have no heart even for looking out? That seemed more likely, judging by the change in her. The ivory clothes she was wearing were as beautiful as usual; out of habit she had even put on jewellery; but everything looked loose and crumpled, as if she'd slid into them in a slow stupor. The straight grace with which her body held itself up was gone; she would never have let anyone see her slumped despairingly forward as she was, her feet splayed limply under her chair.

And her hair was up, although in only a rough approximation of the smooth dark tower, and he was a little disappointed, for he liked uncoiling the length of it from its pristine height; he could never understand how she made it do that.

When he came into the room she started up, crying, '*Drusus* – you have to help me. You *will* help me—'

They rushed at each other, they were both in tears. 'They will hear—' she said once, but he answered, 'I don't care, I don't care,' kissing her desperately, as they broke down onto the carpet together. They inflicted small pains with teeth and fingernails, without design, gasping and sobbing, clawing at bare skin through clothes hurriedly pulled apart or pulled up, they never made it into full nakedness. It was fast and hopeless; he couldn't tell the pleasure when it came from the anguish that seemed gathered into his every muscle, only that whatever it was at last it would stop, and there would be emptiness and peace. And just before it happened he thought of an animal, lashing around when it was already mortally hurt, a fish jumping on a deck.

Afterwards, they sat shaking together on the floor, as if all the furniture had been destroyed by a bomb.

'You haven't said anything?' he asked her.

'No, of course not,' she whispered. She gripped his hands. 'You will get me out, Drusus.'

Drusus began to straighten his own clothes, and, after a moment, hers.

'What do you think I can do?' he asked quietly, pulling her neckline into place. A brooch fastening at her shoulder had ripped the white cloth a little, but he adjusted it, and the tear did not show.

'Tell Titus—'

He never liked to hear her mention his uncle. His mouth tightened. 'What? To forget about it? Of course I wish I could, but how can I?'

'*Convince* him, you've got to. I won't, I can't – I'm not going on trial. I'm not going to be executed. *Drusus*.'

She was crying once more. 'Hush,' he murmured, stroking her, letting her huddle against him, comforting her simply with the warmth of his body, until the tears left her quiet again.

She whispered, 'I heard about Gabinius.'

'He was stupid, he should have given himself up.'

'Why?' she asked, wiping her eyes. 'It would have come to the same thing. Maybe he decided it was better like that.'

'Maybe you're right,' he agreed.

Tulliola hesitated, and breathed into his chest, 'Or did you do it?'

Drusus said nothing. He went on stroking her hair.

She said just as softly as before, 'You got in, so some of the guards must be yours.'

'I was never here,' he told her emphatically.

'But exactly, so I can get out of the house, too, can't I, can't I? All I need is somewhere to go after that. I can vanish.' She hesitated again. 'We don't need to separate. You could come with me.'

'Tulliola, I'm sorry – it's impossible, it's too dangerous.'

Tulliola didn't move but her hand on his chest tensed, he could just feel her nails again. 'Then, *what are you going to do?* You cannot let this happen to me, you owe me—'

Drusus drew back from her a little. 'What do I owe you?' he asked quietly. 'What have I gained from this? I have less chance of being Emperor than I ever did before.'

Tulliola sat up, staring at him. 'But *I* took the risks, *I've* done everything. *For you*. Why am I the one paying for it, for things I've done *for you*?'

Drusus whispered, 'Everything is ruined, and it doesn't make any sense. I was *told*—'

'I *know*,' she said, groaning.

'She was so clear. I thought and thought if it was a trick, but she said – when there was no one else left—'

He remembered the state he had been in; he could feel it

coming back now: he'd already been obsessed with Tulliola, it had begun at her wedding and every day, as it got worse, he was the more wracked with his father's ridiculous secret, and with rage about it. Because, he told himself, that's always going to count against me, I can't ever make up for that. And yet he could not bring himself to give Lucius away – even if I did, he thought, it's too late, he's never going to be like Leo. And Leo's popularity seemed ostentatious and brazen to him, unnecessary. You don't need to smarm around like that, he would think, bitterly, every time Clodia found Leo another audience to entrance. You've already got what you want.

He did not always think of these things, or know why he felt so daily panicked, a breathless, scuttling, awful feeling. Sometimes he thought it was the madness starting. He didn't know if he believed in the Pythia, but he wanted someone to look at him and know what was wrong, someone had to tell him something or he thought he might die.

He had pictured Sibyls as always haggard and manic. In the dark, perched high on a spindly tripod, this one had been stately and plump, but still compelling, with wolf-like, yellow-green eyes in a round sallow face.

The relief that he'd felt at first, that his father hadn't after all spoiled everything for him! And then he was frightened, because it was as though she had answered the impossible thought that already kept circling back to him: that there *was* something he could do, his situation *could* be changed. He knew there were people who would want to help. Not everyone liked Leo. And this must mean it was going to happen, as all along until now he'd known it couldn't.

The Sibyl had said, all at once, before she could even have looked at his face through the fumes and recognised him, in a long loud drone, without pauses for breath, so at first it was hard to separate the words into sense:

When there is no one else left to take it you will have what you want it will be you the last one Novius it will come Emperor of Rome you.

571

And almost at once it had seemed to start coming true. He had been promised what he *wanted*. It was only a few weeks after his return from Delphi that he was alone with Tulliola by a fountain in the palace garden. 'How was Greece, Drusus? Did you see Makaria?' she'd asked serenely, smiling. And almost at once he'd found himself pouring out to her what the Sibyl had told him, finishing – nervously – because she frightened him a little back then, she was so effortlessly dignified, and a few years older than him: 'Of course – I just went out of curiosity, you know – for the experience. It was striking at the time, that's all, I'm sure it doesn't mean anything.'

And they had looked at each other in silence and then she had said, 'No. I'm sure it does,' so that he was not frightened at all any longer, he had known he could kiss her. She took the kiss coolly and without comment, and glided flawlessly away, but he knew he could go after her, he followed her up into a guest bedroom, where she met him with a frustrated excitement as violent as his own.

'And *have you told anyone*?' he asked her again now.

'*No*,' she cried, but with a jaggedness in her voice that he'd been expecting to hear, and understood. She would, if he couldn't help her, even if telling would do her no good.

'All right.' He pulled her back to him. He was smoothing her hair, trying to arrange it upwards, but he couldn't do anything with the subtle cords and pins, he didn't even know how to make a plait, although he had pulled the thick strands apart often enough.

A golden hairpin of hers lay on his knee. It was seven inches long, a sharp slender cone or spike, crowned with a pear of blue tourmaline held in a little circlet of gold teeth, above a row of tiny studded pearls and beads of lapis lazuli.

She had left it in his bedroom once, and he had never given it back to her or told her he had it; not from forgetfulness, but because he liked to have it. He had that at least, he would think, picturing her all too clearly in Faustus' bed. His jealousy sometimes confused him; it wasn't reasonable. He knew she didn't love Faustus, and he couldn't expect her to leave him, that would ruin everything. They were very careful. But he wished she wouldn't always look so placid. It was a strain on him, always, terrible – was it nothing at all for her, didn't it make any difference? When Faustus kissed her or laid his hand on her hip, he wanted her face to change – only for him, no one else would be able to see – just a flicker of disgust to show that she hated being touched by Faustus and wanted *him*, that it was torment to her to be made love to by anyone else. He was never sure she truly wanted anybody. He thought, wrongly in fact, that Faustus might have given the jewelled hairpin to her, and now *he* had it, and nobody knew. It was as if the little shaft of gold was a totem, and he believed it gave him power over her. And so it did.

'Oh,' she said, blankly, recognising it, 'you've got that.'

She must have thought at first that it had just come out of her hair, and then realised that it had been months, almost a year, since she'd seen it.

And then her eyelids lifted a little with doubt, and he whispered soothingly again, 'Hush,' and kissed her before she could worry any more, swallowing the cry she made when he pushed the gold pin into her heart.

When he pulled the pin out of her she tried to struggle and fight him, but she was already weak with shock. And as her blown heart strained and bled, and her strength faded, he lay down with her again on the floor, stretched out on top of her, muffling the sounds she tried to make with his hands and mouth, murmuring, 'There, shh, quiet, I love you, I'm sorry, I have to, hush . . .'

He'd never killed anyone before, not himself. He waited to feel some great change come over him, but nothing seemed to come. He did not seem, at least not yet, to feel any guilt, only bewilderment and grief, because Tulliola was dead. It was as if someone else had killed her, as if she really had killed herself. He curled her fingers around the hairpin, laid her warm hand over her breast beside the wound. He had sharpened the tip slightly that morning, it hadn't needed much and the metal was so soft that it wasn't difficult, anyone – she – could have done it. He kissed her again, kissed her throat and the tops of her breasts, all still so warm and soft – it was almost as if what had happened didn't make any difference, she was still the same – neither of them had changed. He rearranged her a little and lay quietly for a while, stroking her hair and whispering to her, as if she were still crying and he were still comforting her.

Finally he got up and went into the next room. He'd left a change of clothes there, and when he'd put them on they made him feel even more as though it couldn't really have happened, although he still knew what to do.

He bundled up the bloody clothes into the bag. He told the guard in the hall, 'Make sure she is not disturbed until supper.' The man had been at the Galenian, Drusus had already paid him for this. Soon he would have to fade quietly away from the investigations chewing through the vigiles and the Praetorians Guard, and Drusus knew wearily that he would always be a worry, in spite of the money, although he would have no proof, unless Drusus could think up some way of making utterly sure of him. But for the moment he couldn't be bothered with it. As he rode away in the car he looked at the daylight with a kind of boredom. What a waste of time the whole thing has been, he thought. But what else would he have done with the time, what could he do now?

At the Quirinal villa that was home for the moment, he burnt the clothes and floated in a deep bath, drugged with hot water, for a long time.

Later Faustus called him to tell him what had happened. His voice was hoarse and weak: 'They should have taken those hair things off her, of course. Still I can't help feeling it's better than it all happening in public: she must have had some sense of honour after all, but—'

'But it must be terrible for you, Uncle,' said Drusus. 'I can't tell you how sorry I am.'

He sat for a while longer downstairs. Marcus would be back in Rome soon. He couldn't bear it. He'd never lived outside the city for long; well, he'd have to now.

Then he closed all the curtains in the house, although it was still light, and got into bed, gathering up all the bedclothes in one violent movement and embracing them, and cried himself to sleep.

[NOTE]

THE EMPEROR'S HEIR

Formally each new Emperor was appointed by the Senate; in reality, the Senate's role was reduced to rubber-stamping either the existing Emperor's choice or whoever had ousted him. There was thus no automatic right of primogeniture; in fact, before the Byzantine period, power passed from father to son only rarely – although this was generally either because (for whatever reason) there was no son available, or because the succession was disrupted by violence, not a matter of design. If he could, the Emperor would certainly be likely to choose someone from within his own family – though it might be a brother or a nephew – as Caesar, a term which came to mean something like Crown Prince.

DATES

The Romans counted the years from the founding of the city *ab urbe condita*, taken as 753 BC. So 2005 AD = 2758 AUC.

NAMES OF PLACES AND PEOPLE

In writing this book I wanted to find a balance between the familiar and the strange, and because of this there are inconsistencies in my rendering of place names.'Londinium', for example, sounds fussy and archaic, to me at least, and as no English-language book ever refers to Rome as 'Roma', I felt free to use the city's modern name. Similarly, I have called the town of Tivoli by that name rather than its ancient one, in order to avoid the homonym of Tibur/Tiber. However, I have preserved other Latin names, sometimes for their own sake, sometimes because I thought the modern French or Spanish name would break the impression of a Latin-speaking world, so Tolosa and Nemausus, not Toulouse and Nîmes. I have translated 'Passus Lupi' (a fort in Pompey's time, now the site of a village called St Beat) into English – 'Wolf Step'.

I have also had to deal with names that the Romans never encountered at all, from the Far East and the Americas. The first syllable of Kyoto, for example, contains a sound impossible in Latin, but the Romans might well have coped with it by inserting an 'n': hence 'Cynoto'. Japan, meanwhile, appears as Nionia – a Latinate elaboration of the Japanese word.

Sometimes it seemed that the difference between an English and Latin rendering of an indigenous name for a place or people would have been negligible. Sometimes I changed a 'ch' (which Latin does not use) to an 'x' or a 'ts'. Sometimes I simply used the alternative form of a name ('Mexica'). The Latin word for the Chinese adapted the name of the Qin or Ch'in dynasty into 'Sinae'. The English name for China comes from the same source, so 'Sina'.

I thought older, non-Roman personal names might be most likely to persist among slaves and those born far from the Empire's heart. Una's name sounds Latin but is actually Celtic, as is Sulien's. Delir and Lal are, of course, Persian.

Of course, any language would change over the centuries – which I hope accounts for anything that might otherwise look like a mistake.

A SHORT HISTORY OF THE ROMAN EMPIRE
933 AUC TO THE PRESENT (180 AD–2004 AD)

'To heal, as far as it was possible, the wounds inflicted by the hand
of tyranny, was the pleasing, but melancholy task of Pertinax'

Decline and Fall of the Roman Empire, Edward Gibbon

AD	AUC	
180	933	Death of Marcus **Aurelius**. His son Lucius Aelius Aurelius **Commodus** succeeds as Emperor.
192	945	Commodus' bloody and extravagant reign leaves Rome impoverished and riddled with corruption. He is murdered by a group of conspirators including his chamberlain, concubine and Laetus, the head of the Praetorian Guard (the urban army whose formal function was to protect the Emperor). The conspirators claim that Commodus died of apoplexy, and install as Emperor 66-year-old Publius Helvius **Pertinax**, the son of a freedman who had risen through merit to become a General, a Senator and minister of justice.

HELVIAN IMPERIAL DYNASTY

192–204	945–957	Early in Pertinax's reign, Laetus, disgruntled by Pertinax's independence, encourages a plot by the Praetorian Guard to assassinate him. The plot is discovered,* and Laetus banished.

* This is where my history of the Roman Empire departs from the usual one.
In reality, the plot was successful. The talented and conscientious Pertinax
(who planned many of the reforms indicated here) was murdered after only
eighty-six days in office and the Praetorians auctioned the throne to the
highest bidder. Didius Julianus bought the title of Emperor, but was deposed
and executed shortly afterwards by Septimius Severus, who returned to
Rome from Pannonia to avenge Pertinax.

Severus corrected many of the problems facing Rome and at the time his
reign could be viewed as a success. But he stripped the Senate of authority
and allowed corruption and indiscipline to flourish in the army, whose power
undermined the stability of the Empire. Gibbon says of Severus 'Posterity,
who experienced the fatal effects of his maxims, justly considered him the
principal author of the decline of the Roman Empire.'

Pertinax disbands almost all of the Praetorian Guard, hand-picking the remainder for loyalty. At the same time he increases the powers and numbers of the Vigiles to create a counterweight police force, reasoning that any future conspiracy against the Emperor in one body will be detected and exposed by the other.

Pertinax remits Commodus' oppressive taxes. He halves the expenses of the Imperial household, grants tax-breaks to farmers and lifts restrictions on commerce.

He taxes the urban aristocracy more heavily, but the cities benefit from the wealth generated by the farms, and he restores to the Senate some of the authority it had lost.

204	957	Death of Pertinax. After the disastrous succession of Commodus, Pertinax was reluctant to name his young son Publius Helvius Pertinax II, '**Venedicus**', as Caesar and heir to the Empire until just before his death. The senate approve the succession.
204–220	957–973	Pertinax II continues his father's economic reforms, gradually rebuilding the Empire's finances. When the economy permits it he restructures the army, detaching the legions from the frontier garrisons to create a mobile force. He ties pay to the rate of inflation, stabilising the income of the soldiers and rendering them less susceptible to bribery, whilst attracting a higher standard of recruit.
225	978	Ardashir, the Persian king, kills the last king of Parthia and creates the Sassanian Persian Empire, with Zoroastrianism as its state religion.
238	991	Renewed attacks from Germanic tribes along the Rhine and Danube. The

revitalised army resists and pushes the barbarians back. To deal more fully with the threat, and despite protests from Roman Britons, Pertinax II pulls the legions out of Britain and leads a massive force into Germany and Sarmatia.

230–240	983–993	Ardashir invades India, and Roman territory in Syria. In 240, his son Shapur succeeds to the Persian throne.
238–242	973–978	Pertinax II completes the conquest of Germany and Venedia, pushing up into Fennia and Gothia.
242–256	978–992	Skirmishes with Persia over Armenia. Roman recapture of Syria.
256	992	Death of Pertinax II, accession of Lucius Helvius Pertinax **Sarmaticus**. Rome's victories over the Eastern European tribes continue into Sarmatia and Alania.
260–265	996–1009	Still feeling the elation of their German victory, Roman troops, augmented by huge numbers of German barbarians and with support from Palmyra, attack and conquer Shapur's Persian Empire.
265–291	1009–1044	Occasional Persian uprisings and fluctuating borders in Roman Persia, but Rome's grip remains generally firm.
291–313	1044–1066	Under Sarmaticus' adopted son Gaius Flavius **Sulpicianus**, Rome loses Persia and Mesopotamia.
313–345	1066–1098	Marcus Flavius Sulpicianus **Cruentus** reconquers Persia and Mesopotamia. Slaughter and enslavement of thousands of Persians. Persecution of Christians, Zoroastrians and Jews throughout Empire. Invasion and conquest of Arabia. Cruentus exports the Roman religion, or

a Roman interpretation of local deities, to the enlarged Eastern Empire.

347–447	1100–1200	From here on it will be convenient to summarise the major gains, losses and technological advances of each century.

SECOND FLAVIAN DYNASTY
1066–1234 AUC

Reconquest of Britain, with Hibernia and Caledonia. There has been a revival of Celtic culture, but a sustained British nostalgia for Roman rule makes victory fairly easy. Sporadic incursions by Huns, but they are either repelled or absorbed by Rome, resulting in gradual, unsystematic Roman expansion into Scythia.

447–547	1200–1300	ACILIAN DYNASTY 1234–1618 AUC

Continued conquests of territory in Scythia. Expansion through Persian territory into India. Lengthy wars to secure it. Romanisation of Indian Gods.

547–647	1300–1400	Quelling more uprisings and rebellions in India and resulting instability in the region keep the military fully occupied – no expansion.

647–747	1400–1500	Attempted expansion into Sina (China) unsuccessful, and there are continuing problems in Syria, Persia and India.

747–847	1500–1600	Border disputes with Sina. India and Persia subside into uneasy peace, but tensions will flare up at any sign of weakness in the Empire for centuries to come. By this time the once-significant Christian sect has more or less died out of existence. Active persecution of Jews and Zoroastrians has ceased, although they are still denied full citizenship.

847–947	1600–1700	CORDIAN DYNASTY 1618–1836 AUC

Libya and other Roman states in North Africa attempt to devolve peacefully from the Empire, but Africa is essential to feeding the Roman world. Heightened military presence there.

947–1047	1700–1800	Song Dynasty unifies and stabilises Sina.

Rome is initially concerned about Sina's growing power, but the Emperor feels that Rome is now unassailable, re-attempted conquest of Sina would be costly and futile, and that therefore there is no need to jeopardise profitable trade with Sina. Relations remain cordial – especially since Sina supports Roman rule in India.

1047–1147	1800–1900	BLANDIAN DYNASTY 1836–2176 AUC

The Romans defend the Song against the Jurchen uprising.
Rome introduces various Sinoan innovations, such as paper money, banking, Romanised versions of certain fashions in clothing – and gunpowder.

1147–1247	1900–2000	

Quicker to see the military application of the new discovery than its Sinoan inventors, Rome sides with Sina against the Mongols, saving the Song Dynasty.
First Roman contact with Nionia (Japan). Rome welcomes the new source of coveted oriental goods, but has little political interest as yet in the chain of islands, which is riven with internal divisions and wars.

1247–1347	2000–2100	

Armed with cannons, Rome invades Ethiopia in Africa. Sina watches this new phase of expansion with concern.
The Nionian Emperor Go-Daigo visits Rome, learns about Roman exploration and conquest, and brings the secret of gunpowder back to Nionia.

| 1347–1447 | 2100–2200 | Go-Daigo leads the Kemmu Restoration, using firearms against the powerful Hojo regency. The new firepower helps him to see off opposition from his erstwhile ally, Ashikaga Takauji. He restores the powers of the Emperor and unites Nionia. Continued exploration/conquest of interior Africa runs into difficulty when Roman African states unexpectedly turn against Rome. |

Roman explorers return from an attempt to circumnavigate the globe with news of a brief landing on a huge landmass in the West. They call it Terra Nova, but this is no time for a military adventure there.

Plague in Europe and in parts of Sina. The Emperor Blandius **Postumus** dies suddenly and there is a struggle for power unprecedented in over a thousand years.

| 1447–1547 | 2200–2300 | The first electrostatic machine. After a succession of short-lived Emperors, the Senate votes Sextus Vincius **Sacerdos** into power. |

VINCIAN DYNASTY 2204–2509 AUC

Sacerdos is still trying to secure his position when Nionia invades Corea and attacks Sinoan territory. Sina appeals to Rome for help, but the call comes at exactly the wrong time. Rome is struggling to survive in the face of its internal rifts, African entanglements, renewed Indo-Persian problems and the decimating effects of plague. The Empire is in no position to assist.

Sina battles Nionia alone but concedes large tracts of territory. Roman relations with both Sina and Nionia are damaged. Rome tries to repair the damage of the last century. In an attempt to rebuild Roman solidarity, Sacerdos extends full citizenship to all free inhabitants of the Empire, regardless of nationality or religion, withholding only the right to hold office from freedmen.

1547–1647	2300–2400	Meanwhile, Nionia is still in the ascendant. Nionian explorers sight the Southern island continent and call it Goshu.

When Nionia begins to colonise Goshu, Rome becomes seriously alarmed. Nionia is beginning to look like a serious rival to the Empire. Rome puts pressure on Nionia to cease expanding and urges Sina to do the same, but since becoming a buffer state between Rome and Nionia, Sina has become increasingly introspective, and the Sinoan government refuses to get involved.

Rome completes the conquest of Africa. More experiments in electricity and magnetics.

Rome at last begins a serious invasion of central and southern Terranova, spreading cautiously into Mexica, Maia, and inland into Aravacia. Nionia follows suit, entering Terranova in the far north. Rome is more uneasy than ever and begins seriously to debate war but for the moment, and to the dissatisfaction of many, does nothing; there is still a huge amount of land, with its own peoples to contend with, between the two powers.

1647–1747	2400–2500	Nionia pushes south, until Rome's fears that she is not only allowing her rival to claim valuable territory but that her existing Terranovan provinces are under threat become intolerable. Conflict is now inevitable and is to dominate the next century.

The two armies sweep towards each other across the country – the Romans pushing north from the south-eastern coast of the northern continent, each trying to cajole or force the indigenous peoples to side with them.

The ensuing sequence of wars, although they vary in intensity and are divided by short, unsuccessful peace agreements, is brutal and often chaotic, with naval battles in the Atlantic and around Nionia itself. Tracts of land change hands several times, at vast cost in Roman, Nionian, and Terranovan lives. The Camian peninsula in Mexica is of particular importance since for Rome to allow the Nionians to claim it would amount to their being permanently flanked.

The Emperor Vincius **Arcadius** dies in suspicious circumstances and his brother, **Nasennius**, seizes power.

The Roman military and economy has been damaged. During a brief lull in the Roman-Nionian conflict, the final years of the 25th Century, the first African Uprising takes place in the province of Lundae in Africa.

The first – very slow and inefficient – electrically powered vehicles to run on magnetic rails.

| 1747–1847 | 2500–2600 | Madness first appears in Novian family. The Africans are temporarily subdued. In the second African Uprising of 2503, a poorly equipped Roman legion is massacred near Musitania (Mosi-oa-Tunya) Falls. Nasennius is widely blamed for the disaster. |

Oppius Novius, Nasennius' nephew-by-marriage, gains in popularity in the Senate.

After an outbreak of smallpox in Rome, Nasennius commits suicide leaving no children. Oppius Novius takes power.

Rome secures Northern half of Africa.
Southern Africa claims independence.
Although bringing the conflict to an end
and holding onto Northern territory are
significant successes for Rome, this is the
first serious loss of territory for the
Empire in centuries. Cracks appear
elsewhere in the Empire: there is conflict
in Terranova, and old tensions in India
stir again.

In 2512, Oppius' brother Servius
succumbs to family madness.

Oppius works to rebuild international
stability. He succeeds in reversing Roman
fortunes in Terranova, where the Romans
advance north. His task is eased by new
technology such as longscript – a method
of transmitting codes through electric
pulses invented in 2511. This allows
direct government of overseas territory.
Longscript lines are laid under the
Atlantic, and through Africa. Thirty years
later come longdictors. Rome will be able
to respond far more swiftly to any future
unrest.

There are accelerated attempts to find a
reliable form of air-travel.

Rome's military might is, just, superior to
Nionia's, but it looks as though it will be
impossible to ever expel the Nionians
from Terranova altogether. Therefore,
Rome finally comes to grudging terms
with Nionia and northern Terranova is
divided between the two Empires. Under
the Mixigana Treaty, a huge wall is built
across the continent to separate them.
Trade between Nionia and Rome resumes,
but there is a persistent distrust and rivalry.
Rome develops new high explosives.
Nionia seems always on the verge of
catching up with Roman technology.

		Rome begins to expand through Southern Terranova. Rome works to improve the network of roads, whilst simultaneously building a vast system of magnetways throughout the Empire.
1847–1947	2600–2700	Development of flight using circling wings powered by engines – the first spiral-wing. Continued colonisation of North and South Terranova. The arms race with Nionia goes on.

RECENT HISTORY

1943	2697	Titus Novius **Faustus** born.
1949	2702	Lucius Novius Faustus born.
1958	2711	Tertius Novius Faustus born.
1969	2722	Titus marries Julia Sabina.
1971	2724	Julia gives birth to Novia Faustina ('Makaria').
1977	2730	Lucius marries Drusilla Terentia.
1979	2732	Drusilla gives birth to Drusus Novius Faustus.
1981	2734	Lucius succumbs to hereditary madness.
1982	2735	Gaius Novius Faustus **Rixa** dies. Titus succeeds as Emperor. Tertius Novius posted to central Terranova. He quells an Aztec uprising and his courage gains him the agnomen 'Leo'. He is hailed as a hero, but sees hundreds of previously free Aztecs enslaved and is shocked by the experience.
1983	2736	Faustus divorces Julia.
1984	2738	Leo marries Clodia Aurelia. With Senatorial approval, Faustus names Leo as Caesar and Imperial heir.
1988	2741	Clodia gives birth to Marcus Novius Faustus Leo.

| 1996 | 2749 | Faustus marries Tullia 'Tulliola' Marciana. |
| 2004 | 2757 | In mid-August, Leo and Clodia are killed in a car crash in the Gallic Alps. |

[1]

YELLOW FIRE

She had barely slept. The single damp sheet that lay over her was smothering, a pelt, but when she pushed it off she felt exposed, a little panting grey animal, curled up in the heat. The windows were all open but when the air moved it made no difference; it was like moist wool brushing over her. Summers had not always been like this, had they? She thought she could feel the bricks of the house, the trees outside and the miles of ground, hurt with heat, straining and creaking.

But after all she must have been more than half asleep, or stunned with the nights she had already lost, though she kept moaning and shifting in the bed; for she was very late noticing the sound, or the scent.

She thought that possibly something had moved in the corner of the room, near the door: an animal, or a person. She blinked heavily and pressed her cheek to the pillow, not afraid; it did not really occur to her to believe there was anything there. She lay possibly asleep, possibly with her eyes shut, she could not tell. The heat puffed and crept.

Then again she had the impression of motion; in the air above her this time; a dark ripple, and she smelt it now.

She sat up, the gasp she made brought the bitterness in the air far more clearly into her throat. She had seen smoke moving, and there were flames like small creatures on the floor.

She ran shufflingly across the room. The door led into her sitting room, the stairs down into the rest of the house were beyond it. The little flames by the door were not, in themselves, terrifying, but she pushed the door open and the room was bright with yellow fire, and a thick, hovering flood of hot gas and dust struck her face.

She choked and cried out, backing away into the bedroom. She groped towards the window, at first only for the air that now seemed clean and cool. Then she looked down and saw the thick red flames, gushing like a liquid, like blood, upwards out of the lower windows. Her brother and sister-in-law, and their children – they were out, weren't they? She could see dim figures in the garden, but there was no light except that of the fire.

She could not climb down or jump. Her rooms were on the third floor, out of the family's way. She had not meant to end up surviving on goodwill like this, but she'd always lived in this house, and now, even as she leaned out, calling for help, she wanted to weep with grief for it, for the *things* – furniture her parents had bought – pictures—

A rich fountain of black smoke, fast and bloated, rolled up to her window from below and forced her back into her bedroom.

The vigiles, surely, must be nearly here.

She stood for a moment, coughing, clasping her hands near her face, crying with helplessness – and then plunged through the burning doorway into the other room. Down near the floor there was still some air, though her palms and knees were seared at once. She crawled into the cavern of heat, whimpering with pain and horror, and at the sight of her own possessions blazing – oh, hidden in the drawers of the burning writing-desk – her bundles of *letters*. Some of them thirty years old, some of them she could almost never bear to read over, but terribly important, necessary.

It was dark, cavernous. She could not understand how the familiarity of the room's shape could be burning away with everything else, how hard it was even to remember the way to the door, but she saw in despair that even if she reached it, it would be no good, of course the stairs would be impassable with flame. And she could not breathe, and the fire enroached towards her from all sides, it steered her, so that she had to scramble backwards again, and could barely make it into the bedroom once more, in pain, her hair already singed and eaten to rags by the fire.

But this room too was soaking up with heat and poison, and she could not even try to get near the window again: the curtains were moving murderously and dropping away in flakes as they burned. Flame was beginning to pool on the ceiling.

'If there is ever a fire, don't hide, children die in fires because they hide from them.' Her parents had told her this. She crept under her bed. It was decades since she had been a child, and there was nowhere else to go. She lay there on her stomach, and saw the carpet steam or smoke, and she could feel that she would probably lose consciousness soon, and she was afraid that even if the vigiles came in now they wouldn't find her; they wouldn't know she was there.

But nothing ever was found of her. She was dead before the orange flame burst everywhere from the floor, from the bed, before the roof fell through, crushing the shell of her body into black crumbs of bone, that later could not be told from those of the slaves, or even, at first, from the scorched chips of plaster and wood.

KANANOKUNI

The heat exhausted Faustus, heaped viscously over his body, gripped his head, a bottling, fermenting feeling. It was hard to think clearly, but the month's meetings kept multiplying, swelling: there were forest fires, more this year and worse than any he could remember, huge red flotillas, crescent-shaped on Terranova, advancing on tall sails of smoke towards the cities on the west coast. And also in Gaul, and even in Italy itself, to the north. And Nionia – how serious the threat was, how fast it was growing – just for an hour he should be allowed to forget about it – but he could not, and he could not sleep, for that and the heat.

His eyes pulsed redly against his shut lids.

The woman trying to rub the ache out of his shoulders was young, with long dark hair which he sometimes felt whisk against his skin. Not really like Tulliola, except in that. A slight pleasure glowed in his scalp as her fingers moved up into his hair, but the tiredness had only retreated from her a little, she could not do more than just touch the surface of it.

He felt a very faint, very perfunctory excitement, mingled with a stronger boredom, at the fact that, if he wanted, he could turn over, reach for her. He was the Emperor, she would have to . . .

He was sad. He did not want to. Because of Tulliola, and because he was so tired.

There was a slight noise, a tap, a warning, recognisable clearing of the throat at the door – it was Glycon – to which Faustus uttered a vague grunt of mingled assent and protest.

The girl draped a towel over him, and he raised himself, embarrassed not by his nakedness, but by the slowness with which he did it, the little groan, a creaking 'mmm . . .' His eyes were still shut.

'Sir.'

Faustus opened his eyes, knowing the tone of voice. He had of course heard it several times, but worst of all and most repeatedly during the terrible summer and autumn of three years before, beginning with the news that his youngest brother was dead. Then everything with his nephew Marcus, and finally that they had found Tulliola, dead under house arrest—

How should he think of her now? As little as possible, and not, if he could, as having been his wife; he was so ashamed of her. He did not know why she had done such terrible things, and he never wanted to find out; and she had been so beautiful, and he was almost grateful to her for having killed herself. It was better than having to have her executed.

So his first thought was that, again, he was going to hear that something had happened to one of his family. Marcus, who was his heir now. Or even worse, his daughter Makaria – no, please not her. Or it could be both of them, they were both in Greece.

'We need you downstairs,' said Glycon, 'there has been a massacre.'

Oh, thank goodness for that, thought Faustus, disgracefully, glad that no one would ever know. He sat up and punitive pain flowed back into his head

It eased off. 'What do you mean by a massacre? How many people?'

He felt sorry for Glycon: he knew he would hate answering that. He saw Glycon flinch, resist the urge to dodge the question altogether, settle on saying softly, 'The lowest figure I've heard was a hundred, the highest was four hundred. Yanisen can tell you more.'

'This is on the Wall, then, of course?' Yanisen was the governor of Roman Terranova.

'The Wall has been breached,' said Glycon, just as gently.

Faustus felt a sharp twang of real shock, for the first time. 'The Wall has been *breached*? Are you telling me about an invasion?'

Glycon again recoiled a little. 'It's a matter of the last few hours, it's very unclear. I think they are still fighting. I wouldn't like to speculate. But you will need the military options before you: I have General Salvius waiting with Probus, and Memmius Quentin, because obviously the impact on the public will become important very soon.'

'Good,' said Faustus heavily. 'You'd better get, ah—' for an odd moment he could not get the name to form, either in his brain or on his tongue. 'Falx,' he said finally. Falx was an intelligence specialist on Nionia.

'He's on his way.'

He walked with Glycon through the palace. The massage seemed to have done no good at all. He was just as sluggish as before. He felt oily under his clothes.

'We can talk to Nionia through Sina or our trade contacts,' said Glycon, because for eighteen months and more there had been, officially, only bitter silence between Nionia and Rome. The last Nionian ambassadors had been spies, or at least, the danger that they were spies was too strong to take chances.

'Sina,' answered Faustus dully. The light through the gold-tinted glass hurt his eyes.

In the private office the doors were almost invisible when closed: carved leaves obscuring the edges, even the hinges and little handles concealed among the unbroken ivy and clematis painted in fresco round the walls, so that once inside you seemed to be within a large, cool, motionless garden, beautiful, with no way out. But there was a bright, flat aperture now in the green wall opposite Faustus' desk, where the doors or shutters that covered the longvision were folded back, displaying Yanisen.

Yanisen was Navaho, but looked – was – as essentially Roman as the men in the room: dressed in crisp white, his stiff, lead-coloured hair cut short and square above his elegant long face. Terranova was one of the few regions left in the Empire where languages other than Latin still had much currency; but the governor's full name was Marcus Vesnius Yanisen, and he would probably have dropped or altered even the Navaho cognomen, if it had not run easily enough off tongues used only to Latin.

He and Probus should have been preparing what they would say to Faustus; instead they were in passionate argument: 'If you had given me the resources—'

'Do you – think – this is – n'appropriate time to be scoring *points*?' said Probus, in a series of low, dry, furious gulps.

'I think it's a time to remember that I've been warning about this for years!'

'Yes, we are all very aware of *that*, you've spent less time—' he swallowed again, '– actually *doing* anything about it.'

Probus was thirty-six, a short but upright man with dark hair and a square face. He was precociously high-ranking, the youngest person in the room, and the most afraid for himself; for it was true Yanisen had often complained to him, as the tension on the Wall grew and the skirmishes got worse. It was also true that Salvius and Faustus himself were just as responsible for refusing Yanisen everything he had wanted, but Probus must know he would be the easiest to blame, if it came to that.

Yanisen opened his mouth, incensed, but cut himself short, seeing Probus react as Faustus entered. The appalled, argumentative look of them brought the ache and the weariness to a peak again in Faustus. The lovely green room felt inexplicably stuffy.

Salvius made him tired, too; he was sitting on one of the green couches, scowling at the argument but taking no part in it; he sprang up to greet Faustus with the energy of a charge going off. He was white-haired, but the hair was still thick, and combed to a snowy gloss, and he was as muscular and handsome as he had been at twenty-five. Leo, Faustus' dead brother, had been similarly careful of his appearance, and yet Faustus did not believe Salvius was really vain at all, as Leo certainly had been. Salvius had simply realised at some stage that to look this way helped him extract respect. He certainly had none of Leo's loucheness – he seemed to have been happily faithful to his wife for thirty years. Oddly, though, for politically they must have violently disapproved of one another, Leo and Salvius had got on quite well, not only out of military fellow-feeling, but also the conscious shared possession of a certain kind of strength.

Salvius bowed; Faustus took his hand, and felt that though it gripped firmly on his own, it trembled too, not with fear like Probus – Faustus looked into his face and saw the spontaneous, wounded outrage there, and was surprised. He felt again rather ashamed of himself; he just did not feel as if he personally had been attacked, when presumably of all people he ought to.

Salvius burst out: 'That's the last shred of Mixigana gone, Your Majesty, and frankly it's been a farce for years anyway: we've got no choice but to show we won't tolerate this.' Mixigana was the peace treaty that had established the Roman–Nionian border more than three hundred years before.

'That's probably the best way to let this out, it makes it clear you're still in control,' agreed Quentin, although Salvius did not seem to relish the advisor's support, and glanced at him with minor distaste. Quentin was in his forties but plumply boyish-looking, round-faced, with smooth chestnut hair; he did not look particularly shocked by what had happened.

'Quiet. You may think you know what this is all about, but I don't. Yanisen.'

It was principally for Salvius' benefit that Faustus tried to sound forceful, pulled his protesting body up as straight as he could. You've got to watch people like that, he felt, deeply and instinctively. The Novii might have ruled in Rome for two hundred years now, but it would never be long enough to be completely certain they were safe; not for any Emperor.

Salvius looked at him broodingly, and he and Quentin subsided. Probus stood and clenched his teeth.

Yanisen nodded. 'Sir. Our troops came under the kind of attack they've experienced *many times*, especially in the last four years—'

Probus grimaced, longing to interrupt.

'Where?' said Faustus.

'This was in – that is, it began near Vinciana.'

'I've never heard of it.'

'No, there's no reason you would have done. But it's in Arcansa, very near the Wall, close to where it intersects the Emissourita. Of course, our troops retaliated. I think we lost four or five men at this point, sir. You must understand that with all of this – because of the way things escalated, it's hard to be precise. A detail in armoured vehicles advanced a little way into Nionian territory to disperse the enemy. It appeared they had done so successfully. But on the return they were attacked again. Sir, the Nionians must have reinforced at some point in the last month; it was much more sustained, the numbers were such that the Roman soldiers were all but wiped out. We haven't been able to recover the bodies.'

'But that can't have been a hundred people?' asked Faustus.

'No. The Nionians pursued the remnants back. And this is when they fired explosives at the Wall itself. Of course by this time our surviving troops had called for support, but it didn't come in time, there was no way they could hold the breach. The fighting spilled into Vinciana. And then – I think they – the Nionians – must have begun simply killing people indiscriminately.'

Faustus exhaled heavily; he hadn't realised so many of the deaths were civilian. He understood Salvius' indignation better now, but he still couldn't share it, not really; he felt more depressed than anything.

'But they were driven back or killed after that? They're not still there?'

'No. The back-up from the next fort arrived; it doesn't seem there's been any more gunfire.'

'And the breach itself?'

'They've got it contained for the moment.'

'But how big is it? What does the town look like now?'

'Well, it's – the damage must be – I'm not there.'

'Then go there, but first find me someone who's there already, and decent pictures, and some idea of where these numbers are coming from.'

'Very well,' said Yanisen, his voice strained. Then, seemingly trying in vain to stop himself, he continued through his teeth, 'The town is still vulnerable, of course, and will continue to be. I am sorry, Your Majesty, I feel I *have* to say, this could have been prevented—'

'Yes, *you* could have prevented it,' exclaimed Probus savagely. 'Don't you try and lay the blame here because just because we weren't prepared to throw good money after bad.'

'Stop,' barked Faustus, acting being furious easily enough; after all these years he could produce the right voice and expression on demand. 'You can continue this in person, Probus; you should be out there too.' Probus nodded shakily, but Faustus added, '*Now*, go now,' and felt, as vague as his desire for the girl in the bath-suite, a pang of pleasure at being able to flick Probus so across the globe. Infantile, really. Probus left, still swallowing drily; Faustus thought, with mingled scorn and pity, that when he was alone he might even burst into tears.

He gestured at the screen and a slave turned it off. An aide had entered and whispered something to Glycon.

'What's happening with Cynoto?' Faustus asked.

Glycon looked disconsolate. He was training a quietly tormented, imploring expression on a cherry-tree painted on the wall, and he had to lower his hand from his mouth to speak: unconsciously, he'd been biting the flesh of his index finger. 'It's taking time,' he replied.

'They're not refusing to speak to us?'

'No. Possibly keeping us waiting to make a point.' He slipped out of the room.

Faustus and Salvius exchanged a silent look now, not

quite of guilt, but both aware that for years they had considered quietly, why lavish money on the Wall when a war with Nionia might be coming, when after such a war the Wall would be pointless? Yanisen must have known as much.

'All right, now you can talk.'

'We have almost the numbers on the Wall to head North already; we can reinforce them within weeks. I don't believe it would take more than four months to take control of the territory.'

Faustus nodded. Glycon re-entered to interject, 'Falx is here.'

'In a minute. But could we keep the war contained in Terranova?'

'Obviously we would attack Cynoto from the air at the same time,' said Salvius.

'And their bases in Edo?'

'It goes without saying.'

Faustus nodded again, but he looked at Quentin. 'Are you sure this looks like being in control? Because you could equally well say the opposite.'

'Well,' said Quentin, 'people will want to feel *something* is being done.'

'But – not to belittle what's happened today – we don't need to overstress it to the public, do we? People are used to hearing about skirmishes.'

Quentin looked thoughtful. 'It's true that it's a long way away for most people. But it's not as easy to keep things quiet these days; and even if we were successful, they might then find it harder to accept if you did decide war was necessary.'

Salvius was looking overtly disgusted by this time. '*What*?' demanded Faustus, loudly, finding with some surprise that he was contemplating Salvius almost with hatred. Oh, you think you'd do so much better, he thought sourly.

Salvius hesitated, bristling warily. 'I suppose it seems like a question of right or wrong to me. A question of the interests of Rome, at the least: I'm a little surprised it's being considered in these terms.'

'We're considering everything, I hope,' Faustus snarled.

'Of course,' said Salvius, trying to sound dispassionate.

Faustus wanted Salvius out of the room so he could release his body from the straight posture he'd hauled it into, knead his face with hands. He said, '*You* talk with Falx. Come back and tell me what we can expect from the Nionians, and what we need to do to be ready.'

Salvius was even a little appeased by this. When he and Quentin were gone, Faustus let himself sag, as he'd wanted to. He rubbed at the back of his neck and head, trying to mimic what the girl had been doing, but holding his arm aloft like that only seemed to make the muscles stiffen even more painfully and he let it drop.

He noticed Glycon. He had retreated diffidently into a chair at the edge of the room, but as the conversation went on, he wound himself by subtle degrees into a position that looked agonising: his legs twisted round each other, his shoulders skewed, his hands up at his face with the interlaced and steepled fingers spikily protecting the lower half of his nose, his thumbs under his chin, jutting into his neck. He might be unaware he was doing it, but still Faustus was sure Glycon wanted him to say, as he did now, 'You're looking very gloomy.'

Glycon separated his hands to hold them splayed in mid-air. 'Of course,' he murmured.

'No, don't give me that,' said Faustus, tersely gentle. He dragged a chair into place to sit opposite Glycon.

Glycon unknotted himself fully, sighing. 'I think the General reaches decisions so fast,' he confessed. 'I think it . . . it's possible he underestimates the cost – financially, apart from anything else. And in – destruction.'

This was an unusually strong word for Glycon: having said it he blinked and made a mute gesture, as if to rub it out of the air.

'Of course, he may very well be right,' he added quickly, which almost made Faustus want to laugh, but Glycon went on again gravely, his eyes distant: 'But if Nionia is stronger than he thinks, then this would be something we've never seen before. A world conflict. It doesn't bear thinking about.'

'*I* haven't decided anything yet,' Faustus said quietly.

As the afternoon wore on, however, he became increasingly angry with Nionia, for still all they heard through Sina were imprecise promises that the Nionian Emperor would be ready to speak with them soon. Faustus found himself roaring at Glycon, as if it was his fault, 'Make sure they know they're taking a damn stupid risk playing this game! He should be glad I'm willing to talk to him at all!'

Glycon only nodded, unflinching. At last he came into the private office again to tell Faustus, 'The Nionian Prince will speak with you, if you want.'

'Which one?' asked Faustus. He found the workings of the Nionian court confusing; he knew the Emperor had a lot of children. Faustus felt envious. It was curious and regrettable that he and his two brothers had only managed to produce one child each. He thought again of his daughter Makaria, and of Marcus. If Makaria had been a son – if she had married and had children like a normal woman . . . how much easier everything would have been. Of course, it was still not impossible; though she was thirty-six now. But he no longer seriously expected it to happen.

If he had had a son with Tulliola – a child of six, at the oldest, now? He imagined such a boy, briefly: with black hair, and a crooked Novian mouth. But the idea of Tulliola jabbed at his head again, and in honesty, did he remember what you were supposed to do with a child that young? A grandchild would have been different.

Very occasionally he heard rumours that Makaria had a lover out on Siphnos; if so, he wished she would produce him; Faustus would really not care who it was.

'Tadasius, the crown prince,' said Glycon.

But of course the Prince did not call himself Tadasius, that was only the Latin rendering of it. His name was Tadashi.

603

Faustus exhaled at length again, trying to puff the anger out of himself so that he could think clearly, 'Suppose that'll do,' he muttered.

The aides adjusted the longdictor and Faustus took it. 'Your Majesty,' said a voice.

For a moment Faustus thought this must be some Roman intermediary, for the Prince's Latin was disconcertingly flawless. Faustus was thrown, not only by this, but by the Prince's age; older than Marcus, true, but what – twenty-two, twenty-four? 'Your Highness,' Faustus said, 'can I not speak to your father?' and realised it sounded, absurdly and offensively, like something one might say to a child – 'Is your daddy there?'

In response he heard a quiet, sharp intake of breath. 'My father trusts me to represent him accurately; I hope and believe he is right to do so. May I pass on to him your condolences for the murders of our people today? Shall I say Rome feels at last some degree of remorse for her actions?'

Flawless was almost an inadequate word for the Prince's fluency. And yet Faustus no longer thought he would have mistaken him for a native speaker: though the accent was exhaustively correct, it was somehow clearly not intended as a pretence or disguise of being Roman; the structure of each sentence, the resonance of the voice were all deliberately, even insultingly perfect. Faustus felt uncomfortably aware of the very few, very faltering words of Nionian that had survived in his memory through the fifty or fifty-five years since his schooldays.

'Oh, come on,' he said, irked, 'your troops attacked the Wall. Did you authorise that or not?'

'Our soldiers are authorised at all times to respond to Rome's persistent incursions into *Kananokuni*.' The sudden, soft foreign syllables, spoken so naturally, sounded bizzare to Faustus, resting incongruously on the familiar frame of his own language. There was no established Latin interpretation or taming of the Nionian name for the land north of the Wall – Cananocyne, perhaps, it would have been, but Romans would only speak grudgingly of 'Nionian

Terranova'. But he still remembered – Kananokuni, the Gold Country. That was what the Nionian name meant.

'Yes, and you've sent in more. Even aside from what happened today, they are in violation of Mixigana simply by being there.'

'We see Rome violate the treaty daily. We see infringement on Nionian territory, kidnappings, murders, rapes committed by your soldiers, or by your citizens with their protection—'

'All that's rubbish.'

'It is possible,' suggested the Prince, with pointed, forbearing courtesy, 'that your subordinates prefer to keep these things from you, in which case your reaction is understandable. But I can give you specific instances.'

'If I'm not supposed to believe my people, why should I believe yours? Look, the point is that explosives were used on the Wall, I assume you don't dispute that much. Did this happen spontaneously, in which case we will expect the men concerned to be punished, or was this an intentional act of war?'

'They were repelling your army's assault. They were responding to the destruction of a village. The murders of children. Did *you* authorise *that*?'

Faustus hesitated. His head beat. He began, 'Deaths in a battle provoked by your troops—'

'A village *ten miles* away,' cried the Prince.

Faustus was silent, blinking, thinking first, I don't have to believe that; then: but *he* believes it, that much is obvious. He pulled at his neck-cloth, which had begun to feel smothering, finally unpinned it and took it off altogether. He said quietly, 'Tell me what your intentions are.'

'The Emperor's intentions have always been to protect and uphold Nionia's side of the Mixigana treaty, despite Rome's evident contempt for it; after today, of course, he may be forced to reconsider,' said the Prince, performing the sentence with a kind of restrained, hostile flourish, and so beautifully that he was almost singing.

'This isn't helping anyone,' snapped Faustus. 'My generals

are fully prepared to respond. I thought you would appreciate the chance to give me your side of it.' He glowered, angry with himself, and with the Prince for goading him into this. He had not meant to sound so schoolmasterly. It would not have come out so if the Prince had been older.

There was a silence, which he thought he could hear ringing with both rage and satisfaction. The Prince said finally, politely, 'Thank you. I *have* appreciated it. Goodbye.'

'Sir, are you all right?' asked Glycon, watching him.

'Yes,' said Faustus thickly. Shouldn't have drunk so much, he thought. What was that supposed to mean? He hadn't had a drink since the night before – he shouldn't still be feeling that, should he? How much had it been? He couldn't remember. 'Get Salvius in here again.'

Salvius listened impassively while Faustus told him what the Prince had said. 'I think it's a good sign he felt the need to justify it. It shows they know they're in the weaker position.' Talking with Falx had made him calmer, more confident that the right thing would be done.

'You don't think there's any truth in the story about the village?'

'Well,' Salvius did lower his eyes briefly, 'I might not go as far as *that*, but you can't trust his account of it.'

'No, I suppose not,' said Faustus bleakly.

'In any case it hardly makes a difference. However today began, the fact is that the Nionians have proved themselves a threat, and neither the Wall nor the treaty is strong enough to protect us. And this is not just a matter of our territory in the West, sir, it's a question of whether we're willing to let Nionia overtake us as an imperial power. Because if not, this could be our last chance to stop it.'

'Wait a minute,' said Faustus, and could see that something had gone wrong; he hadn't said it properly. He rose from his seat and tried again, 'Just wait.'

And made for the hidden door because he felt it was the room that was wrong: the beautiful green room was so full of detail, and of the past, a minute or two anywhere else and he would be all right again. He reached the door, but fumbled at the familiar handles among the painted foliage.

'Sir,' Glycon was saying, coming towards him, his voice full of concern.

Then abruptly the door opened, and before his foot could fall in the doorway the impact came; a huge, soundless thud, a detonation so total that he could not immediately tell that it was not within the walls of his own skull, for it knocked half the floor away, so that he stepped off the remaining ground into dark air, and fell.